# Mark Trapino

## Res Publica

### *The Gift of Mars*

# About the Author

Mark Trapino is a retired high school English teacher and an admitted Italophile. He spent ten years researching the Roman Republic before putting pen to paper, and wrote the novel, Res Publica, while living in the area in which it takes place.

# Dedication

To my wife, who contributed the cover art and whose unflagging support made this book possible.

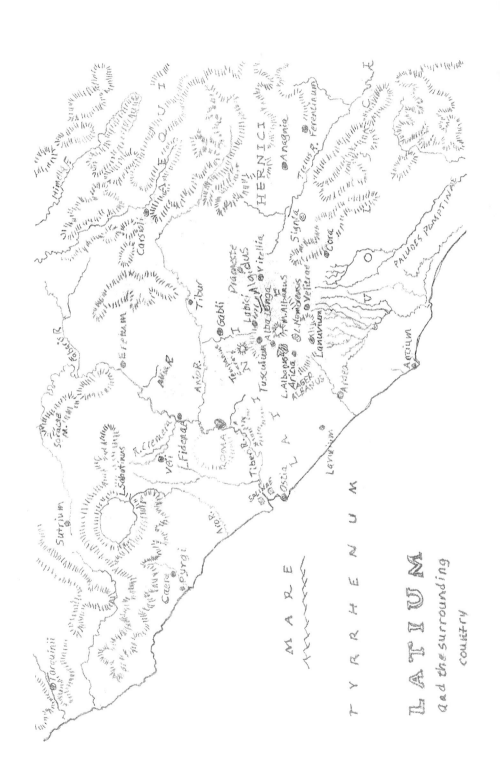

# Table of Contents

# PART I

## I

### July 476 BC

One by one, meandering desultorily in single file, laden two wheeled carts hauled stacks of Fabii dead like human cordwood into the city. A thin pall of dust, lifted into the air by a ragged wind, hung like gritty tears above the slow-moving wagons. Plodding oxen, lashed by the keening wails of the newly widowed, lowered massive horned heads beneath crude wooden yokes and dragged their dire cargo from the killing fields.

Awed by their sacrifice and stunned by a horrible foreboding, Romans lined the Via Salaria to stare in shock and disbelief at the stripped and mutilated bodies of the men they had come to see as invincible. Three hundred and six dead. The pride of Rome. An entire clan along with their clients wiped out in a single day. A day that, coinciding with another disaster on the same date nearly a century later, would forever be declared unlucky on the Roman calendar.

Others, more sanguine, shared a different perspective. It was not so long ago, these plebeians recalled, that they cursed the name Fabius. Too bad the Veientes left one alive. Three years running the Fabii had dominated the politics and the consulship of Rome, disputing, disrupting, and denying every plebeian attempt at civil reform. Why should their passing be mourned?

In the Tusculan foothills, twenty Roman milestones south of the battlefield, in the middle of ten acres of good arable land on Rome's southern frontier, Marcus Tempanius heard the news with a solemn ambivalence of his own. He was no admirer of the Fabii, but they were Romans, and the death of a Roman at foreign hands could not be tolerated. The soldiers and inhabitants of Veii would have to pay.

He ran a thick hand over the wide jagged scar that bisected his left shoulder, a reminder of twenty years before when he

1

had fought against Rome as a citizen of Tusculum. The scar, acquired at the battle of Lake Regillus, symbolized not only the loss of that battle by Tusculum and her Latin allies, but also the annexation of part of her territory and citizens into the Roman state. Marcus had been annexed.

A quick glance at a cloudless azure sky told him the day was fast dissolving, and he still had much work to do. Northwest over the plain below a blue mist spread, obscuring Rome like a mystery. In the morning one could see all the way to the sea. But then the vapors began to rise and creep slowly over the flats until the hills of Rome were but a blue-green shadow behind a gauzy veil by late afternoon. There was a kind of poetic justice in the view, Tempanius thought, because down there the basics of life were shrouded in the shifting mists of politics, of ever-changing loyalties and policies. Up here on his hill all was clear and straightforward. There was the land, and the crops, and the work it took to make the one grow the other.

He called to his son Antonius, weeding between furrows of wheat forty or fifty yards away. Around Marcus lay bundles of stakes, each about six feet in length. Next to these rested small grapevines wrapped in wetted sackcloth, and a large clay urn containing a mixture of ox and human urine.

"These won't keep," he said, more to himself than to the messenger who stood before him. As he reached down for a scuffed and dented iron field flask he grunted with pain. "I'm getting too old for this," he said, wiping his hands on his stained tunic.

"Have you no slaves?" Publius Anuncius offered between deep breaths. Though only one hundred feet in altitude the steep ascent up the north face of the knoll the Tempanius farm occupied had winded him. Billowing up behind like a dark green cloud the first range of mountains forming the Alban Hills climbed swiftly fifteen hundred feet. Atop the peak to the southeast sat the Latin town of Labicum, and hidden just on the other side of the peak to the southwest lay the city of

Tusculum. Dense forest of oak, beech, and chestnut trees covered the slopes, unoccupied save for the few goats and pigs the Tempanii grazed within its cool environs. Technically part of Tusculum, it served as a nearly impenetrable buffer between Rome and that city when it was a rival and a threat.

Marcus looked the crier over with a critical eye. He was tall enough, and although not visibly soft lacked the hard muscled body of someone who worked his land. He doubted that the man had served much time in the legions, though obviously younger than Marcus' forty-one years. He belonged to the college of criers paid by the state to announce all public business both in Rome and her outlying communities.

Publius Anuncius wilted a little under Marcus' appraising eyes. They were strange eyes, nut brown with a gray ring circumvallating the iris like a palisade. They seemed to look directly into his heart and assess his courage. He drew himself up, for he stood taller than Marcus and gazed over his head at the farmhouse on top of the knoll.

"You appear to be doing well enough to afford one," he said, trying to sound authoritative. Indeed, he thought Marcus Tempanius was doing quite well for himself. He had a two-story brick house with a tile roof, two or three pigs in a pen to the left of the house with their own wattle and daub shelter, and to the right a pen with goats and an ox lazily grazing on fodder strewn about their enclosure. These animals were stabled in the lower level of the farmhouse.

"Why should I have slaves when I have sons? A man does not have sons just to provide Rome with soldiers." Marcus offered the canteen to Publius, who refused politely. As he drank Marcus knew his words were a lie. And he knew his view of life on his hill was fanciful as well. Because everything that was done within Rome's mist enshrouded ramparts had some influence on life on his hill. He or his sons were sent off to war; enemies ravaged his fields and home; the state demanded a greater share of his labor. A thousand variables besides the weather affected his little farm. There was a multitude of obligations; to the gods, to family; to tribe, to patron, to state. Ultimately it was these that caused parents to send their sons off to war. And, he reflected, these bonds had nearly brought the republic to an end in only its second decade.

In his mind it did not seem as if eighteen years had come and gone since that time. Only his body recognized the passage of years. A cool stirring touched his cheek, and he turned his face to the west to welcome the late afternoon breeze from the sea. The mind might be easily fooled, but the body told the tale of one's life accurately. How simple his mind had been, he thought, as he fixed his memory on that moment in time eighteen years before....

# II

## October 1, 495 BC

## The Sister's Beam

Tarquinius Superbus, exiled king of Rome, died at Cumae on the Bay of Neopolis one hundred miles south of Rome. Marcus Tempanius greeted the news with harsh joy. From everything he'd heard Cumae was a beautiful spot, and he resented the pleasure it must have given the deposed king. Rubbing the scar he'd named Tarquin's Folly on his left shoulder, a fresh wave of resentment swept over him, just as Tarquin's ambition had swept Tusculum and the rest of Latium into war with Rome. He supposed he should be glad the Romans annexed his farm and granted him citizenship, rather than confiscate it and sell him into slavery. But he missed being a citizen of Tusculum.

Tusculum was the antithesis of Rome. Though she had her conflicts from time to time, she did not have to endure the destructive raids and attacks on her territory that Rome suffered perennially. Whether her position across the trade routes to Etruria, or her control of the saltpans on the coast made Rome a tempting target or whether jealousy of her size and prosperity motivated others to attack her, Rome seemed never at peace. Tusculans watched from their hilltop city as the legions debouched from Rome every March and returned every October year after year in unending turmoil. Now he had become a part of that cycle.

"What's the sigh for, Marcus?" asked Publius Opimius, breaking into his reverie.

"Nothing. Just wondering what happens tomorrow." He dipped a wool cloth into a clay pot of grease and began cleaning the blade of his sword.

Opimius pulled a stool up beside him and sat down. "This your first campaign?"

"As a Roman." Marcus examined a spot on the blade closely, rubbing it hard with the greased cloth.

"Anxious to get home?" said Opimius.

5

"Sure," said Marcus. He wiped his forehead. "It's been a long summer and my farm needs work."

"Well," said Opimius, looking up at a blue sky studded with clouds like white rivets. "Tomorrow we pass under the Sister's Beam."

"And that is?"

"Haven't you heard of the Horatii and the Curiatii?" said Opimius.

"Sure," said Marcus. "Everyone knows the duel of the Roman and Alban triplets to see which city would rule the other."

"Exactly," said Opimius. "Well, when Publius Horatius, the only survivor, returned victoriously to Rome at the head of the army he was carrying the armor of the three Curiatii he had killed. It just so happened that his sister was betrothed to one of the brothers. When she saw the cloak she had made for her lover slung over her brother's shoulder, she burst into tears, cried out her dead lover's name, and pulled her hair loose in mourning. Needless to say, Publius Horatius was enraged, and right then and there pulled his sword and stabbed her through the heart."

"That seems a little harsh," said Marcus, laughing. "Is this true?" A rising breeze slapped the sides of the leather tent behind them. Suddenly chilled, Marcus looked around for his cloak.

"Certainly," said Opimius. "Her grave is on the Via Albana with the Horatii."

"So what does that have to do with the Sister's Beam?" asked Marcus as he wrapped a faded red cloak around his broad shoulders.

"Ah, well, no one knew what to do. It was a ghastly murder, but no one was willing to convict him after his heroism in the service of Rome. Not King Tullus, not the people, and not his father, who actually pleaded for his life. So they made his father perform some rites of expiation and mounted a beam over the roadway at the Carinae. Horatius then had to pass under it with his head covered as if passing under the yoke of submission. Since that time, it's been deemed proper for all soldiers to perform the same ritual so Terminus will bless our return to civilian life."

Satisfied that all deposits of decay had been removed Marcus pulled a whetstone out of a leather satchel next to him and dressed the sword edge, scrutinizing it for any chips, indentations, or flat spots.

Publius Opimius, out of boredom, retrieved his spear from those stacked in front of the tent. He laid the spear across his tree trunk thighs and began absently rubbing it with the cloth Marcus had set down.

"What will you do with your share of the booty?" he asked after a short silence.

Marcus looked at the other man he thought he could call a friend after sharing a tent, and the dangers and boredom that came with it, for an entire summer. His wide ingenuous face and crooked nose displayed no guile.

"I hope to buy some land," he confided.

Publius snorted. "Not much of that around."

"True. Nevertheless," said Marcus, clipping off his words as if pruning a vine.

"Have you got some picked out?"

"Not specifically," Marcus said guardedly. "But I'd like it near my present property or it'll be too hard to work."

"Not really," Publius said. "All you need is an overseer. And those are easy to come by these days."

"Why would I want someone else to work my land?"

"For the simple fact, my friend, that the Aequi and Volsci will make it impossible for you to do it."

Marcus grunted and nodded in chagrin. "You have a point there, Publius. And if not them, the Sabines."

"Ah, well, maybe Appius Claudius, having been one of them, can keep them quiet as consul. If he's elected."

"Nevertheless, I don't like the idea of someone else working my land."

Opimius regarded the long earnest face of his friend. "Don't be so squeamish. There are plenty of men who would be happy to have any work to do."

"It's not that…"

"Certainly it is," Opimius said, clapping Marcus on the back with a bear paw sized hand. "You're afraid of taking advantage of someone else's misfortune. But believe me, most of those loiterers around the Forum would prefer plowing the land, regardless of whose it is."

"That may be. But will they do it with the proper care?"

Publius shrugged his wide shoulders and scratched his thinning hair. "If not, find somebody else."

Marcus laughed. "Now there's a patrician attitude."

Opimius didn't exactly take offense, but his wide smile fell, and his almond colored eyes appraised Marcus closely. "I think," he said slowly, "that it's simply reality. It may sound callous, but there are too many Romans and not enough land. Everyone's feeling the pinch."

At that moment Aulus Vibulus emerged from the tent behind them. Long fingered hands pulled the weathered skin of his bovine face downward. He yawned, gap toothed and loud. He stood a head taller than the other two, and lean as a string bean, which was the nickname they'd given him. He had overheard much of the conversation and could no longer resist involving himself in it.

"Of course," he said, "some are feeling the pinch more than others." He adjusted his dingy red tunic and retied the belt, checking the tunic's length in relation to his bony knees.

"That's the way it's always been, Legumenus," Opimius said.

"And so of course it must always remain so," Vibulus responded.

"Oh, oh," said Marcus, with a wry chuckle. "Now you've aroused the beast." He flipped his sword over and resumed working on the edge.

"No, no," protested Vibulus further, "I also think it's important to maintain traditions like throwing men off their land."

"Men who didn't pay their debts," said Publius.

"Yes, the slackers! Why, anyone with the least ambition should be able to make more than enough on two iugera to feed his family, buy shoes…what am I saying, they don't need shoes. Let them do without shoes, I say. In fact, let them do without tunics or togas as well. We all know they're little better than beasts anyway. I say, let them go naked."

"Very well, Legumenus, what's your answer?" asked Opimius, exasperated.

"Despite protestations to the contrary, there is land. The problem is that the largest share of the land is in the hands of the smallest portion of the population."

Publius Opimius set his wide jaw. "We overthrew one king because he thought he had a right to someone else's property."

"May he be condemned to eternal torture in Hades," said Marcus.

"Yes," said Vibulus. He kicked a stool into the sun and folded his long legs to sit down. "We got rid of one king so we could have two."

"You should watch how you talk," hissed Opimius. "You're still under oath."

Vibulus heeded the warning. The consul held life and death in his hands without appeal as long as the men were under military oath. Any whiff of sedition and he could execute the suspects without trial. "The point is, Publius," said Vibulus, modifying his tone, "there is plenty of public land. Or at least enough, if the patricians would just allow equal access to it."

"Is there some law limiting the use of public land?" asked Marcus with concern. As a relatively new citizen of Rome he had no desire to run afoul of the law out of ignorance.

"None," said Opimius.

"That we know of," said Vibulus. "But even so, in practice that is most certainly the case."

"There might be isolated abuses," conceded Opimius.

"Wide spread," said Vibulus.

"Well," said Marcus, sheathing his sword in a leather scabbard. "You two work it out. I'm going to bathe and get ready for tomorrow."

Passing under the Sister's Beam, Marcus found, was more than symbolic. They entered the city on the Via Albana following the shallow stream up the Murcia Valley, green with fresh sown winter wheat. In solemn order they passed the cone shaped tomb of the Horatii, then triangular Lake Camenarus. At the east end of the Circus Maximus they made a sharp right turn onto the Vicus Cyprius and passed through the portal in the earth rampart between the Palatine and Caelian hills. Here, where volcanic flagstones paved the road, their hobnailed boots rang with martial ardor as they crossed the Via Sacra and passed behind the small hill of the Velia. Marcus imitated his comrades and covered his head with his cloak as he passed under a rough-hewn 6x6 beam stretched across the road. Like a mist burned away by the morning sun the killing, maiming, and destruction evaporated, discipline disintegrated, and before they reached the forum they were no longer an army. Marcus turned right at the Vicus Suburanus and left the city on the Via Labicana.

+ + +

Marcus Tempanius, while suffering many misfortunes in his childhood, had nonetheless been blessed by his ancestors. He lost his mother soon after his birth. An only child raised on the milk of other women he received an independent spirit and a strong physical constitution. His father had been a willful man of strict habits and expectations who honored the gods fastidiously and worked his farm assiduously. To his son he devoted time for his education that he might not be ignorant in the knowledge of reading, writing, and mathematics, nor weak in self-defense and the rigors of war. He considered every day advantageous for the education of his son, be it preparation of the soil for planting, or calculating weights and measures on market days. He was unable to complete his son's education, however, being killed at the hands of an Aequian raiding party soon after Marcus' fifteenth birthday. Survival left in his own hands, Marcus had little time for grief, and set about working his inheritance as his father had taught him.

This inheritance consisted of five iugera of land, a small stone cottage, two oxen, three goats, one of which was male, a sow, and assorted chickens. About average in size the property fell under the covetous eye of an uncle who had been appointed his guardian, since Marcus had yet to take the toga virilis of adulthood. Here the tenacious independence he had suckled at the breasts of ever-changing nursemaids proved stronger than his uncle's persuasive temptations, and he kept his inheritance firmly in his grip.

It was to this little plot of fertile land that he marched when his season of service ended. One by one, walking companions turned off on small, unimproved lanes to their own farms until Marcus climbed the high knoll on the outskirts of Roman territory alone.

The first to greet him were the dogs, one a large dirty white shaggy male with a benign and quiet temperament, the other a sleek female with lissotrichous short fur of a murky color and impetuous temperament. Faustulus, shaggy coat fanning with the breeze, came unhurriedly on while Tibia leaped and nipped at him all the way down the lane. He petted them affectionately, giving each a hearty scratch behind the ears, then finished his walk between the poplar and elm trees that lined the drive.

At the door of the house his wife Drusilla waited, their son Lucius clinging for balance to her plain brown stola. In her hand was a terracotta cup with ear-shaped handles on either side.

"Hail husband," she said as he approached. Full lips and substantial mouth smiled invitingly. Her ink black hair was pulled back and held up with a simple bronze comb.

"Hail Drusilla," he said, the beginnings of a grin on his long dour face. Lucius tottered out to him with hands upraised and Marcus swung him up to look him in the eye. Lucius gazed back unwaveringly, baby teeth grinning with delight.

"We're glad to have you home," said Drusilla, her voice singing in his ears.

"I'm glad to be home," he said. Under black swallow-wing eyebrows her large almost oriental shaped eyes looked him up and down, inspecting him with a mixture of hunger and worry. "I'm fine," he said, a satisfied smile opening his small mouth beneath a large drooping nose. He took the proffered cup from her hands and stepped through the doorway. He poured a milk libation on the small wooden altar to the household gods, the *lares*, just to the left as he entered the one room house. What could possibly change in a room twenty feet by twenty feet he couldn't have said, yet he stood looking to see if everything were still in its place. That didn't amount to much. The furniture consisted of two wood frame beds with straw mattresses, and a cabinet that separated them against the wall on the right. In the center of the room just enough space for a table and a loom remained. On the left wall were storage cabinets and the cooking hearth on which a pot of porridge bubbled. A garland of laurel made in honor of the kalends, the first day of the month, hung over the hearth.

"I've prepared something for you to eat," Drusilla offered.

Marcus Tempanius, twenty-three years old and just returned from months of hardship and deprivation, should have been hungry. But he had no appetite for food. He put Lucius outside to play with the dogs.

Time was short. The calendar, though not full, still contained obligatory days of religious observance. Golden wheat swaying in hairy ripe clusters, and a garden overgrown with beans, peas, cabbage, asparagus, and chard cried out for his attention. They rose with the sun, sacrificed cakes and milk to Jupiter, Janus, Juno, and Ceres goddess of grain, and set to work. As he slashed at fistfuls of wheat with the curved edge of a scythe he realized his friend Opimius had been right about one thing, he would not be able to work any additional land by himself even if it were contiguous. With each swing of the scythe the thought that he would have to pay someone drove doubt into his mind about purchasing more land. He saw the fruits of his labor flowing out of the storehouse like sweat from his pores. Yet how could he provide a decent future for his progeny if not by enlarging their inheritance? As he labored, stopping only long enough to straighten his back and eat some unleavened bread at midday, the land he wanted lay before his eyes in weeds and wild flowers---going to waste.

For days on end they labored without ceasing, falling exhausted into bed, sleeping like stones. By the Ides (marking the full moon or middle of the month), Marcus had firmly resolved to try to purchase the land surrounding his. The acquisition would double his holdings, and if Juno made the children live there would be plenty of hands to work it in the future.

Bathed and dressed in their finest clothes, with a prayer and sacrifice to Janus to bless this beginning of a new venture, they yoked the oxen to a two-wheeled cart and headed for Rome and the celebration of the October Horse.

Accommodations were difficult to find with the city bursting with excited people, but they finally found a room at a tavern in the Subura district, not exactly the best part of town. Revelers made merry long into the night. Shouted conversations, loud laughter, raucous scuffling and raunchy bantering echoed in the narrow alleyways.

At first light Rome's inhabitants migrated toward the Forum. Marcus and Drusilla joined the cavalcade of people flowing onto the main arteries from the small streets and alleys where they lived. On the Vicus Suburanus they followed the Cloaca Maxima, the open sewer that drained the low-lying areas north of the Forum, and in times past the Forum itself. Marcus sauntered next to Drusilla, secretly pleased at the stolen glances he caught other men casting at her. Dressed properly in a light colored stola that fell in graceful pleats to her feet, exposing only her toes in open sandals, she garnered plenty of attention. Over the stola she had wrapped like a shawl a pale blue mantle, or palla, that modestly covered her head. Hidden beneath the palla her jet-black hair, woven into eight thick braids, each two of which were bound together, cascaded down her neck. Despite the modesty of her dress her voluptuous figure sent ripples of sensuality through her clothes with every movement.

Marcus walked beside her in open sandals, and light brown toga under which he wore a woolen tunic. His black curly hair had been cut to the top of his ears and his flat cheeks freshly shaved. He thought they made a handsome couple.

Observing Lucius, swinging from their hands between them, one would not have thought him to be their child. He had neither his mother's high cheekbones, nor his father's long thin face. Rather, he had a large, round head and a face full of merriment. His child's short-legged body already showed signs of power under the purple-bordered tunic of childhood.

"Papa," Lucius said, picking his legs up and suspending himself from his parents' hands. "I jumping." He slapped his feet down on the street like a long jumper.

"Very good, my life," said Drusilla.

Lucius laughed. "Girls non't jump," he challenged.

"And why not?"

"'Cause, Mama…"

"Don't call your mother, Mama," Marcus admonished. "You call her Domina." He looked sternly at Lucius, who stared back stubbornly.

"It's all right…" began Drusilla, her large dark eyes reflecting softly with concern.

"No, it's not," insisted Marcus. "My sons will show respect to their mother."

Lucius tugged at his mother's hand and pulled her down close, stopping their progress. Lucius tugged again, pulling his mother's face down to his. "I love you, Mama," he whispered loudly.

Drusilla laughed a river of delight and swept him into her arms, kissing both his cheeks. Marcus turned away in resignation, a warm smile secretly spreading in his heart. There could be no greater difficulty than raising a boy in the stern necessities of Roman life in direct opposition to the love and adoration of his mother.

Nearby, gray blocks of squared stone were piled in readiness for the pedestal of the new Temple of Castor and Pollux. "This looks like as good a place as any," he said, indicating the blocks of stone. They sat, waiting for the parade to begin.

Situated at the southeast corner of the Forum Romanum the Temple of Castor and Pollux, the twin gods who helped the Romans defeat the combined forces of the Latins, had been vowed by Aulus Postumius at the battle of Lake Regillus. Marcus felt acutely aware of his ironic status sitting on those holy stones, a Roman now, an enemy then.

The Forum steadily filled with citizens and visitors alike. They flowed expectantly around the sacred olive trees that divided the Forum into northern and southern halves. With women and children mixed in, the atmosphere became truly festive and colorful. Most of the men wore the more relaxed tunic, eschewing the toga as too cumbersome and uncomfortable. Still, it was the women who provided color, with stolas of blue, yellow, or red, while the men's clothes ranged from off-white to dull brown. Marcus changed his mind.

"Let's see if we can find another spot," he said.

He led them through the milling crowd up the south side of the Forum, past the Temple of Saturn, and took a left on the Vicus Iugarius that ran below the Capitoline Hill. Passing through the Porta Carmentalis they came out on the Forum Boarium that smelled of the animals daily bought and sold there---some on the hoof, some butchered. Where the road curved past the mossy squared stones of the ancient Temple of Fortuna in the shadows of the Tarpeian Rock they found a place from which to watch the parade. Behind them Tiber Island floated in the turgid green river like a barge at anchor. In front of them, scrunched between the Peteline Wood and the back side of the Capitoline Hill, the Flaminian Meadow, newly adorned with temporary wooden bleachers, waited like a flower bedecked bride for the people.

The parade began at the Capitol led by the two newly elected consuls, Appius Claudius, and Publius Servilius in magnificently caparisoned two-horse chariots called bigae. The broad purple borders on their togas, signifying the dignity of their office, flashed in the sun like wild flowers as their matched pairs of stallions, two white, two black, high-stepped down the Clivus Capitolinus into the Forum. Behind them came all the youths of Rome who would turn seventeen within the next two years. Next came the sacred pipers playing nonstop along with lyre players and other musicians. Following them dancers, dressed like warriors in red tunics belted with brightly colored sashes, lunged and slashed, imitating the movements of battle to the rhythm and beat of the pipes, lyres, and drums. On their high-kicking heels came the colleges of priests, led by the Pontifex Maximus, the Rex Sacrorum, and the Flamen Dialis, the priest of Jupiter Best and Greatest. Stately and solemn in their saffron colored robes, the augurs--readers of entrails--brought the silence of awe to the people as they passed. Then, as if in counterpoint, a stupendous roar rent the air as four teams of chariots pranced by in splendid array. Each biga, sleek with womanly curves and guided by the deft hands of its charioteer, elicited cheers from the highly partisan crowd. The charioteers were dressed in short tunics belted by leather straps wound from waist to chest, leather leggings, and leather caps with cheek pieces tied under the chin. Each wore a different colored tunic, white, red, green or blue, and throughout the city bets had been laid with religious fervor on the outcome of the race. Wrapped in perilous heroism like the reins around their waists, they waved to the multitude with the slightest tilt of the whip in their right hands.

Lucius clapped his pudgy hands in glee from atop his father's shoulders. "Look," he cried. "Those mens."

Marcus thought they were magnificent also. Astride their sensuously shaped chariots they held back their straining chargers with confidence and poise beneath the sun that poured in golden streams over their brightly colored livery. Brushed to a brilliant sheen the horses flashed like lightning bolts, and the power of the wind rippled in every twitch of muscle.

They followed the final team to the course on the Flaminian Meadow where spears driven into the ground at either end marked the turns. Along with thousands of spectators the Tempanius family found seats and watched the chariots circle the track with stately magnificence. As the charioteers gave their teams a look at the track, acclimating the horses to the sounds and the view, spectators tossed pieces of terracotta inscribed with prayers or curses. Beneficial or injurious enchantments rained down from the stands onto the temporary track in hopes of bringing victory or defeat to the chosen teams.

The track was laid out in a roughly north-south direction so that the sun, now well up, would be no factor as the teams made their left turns. Marcus found a spot half way up and near the middle of the west grandstands. Across the way the stands reserved for senators and their families filled with color. Drusilla eyed the wives dressed in the finest linen dyed in blues and greens, the richest reds and yellows, their hair, arms, and fingers flashing and glittering with precious jewels and metals, as they gesticulated grandly, pointing out this or that person or point of interest. Like flowers they reflected the light and gave it even greater glory. What their lives must be like, she speculated enviously.

All around him conversations rose and fell like whitecaps on a sea of noise, but Marcus had his whole attention on the charioteers and their wonderful horses. He missed the rude jokes, the latest gossip, and even the knowledgeable comments on the horses and drivers. Instead, his eyes fixed on the arched necks, and the rolling angry eyes of the horses as handlers guided them into makeshift starting gates at the north end. He thought it strange how much these animals wanted to run, yet pranced sideways, chafing at the force that made them do so with slaps and jerks, and angry words.

While he watched, Gaius Opimius and Aulus Vibulus shouldered their families into position nearby and sat next to him.  Lucius looked wide-eyed at Aulus and bruited an observation to the assembly of people as the men exchanged greetings.

"Him tall, Papa," he said.

"Yes," laughed Opimius, "and it makes his head light so he's always dizzy."

"Why?"

"You always start conversations you can't finish, Gaius," Vibulus said.

"It must have something to do with the company I keep."

"Absolutely," laughed Vibulus, "they're too smart for you."

Opimius sneered, ignored the comment and turned to Marcus. "So," he said, "who did you bet on?"

"No one," Marcus replied. He immediately returned his attention to the horses.

"You must have bet on one of the colors," Opimius insisted.

"No. I never pay for expectations."

"We thought it wiser to put our money into land," Drusilla interjected.

"Ah, well, your husband's a cautious one, certainly."

"Except when it comes to battle," Vibulus said, leaning over to look past his friends. "He's more like a cornered badger then."

"Yes," Opimius agreed, "he acquitted himself well.  Didn't he tell you?"

"Not really," said Drusilla.  She didn't know whether to be thrilled or afraid.  She swelled with pride at her husband's bravery, but cringed with the fear he might be careless with his life.  "He said it was mostly raids.  Nothing very dangerous."

"Sometimes that's the most dangerous," said Vibulus.

Marcus, as if in a stupor, came alive to the conversation. "Enough," he said. "Quit trying to scare my wife with tall tales."

Vibulus, unrepentant and undeterred, went on. "There's less organization on raids. That leaves more chance for surprises."

"I wan' a soprise," Lucius insisted.

"We're not talking about those kind, my heart," Drusilla said, smiling and stroking his curly black hair.

"What kind of surprise would you like?" Opimius asked him.

"One of 'dose," said Lucius, pointing at the chariots neatly lined up awaiting the starting signal.

"Which do you like best?"

"Red."

"Ah. I think green will win."

"Red," insisted Lucius.

"There you go," Vibulus teased, shaking his equine head, "arguing with superior intelligence again."

The position on the starting line had been determined by pouring colored balls out of an urn into bowls marking the places. Green received the advantageous position on the inside. Next to him the white team, then red, then blue. Quiet suddenly hung over the spectators like the white cloth fluttering in the breeze with the hopes and fears of the bettors dangling from the consul Servilius' upraised hand. A tense silence, disturbed only by the impatient snorting and pawing of the horses, descended on the crowd as the consul suspended each individual's fate in his fingers. Then released it.

The chariots spurted from the starting gate with an exultant roar from the crowd as it screamed to life. Pulled at astonishing speed the chariots seemed like fragile wooden boxes tossed precariously by every bump. The reins wound round the charioteer's waists kept them from falling out the open back as they hurtled down the track. They reached the southern end in the order of the start, green, white, red, and blue, negotiating the tight left turn without mishap. Like the constancy of the sky above, the screaming exhortations and curses, the calls of unheard advice became like a vast silence in Marcus' ear as he focused on the race. The charioteers guided their powerful chargers now in, now out, surging forward, hanging back. Pounding down the track side by side two teams of horses strove against one another. Oblivious to the whip or the reins the horses, fiercely competitive, battled each other for the lead without encouragement as if the drivers scarcely mattered. Clods of dirt and grass, torn and shredded by the skidding wheels and sharp hooves, spewed into the air. Numerous lead changes occurred as the teams jockeyed for position for the finish. Intricate stratagems were employed to tire out the opponent while saving one's own team. Feigning a charge, swinging a little too wide in the turn, showing a false opening in hopes the opponent would whip up his team to extra effort only to expend it in abortive lunges.

The wooden egg marking the tenth lap fell and the race became violent. Blue slid wide through the north turn, lost precious time, and endured a humiliating chorus of boos as he fell to the rear. A white froth covered the horses' mouths, and their glossy coats shone with sweat. Four more excruciating laps were required of them. Wrapped perilously in the reins, knees bent, left foot thrust forward to the front of the *biga*, right foot splayed sideways for balance against the rope net that prevented their feet from sliding out the back, the drivers leaned hard against the reins and urged their steeds to a last ditch effort. Green pulled up behind white with the encouragement of the whip, while red moved up on the outside. A fearful excited glance backwards informed white of his danger and he flailed at his horses with the whip to gain space. One hoof striking the back of his chariot spelled imminent disaster. His horses' hooves pounding at the very edge of white's chariot, green reached back with his whip for one more burst of speed. With all his concentration focused on white inches away, sudden disaster caught him up as red crashed into him from the side, shattering his world. Green's chariot jumped into the air, hung suspended momentarily then crashed to the ground and splintered. Too late he reached for the knife tucked into the leather bands around his waist, and as his chariot disintegrated his horses dragged him through the wreckage, unable to disengage himself from his calamity.

"Capsized!" cried the spectators in joy, heartbreak, awe.

Red and white raced for the final turn abreast, white on the inside, red just off his wheel. White whipped wildly at his chargers as he eyed red intently. The matched roans of red, looking fresher, surged ahead by almost a length as they neared the turn. White tried to force him wide, but red's courage held, and at the last instant he dove inside to take the turn. Forced into too tight a turn white's biga flipped sideways. Horses, driver, and cart went down in a jumble of harness, splintered wood, and broken man-flesh. "Capsized," roared the crowd with delight as red trotted home the winner. Immediately officials ran to the downed drivers and carried their broken bodies from the field.

In a slow stately walk, right hand upraised to the accolades of the crowd, the victorious charioteer circled the track one more time. Victory lap completed the lathered horses were unhitched and separated. The right side horse followed the Flamen Martialis-the priest of Mars-with the docility of exhaustion, head hanging, to the altar of Mars.

At first Marcus didn't notice the commotion in the stands with his eyes fixed in fascination on the wonderful horses. Finally, his attention was pulled away by two lines of young men forming at either end of the racecourse. On the south end, red tunics bright and martial in the sun, young men from the wealthier class of society organized themselves. On the north end, wearing yellowed natural wool tunics, residents of the Subura district formed up in line two deep.

The short, strangled neighing of a horse shifted his eyes back to the temporary altar where the victorious horse now lay twitching with a javelin in its heart. A young patrician, the son of Appius Claudius, held aloft the tail dripping blood, and ran back into the city as fast as he could, to sprinkle the floor of the Regia, once the royal palace, now the home of the Pontifex Maximus. Moments later the horse's severed head was brought into the center of the field between the two groups.

21

Cakes of wheat, and a garland of flowers were placed upon the head, and once again the consul held high the white cloth and let it drop. With a shout the two sides charged for the head and a violent fight for its possession ensued. Marcus thought he should cheer for one side or the other, but he didn't know which. He tried to take his clue from Vibulus and Opimius, but found they were on different sides, Aulus for the Subura district, and Gaius for the Palatine. He laughed at himself, decided he didn't have to choose a side, and instead enjoyed the spectacle of the melee. A helpless sadness for the horse lingered in his heart as the Palatine won possession of its head. The next time he saw it, it would be mounted on the Regia. Mounted as a harbinger.

# III

October 19, 495BC

## The Armilustrium

Marcus Tempanius shivered in the predawn cold of an October morning. He shivered, not from the cold, but from a fear greater than any he had ever felt before battle. Shuffling his feet nervously, he yawned widely before the door of the great Scipio home, glancing furtively at the other men gathered there. Some sought favors, others their daily bread. He had been first to arrive, and for that he felt good. It showed the ultimate respect and the head of the Cornelian clan would not be too tired to be benevolent. Or so he hoped. He greatly needed Publius Scipio's help.

To his relief the sky finally began to lighten and the first hour of the day approached. He did his best to make himself presentable—slapping the dust from his beige toga, smoothing his curly hair with callused hands. He checked his clean-shaven chin and hoped the irritation didn't make him look ridiculous. Still, nothing happened. Would Scipio wait until the second hour before seeing anyone? The unbearable thought paralyzed his brain. He pretended to be cold and paced in front of the door, mindful not to let anyone snatch his place in line. Some fifty anxious faces had gathered, nearly all of them clients of the Scipios. Including Marcus Tempanius. For Publius Cornelius Scipio had been instrumental in making him a citizen instead of a slave after the battle of Lake Regillus. Marcus put a scowl on his face as if angry at the inconvenience of waiting now that daylight had come. After all, his dour face declared, he had important work to do as well.

He was attempting to glower even more darkly when the latch on the door slid free with a snap. He jumped in surprise. A snicker of suppressed nervous laughter rippled through the assembled ranks. Marcus flushed hotly in indignation.

"Whom shall I announce to Publius Cornelius Scipio?" asked the doorman archly.

Marcus drew himself up to his full five feet seven inches and cleared his throat. "You may tell Publius Scipio that Marcus Tempanius has come to see him on urgent business."

While he waited, Marcus silently rehearsed the speech he would make to Scipio. Before he could complete it, the doorman returned and ushered him into the presence of the man himself.

"Good morning, Marcus. How are you?"

Marcus Tempanius spluttered, coughed, and cleared his throat. The sight of Publius Scipio did not awe him. His small thin face and pointed chin surmounted by a bulbous bald head inclined in expectation. Slightly taller than Marcus the taut, smooth skin of his tanned face and his economical build belied the forty-six years that flowered in penetrating dark eyes. Marcus choked on the magnificence of the house, and the importance of his mission.

"I am well, thank you. And you?" The reception room, or tablinum, could have held Marcus' house with room to spare. Brightly colored frescoes covered the walls depicting battle scenes that Marcus assumed held historical significance to the family's history.

"I'm well, thank you. And how is your family?" His solicitous brown eyes posed the same question sincerely.

"They are well. My wife is a bit weak. She thought she was to have another baby but..." Marcus shrugged his powerful shoulders beneath the toga.

"I'm sorry to hear that," said Scipio, opening his hands in a gesture of sympathy.

"Thank you. It's a small matter really. We'll have others."

"Of course. But even so, it is especially hard on the women. They have such hopes; do they not?"

"True," said Marcus with a small smile.

"Now," said Publius Scipio, ending the pleasantries, "please allow me to be of some help. If I may."

Now that the time had come to make his pitch, Marcus could not think of a single word he had rehearsed. He stalled, clearing his throat, coughing. Scipio looked on solicitously.

"It's a small matter, really," he said, forging ahead and hoping his brain would catch up with his mouth. "I wouldn't bother you with it, but my wife insisted I seek your help. And in her present condition..." his voice trailed off, and he suddenly felt he'd committed a terrible gaff—appearing at once uxorious and inconvenienced by having come to ask for help. "Forgive me, Publius, I didn't mean to sound ungrateful. What I mean is, I know you're busy with many important matters, and I'm sure mine will seem trivial in contrast."

"Fulvius," Scipio said, indicating his secretary, "said it was 'urgent'."

"Well, of course, for me it is urgent."

"Speak to me."

"I would like to purchase another five iugera of land next to mine. But it's owned by one Quintus Caprollius who seems interested in selling only to someone of patrician stock. I suppose to gain influence in some way."

"I see. And so you've come to me."

"I thought that if you...sponsored me, the weight of your ancient and storied name might induce him to sell me the land." Marcus ran a sweaty right hand through the black ringlets atop his head and cursed the toga that imprisoned his left.

"What would you like me to do?"

"If possible, perhaps you could write me a letter of introduction." He indicated the secretary with a nod of his head, who as a slave would perform such menial though necessary tasks. Unconsciously he scrubbed the red tiled floor with the toe of one sandal.

"Listen, Marcus," Scipio said, slapping his hands on his knees and leaning forward. "I think a letter would have a very small impact in this case."

Marcus Tempanius' hopes fell like sawdust, and he saw his dreams scatter in the wind. He felt like a man condemned and dreaded explaining his failure to his wife.

"What you need," continued Scipio, "is a personal introduction. In fact," a note of anticipation filled his voice, "what you need is someone to negotiate for you."

The heart of Marcus Tempanius leapt like a stallion spurred toward the enemy. He nearly cried for joy.

"I know this Quintus Caprollius," continued Scipio. "He is a grasping conniver of the worst sort. He made his money buying and selling merchandise from the Greeks and the Carthaginians. So now," he spoke more to himself than to Marcus, "he thinks to make a fortune buying and selling land." Scipio looked intently at Marcus already seeing the confrontation in his mind. "Have you any bronze?"

"Yes," said Marcus, hurriedly fumbling with the folds of his toga for the leather purse around his waist. "Ten asses," he said.

Scipio waved his hand. "No need to show me." He paused a moment more, resting his chin in his hand. "Come back about the sixth hour. Fulvius, make a note. We'll go visit Caprollius together. In fact, Fulvius, send someone with a note to Quintus Caprollius and inform him of our desire to pay him a visit." Fulvius scribbled quickly on a wax tablet.

"How can I ever repay you?" gushed Marcus.

"It's nothing," said Scipio with a dismissive wave. "Perhaps someday you will be able to perform a favor for me. Now, if there is nothing else I must see to my other guests."

The day dragged without mercy. A beautiful day of warmth and sunshine he could not enjoy. He searched the Forum restlessly for nothing, and tried not to spend his precious money. It would have been easy to head for the Subura where there were taverns and cheap women, but he needed every uncia so he denied himself. The temptations of Rome were many, and sweet. He envied those who could partake of them. Like Scipio, though he was said to be austere and disciplined. A cold shiver of excitement raised goose bumps over his flesh as he thought of the honor of Publius Scipio personally helping him. Of course, his help did not come without a price.

Thinking it couldn't hurt to have the assistance of the gods as well as the Scipios, he wandered over to the foot of the Argiletum to the temple of Janus, god of beginnings and openings. He bought some incense from a vendor outside, and paid a small admission price to enter the temple. Passing through the brick faced wood columns of the portico and into the sanctuary he came face to double-face with the terracotta statue of Janus standing with hand outstretched, two faces looking in both directions at once. He crept close to the statue elevated imposingly on a stone pedestal inscribed with sacred words, and lit the incense. With palms upraised he whispered a prayer for success of this new enterprise, asking the god's blessing and protection, then exited in the same stealthy manner in which he entered.

Outside he found a bench in the shade of a tree on the side of the temple. Casually watching customers going in and out of shops specializing in shoes, sandals, slippers, flax, wool, pillows, and a host of luxurious items for which the Argiletum was renowned, he idly considered the cost of products in relation to the land he hoped to buy. His conjectures led him directly to the cost of Publius Scipio's help. He tried to imagine what Scipio might demand of him in the future. Would he run for consul at the next elections? And how could he, Marcus Tempanius, a man of no influence be of help? He doubted he could persuade anyone in his tribe or his century to vote one way or another. Perhaps Scipio would require him to be part of the retinue that accompanied him to the Forum. But that would be nothing new. He performed that duty often when in Rome.

As he ruminated the sun approached its zenith, the sixth hour, time for him to return to Scipio's home. He entered the Forum from behind the Curia on the northwest end, crossed diagonally past the roundly fecund temple of Vesta where the vestal virgins tended the city's eternal hearth fire, and crossed to the Vicus Tuscus. At the statue of the Etruscan god Volturnus in the Etruscan quarter he turned west and followed a small street to the Scipio abode behind the shops on the south side of the Forum. This time Fulvius ushered him in only as far as the atrium. Sunlight poured through the rectangular opening in the tiled roof, splashed into the impluvium, and spilled out onto the stone floor. Closed doors to the rooms that lined both sides hid the family from prying eyes. At the far end the doors to the tablinum where Scipio had received him previously were also closed. Marcus waited, assuming Scipio would come from his private rooms at the rear.

When he came out Scipio greeted Marcus warmly, and they left the house together, followed by two slaves. Marcus started to fall in behind him, but Scipio shook his head vigorously and waved him forward to walk on his right side.

"No, no," he said. "We must show a united front to our friend, Quintus. How else is he to know that we have come together?"

At first Marcus walked timidly next to his illustrious patron as they descended the Palatine and stepped onto the Via Sacra and turned right. By the time they ascended the Caelian Hill he assumed his normal stride and upright posture, proud to belong next to Publius Scipio.

Quintus Caprollius lived in a fashionable house near the grove of old oak trees on the eastern prominence of the Caelian. Plain heavy oak doors opened to admit them to an atrium of elegant simplicity. Marcus admired the floor tiles, alternating squares of midnight blue and white. The opening in the roof was supported in Greek style with four graceful columns that seemed to buttress the sky itself, a marvel that Marcus had never seen. Casting a quick glance at Scipio he saw the house made an impression on him as well, though he detected disapprobation as well as appreciation in the observant brown eyes of his patron. The unadorned walls were painted white, cheerfully brightening the inside as if they were under open skies.

Caprollius did not wait for them in the tablinum as he would have done if Marcus had come alone. Instead, he hurried across the atrium as they entered and greeted them effusively.

"Publius Scipio," he said, in a voice unpleasantly hoarse. "It's an honor to have you in my home." He turned to Marcus. "And Marcus Tempanius, how nice of you to come by."

Marcus shifted his feet and bumped into a finely carved wood altar to the household lares of the Caprollius family. He turned to look at it, thought that might be rude, and turned back. Though physically superior to both men, he felt painfully inferior. To overcome the feeling, he decided to analyze Caprollius.

Caprollius stood about the same height as Scipio, but with fleshy jowls, and a luxurious paunch that spoke of soft food, and softer living. His graying hair grew in thick coarse curls. His toga was of the finest wool and appeared to have been whitened, though not as to imply his candidacy for office.

Quintus Caprollius lived in limbo. Wealthy, a member of the class of equites, his family was neither patrician nor common. As an equite he or his sons served in the cavalry, and were provided a horse at the public expense. A source of great pride, it still rang hollow due to the inability to gain the highest offices of state. To make matters worse, his fortune had been made by buying and selling imported goods from Greece, Carthage, and Etruria. Only later had he purchased land and become a respectable Roman.

"Come," Caprollius said, "let us retire to the garden. It is so much more conducive to pleasant conversation."

From the atrium they skirted the tablinum, and passed through the private quarters. To either side were bedrooms, a study, and the kitchen off in a far corner to the right with a bath next to it. Straight ahead they passed through a door and into a walled garden. Marcus had been unable to keep his eyes to himself, feasting on the wealth that surrounded him. His imagination flamed with visions of himself living in like sumptuousness, then immediately recognized the desire as transitory. A persimmon tree and a pomegranate tree were the centerpieces of the peristyle, around which were planted varieties of flowers and herbs. Stone pathways woven throughout provided convenient access for both maintenance and enjoyment. They sat on an L-shaped tufa stone bench under the persimmon tree.

Two female slaves entered, one bore a tray of fruits and nuts while the other opened a bronze tripod with lion paw feet on which the tray was set. On the tray an array of apples, figs, shelled pine nuts, roasted chestnuts, large green grapes, and smaller purple grapes demanded their attention.

Caprollius inspected the persimmons on a few of the lower branches and pronounced his verdict. "Not quite ready yet," he said. "Another week or two. Shall I send a basket to you when they're ripe?" he offered Scipio.

"That's very kind of you." Scipio looked around the garden briefly. "This is a very pleasant space."

"Thank you. It is a nice place to relax after the rigors of the day. Please," he said, indicating the tray, "help yourselves."

Marcus scrutinized Caprollius with further diligence, unsure of when the moment for him to speak would come. He noticed that Caprollius had a squashed face, as if a sculptor had not liked his work and pushed it in disgustedly, then fired it out of spite. The nose was distinctly not Roman—short and pugnacious. His close, dark eyes protruded avariciously, and Marcus thought he saw a flicker of doubt flash on the lusting surface now and then. When he spoke in that strangled voice, the small beard on his chin waggled like a hand shooing flies.

Silently sampling the delicacies, Marcus felt the time drip by like water in a Greek water clock he had once seen in a shop near the docks along the Tiber. Why anyone's day should be measured out in tedious drips he could not understand.

"Well then," Caprollius finally said. "How may I be of service to you?"

Scipio took Marcus' large callused hand in his own and patted it affectionately. A glimmer of surprise swept his eyes, and he glanced quickly down at the rough texture of the skin. "I have come with my good friend, Marcus, to introduce him to you. He has expressed a desire to purchase a piece of property you have for sale."

Caprollius shot an appraising glance at Marcus, seeking in his mind for a connection. These two vastly different men, one a patrician of ancient lineage, the other a commoner, a rustic bumpkin, could not possibly be friends. He recognized the relationship for what it was—a powerful man extending his help to a client. He wondered what interest Scipio could have in the transaction.

"And you have an interest in the same parcel?" he asked, forcing suspicion out of his voice.

"Ah!" exclaimed Scipio, slapping his thigh with his free right hand. "I see you have misunderstood. Let me explain my position. Marcus over the years has performed many unselfish services for my family and me. Out of respect for our mutual ties he sought my advice."

"I see. He is a man of great fides." Caprollius nodded slightly towards Marcus.

"Indeed," Scipio said, as he peeled a chestnut. "He has proven his faithfulness to family, friends, and gods on many occasions. It is only because of his excellent character that I am here."

Marcus listened carefully for the moment when he should speak. That moment had yet to arrive, and he felt a trifle nervous about it. He picked at the food to busy his hand, which he feared would otherwise flutter inanely like a butterfly. It seemed like they'd been there half the day and the hot, heavy toga wearied him. He cursed himself for wearing a tunic underneath it, adding to his discomfort. He shifted on the bench and looked up to check the sun's position. Still high, it had begun its westward arc, turning the sky so pale it appeared translucent. He silently thanked Caprollius for the shade of the unripe persimmons.

This seemed like an auspicious moment to say something, so as not to appear a complete oaf, so Marcus cleared his throat as if embarrassed by Scipio's accolades.

"Publius Scipio does me great honor," he said. "But in reality I have only done my duty as any Roman would."

"You are too modest, Marcus," said Scipio. "Listen, Quintus, I want you to do me a personal favor."

"Anything within my power." Caprollius peeled an apple with a delicate bone handled knife. "These apples are excellent," he said. "You must try one."

Scipio acknowledged the offer with a faint smile and discreet nod of his bulb shaped head, but did not partake. "As I have said, Marcus is an important and loyal asset to the Scipio family, and I want to ensure that he has every advantage in life that is within my power to arrange. Since I know you to also be an honorable man, it was my intention to bring the two of you together so that you might dispose of your property for a fair price, and my trusted friend might extend his modest holdings to provide better for his family."

"Well then," said Caprollius, "let's see what we can do. May I offer you refreshments? Wine? Water?"

The magnitude of the moment suddenly fell on Marcus like a cartload of roofing tiles. He knew that to both of these men ten iugera of land was a trifling amount. To him it offered a potential for prosperity his ancestors could never have dreamed of.

"Wine for me," he said, suddenly desperate for a drink. He popped pine nuts nervously into his mouth. Scipio shot him a disapproving glance, and he restrained his anxiety.

A pitcher of chilled white wine magically appeared from the house, and Caprollius filled three modest bronze cups. The men saluted each other with raised cups then sipped the wine. It tasted bright, sweet, and clean with a hint of anise.

Amazed, Marcus said, "It tastes like water."

"I'll take that as a compliment," laughed Caprollius.

"It is delightful," agreed Scipio. "Where is it from?"

"I have a cousin in Gabii who has a vineyard. The area is overrun with fennel, so he makes use of it in some of his wines. This batch came out exceptionally well, I think."

Scipio took another small drink. "Well then," he said, smacking his lips appreciatively, "first let me ask how much you are asking for this property."

"I am asking twelve asses, which is very reasonable considering the quality of the land. But I believe Marcus is well aware of that." He smiled knowingly at Marcus without exposing any teeth. "Since we are neighbors."

"I understand the property adjoins Marcus', but I didn't know there was a house on it."

"Well, no, there's not…"

"Then the land is already cleared?"

"Well, no…not entirely."

Scipio gave Marcus a long intense look. "Do you still wish to pursue this? It will take mountains of work before the land is productive."

"I'm used to hard work," said Marcus, staunchly.

"The price is eminently fair," Scipio said, turning back to Caprollius, "if the land were ready for cultivation. Or even if it were a bit closer to Rome." He shrugged, raised his hands palms up to the sky, "but Marcus will have to spend the entire winter clearing it. Even at that, he will probably have to hire laborers. The risk is…large."

"Risk is always an element of investment; is it not?"

"Of course. But the risk should not outweigh the prospect of success or it becomes gambling. I know Marcus Tempanius to be a diligent man. But even the most assiduous of men can be overcome if the burden is too great. Perhaps you could lighten the burden."

"Naturally I am not out to profit at the expense of another's future. Perhaps I could let your client have it for ten asses."

Marcus nearly jumped up and grabbed Caprollius' hand to seal the bargain. But as if he could sense the swell of excitement, Scipio laid a restraining hand on Marcus' thick forearm.

"I'm sorry," Scipio said. "Perhaps we shouldn't have come. I had hoped you would understand my friend is not a wealthy man. Added to that the cost of labor, and the constant danger from Volscian and Aequian raiding parties…" He tossed his hands helplessly in the air. "I can not, in good conscience, let him pay this much." He started to rise.

"Rather than feeling my way in the dark," hastened Caprollius, "perhaps you could give me some idea of the price you have in mind."

Marcus breathed a silent sigh of relief, having seen his land come and go in a twinkling.

"I thought six asses would be fair remuneration."

Marcus watched the land slip through his fingers again. He would never have dreamed of beginning the negotiations at such a low price.

Caprollius fidgeted. "Publius Scipio," he began, "I do not wish to offend you. I have the utmost respect for you and the greatness of your family. But such an offer, you yourself must realize, is absurd. I may as well give the property to Marcus Tempanius. In these times any available land is at a premium. Were it anyone else I would be asking twice the amount. However, out of respect for you, and as a personal favor, I will sell it for nine asses."

In the silence that followed, the drone of a gigantic blue-black bottle fly as it honed in on the tray of fruit sounded like the shout of ten thousand voices. Marcus curbed his enthusiasm by reaching for a fig. For a moment the land was his again, but this rising and falling of emotions was as exhausting as walking the Tusculan hills around his farm. As he bit into the sweet chewy fig he realized that Scipio was looking expectantly at him. He turned his head in mid bite. "Well, Marcus, it seems you have a decision to make. Yes or no?"

"Yes!" said Marcus quickly, fearing one or both of them would change his mind before scales could be brought out and his bronze weighed against stones culled from the property he coveted.

Before witnesses Caprollius asked three times, "Whose land is this?"

"It's mine," exclaimed Marcus, and rang the scales with his piece of bronze.

# IV

In an ebullient mood Marcus Tempanius descended the Caelian Hill and took the Via Sacra back toward the Forum. He planned to find Aulus Vibulus who had offered to put him up for the night in his house on the Viminal Hill. Despite the cumbrous toga he stepped lightly, with a joyous bounce. He congratulated himself on his wisdom in seeking the help of his patron Publius Scipio as he passed the uneven rectangular portico of the Regia on the eastern edge of the Forum.

With a self-satisfied smile he took in the crowded, busy atmosphere of the great square. As the center of public life the flagstones of the Forum were always covered with sandal shod feet holding up gossips, rumormongers, candidates in chalk whitened togas, malcontents and beggars, social climbers and those who were simply sociable. Marcus enjoyed the afternoons in the city's main square far more than the mornings, which were given over to official business, trials, politics, and assemblies. The mornings could be interesting, even exciting, but seldom fun. In the afternoons, however, people gathered simply for the joy of talking, of expressing their common bond of community.

This day, as he picked his way through the throng of togas ranging from yellowed off-white to dark brown and women in stolas dyed in all the colors of the rainbow, he noticed a strange directness and urgency to the normally desultory conversations. A large knot of people gathered near the shops on the south side of the square attracted his attention, so he turned in that direction. He pushed his way into the crowd until he saw a bedraggled man in shabby tunic, shaggy, greasy hair and unkempt beard. A musty, decayed smell emanated from his emaciated figure.

"Who is he?" Marcus asked one of the bystanders.

"Publius Scroconius," the man answered. "At first I didn't recognize him, his appearance has changed so much," he added.

"You know him then."

"Certainly. He was once centurion in the legions. A brave man."

"Publius," someone called, "how have you come to be in such a state?"

Scroconius sniffed, wiped his large hooked nose with the back of a dirty hand. "Where to start," the old man moaned. "While I was on service against the Sabines they raided my farm, which was near the Anio River. They ruined my crops and burnt my house taking everything they could carry. Then they drove off all my livestock so that when I returned, I had nothing left." He scratched his bony scar-stitched ribcage with untrimmed nails. "Naturally I had to borrow to start over, so I went to Quintus Caprollius who loaned me seed, and tools…"

At the mention of Quintus Caprollius, Marcus' blood ran cold. He suddenly felt as if he were an accomplice to the debt bondage into which the old man had fallen. He was intensely relieved that he had not in fact bought the old man's farm, but that seemed a minor qualification. He looked down guiltily as the man went on to describe how, despite working day and night his crop yield had been insufficient to repay the debt, and he had fallen further and further behind, until Caprollius had him hauled off into bondage. Which state, he ended lamentably, was a slow form of execution.

Now it seemed as if everyone in the Forum had a friend who had fallen into the same condition, and like fire in desiccated grass sympathy and anger spread through the city. Suddenly the streets filled with people, even debtors in bondage took every opportunity to display their wounds, stripes, and fetters.

Crammed elbow to elbow with contentious citizens, Marcus felt claustrophobic and vulnerable. On his person he carried the bill of sale for the property he had just purchased, as well as what bronze he had left over. Any thief would find him an easy mark, he thought, and began to squeeze his way through the crush along the southern edge of the plaza.

He soon found himself back in front of the Regia ghoulishly confronted by the severed head of the horse from the chariot race a few days before. It struck him that a city that had just put away the weapons of war and should have been enjoying the respite of peace, suddenly verged on internal strife. All over the sight of one beggared man.

Rooted to the spot he stared at the deteriorating head as if to divine the answer in its fly encrusted eyes, blackened, swollen tongue, and nauseating stench of decay that stained the air. He reconstructed the events of the month to see if a clue to this present behavior lay hidden there. First, they had put aside violence and bloodshed by passing under the Sister's Beam, once more entering civilized society as citizens. They had further celebrated this transition by the festival of the October Horse, in which the ultimate beast of war had been sacrificed. On the nineteenth the weapons of war were purified at the Armilustrium, and the doors of the temple of Janus closed, officially bringing the season of war to an end. That had been two days ago. Now it seemed as if war were about to break out again, only this time not against a foreign foe. And maybe therein resided the clue; once foreign wars ended the Romans engaged in domestic political wars. Perhaps, as a relative newcomer to republican polity, it just took some getting used to on his part. But the nascent violence surging like a consuming flame left him uneasy.

Apprehension that events might get out of hand made him acutely aware of the restrictions a toga imposed on the human body. Wound from shoulders to feet in one large piece of wool, left hand gripping the loose end to keep the whole thing together, one had only his head and his right hand free. Self-defense was next to impossible. Jostled and bumped repeatedly by the thickening crowd he considered stripping to his tunic. Simultaneously, he entertained two other internal arguments in his confusion. He tugged uncomfortably at the wool crossing his shoulders and considered the argument that he should go home, work his land, and leave behind this fruitless strife. On the other hand, his future lay there in the Forum; to be ignorant was to be at someone else's mercy.

But he could not think in all that noise. The whole of Rome seemed to be emptying into the streets. Debtors poured out of houses decrying their virtual enslavement and lack of protection.  People swirled around him like ten thousand tops spun loose all at once.  Unable to resist the flow he followed the path of least resistance and found himself near the center of the Forum amongst a crowd of people listening to a speaker railing at them from a platform erected for the hearing of trials.  How he could have missed him before he didn't know, but he looked up to see Aulus Vibulus atop the tribunal.

"They call us citizens," he was saying, "then deprive us of our land.  While we spill our blood to extend their power we are left without the most basic protections."

Atop the dais Vibulus was like a giant, visible from every corner of the Forum.  A large gathering, clearly dominated by the poor stared up attentively to hear his words.  Most of the men wore patched and mended tunics, and what few togas there were appeared shabby, threadbare, and discolored.  Marcus felt self-conscious though he was by no means richly dressed.

"When did you become one of us, Legumenus?" a heckler cried.

Vibulus laughed heartily with genuine good humor.  "Perceptions are only reality in minds closed to truth," he said.

"What in Hades does that mean?" someone close by muttered.

"Those of us who work our farms with our own hands and risk our lives in the legions," Vibulus announced, "are but one misfortune away from sharing your fate.  This, my friends, is the truth of free Rome.  We work and fight so that others might reap the rewards.  You may perceive that my class has nothing in common with yours, but in truth, we have more in common with you than with our masters in the senate."

As Vibulus harangued the crowd the demographics began to change.  Marcus suddenly felt afraid of who might see him in this crowd and attempted to work his way out as more men in fine togas worked their way in.  His retreat was arrested when Appius Claudius, the consul, preceded by his twelve lictors bearing the rods of his authority, pushed his way up and onto the dais. A great crowd of clients followed, and the complexion of the multitude changed immediately. A thrum of menace hung in the air, and a murmur of concern passed through the crowd. Appius Claudius flushed red with anger, his oblong face set in hard flat lines. Aulus Vibulus was not intimidated.

"You see how it is," Vibulus proclaimed, indicating Claudius with his open right hand as the clients of the consul tried to shout him down. "Who will protect me now, and my rights as a citizen? This is the freedom and protection Rome offers her citizens; to be shunted aside like refuse by those who can command others to do their bidding."

Now Claudius took control of the dais. "Has our Republic so soon come to this?" he shouted. "That the urban mob, this mass of unwashed plebeians should demand immunity from the law? Which rights, exactly, do you require? The right to renege on your debts? The right to land the Roman state does not possess? Perhaps, in your minds, you have a right to other people's property. I say, the right of appeal was more than these plebeians deserved, and more they shall not have!"

A confused roar encompassed the crowd as various factions shouted at each other. Pushing and shoving moved through the crowd like cats fighting in a sack until Aulus Vibulus once again moved forward to speak.

"Appius Claudius calls us plebeians and expects us to take offense, or be cowed by such pejorative terms. But I, for one, will bear the name plebeian with pride. If we are unwashed it is only because we cannot afford the price of a bath. And if we are a mob, it is because that is our only form of protection from the arbitrary treatment of the wealthy. Do we ask to be freed from the laws of debt? Not at all. But it might be nice to have a trial before we're condemned to servitude. Appius Claudius calls us a mob, but which one of you moved to Rome with five thousand dependents and immediately commanded a seat among the ruling class as he did? Which one of you came to the Forum today with an army of clients to protect you? Wait! Wait!" cried Vibulus, holding his hand up like a spear for quiet. "Perhaps the difference is that we, the cursed plebs, are disorganized, while they," he pointed at Appius Claudius, "are as organized as the legions."

As he spoke the last few words Vibulus hurried off the dais, for Claudius obviously found his diatribe seditious, and would have had his lictors seize him. An aroused crowd formed around their new champion and prevented the lictors, despite the authority of the bundled rods they carried, from touching him. The word plebeian spread like oil on water, and soon everyone of the lowest property rating hailed his fellows with the satirical appellation of pleb. Vibulus was escorted by the mob, including Marcus Tempanius, to the Subura, ensconced himself in a tavern and promptly proceeded to get drunk for the sheer joy of his combat of words with Appius Claudius.

"What are you doing?" asked Marcus, incredulous.

"I'm enjoying myself. Why don't you join me?"

"Aren't you worried about tomorrow? Shouldn't you be preparing something?"

Vibulus shot Marcus a curious glance, a smile creasing the joy-flushed length of his equine face. "Tomorrow's another day. Today, I'm celebrating my victory against Appius Claudius in single combat." He clapped Marcus on the shoulder. "Postumus! Another glass for my good friend."

# V

## FEB. 22 & 23, 494BC
## Festivals of the Caristia and Terminalia

He used the excuse that he had no Roman family other than Drusilla and Lucius. Well aware that it was a mere technicality and only his own prejudice prevented him from celebrating the Caristia with family members from Tusculum, he nevertheless refused to change his mind.

"If it was up to them," he reminded Drusilla, "we wouldn't be sitting here now."

Drusilla arched her thick black eyebrows like a bird about to take wing, plucked a dried fig from a bowl and held it briefly in front of her full lips. "Isn't that the idea of the Caristia? To mend fences and rebuild family ties?"

"You and Lucius are all the family I need."

Lucius, seated at the end of the table, followed the conversation as if it were a ball being tossed back and forth on the field of Mars. At the ripe old age of two he considered himself grown up. Although most Roman children were weaned at three, he refused his mother's nipple and insisted on solid food. If he drank milk it came from a cup like his father.

"Jus' us, huh Papa," Lucius said sternly.

"Yes, Lucius. Just us."

"Oh yes," scolded Drusilla, "you're just as stubborn as your father."

"You don't seem to have suffered too much from it," Marcus said.

"No man should presume to understand the suffering of women."

"No man would need to if he remained unmarried."

"That's uncivilized."

"Nevertheless."

"Nevertheless," Drusilla mimicked. "It dishonors the gods to twist the meaning of things like this."

Marcus shoved his chair back angrily. "I am the head of this house. No woman shall presume to tell me how to honor the gods. If this much family is not good enough for you, we can talk to your father soon enough." He spun and slammed the door behind him.

"Mama? What's cibilibed?"

"Drink your milk, my heart."

The threat of returning her to her father held no authenticity, Drusilla knew. In the first place, theirs was not a loveless marriage. In the second, she was pregnant again, and Marcus would be loathe to give up his child. She picked up the dishes and put away the food, then puttered around to give Marcus time to cool off. On the other hand, she reasoned as she cleaned the cluttered confines of their constricted cottage, she could probably do better than this. She swept the dogs out of her way. They yawned, stretched laconically then lay back down only a foot from where they had been. Frustrated, she put a wooden sword in Lucius' hand and shoved child and dogs outside. Calmed by the solitude, Drusilla threw some charcoal onto the bronze brazier, then sat down and put her feet up on the wooden frame of the brazier to warm them. Outside unseasonably warm weather held out the false promise of spring. Inside the house the cob walls, persisting in unbelief, clung to the cold. Regardless, she endured the cold a while longer in anticipation of the right moment to make amends with her husband. In this as in other things nature endowed her with perfect timing. To have called it a sixth sense would have made her bristle indignantly, for there is nothing supernatural in knowledge. And it was this, the knowing, that gave her understanding of the timing of things.

She dropped her feet to the cold stone floor, pushed up from the chair, and smoothed the flowing folds of her stola. Grabbing a pitcher from the shelves by the hearth she stepped calmly outside. A bright sun showered warmth on her from a cobalt sky and she hesitated momentarily to soak it in. Birds chirped happily, and premature bees searched the dandelions already sprouting in brilliant yellow profusion. Two black flies coupled in flight buzzed past her face. "Thank you Juno for this sign of fertility," she said, quickly appropriating the event as a good omen. From below came the steady rhythmic sound of chopping, interspersed with the lighter thwack of imitation as Lucius attempted to chop down a tree with his wooden sword.

Inhaling the ripening smells of spring, vaguely tart with pine, Drusilla looked out over the Roman plain below their farm and felt a quiet contentment warm her as the sun had done. Within the warmth the knowledge grew that she also harbored false illusions of a better life. For the knowing inside told her that contentment was the treasure most sought after. That beside this, all the wealth and honors the world had to offer paled in glory as the moon compared to the sun. In the recognition of this she knew lay wisdom, but also luck. Because the knowing also told her that the life growing inside her might very well kill her. And in her wisdom she accepted the possibility as just and right. For life and death were a single thing, and only through one could the other exist. If then, at so young an age fate decreed she leave this life, she would go bearing her contentment like an amulet of honor.

Behind the house, shaded under a cool canopy of pines, a spring spilled forth sweet, cold water that quenched the thirst of the entire Tempanius farm. Drusilla knelt on the moist earth and filled her pitcher. Murmuring a blessing to Neptune for the spring from which their lives flowed she poured a small amount of water back into it as a libation.

Yet she lingered, picking daisies, sprung up in gay profusion, opening wide their tender white fingers to gather the sun to their golden center—which seemed to Drusilla an exact copy of the sun.

"It's too early for you, my children," she whispered, caressing her lips with the soft petals, and inhaling the sweet fragrance. With a look at herself in the smooth surface of the spring she placed the flowers in her hair, laughing self-consciously.

She made sure the wood stopper was tight in the oval jug she cradled in her arms. It had a single handle on the side and the mouth protruded at the point where the handle ended. The oxen eyed her closely, and the goats bleated at her as he walked by.

"I have nothing for you, selfish ones," she admonished. Reaching into the pen constructed of cane stalks tied closely together, she petted the soft black wool of the most earnest of the female goats. "Why don't you have twins and make us happy," she told the goat. The goat bleated plaintively, and Drusilla admitted she knew it was not the animal's fault.

The bitter odor of the manure pit close by kept her stay at the pen brief. She passed by the garden, blooming with confusion in the warm weather, traversed the wheat fields sown with legumes and clover for the winter, and exited the gate of the low stone wall that marked the perimeter of the original farmstead. A short descent took her to the flat crown of the second step of the new property.

Marcus, Lucius, and the dogs were down at the far end. Most of the trees had been cut and stacked as they cleared the land and a kiln built to make the wood into charcoal for the winter. Many stumps remained to be pulled, and wild grasses and thorny vines grew in thick tangles along the ground. The dogs suspended their operations in the dense underbrush and rushed up to greet Drusilla. Marcus and Lucius halted their exertions also, and waited for her arrival.

"Papa make me a biga," Lucius proclaimed, walking unsteadily towards her on short stocky legs.

Drusilla steadied him against her legs. "Ah," she said, smiling down at him. "And what color shall I make your tunic?"

"Red 'course," Lucius said.

Marcus, hair matted with sweat, his face scarlet from exertion, sank his axe into the trunk of an oak tree. "I didn't promise," he said. He rubbed one shoulder, and his biceps twitched and bulged, stretching the skin so tight Drusilla thought it must burst. His muscular physique seemed almost animal to her, like the oxen in the pen up above.

Holding out the jug of water to him she said, "I came to tell you I'm sorry."

He rinsed his mouth out and spat a stream of water onto the ground. "No need. I figured it was probably just your woman's time." Raising the pitcher again he took a long drink, and then knelt to help Lucius take one.

Lucius copied his father and inexpertly spit a mouthful of water down the front of his tunic, garnering a chuckle from his parents.

"Actually," said Drusilla, nonchalantly, "I haven't had one of those for over three months."

Marcus paused, suspending the jug in midair, and gazed at his wife with frank gray-ringed eyes. "Well," he said, "it's nearly the same thing." Pouring water into his hand for the dogs he looked up, a smile furrowed his planiform cheeks. "But it's a happy difference."

"I think so too. You have done well," she said, swiveling her head to view the cleared land. "At this rate it will be ready for planting in spring."

"If it weren't for all the interruptions. But tomorrow is the Terminalia—that's a complete day wasted."

"Yes," she agreed. "Still, it's a good thing to make friends with our neighbors. They'll be more willing to help if we need it."

"Nevertheless," he said, dismissing the practical nature of the boundary festival, "after that is the last nundinae of the month. I'll have to go to Rome for that. Then it's the new year and we'll have even less time to work." He ticked off coming events on his fingers. "There's the dance of the Salii, the Matronalia, Anna Perenna, the Equirria..."

"Well," Drusilla said, cutting him off, "we'll just have to do the best we can. At least you have help."

"Thank the gods for that."

The following day, the 23rd of February, they solemnly met their neighbors at the boundaries of their respective properties, sacrificed a young pig and some cakes to the boundary god

Terminus, then the three families sat down to a feast. Marcus also invited the two men he employed, Didius Crispus, and Petronius Tuscus, along with their families. He sought in this way to incorporate them symbolically into his own family in the hopes that he could procure their loyalty and constancy. In his guileless way he failed to realize that he had also created a clientele, albeit a tiny and loose one. So that it surprised him to be addressed in such terms when he left for Rome two days later.

"In the mouth of the wolf, Patronus," Didius said as he heaved a last basket of charcoal onto the wagon. The expression meant 'good luck'. A sliver of pale blue over the dark hulks of the mountains announced the coming of dawn as delinquent stars tarried in the heavens.

"But why do you call me that?" Marcus asked, climbing onto the wagon and adjusting his woolen cloak around him. Drusilla handed up a large basket containing his toga and food.

"Because that's what you are," said Petronius simply. From his callused hands he fed the ox that had drawn the duty of pulling Marcus to Rome. The ox nuzzled him like a pet each time his hands emptied of hay.

"There are certainly more worthy men than me to attach yourselves to," Marcus insisted. He patted the seat next to him and Tibia, the female dog, jumped up and leaned against him.

"Then we would have done so," said Petronius. He spoke in a voice deep as thunder and soothing as slow water.

"Certainly," agreed Didius. "And there are many men in Rome still seeking them out. Meanwhile you have made it possible to feed our families." Didius uncoiled a length of rope made from broom. His small hands were like dark knots connecting his sinewy rope-like arms to the cords with which he lashed and secured the baskets of charcoal in the bed of the cart.

"Truly," said Petronius, emphatically. He patted the ox's great white head, scratching the tight curls between the short horns, then moved around to the side. The ox swung her head to follow him but the yoke prevented her. Snorting her discontent she lowered her head to nibble at the grass at her feet.

Didius finished securing the load, brushed his simple sleeveless tunic with his hands and walked with springy steps to the side of the wagon. He was even shorter than Petronius, and thin as the cane that grew along the stream at the bottom of the hill. Both were closing in on thirty, but Petronius, almost bald, looked as if he'd passed it. His thick coal black beard grew uninterruptedly down his neck to his chest.

"Nevertheless," said Marcus, "you've cast a net of responsibility over me I didn't seek."

"Think nothing of it," said Didius with a crooked smile.

"Hmm. Well, if all goes well I'll see you in three days."

"Don't forget," said Petronius, "stress the idea of false spring. People will be more apt to pay your price for the charcoal if they fear it's going to get cold again."

Marcus shook the reins and the ox took her first disgruntled steps of the long walk to Rome. "Don't forget to pull the stumps at the south end," he called back over his shoulder.

In Rome he took lodgings at a tavern in the Subura district. The small stable in the back provided a warm place to bed his animals, after which he went to bed early…in the same stall as the ox. The better to keep a wary eye on his wagon and livestock. Tibia slept with her head across his ankles.

Before the sun could find its way through the maze of buildings into the stall where Marcus slept he found his way out. By the time it streaked the ground with its waking flames he had already set up his cart along the road where it curved around the Capitoline Hill and crossed the Flaminian Meadows. He found a stall for his ox in the Forum Boarium nearby.

"What's her name?" asked the stable master.

"Who?"

"Your ox."

"Regina. She thinks she's a queen."

"Doesn't she know kings and queens aren't accepted in Rome?"

"I threaten her with sacrifice daily, but she knows she's impure and pays no attention."

Across the Forum Boarium at the southwest end of the Circus Maximus workmen began to crawl over piles of bricks, hewn squares of stone, wooden beams, and barrels of nails as construction progressed on the temple of Ceres. Behind him the warehouses on the docks came to life as they were prepared to receive barges from Ostia, or opened to disgorge their contents from the previous day's shipments.

Marcus hurried to his cart prayerfully hoping the day would be cold. He hoped to sell charcoal for Rome's braziers that he, Petronius, and Didius had made from the trees they had fallen. Whether he received bronze or other goods he didn't much care as long as he could make use of it. He praised Tibia for staying put and watching the wagon.

The gods were not as faithful. The sky brightened to a polished blue and limpid as the spring behind his farmhouse. He praised himself for arriving early and procuring a good spot, for on either side a crush of carts and temporary stands spread out beneath the warming sun. He couldn't resist the temptation to bask in it with eyes closed.

"Oy, oy," he cried suddenly. His wandering mind jolted back to the present by a cartload of cabbages trying to park right in front of him. "Are you blind? I'm here already."

"Eh! There's space."

"There is not space. No one will see me behind this ugliness of yours."

"Bah! Who needs your faggots in this weather?"

"Did you ever hear of cooking your cabbage—or is that all that's between your ears?"

"You're an insulting one."

"I'll be more insulting if you don't move that cart." Reluctantly the cabbage seller moved farther west along the road. "Hercules! The gall of some people," Marcus said, turning to the leek vendor next to him.

"Old Titus? He's always late and always trying to sneak in front of someone. But he grows excellent cabbages."

"And how's the leek business?"

"Actually, with the shortage of wheat it's been quite good."

Which proved to be true as Marcus saw, for soon the man's wagon was surrounded with customers. Marcus' charcoal did not sell so well, yet he bawled out his prices and sales pitches, importuned passersby, and entered into the spirit of the market day with a certain joyous abandon. Out of the swirling sea of people suddenly appeared Aulus Vibulus, a head taller than everyone. His hooked beak of a nose glowed red, and Marcus felt pretty sure it wasn't from the sun.

"Hail, Marcus," Vibulus greeted him jovially.

"Well met, Legumenus. How are you?"

"Never better. Everything's exciting in Rome. Have you sold anything?"

"Some. It could be better."

"No wonder. Selling charcoal in this weather."

"What, does no one cook? And how long do you think this weather will last?"

"Well, Marcus, you know people live for the day. So how much have you made today?"

"Why?" Marcus narrowed his eyes.

"Just friendly concern," protested Vibulus. He chuckled, holding his hands up in surrender. "So suspicious."

"I've made one bronze as, a pair of shoes for Drusilla, a rope from Lucius Tunnius, and some pots and jars."

"Well then, not so bad." Vibulus stretched his long neck and looked around the market area. "You know," he said, perplexed, "I thought Gaius was right behind me."

"Don't you two ever work?"

"Well of course we do. But some days are just not made for it."

"And today…"

"Is one of them. Exactly. Marcus, you are a sad person. You just don't understand the true meaning of coming to Rome."

"Certainly in your view it's not to make a living."

"Of course commerce must go on. But there are many forms of commerce, of which this," he swept his arms across the temporary market, "is just a small part."

"Yes. Unfortunately for me it's the part that puts clothes on our backs, or seed to put food in our bellies."

"Ah, but it doesn't put fat on your bellies, and that," Vibulus punctuated the word with a long finger, "is where the real commerce is."

"Uh huh." Vibulus had lost him. "So where's the excitement today?"

"It's always in the Forum, Marcus. The Forum proper. Not here in the vegetable market where you while away your day." He swung around to point in the direction of the Forum Romanum, and nearly knocked a passerby down. "Today," he said, "the friends of our consuls in the senate are mediating an argument over which of them should dedicate the temple of Mercury."

"That's a ways off, isn't it?"

"They think to dedicate it on the ides of May. And of course there are a great many preparations to make."

"Of course."

A man in a ragged tunic cautiously approached. Thin as a vine his ears stuck out from his gaunt head like leaves. Marcus said nothing as he eyed the charcoal filled baskets.

"How much the basket?" he finally asked, exposing a mouthful of rotting teeth.

"An eighth of an as," said Marcus.

The man fingered a pouch inside his tunic. "Hmm, better to eat raw lentils than boiled water, I suppose," he muttered, and started to walk off.

"Here," said Marcus, pulling one of the baskets from his cart.

"No," said the man. "I can't pay and I won't take charity."

"It's not charity," Marcus said. "I expect you to pay when your fortunes change, or when you can do me a service."

"I accept your price." The thin old man extended his hand. "I am Faustus Ventriculo."

"Marcus Tempanius," said Marcus, taking the emaciated hand.

"I am in your debt."

"Yes."

As he walked away, legs bent and back arched under the burden, Aulus Vibulus gave Marcus a wizened look. "His fortunes will never change," he said.

"You think I was born last night?"

"Then why say you expect him to pay?"

"Because a beggar has no dignity and comes to hate those he begs from."

"Well, a philosopher. Just remember; no one is more hated than a creditor."

Just then Gaius Opimius plowed his way through the aimlessly wandering crowd. "Ah, you should have heard it Legumenus, bitter rancor between our consuls."

"So that's where you've been," said Vibulus.

"Yes. It's a regular festival of chest pounding in the curia."

"And who emerged victorious?"

"No one, they've postponed the decision."

"Our consuls and their advisors in a nutshell," said Vibulus.

"Hasn't the Aventine been traditionally the cult center for the commons?" Marcus asked.

"Plebeians," corrected Vibulus. "We're proud to be the mob."

"Fine. Just answer."

"Yes, exactly as you say."

"Then why is Appius Claudius so interested in dedicating a plebeian temple? Given his dislike for their class."

"Of course it's prestige," Vibulus said. "And it improves his image."

"From what I've heard that's not possible," said Marcus, chuckling.

"People always grouse," Opimius said. "It's human nature. Especially when times are a little hard."

"Times are a little hard for some," said Vibulus, "and something much worse for others."

"One's responsibilities don't end just because things become difficult," Opimius said.

"And which responsibilities would those be, Gaius?" demanded Vibulus. "To die for the glory of Appius Claudius and his yes-men in the senate?"

Gaius Opimius shook his block shaped head and laughed. Marcus thought he detected a note of menace in his laughter. "Have you ever seen anyone as negative as Legumenus?" he asked Marcus. "He never sees any good in anything."

"Of course, I knew it was my fault," Vibulus broke in.

"You two are driving my customers away," Marcus said. Their uncompromising arguments tired him out more than a day of work in the fields. "But thanks to you I think I know exactly what's going on in the senate."

"Oh, he's a sly one, Gaius," Vibulus chortled. "The country bumpkin is just an act."

Marcus bristled at the comment. "And what makes you so sophisticated? The fact you spend more time in Rome than on your farm?"

"Oh, a low blow," exclaimed Vibulus, showing the gap in his front teeth while Opimius laughed heartily. "However, duty calls, and I must be off to the Forum."

"Yes, to stir the rabble," Opimius said.

"No need, they're already stirred. The consuls and their henchmen have seen to that."

The two men began walking off together, still arguing.

"But why do you talk about the senate this way? Wouldn't you appoint your friends if you were consul?"

"Only those who didn't agree with my every thought. Like you. You'd tell me what you honestly think. But these senators, they're so worried about getting elected to the office themselves, they're no better than clients to the consuls."

Their voices faded into the crowd along with their bodies, though Marcus could see Vibulus' head, as if hoisted on a pole, for some time. He called to Tibia, asleep under the wagon. She yawned, stretched her sleek body, and came out wagging her tail with an inquiring look on her sharp face. Marcus patted the wagon. "Up," he commanded. Tibia jumped into the wagon effortlessly, sidled next to him and reached out her slobbery tongue for his face. Marcus recoiled from this advance but scratched her ears affectionately. "Stay," he commanded again.

Behind his cart the Tiber River ran past steep banks shaded by oak, plane, and pine trees. Marcus sought out the solitude of the underbrush both for natural purposes and for a place to think. He brought with him one of the terracotta bowls he had taken in trade to fill with water for the dog. As he descended the bank the sounds of the market fell away like the earth fell to the river. He listened instead to its unintelligible yet soothing voice.

In the shade by the banks a thick, damp odor, tangible as mist, perfumed the humid air. The season seemed as confused as he felt. Plane trees, mottled bark looking strangely reptilian without leaves on the branches, and barren oaks waited for spring while below them green grasses and wildflowers thought it had already arrived. Long-needled pines, dark as the green water that flowed unceasingly by, regarded not the weather, but were as constant as the river. He found a dry spot and sat down close to the river. Picking absently at grass, twigs, and rocks, he flipped them into the water and let his thoughts drift by.

In the back of his mind the fear grew that he would be forced to choose between the voluble and volatile Legumenus, and the steady, conservative Opimius. Their friendship amused him, constantly at odds yet inseparable. However, he felt ultimately it must lead to tragedy, and he would be compelled to be a party to it. He was loathe to take sides. The pressure building in Rome would surely divide friends, perhaps families. He had seen the beginnings of it in the riot over old Scroconius the debtor. Since then tension had risen and fallen, but on the whole continued to build.

With the calendar broken up by festivals, and days when no public business could be done, with a populace constantly sifting in and out of the city to work the farms that needed their attention, political emotions were difficult to sustain. One day the entire community feasted together in honor of one or more of the gods. Another, for reasons known only to the priests, no public business could be allowed because the day held ill omens. Then another might be marked *comitialis*, and assemblies could be held, laws passed, trials conducted. These were the days when Rome reached a fever pitch. Agitated crowds might chant slogans or accusations, magistrates got jostled angrily, and the whole city would be in ferment.

A sparrow landed nearby, eyed him inquisitively and chirped insistently, as if trying to tell him something. A common man addressed by a common bird, he thought. It seemed to say, "look up". Tiber Island, overgrown with wild brush, willows, and cane floated like a corroded spear tip in the river. The brown sparrow cheeped peevishly and hopped farther to his left. Obediently Marcus raised his eyes higher. Downstream the Sublician Bridge joined Rome to Etruria. Towering above the bridge the Aventine Hill stood guard over the river. Out of his line of vision on its lower slopes the disputed temple of Mercury received its finishing touches. The sparrow flew off in that direction.

He grunted appreciatively at the wisdom of the sparrow. In a sense the Aventine did symbolize the dispute between the commons and the patricians. Outside the sacred *pomerium* of the city all the temples on the Aventine were either Latin, like the temple of Diana on the summit, or plebeian like the temple of Mercury and the temple of Ceres, now under construction. These latter two temples had been dedicated in response to economic hardship and famine. A guild of merchants was to be set up in the temple of Mercury in the hopes of stimulating business. The temple of Ceres, though dedicated at the battle of Lake Regillus, was being built in the hopes of alleviating persistent food shortages. Without doubt the Aventine was indelibly associated with the plebeian class. Yet ironically the hill fell under the domain of the state as *ager publicus* which leased grazing rights on sections of it, and prevented squatters from taking up illegal residence on its slopes. No wonder, he thought, that the consuls desired to associate their names with the temple of Mercury and thereby exert influence over development on the Aventine.

Just then the sound of Tibia barking interrupted his cogitation, and he clambered up the bank in alarm. Instead of thieves he found people hurrying off to the Forum.

"Good dog," he said, patting her smooth head. She pushed her head against his chest so he would scratch her ears, moaning with pleasure as he did so. The vegetable market had grown quiet. A few people wandered from cart to cart sampling the olive oil, having their hands slapped as they groped a cabbage, or arguing over the price of dried figs. But the commotion in the Forum had stolen the interest of the majority.

Marcus made up his mind. He placed the bowl of water on the cart, which Tibia lapped gratefully. "Now you stay here and watch things," he instructed gravely, gently lifting her sleek head to look her in the eyes. Backing off a step he raised his hand in salute. "Hail, Tibia," he said. Tibia sat, raised her right paw, and barked in response.

The consuls, unable to reach agreement on which of them should dedicate the temple of Mercury decided that dispensing justice should occupy the remainder of the morning. The sun passed the third hour when they mounted their respective tribunals, Appius at the west end near the comitia, Servilius at the east end near the temple of Vesta.

The two men could not have been more opposite in character. Servilius had a self-deprecating, conciliatory nature, a little too eager to please. His generous nature was not enough to offset the equivocal side of his personality, and he often found himself distrusted by patricians and plebeians alike. Appius Claudius was all patrician. A Sabine by birth, he had moved to Rome ten years earlier bringing with him five thousand personal dependents. He settled them on lands north of the Anio River and immediately became a citizen and patrician. He exerted his influence just as immediately and championed the aristocracy vehemently and unwaveringly, a trait he would pass on to generations of his descendants and earn them the same undying enmity the plebeians held for their progenitor. Thus the dais on which he sat in his curule chair of office drew the largest crowd, and that is where Marcus headed. Besides, as he entered the Forum he could see the hawk-beaked head of Aulus Vibulus protruding above the crowd like a pimple on a nose.

Aulus Vibulus itched to get involved in the trial. Marcus could see it in the strained tight lines of his thin face, and his intense stare focused on the tribunal. He squeezed between Vibulus and Gaius Opimius, and asked what was happening. Opimius turned his pugnacious face towards him.

"This man has not paid his debts, and must now give up his freedom for it," he said. "Despicable," said Vibulus, without shifting his gaze.

In a clear space before the dais two men stood. One, impeccably barbered and dressed in a fine toga, stood relaxed and at ease. The other, a lean man with unshaven, haggard face and dirty brown tunic, shifted from foot to foot, and could not decide what to do with his hands. The man in the toga ticked off the counts against the defendant in measured tones, keeping cadence with his right hand.

Appius Claudius sat listening imperiously with all his lictors in attendance. The folds of his toga fell elegantly to the wood planking, the purple border conspicuously displayed. Three patrician senators sat behind him to observe and offer advice. Marcus could not fail to notice Publius Scipio among them.

The sight of Scipio gave Marcus an immediate sense of insecurity. He felt guilty, and didn't know why. He thought of the favors Scipio had done for him and the promises he made to Scipio. In fact, he had planned on accompanying him to the Forum the next day to show his respect. So why should he feel guilty? Just because he came to watch a trial didn't mean he had violated the principles of fidelity which bound client and patron. Then he realized his fear arose from being seen with Vibulus. But so what if Legumenus played the role of reformer. Didn't Romans have the right of free association? And just because the gangly Legumenus opposed the likes of Appius Claudius didn't necessarily mean that Marcus did. His thoughts existed independently of their friendship, which had been founded on the basis of shared dangers and hardship, not ideology. Nevertheless, he felt guilty, and had to resist the urge to disappear through the crowd and go back to his cart, and Tibia's fawning company.

"I offer a prayer to Jupiter Best and Greatest, and all the gods and goddesses of Rome to protect us from the impiety of injustice," the prosecutor said. Vibulus snorted derisively, and a few others muttered at the invocation. "But can it be injustice to ask for repayment of that which was loaned? People will say that debtors should have rights. But should not lenders also? It only makes sense that if lenders have no recourse to recover their loans plus the agreed fee that there will cease to be lenders. Judgement may seem harsh, but harsher still would be the plight of the common man if he had no access to loans..."

"Who's speaking for the defendant?" Marcus whispered.

"He has no one as far as I know," Opimius said.

"He has no patron?"

"That's him prosecuting."

Marcus gasped. "Speaking of impiety..." he said, appalled.

"I'm defending him," Vibulus said, striking his friends dumb. "I arranged it only this morning when he was brought to me by one of my clients."

"You've been drinking," Marcus said finally, dumbfounded by his friend.

"A little wine makes the mind flexible," said Vibulus.

"Are you crazy, Legumenus?" Opimius uttered vehemently in a hoarse whisper. "You'll make enemies of the wrong people," he warned.

"They've made themselves enemies. I had nothing to do with it," responded Vibulus blithely. Then seriously he bent his head, looked them each in the eye and said, "I release you from all obligations of friendship if you find this too uncomfortable." Receiving no response, he stepped into the open space before the dais.

A look of equivocal relief passed across the defendant's grizzled face as Vibulus stepped forward. The poor man's shoulders sagged and his hands hung in resignation to the will of the prosecutor as he finished speaking. His deeply creased eyes displayed, not hope, but gratitude that someone would try to help him.

It cost a small fortune in wool to make a toga long enough for Vibulus, so that he always looked as if he were about to walk through standing water. A rustle of snickering went through the spectators at the sight of him. Amusement and surprise lit the craggy features of Appius Claudius as well.

"I have agreed to speak on behalf of Spurius Galinus," Vibulus began, "because the man who swore an oath to defend him, to explain the law to him in exchange for services rendered, is today prosecuting him. To render unto himself the only thing Spurius Galinus could deny him; namely his farm and his person in perpetuity. Publius Licinius would have us believe that loans to the commons are an act of benevolence and that onerous and exorbitant fees are simply fair recompense for the strain such loans put on his own resources.

Yet it is perfectly clear that he is only too eager to seize not only his property, but Spurius Galinus himself. It is equally obvious that these loans were made for this express intent!"

The amusement fell from Claudius' face and the flush of anger tarnished his silver hair. A swift motion of his hand brought his lictors instantly forward to his side. Divisive voices surged through the multitude, but it became quickly apparent Vibulus was winning the majority to his side. A nascent hope lit the rugged features of Spurius Galinus as he felt the crowd's reaction. But Appius Claudius would have none of it. He quickly stood up and pointed at Vibulus.

"You have no right to speak before this court," he shouted. "I command you to desist."

For a moment Vibulus stood silent, hesitating, unsure of his position. Then he cast caution to the wind. "I have every right," he proclaimed. "I am a Roman citizen."

"This is not a capital case," Claudius shouted above the increasing volume of the spectators. "The court will hear the evidence and render its verdict. An advocate for the defendant in not required. By law."

"Where is this law written that we may all see it?" demanded Vibulus. Voices from the crowd echoed this sentiment.

Claudius ignored his statement and pointed at Galinus whose face had fallen into a look of abject dismay. "Go, lictor, and bind his hands," Appius uttered the formal decree.

One of the lictors detached himself from the others and descended the three steps of the tribunal to take hold of Galinus. Galinus stretched out his hands to his fellow citizens imploring them to come to his aid. A confusion of voices filled the air like swallows as the crowd began pushing and shoving. Someone shoved the advancing lictor. Before he could regain his balance another man shoved him and sent him sprawling. The gravity of attacking one of the consul's lictors, the agents of his authority, suddenly impacted the crowd and the threat of violence momentarily dissipated as everyone backed away from the fallen man. Galinus inched his way backward as if ready to flee at any moment as the lictor gathered himself and stood. One of his elbows dripped blood liberally, but he paid no heed. Apparently disoriented he searched the crowd for his prey, only to find the lengthy Legumenus blocking his path.

"See citizens, the rule of law bruited about so self-righteously by our 'fathers'. It is a law they keep hidden inside their purple togas. It is a law that says—apparently, for we are not able to read it anywhere—that a man whose liberty is threatened has no right to defense before the court." Vibulus paused momentarily. Silence hung like an axe in the air as everyone, including the lictor, waited for his next utterance.

Pressed on every side by the multitude, Marcus awaited Vibulus' words with excitement and trepidation mixed. Looking around he found Opimius had left his side and could not find him anywhere in the crowd. He wondered if he shouldn't have escaped also while he had the chance. But the high-handed judgement of Appius Claudius also angered him. It was one thing to fairly hear both sides of a case and dispense a verdict in favor of a creditor, quite another to pass judgement without both sides having equal opportunity to present a case. How could justice be one-sided and called justice? All this flashed through his mind as he waited for the words Vibulus would fling like a gauntlet.

"Therefore, plebeians of Rome," Vibulus stressed, "it is obvious that we must protect one another, since we have no protection from the state."

Livid with indignation, Appius Claudius nearly hurled himself off the dais at Vibulus. "You dare speak sedition before this tribunal?"

"Only those who seek to enslave others view equal protection under the law as sedition," Vibulus shot back. "The liberty of the common man in Rome is threatened more by his fellow citizens than by any foreign enemy. If the state will not dispense justice, then we will insure it for ourselves!"

"Seize that man!" Claudius ordered. But before any of his lictors could dismount the dais a crowd of plebeians had closed around Vibulus and Galinus breathing threats at anyone attempting to lay hands on them, and escorted them out of the Forum. Once again Marcus Tempanius found himself in a body of men escorting Aulus Vibulus out of the Forum and danger. As they climbed the Argiletum he congratulated Vibulus on his heroics.

"You were magnificent, Legumenus. I didn't know you had it in you," Marcus said.

"Yes," Vibulus agreed, exulting. "Someday a Vibulus will be consul."

The comment mystified Marcus, and he fell into silence; then he fell out of step; finally, he fell out of the clot of supporters entirely. People's motives were altogether too confusing.

# VI

## Ides of March 494BC
## Festival of Anna Perenna

Though tantalizingly close, the Sublician Bridge might as well have been a hundred miles away. He cursed them as fatherless when individual horsemen or people on foot went by his loaded wagon and threaded their way onto and over the plank bridge while he waited, as good as anchored to the spot. Two lines of wagons, one from the direction of the forum, one from the area of the Aventine intersected at the crossroads shrine before the Sublician Bridge---the only way across the Tiber. Rather than proceed in an orderly fashion people vied for entrance onto the bridge like charioteers in the circus, whipping their teams forward, locking wheels and cursing each other in the most explicit manner. Oxen bawling, horses whinnying and snorting, and the hideous laugh of mules mixed with the angry voices of humans as the city vomited its occupants. The rising smell of dung putrefied the air. Marcus stood up to see what the holdup was, but all he could see were wagons and carts clustered like shards of smashed clay pots swept into a disorganized pile. The movement of one wagon across the bridge caused a recoil through the lines of waiting carts, and a hundred whips ripped the air. Creaking like a flock of crows the wagons lurched forward a few paces then halted again.

"I told you we should have gone by way of the crossing at Fidenae," Gaius Opimius called from the wagon in front of them.

Marcus ran a hand over his long face in exasperation and said nothing. Originally the idea seemed ludicrous. Inclined towards the straight approach, he had agreed with Aulus Vibulus and come straight into Rome on the Via Labicana. After all, it practically ran straight by his house, and entered

Rome at the Esquilline Gate. From there it was a straight shot down the Vicus Suburanus, across the Forum, through the Porta Carmentalis, past the Velabrum and the Forum Boarium, and onto the bridge. Or should have been. Instead, like wine poured through an innkeeper's funnel, two and four-wheeled carts, mixed up with revelers on horse, foot, or carried in litters, flowed into the Forum and spilled over. Their first halt came between the two bridges connecting the Subura with the Argiletum, beside the aromatic banks of the great open sewer, the Cloaca Maxima. Drusilla wrinkled her nose distastefully and from the back Lucius complained that something smelled.

In the forum chaos reigned. Two roads, the Vicus Tuscus and the Vicus Iugarius, led south out of the Forum exiting the wall that connected the Palatine and Capitoline hills. The Vicus Iugarius ran behind the Temple of Saturn on the west end of the forum, skirted the sheer cliffs of the Capitoline Hill, exiting at the Porta Carmentalis. The Vicus Tuscus followed the Cloaca Maxima, that re-emerged after passing beneath the north side of the Forum, curved around the Palatine Hill, and became the Via Albana near the Circus Maximus. Naturally, some wished to take one, some the other road. Marcus, entering along the Vicus Suburanus, thought to cross the forum diagonally, and travel along the Vicus Iugarius. At cross purposes with those of the other mind a hundred conflagrations burst out at once as a conglomeration of conveyances attempted to negotiate in the Forum's confines. Extricated at last from that confusion, they now found themselves pinned between the Forum Boarium (the meat market), and the Velabrum—a malodorous holding pond for the effluent of the Cloaca Maxima before it spilled into the Tiber near the docks.

"Is it too late to turn around?" Drusilla called back. She turned to look behind her. "Oh Juno, what a mess."

"Where going?" asked Lucius from behind the seat.

"Across the river," Drusilla answered her son in a singsong voice. Adjusting her stola and shawl she turned back around to face forward.

"Why?"

"To celebrate the returning year."

"Why?"

"To have a picnic, my heart. Now play with your biga."

"It bwoken," Lucius said, holding up the chariot Marcus had painstakingly fashioned for him, now missing a wheel.

"Here," said Petronius, reaching out a battered hand. "Let me see if I can fix it."

Lucius scrambled back to the rear of the cart where Petronius sat with legs dangling. Marcus fumed in silence, the reins hanging loosely, watching balefully as Vibulus came towards them from up ahead. As he passed Opimius' wagon Gaius hopped down and stomped alongside gesticulating angrily. A tolerant smile widened the thin face of Aulus Vibulus as they came up to the Tempanius cart.

"Yes, yes, you're absolutely right, Gaius," Legumenus said. "We should have gone by way of Fidenae. But it's too late for that now, so let's figure out another course of action."

Looking into the gray ringed eyes of Marcus Tempanius was like looking into a pot about to boil. He could practically see the steam rising. "Why don't you hand the reins over to your man, there," Vibulus suggested, "and the three of us will go sort out the congestion at the bridge."

The suggestion placated both Marcus, and Gaius Opimius. Petronius moved up to the driver's seat, and the three men went up to the bridge to direct traffic. At first their administration met with derision and resistance, but as wagons began to move more freely and the traffic flow over the bridge became smoother, cooperation increased and progress was made in getting the multitudes across the Tiber. Even so, the sun was well up by the time they found their campsite.

Didius Crispus had done well. In a shady bower below the Janiculum Hill he had built a hut of rushes, cane, and branches. A pile of wood was stacked nearby and a fire crackled in a shallow pit in front of the hut. Two forked sticks flanked the fire, providing a spit for cooking. Hard by the river, Didius had even managed to dig a trench to divert cold water into a shallow pool to cool the wine. How so much work could be gotten out of such a short, skinny body never ceased to surprise Marcus.

"You amaze me, Didius," Marcus said, as they unloaded the cart. "You did all this?"

"With the help of my wife and the two youngsters." He looked up at Marcus, and his light green eyes flashed with pride. He smiled crookedly, the left side of his face frozen, allowing only the right side to move. "It wasn't that much work. We started on it yesterday, and finished today."

"I'm just sorry I wasn't here to help," Marcus said, pulling an amphora of wine onto his shoulder.

"Forget it. It looked like you had a little trouble crossing over."

"Ah! Rome needs another bridge across the river."

"Then we'd have needed two Horatius Cocles to keep Lars Porsena from capturing the city," Didius said, handing a small basket to his seven-year-old son, Quintus and grabbing another himself. The boy waddled proudly off under the load, his younger brother Sextus trailing behind. Marcus and Didius followed.

Vibulus and Gaius Opimius had brought leather tents and these they were in the process of setting up. Opimius set his up opposite the hut constructed by Didius. Vibulus set his up in the space between the two so that the three structures formed a U with the open end facing south. This end they closed with a long low table that, after directing the children to clean the area, they then surrounded with cushions. This luxury surprised Marcus and Drusilla, but no more than the Opimius and Vibulus families themselves.

Marcus thought he knew his friends well, but that thought dissipated immediately upon meeting their wives. Vibulus was married to Aemelia, daughter of the patrician Lucius Aemilius, a man everyone expected to gain the consulship. She was not pretty, a little chubby with a plain face and slightly bucked teeth. But she must have come with a hefty dowry and Marcus no longer wondered how Vibulus could spend so much time in Rome.

Opimius was equally well connected having married Veturia, daughter of Veturius one of the consuls during the battle of Lake Regillus. While everyone else lifted and hauled jugs and bowls, baskets and stools, she held her petite body aloof and gave directions on their placement. Opimius had also brought a freshly butchered suckling pig which Didius and Petronius quickly spitted and began turning over the fire.

When everything was in place, they gathered around the table laden with sweet cakes, figs, nuts, raisins, and most importantly jugs of wine. For the more cups of wine one drank the longer one lived, according to the tenets of Anna Perenna.

"Let us first," Gaius Opimius said, standing, "pour out a libation to the goddess Anna Perenna and then pray to Jupiter Best and Greatest to make the new year profitable for us all."

Everyone poured a small amount of wine onto the ground.

"Here's to living forever," said Aulus Vibulus, raising his cup.

"I don't think I can drink that much," Marcus laughed. "But let's try." As one they tipped their cups and let the sweet wine flow over palates that would soon be beyond tasting. Marcus, with a sudden exclamation of remembrance ran into the thatch hut and came out with a bundle of tawny wool over his arms. He separated it and the wool became two tunics. "These," he said as he approached the table, "are for my two friends without whose expert hands my land would still be a forest." He handed the tunics to Didius and Petronius, who instantly put them on over their old tunics and admired each other proudly. Then, embarrassed by their poor manners, profusely thanked Marcus and Drusilla for their generosity, sentimentally pledging their undying loyalty to their household.

"You're a sly one," Vibulus said, looking at Marcus over the rim of his cup. "Building yourself a clientele for the future?"

Marcus laughed. "If you call two men of the infra classem a clientele."

"You have to start somewhere."

"Legumenus, you have the suspicious mind of the schemer," Marcus said. "You see your own intentions in others."

Behind them Didius and Petronius turned the pig on the spit while the three men reclined, drinking wine and eating the fruits of their labor. As they made small talk Marcus felt a twinge of guilt. Didius and Petronius fell so easily into service while the others, so used to being served, took no notice. Thinking to make a point he filled two cups of wine, stood up and carried them to his two men.

"Here," he said, holding out the cups. "Add a few years to your lives. Legumenus, come and help me turn this pig."

Across the table with the women and children Drusilla smiled broadly at him, knowing his thoughts exactly. Legumenus, for all his apparent idleness was no stranger to hard work, yet his immediate reaction was the same look Lucius gave when required to work instead of play. Drusilla burst out laughing and nearly fell off her stool.

"Don't pout so, Aulus Vibulus," she said. "It'll help you drink more."

"That's not the problem," Gaius Opimius said. "It's getting that long body off the ground. It takes twice as much effort as a normal person."

"You're just jealous," Vibulus said. "Tall people command more respect."

"Not me," proclaimed Didius. "Short people live longer."

"Certainly," Opimius said, "because they're not permitted to serve in the legions."

"Perhaps not in the hoplites," Petronius said. "But there are no such restrictions for the velites."

"Of course not," Vibulus said, rising like a crane from the water. "They don't have to carry all the heavy armor." He grabbed an end of the spit, and he and Marcus rotated the pig.

"In fact," Didius said matter-of-factly, "we're afforded no protection at all."

"Yes, but then, you're not long in the battle either," Opimius said. "You throw your javelin or sling your stones, and then you're gone."

"While we hoplites slug it out in the phalanx with the enemy's best men," Vibulus pontificated.

"Perhaps we are not necessary then," Petronius said. His deep voice could not bury the peevishness beginning to well inside him. He resolved not to drink too much wine regardless of how many years it might add to his life. If he got into a spiteful exchange with these men a longer life would only mean more misery.

"Don't speak foolishness," Marcus said. He displayed the scar on his left shoulder. "I got this from one of your javelins at Regillus," he said. "I was out of the battle before I could strike a blow."

"Fortunately for us," Vibulus said. "Give me another year, here." He held out his cup, shaped like a bent leg with a face on the thigh.

"No, you were quite safe Legumenus. No one else can fit in your armor so there's really no point in killing you for it."

"So much for the theory short people live longer."

"I've heard there are a people north of Etruria among whom even the short ones are taller than our Legumenus," Gaius Opimius said.

"They must be giants," Aemilia exclaimed with awe.

"Yes," agreed Opimius, "and it's said they fight completely naked."

"Disgusting," said Veturia.

"Then they give up the advantage of their size," said Marcus. He filled his cup from a pitcher in the pool Didius excavated. "We would have nothing to fear from such a people."

"I've heard they are extraordinarily fierce, though," insisted Opimius.

"Well, of course, anyone who fights naked would have to be, wouldn't they," said Vibulus. Everyone laughed and they continued to discuss warfare and exchange tales of feats of bravery or deceit.

Scattered about the Janiculum hill under a limpid sky, flimsy tents and stick huts sheltered drinking Romans of every class. The smell of roasting flesh filled the air and birds chirped in competition with human voices rising and falling in laughter or bursting into song. Children crawled about the hill collecting wildflowers or chasing bugs. Here and there young men competed in games of skill, or wrestled drunkenly while their fellows loudly denounced or applauded each throw or escape.

Marcus was at last content and at ease. He was also drunk. The women had taken the children on some expedition, the nature of which he couldn't remember, and Didius and Petronius had gone along to serve as protection. As long as they encountered nothing more dangerous than a mouse they should be all right. He giggled to himself. Looking up at the westering sun his brain told him the air was cooling, and he should wrap a cloak around himself, but the wine made his body lie, and he felt nothing.

"I think one of my goats is going to have twins," he said out of nowhere after a long silence.

"That's good," Gaius Opimius said. "You'll want to keep the male if there is one."

"Yes. The buck I have now is almost five. I'd like to sell him soon."

"Mm," Opimius said. "Best time; before he's worn out. You'll have to guarantee he's sound of body."

Aulus Vibulus scoffed, like a horse blowing. "No man in his right mind would do that. Goats are always sick with fever, or ripping themselves open on thorn bushes."

"How do you sell them then?" asked Marcus.

"Best just to eat him," said Aulus. He tipped his head back and lowered a strip of pork into his waiting mouth.

"Nonsense," Gaius Opimius said. "You don't have to guarantee it for life. What color is it?"

"White."

"That's best," Opimius asserted.

"Black," Vibulus contradicted. "Black is best."

"If I'd said black, you'd have said white."

"That's ridiculous."

"Do you even have any goats?" Marcus asked.

"Of course," Vibulus said. "Twenty-five or thirty head."

"I suppose they're all black," said Opimius.

"Don't be ridiculous. But I always keep three bucks for mating that are." Rising up on both elbows he said, "You know, there's a curious thing about goats. My goatherd has observed that unlike other animals, goats breathe through their ears."

"Your goatherd has been taking too much wine with him," said Opimius.

"I suppose," said Marcus, "they hear through their noses."

"I didn't think of that," said Vibulus. "But I suppose they'd have to if they breathe through their ears."

"Now that is ridiculous." Gaius Opimius shook his head. He poured another cup of wine. How much wine did it take, he wondered, to dispel disbelief.

A blooming mimosa tree glowed like molten gold as the slanting rays of the sun set it afire. A weak breeze from the west lifted and dropped the branches so they shimmered in undulating waves of windswept light. It appeared to Marcus as if the tree were breathing, but instead of air it inhaled light and exhaled a glorious effulgence of golden blooms.

The children returned bearing fistfuls of these blooms along with white daisies, dandelions, and purple hued bluebells. Except Lucius, who had instead found a branch suitable for use as a sword, upon which he impaled imaginary enemies, or assaulted Gaius Opimius Jr. and Quintus Crispus and his brother Sextus.

"You have a born soldier, there," Gaius Opimius observed approvingly. His large catapult stone face was red as the sunset, and his speech thick as porridge. He sloshed more wine around his teeth to extricate his tongue from the roof of his mouth. "I'll bet he wins the civic crown."

The corona civica, a crown of oak leaves, could only be won by saving the life of a citizen. It was a great award, second only to the corona obsidionalis, awarded for the rescue of a besieged army. While Marcus felt grateful for the compliment, and genuinely hoped his son would show courage when called upon to serve, his heart darkened with a different fear. Not so much for his son's safety; only valor, luck, and the favor of the gods could secure that. No, he lived in fear that his son would love war too much. "I'll be content if he never has any scars on his back," he replied. "I just wish he was a little more of a born farmer."

"Rome has plenty of farmers," Opimius observed. His matter-of-fact speech displayed no derogatory implication. "What she needs now are exceptional soldiers."

Vibulus, lying face up, fingers laced behind his head, laughed cynically. "We won't have enough of either pretty soon."

"Don't start with your demagoguery again Legumenus. Your political aspirations have clouded your judgement."

"I'm amazed you could say that after all that wine," Legumenus chortled.

"Don't try to change to subject. You know as well as I do we're hemmed in on all sides and under constant attack from our enemies. There is no land to distribute to the poor."

Legumenus clapped his hands in explosive applause. "Wonderful. Really, a wonderful speech. You have the vote of my tribe!"

Opimius spat in disgust. "I need some water," he said, rising slowly and unsteadily to his feet. At the little pool Didius had made to cool the wine he got down on all fours and took a long drink, then dunked his whole head in the water. Glaring up at them on hands and knees, his black hair matted and dripping, he resembled a wild boar about to charge. The short muscular arms, stub-fingered hands bunched into hooves, and powerful shoulders rolled forward aggressively.

Marcus and Vibulus simultaneously burst into laughter. There he is," cried Vibulus, mocking Opimius with a pointed bony finger, "the champion of the patriciate."

"Why are you so against them?" asked Marcus when his laughter subsided. "Publius Scipio has never failed to help me. And I can think of many others who've been given seed, or bronze for dowries; or gotten help with some dispute—whatever."

"Because he wants to be one of them," Opimius proclaimed. He attempted to point at Vibulus and rise at the same time, lost his balance and fell over on his side.

"Of course," said Vibulus, laughing at his friends' struggles. He felt no need to deny it, or pretend his aims were wholly altruistic—if at all. "And who doesn't? They hold all the priesthoods, and if they get their way only patricians will be consuls. As if they alone have the right—or ability—to earn glory and honors."

"But Servilius is not patrician and he's consul," protested Marcus.

"Not entirely true," said Vibulus, "his mother was not patrician. But even so, look how they treat him. They scorned him when he proposed his reforms of nexum, and so vilified him that even the friends he appointed to the senate wouldn't support him."

"He's weak, and caters to the whims of the 'plebs'—as they call themselves—just to avoid conflict," asserted Opimius.

"That's ridiculous," said Vibulus. "All he proposed were the most basic protections of property rights. How in good conscience can you deny to any Roman the security of his property when he is away on service?"

"A debt is a debt, Legumenus. Either it's paid or the debtor must suffer the consequences. What does it matter if he happens to be serving in the legions at the time?"

"What matters," said Vibulus, "is that while he's off giving his blood to the state, his creditors are safe in Rome currying the favor of consuls and senators. So that the full weight of the law is brought down on the unsuspecting head of this plebeian before he so much as passes under the Sister's Beam."

"You make it sound so tyrannical," Opimius said.

"You said it, not me," Vibulus retorted.

Reclining on the ground, recuperating from their labors with the women and children, Petronius and Didius listened to the conversation with a disturbing equanimity. They sipped cups of wine, exchanged glances now and then, but said nothing. Marcus, frustrated by his friends' constant bickering over the subject, and perhaps more so over his inability to make up his mind over who was right turned his attention to the two observers.

"What do you think, Petronius?" he asked. "After all, of all of us here, these questions affect you the most."

Petronius scratched reflectively at the thatch of beard under his chin. "It would seem," he said in his resonant voice, "that you are the first person to ask."

Didius laughed, slapping his thigh and shaking his small head in chagrin. "Isn't that the truth."

"But the fact is," Petronius continued, "both Gaius Opimius and Aulus Vibulus are right. And wrong."

"There's clarification for you," mocked Vibulus.

"It's not cancellation of debts the plebeians want," Petronius said, undeterred. "As Gaius Opimius said, a debt is a debt."

"Nor," interrupted Didius, "is it nexum that we object to. After all, who would choose slavery over a chance to work off our debts and remain citizens?"

"Hah!" exclaimed Opimius triumphantly. "You see; even they agree with me." He quaffed another cup of wine in celebration of this moral victory.

"On the other hand," Petronius started again, "we did not join in the overthrow of one king just to substitute him with a group of kings."

"Exactly," agreed Didius. "In fact, we seem to have less protection under the republic than we did under the kings."

"Did the kings give you the right of appeal?" demanded Opimius.

"No," admitted Didius. "But then, our patrons didn't prosecute us either."

"You're speaking around the question," said Marcus, still frustrated. A straight answer in Rome seemed all but impossible. "What is it the plebs want?"

"We want protection of the law," said Petronius. He scratched the balding crown of his head. "If I owe a debt I can't pay and must be bound over to my creditor, at least give me a trial before the people, and set the limits of my bondage. As it is now, the creditor determines the sentence—which more often than not never ends. Is that justice?"

"You talk of law," accused Opimius, "but gangs of plebeians have assaulted and beaten creditors in the middle of the Forum. Even the consuls have been threatened if they try to interfere."

"We have been forced to protect ourselves," Didius said. He rose and brought wood to the fire, feeding it a piece at a time.

"And who will protect the Republic?" asked Opimius.

"Let the patricians do it," Didius snarled. "They want it all to themselves anyway."

Aulus Vibulus enjoyed himself immensely. He liked nothing better than discussing civic affairs. Many of his happiest hours had been spent in taverns in the Subura district doing just that with the peers of Didius, and Petronius. All their arguments were familiar to him. His gladdened ears drank in the discourse like sweet Greek wine. When he could listen no longer, he added a little goad and sat back.

"Let me ask you this, Didius," Vibulus said. "What about your patron, Marcus, here? He is neither patrician nor plebeian. Of course, there certainly seems to be not only loyalty but also affection on both your parts. Would you not defend him and his family?"

"With my life," Didius and Petronius said in unison.

"And what about you, Aulus Vibulus?" Didius shot back. "The bonds of friendship are no less sacred. Will you defend him when the time comes?"

# VII

## March 17, 494BC
## The Agonium Martiale-Purification of
## Weapons

Unable to resolve their differences the consuls called the people together in the comitia centuriata to decide which of them should dedicate the temple of Mercury. The people gathered on the Campus Martius in their sixty centuries, summoned by trumpets. From the Capitol and the Janiculum Hill red flags flew, signifying the people in arms were in session, and guards were posted to warn of the approach of the enemy. As a 'military' organization, the comitia centuriata was required to meet outside the sacred pomerium, the boundary of the city proper.

Appius Claudius, arrogant, self-possessed, confidently stalked the campus visiting the centuries, extolling his virtues and the weakness of his colleague. Servilius openly begged for their support, recounting the many favors he had performed. A train of supporters that included the men they had appointed to the senate followed the consuls. Appius Claudius had the greater support among the patricians, as well as a huge clientele that he counted on to sway the vote in his favor. Publius Servilius placed his hopes on the men of the first class, or classis, who voted first. The patricians, primarily located in the six centuries of cavalry, voted afterwards and were in that respect less influential.

Neither consul counted on the influence of the plebeians. In fact, they disregarded them completely. Relegated to the second class, or *infra classem*, they had little or no weight in the voting. The issue should have been decided before the vote reached them. But the plebeians had been organizing. They lobbied their patrons and friends in the first class so diligently that when they crossed the special polling bridges and announced their selection to the official vote takers, an unknown named Marcus Laetorius, a centurion and member of the first class, won election to perform the dedication. Mercury being the patron god of merchants, he would also be responsible for setting up a merchants' guild whose offices would be in the temple. In conjunction with this his duties were to include supervision and distribution of the grain supplies for the city. Duties which, by class, he was unqualified to perform.

Claudius and Servilius stomped off the Campus Martius enraged. They promised retribution. The insult to their dignity, they claimed, would not be forgotten. The people hoped not.

Shortly after the vote, Marcus met with his friends to share a cup of wine at a tavern in the Subura. Excitement still ran high, and the day's events were the main topic of loud discussion. Marcus laughed at the memory of the outraged faces of the consuls and their supporters.

"Did you see Appius' face?" he chortled. "It was so red I thought he would burst."

"It was better than I could have imagined," Vibulus said in genuine wonderment.

Five of them gathered around a small round table, seated on low stools. A half empty pitcher of wine, and bowls of raisins, figs, and a variety of nuts filled the center of the table.

"Well they deserved it," said Opimius. He spat on the floor as if the whole event had been distasteful to him. "Their dignity was lost when they argued over who would dedicate the temple. I've never seen such a mockery as these two."

"Now we've got to keep them on the run," said Vibulus. "For all their blustering about getting even they've got to feel they're on the defensive now."

"Over this?" said Petronius. "Forgive me Aulus Vibulus, but this is but a pebble in the shoe to them."

"In what way?" asked Marcus. Petronius and Didius had worked Marcus over hard trying to enlist his support for the day's vote. That didn't constitute the end of their machinations. Despite his membership in the first class, they had invited him to attend a meeting that night on the Aventine. They assured him of their apolitical intent, claiming they simply wanted to be sure nothing they did would be construed as detrimental to his family. They withheld the same invitation to Vibulus and Opimius. The day's events heightened his inclination to listen to what they had to say.

"They'll take the offensive," Petronius said simply, stating the obvious. "We can expect sterner sentences in court, and stricter discipline in the legion."

"I agree," said Didius. "They'll test our resolve now."

"Our resolve to what?" demanded Opimius. "I agreed to this vote because of their puerile behavior. But that's all. I'll oppose any seditious actions, I assure you."

"We'd expect no less, Gaius," Vibulus said heartily, clapping Opimius on the back. "Of course, in some circles what we're doing now is considered seditious behavior."

A worried, doubt-stricken look crossed the round features of Gaius Opimius, and the whole table laughed at his sudden discomfiture. "I expect a lot less from you, Legumenus," he said crossly. "Well, I have to go." He rose hastily from his chair and looked anxiously around the room. "I'll see you next market day, I suppose."

A short while later Didius and Petronius also took their leave. Vibulus and Marcus remained to finish the wine.

"Why don't you spend the night at my house?" offered Vibulus. "No sense in paying for a room."

"Thanks, Legumenus. I wish you'd offered sooner. I've already accepted an invitation from another acquaintance."

"Ah, too bad."

"Certainly. I'd much rather spend the night at a friend's."

"I appreciate the distinction."

They drank quietly for a while, though it was hard to think in the tumultuous atmosphere of the tavern. Dozens of men crammed themselves shoulder to shoulder in the small room.

A rank smell of spilled wine mixed with men's sweat stained the air like a pestilence.

"Politics is always good for business, eh Marcus?" said Vibulus, observing Marcus' roving eyes.

"Is it always this busy on comitial days?"

"Oh, it's much worse during the consular elections. Everyone comes to Rome then." Vibulus poured the last of the wine, dividing it between them. "So, do you think your men are right?"

"About what?"

"Things becoming worse."

"You'd know the answer to that better than I would. I'm a farmer, not a politician."

"Of course, you have no opinions," said Vibulus, taunting his friend.

Marcus raised his thin lips at one corner in a knowing half smile. "Don't worry Legumenus. When I have one, I'll let you know." He drained his wine and stood up to leave.

Outside, evening drifted lethargically across a pale sky obscured by clouds. A cool breeze tickled his arms and legs with misty fingers. Marcus liked this time of the day best. Serenity fell like a woolen cloak over the earth, causing stone blocks to look soft and malleable in the declining light. The city grew quiet as people took themselves indoors in preparation for vesperna, the evening meal. Even the smells of the city seemed to fade with the day into a kind of humidity deprived of scent. Marcus drifted through the tortuous alleyways of the Subura, followed the Vicus Cyprius behind the Velia and the Palatine, and exited the sacred boundary of the city at the portal in the earthen rampart connecting the Palatine to the Caelian hill. Near the altar of Consus he descended the sloping sides of the Circus, crossed the flat empty meadow, and climbed the south side at the site of the nearly completed temple of Mercury.

"Marcus," a voice hissed from a clump of trees on the rising slopes of the Aventine.

Startled out of his drifting reverie, he flinched, and stepped back.

"It's me, Didius," the disembodied voice said. Then the body stepped out from behind a tree.

"Sorry," said Marcus. "My mind was elsewhere. Where are we going?"

"Not far. Just up the hill a ways." With that the diminutive man disappeared wraithlike into the woods.

Marcus followed hurriedly, afraid to lose him. Didius moved like a shadow. He picked his way quickly and silently up the hill, following a ridge through the trees. They took a small footpath and climbed a second ridge through oak and beech trees to the crest of the hill. At the edge of the trees Didius stopped, and waited. A dilapidated cottage nearby gave evidence of previous habitation. Satisfied, Didius rose again and led them off along the edge of the ridge southwards. He stopped as they approached the Clivus Publicius, the road that cut across the top of the Aventine. Searching the road repeatedly he finally rose and trotted across, waving for Marcus to follow. Once again he melted into the woods and led Marcus through budding thorny cyclamens, thick pines, and sopping wet grass. Another trail led them back northwest to a clearing by the temple of Diana. Once again Didius squatted in wait. He pulled a dark cloak around him to blend into the underbrush. Marcus imitated him. Apparently satisfied, Didius skirted the edge of the temple grounds, moving stealthily through a grove of oak trees along the south wall of the grounds. Marcus began to have doubts. Anything this clandestine could not be legal, he reasoned. Perhaps the plebs really were plotting treason. As the sky darkened to night his apprehension increased.

"Where are we going?" he hissed at Didius' back.

"We're almost there," Didius whispered.

He led them into a small clearing where a modest stone house bled weak light through closed shutters. Didius knocked on the door once, then twice quickly. An aperture slid open and two baleful eyes looked out. Wordlessly the door opened to admit them.

The doorman led them through a small atrium, the opening to the sky barely larger than the cistern that caught rainwater beneath it. Directly behind the atrium twenty-one men cluttered the tablinum, conversing by the light of four oil lamps mounted on bronze tripods. Their frugal light, cast at the expense of precious olive oil, wavered from drooping tapers. Didius first introduced Marcus to the host, Gaius Sicinius, then to others until Sicinius called the meeting to order.

"Gentlemen," Sicinius said. His high-pitched voice matched his aquiline face. "Let us come to order." As conversation died, he stood before a chair at the back of the room, hands immobile by his sides. Stiffly waiting for the last voice to fade, his stern posture, erect as a palisade, brought them to attention. "Thank you. We have been called here tonight to draft a contingency plan based on the assumption the consuls will be madder than infernal demons." A small, tight smile flashed and was gone. "I trust that you have spoken with members of your tribes and have come equipped with some of their thoughts.

"What's he talking about?" Marcus whispered in Didius' ear.

"Each of us is an elected tribune of our tribe," Didius whispered.

"You're a…"

Didius nodded his head at the unfinished question, a thin smile tugging the right corner of his mouth downward. Even to the best of men, a plebeian was a body without a mind capable of any thoughts beyond the work at which they were normally employed.

"The first order of business under discussion is the likely nature of the consuls' reprisals." A hand went up. "I recognize Gaius Limonius," Sicinius said.

"The consensus seems to be that they'll be exceptionally harsh in their judgements in court. I think we should be prepared for them to contest any appeals."

This comment met with general approval. Sicinius' high voice cut short the clamor of discussion circling the room.

"Gentlemen, let's maintain order," he said. The room quieted. "Thank you. Do we have any motions on actions to resist this eventuality? I recognize Quintus Annius."

"Everyone seems satisfied that the tactics of disruption and direct intervention should be continued."

Numerous voices assented and a vote taken to confirm the continuation of present policies.

"Good," said Sicinius. "Remember to keep your groups mobilized and ready. Now is not the time to grow lax. Fine; what else then? I recognize Julius Longus."

"It seems most obvious that they'll try to call us up for the legions," Longus said, to a buzz of agreement. "Once we've taken the oath we'll be powerless to resist them."

Didius raised his gnarled hand. The whole scene was surreal to Marcus. Order and calm reigned, unlike the tribal and centuriate meetings he'd been to. And in reality it seemed a tremendous contrast to the behavior of the consuls as well.

"I recognize Didius Crispus," Sicinius called.

"In the event of a levy there is only one way open to us. We must refuse." A host of hands shot up like spears, but Didius had not finished. "Not only must we refuse, but we must secede altogether." Suddenly all the hands fell, and waves of agreement swept the room.

Marcus could not believe his ears. He thought they must have lost their senses. Self-consciously he raised his hand. Around him men stared as at an interloper. He represented no one so far as they knew, and had been brought on the sufferance of one of their members. Even so, Sicinius recognized him.

"I know," Marcus began, "that I have no legitimate right to speak here. I am not of your class, nor do I represent anyone of your class. I am here only as a concerned friend of Didius Crispus and ask you to listen. I believe that secession would be a mistake. Today you proved you have influence with the people. Continue working on that, and you will win the reforms you want. But if you secede you'll destroy the good will you've created. And to what purpose? I don't mean to offend, but the truth is Rome can raise an adequate army without you. I doubt that many in the first class would support you, and even if they did the patricians would simply call on their clients. Appius Claudius himself could raise three or four thousand men out of his personal clients. And who can refuse that call without bringing down the anger of the gods on his house? My friends, if my patron Publius Cornelius Scipio calls, how am I to answer?"

"I would like to answer my patron, Marcus Tempanius," said Didius with his hand in the air.

"You are recognized," Sicinius allowed.

"First of all, Marcus Tempanius, we have no hope, at least in our lifetime, of gaining our liberty through the consuls or the senate. And while we have no wish to destroy any good will with those of the classis, like yourself, we must ask your indulgence because we have no choice. As to the legions, well, it's true that Rome can do without us on a basic level. But who will they find to act as teamsters, mechanics, cobblers, ironworkers, porters, and the hundred other tasks we perform to free you to fight? And again, who will finish constructing the temple of Mercury, or Ceres, or Castor and Pollux? Who will plow, sow, and reap their fields, guide the sheep to pasture, prune the vines and the olive trees? No, we will show these patricians just how worthless we are. As to your last question, I have pledged you my faith. I will not dishonor it while I have breath. That's the best I can do."

Orion had traversed much of the sky by the time the meeting broke up. The heavy clouds rolled back leaving a clear, planished sky studded with bright stars. Marcus and Didius eschewed their surreptitious ways and descended the Aventine openly along the Clivus Publicius in the direction of the port. No moon illuminated their way. Tall cypress trees, shadowed against a dark sky, lined the road like spear points in close formation. At the bottom of the hill by a crossroads altar they stopped, deciding whether to take the Vicus Tuscus into the city, or turn right along the Circus Maximus and take the Vicus Cyprius. The gurgling of the Tiber as it flowed around the supports of the Sublician Bridge wetted the air. Ahead they could see the faint glitter of the Velium beyond the dark smudge of the Grove of Hercules. As they crossed the road, having decided to go straight into the Forum, the clatter of footsteps coming from the copse of trees surrounding the altar of Hercules surprised them. Suddenly five men blocked their way. In the dark Marcus could make out nothing of their features, but could clearly see they each carried something in their hands. He looked for the glint of iron but saw nothing. So, it's clubs, then, he thought.

"Where are you going at such a late hour?" one of them demanded.

"We've just come from a friend's house," said Didius easily.

"Without so much as a torch to light your way?"

"What's your interest?" asked Marcus, tightly. He could feel his anger rising.

"A citizen is always interested in those creeping about in the dark."

"You've described yourselves very well," snarled Marcus. "Now let us by."

"Not until we know exactly what you've been up to tonight," said the leader. Something slapped rhythmically into the palm of his hand.

A hot surge flooded through Marcus. "Don't threaten me," he said tersely. "I'll come and go as I please, and answer to no one."

"So you can plot treason against the Republic?"

The vigilantes moved into a semicircle around Marcus, and Didius. Didius took a step backwards, as if to make a run for it, but Marcus grabbed his arm and pulled him closer to him. Forward, he thought, was the way to go. His voice choked on welling anger, and the recklessness of battle gripped him like a monster.

"Out of our way," he said, in a strangled, feral voice. He took a small step forward, placing himself directly in front of the leader, and felt him flinch.

"Not..."

Marcus didn't wait for him to finish. Springing forward he dropped to a knee, then brought his left leg around as he wrapped his arms about the man's waist. Driving forward he threw him down hard on the paving stones, cracking his head. Didius shot through the gap, pulled a knife hidden under his tunic and sheathed it under the fifth rib of the nearest assailant. In one fluid motion Marcus crawled over his sprawled opponent and wrested the club from his slack fingers. Two men were down, one laid out unconscious, the other sitting on the stones with his hands clutching at the blood draining from his side. Their three companions now had their backs to the Aventine, while Marcus and Didius had theirs to the Forum Boarium. For an instant no one moved.

"Run!" commanded Marcus, and he and Didius spun about and ran as fast as they could toward the Forum Romanum. No one followed.

# VIII
## March 23
## The Tubilustrium—Purification of War Bugles

A mockery, pure and simple. They sacrificed a bull, paraded around the city in their finest togas, and acted as if everything were fine. The tubilustrium took place as usual on the twenty-third of March, following yet another day of violence in the Forum. Gangs of patricians and plebeians filled the Forum waiting for a trial, or for a creditor to appear before the courts. A fight would ensue, which so far the plebeians had had the best of. They shouted down the consuls, assaulted their lictors, and beat creditors. The miracle of it was that no weapons had been drawn. Although weapons were outlawed from the sacred pomerium of the city, the fighting had escalated to such an extent that it seemed only a matter of time before someone drew dagger or sword.

Tense with expectation, the populace waited for the moment everyone knew must surely come, as it came every spring regular as the flowering of mimosa trees, and the leafing of grape vines. Then, like the sunrise, there it fluttered, the red flag flying from the capitol. Soon a crier came marching out calling the people to gather in their centuries. The Sabines had invaded.

Under a stone gray sky Marcus gathered with his century below the Capitoline Hill. Thousands of men, aged seventeen to forty-six crushed together in the Forum. All sixty centuries had been called, a fact that met with skepticism by some. Red flags flew from the citadel and the Janiculum. The consuls, surrounded by lictors in red tunics, were dressed in full military regalia. Sixty tall poles held by the consuls' men, each bearing a number, informed one where his century was to form up. Marcus Tempanius located the fifty-first and immediately set about looking for Gaius Opimius, and Aulus Vibulus. Not a difficult task given Vibulus' height. Or shouldn't have been, except that when he finally found them, they were on their hands and knees playing a game of latrunculi for money. The game board had been made from a piece of paving stone that one of them had inscribed with squares. Bits of broken clay were rounded off on a stone and used as the playing pieces.

Vibulus gazed intently at the board, raked his hair with long fingers, moved his pieces with triumphant impetuosity, and cursed heroically when his opponent took them from the board. He lost in a hurry.

"Don't ever run for consul, Legumenus, if that's the best you can do. You'll be throwing away men's lives faster than they can be born." Marcus clapped his friend on the back as they stood to watch Opimius challenge the winner.

Vibulus stretched, bending his long back painfully. "It's the posture," he said, sucking air through the gap in his front teeth. "It puts me in a hurry when I'm all folded over like that." Suddenly he grabbed Marcus by the elbow and spun him away. Glaring excitedly, his big hooked nose red with anticipation, he found an open space.

"So?" he said. "Will they answer when called?"

"I don't know for sure," Marcus said. "But I don't think so."

"This whole Sabine invasion is a hoax. The consuls are trying to force the issue."

"How do you know?"

"Of course everyone talks. You only need to keep your ears open. Not only that; did you see any smoke? See any refugees? I haven't heard a single story of anyone who's seen them."

"Maybe we got an early warning."

"Of what—invisible Sabines? Jove, Marcus, you live right out there. If anyone would have seen them it would be you. Unless they're the dead come back to earth."

"Don't talk like that," said Marcus, shaking his shoulders as if he'd shivered.

"Well, it's about as likely. Don't you think?"

"To be honest, Legumenus, I'm afraid of what I think."

"I know what you mean. But that's the way it is with politics…everything to gain and everything to lose. There's no middle ground."

"Maybe that's the problem."

"No, that's the glory."

The blast from a purified trumpet split the air. Men moved towards the dais which had been set up by the ancient open air altar to Saturn next to the newer temple at the west end of the Forum. All the majesty of the Capitoline hill topped by the great temple of Jupiter stood as backdrop.

"The moment of truth," exulted Vibulus, rubbing his hands with glee.

"Legumenus," Marcus said, "I think truth is the last thing you care about."

"I'll take that as a compliment," said Vibulus, staring down hard at his friend. "Although I doubt you meant it as one."

"It was a joke," Marcus said. "I meant you're more interested in the excitement than the results."

"Listen, Marcus…" Vibulus, straining to see the front of the dais, had already forgotten Marcus' words. "What if you were the first name called? Think of that! It all depends on you, what you do. If you go, who would have the courage to refuse? But if you refused…"

"If you refused, you'd better be sure you have enough friends to resist the lictors when they come with the hook for your neck."

Spread out below the Capitoline Hill under a thickening sky, eighty-four centuries waited with quivering expectation as two corniculars sounded the assembly on their circular bronze horns. The consuls had taken every precaution to keep the centuries divided, especially those of the infra classem, who made up the plebs. Thus they had split the twenty-four centuries of the infra classem and placed them on either end, with the sixty centuries of classis—those who made up the heavy infantry, in the middle. Behind the plebs on the wings, the six centuries of cavalry were stationed, as if to guarantee their behavior.

Clerks and record keepers occupied the temporary wooden tribunal with the consuls Claudius and Servilius, who sat through the proceedings on their ornate ivory curule chairs of office. Armed with lists of names for each of the centuries, they provided them as the consuls required. Arrayed below the tribunal twenty-four lictors, dressed in blood red tunics and white sash belts, held their bundles of rods. From their boots, red as poppies and laced to mid calf, dangled small pieces of whitened bones. Ranked on either side of the dais were twelve military tribunes, six for each legion, and chosen by the consuls to command a thousand men.

Appius Claudius, finely outfitted in bronze cuirass, purple bordered white tunic, horse hair plumed bronze helmet, and sparkling bronze greaves covering his legs from ankle to knee stepped forward to call the first name. Ten thousand men strained their ears to hear. One of the tribunes strode forward to the century selected and called out a name. No one answered. Another name was called. Still no one answered.

A profound silence of anticipation hung over the assembled warriors. Over their heads lowering clouds compressed the atmosphere until it seemed as if the pressure of the gathering sky would hold everything absolutely still. Nothing moved. No birds sang. Publius Servilius, thought to hold more favor with the plebeians, attempted to call them by name. No one answered. Appius Claudius leaned over the tribunal and spoke to one of his lictors. Again he called a name, this time pointing at an individual. The man did not step forward. But a lictor did.

"War has been declared," observed Vibulus.

As the lictor neared the chosen man, his red tunic bright under the gray sky and muted colors of the assembly, several men stepped in front of their comrade. The lictor attempted to slide between them but was pushed back. He tried again, and again they pushed him back. A third time he tried, taking a running start, and again they repulsed him. But now a ball of men shoved him, and continued shoving him, propelling him backwards until he reached his fellow lictors. Behind this fistful of men suddenly poured all twenty-four centuries of *infra classem*, crowding the tribunal, shouting, gesticulating, shaking fists in the air. Publius Servilius waved his arms, appealing for quiet, while Appius Claudius shook his fist in return and appeared ready to dismount the tribunal and wade into the seditious mob himself. His men restrained him with difficulty.

Marcus Tempanius, along with the rest of the *classis* centuries looked on as if the plebs were a separate people. As in fact they seemed to be. Since he and Didius had been attacked, Marcus' sympathies resided firmly with the plebeian cause. Yet his body did not, and somehow this made all the difference in the world.

Rome divided her citizens, not including the centuries of engineers and musicians, into four classes. The *equites* were made up of patricians, and the wealthiest members of society and served in the cavalry. The *classis* comprised those who could afford to equip themselves as heavy infantry—typically small to medium landholders. The *infra classem* incorporated small shopkeepers, artisans, small shareholders, and landless peasants who served as light infantry, and performed a host of other tasks for the legions. Finally came the *proletariate*, those whose property rating was so low they had no share in the dangers or spoils of Rome's military adventures. Yet all could claim citizenship. And it was this unity of division that held Marcus aloof from the class of Didius, yet sympathetic to their cause.

Aulus Vibulus, his equine face glowing exultantly, did not take his eyes off the tribunal. There the strangest conflict he had ever seen was taking place. Three thousand men arguing with two consuls, while over six thousand spectators looked on. They shouted for redress of grievances, while the consuls bitterly accused them of extorting reforms out of the state in a time of danger. Unlike Marcus, who saw irony and confusion, Vibulus saw opportunity. He had no doubt that he was right in his assessment of the patrician class. One had only to look at history to discern their intent. In the time of the ancient kings they had been lords, leaders of clans, and the kings ruled at their sufferance. Then came Servius Tullius who, with the backing of the infantry (by this time indispensable to Rome's defense) reformed the tribal organization, and created the comitia centuriata. By dividing the people into centuries and levying troops from them, rather than the tribes, he broke up clan and regional loyalties and weakened the power of the aristocracy. Now, while they remained the privileged class, controlling the priesthoods and dominating the consulship, they sought to regain the power and exclusive influence of their ancestors in the governance of Rome. Vibulus entertained no doubts of their ultimate success. He also had no doubt that a new avenue to power was about to be opened, and the plebeians, whose creation it would be, didn't even know it.

Like Marcus, Vibulus, because he had publicly championed reform, had been privy to a number of clandestine meetings in which the plebeians laid down the groundwork for a completely new organization designed for their protection. It would be, to all intents and purposes, a government within the government. This very demonstration was the final attempt of the plebeians to get satisfaction from the ruling class.

Gradually quiet fell over the gathered plebs. Backing up a few paces they cleared a space in front of the tribunal into which Gaius Sicinius stepped. Dressed as all the others in tawny tunic, and sandals laced up the calves, he carried his spare frame with a dignity that set him apart. The consuls made no attempt to silence him though Claudius openly fumed on the dais.

"It would appear," Sicinius began, "that we have no reason to expect justice at the hands of our consuls." His high keening voice echoed like the cry of a hawk off the steep face of the Capitoline Hill. "To say that we expected better of them would, I am sorry to say, be a lie. In fact, citizens, we have received exactly what we expected, dissembling, denial, denigration, and dismissal. To what purpose have we worked the fields until we had not strength to lift a cake to our lips; or been crushed by blocks of stone building temples we helped pay for with our blood fighting the Latins, Volscians, and Aequians? To be called traitors and extortionists!

"Publius Servilius, who promises everything, promises that if we will but save our country in this time of dire peril he will see to it that our grievances are taken up. But I find it curious that the lowing of cattle or the bleating of refugee sheep in the Forum Boarium does not tickle my ears. Nor are these clouds above our heads the thick black plumes of crops and houses burning, but are those sent by the gods to bring rain to nourish our budding fields. And in any case, Publius Servilius thinks we are more dense than these clouds and will forget the promises he's made by the time the sound has left his mouth." A ripple of laughter greeted his words.

Marcus looked at Vibulus who seemed to be wearing a secretive, conspiratorial smile. "Did you write this?" he asked.

Vibulus waved him silent, eyes gleaming with delight.

"Well, then," Sicinius said, "is Rome in danger? Indeed it is. It is in danger of becoming the sole possession of a small group of men who speak of liberty and mean the oppression of everyone but themselves. It is no exaggeration to say that we have more to fear from our fellow citizens than from foreign enemies. For we are sold into slavery by acts of connivance, and handed over by a law kept secret by those who render judgement. What good, then, is citizenship?

"Appius Claudius, whose lineage as a Roman isn't as old as my son, calls us traitors, good-for-nothings. In fact, citizens, this great Roman, a patrician by virtue of bringing out of the Sabine hills an armed contingent of brigands, claims that we, the plebs sordida, are not needed by Rome in any case.

"Well then, Plebeians, let us take ourselves out of this city and create for ourselves a just society, and see if Rome does not need us in truth."

A roar went up from the crowd of men near the tribunal, startling pigeons to flight, and putting seagulls into evasive glide patterns. Stunned to silence the remainder of the centuries looked on with widened eyes as the plebeian centuries marched out of the Forum in a body. In column of fours they climbed the Quirinal on the Vicus Ficus. From every door, excited inhabitants poured out to watch an entire class of citizens march out of the city.

Nonplused, the consuls informed the remaining centuries that the levy would be postponed for one week, and dismissed them.

"Some emergency, eh?" sneered Vibulus.

"What's next?" asked Marcus.

"Let's follow the plebs and find out."

Like a swollen river running thick and muddy the self-proclaimed plebeians marched out the Porta Collina, and followed the river northeast to the confluence of the Anio River, about three miles from Rome. From a distance the line of men resembled a fat caterpillar climbing the small hill they called the Sacred Mount.

Marcus and Vibulus were among a small group of men who followed the plebs out of the city. On a hill no higher than the one on which Marcus had his farm, the plebs laid out a square camp in the finest military style. Not willing to be called lazy they set to work digging a regulation ditch, twelve feet wide and nine feet deep, around all four sides. Cut turves piled on the inner edge of the ditch formed a mound four feet high. On top of this earthen wall, which measured thirteen feet from the bottom of the ditch, they sank sharpened three-pronged stakes that each man carried for this purpose. Like the soldier ants they were, they labored with mattock and shovel, filling wicker baskets with earth, passing them up to be dumped on the rising wall, while others reinforced the earth rampart on either side with stones and wood.

When the camp had been fully erected, and hide tents pitched in orderly rows along broad avenues, the men settled down to a plain meal and rest. They spent the night under leather. At first light they rose, washed, ate a simple breakfast, and met in the 'forum' of the camp.

After the exhilaration of work cooled, after the brotherhood of sweat evaporated, as Marcus sat in repose, doubts filled his mind like ants marching out of an anthill. He wondered if any lasting victory could be achieved. He doubted, as he listened to a steady stream of debates, that true justice or liberty could be won. Perhaps the inevitable defeat could be postponed. It might even be possible to force the patricians to retreat. For a time. But in the end, he knew, with a certainty that grew even as the structure of a new plebeian organization grew, that the patricians would regain what they lost, and seize yet more. Not, he reasoned, as he listened to a debate on establishing plebeian officers, that mystical, diabolical, or even political forces dictated the growth of patrician power. As he saw it a natural law held sway. The patricians have the resources, he thought. What did the plebs have but their bodies? No, resistance was hopeless because the tide of wealth and privilege would ultimately wash away hope and struggle. It was a natural law.

Later that night he broached the subject to his tent-mates, Vibulus, Didius, and Petronius, as they lay in the dark. Cool air, damp and clammy, slithered under and between the tent flaps, crept inside their wool cloaks, and made them squirm against its gelid fingers. The laborious warming of March seemed too slow. Marcus inhaled the humus greening smell of the earth and wished he'd had the sense to go home. There he felt a permanence and satisfaction that contrasted directly with the ethereal nature of politics.

"A man can sink his fingers like roots into the ground," he said. "But this," he waved his hand invisibly through the blackness, "is like trying to catch your breath in the winter. You can see it, but your hand comes away with nothing."

"But the alternative is slavery," said Petronius in his deep as night voice. Though not so sanguine as to believe his class would ever achieve anything like equality, Petronius felt more alive and optimistic about the future than he had in years. The events of the last few days as the plebs hammered out a protective organization had given him hope that the liberty of his progeny would be secure.

"You're too much of a pessimist, Marcus," pronounced Vibulus. "This is just the first step. Others will follow, as with any journey."

"Those are just words, Legumenus," Marcus protested. "Just as these tribunes and aediles are words as long as those in power refuse to recognize them."

"I disagree," said Didius.

"What will you do then?" demanded Marcus. "Set up a new state? How long do you think that would last?"

"If you mean, can we build our own city, of course not," said Petronius. "But whether or not they recognize our assembly and our officers actually makes no difference. They will function regardless."

Marcus snorted into the darkness. "How?"

"Because," said Didius, "we will swear a sacred oath to defend them."

"And eventually," added Vibulus, "the other classes will be forced to recognize them."

That, at least, was Aulus Vibulus' goal. In fact, the nature of the debates and resolutions had surprised and discomfited him. The plebs had adopted the Greek method of democratic voting, and shunned the traditional group vote system. Secretly he saw this as a dangerous precedent that would have to be abjured. But that too could wait. In fact, it would make a nice bargaining chip when the time came.

"They will never recognize the tribunes," asseverated Marcus. "They are a threat to their authority. We'll see blood in the streets before this is over."

"You forget, Marcus Tempanius," Petronius said, "this is Rome. We may have our squabbles as any family, but we don't shed each other's blood to solve them. That would mean the end of our city. And without the city what is a man? He is no better than a beast, a wolf. Without the society of other men, a man has no soul. Is that not so?"

"Certainly that's true…" began Marcus.

"Then how can Rome not accept our tribunes, our assembly, and even our aediles?"

"He's got you in a hold, there, Marcus," laughed Vibulus into the inky confines of the tent.

"Nevertheless," insisted Marcus, "they will never agree to share power. As it is, they regard the comitia centuriata as an affront to their dignity."

"Power?" said Didius. "But this is where you continue to see things wrongly. We don't want to share power. What we want is protection, and this is exactly what the tribunes provide."

Aulus Vibulus, keeping his own dark council, did not wholly agree with this assessment. To him power would most definitely be gained through the organization of the plebs. It would take time, and it would take those with intelligence to use it properly, as the use of any weapon must be learned, but it would be the way to power. He couldn't be sure if it would be the tribunes (it appeared the plebs would elect two in opposition to the consuls) or the concilium plebis (the plebeian assembly) that would be the focal point for the assault on the offices of state. But that mattered little. It might even be the most innocuous looking position, that of aedile, which the plebs created to oversee the markets, keep records of all laws passed and posted by the consuls, and hold annual games that opened the door simply because it would face less opposition. He thought it ironic that these men, so despised as inferior by the likes of Appius Claudius, were formulating a far more intricate system of government than that of their 'betters'. Yet as Marcus pointed out it would not even be recognized. Yet.

As the days passed delegations from the senate came out to meet with the leaders of the plebs to see if some form of agreement could be worked out. Neither side would budge. The senators held out a promise that grievances would be looked into and would go no further. The plebeians demanded recognition of the organization they had ratified amongst themselves. That is: two tribunes with the power to intercede on behalf of citizens on trial, two aediles to oversee the markets, record the laws, and put on annual games, and the concilium plebis to elect both sets of officers strictly from the plebeian class.

In desperation the consuls and senate sent Menenius Agrippa. Well advanced in years, he had once been consul and celebrated a triumph against the Arunci. He was neither patrician, nor exceedingly wealthy, though anyone on the Sacred Mount would have happily exchanged lots with him. Still, the commons liked him and welcomed him to their camp.

Agrippa came dressed in a simple tunic, open sandals, and a red cape thrown around his broad shoulders and held by a simple bronze clasp. In the bright sunlight his full head of silver hair glistened like the snowy peaks far to the east. Under courteous escort he forced his heavy frame up the three steps of the dais with slow ponderous steps. At first he didn't speak, looking over the men gathered in their camp with bright green eyes sunk in deep folds of flesh, like satchels under his eyes to hold all the things his life had seen.

In a gruff voice, swollen with age like his bulbous nose, he addressed the men. "My compliments on a fine camp," he began, waving a massive hand, the thumb of which made an arthritic forty-five degree angle at the knuckle. "It makes me proud to say I have served with many of you in the legions. And on that point, may I say, let us not sever such a grand relationship."

Polite applause greeted this pause in his opening remarks.

"As you know," he continued, clearing his throat, "I was asked to come here to persuade you to return to your city. I did not come here to negotiate." More applause mixed with laughter underlined his words. He cleared his throat again. "Because what I think you need to know is how important you are as a part of our city. But, and here I will not lie or coat with honey my next words, you are indeed only a part. Our city needs you just as you also need the city.

"Let me express this in a parable. Long ago, when man was first formed and everything was new, the different parts of the body were not always in agreement. After all, they had not been working together that long yet." Laughter fluttered like a black butterfly over the assembly. "As seems natural, there arose, out of mutual jealousy and mistrust, a controversy. It seems that the various parts began to resent the fact that their time was spent in providing for the stomach, while the belly received everything in idleness with not a word of thanks. So, the discontented members plotted amongst themselves how they should get even with their pleasure-seeking belly. It was decided that the eye would see no good thing to eat, and that the hands should carry nothing to the mouth, and that the mouth should take nothing offered to it, and that, finally, the teeth should accept nothing to chew.

"At first their plan seemed a good one, and they rejoiced to hear the belly grumble and moan for food. But as time went on, they found themselves growing weaker and weaker, until the whole body wasted away to nothing. And so they discovered that although the belly seemed like a parasite, he also had a service to perform. It received food indeed, but it also nourished the members by giving back through the veins of the body all the blood it made by digestion. For it is upon this blood our health, and our very lives depend."

Maybe the comfort of a warm sun, a clear sky blue as the waters of Lake Alba, and pullulating wildflowers spreading cheerful colors on the ground loaned the parable an air of reason and hope. Whatever its charm, Marcus made up his mind that he had spent enough time on the Sacred Mount. A flight of birds flew towards the city and he lifted his eyes to watch. The message, the omen was clear. Other men voiced the same idea simultaneously.

Gaius Sicinius stood up and addressed the crowd as well as Menenius Agrippa.

"Thank you, Menenius," he said, "for a moving and entertaining story." He smiled as widely as his thin face would allow. "We will take your parable to heart. We have but one request of you, to take back to the consuls, senate, and our fellow citizens this message. When we return, we will have, recognized or not, our own plebeian assembly. We will elect two tribunes whose persons we have sworn to protect. If anyone should violate their sacrosanct persons, we will avenge them before the gods without bloodguilt. We have sworn it before the gods.

"Tell them, Menenius Agrippa, the plebeians are returning to Rome!"

# PART II

## IX

### July 476 BC
### The Neptunalia

Marcus Tempanius released his memories as one releases a captive bird, with sadness and hope intermingled. The years he had shed in reminiscing fell with the weight of dread on his aching back. War with Etruscan Veii would be serious and prolonged. She was a large, well-organized, and powerful city.

A quick gust of wind set the cane rattling along the stream below, rustling like a thousand voices of warning. He looked at Publius Anuncius the crier who waited expectantly as inchoate fear spread from his extremities. "I will inform my son of the call up," he said, vacantly. A polite, enigmatic smile furrowed his planiform cheeks, bronzed by the sun. "Is there anything else?"

Clouds congealed over the sea, pushed against the coast, threatening Rome. Publius Anuncius followed those strange, gray ringed eyes of Marcus Tempanius thither and decided he should hurry on. Marcus sighed, glancing around him at the vines and tools scattered on the ground.

"Nevertheless," he muttered, "these won't keep." He picked up a spade and forced its tip into the soft loam, inhaling the moist fecund smell of it as he turned the dark brown earth over. A worm, its glistening reddish brown body thick as his index finger, squirmed and writhed to escape the scalding rays of the sun. War, thought Marcus, was like that worm, desperately seeking to bury bodies in the cool loam, never to feel the sun.

How many sons would he give to that awful worm? Lucius, his oldest, was already serving under the consul Menenius, son of Menenius Agrippa, long dead. Now Titus, who had just taken the toga of manhood that month, was also to be called. He discounted the fact that at forty-one years of age he remained eligible for five more years. No, the killer worm liked the young. The old were too bitter and tough. It was the young, with dreams and futures, the worm found most delectable.

Gently Marcus lowered the tender vine into the hole, carefully scooping the dark soil around it, and then dipped a ladle into the urn and poured the urine mixture around the freshly planted vine.

"Where is that boy?" he asked himself. "Antonius!"

Antonius, the youngest of his three sons, answered from far up the hillside. "Coming." When he arrived, he had his older brother, Titus, in tow.

"I thought you'd probably want me to get Titus," he said.

Marcus shook his head. The boy knew his mind before he himself did. "You're too smart for your own good," he said.

Antonius did not resemble his brothers. He had neither Lucius' stocky build, nor the bulging musculature of Titus, but the lithe, long muscled build of a deer. In every way he was lighter; lighter complexion, lighter nut-brown limp hair. The image of his mother, Marcus thought guiltily that he would miss this child most if something should happen because of this resemblance. He had her large, dark olive shaped eyes, wide smile, quick wit and equally quick temper.

Help me get these vines planted," Marcus said, "then we'll discuss what the crier had to say."

Titus knelt down by his father. "Antonius said the Fabii were wiped out," he said excitedly.

When Antonius looked at his brother, he saw his father twenty years younger. They shared the same gray ring encircling the brown iris of the eye, thick wavy black hair, long drooping nose, and flat cheeks. Though Titus had yet to fill out, it was obvious he would have the same build, with shoulders like axle hubs and forearms as big as Antonius' thigh. He wondered why he had been made so small.

They worked until nightfall planting vines in the rich volcanic soil. Over the years Marcus had added more grapes to the front section of his property hoping to make the land more profitable. Yet wheat and barley remained the main staples of their income. Satisfied with the day's work, Marcus could no longer put off telling his son Rome expected him the day after the furrinalia in ten days time. His first campaign as a Roman legionary within sight, Titus could not have been happier.

+ + +

"It must fit snugly enough that it can't be grabbed easily, but loose enough to give him freedom of movement."

"Marcus, you may recall that I have made quite a few red tunics for you over the years," replied Drusilla. Stretching a length of knotted yarn she measured across Titus' shoulders, a slight trembling of her hands the only sign of an emotion she dared not display. With a certain detachment she marveled at the width of her middle son's shoulders. Her voice caressed him with motherly pride. "I hadn't noticed how big you've gotten. Your father was much smaller at seventeen."

Marcus snorted with false indignation from a stool nearby. "If you hadn't cut up my first red tunic we could compare." He slapped his hands on his knees and pushed himself up to walk over to one of the open windows. Two windows illuminated the room in which Drusilla kept her loom, one in the south or back wall, the other in the west wall. From the south window Marcus watched the grandson of Petronius lead a flock of goats down the narrow track descending the south side of the hill towards the dark woods of the Alban massif.

"Is it possible they could select you both?" asked Drusilla. Her husband's nervousness made her edgy as well.

"Possible," said Marcus. He picked absently at the wood of the windowsill. "But unlikely. They think men my age are better suited to stay with the women."

"War is for young men," said Titus. He held his left arm out for his mother to measure the short sleeve of the military tunic. "You've done your part. Why should you risk your life further?"

"For the simple reason that I know what the risks are. When you're young you think you're invincible. If you're lucky you'll live long enough to realize you're not."

On the cone-shaped peak to his left the fulgent city of Labicum received the first rays of sunlight like a diadem sparkling in the early morning. Strafing only the peaks with its glory the sun left the dense green-black forests in shadow. No breeze stirred the humid air. From the plane trees behind the house the strange, incessant creaking of cicadas filled the motionless air. Rome would be a misery of insufferable heat today, he thought.

"Your father is just worried you'll be like him," Drusilla teased.

Titus laughed, his mind on the collection of medals his father kept in a cabinet in his office. How often as a child he had fingered them with awe and made his father recount endlessly how he won them until he knew the stories by heart. "Like when you won the corona muralis at Velitrae?" he said, mentioning his favorite story.

"Hm," said Marcus, watching the last of the goats disappear in the field of tall, golden wheat growing on the *ager publicus* behind the farm. "I was angry they killed Petronius' son. I lost my head."

"That seems to have happened a lot with you," said Drusilla. "Hold your arms out straight," she ordered Titus, a little testily he thought.

Marcus left the window and returned to his stool. From his seat he appraised his son, who so remarkably resembled himself. "Remember what I've taught you," he said, "and the training will be easier. But don't expect it to be easy. Handling a sword and spear out here in the yard is one thing, doing it with a hundred others around you in battle is another."

"Yes, Father," Titus acknowledged.

"You've got the legs for it," Marcus said, eyeing Titus' bulging thigh and calf muscles. "But it's the head," he said, tapping his own with a gnarled forefinger, "that makes the difference."

"Yes, Father," Titus answered stiffly. Titus could lay claim to the title of most obedient son. And willingly so. But his father's nervousness irritated him.

"Have you checked your equipment?" asked Marcus, rising again from the stool. Without waiting for an answer, he said, "I'll do it."

Titus began to protest, but Drusilla gave him a discreet tug, wordlessly telling him to allow his father these small attentions. They were his method of expressing both his love and his concern, just as taking her son's measurements, when she could easily have laid out one of his tunics as a pattern, was her way of keeping him close to her one last time.

Marcus crossed the hall and entered the narrow, windowless room that was Titus' bedroom. Laid out in orderly fashion on the straw-stuffed mattress were a round, leather covered shield, bronze breastplate, leather jerkin, and bronze helmet with three black feathers standing straight up from a conical knob on the top. On a small table against the opposite wall lay a sword, sheathed in a leather scabbard studded with bronze rivets. Next to it a leather satchel awaited the polished bronze cook pot, bronze bowl, and iron canteen stacked on top of it. In the corner leaned his spear, six and a half feet of hardened wood and tempered iron sharpened to a vicious point. Grabbing the sword and spear, which was heavy and awkward in the close confines of the bedroom, Marcus went out and down the stairs to the front yard. Descending the stairs, he saw Didius and Petronius look up at him from their work repairing a wagon. Into the tool room he fled, ignoring their amused gaze. He stalked back outside encumbered with a whetstone and stool and dropped everything into a pile in the sun filled yard. Righting the stool, he sat, picked up the whetstone and unsheathed the sword. Wordlessly he began working over the edge of the curved blade.

As much as anything the expense of the equipment drove him to fastidiousness. It cost him precious pigs, as well as bronze *asses*, damaging the fragile economy of the farm. He had been forced to equip two sons, and there would yet be a third in a few years. He leaned close to the blade to inspect a spot, drew the whetstone over it in precise strokes, then flipped the sword over and worked the other side in the same location. He hoped his sons could make up for the expense of the weaponry by coming home with valuable booty. So far, fortune had not favored them in this regard. His eldest son Lucius, now serving in his third campaign, had proved himself a courageous and determined warrior. Together they had celebrated a triumph under the consul, Marcus Fabius, parading through the streets of Rome behind rows of captured Etruscans, and wagons filled with their armor and weapons. The rewards, however, amounted to little.

Should either or both of his sons be killed the loss would be catastrophic. This thought had to be rejected, and a prayer spoken to Mars immediately to protect his sons. To ward off the evil eye he made the special sign of placing the tip of his thumb between the middle and index fingers. Still, something unidentifiable left a vacant feeling in his guts, something left undone, something missed, something neglected.

Petronius and Didius sidled over as his morbid ruminations darkened his complexion. A cluster of black winged chickens scurried out of their way, ruffling the reddish-brown plumage on their backs in umbrage at the intrusion.

Petronius and Didius, both widowers, had taken up residence on the farm. They lived in the old part of the house, which now comprised half of the lower level. A complete set of stalls and storage rooms had been added off the back wall, and the Tempanius family's living quarters had been added as a second story.

"Tomorrow is the Neptunalia," Petronius reminded Marcus. His deep voice was soothing as ointment, calm as deep water.

Marcus grunted acknowledgment but said nothing. A black insect as big as his thumb inspected him briefly then flew off. One of the offspring of Tibia's last litter ambled up, sniffed his leg with a cool wet nose, and lay down next to him with a groan. He reached down and patted her heaving side.

"We've already built three umbrae behind the spring," said Didius. Mumbling out of the sagging right side of his mouth. He stirred the dirt with a bare toe, toughened to shoe leather.

Umbrae were huts constructed of foliage and erected as symbolic shade for protection from the heat. Neptune, honored as the god of irrigation and fresh water, protected irrigation gates and canals. Two days later the *furrinalia* honored the god of the source, or of deep water. That is, wells and springs which brought sweet water from deep in the earth.

Marcus could not stir up any enthusiasm for the occasion. The thought of irrigation conjured up an image of rivers of blood flowing into the ground. Again he made the sign against the evil eye.

Didius and Petronius noticed and both began to speak at once. Petronius deferred to his older friend. "You seem more worried than usual," Didius said.

"What do you think about this war with Veii?" asked Marcus. He sheathed the sword and picked up the spear.

Petronius rubbed his sweat shined bald pate. "War is war. It's never good. One can only hope it's not too bad."

"I think you're wrong," said Marcus. "Veii is a powerful city—as strong or stronger than Rome. A lot of widows and orphans will be made in this one."

"Then we should prepare the farm for raids," said Didius, his direct green eyes chastising Marcus. "Hide what we can, move the stock into the forest, and prepare to defend or evacuate the farmstead."

Marcus suddenly brightened. "That's what I like about you, Didius; you're a practical man."

+ + +

Summer drove forward with fierce, unremitting heat. So did the Veientes. They drove a legion led by the consul Menenius from the field at the ford of Fidenae and chased them ignominiously to the walls of Rome. There, in a desperate battle fought in front of the Colline gate, the Romans barely kept the city out of enemy hands. Denied the ultimate victory, the soldiers of Veii did not despair but fortified a camp on the Janiculum Hill across the Tiber and instituted a policy of plunder and destruction. Denied food, Rome could either capitulate or give battle.

On the Campus Martius, Titus and the other recruits drilled daily. Over and over they practiced advancing in line, using the spear, and setting up camp. They fought mock battles, which differed from reality only in the use of spears without points, returning to their tents bruised, bloodied, and sometimes broken. The proximity of the Etruscans spared them the long training marches of previous recruits. They accepted the reprieve, based on the assumption they weren't ready to fight, with ingratitude.

Lucius Tempanius served with the consul Menenius and distinguished himself in the fight before the Porta Collina. Though two legions were encamped before the dirt ramparts of Rome, one or the other was usually dispatched to protect the surrounding country from the depredations of the Etruscans. Lucius logged a lot of miles on his feet. Regardless, Roman stomachs grumbled with hunger, and every day the number of refugees from the country increased.

Out on the Tempanius farm things remained quiet. A surreal tranquillity, like false spring, hung over the little hill. Yet Marcus kept them all busy. From the fields stones were gathered and mortared into the north wall that bordered the original farmstead, raising its height to nearly six feet. They felled trees in the forest behind and from the lumber constructed a heavy gate hinged to towers ten feet high at the main entrance. An abatis of felled trees barricaded the main drive. Lopping off the branches facing the house, they sharpened them into stakes and seeded the vineyard with deadly spikes to deter cavalry and slow infantry.

For the defense of the farm there remained Marcus, his youngest son Antonius, Petronius, his grandson Primus, and Didius, whose two sons Quintus and Sextus were serving with the legions. Despite the fact that Antonius was only twelve, and Primus fifteen, Marcus felt confident that the five of them could hold off any band up to double their number. Antonius and Primus trained daily in the use of the sling and spent hours collecting stones for ammunition. Petronius and Didius could handle slings as well as javelins, and were passable swordsmen. Marcus, as an experienced heavy infantryman handled spear and sword well, and had also trained himself in throwing the javelin. He, Didius, and Petronius each had three of these, thanks to the stealth and scavenging ability of his two men, who managed to 'requisition' five of them from the Etruscans.

Drusilla had her doubts. She felt sure they would be safer in Rome. There would be at least two legions defending the city. Living conditions might be cramped, but living in quotidian fear was worse.

Finally, as paterfamilias, Marcus called a meeting. Though technically free to impose his will on all his dependents, to do so was considered an abuse of power, and it was expected that the paterfamilias would first seek counsel from other members before making important decisions. To this end, after *vesperna*, the evening meal, they remained in the dining room to discuss the situation. A jug of hot spiced wine sat untouched on a warmer in the middle of the table. The diners picked desultorily at a bowl of figs.

"You would soon be afraid of where your next meal was coming from," asserted Marcus, peeling away the green skin of a fig and biting into the sweet pink and white flesh.

"There are grain stores in the city," said Drusilla. "And supplies are still getting through."

"Nevertheless, every time a farm is abandoned that's one less source of food."

"That's true, Domina," said Petronius. "Plus, you must add to that the crops destroyed every day by the Veientes."

Drusilla looked to Didius for support. Embarrassed, he bent his silver head and stared at his callused hands. By the gauzy light of sunset streaming through the open north window his hands looked just a shade lighter than a chestnut. This observation led him briefly astray to look at his arms as well. "Maybe it would be best if you and young Antonius go to Rome, and us others stay here and watch after the place."

His attempt at tact backfired. "I will not desert my family," said Drusilla hotly. "And if it comes down to it, Antonius will do his duty as any other Roman."

Didius ducked his head as if she'd just slung a stone at him. "Forgive me, Domina. I was only concerned with your safety."

"Don't put on that meek and humble act with me, Didius Crispus," she fumed. "I know you too well."

"No," said Marcus, rubbing his square chin reflectively, "I'd rather hide you in the forest than send you to Rome by yourself."

"But what if," she paused, "what if Primus is in the forest with the goats, and Didius is working the south wheat field, and Marcus you're working the vineyard and the Etruscans come? How will you all get here in time to defend the place?"

"That's why someone must always be up here to sound the warning."

"But what if you can't see them from here until it's too late?"

"There's the tower," volunteered Antonius. "You can always see that."

"The tower?" asked Drusilla.

"You know, the one about two miles away to the northeast," Petronius said. "They built it a couple of years ago to give advance warning of enemy forces."

"I'd forgotten," said Drusilla softly.

"The boy's right," said Marcus. "It's still manned, and if there are any Etruscans in the area they'll light a fire. You can see it right from this window." He pointed over his shoulder with his thumb.

"Plus, we have the dogs," said Primus.

"But there are thousands of Veiente soldiers out there," insisted Drusilla. "How can you possibly hope to defend our farm against them?"

Marcus stared at his wife, mouth open in disbelief at her tenacity. He tried to force exasperation out of his voice and replace it with calm, understanding, tutorial tones. "Drusilla, listen, most of their soldiers are on the other side of the river. If they cross and come this way their line of retreat will be cut off. Believe me, the consuls have tried any number of ruses to get them to do just that."

Didius and Petronius nodded their heads vigorously in agreement. "They let a whole herd of cattle graze practically unattended on the Circus Maximus trying to entice them," said Didius. "But to no luck."

"Truly Domina, it's only their cavalry that's able to cross over and do much damage," said Petronius.

"I see," said Drusilla, flashing her dark olive shaped eyes around the table. "We're only afraid of large bodies of infantry." Everyone smiled at her sudden understanding.

"Large bodies of cavalry are somehow no threat whatsoever."

"Large bodies are intercepted by our cavalry," said Marcus, wearily. "It's the small raiding parties we have to worry about."

"And will our tower notify us of them?"

"I don't know, Drusilla. What do you want me to say?"

"That it's safer here than in Rome."

"The only safe place in war is the place where it isn't."

+ + +

Titus walked towards her, all the while telling himself he shouldn't. His legs felt leaden with fear, but his eyes were captivated with delight, drawing him on. Never had he seen anyone like her, hair the color of ripe wheat, lithe figure draped in a flowing almost sere stola. She beckoned to him with a slender arm and calmed his fears with laughing eyes the color of the sky. As he drew close she spread her arms as if to embrace him, then opened her mouth to speak. In an instant her mouth became a deep cavern, her teeth moss encrusted blocks of stone. Titus stood riveted to the spot, his legs too heavy to move, staring into the black grotto of his lover's mouth. He felt as if he were slowly turning to ice from the feet up, and looked down to see if it were true. When he looked back up a gargantuan red worm uncoiled like a tongue from the back of the cave mouth, flailing about in search of him, yet somehow missing though he stood rooted, unable to move. 'It's not looking for me,' he thought. 'Who is it after? Who is it seeking to devour?' He turned his head to look, to yell a warning, but could not. Then he woke.

Disturbed by the fact he could not see who the worm was after in his dream, yet certain he knew them, he could not let it loose. All through the day he told himself to forget it as just a stupid dream. Yet it clung to him and would not give him peace. That afternoon when his duties were over, he sought out his brother, Lucius, encamped with the legion of Menenius along the Via Salaria on the north end of the city just outside the Porta Collina.

"You worry too much," chided Lucius. A wide easy grin made his large head seem even more round.

"I don't have your carefree attitude toward life," observed Titus.

"Why shouldn't I? Life's a bubble."

"I hear rumors you're to receive an armilla for the fight at the Porta Collina."

"That's what they say," said Lucius. He held out his two massive arms like tree limbs. "Which arm do you think it'd go best on?"

Titus, who had seen his brother intermittently over the last few months, gawked openly at the size of his brother's arms. "Army life seems to agree with you," he said.

Lucius chuckled. "That's a lot of boring ditch digging," he said. "But when it's exciting there's nothing like it. You'll see, Titus. You can't drink enough wine to get the feeling you have in battle. So, what do you think?" he reiterated. "Which arm?"

"Your right," Titus said. "It would be a little extra protection, and put a little fear and doubt in the enemy when he sees it."

"Perfect. Exactly what I was thinking."

Darkness gathered over the high mountains to the east. Nestled in the front range, the last rays of sun lit the city of Tibur like a taper flaring brightly before it burns out. Titus and Lucius sat on stools in front of Lucius' tent, warm in their red tunics, silent within their thoughts.

"I still think we should ask for leave to go check on the farm," said Titus.

Lucius shrugged his mountainous shoulders indifferently. "If anything happened, we'd have heard," he said.

"How?"

"Someone—Petronius, Didius—someone would find us."

"What if they were all…"

"You worry too much."

"Well, whether you go or not I'm going to try."

"You do that." Lucius laughed, showing square white teeth. "And after Father gets done kicking your backside just remember I told you so."

The next day his legion marched south, carrying Titus away. It would be some months before he talked to anyone in his family again. If ever.

+ + +

Beyond the boundaries of the known world it formed. Carving indolent whorls and eddies, seemingly aimless and harmless it spread, gaining force by accretion. Flying low over the deserts of Africa it grew stronger even as it grew sere, desiccated, pulling up the desert sands, hurtling over high dunes, screaming through rocky canyons. The wind. The moisture sucking, howling torrid wind swept out of Africa, crossed the Mediterranean Sea, dropped its load of sand on Sicily, and hit Latium like a firestorm. Rome roasted, crops shriveled, rivers and streams shrank like rabbits before a ravenous wolf.

On the farm the wind swept all thoughts of the Veientes away as they labored to defend the crops. Days of arduous work at the end of a shovel or mattock blistered their callused hands as they dug irrigation ditches to bring water from the spring to thirsting crops. Drusilla, whipped by the scalding desert wind, carried water until she could not straighten her back and quenched the thirst of each grapevine as if it were her child. And when they deracinated the last piece of sod, and opened the floodgate to spill water in life-giving freshness onto the fields, they rejoiced.

They sat right where they were in the shade of a plane tree, resting their backs against its mottled bark. Drusilla went to the house to put together a meal to share there at the literal end of their labors. She brought out a simple meal of wheat cakes, figs, cheese, and salted pork on a ceramic platter, and then returned to the house for a pitcher of wine.

"Don't eat it all before I get back," she admonished with a laugh as the men dove ravenously into the food. Upstairs she went into the dining room for the pitcher she'd left there. The beautiful view from the window arrested her, and she paused a moment to take it in. To the north, distant Mount Sabinus hulked solitary, cone shaped, like a tower guarding a gate. To the right the first range of the Apennine Mountains invaded the turquoise sky with sheer peaks of dark green and gray. On the lower slopes, like mosaic tiles set into the dark background, the city of Tibur reposed, overlooking the tawny plain, for possession of which Rome and Veii locked horns in bloody war. She wondered what the citizens of Tibur thought, macabre spectators of a deadly drama.

As she turned away from the window a puff of smoke caught her eye. With swift realization that the smoke came from the warning tower she dropped the pitcher. It smashed on the wood floor. "They're coming," she screamed out the window, then raced for the stairs, shards of pottery snapping under her feet.

The men were already on their feet when she turned the corner. "They're coming," she said again into their bewildered faces.

"Are you sure?" asked Marcus. His utter calm passed to Drusilla.

"I saw smoke from the watchtower."

"All right. Didius, Petronius, call Primus from the woods. Drusilla, gather your things and go find him."

"But Marcus…"

"Stick to the plan, Drusilla. Someone needs to stay with the goats, and we need Primus here. Now hurry!"

Didius and Petronius ran down the south side of the hill to the wheat field planted in the saddle between the hill and the mountains a quarter of a mile away. Together they whistled a shrill, ear-splitting signal that Primus had never failed to hear.

Marcus immediately entered the tool shed and put on his helmet, securing it to his head with a leather thong that passed from a loop at the back to brazed loops on the cheek pieces, and tied under his chin. Antonius helped him with his breastplate, simply a square piece of planished bronze covering his chest, held in place with four leather straps. When Didius and Petronius came running back Marcus handed out the javelins, wicker shields, and short swords. He belted his own Greek kopis style sword around his waist, grabbed his long thrusting spear and round shield, and led them to their positions.

Marcus, Petronius, and Didius hid in the fallen trees blocking the drive. Lanes for withdrawal had been prepared in advance to a second line of fallen trees where Antonius and Primus would cover them under a shower of stones. The battlefield had been prepared. They hoped, as Primus came puffing up, it would be good enough to save them.

What seemed like hours passed as they waited. The sun, arcing towards the sea, blistered the air and the southern wind stirred up the desiccated earth in small cyclones. Still, no one came. Inchoate hope the Etruscans had taken another direction invaded their brains like the delirium of thirst. They relaxed. Wished they'd brought water. Wished they'd brought the food. Still, they waited.

Then the Etruscans came. Rounding a hill to the southwest they rode into view in a swirl of dust pulverized by the hooves of their warhorses. Now they saw the lane at the bottom of the hill and turned up. Peering out between once leafy branches Marcus tried to count the riders. There must have been twelve or fifteen, but he couldn't keep track. When they saw the barricade, they stopped. He heard derisive laughter as the lead riders pointed and swept their arms in an arc. They rode closer and Marcus crouched lower, wishing the tree had more foliage.

He could see them clearly now. They wore short tunics of fine white linen. Protecting their chests and bellies were polished bronze cuirasses fashioned in three round discs, one over each breast, the third covering the upper abdomen. On their heads they wore helmets with horsehair plumes, large cheek pieces and protective nose guards, giving their eyes a large, vicious appearance. Dusty bronze greaves gave their legs a long elegant look hanging down the sides of their restless mounts. In one hand they carried a long lance, while the other held the reins and a small round shield.

Marcus waited, hugging the trunk, watching closely for the moment when the riders crushed together. Didius and Petronius, on either side of him, cast worried looks his way. The voices of the Etruscans were easily discernible only ten yards away. Still, he made them wait.

For the Etruscans of Veii the dilemma was the vineyard. The vines there were yoked, that is, each grew up a vertical stake then across a horizontal one, creating a leafy canopy over the ground. They had either to hack their way through this, pull the trees from the road, or dismount to plunder the house. The commander swiveled in his saddle to give an order and Marcus could clearly see the ornate embossing on the bronze covering of his shield. He turned back and seemed to appraise the farmstead again.

"This would make a nice addition to my property," he mused to a subordinate.

"It looks well tended," responded the man on his right. "It's a pity to have to burn it."

Marcus fumed as he listened to them discuss the fate of his farm with the casual air of proprietors. Reining in his anger he waited as three riders approached, waved forward by their commander. As one of them reached down to grab hold of a branch his eyes widened catching sight of Marcus crouched behind the trunk. Before he could react, Marcus leapt to his feet with a shout and hurled a javelin into his guts. The rider went down with a scream as Didius and Petronius jumped up and launched their javelins into the bodies of the other two riders simultaneously. They hit the ground, raising clouds of dust as their comrades fought rearing mounts, yelling at one another in confusion. Another volley of javelins flew from the abatis and another man thudded lifeless to the ground, but Marcus and Didius both missed.

The captain, his shield impaled by Marcus' second javelin, threw the now unwieldy device to the ground and ordered his men to dismount with a hoarse cry.

"Let's go," shouted Marcus. As the Etruscans milled about, he, Didius, and Petronius fell back to the second line of defense where Antonius and Primus covered their retreat with a hail of stones.

"I hit one, I hit one," shouted Antonius jubilantly as yet another Etruscan hit the hard packed earth.

The Etruscans regrouped out of range, Antonius' victim supported on wobbly legs to the rear. Four of their number lay on the ground dead or dying, a fifth had no idea where he was. Nevertheless, the captain regained his confidence in the superiority of his numbers and his arms, and ordered an assault. Assessing the situation coolly he concluded that five men opposed him, only one of whom had been heavily armed. While he couldn't be absolutely certain no one waited behind the wall he thought it unlikely. He ordered one man to watch the horses and divided the remaining seven, intending to attack the peasants from the flanks with his trained soldiers.

"Vipinas, Laris, and Rasce come with me, the rest of you go around the left side." He surveyed the terrain again. "Swords only. Spears will be useless in the vineyard."

Adrenaline coursed through Marcus in tremendous surges like jagged bolts of lightning. Suppressing the urge to rush upon the enemy in a mad joyous fury he ordered Antonius and Primus back to the wall. Didius again took a position on his left, Petronius on his right. He watched the Etruscans divide and enter the vineyard. The captain picked up the shield of one of his fallen men.

"All right," said Marcus through clenched teeth, "throw your javelins and retreat to the wall. Unless you have a clear advantage do not get in a sword fight. Didius, take my javelin." He tossed it to the little man. "Make them count."

They too entered the vineyard, keeping the sharpened stakes between them and the enemy. Didius and Petronius went a short distance, hoping for a clear view to throw their javelins and retreat. Marcus went wider, planning to take the enemy in the flank. In his heart he did not want this little fight to reach the wall. He raced through the shady arbors of his vineyard. Ripening green grapes hung down in fat clusters giving off a fruity perfume. In the cool shade of the wide green leaves, he searched for the end of the stakes they had planted in a swath twenty yards wide on either side of the drive. Reaching the end of this malicious planting he quickly turned right and stopped, waiting for the enemy. Just as he hoped, the stakes slowed their attack, catching them by surprise. Marcus heard a howl of pain far to his right, then another nearer. Didius cursed, his second javelin nicking a stake and shearing off target. Suddenly one of the Etruscans came into view. With a howl of rage Marcus attacked him. Startled, the soldier looked around, his black horsehair plume wagging in confusion. At the last moment he saw Marcus and turned to engage him. Before he could square his feet Marcus hit him, charging into him with his shield up and close to his body. The Etruscan went down with a grunt. He raised his shield and tried to scramble to his feet but Marcus was on him, raining furious blows on the upraised shield, pinning the man to the ground. From the corner of his eye he caught movement and instantly aimed his next blow at his adversary's extended left leg. Bronze, flesh, and bone parted, blood spurted dark red geysers onto the earth. The soldier screamed, dropped his shield arm and Marcus plunged his sword into his bowels.

117

Two men were coming at him now, ducking beneath the vines. He wanted them both. Blood lust raged through him, but he conquered it and turned tail and ran, making for the stone wall. "Stick to the plan," he told himself fiercely. "Stick to the plan."

"Close the gate," Marcus shouted as he ran toward the wall.

Petronius and Didius manned the wide-open gate, ready to close it as soon as he got there. Antonius and Primus were behind it, slings whirling, flinging rocks like brimstone through the air. The Etruscans slowed. There were only five of them now.

"Close the gate," Marcus ordered again. "I'm staying here." He indicated a spot in front of the gate.

The Etruscans regrouped in the road near the fallen trees, out of range of the slingers. Their captain flew into a rage, infuriated by the sight of Marcus standing alone in front of the gate.

"The key to the gate is in front of it," he said bitterly. "Let us go take it."

"What about the others?"

"They are mosquitoes."

"They've drawn a lot of blood today."

"Forget them! They're out of stingers now. There," he pointed angrily at Marcus, "is the key to the gate."

Marcus stood before the gate like a legionary at attention. Three black feathers attached to the top of his helmet ruffled in the wind. Pulsing with adrenaline the gray ring circling his eyes seemed to shine like silver. He was sweating and thirsty as the dry earth. Yet he refused to listen to Didius and Petronius as they implored him to come inside the wall.

"Maybe they'll get discouraged and go away," Petronius said.

"No," Marcus replied. "They'll just come back with more men. I want them to come now." He clenched his teeth. "Come and die," he cried hoarsely to the Veientes. "There is nothing better for Roman soil than Etruscan blood." He clashed his sword against his shield, sending out a ringing challenge, then sheathed it and hefted his long thrusting spear, the hasta.

Hoisting their shields high to ward off stones, the Etruscans hurled themselves at him, obeying his challenge. From behind the wall a hail of stones filled the air, intended to break up the charge. Marcus stood rooted to the spot in front of the gate until the charging Etruscans were strung out ten yards from him. With his long hasta leveled he exploded into them at a dead run, impaling the first man with such force the spear came out his back. The shock of his counter-charge momentarily stunned and slowed the Etruscans. Immediately he pulled his sword. He crashed into the captain, who lost his balance and half turned away. Marcus brought his sword down with tremendous velocity on the Etruscan's sword arm and chopped it off. Blood poured like a fountain onto the ground. Marcus spun, was hit, stumbled, regained his footing.

"Sally, sally," cried Petronius. The gates flew open and Didius and Petronius, with their flimsy wicker shields and short swords threw themselves on the remaining Etruscans. The enemy broke and ran. Marcus gave chase, gained on the lead man. Suddenly something hot slammed into him, tore like fire into his side. He stumbled; the ground rushed up and hit him in the face. He spit dirt from his mouth, tried to push himself up, tried to move his legs but couldn't get his face out of the dirt. What was happening? He heard voices retreating, then rushing footsteps coming at him. He attempted to rise to defend himself but his body wouldn't respond. Suddenly he rolled over, not knowing how, and was facing the aqua blue sky. It felt good on his face. Antonius and Petronius were over him now, looking with worry carved faces at him. He tried to smile.

"Papa, Papa," cried Antonius, tears starting in his eyes.

"We won, eh?" croaked Marcus.

"Yes," said Petronius. "Be quiet now. Where are you hurt?"

"My back. I can't move. I think they cut…"

"Shh," Petronius soothed. He turned Marcus over slightly to look at the wound in his back. Blood saturated his tunic and ran in rivulets into the greedy earth.

Marcus laughed weakly. "Well," he breathed, losing strength, "we irrigated the ground good today, eh?"

"Yes," choked Petronius, his eyes blurred with tears. "Yes we did."

Marcus Tempanius didn't hear, instead he stared at the blue, blue sky forever.

# X

## March 19, 475 BC
## Festival of Minerva

Out of the southwest, spawned by the sea the winds came, growling fiercely, tearing with water-filled claws at every loose thing. Roof tiles flew with perilous precision, boards groaned as soggy wind-fingers tore them from their nails. Hides took wing like giant disoriented bats. Trees bent, then broke as the merciless wind launched branches like blunt spears, bludgeoning tender new crops that lay down and died. Shivering with cold, artisans and tradesmen filled the temple of Mercury to celebrate the festival of Minerva their patron goddess. Inclement weather having forced them to abandon her open-air shrine on the Aventine, a lean and subdued celebration took place.

Of all the months in the year, Lucius Tempanius disliked March the most. The anticipation of spring and warm weather made every cold day a personal reproach. This March particularly riled him. He had been under hides for a full year, had gone through a bitter cold winter, and was impatient not only for spring, but for a chance at the Veientes. They still occupied the Janiculum Hill. Revenge occupied his mind.

He and Titus had been given leave for the full period of mourning after their father's death. The little battle had taken on heroic proportions at Rome, second only to the near destruction of the Fabii. But in the Tempanius household grief reigned. Antonius, who had watched his father get stabbed from behind, blamed himself and maintained a morose, inconsolable silence. Drusilla honored her dead husband, mourned him, and said only once that she had begged him to go to Rome. Didius and Petronius extolled the courage and virtue of their patron, and pledged the same loyalty to Lucius, the new head of the family. They also reminded him that the family had increased its wealth by five horses along with the armor and weaponry of the dead soldiers of Veii.

Publius Scipio, Aulus Vibulus, and Gaius Opimius insisted on helping to pay for a public funeral in Rome, and helped carry the bier. Lucius delivered a nervous funeral oration, then set aflame the pyre on which his father was cremated. His anguish was mitigated by the dignity, honor, and gravitas he gained by the public homage Publius Scipio paid to the dead Marcus Tempanius.

At twenty years of age Lucius neither desired, nor felt prepared for the position of head of the household. So, his first decision was to postpone any family meeting on the matter until after the war with Veii. At the time, he thought he had given himself two or three months reprieve at most. Now, eight months later, Rome still huddled under the threatening eyes of Veiente soldiers.

The harsh winter brought a sack of miseries. Pneumonia and other diseases swept away hundreds of legionaries. Rations were thin, and so were tempers inside the camp along the Via Salaria. Four thousand feet churned the sodden ground into a muddy quagmire. The air reeked of it, and it clung disgustingly to one's feet.

The wind flung a cloudburst against the leather tent with a ripping sound. Lucius, mercifully free of duties, lay on his cot covered by a thick woolen cloak on top of which he spread a leather rain cloak also. The sound of sucking footsteps stopped outside the tent and a blast of cold air invaded the tent as the flap opened. Gaius Opimius Jr. stuck his head and shoulders in.

"Hail, friend," he greeted Lucius.

"By Jupiter," yelled Lucius, "either come in or get out, but close the flap."

Gaius Opimius Jr. pushed through the tent flap like a barge. He was all torso, with thick short legs, earning him the nickname Truncus, or stump. He could easily have been called 'block' since his body seemed all one thickness from shoulders to feet, resembling a squared block of stone. He shook his big head vigorously, sending a fine spray of water from tight black curls. His clean-shaven face swelled strongly at the jaws and joined his shoulders as if without a neck. Dropping his gear next to an empty cot across from Lucius he put his hands on his hips and smiled at him.

"Well, is that any way to greet your friend and tent-mate," he said. Full lips pulled back in an arrogant smile, and his dark eyes challenged Lucius.

Their friendship was not wholly ingenuous. A competitive aspect left a dissatisfying taste---at least in Lucius' mouth. Lucius locked eyes with his erstwhile friend. He remained supine under his stack of cloaks.

"How are you, Truncus?" he said. "Did your father use his influence to get you billeted here?" He laughed ironically.

"As a matter of fact he did," Opimius Jr. said. "They wanted me to be military tribune with Verginius. But I insisted on serving with my famous friend, and Father arranged it."

Lucius shot him a sneering half smile. "Very funny."

Opimius Jr. lowered his square body onto his bunk. His faded red tunic, not so much covering his body as restraining the musculature of his vast chest, barely moved to accommodate the change of position.

"Is it dark yet?" asked Lucius.

"Almost. Another hour."

"Hm. Have you eaten?"

"What is there to eat?"

"Didn't you bring anything from home?"

Opimius Jr. gave a strangled laugh. "You should know my father better than that." He straightened his back and deepened his voice in imitation. " 'Soft food makes soft soldiers.' I have wheat and hard tack."

"Let's wait," Lucius advised. "Maybe Considius and Vopiscus have found something."

They chatted desultorily for a time, comparing family notes, news, women, and horses. As the fugitive sun hid behind the sea the tent grew yet colder. Soon Opimius Jr. pulled his cloak tighter and shook himself like a dog.

"Don't you have more charcoal for this brazier?" he asked, looking around the tent. He rubbed his hands over the barely smoldering brazier.

"Soft living makes soft soldiers," parodied Lucius. "Well, I guess we'd better make something to eat before it's too dark to see." He threw off the cloaks covering him and swung his feet to the ground. From beneath his cot he pulled a cook pot, a terracotta urn with a wide mouth and lid, and a metal canteen. He pointed to a corner of the tent that sheltered one hundred men. "There's some charcoal under Considius' cot, there."

While Opimius stoked up the brazier, Lucius poured water into a bronze cook pot and when Opimius had a glowing bed of coals set it over them on a small tripod. As soon as the water boiled, they poured in equal amounts of wheat, a large pinch of salt, and waited. When it finished cooking, they divided the porridge and ate in silence.

Squishing footsteps, competing voices, and two wavering shadows cast by a wildly guttering torch pushed aside the tent flap and entered. The smaller of the two planted the torch in the muck outside the tent.

"Well," Lucius said, "the scavengers return at last."

The two men stood shaking the rain off their foul weather cloaks. "Who's the new resident?" asked the torch-bearer. He held his thin frame straight as a knife blade.

"I thought everyone knew Gaius Opimius," said Lucius. "Truncus, meet Attius Vopiscus, and Cnaeus Considius."

"Ah, yes," said Vopiscus. Though the same height, the gargantuan dimensions of Opimius diminished the lean Vopiscus considerably. Vopiscus extricated his hand quickly from Opimius'. "I can see how strong you are," he said, shaking his hand. "You don't have to prove it."

"Glad to have you," said Considius. The tallest of the four, the shortage of provisions arrested his propensity to obesity. "Bad luck," he announced, his accommodating gray eyes registering both apology and disappointment. "There wasn't so much as a loose chicken in Rome." His plump round face flushed bright red.

"Look at him," laughed Lucius. "Red as an apple. What's he hiding?"

"Don't mention food," despaired Considius.

"I'll bet you made it to the Subura, eh?" taunted Lucius.

Vopiscus grinned thinly as he lifted the leather scabbard strap over his head. "We had to make sure there was still some wine left over from your last leave."

As night closed around them the rain ceased, the wind fell, and suddenly a still quiet blanketed the camp. The tent began to fill as men came off duty and the low murmur of conversation hummed like the low notes of a pipe. They fell to talking about what all young soldiers talk about—women, and their new commander Servilius. A game of latrunculi began at the opposite end of the tent and they went to join in.

Five miles up river the little city of Fidenae slept. It had the honor or misfortune, depending on one's point of view, of guarding the best ford across the Tiber River. Veii and Rome coveted this ford because it controlled traffic moving north and south along the main trade route between Etruria and Campania. To bypass the ford at Fidenae meant to take on the perilous wilds of the Apennine Mountains. No one's product could withstand that kind of price increase. Yet for all that, Fidenae could never rival her two covetous sisters, and so fell to being the spoil of their vile affections. So the ever-coveted citizens listened to the soft clop of pitch smeared horses hooves, the tramp of soldiers marching, the clinking and rattling of equipment. They endured a rear guard posted to secure a line of retreat if necessary, and the Veientes moved into Roman territory.

Rome slept. No one was going anywhere in the driving rain, on mud sucking ground in gale force winds.

Quintus Crispus, son of Didius Crispus, patrolled his assigned section outside the stockade wholly engrossed in the pursuit of warmth. He wore every piece of clothing he possessed; two wool tunics, a leather skull cap, and shoes. On his back he wore a wolf pelt, the front paws tied over his shoulders and laying on his chest, the rear legs tied around his waist. The wolf's head covered his own so that it appeared as if his blade thin face were sticking out of the wolf's mouth. Over all of this he wore a thin hooded cloak. But he still could not get warm. At least he had no fear of falling asleep on guard duty.

Then like the floodgate of an irrigation ditch being closed the wind ceased abruptly, the sky cleared and the vast star filled heavens spread out above him. Orion stalked the western sky dragging the big dipper after him. Quintus reckoned his watch must be nearly up and thought longingly of the twig and leaf mattress awaiting him in his tent. He stood still for a moment gazing up at the stars that looked like bright seeds sown into the black loam of heaven. From his right the muffled sound of someone choking and spitting followed by sniffing informed him of the presence of one of the other guards. It crossed his mind that a centurion might be making inspection rounds so he let his cloak fall open to free his arms, and adjusted the long dagger belted around his waist. He brought the hide bound wicker shield slung over his back into his left hand, gripped his javelin firmly in his right and straightened his posture. This last did not increase his stature much but at least gave him a more military bearing. Like his father, Quintus stood a short five feet two inches, with a scrawny build that completely hid the strength it contained.

Sure enough soft footsteps moved towards him. As they grew in volume he could make out the shadow of someone approaching like a smudge against the dark background. A vague apprehension took hold of him and he decided on strict military behavior as his best course of action.

"Halt," he said.

The man stopped twelve yards away, still obscured by night. Quintus saw only that the man had several inches of height on him, and carried no shield —like many velites who could afford only the barest equipment. Under a dark hooded cloak his inscrutable visage gave no clues. He cleared his throat and said, "Hail friend," coughing behind his hand. "I've come to relieve you." Despite his best efforts to hide it behind his hand the man's accent was certainly not Roman.

Quintus felt a cooling tightness tingle across his narrow forehead, and high cheekbones. The hair on the back of his head rose in alarm.

"Password," Quintus demanded loudly. Behind him the ditch, nine bottomless feet deep, suddenly gaped like an open grave. His. He doubted any of the sentries inside the palisade had heard him. He demanded the password again in a louder voice.

Again the man coughed, took a few steps closer and said, "Patience friend, let me get the…" He reached his hand inside his cloak.

"Attack!" screamed Quintus. Fearing retreat more than death he threw himself at the stranger with shield raised and javelin poised to strike. Ten yards separated the two but Quintus reached full speed within three and his adversary had just time to clear his sword when Quintus hit him. With shoulder lowered into his shield Quintus struck the Etruscan at full speed, deflecting a glancing sword blow from the much taller man, and knocked him off balance. As the Etruscan fought to regain his footing Quintus brought the javelin forward with all his strength. The Etruscan fell with a strangled cry, nine inches of razor sharp iron severing arteries, vocal cords, and muscle in his neck.

Swiftly falling footsteps approached him. Quintus left his javelin in the enemy's throat, grabbed the man's sword, and ran for the north gate of the camp hollering, "attack" at the top of his voice, with Etruscans hard on his heels. A great shout came out of the darkness and suddenly confusion erupted everywhere.

Like a blast of cold air, the trumpet brought Lucius awake with a jolt. From the mannequin at the head of his cot he grabbed his helmet, pushed it down on his head, ducked under his scabbard strap and carried his shield to the tent opening. Like a mother hen his centurion calmed and directed the men into position along the palisade. He scoffed at cries the Etruscans were in the camp, forcing the men to hurry in an orderly fashion along the broad avenues of the camp.

"Tempanius," he said, as Lucius pulled his spear from the orderly rack outside. "Where's your breastplate?"

Lucius felt his chest with his free hand. "In the tent."

"Get it on," the centurion ordered. "This could be a long fight."

Lucius hustled impatiently back into the tent to put on his breastplate. Outside the cacophony of voices, trumpets, and clashing arms, of pounding footsteps and excited shouting reached his ear with an inciting persistence. He fumbled with the straps of the 'heart protector,' cursing his fingers. As he burst out of the tent the centurion still stood shouting, directing, encouraging. He pointed to the north wall.

"Go, go, go," he commanded.

Lucius took off at a dead run for the north wall and took up his position between Gaius Opimius Jr. and Cnaeus Considius. Next to Opimius, Attius Vopiscus looked anxiously into the dark beyond the stockade.

"Where in Hades are they?" he wondered, straining his eyes against the night.

To their left a growing tumult roiled near the gate. A missile thudded into the wood stakes of the palisade. Another hissed by their heads and skidded in the dirt behind.

"Jove!" exclaimed Lucius, full of anger and frustration. "They're hitting the gates. Why are we stuck here?"

As if in answer the centurion of their century strode down the line ordering them off the wall. "Four wide!" he ordered. "Follow me; double time."

Expertly they formed up four wide, spears held vertically, and took off at a brisk trot behind Petronius Albinus the centurion. When they reached the north gate, he formed them up six wide and ten deep. Lucius, Opimius, Vopiscus, and Considius made part of the front line.

"Alright," Albinus yelled, "when I give the order we go at full charge."

In front of them furious waves of sound and a vision of hellish chaos widened their eyes. Lucius waited like a javelin to be flung into the fray. A ferous urge to crush the enemy welled in him. He twitched his shoulders and rolled his head to loosen his neck, and itched everywhere. Around him missiles of all kinds flew; rocks, spears, arrows, whatever came to hand. Velites and legionaries mixed like rocks and dirt as they fought to keep the Veientes out of the gate. Now suddenly the white tunics of the Etruscans became more numerous, on their faces Lucius saw jubilation. He tensed with expectation.

"At the run," Albinus exploded into his ear. "Charge!"

Spears leveled in the front ranks the Romans charged at the opening that was their gate. Like a boulder rolling down hill they smashed into the leading Etruscans, felling them like grass beneath the stone. Lucius drove with his legs, his spear couched with an underhand grip. From behind he could feel the weight of ten other men pushing him forward. A man fell beneath him, and he stepped in the middle of his chest. Another rose into his vision and he aimed the point of his spear. He felt more than saw a blow aimed at him and took it on the bronze boss of his shield, but kept his legs driving, pushing. Then his spear hit the target, his arm moved backwards but he shoved forward driving, driving, churning his legs, don't let up, stay in contact, a face exploded in his vision mouth wide in terror agony horror death. Lucius saw everything and nothing, he slowed but the man behind leaned hard against his back pushing. He drove forward, his spear glanced off a shield, was shoved sideways but on he went. Another blow rattled off his shield sending shock waves to his elbow. Now he smashed into the enemy in front with his shield, driving with his legs, pushing, bearing down, propelling the enemy backwards.

"Drive," he yelled. "Drive!"

Beside him, locked elbow-to-elbow Gaius Opimius exalted, laughed, grunted, swore. Behind him his century yelled encouragement without words, emitting barbaric guttural sounds as wild as lions. All around blood, bone, and sinew raged in boiling combat. His spear point found an unprotected belly and he jammed it home, only to have it yanked from his hands by the falling, flailing body. With a cry of rage he pulled his sword and cleaved the sword arm of an adversary. Red, reeking blood sprayed his face. Charging forward he took sight of a terror filled face in front of him, his lips curled in a vicious bloodthirsty laugh and the man bolted. Now, like a weak dam, the Etruscans broke, ran, fled for their lives. Lucius caught one from behind and slashed at his shoulders, cutting through the collarbone, yanking his sword free by the momentum of the man's fall. "Yah!!" he cried in unintelligible lust, anger, joy, and the Etruscans of Veii ran before him, ran like stags chased by the dogs.

Bodies littered the ground all the way to the crossing of Fidenae. There the Etruscan rear guard held up the disorganized pursuing Romans long enough for their comrades to regroup on the other side and retire in order to their camp on the Janiculum Hill. The Romans followed and built a camp at the bottom. Exultant, flush with victory, eager for the morrow.

Spurius Servilius, the newly elected consul, paced joyously in his tent. He could not have hoped for a more propitious sign of the gods' favor. One more victory and a triumphal parade must surely be his. He immediately sent a dispatch with a squadron of cavalry to his colleague's encampment in the vicinity of Alba Longa requesting they link up and make a crushing joint assault on the Etruscans.

+ + +

The more he marched, sixty pounds of pack and equipment breaking his back, the more work on the farm seemed light, peaceful, and relaxing to Titus. After months of fruitless trudging around the countryside, nothing appealed to him more than breaking ground behind a powerful ox, straining against the reins, holding a lurching plow deep in the furrow, guiding a willful beast in a straight line as it broke wind or defecated a few feet from his face. Anything but this dreary, monotonous, bone- wearying chase of an ephemeral enemy.

In the early hours before dawn the sound of pounding hooves alerted the soldiers to new developments. In moments the camp flared into activity. "What's happened?" Rumors spread like wildfire. "There's been a great victory." "We're marching on Veii." They broke camp and were on the march soon after first light. At last the pack felt light, the road short, the soldiering exciting. Titus Tempanius had yet to see battle.

Brutal is the best word to describe the march. Thirty miles to cover in a few hours. Impatient and impetuous, Servilius wanted to put the Etruscans between the hammer and the anvil before they had a chance to reorganize, or get reinforced. Verginius had to cover the distance yet not exhaust his troops, a delicate balance he considered virtually impossible to effect if they had to fight the same day. He sent couriers to Servilius recommending a delay of one day.

Legio II marched under cloudless blue skies. Not a breeze nudged the wild flowers springing up in gold, red, purple, and blue along the roadway. Small brown lizards sunned green-striped bodies on the hard packed earth, scurrying into thorny vines as the legion hurried forward.

Anxious of security Verginius sent one squadron of cavalry ahead, and one to the east to screen his movements. Dismounting he marched his legionaries relentlessly, driving them on, varying the pace from standard to quick-time, even running for short bursts. After three hours and ten miles he called a halt for rest. Titus fell out with his century like a lead weight carelessly dropped. His tunic hung heavy with sweat, his shins ached, and his shoulders were in open rebellion. Above his dripping head the sun bore down, promising more heat. In one draught he drained half his canteen.

"Is he trying to kill us before the Veientes have the chance?" he said, swiping his forehead beaded with moisture.

"Ah, it gets easier after this," one of his comrades said, reclining against a mound of dirt.

"Sure," said another. "You'll catch your second wind after this."

"I think I caught it and lost it about an hour back," laughed Titus. Squinting up at the sun he tried to gauge the time. "It must be about the fourth hour," he said. "Do you think Servilius will wait?"

His companions all raised their eyes to the sky to verify the time for themselves. Shading his green eyes against the brilliant sunlight Lucius Gallio laughed darkly. "Not that one," he said. "He's too hot for glory."

"All right. Form up. Column of three. Let's go," came the command from their centurion walking up the line.

Groaning they rose on weary feet, formed up and started off again. The crossing at Fidenae lay a long way off a step at a time.

+ + +

Spirits ran high in the Roman camp at the base of the Janiculum. Even a meager breakfast could not dampen the enthusiasm washing over the legion. Lucius sharpened the curved edge of his sword with a weary satisfaction. With his thumb he tested the point and traced the edge from the curved swelling near the tip to the narrow waist at the hilt. Satisfied, he sheathed it and picked up his heavily damaged spear. The point was nearly flattened, and the shaft had cracked when jerked from his hands. Quintus Crispus coated the crack with hide glue, wrapped it tightly with linen strips, and bound the shaft tightly with thin filaments of twine six inches on either side of the crack. But Lucius still worried over its reliability. Seated on stools outside Lucius' tent in bright sunshine they inspected the spear together.

"Perhaps you should take it to the armourer," Quintus suggested. No trace of offense occupied his earnest face though he had labored assiduously over the repairs.

"There's no time," said Lucius.

"Well, we'll make a new shaft when the war's over," said Quintus.

"You know," said Lucius quietly, "you saved the camp last night."

Quintus fingered the sword and scabbard belted around his waist. Styled like the Greek kopis that Lucius used the sword had an enclosed bone grip. The scabbard, which he had 'liberated' from his dead adversary after the battle, was of finely crafted leather with four wide bronze bands. "Perhaps you should keep this sword. It's too fine for one of my class, and I doubt Servilius will let me keep it."

"By Jupiter he had better. Listen, Quintus, it's yours by right. You won it in single combat. In fact, there should be some award in it for you."

Quintus smiled, his front teeth a narrow arch in his small mouth. "You have a generous spirit like your father," he said. His light green eyes filled with respect.

Lucius smiled in return, a broad flat thing—his teeth like paving stones. "And you're loyal to a fault...like yours."

"Can loyalty be a fault?" Quintus asked. Now his olive green eyes flashed with mirth.

Though technically patron and client, the two men had grown up together. Quintus, five years older than Lucius, had first treated him as a little brother, then as an equal, and finally with deference. Lucius squirmed uncomfortably within the vestments of this part of the relationship. Not because he regarded the client-patron system as strange. Certainly, no discomfort obtained because of nascent altruistic or egalitarian convictions. Instead, his responsibility as patron to a man he esteemed caused him trepidation. In truth, he did not want the responsibility.

Lucius scrutinized the battered head of his spear. The edge was chipped and flattened in spots, but still serviceable he concluded. From a small jar he poured out a thin stream of amura, watered down olive oil, onto the head. Slowly, deliberately he spread the oil along the edge and drew a soft, gritty whetstone held at a precise angle across it, working from point to barb.

Quintus, assigned guard duty along the stockade, pushed himself reluctantly off the stool. Just then Vopiscus and Considius strode up fully armed, having just come off guard duty at the consul's tent. They stopped abruptly in front of Lucius and came to attention.

133

"Hail, hero," they said in unison, raising their hands in salute.

A sardonic smile stretched the right side of Lucius' mouth. "Hail yourself," he said. With his thumb he pointed at Quintus. "There's the real hero."

"Yes," Vopiscus said. "He performed his duty admirably."

"No," Lucius said, eyeing his tent-mates. "We performed our duty. He killed a man in single combat, and stripped him. He alerted the camp."

"We don't mean to…demean the importance of Quintus Crispus' actions," said Considius. His splotchy complexion reddened, and he spoke hesitantly, his porcine eyes shifting weakly. "It's just that, well, you and Gaius Opimius really led the attack. At least, that's how Servilius sees it."

Lucius chuckled, nudged Quintus, and said, "What do consuls know? And how do you know all this?"

"We were on guard duty at his tent; remember?" said Vopiscus. "And just why did you think you were exempted?"

"I thought Albinus changed the rotation. It wouldn't be the first time."

Quintus smiled self consciously, edging away. "Excuse me," he said, "but speaking of guard duty I'd better get going before they think I've deserted."

Lucius looked up from his honing. "Just make sure you come and get me first if you do." His square jaws spread in a smile of intimate friendship.

"You two are peas in a pod, I see," said Vopiscus.

"We grew up together," said Lucius.

"Speaking of food," moaned Considius, "is there any to be had?"

"That stomach of yours is going to be the death of you," said Vopiscus. His laughter carried a stern undertone.

Considius cast his porcine eyes sideways self-consciously. "A man's got to eat, true?"

"Absolutely, Cnaeus," Lucius agreed heartily. "If you're going to go, it might as well be on a full belly, protecting an amphora of sweet wine.

"Don't forget the women," said Vopiscus, his thin voice dripping disdain like hot wax.

"Women?!" scoffed Lucius. "Fine wine is much harder to come by."

Considius laughed, a high-pitched mulish sound. "You're a man after my own heart, Lucius," he gasped. "But seriously; have you any food?"

"Sorry Cnaeus," said Lucius, turning his attention to his spear. "Now leave me alone and let me finish this."

The conversation with Vopiscus and Considius bothered Lucius. He believed strongly that Quintus deserved recognition for his bravery. Much as he disliked the role, as the little man's patron Lucius felt obligated to do what he could to insure that recognition. With that in mind he went to see his own patron, Publius Scipio, serving as military tribune. After he laid out his case, Scipio agreed to speak to the consul on Quintus' behalf. Lucius returned to his tent seething with anger from the nervousness he had felt in requesting such a favor. Especially since every favor came with a price.

"I'd like to thank you both for what I just had to do," he said vehemently as he pushed through the flap.

Nonplused Considius mumbled a quick apology before he even knew why. Vopiscus gaped, looked at Opimius, and finally found voice. "What are you talking about?"

"I had to go see Publius Scipio—who happens to be my patron—and plead the cause of Quintus Crispus. I hate it."

"And what did we have to do with that?" insisted Vopiscus.

"You convinced me that no one was giving him credit for saving the legion."

Inquiring eyes pried into the conversation from nearby bunks. Lucius squirmed under the scrutiny.

"So, he's your client, eh?" Opimius said.

"He feeds at the Tempanius trough. For what it's worth."

"And do you have many such clients?"

135

Lucius regarded Opimius with a quizzical expression. Why did he ask these questions? He should know the exact structure of the Tempanius household, since their fathers had been close friends. "It's a small trough," he said instead.

Opimius gave him an unctuous smile. "Then why this grave concern for the dignity of one seasonal laborer?"

"Because as you should know, Gaius, I've known him nearly all my life. It seemed like the right thing to do."

"Well," said Opimius, "you don't want to be too soft with your clients or they'll come to expect it." Vopiscus and Considius nodded their heads in agreement.

"I see," Lucius shot back. "Loyalty should only be one way."

"Not at all," said Vopiscus. "It's just that if you are too generous they soon forget to which class they belong."

How he had gotten into this conversation Lucius didn't know. He did know that he wanted out of it. The entire episode became more distasteful as the day progressed. Clamping his mouth shut, he went to work polishing his breastplate, ignoring his quondam friends. Moments later the order to parade sent them all into a flurry of activity.

Sixty strengthened centuries of hoplites, roughly thirty-six hundred men, and fourteen hundred velites or light infantry, lined up in parade formation in the open space next to the consul's tent. A small podium had been erected so he could be seen and heard.

"Yesterday," Servilius said, "you acquitted yourselves like true Romans." Stiffly, as if carved in relief from the background of the camp and the Janiculum Hill rising behind, the consul stood addressing his troops. His slight build and average height belied the imperious and imposing figure his exaggerated mannerisms were meant to portray. Yet his soldiers liked him for his daring aggression.

"Today," he emphasized," we will continue to press the enemy, to take the battle to him. Today, we will seize him by the throat and cast him from that hill." He turned woodenly and pointed in the general direction behind him.

"Roma!" responded the legionaries, clashing their spears against their shields.

Servilius smiled, held up his hand for quiet. His muscle cuirass flashed reddish gold in the sunlight, and the purple border of his white tunic glowed joyously. "First, we will honor those soldiers who fought with particular courage. In this way we may all have examples to emulate, and incentive to gain honors and glory for ourselves."

Starting with the officers he called out two of the six tribunes, including Publius Scipio, and awarded them each a *vexilla*, a small symbol of Rome mounted on silver. Then he called out five of the sixty centurions, including Albinus, and awarded each of them a small silver spearshaft called a *hasta pura*. Finally, he came to the men in the ranks. Lucius stood proudly at attention, bronze helmet and heart protector polished splendidly, waiting for his name to be called. His red tunic had been brushed and beaten so that the color glowed like fire in the hot sunshine, and the *armilla* on his right arm reflected like a mirror.

"Quintus Crispus, for killing and stripping an enemy in personal combat, a cup. Gaius Opimius…" Opimius stepped forward. "Lucius Tempanius." Lucius stepped forward, heart pounding, chest swelling. "For leading the sally against the enemy with such ferocity that you drove completely through their line, the Roman people today award you with *torques* in honor of your exemplary valor." He placed the brazen necklaces over their heads and shook hands.

Lucius stepped back into line, resisting the desire to finger the links of chain. 'At this rate,' he thought, 'I'll have more medals than Father.' The thought saddened him as it brought the bitter bile of vengeance into his mouth.

When Servilius finished handing out awards he marched the legion out of camp and formed it into battle formation. Once again, each century formed up six wide and ten deep. To look at it, one would not recognize any individual groups of men. From a bird's view the legion would have appeared to be formed in ten long straight lines without a break. So it was.

On either end one hundred-fifty cavalry sat their horses, protecting the flanks. In front two lines of skirmishers would prepare the way. Their armaments consisted of either slings or javelins. Some, like Quintus Crispus, carried hide covered wicker shields. None had any type of protective armor, and at most carried a long knife for personal protection. Only half of the fourteen hundred fought as skirmishers, the remainder followed to aid the wounded or dispatch the enemy wounded. In front of them the consul Servilius sat astride a brilliant white stallion. The fourth hour of the day commenced.

The legion waited. Climbing like a hot coal off a blacksmith's anvil the sun ascended in the sky. Not a wisp of a cloud scratched the smooth cobalt blue surface. Like long rows of blood red poppies waiting for the scythe they stood, black feathers protruded like stamens from their helmets, unstirred by any breeze. Still they waited.

Above them the Etruscans filed out of camp, formed up their phalanx and waited. Their formation mirrored the Roman's, skirmishers in front, cavalry on the wings. The heavy infantry, the hoplites, drew up in a longer, shallower line.

Lucius, in the second row in the middle of the Roman line admired the enemy's look. Unlike his tunic, which came down to about three inches above the knee, the Etruscan's tunic barely reached the top of the thigh, and was a gleaming white. While he wore a leather sleeveless jerkin and a square bronze chest protector, they wore beautiful molded cuirasses of leather and bronze with linen pturges hanging down to protect the groin. A variety of helmets adorned the enemy warriors, some with wing-like protuberances angling up and outward from just above the ear, some with completely open face, some with cheek guards that left only the eyes, nose, mouth, and point of the chin exposed. All unfailingly had a high center crest of bronze or horsehair dyed in varying colors. In armament the Veientes resembled the Romans, carrying the long thrusting spear, short sword, and round *clipeus* shield. In their sparkling white and bronze they appeared to glow as if an aura of heavenly light surrounded them.

"They sure look pretty, don't they?" he muttered to Opimius beside him. A rivulet of sweat rolled down his strong nose, and his stomach growled loudly.

"Hungry?" chuckled Opimius through his teeth.

"Yes. I wish Servilius would decide what he's going to do."

"Me too," whispered Considius on his left. "I'm starving."

The fifth hour came and went. Still they waited.

+ + +

Billowing dust from a thousand pairs of feet mixed with the sweat streaming down his face, ran muddily into his tunic, and found every possible crevice where it could rub and irritate his skin. His canteen clanked uselessly against his hip, an empty reminder of a gargantuan thirst. At this rate, Titus was sure he'd never make it to battle. He envisioned his bones drying white along the roadside. The sun beat down mercilessly, and as if all the gods were holding their breath, not the weakest breeze cooled them. At the sixth hour they fell out for another rest.

"Is this really March?" someone exclaimed wearily.

Lucius Gallio plopped his muscular body down next to Titus. "Not for long," he said. His voice, gravelly at best, came out thick and harsh from dust. "In another hour it'll be July."

Weak laughter floated in the air like mist and burned away. Gallio rubbed the back of his columnar neck and scratched his head roughly. He lay back with both hands behind his head, surveying the surrounding countryside. "It's going to be a long summer if we don't get some rain soon."

Titus looked at him with disbelief. "It just rained two days ago." With a playful index finger he poked Gallio's high forehead, expanding as the curly black hair receded. "If you weren't so old you'd remember."

"If you weren't so young I'd take offense," retorted Gallio, laughing.

"Maybe your memory is going along with your hair."

"Look at it," said Gallio, sweeping his hand across the countryside. "Empty. Nobody working."

"Most of them are in Rome, I suppose," Titus said.

"Hm. Going to be a lot of work to do when we finally get these Etruscans off our backs."

Titus looked around him. All ready weeds and thorny vines reclaimed portions of the fields. Evidence of burning could be seen in the dry scorched remains of plants and destroyed farm buildings stood out like broken teeth. War offered nothing but devastation.

"What a waste," he said.

"Eh!" Gallio grunted in agreement. "We have to quit waging these wars on our ground. Look how close we are to Rome," he said, pointing west.

Titus followed Gallio's finger to the shadowy outlines and red roofs of Rome only a mile or so due west. Turning his eyes eastward the wide upswept blue-gray peak of Mt. Janus stood watch over the undulating plain. So peaceful from where he sat, range upon range of mountains marched away into the hazy distance. His feet had traversed much of it. In fact, the whole of pullulating Latium had passed quietly beneath his feet in just a few weeks. From Rome they had followed the Via Gabina east across the rolling verdant plain to Gabii. One of a string of Latin cities on the eastern boundary of Latium, Gabii guarded access to the plains from the mountains looming mysteriously behind her. Tibur lay to the north flanked on the west by three small pointed hills. Encamped near a stream flowing from the Alban Hills, Titus imagined he could see his home just below the hilltop city of Labicum clearly visible fifteen hundred feet above the plain. From Gabii they had turned southeast, past limpid Lake Regillus, following the valley that flowed around the forested Alban annulation like water around a moss-covered boulder. The legion passed under the watchful eye of Praeneste's high walls soaring protectively up the side of a mountain directly across from Algidus, the cleft entrance into the center of what had once been the cone of a giant volcano.

As they swung farther south the situation became surreal, for here the war had not reached, and people went placidly about their days as if men were not slaughtering each other just one or two days hike away. Fields were being plowed, cleared, and planted. Vines were trimmed, trenched, staked, and pruned. Everywhere people buzzed about like bees readying their fields, stopping momentarily to gawk at the dusty red and bronze soldiers as they marched inanely by. Rounding the southern curve of the Alban Hills they had passed through Vellitrae on the edge of Volscian territory, and were themselves on edge. But the Volscians were not to be provoked and the Romans swept around the great ring turning north toward Rome. At Aricia they had climbed into the ring, skirting the two lakes set like sapphires in the emerald green mountains. Lake Nemorensis, where the slave-priest of Diana guarded her temple, and its larger cousin to the north, Lake Alba. There on the east slopes of Mount Alba the couriers from Servilius had found them and begun this miserable march.

"Well old man," Titus grunted, rising stiffly to his feet, "try to keep up." He put a last bite of hard wheat cake in his mouth, hardly able to work up enough moisture to masticate it.

"I'll do that," Gallio laughed. "Here." He passed his canteen to Titus. "Try not to drink it all."

+ + +

At the sixth hour the sun reached its zenith and began the long descent to the sea. Still the two armies waited. The Romans had taken the field at least an hour earlier and stood in long exasperated lines, sweating and hungry, their last meal some four or five hours behind them. Servilius wrestled equally with impatience. The day was waning; where was Verginius? He pounded his fist against his thigh, yanked the reins of his white charger, and faced his men.

"Men," he yelled, and pointed up the hill. "There is the source of all your discomfort. There is the reason our wives and children waste away to skin and bones. There is the reason our fields lie empty, waiting like hungry children for hands to nourish them. There is the reason your stomachs growl and your tongues cleave to the roofs of your mouth. Let us expunge the bitter taste of our enemy's arrogance. Let us drive them now from the sight of our city. Men, be valorous and they will flee before you as they did last night. For Rome!"

"Roma!" thundered five thousand voices.

"At the walk!" ordered the tribunes. "Advance!"

Like a bristling centipede with ten thousand legs the legion stepped out, advancing uphill against the Etruscans. The uneven terrain, steep here, level there clogged with trees and rock outcroppings forced the lines to flex, compress, break apart and reform on the other side. Lucius shifted his eyes nervously, checking his interval with the man in front, and Considius and Opimius on either side. Up and down the line men talked to each other while centurions needlessly yelled at them to maintain formation. Lucius shifted his spear in his hand, trying to find a comfortable spot to grip it on the repaired section.

Inexorably the lines moved forward. One hundred fifty yards separated the two armies. Lucius squinted into the sun, looking unsuccessfully for Quintus with the velites thirty yards ahead, and then checked the Etruscans on top of the hill. They had yet to move, their spears planted vertically in the ground. 'Guts' he thought. 'They've got guts.' Again, he checked his interval forward and on each side, stretched his neck against the helmet strap, and inspected the two shield straps that crossed over his thick forearms. Flexing his left hand around the shield grip held in backhand fashion, he tried to relax himself. Now the order came to pick up the pace. His legs strained against the incline, burning thighs. One hundred yards now. The Etruscans lifted their spears and brought the points down. Now it begins. Focus. Check the interval. "Where are you Truncus?" Closer, closer. Unconsciously his breathing became quicker. Now the slingers from both sides let fly. Stones filled the air. Javelins impaled shields, men. Raise your shield. "Keep up, Cnaeus!" Don't worry about the stones. All right, here they come. Anticipating the order, he began to run as the centurions cried, "Charge!" A great anger burst suddenly in his chest as he leveled his spear. Now the light infantry from both sides peeled off to the flanks.

"Drive, Truncus, drive!" he cried. "ROMA!"

In good order the Veientes attacked down hill, meeting the uneven Roman advance that hit the Etruscans in segments instead of in a solid contiguous line. The Etruscans downhill movement added impetus to their charge and halted the Roman advance. Lucius leaned against the legionary in front of him digging his hobnailed shoes into the ground and pushing. The legionary behind him did the same thing, and so on all the way back to the last man. Pushing, shoving, grunting, exhorting, cursing, sweating, dying. A man fell, immediately someone stepped up, closing the breach. Now they went forward, now back. Exultation and fear mixed with adrenaline in a deadly philtre. Straining, sweating, legs burning, he leaned into the back of the legionary in front of him, willing, propelling him forward. Spear tips flashed, he thrust back in retaliation, eyes up, find an open spot, a flash of unprotected white, thrust, soft resistance then penetration, he's falling push harder, drive, a hot flash ripped his stomach but everything is burning, sweat pouring into his eyes. A face, a crest, a glint of dirty bronze, he sees the straining vein-popping exertion on the ruddy face of the enemy and wants to laugh, wants to smash it. Reaching down inside he pulls energy from some hidden reserve and with a mighty shove pushes his man forward thrusting with his spear at an Etruscan's uncovered side. "Drive!" Legs churning, pumping, forward, forward, punch a hole in the line. The air is filled with spears, high crests bobbing, flashing armor, cries, shouts, cursing. There are not many dead yet. Now it is a shoving match to see who has the most strength, looking for a weak spot to punch a hole, then the line will collapse, cave in, explode like a scroll set on fire in the center—destruction racing outward to the edges. Then the dying truly begins.

Suddenly Considius goes down with an agonized cry, clutching at his knee. His comrade pushing from behind stumbles, falls face down, now the soldier in front is hurled backward onto a confused heaving pile of Roman bodies. A joyous cry escapes the throats of the Etruscans as they pour into the breach. Lucius decides instantly, sliding left, dropping his spear and drawing his sword. "Hold Gaius!" he yells, implores, exhorts, and then crashes into the lead Etruscan, knocking him off his feet. With his shield he parries a spear thrust swings his sword at a face and charges forward. All is confusion, like the tide flowing in and out crashing against a rock outcropping, the battle rages all around him. Romans push forward, are driven back; now around him are burnished, smashed bronze and red, now the white short tunics of glittering bronze clad men; a swirling mass of bulging powerful muscles, bloody swords and spears, dark red splotched tunics, faces smeared with grime, sweat, blood, anger, fear. Lucius feels nothing but rage, great consuming unrelenting dominating rage; like an island he stands, legs spread unyielding, delivering blows with shield and sword, pushing stabbing, slashing. Now Opimius is by him and they are screaming, taunting, howling like rabid animals, cursing the Etruscans as they slash them to ribbons. Bodies pile up around them but they are oblivious. Vopiscus fights his way up to join them; maddened by fear of defeat they form a small outpost in a retreating frontier. Etruscans gush around them pushing the Roman line back, but here, like a wedge, like the point of a spear the fighting rages with ferocious fatalistic fury. The centurion, Albinus, leads a charge, and for a moment the line is restored, then Albinus is hewn down and the line collapses again. Lucius, Opimius, Vopiscus, and a few others, anchored by a ferreous refusal to retreat hold a four hundred square foot abattoir in the center of the battlefield.

Lucius becomes aware of a growing, seeping wetness around his stomach, oozing down his legs. His breath comes in great gasps of weariness; weakening, each swing of the sword drains more strength from him. An Etruscan looms large with upraised sword. At the last moment Lucius jerks his shield up, takes the blow, absorbs it with his whole body and goes down, rolling off a pile of bodies face down on the ground. As he frantically tries to push himself up someone falls on top of him and he expects any moment to feel a sword invade his inner parts. He struggles to rise, refusing to die now in this way. "Get off me!" he screams in feral rage.

+ + +

The sight to the soldiers of Legio II as they formed up in line of battle was awesome, fearful, hideous. Before them the Roman line disintegrated into a ragged bloody wedge. Dead and dying lay strewn upon the hill in grotesque heaps. In their exhaustion they looked on almost with indifference, deadened by their own weariness. Verginius exhorted them, reminding them that fathers, brothers, and friends faced death in that faltering legion. He led them on foot, at the charge, hurling them into the flank of the surprised Veientes. The Etruscan advance collapsed, retreated up the slope the way it had come, then lodged stubbornly in front of their camp, repulsing the Roman attack. Leg-weary from the march, they could not push the Etruscans from the hill.

Then like a splash of cold water the sun dropped, the armies separated like two doused cats and retired to their respective camps to lick their wounds.

+ + +

Quintus Crispus searched frantically by torchlight for Lucius Tempanius. Searching through the gore and slaughter, turning over bodies hacked to pieces, entrails poured out on the ground, lolling heads barely attached by a few sinews, he wanted to retch. Then he heard someone call for help and turning in the direction of the sound found Cnaeus Considius crawling away from a heap of bodies.

"Have you seen Lucius Tempanius?" he asked urgently.

"Help me," implored Considius, reaching up a hand. "I can't walk."

"Where is Lucius?" Quintus repeated.

"I don't know," gasped Considius. "My leg…"

Didius held the torch close and saw Considius' knee swollen to three times its normal size, but he seemed otherwise unhurt.

"Where did you see him last?" he demanded, disregarding Considius' pleas.

145

"Over there," Considius wailed, waving his hand in the general direction of the pile of bodies from which he had emerged.

Quintus found Lucius face down under a pile of awful carnage. Stacks of dead, like mown wheat on the blood soaked earth, lay rigid where they fell. Included in the dead heaped on top of Lucius he recognized Gaius Opimius and Attius Vopiscus. Lucius moaned as Quintus pulled him free, and his heart leapt. Though half his weight the little man crawled under him, levered Lucius onto his back and carried him down the hill.

Quintus stumbled into the surgeon's tent where two attendants helped him lower Lucius onto a table. Stripping off his breastplate and leather jerkin they discovered a four-inch gash low on the right side of his abdomen. It had not punctured the inner cavity so the surgeon flushed the wound with water, and with pliers and a bronze needle stitched it up.

"Feed him chicken or beef liver, endive, and watered red wine to rebuild the blood," he advised. "And keep him from pulling out those stitches."

The only item Quintus could readily lay his hands on was the wine. For the rest he contacted Titus and made arrangements through him to transport Lucius home.

Rome and Veii were exhausted. Two days later, accompanied by high winds, a freak snowstorm blasted Latium. Both sides saw it as an omen, a message from the gods. They called a truce that went unbroken for forty years.

Lucius went home to heal. He had been awarded a phalerus for bravery. His stand in the center had saved the legion. Veii still held Fidenae.

# XI

## April 21, 475 BC
## The Parilia

Although the wound in his belly healed nicely Lucius did not respond as well. Everyone attributed his uncharacteristic depression to the loss of his friends Gaius Opimius, and Attius Vopiscus. True, he felt sadness for the fate that overtook them, but men died in war, an immutable fact. Opimius and Vopiscus had covered themselves in glory—no Roman could ask for a better death.

As he convalesced and thought of these things, he considered the possibility that he felt cheated by having survived. He discarded the ridiculous thought immediately. In one campaign he had won an armillus, a torque, and a phalerus for bravery. Some even thought he should have been awarded the corona obsidionalis for he had by all accounts saved the legion. Others quibbled that the army had not been besieged and so the obsidionalis did not apply. Lucius laughed at the controversy from afar. No, the honors were sufficient, he thought as he turned the embossed bronze disc called a phalerus in his hands. Truth be told, in his heart of hearts, two things oppressed him, the absence of war, which time would heal, and his assumption of duties as head of the family, which would bind him forever. He wanted to make war; the rest of the world could cross the river Styx.

With a resigned sigh he swung his legs off the bed, returned the disc to the shelf with his other medals, and went out. Drusilla, in her spinning room across the hall, saw him instantly.

"Lucius," she called, trying to keep any trace of worry from her voice.

"Yes, Mama." Lucius veered off into her room and stood in the doorway expectantly.

Drusilla sat at her loom weaving a new toga that she hoped would be Lucius' wedding toga. As head of the household the time had come for him to get married and start producing heirs. Without being told, Lucius knew exactly what his mother was doing. It drove him to despair.

"How do you feel?" asked Drusilla. Her strong fingers stopped long enough to pull a dark red shawl made from remnants tighter around her shoulders.

"Fine. I thought I'd go out and help Antonius with the work." A chill breeze poured in the open west window. "Why don't you close a window?"

She ignored his concern. "Are you sure you're up to it? You don't want to reopen your wound." Her hands worked in perfect concert to swiftly weave the horizontal threads through the vertical, draw them tight and start the next row. Beneath her chair a brazier sent ripples of heat upwards, flaring brightly as the breeze excited the coals.

"I'm fine," he said. "Don't worry about me."

"Why do sons find that so easy to tell their mothers?" She stopped her hands and looked at him with large oval eyes darkened by love and amusement. Her full lips compressed in a half smile, a full smile requiring complete forgetfulness of her husband's death. She missed Marcus and would gladly have sacrificed his renown for his presence.

"Domina," Lucius said formally.

She raised her black arching eyebrows and looked at him down her proud straight nose. "Yes?"

"You are still the most beautiful woman in the world to me."

"Thank you, my heart. But?"

"I am not ready to wear that toga." He pointed at the loom. "At least not yet."

"That's good," said Drusilla easily. "It's not finished yet."

The implication that she and time would change his mind hung between them like a wall. If he threw up the one scaling ladder he possessed that could surmount the wall, his refusal, the whole family might very well be thrown down. The alternative was unbearable. The ladder had to go up.

Disguising his fears with anger he said, "As soon as Titus returns, we'll have a family council. That's my decision."

That Lucius as *paterfamilias* could make any decision unilaterally and the rest of the family would have to abide by it meant almost nothing. To do so without calling a family council would have violated tradition, and brought dishonor on the family. He knew that what he wanted was, in and of itself, scandalous to some degree and would bring disruption and possibly division to his family. Most of all he felt concern for the feelings of his mother, on whom his decision would have the most detrimental emotional effect. He held the meeting in the kitchen, and besides his mother and two brothers he asked Didius, Petronius, and Quintus to attend. The seven of them gathered around the table seated on low backed chairs with Lucius and Titus on the ends. Drusilla and Antonius took the side closest to the hearth. A black pitcher of wine, with a scene depicting Aeneas escaping Troy around its circumference, sat on the table. Lucius filled his cup and tasted the sweet white wine that had been cooling in the spring out back.

"Well," he said, after small talk had dribbled away to silence, "the reason I called this meeting is to discuss the best plan for the future of the family." He played absently with the two ear-shaped handles on his cup.

"I think the first thing we should do is sell those horses," said Titus without hesitation. "We can't afford to feed them and we really get no work out of them."

Lucius held his hand up. "Yes, they're a luxury," he agreed. "But what I'm talking about is the distant future. Not what needs to be done for today, but what needs to be done for five, ten, twenty years from now."

"That's a long ways to look, Lucius," said Drusilla. "No one knows what the future holds."

"I know, Mama, but we still must plan as best we can."

"He's right, Domina," said Titus. "That's why Father put in the vines down below. He was planning for the future."

"I'm glad to see my sons are as wise as their father," she said in a voice icy with irony and bitterness.

"The point is," said Lucius, plunging ahead, "I don't feel like I'm the one to do it."

"Of course," said Petronius. "You're young. But you'll grow into it, and you can count on Didius and me to help in whatever way we can."

Didius nodded affirmatively but kept his own council.

"You want to leave us," Antonius said. Accusation fired his charcoal eyes, and his black swallow wing eyebrows gathered furiously.

"What I want," Lucius said, filling his voice with persuasive reasonableness, "is to do what's right for the family."

"I suppose you call running away right," Antonius persisted.

Antonius' unrelenting allegations pushed Lucius to bluntness. "Listen," he said, "right or wrong all I know is I don't want to be responsible for this whole family."

"Lucius," said Titus, "I know it seems like the whole weight is on your shoulders, but it's really not. There are all of us here to help with the work and the decisions."

"It's not that simple and you know it, Titus. Mama is already weaving a wedding toga for me. Talk about planning for the distant future." Light laughter traversed the table.

"But she's right," Titus said. "You need an heir."

"What about you? Why don't you get married?"

"I will. But you're paterfamilias."

"Exactly," stormed Lucius. "And that's why I don't want to be. I don't want a wife, children…this farm." He waved his arm dismissing, as it were, his entire life to that point.

"What **do** you want, Lucius?" asked Drusilla coldly.

"I want to fight, Mama," he said with passionate honesty. "I've never felt so alive. And I'm good at it." He reached into a leather satchel dangling from the chair back and spread his medals on the table as evidence. "You know as well as I do that Father always forced me to do chores. I hated it. But Titus, he can't wait to get to work."

A clearing field took shape in Titus' mind. He suppressed his immediate negative reaction to the lay of the land and sought more information. "What are you proposing?"

"I'm proposing, Titus, that we find you a wife, make you and Antonius sole heirs, sell the horses and split the money, and I'll move to Rome as soon as practical."

"Will you want a stipend?" asked Titus.

"You talk as if this is agreed," challenged Drusilla.

"Mama, it's the best thing," said Lucius. Looking at Titus, he said, "No. I'll just expect a home if I need it. And I keep any dowry I negotiate."

"This will always be your home," asserted Drusilla.

"Yes," Lucius agreed, "I just want to hear Titus say it."

"Of course," said Titus. "You'll always have a home here." With the last stump cleared from the field, Titus could not say the view pleased him. He harbored grave doubts that such a decision could benefit the family. "My dream has always been that you, Antonius, and I would all raise families together on this place." He looked directly at Lucius, unblinking, his long face open and ingenuous. "That's the truth."

"Good, it's settled then. We'll record it in the comitia curiata and then it's finished. Now, about you getting married..."

"I'd like to go with you, Lucius," Quintus suddenly spoke up.

Didius shot him a look and their matching lichen green eyes met, clashed. Quintus defiantly turned back to Lucius. "That is, if I could."

"Listen Quintus, I have nothing to offer you. But you can be sure that wherever I am you'll be welcome."

Didius burst into a squawking laugh. "That's the best patrician answer I've heard in a long time. Stick with him, Quintus. With talk like that he'll be running for consul soon."

The tension eased and they fell to discussing possible marriage matches for Titus. Drusilla and Antonius remained unhappy, though for different reasons. For Antonius, who looked up to his eldest brother with something like hero worship, the decision by Lucius was pure abandonment. As if Lucius were renouncing brotherhood to he and Titus. He could not and would not understand.

To Drusilla the connotations went deeper. In her mind Lucius, in denying his role as head of the family, denied the household gods (the *lares*), tradition, custom, and the proper cycle of life. Already the delicate balance had been upset with the division between Didius and Quintus. By stepping outside the family how could a man be civilized? And wasn't his love for war symbolic of a descent into animalism? She reassured herself that he would be in the city, so that his soul would not become completely wild, but she could not extirpate her fears by such rationalizations. The foundation of the family held up the entire structure of civilized society. If a man could deny his family surely civilization could not be far behind. And if the city should devolve into animalism? She shuddered at the thought, sure the household *lares* would not look favorably on her family, might even desert them altogether and leave them unprotected. She shivered and quickly checked the hearth to see if the sacred, eternal fire had suddenly gone out. Not content with the glowing coals smoldering hotly, she threw more wood on, stirring it into flame though the room did not need the heat.

Lucius could only imagine his mother's thoughts at that moment. He knew he had upset her, could see the anger in her stiffly controlled movements and the disappointment in her dark eyes. Painful regret thudded like a cold stone in the pit of his stomach. To disappoint his mother, whom he cherished above all else, brought anguish to his soul, and second thoughts to his brain. Maybe he loved himself too much, was innately selfish and cruel. The impossibility of explaining so she would understand wrenched his heart with remorse.

"So, who is this Duellia?" Titus asked, breaking Lucius' reverie.

"Hm? Oh, the daughter of Marcus Duellius. You should know him; he was a centurion with Legio I. It would be a perfect match for you. You'd be well connected."

Didius whistled between his teeth. "No offense," he said out of the side of his mouth, "but that would be a real step up."

"Yes," agreed Drusilla. Putting aside her disapproval she entered into the practicality of alternatives. "Are you sure he would accept?"

"Am I sure? No. Am I confident? Yes. Our family has gained some recognition lately. Even Antonius is famous in Rome. We should take advantage while we can."

"The sooner the better," said Titus. "When can you arrange it?"

"I need to see a calendar."

Antonius, appeased by his 'fame' jumped up and took a calendar, painstakingly copied on a scrap of leather from the official one mounted on the Regia, off the wall.

Based on the lunar cycle, the Roman year had 354 days. There were twelve regular months, and one additional intercalary month inserted every other year adding eleven days to catch up with the solar cycle. The chief priests of the city, the college of pontifices, were charged with putting the calendar together. During an intercalary year they arranged the calendar in thirteen columns, inserting the additional days after February, the last month of the year.

The days were listed from A to H, there being eight days in the Roman week. Each day was designated with an additional letter or set of letters; F-*fastus*, meant an ordinary working day; C-*comitialis*, was particularly propitious and therefore assemblies, trials, and other public business could take place; N-*nefastus*, was wholly unlucky and no work could commence, though some work might be continued; EN-*endotercisus*, meant the day was divided, the morning and evening declared *nefastus*, but the afternoon *fastus*; NP-*nefastus publicus*, signified public festivals, and carried an additional abbreviation for the particular festival. No public, and in many cases no private business could be undertaken on these days.

Finally, the calendar fixed three other points in the month; the *kalends*-the new moon and the first day of the month; the *nones*-marking the first quarter, and the day the *Rex Sacrorum* published the religious calendar for the month; and the *ides*-marking the full moon and midpoint of the month.

So when Lucius consulted the calendar that fourth day of April (a day marked *comitialis* and thus the reason for the family meeting) he knew two things instantly; exactly which days he might meet with Marcus Duellius, and that there were only six of them left in the month. A festive month, April.

"Well," he said, leaning back with a sigh, "it looks like we'll have to wait until after the Robigalia on the twenty-fifth."

April contained twenty-nine days, only twelve of which were either *fastus* or *comitialis*. Eight different festivals broke up the month yet the farm required constant care. The fields needed weeding, and harrowing, vines dressed, pruned, and trenched. Primus now had twenty goats to care for, and the sow gave birth to a brood of piglets. Didius worked diligently at constructing a chicken coop; there were horses and oxen to feed, and repairs to tools, fences, and buildings that couldn't wait.

Obviously, they could not faithfully observe every festival. Fortunately, the *Flamen Dialis*, forbidden to see anyone working (or dead), did not often make it out their way. They decided to observe the *Parilia*, however, since their flock of goats had prospered. To this end Lucius went to Rome during the *Fordicidia* to procure the ashes of an embryo of a pregnant cow burned on the sacred hearth in the temple of Vesta. At the same time he paid a social call to Marcus Duellius and they planned a meeting to discuss unspecified business on the twenty-fifth.

The *Parilia*, celebrated on the twenty-first, and dedicated to *Pales* goddess of herds, began at first light and ended in the dark. As the sun climbed above the mountains and splashed light the color of mimosa flowers on their little hill, Primus and Antonius let the goats out of the pen, and with bundles of twigs tied into brooms swept out the pen. As they performed this task Titus fought one of the females for her milk, and Drusilla made wheat cakes to be sacrificed later. Didius, Petronius, and Sextus spent the morning weaving beautiful garlands abounding with purple, red, and yellow wildflowers, and cutting boughs to adorn the sheepfold. Lucius did what he did best, lounged in the grass with the dogs, and kept the goats from eating what they weren't supposed to while their home got cleaned. Quintus joined him.

"Do you ever wonder what's in those mountains?" asked Lucius, staring with faraway eyes at the mountains that scaled the azure sky in dark gray rows as if they had no end.

"Aequi, Sabines, and Samnites I guess," said Quintus.

Lucius chuckled. "Don't forget the Hernici and the Volsci," he teased.

"The Volsci are south," said Quintus.

"Eh," Lucius grunted. Scanning Quintus with wide spaced sarcastic eyes he nodded his big head several times quickly. "I know where Volscian territory is. What I mean is, don't you ever wonder what those other peoples' lands are like?"

"I suppose," said Quintus, sticking his lower lip out noncommittally. "But Why?"

Lucius picked up a golden buttercup and brought it to his nose. "I don't know," he said. "Just to see it. If you think about it the only way a lot of Romans will ever get land is by taking it from someone else."

Quintus scratched at his thin arms, then pointed at the spot on Lucius' belly where his latest scar served as a livid reminder. "Seems to me we have enough trouble keeping hold of our own."

Lucius laughed, threw the flower to the ground and kicked his legs out straight, bracing himself on his hands. "You're right about that. But maybe the best way is to fight on someone else's ground."

"I'm sure you're right, Lucius. The problem is, they don't let us off ours to fight on theirs."

"Maybe we could make a treaty about it. You know, one year they fight here, the next we fight there," said Lucius. They laughed cynically.

Lucius tilted his head back, luxuriating in the pressure of the sun on his face. The pores of his skin, like the little four petal violet flowers around him, seemed to open up to the sun. Migrating eastward a quick puff of wind carrying memories of cold salt seas chilled him, then departed, leaving the heavy scent of pine and delicate wildflowers in its wake.

Titus came down the gradual incline behind the house, a scowl on his canine face, then stopped, arrested by the view. Before him, glittering saffron patches of spring foliage lit the mountain, casting light into the sapphire sky as if emanating from within. Coming back to his purpose he glanced down to locate his idle brother. Quintus rose hastily to his feet when he descried Titus coming down the hill, but Lucius remained indolently supine. Goats browsed unperturbed, kept from straying by two attentive dogs.

"Are you two flowers going to sit here soaking up the sun all day?"

"I can't think of anything better," Lucius said, stroking the sateen brown fur of one of the dogs curled up beside him.

"Are you ready for the goats?" asked Quintus helpfully.

"We've been ready," Titus said curtly.

Lucius turned his dark eyes on his brother. "Don't try telling me what to do, Titus," he said. Latent violence chilled his quiet voice. "And if Quintus is with me, you can assume he's doing exactly what I've told him to."

Titus cooled. Lucius had been proving his superior strength for nearly eighteen years, and Titus had good reason to fear him if provoked. But just as suddenly amusement illumined his brother's wide face and he pushed himself up off the ground. The dog groaned.

"Come, Falca," said Lucius. "I guess it's time we did some work." Falca stretched, yawned widely and looked at him. "Home," he commanded. In a moment she had the bleating goats moving up the hill.

In the middle of the pen Antonius and Primus protected a shallow pot of sulfur. As soon as the goats were safely in Titus passed Antonius a lighted torch and he touched it to the sulfur. A blue flame snapped, and the stench of rotten eggs flowed out with the smoke over the startled and terrified goats. Bleating in protest and fear they retreated to the farthest edges of the fold, milling nervously with wide rolling eyes and twitching ears. As this act of purification progressed the men intoned a prayer for the health of the flock. After which Drusilla called them to dinner.

"Finally," said Lucius, to chuckles from the others. "I'm famished."

The men divided. Lucius, Titus, and Antonius went upstairs, while Didius, his sons, and Petronius and Primus retired to their quarters in the old part of the house. A three hour period of repose followed. They emerged to the sun casting long slanting shadows across the fields. The sky paled, preparing for its fiery change to night, and a steady breeze kicked up from the sea. Lucius entered the goat pen with a wide mouthed pot of water and a small bundle of alder twigs. Dipping the twigs in the water he sprinkled the goats, ensuring that each received a few drops, reciting a prayer for health, safety, and fertility.

Simultaneously, Didius and Quintus hung the garlands and other greenery around the pen, making an attractive home in which *Pales* might be pleased to dwell. Titus and the others built two fires in the main yard in front of the house.

As the sun drove itself like a hot spike into the sea Drusilla came out with an array of sacrifices on an earthenware tray. Lucius took them one at a time, said a prayer over each, and gave them to the fires. He threw precious wheat still in the sheaf, barley and wheat cakes, olives, beanstalks without pods, and the ashes of the embryo on one fire. On the other he poured libations of goat milk and horse blood.

When the fires had burned down to low licking flames each man leashed a goat, and despite much bleating and stiff legged refusal leaped over the fire three times in tandem. The blessed and purified herd returned gratefully to the safety of the pen.

Lucius breathed a sigh mixed with equal parts of relief and impatience. Soon he would be able to contract the marriage for Titus. But first the *Vinalia* and the *Robigalia*. Would April never end?

+ + +

Marcus Duellius and Lucius Tempanius met at the temple of Mercury to discuss their business. It seemed appropriate to both since the temple was the cult center for a host of merchant guilds. In his mid-forties, Marcus Duellius had sons the age of Lucius, yet he retained a vigorous physique to lend distinction to the gray hair streaking his temples.

Lucius, whose physical courage was beyond doubt, felt insecure when it came to business or public affairs. His training as a soldier and farmer had not prepared him for the more subtle arts. The fact that he had served under Duellius, had taken orders from him added to his discomfiture. He found it difficult now to treat with him as an equal. He steeled himself, and fought to keep the wavering of anxiety from his voice. His eyes shifted self consciously to passersby, as if they would know intuitively everything he thought or felt.

"I had hoped," Marcus Duellius said, "that you were speaking of yourself when you asked about Duellia."

"Ah, well, my brother is more the marrying type." Lucius tried to sound insouciant. "However, when it's done, he'll be the head of the family as far as inheritance. So actually Duellia will be in a better situation than if she were marrying me."

Duellius raised his eyebrows questioningly, and regarded Lucius with interest. "And why is that?"

"Because truthfully, I prefer soldiering. I find the country life tedious."

"Yes, but to give up your inheritance seems extreme. Why not simply move to Rome and take a small stipend?"

Lucius shrugged his broad shoulders. "Maybe I didn't want anyone to have any kind of hold over me. This way I'm completely free."

"Has the inheritance change been registered with the comitia curiata?" Duellius asked.

"Not yet. But it will be soon."

"And Titus?"

"Titus is the perfect match. He's a good soldier, brave and strong. And he's a better farmer because he enjoys it. He'll provide well for Duellia and your grandchildren."

Duellius laughed. "Anxious as that, is he?"

"Well, you know," said Lucius, wizening his husky voice with sophistication, "when you're seventeen that's all you think about."

Duellius reflected a few moments. "And a dowry? What did you have in mind?"

"Not much," said Lucius. Insecurity unmasked itself in his voice. "I'm more interested in creating a bond between our families. Something symbolic." He attempted an off-hand tone. "Say, a hundred and fifty *asses*."

Duellius smiled, nodded politely. "I think that's a little too symbolic," he said gently. "Fifty might be considered appropriately symbolic, however."

Lucius guffawed at the light satire. "I suppose," he said through his laughter, "I should make a symbolic counter offer. But I won't. Fifty sounds perfect."

"Well," said Duellius abruptly, "may the gods bless the match; I'm willing." He stuck out his hand and Lucius engulfed it enthusiastically in his. Free at last.

+ + +

What could be more auspicious for a wedding than pellucid skies, a beaming sun, and peace across the land? Drusilla gave up her anger at Lucius and entered into the joy of the occasion for her second son. She consoled herself with the thought that all things change, and Lucius and Titus were young. What had Lucius done, really, but bequeath his share of the inheritance

159

to his brothers? He remained, by birth, titular head of the family. To have abjured all would have put him with the *infraclassem*, and left him without prospects. Thus, their agreement that Titus should be head of the family had no legal standing and rested strictly upon their honor. That they would scrupulously adhere to their word she had no doubt, but she also knew she had influence, and hoped in time to exert it in order to restore things to proper balance. Time and maturity were on her side.

Lucius found two rooms at an inn in the Subura district called the Boar's Tusk for himself, Drusilla, and Antonius. He awoke in an expansive mood, and visualized living there when all the sediment of events settled out.

The Boar's Tusk was a solid two-story gray stone edifice with a rust colored tile roof. Both floors were divided lengthwise. The bottom floor combined a tavern and kitchen in the front half, and stables in the rear half. Upstairs the owner's living quarters occupied the front half, with five small rooms to rent in the back. The entrance faced a small market square built around a central public fountain. A nearly impassable warren of small huts, and workshops isolated it from the Vicus Suburanus at the rear.

Taking the stone steps two at a time Lucius landed hard on the ground floor with both feet, and strode joyfully into the kitchen. The proprietor Pontius Cominus, bald as an egg, looked up dourly from a steaming cup. Before him a scroll lay unrolled, a shard of pottery holding one end open.

"Good morning, innkeeper," Lucius drawled.

Cominus scrunched his puffy eyes and grunted lowly. Without a word he took a drink from the steaming cup and returned to his reading.

Lucius came around the table and looked at what Cominus was drinking. "Listen," he said, "it's no wonder you have bird's nests under your eyes when you drink water made from them."

"They are herbs," Cominus said. "And they're good for the blood. If you want something to eat there are cakes and eggs on the counter. Plates are on the shelves over there." He pointed without looking up.

Lucius put two of each on a plate, grabbed a pitcher of milk, and sat down opposite Cominus. He cracked the eggs on the table, rolling them over and over, cracking the tawny shells again and again, oblivious to the annoyance the repetition caused the innkeeper. "What are you reading?" he asked, with an egg stuffed whole into his mouth.

Cominus ignored the question. "Are you always so cheerful in the morning?" he countered.

"Why not?" said Lucius.

"Because usually one likes peace and quiet to start the day."

Lucius shrugged indifferently. Observing him, Cominus decided a streak of greed and avarice were evident in the way the young man gobbled one bite after another without pause, barely chewing the food. "You didn't answer my question," he said at last.

"I'm sorry," said Lucius, ingenuously. "What was it?"

"Are you always so cheerful in the morning?"

Having polished off the food, Lucius poured himself a cup of milk and drank it in one gulp. He wiped his mouth with the back of his hand and cleaned his hand on his tunic. "Not always. It depends," he said. Light laughter came guilelessly through his square teeth, carefree and self-deprecating to Cominus' ears.

He decided he might like the young man. "Today's a good day?" he asked.

Lucius regarded portly Cominus, wondering why he should tell him the thoughts tumbling in his head like the wheel he kept rolling with a stick as a child. He liked the attentive expression in his sea green eyes, liked the fact he kept a short stubby finger on the spot where he left off reading, liked that he was neither rude nor ingratiating.

"Yes," said Lucius, "it's a good day. My brother's getting married."

"But," said Cominus, perceptively, "that alone is not what has made you so happy."

"No," Lucius admitted. "It's also the day I get my freedom."

"What can that mean? You're a Roman citizen, you have your freedom in your hands."

"Now, yes. Before I was tied to responsibilities I didn't want. After today," he brushed the palms of his hands, "I'm free."

"And what will you do with this…freedom?"

"Perhaps," said Lucius with a big adventurous smile, "I'll come here to live."

Cominus flinched in surprise. "Perhaps the rooms will be full."

"Then I'll be sad. But I think you'd find me an asset."

"And how would you pay the rent?"

"I have money enough," Lucius hedged.

"I see," said Cominus. Instantly Lucius personified hedonism and indolent sensuality and Cominus lost interest in him. "So, you have no ambitions other than to enjoy life," he said, showing his bald pate to Lucius as he looked down to his reading.

"Oh no," disavowed Lucius. He leaned forward conspiratorially on crossed arms. "My ambition is to be the finest soldier Rome has ever known."

Cominus reconsidered his judgement. He gazed into the earnest brown eyes and wide ingenuous face, and flashed small worn teeth. "Then perhaps the rooms will be empty soon after you take them."

Lucius laughed and straightened up. "I hope not. I need to live a long time to accomplish my dream."

"Indeed." Cominus bent his head to the scroll. "Come see me after the wedding."

Lucius pushed the chair back and stood up. "You didn't answer my question," he said, a sardonic grin stretching his lips.

"What was that?"

"What are you reading?"

"Ah. It's called the Iliad, written by a Greek named Homer."

+ + +

Duellia solemnly regarded her wavering visage in a polished bronze mirror. Her eyes were large enough, and a rich chestnut brown, but perhaps too widely spaced. She rubbed her hooked nose with an index finger as if hoping to smooth it out, or if by feel she might give lie to the reflection in the mirror. A soft sigh of acceptance escaped her lips. She had, she decided, a nice small heart-shaped mouth with supple lips. But alas, her chin dropped away in embarrassment below that pouting lower lip. Daubing her finger in a small cobalt blue clay jar she applied a touch of rouge to her high imperial cheekbones and the bridge of her nose. From another jar a darker red paste accentuated her lips. Now she turned her head left and right to glimpse a side view, but her eyes would not cooperate to allow a complete profile. Again, she sighed, shifted the mirror to her right hand and inspected her jet black hair. With delicate fingers she touched each of the six braids into which her fine textured hair had been twined. A red ribbon held each braid, and a spear shaped bronze comb gathered them on top of her head to fall straight back to her shoulders.

Despite what her mother said, she knew that she would never again look as pretty as she did this day. Maybe that was the reason for her banishment to the far reaches of Rome. Except on special occasions the city would become a stranger to her. Her friends would forget her, and the gay life of society would be lost to her. She wanted to weep. Tears welled, and a hollow ache drummed in the pit of her stomach. Why did he have to live so far away? Why couldn't he have a house in town like other men? By all accounts his property would afford a home in the city if he wanted. Oh, who was this Titus Tempanius? Of course, she had met him two or three times since their betrothal. He looked handsome enough, though he had a rather long, sorrowful appearance. At least their ages were only four years apart. She could have been married to some old man on the edge of death and been a widow most of her life. But she didn't **know** him, didn't understand him.

Fear of the unknown caused her to look nostalgically at her simple little room. She would never see it again. Never sit at the small wooden dressing table; never again lie on the short bed and straw-filled mattress. Never, never, never.

Her mother breezed into the room, thankfully interrupting her dark cogitation. "Well," she said brightly, "aren't you lovely." She pulled Duellia to her feet and examined her as if she were a piece of cloth, or a fine Greek amphora. "Come, we must finish making you ready."

Her mother's sumptuous private room awaited her final preparations. A Sabine slave girl came forward solicitously as she entered the room. Smiling encouragement, she took Duellia by the hand and guided her to the center of the room. Deftly, like a caress, she unclasped the brooch holding her palla together and unwrapped the trembling girl.

"Now," she said, cooing pigeon-like, "lift your arms so we can take off this tunic. We don't want to leave too much in the way for a clumsy husband."

Duellia obeyed, tittering nervously. From a chest her mother brought forth a fine white linen shift, simple yet elegant. Made in one piece, it had holes for head and arms. It fell over Duellia's slim shapeless body as if made for her. The material was fine and soft, but not so sheer as to be immodest.

"I wore this for my wedding," her mother said. She bent down and rummaged around in the chest again, talking to herself as she looked for the object of her search. Suddenly a braided woolen belt, red as forest orchids dangled from her hand. She shook it impatiently behind her, waiting for the slave to take it, as she continued pawing through the chest.

"Ooh, beautiful," said the slave, her round face lit up with pleasure at the sight of the intricately woven belt. "You will be irresistible in this," she said, as she reverently wrapped it around Duellia's small waist. "Now we must tie the Herculean knot." She hummed melodically as her fingers constructed the many-layered knot. "Oh, won't he have trouble with that!" She wrinkled her short, squashed nose at Duellia, and they both giggled as they examined her handiwork.

"Ah, here it is. Finally," said Duellia's mother, straightening. Before her she held a long veil, red as sunset. It seemed to vibrate with color, as if it contained its own light. Duellia gasped and suddenly thought that just the wearing of such a beautiful thing made the rest of her life, come what may, worthwhile.

Dressed at last, her mother escorted Duellia to her room. On her bed lay her favorite toy, a wooden doll with hinged knees and elbows, and shoulders that rotated. Now, as the entire family gathered, she presented the doll and her maiden's toga to the household *lares* as a symbol that she took leave of her childhood. As she lay the doll on the altar the full realization of what was transpiring hit her. She glanced quickly around the atrium as if to record every detail in her memory, and again cold fear took hold of her. Fear of living with a man. Fear of living in a strange home among people she hardly knew. Fear of her mother-in-law. Fear that if she spoke she would dissolve in tears and dishonor herself and her family.

Reading her mind, her mother wrapped a reassuring arm around Duellia. "Come daughter," she said huskily, sotto voce, "there is nothing to fear. When you visit, we'll laugh about this day."

Duellia gave her a wavering, endearing smile full of trust and trepidation as they stepped out into the sunshine. Her mother pulled the flaming red veil over her face. My but Rome looked beautiful in the sunshine.

Titus ceased pacing outside the front door the instant he heard the latch lift. Straightening to attention he brushed at his new toga with his right hand. It felt incredibly smooth. Unlike the toga for which he had exchanged the toga *praetexta* of childhood, this one the fuller cleaned, bleached, teased with combs and cut the nap with shears to give it a soft, luminous quality. He felt like a candidate for office, ostentatious, even outlandish. If the toga hung more comfortably than normal, he felt less so from the false refinement it lent him. His face shone with a ruddy complexion after the barber shaved him and cut his thick wavy hair. He regretted the expense of the wedding, but his mother and Lucius had insisted, stressing the importance of the match.

Marcus Duellius laughed at his first glimpse of Titus' rigid appearance. Obviously, the young man felt more comfortable with a plow in his hand than one end of a toga. "Good morning, Titus," he said heartily. "How nice of you to escort us to the temple."

Titus cleared his throat, then tried to fit the words he'd rehearsed on his way up the hill to the unexpected greeting. "We...I...thought it was the least I could do considering the great honor you have done our family today." He stole a glance at Duellia, invisible behind the fiery veil.

Tall maritime pines, like stately feather parasols, lined the walk from the Duellius home to the street. The Viminal Hill, Titus noticed, bore a resemblance in grander proportion to the hill on which the Tempanius farm sat. Shaped like the point of a spear it descended in two tiers in a southwesterly direction, the tip aimed at the heart of the Forum. The Duellii lived on the upper tier separated from their neighbors by a small wooded area, not far from the Vicus Ficus.

The long walk down the street, through the Forum, and up the Clivus Capitolinus to the temple of Jupiter added further to Titus' mortification. Duellius enjoyed watching his soon to be son-in-law turn shades of red as people complimented him on the match, on his toga, made suggestive or overtly lewd comments about the wedding night. But he misinterpreted Titus' growing anger as embarrassment. The closer they drew to the temple the more Titus fumed. Lucius had insisted on the most sacred of marriage ceremonies not because of religious convictions, but because it guaranteed the dowry would remain in his possession. The ceremony of *confarreatio* offered no possibility of divorce. So, the wily Lucius bore no risks. The question of the dowry did not make him mad. He would have been happy with the simpler ceremony of *coemptio* in which the bride's father gave a symbolic three coins as a dowry. No, it was the idea of the thing. 'Forget about it,' he thought, shoving the anger aside. 'What's done is done.'

The temple of Jupiter Optimus Maximus (Best and Greatest) soared above Rome on tremendous columns, dwarfing every other edifice on the seven hills. A single row of muscular columns ran the full 183 feet of its length, while a double row supported the red terracotta tiled roof that extended past the front of the sanctuary and covered the entire 165 feet in width. Atop the pinnacle of the roof a statue of Jupiter whipping a four-horse chariot to full gallop stormed to the front edge of the temple roof, about to take flight. Cosmic winds sheared back the horses' manes, their eyes wild, nostrils flared in the tempest as Jupiter's flowing hair streamed in a whirlwind.

Awestruck, Titus failed to notice the view of Rome's seven sacred hills spread out below him from the Capitoline heights. His eyes fastened on the great altar of Jupiter that squatted with ponderous solemnity in front of the steps to the front portico. Fresh blood thickened in blackening pools on its hard stone surface. Gratitude overwhelmed him as the significance of the setting and the moment made its impact on him. He climbed the steps and walked between the sparkling white columns of the portico in a daze, all anger forgotten.

Inside, Jupiter regally gripped the armrests of his throne, his beard long with justice, his fierce eyes testing the heart. Ten witnesses, composed of family and friends, waited inside with the Pontifex Maximus, and the Flamen Dialis of Jupiter.

Publius Mucius Scaevola, Pontifex Maximus and son of the famous Gaius who defiantly burned his right hand in the fire as a captive of Lars Porsena, whose army was besieging the new republic, and thus acquired the surname Scaevola or 'the left handed', greeted those assembled for the wedding as they took their places around the bride and groom.

"This is both a solemn and a joyous occasion," he said, looking over the small group. "Today Duellia, daughter of Marcus Postumius Duellius, leaves the hand of her father in which she has been nurtured and protected, and enters into the hand of her husband Titus Tempanius. I am happy to say that we have carefully read the flight of birds today, and the auspices are good. We have also made sacrifice of the goat you provided to Jupiter Best and Greatest." He motioned with open hand to two stools, over which the fresh white pelt of the sacrificial goat had been stretched. "Please take a seat on the sacred sellae," he said. Nodding slightly to the Flamen Dialis he went on. "Now in coming into the hand of Titus, Duellia and Titus must ask Jupiter, and the household gods over whom he has dominion, to accept Duellia into the household to worship as one of the family, and to extend their protection to her." Scaevola stepped to one side as he finished.

At this point Gaius Veturius, the Flamen Dialis stepped forward bearing three cakes made of the sacred flour called *far*. He raised them to the likeness of Jupiter. "Oh Jupiter Best and Greatest, accept this sacrifice so that we may welcome into the state the offspring of this union as you welcome Duellia into the house of Titus Tempanius." First crumbling one cake into the fire on a small portable altar he turned and presented a cake to Titus and Duellia. "Enter now into the sacred *far*, Lord Jupiter." Looking seriously at the couple he said, "You must now feed each other so that Jupiter will know you are of one house and one city."

Titus and Duellia took the cakes from the Flamen's hand and turned to each other. Gravely lifting Duellia's flame red veil Titus gazed at his sanctified bride. Her wide oval eyes glowed with pious fear, and her heart shaped mouth trembled anxiously as she opened it to accept the biscuit from his fingers. Reverentially they ate the consecrated bite sized cakes from each other's hands.

Publius Scaevola smiled as he lightly took their hands and lifted them from their seats. A married woman called a pronuba, a friend of the Duellius family, then asked the bride and groom if they consented to the marriage. Each answered affirmatively in turn then she joined their right hands and pronounced them married amidst loud applause.

A piper named Titinius, a friend of Lucius, led the wedding procession back to the Duellius home for the wedding feast. Tables were set out in a walled garden behind the house. Household slaves served kid roasted with thyme and mint, and a pig roasted with rosemary and garlic, on terracotta platters, with a variety of fruits and vegetables in finely cast bronze bowls. Blooming cyclamen and royal purple wisteria hung in clusters against the stone walls, sweetening the air. Drusilla, seated next to Lucius on a long bench admired the fine artwork and vibrant glazes on a terracotta bowl as it passed her way.

"You have made a fine match for your brother," she told him quietly. "How is it you doubt your abilities?"

Lucius drank long from an ornate cup glazed black and umber, around the sides of which cavorted unlikely creatures of the imagination; winged panthers, geese with human heads, and horses with eel bodies. The wine tasted sweet, effervescent. For another moment he looked at the blood red wine remaining in his cup. "It's not that I doubt my abilities, Mama," he said. A smile erupted across his broad face. "In fact, it's just the opposite. I think I'm pursuing what I'm best at."

Drusilla murmured something unintelligible then turned to the wife of Aulus Vibulus. Pressing her son made him the more obstinate. Attacking him made him more aggressive— no wonder he'd become such a good warrior. In this way, she thought, he resembled his father too much.

"So," Aulus Vibulus said heartily, "I hear you're moving to Rome." Seated to the right of Lucius he grabbed a wine pitcher and filled both their cups. "You're going to be in the center of life, now. Are you excited?"

"Yes," said Lucius. "I'm looking forward to it."

"Have you found quarters?"

"I think so. There's a tavern called the Boar's Tusk down in the Subura where I can rent a room or two."

"I know of it," nodded Vibulus. "Pontius Cominus is the proprietor. An educated and honest man. He even reads Greek."

"Exactly."

"It would be more surprising if he didn't know of it," sneered Aemilia, Vibulus' wife. Having overheard their conversation, she now launched into a dissertation on the failings of her husband. "Rather than cultivate people of real influence and standing, he would rather debase himself with the rabble. He spends more time in taverns wasting his bronze and breath talking and drinking with a bunch of know nothing, good-for-nothings, than he does at home."

Vibulus raised a stricken look to the heavens, persecution beatifying his equine face. He drained his cup and poured himself another, but Lucius covered his. "Someday," said Vibulus, nodding his balding head in the direction of his wife, "you'll leave your cup uncovered like I do."

Lucius smiled sagely in reply. Aemilia epitomized his reasons for remaining unbound. She had always been plump, but now she had reached plush. In her matron's stola and palla she resembled a billowing cloud settled to earth. This termagant provided all the inspiration Lucius needed to remain free and aloof from the normal responsibilities of life.

"Of course," continued Vibulus, "you'll need some form of income. Have you made arrangements?"

"I suppose I'll find something," Lucius said, vaguely. "I have enough stashed away until I do."

"The tavern is the last place you'll want to keep money lying around loose."

Lucius narrowed his eyes. Reservation leaked like oil into his voice. "What would you suggest?" he asked.

Vibulus laughed, the gap between his front teeth wide with fond memories. "You are your father's son," he avowed. "He suspected everybody too."

"He always told me to be alert when someone comes offering favors."

"Or advice. Take it or leave it, I only offer this advice for your own protection."

"I meant no offense, Aulus," Lucius apologized.

"None taken," Vibulus assured him. "There are a couple of men in the Argiletum district that have begun a new business of holding people's bronze for them, and paying for its use."

"They would pay me to protect my bronze? What's the catch?"

"As I said, they use it. It's a new business so I don't know all the details. But as I understand it they loan your bronze to others for a fee, and split the fee in some way with you."

"Listen," Lucius averred, "it sounds too risky for me. I think I'd rather bury what little I have in a jar than let someone else loan it to strangers."

"Perhaps you're right." Vibulus rubbed his chin, looking around the garden at the guests. Across the table he heard Gaius Opimius regaling Titus with all the reasons his son would have been counted among the greatest Romans had he lived.

"Think of it," Opimius said earnestly, "at twenty-two years old to have won a civic crown, two armillae, and a phalerus. I don't mean to take anything away from your brother—I know they competed for honors as friends—but by Jove he was headed for great things."

Titus thought Gaius Opimius had aged badly. In his mid-forties the flesh hung on him, his belly sagged, his jowls flapped like chicken skin. Perhaps that's what happened to men who lost sons. "Well," he said, "at least he left a son. Maybe he'll achieve even greater things."

"Yes," Opimius agreed. He drank greedily from his cup, and it appeared to Titus as if his nose actually enlarged and grew a shade deeper purple than the wisteria that hung like bunches of grapes on the wall. Glancing worriedly into his own cup, as if the wine were making him see things, he repressed a sudden revulsion for Gaius Opimius.

"Certainly," Opimius continued. "I'll train him to engage in honorable competition with his ancestors as every good Roman should. But he should have to compete against consulships and triumphs, not just medals…" His harangue petered out into morbid reflection, staring at the empty bottom of his cup as if he'd completely forgotten he was talking to someone.

Titus turned to Duellia, and smiled. He genuinely liked what he saw. No, she was not extravagantly pretty. As she returned his smile, he noticed her eye teeth were extremely small, undeveloped. Her broad forehead, a bit too high, made him think she might lose her hair before he did. But all this struck him as just fine. Really pretty women were too often full of themselves. Duellia had a quiet and demur mien. Unlike Aemelia she did not appear the scolding type, and unlike his mother she did not seem too opinionated or independent. His only worry centered around her slight build, fearing she might not birth children well. 'But she's young,' he consoled himself, 'maybe she'll fill out later.'

"I think we're just the right ages, don't you?" he said. He would turn eighteen in July, and she had just turned fourteen.

"Oh yes," she agreed. "Perfect."

"Yes," he said. "I think we're perfect too." He smiled warmly again.

Duellia unexpectedly found herself maddeningly happy. 'He really likes me!' she thought joyously. She turned and gave her father a quick, surprising peck on the cheek. "Thank you, Father," she said.

To the accompaniment of a lyre, Titinius played his tibia, the two-piece pipe. From the left pipe he poured the wind soughing through the trees, while from the right came the lilting trills and warbles of songbirds. Forcing conversation to cease with melancholy cries, then propelling it on with gay suggestive staccato notes, the musicians fed the party on sonorous sustenance. Happily ribald, or mournfully reflective the lyre player sang popular ballads and plucked strings of emotion as Titinius accompanied him. Soaring and gliding in melodic eddies and updrafts the revelers allowed the music to carry them.

Flowing like sweet rivers wine slaked the thirst and refreshed the spirits of the wedding party. The sun slid smoothly across a clear sky. Warm and slightly liquid, the air worked relaxing fingers into the muscles and sinews of the guests. Marcus Duellius rose and delivered a prayer to Juno to lead their daughter to her new home as her mother clutched her tightly. Titus, as if Duellia were a Sabine of long ago, wrested her from her mother's grip and dragged her from the house.

"Thalassius, Thalassius," cried the celebrants, the reason for this traditional cry long forgotten.

A happy procession followed the couple, led once again by Titinius the piper. In her hands Duellia carried a spinning distaff and spindle. At the same time two small boys with living parents held each of her hands. A third carried a lighted torch of hawthorn and followed Titinius. Behind them the revelers, tongues well loosed of inhibitions, called out obscene jokes and comments about the wedding night. Along the roadside other well-wishers tossed nuts to the little boys leading the happy parade. When they reached the temporary home where they would spend their first night together Titus picked Duellia up with an uncharacteristic flourish, and carried her across the threshold dinned with suggestive hoots.

Duellia endured the long ride to the Tempanius farm the next day under blustering skies, buffeted by an expostulating wind. Her heart sank once again as she watched Rome shrink incrementally behind her. The ardor and jubilation of the previous day drained from her like her husband's juices. Yet she still had rites to perform and duties to assume. At the door she anointed both sides of the doorposts with olive oil and lard, then tied fillets of wool to nails sunk on either side. Titus waited just inside for her to perform these rites, and when she finished asked her the traditional question.

"What is your forename?"

She looked meekly at him, and her voice came out shakily. "Wherever you are Titus," she squeaked, "I will be Titia."

Titus smiled, bent to pick her up in his arms, and carried her lightly across the threshold of her new home. Only strangers crossed a doorstep for the first time. Family members were all born in the home. Thus, carrying her over the threshold symbolized her birth into the family.

Drusilla took Duellia immediately to her room where she dressed in her new matron's stola, then brought her to the household altar to make sacrifice to the Tempanius lares, and penates for acceptance and fertility.

Duellia no longer belonged to her father. The old life passed away, and a new one began.

# XII

## September 13, 475 BC
## Ludi Romani—The Roman Games

Though Lucius possessed prodigious strength and incredible stamina, Titus would not miss the work he did. That he could replace, but a similar sense of humor would be hard to find. Much as he professed to dislike the work, Lucius still managed to perform it with a lighthearted ease that made the days go faster and lightened the burdens. Titus found himself wishing he would stay.

Lucius remained adamant. All the arrangements had been made with Pontius Cominus to move to the Boar's Tusk after the Roman games. As the stifling days of August drifted away, he grew jovial by degrees, an attitude Antonius found insulting. He considered it unseemly that Lucius should be so obviously happy about deserting the family. When he said as much, Lucius laughed, and his mother smiled and dissembled.

Drusilla realized nothing she could say would change Lucius' mind, and if she attempted to exert her influence he would simply remove himself sooner. But more than that she had resigned herself to his departure. Too many duties demanded her attention to waste energy on a recalcitrant son. She found Duellia a mixed blessing. On the one hand, having another female in the house lightened her load significantly. On the other, her immaturity tried Drusilla's patience.

Duellia strove mightily to fit in. Unfortunately, she didn't understand her place or role within the family structure. Roman tradition told her she was a matron, a position of respect and honor, in many ways the one who truly ran the household. But in reality, her mother-in-law ran the house, and her brother-in-law, despite his protests, acted as paterfamilias. Which meant that although married to Titus, Lucius had every bit as much, or more, say in her future. The confusion left her more timid than normal, which got on her mother-in-law's nerves, which made her yet more timid. She soon felt she couldn't do anything right, burst into tears at the least provocation, and grew utterly miserable.

Titus, completely nonplused, ignored her, hoping she would grow out of it. The only woman he'd ever known intimately was his mother, and she seemed, frankly, out of the ordinary. So, he resolved to concentrate on his work and let the females take care of themselves.

"Are you going to wrestle in the Ludi this year?" he asked Lucius.

"I don't think so," said Lucius, rubbing his wet hair with a thick finger. Just come from the bath his dark tanned skin gleamed. He wore a fresh sleeveless tunic and had scraped his wide face clean of several days' growth of beard. A cup of spiced wine awaited his pleasure on the kitchen table.

Titus continued working. Gathered around his chair were an assortment of jars, urns, and small amphorae with cracks that needed mending. Between his knees he mixed a concoction of wax, resin, sulfur, and gypsum into the consistency of plaster.

At the hearth Drusilla and Duellia prepared the evening meal. Duellia, with tentative fingers, made bread while Drusilla dressed a capon for baking.

Antonius, at the opposite end of the table from Titus, was engrossed in weaving a basket from strips of cane. He worked with meticulous attention to detail so that the weave was so tight Lucius teased him that his baskets would hold water. "In fact," he said, "why don't you come to Rome and go into the business? You'd be an equite in no time."

"I'd rather stay with my family," said Antonius pointedly.

"Ooh," expostulated Lucius as if he'd been punched. "You're like one of those little dogs I've seen that once they lock their jaws on something they never let loose."

"I'll take that as a compliment," said Antonius snidely.

"It was meant as one," Lucius laughed. He put one foot up on another chair and took a long drink, eyeing his brother Titus over the rim of his cup. "You see," he said, as he put his cup down, "this is it; I'm ready to relax. We worked hard all day. Now it's time for a cup of wine, a good meal, and relaxation. But you, you're still working."

Titus held a cracked bowl in one hand and with a flat stick smeared the cement he'd made over a longitudinal crack. "I'm no good at relaxing," he said. "It makes me nervous. Besides, there's too much to do."

"There," exclaimed Lucius, "that's exactly it." He jabbed a finger at some invisible point. "Too much to do. That's why I can't live this life."

Duellia poured the flour she had just ground into a bowl. "My father says that idle hands leave minds free to think up mischief," she said. Adding water gradually she kneaded the flour into a thick ball of dough.

"Lucius doesn't need extra time to think up trouble," Antonius said. "It comes naturally as breathing to him."

Lucius laughed. Drusilla scowled as she infused a capon with rosemary and garlic cloves. From a tub of water she lifted a terracotta crock, placed the chicken in the lower half, covered it with a lid and put it in the oven. "He's not like your father in that way," she said finally.

"True," admitted Lucius. "Father was like Titus. Work, work, work."

"You say that like there's something wrong with it," said Antonius. His full lips compressed in accusation, there could be nothing wrong in being like their father.

Titus picked up another jar. "No," he said slowly. "The truth is Lucius is a lot like Father. When it comes to war no one works harder at making himself ready. I've seen him."

"Why do you always defend him?" rasped Antonius.

"Because he's my brother, first," Titus said. "And because I'm only saying what I've seen and know to be true."

Lucius grabbed a cracked pot and a flat stick and scooted closer to the bowl of cement Titus had prepared. "You should be happy," he said to Antonius as he slathered cement on the cracked pot. "Your inheritance has just increased by a third." He smiled widely at his little brother. "Best of all, you'll still have me to kick around."

Antonius snorted. Titus changed the subject. "I hear the tribunes have brought Menenius up for trial."

"Mm," Lucius intoned, offering no comment.

"Good," said Antonius vehemently. "He deserves it."

"Do you think they'll call you to testify?" Titus asked Lucius.

"No," drawled Lucius. "Why? I was just a soldier."

"But you helped save the city," Drusilla interjected. "Everyone says so."

"Listen, I just did what a soldier is supposed to do. Now, they might call Aulus Vibulus. He was a military tribune and would have been privy to whatever planning or discussions took place."

"Oh, Aulus would be in his element there, wouldn't he?" Titus guffawed at the thought.

Lucius chuckled at the idea. "If they let him make a speech," he said.

Duellia, rolling out the dough, said, "My father always said Aulus Vibulus had bigger dreams than hands to hold them."

"Your father has a lot of sayings," joked Lucius, but Duellia flinched as if struck, and he immediately regretted his words.

"Nevertheless," Antonius insisted, "if Menenius hadn't been negligent the war with Veii would have ended much sooner."

Lucius understood that Antonius blamed Menenius for their father's death. It might even have been true. Certainly, soldiers complained often that their officers didn't know what they were doing. But after the fact, when he'd had a chance to reflect, he wondered just what Menenius might have done differently to win the battle. The position had not been bad, and the disposition of the troops adequate. Sometimes the outcome of a battle rested simply on which army was stronger on a given day. But to say all this to Antonius would only make him angrier. Especially coming from the family-deserting brother.

"Well," Lucius said, "the people will have to decide one way or the other, I suppose."

"They're actually trying him for the food shortage," Titus said. "If he'd just lost the battle no one would have said anything. But when they took the Janiculum and cut off the food supply…well, people don't forget that."

"Oh yes," Duellia said. She had formed the bread into a thin round loaf, and now slid it into the oven next to the chicken. "That was awful. Everything was so scarce."

Lucius chuckled. "Yes, even the trees on the Vicus Ficus were picked clean."

Watching his mother, he saw her body stiffen as she jerked down jars and baskets of fruits and vegetables. She slammed a pot angrily on the counter. Lucius rose quickly and hurried to her side. Tears started in her eyes and flowed down her cheeks. She wiped at them furiously with one hand. Lucius stepped close and pulled her to his chest, enfolding her in his huge arms. "It's all right, Mama," he soothed in susurrant tones. "It's all right."

A cloud of embarrassment floated through the room, dampening the sweet smell of baking bread along with the spirits of the family. Antonius looked down at his basket, eyes black with anger and confusion. Only twelve years old he had seen his father killed before his eyes, had watched crops and farms burned and ravaged all over the Roman plain, and even in their isolation well understood the lingering effects on Rome. Someone, he believed should be punished, and in his mind a triad of culprits wore the hook of guilt around their necks. First, naturally, were the Etruscans, whose destruction of the Fabii clan and subsequent attack on Rome had instigated the tragedy. Second came Menenius, the consul whose incompetence led to a Roman defeat. Third, his brother Lucius, quondam hero now turned deserter. How he could be so honorable as a soldier, and so dishonorable to his family Antonius could not understand.

"I don't think it's right to buy food from the Etruscans right after we had a war with them," he said.

"Hungry people don't care where the food comes from," replied Titus.

"Our war was against Veii, not the Etruscans," Lucius admonished.

"What's the difference?" Antonius sullenly asked.

"The difference is exactly what I said. We weren't at war with the whole Etruscan people, just the city of Veii." Lucius released his mother and returned to his chair.

"They're Etruscans aren't they?"

"Yes, but not all Etruscans are Veientes."

Antonius glared at Lucius, his full lips trembled with unspoken words. Inexpressible thoughts slashed through his brain. He bit his tongue, looked down at his fingers automatically weaving fibrous strands of cane, and fell into stubborn silence, unable to argue further or admit his brother's superior logic.

"So," began Titus, hoping he had found a subject less contentious, "shall we stay in Rome for the games?"

"Why not?" said Lucius. "We can all stay in my rooms at the Boar's Tusk."

+ + +

The great games, the Ludi Romani were first held on September 13, on the anniversary of the dedication of the temple of Jupiter during the reign of Tarquinius Superbus, last king of Rome. They were indeed Jupiter's games, given for the whole community. Soldiers returning from the war season, which had been mercifully cut short after the battle on the Janiculum, were returned to the civic fold even though officially they had not gone through the specific rights of purification.

For Lucius it marked his first attempt at hospitality in the two small rooms he rented at the Boar's Tusk. It seemed easiest to separate the sexes, so he put Drusilla and Duellia in the room he used as the kitchen and main salon, and installed Titus, and Antonius in his bedroom.

Nearly the entire city-state of Rome came to the city for the games. Wealthy patrons spent much time and money making sure their clients, from the important to the humble, had accommodations or were otherwise provided for. In every quarter of the city they made sure tables were piled high with culinary delights for public feasting, and they let it be known exactly who had provided it.

The first day's events started with a parade that began on the Campus Martius. A light haze covered the sky as the sun scaled the Apennines. At the northern edge of the Campus, near the altar of Mars, a great host of participants gathered. A heavy cold mist rose off the Capraen marsh in the center of the Campus so that the woods on the south side looked like a patch of night that refused to leave the earth. Musicians, clowns, dancers, and children gathered in unmartial aspect in a ramshackle line from east to west. Clumps of spectators lined the parade route under the Esquiline and Capitoline hills. Lucius, Titus, and Antonius took up positions under a clump of oak trees at the bottom of the Capitoline Hill, in the shadow of the temple of Juno high above them on the citadel.

In purple triumphal robes the consul Servilius led off the parade riding in his ornate chariot of state. Astride the right-side horse rode his youngest son. Behind his chariot came a host of male children of all the men eligible for military service, organized in centuries. Those whose fathers were of equite status rode proudly past on horseback. Following them came the performers. Charioteers, gleaming in brightly colored livery, balanced haughtily behind prancing teams of glistening chargers. Boxers, wrestlers, runners, and other athletes dressed only in loincloth and a cloak marched by flexing their muscles, exhibiting their moves. Lucius suddenly wished he'd entered the wrestling, though he would have had little time to train because of his wounds.

Hard on the heels of the athletes came the *ludiones*, the dancers and sacred pipers who danced and played non-stop the whole length of the parade. Should one of them stop for any reason, the procession was halted and started over from the beginning. Three groups of dancers, men of military age, adolescents, and children passed by wearing red tunics with wide brightly polished bronze belts. Only the adult men wore

181

the feather topped bronze helmets, and they followed the steps of a conductor, lunging, thrusting, parrying with the sword, holding aloft a short spear and making throwing motions or stabbing downward at an imaginary fallen enemy. Circling, spinning, leaping they danced past to the music of the pipers just behind.

Lucius turned to Antonius. "Don't you think Titus should be in this?"

Inspired, Antonius said, "When I take the toga virilis we should all be in it together."

"Why not?!" agreed Lucius, happy that his brother seemed at last to have put away his anger. "What do you think Titus?"

"Oh, I don't know," he dissembled.

Now, mimicking the ludiones that preceded them, bounded bands of clowns dressed in colorful cloaks and goatskin belts. In hilarious imitation of the feather topped helmets they plastered their hair with lard till it stuck straight out from their heads in three stiff spikes. Taking exaggerated steps, they satirized the dancers with absurd, grotesque movements. Thrusting groins, leering painted eyes, lolling tongues, and clumsy pratfalls had the spectators rolling on the ground and clutching their sides with laughter.

"Titus, I think they've seen you fight," teased Lucius, lying back on the grass.

More musicians filled the air with songs, lyre players, harpists, and corniculars. Incense bearers wafting sweet smoke from clay or bronze thuribles drifted by. Following them all came images of Rome's immortal deities, riding in state on biers borne on the shoulders of her citizens.

Rather than follow the parade into the Forum, the brothers cut across the port, and passed the temple of Fortune. Where the fouled Velabrum entered into the Tiber they wound their way through scattered huts and houses near the grove of Hercules, and took the Via Albana to the east end of the Circus. Near the altar of Consus they found a place to watch the games. They relaxed, snacking on a basket of grapes, cheese, and figs, waiting for the parade to pass by them again. It would make a complete circuit through the Forum, up the Capitol to the temple of Jupiter, where sacrifices were made on the great altar outside, and back across the Forum to the Circus Maximus. Every house along the route kept its shutters tightly closed, for it was a sacrilege to view the parade from an open window.

Laid out in an east-west direction in the Murcia Valley, the long oval Circus Maxiumus was a kind of demilitarized zone in the lowlands between the Palatine and Aventine hills. On the lower slopes of the Aventine, the south side of the Circus, two plebeian cult temples occupied the ground—the temple of Ceres at the west end, and the temple of Mercury at the east end. Outside the sacred border of the city, the Aventine also played home to the Latin cult temple of Diana that crowned its summit. Technically ager publicus (public land) and therefore sparsely inhabited, the Aventine nevertheless held clear plebeian associations. Periodically, to exert their authority, the consuls would clean out squatters who illegally occupied the public land, pulling down houses, enclosures, and other structures erected without legal authority. At other times, to relieve social and economic pressures they turned a blind eye to the small plots and gardens that sprung up there. According to tradition Remus chose the Aventine as his site for the new city.

Romulus chose the Palatine. Curiously the Palatine had twin summits, the germalus and the palatium. On the germalus the hut of Romulus still existed, overlooking the Circus from its southern eminence. On the lower slopes of the Palatine a cave known as the Lupercal, shrine to a college of patrician priests the luperci, brooded like a dark eye watching the rival hill. There could be no doubt as to the affiliation of the Palatine. It was, and would remain, strictly patrician.

But the Circus, except for a short section of permanent stands on the north side for senators, consuls, and the chief priests of the Republic, was egalitarian. Politics and social standing were here put aside and replaced by mutual laughter, excitement, and fun. Lucius, who liked to watch the chariots make the turn, had chosen the spot where they sat under clearing skies. The gentle slopes on either side were now teeming with people as thirty thousand Romans squeezed into places surrounding the great oval depression, along with peoples from all over Latium, Etruria, and even Volscian territory.

Now the parade came around the Palatine Hill and entered onto the Circus at the west end, still led by the consul, his purple toga shimmering in the tumescent sunlight. In his hand he clenched the scepter that for this one day made him like a king in Rome.

The brothers laughed at the arm-weary slave, balancing behind the consul, whose face wore a grimace of pain from holding a golden crown over the consul's head for the entire length of the parade route. The procession came towards them, turned and flowed up the south side of the Circus. As the gods were carried past the spot where Lucius stood, one of the bearers on the left side of the litter carrying the image of Mars stepped awkwardly into a depression and the litter tilted. A collective gasp went up from the crowd, and all eyes went to the spot.

Lucius at that very moment had been thinking of the prospect of buying a plot of land sometime in the near future to provide him with a steady income. He thought he could convince Quintus Crispus to work it for him. When the litter bearer stumbled, Mars, Lucius' patron deity, tilted and nodded directly at him. An immense wave of joy at the propitious sign engulfed him. Surely he would survive many battles and win great honors. Throughout the rest of the games Lucius could think of only one thing; his patron god Mars had nodded at him, had endorsed all his hopes and plans. He rejoiced in the confirmation of the god's approval of his move to Rome. Fate declared him invincible.

# XIII

## December 17, 475 BC
## The Saturnalia

Aulus Vibulus, in marmoreal splendor, waited impatiently for late rising Lucius Tempanius. He tapped his long freshly manicured feet and drummed his neatly trimmed fingers in time to an unheard tune. In a strange reversal of convention, the candidate waited for the retinue. He would have liked to sit, but his chalk-whitened toga deprived him of the comfort. So, he stood just outside the kitchen where Cominus snickered behind his cup of steaming herbs, and papyrus scroll.

Weak beams of light filtered through the shutters of the dark interior of the Boar's Tusk. Outside in the gathering light a larger than normal following of clients shivered in wait. Vibulus had contacted as many of his friends and clients as possible, for in a bold move for a man who had worn the gold ring of the equites less than a decade, he formally announced his candidacy for consul.

A black haired girl of eleven came skipping down the steps and stopped in front of him. She stared openly at him for a moment with frank brown eyes.

"Are you waiting for my father?" she asked. A lilting musical quality to her voice brought a smile to his face.

"I don't think so," he said. "I'm waiting for Lucius Tempanius. He's not your father, is he?" His gap-toothed smile remained plastered on his face.

"Heavens no," she said, her voice trilled with laughter.

"Valeria," Cominus called from the kitchen, his voice quiet yet firm. "Come in here and don't bother Aulus Vibulus."

Vibulus thought her no bother at all.

Valeria started to obey, suddenly stopped and said, "If you're here for Lucius Tempanius you might lose miles in waiting."

"Valeria…"

"Yes, Father."

185

"Oh? And why is that?"

"Because he almost never gets up before the second hour."

"Valeria!"

"Coming Father."

"Of course, if you were to go wake him, we could change that."

Cominus edged his portly body around the tall wooden serving tower that separated the kitchen from the public room. "Valeria," he said, "go in the kitchen."

"Yes, Father," she said, ducking her delicate features beneath his chastisement.

"You have a lovely daughter, Pontius," Vibulus said. Looking down at Cominus like a vine arching over its stake, Vibulus smiled, thinking how Cominus with his bald head and rotund body reminded him of the ball he chased around the streets in his childhood.

Cominus looked up at Vibulus with baleful eyes. In that chalk whitened toga he looked like an apparition stretched to near translucence. "Yes," he said, warily. "She is lovely. And that's why I keep her away from the tenants and patrons as much as possible."

"Ah, you don't want me sending her off to roust young men out of their beds. I understand completely."

"Well," Cominus said gruffly, "I suppose I could go up and see if he's awake."

"Don't trouble yourself," said Vibulus politely. "He'll be down soon enough."

"Have it your way." Cominus turned away.

"Wait." Vibulus lightly grabbed his arm. "As you can see," he indicated his toga with a downward sweep of his right hand, "I'm a candidate for consul. Today I plan on visiting the various trade guilds, and I'd like to tell them I have your support when I stop in at the college of innkeepers."

"I see…" Cominus said, trailing off ambiguously.

"Are you committed to someone already?"

"No, you're the first to ask."

"Of course, I ask only as a friend. But as an educated man you could be of immeasurable help to me in your tribe also. The Suburana, isn't it?"

"Yes."

"And I'm sure you're in the first class. Can I count on your vote?"

Cominus rubbed his double chin, hesitating. He had no desire to attach his name to any candidate. Once, during the consulships of Spurius Cassius, he had done so eagerly. For Cassius had a vision of a Rome that ruled all Italy, incorporating her peoples in one powerful state. To that end he made a treaty with the Latins after the battle of Lake Regillus, allying them with Rome, yet always under Roman commanders. Elected consul thrice, Cassius exerted a powerful influence on Roman policies for over a decade, and Cominus gladly attached himself to the great man. Cassius sent him to southern Italy and Sicily, known as Magna Graecia, to work out trade agreements with the Greek city-states there. He learned Greek, and made many contacts over ten years that would serve him well in the future.

But Cassius' vision reached too far. Jealous patricians, especially in the Fabius clan, sought a pretext to bring him down. When he proposed a land reform bill that included Latin and Hernican citizens as well as Romans, they accused him of plotting to seize sole power.

Cominus' fortunes plunged as Cassius plunged off the Tarpeian Rock to his death. In ruins he sought refuge at the Boar's Tusk, which he bought with what remained of his money after the state confiscated his property, and removed him from the class of equites. They pulled down the house of Spurius Cassius on the Caelian Hill, and left a barren field.

The sound of feet hurriedly slapping against stone steps interrupted their conversation. Lucius came around the corner combing damp ringlets of hair with thick fingers. A yawn covered his broad, round face.

"Am I late?" he asked, expelling the last part of the yawn with his words.

"Nothing a good candidate can't overcome," said Vibulus. "I hope."

"I'm sorry," said Lucius sheepishly, twisting his head quickly at the sound of giggling from the kitchen.

"Well then," said Vibulus, wringing Cominus' hand, "thank you Pontius my friend. Perhaps later we can mount a sign outside declaring your endorsement." Before Cominus could agree, protest, or even remark the two men were out the door.

Lucius bundled himself in both of his tunics, a toga, and a cloak clasped over the right shoulder with a bronze pin. Still he shivered against the cold.

"Where to first?" he asked.

"To the Forum, of course. Ah, I can see you're just like your father. He never understood that the center of life is the Forum."

"No," said Lucius, laughing through chattering teeth. "He thought the center of life was the farm."

"I know. Of course, the farm is the foundation of life. But that's a different thing."

Lucius looked up at the low gray sky with disgust. The gelid air felt thick and moist against his face. Why, in the name of all the gods, he wondered, did they hold elections in December? Apparently, the rest of Rome did not feel the same. When they entered the Forum, it teemed with people. Four or five other candidates in whitened togas, each with his entourage of dependents and adherents, worked the crowd. By far the largest following attached itself to Lucius Valerius, great grandson of the revered Publius Valerius Publicola, whose house sat at the foot of the Velia, not far from the Subura district.

Vibulus pointed him out to Lucius and said, "We are not running in opposition to Lucius Valerius. The weight of his family name guarantees him victory."

"So you have to defeat four other men for only one position?"

"If you choose to look at it that way. I see it as one less opponent I have to defeat. After all, I can only win one consulship at a time."

Lucius chuckled and squinted skeptically. "My father always said you were one of a kind."

Vibulus paid him no heed. He threw himself into the crowd and began working it. Grasping every man's hand he came near he pumped it vigorously, bent his lanky frame and implored, "Please vote for me." "I beg you, vote for me." Like a mendicant asking for wheat cakes, he begged and pleaded, debasing himself and extolling his virtues at one and the same time. Now and then he would indicate Lucius and say, "See, Lucius Tempanius, hero of the war with Veii supports me," and he would finger the medals he had asked Lucius to wear. Then he would move on.

Others, far more important than Lucius, joined Vibulus' entourage in the Forum. Men like Gaius Opimius, Gaius Sicinius, and Marcus Duellius not only joined, but also began performing the same act as Vibulus, begging on his behalf for votes. Lucius, unaccustomed to humiliating himself in such fashion, hesitated to duplicate their behavior, then with a shrug of his huge shoulders forced himself to try it. At first, he pleaded insincerely, but with each new encounter he became more relaxed, and soon put his whole heart on display. In every corner of the Forum each candidate and his host of adherents did the same so that once in a while one implored a member of another candidate's party for his vote, which nearly always garnered a laugh, a hearty handshake, and renewed enthusiastic entreaties. Then like an irrigation gate shutting off the water it ended. From the Curia the midday trumpets blared, and the candidates dispersed.

Not that the campaigning stopped. Instead, all the men of importance scattered to every part of the city, or to districts outside the city, to drum up support for their candidate. With nothing of importance to do Lucius entertained the thought of tagging along with Vibulus.

"Where are you going next?" he asked.

"I thought I'd pay a visit to some of the tribal headquarters," answered Vibulus.

"Do you mind if I come along?"

"Not at all. I'd be honored."

King Servius Tullius had divided the city of Rome, according to tradition, into four urban and seventeen rural tribes. The urban tribes, the Palatina, Suburana, Collina, and Esquilina kept headquarters in their respective quarters. The rural tribes gathered their headquarters together at the base of the Palatine hill along the Via Sacra near the intersection with the Vicus Cyprius. It was to these offices they headed.

Once out of the congestion of the Forum, Lucius immediately felt the cold again, and thought with a bitter despair of the three months of winter remaining. The leaden sky seemed even lower now, and he thought with certainty that it would snow. Vibulus seemed impervious to the cold despite his thin build.

"Aren't you cold?" Lucius asked, as they passed the annular temple of Vesta.

Vibulus laughed. "Not a bit. Of course, I'm wearing four tunics under my toga. Let's stop here for a space," he said, pointing at the Regia.

They walked between the columns of the unequal length portico and crossed to the vestibule that separated the temple of Mars from the temple of Consus. As Vibulus stooped his tall frame to read the white notice board mounted there by the Pontifex Maximus, Lucius bought a stick of incense and entered the temple of Mars to make a small offering to his patron god. Vibulus carefully scrutinized the notice board to make sure nothing escaped his attention that might help him sway a vote.

They did not visit all seventeen of the rural tribes' offices. In the twenty-four days before the election, Vibulus would visit each and every tribal headquarters. Like any good politician he could count the votes, and he knew which candidate could virtually be guaranteed the votes of certain tribes. So, he prioritized his visits making sure he visited the tribes he thought he could carry first, then those that might be up for grabs, and finally those for which he held out little hope. In each office he made sure to see two people, the curatore who kept the records and knew all the comings and goings of the tribe, and the divisore who distributed to tribal members such gifts as their wealthier patrons might wish to dole out. If possible, he would try to wheedle out of them the names of members who were influential, and if they were as yet committed or pledged to a candidate.

Lucius looked on interestedly though a bit confused. As they came out of the headquarters of the Perpinia tribe, their fourth stop, Vibulus sighed, rubbed his long cheeks, and said he'd had enough.

"Come," he said, "I'll walk you home."

"Need some rest for tomorrow?" Lucius chuckled.

"Tomorrow? I need rest for tonight. I'll have a house full of friends to entertain."

"And you have twenty-three more days of this?"

"Of course, we won't count the six months prior to the official campaign season."

Lucius whistled softly through his teeth. "Are you sure it's worth it?"

"Honors are always worth the trouble, Lucius. Your father was a man of great honor, but he did not aspire to them. Had he done so he would have left you a tremendous legacy."

Lucius didn't quite know how to take Vibulus' comment. He recognized it as a compliment, yet also a judgement against his father. Lucius knew his father to be a simple, hard working farmer who loved his land. He had heard him speak lovingly to plant and animal alike, had seen him literally taste the soil. Vibulus seemed to regard land, crops, animals as means to social and political ends, and imbued them with no intrinsic value. Ironically, he saw himself as more like Vibulus than his father.

They walked under the heavy timbers of the Sister's Beam. The Velia rose a dirty green on the left. On the right plane trees marched up the steep slope of the Carinae to the Fagutal like a column of lepers, their patchy bark lifeless in the dull light. Lucius and Vibulus wove their way through the street crowded with donkeys, carts, and people as they made their way home for the afternoon meal.

"So, I don't understand," Lucius began, changing the subject. "If the people vote by centuries, why is it important to visit all the tribes?"

"Ah," said Vibulus, rubbing his hooked nose, "good question. The tribes have members spread through all the centuries. You're right of course; the election will be held in the comitia centuriata. But the best way to influence the centuries is through the tribe precisely because each tribe has many members in each century. And it is far easier to visit seventeen tribes than ninety centuries."

"I see."

"Keep in mind, Lucius, that I have many other people to see. There are all the trade guilds; the teamsters, fullers, barbers, the pipers for all the gods' sakes. And of course, not everyone is in Rome. There are many influential people who stay out of the city until the election proper. Then there are signs to put up…well, I could go on for hours."

"Listen," said Lucius, "I think I'll leave you here if that's all right." They had come to the back side of the Subura district in the narrow area between the Velia, and the Oppian Hill, and Lucius, well informed of the anfractuous byways, thought to take a shortcut and get out of the miserable cold.

Vibulus sighed with resignation. "I'll be the only candidate in history to walk himself home." An exaggeration since two slaves and a small group of clients he had hired for the day still trailed them.

"If you'd rather I…"

"No, no, go on. But Lucius."

"Yes?"

"I could use your help in both your century and your tribe."

"Of course," Lucius hastily agreed. "And I'll see you tomorrow."

"In the Forum."

"In the Forum," Lucius repeated with a smile.

The shortcut wasn't. Driven by the penetrating cold to hurry he made several wrong turns and found himself in dead ends, or suddenly back at the place he started. The Subura district formed a roughly triangular shaped section squeezed into the low-lying area between the Velia and Viminal Hill. The base of the triangle faced north, bordered by the Cloaca Maxima. The tip of the pyramid pushed into the valley between the Velia and the Oppian Hill, contained by the intersection of the Vicus Cyprius and the Vicus Sceleratus (Street of Crime). The street acquired its name when Tullia, wife of Tarquinius Superbus and daughter of King Servius Tullius, ran over the body of her murdered father in a gruesome display of impiety. A stone shrine to Diana nearby witnessed the ghastly crime, and still remained on the spot.

Inside this triangle of roads there were no real streets, just a maze of twisting dirt alleys, and pathways lined or blocked by cob houses, round huts with thatch roofs, small shops, taverns, brothels, and flimsy lean-to shacks. Dirty ragged children stared at his blustery face, and listless, unkempt adults regarded him suspiciously. Pigs, dogs, and chickens ran loose, and their excrement along with human garbage mined the roadway. Bone cold, angry and frustrated, Lucius finally saw a recognizable landmark and found his way home.

Valeria tittered teasingly at his ruddy face as he entered the kitchen slapping his arms and blowing into his clenched fist. "You look like a big red ox," she laughed.

Lucius stomped into the kitchen where she sat at the table husking fava beans. Rubbing his hands together over glowing coals on the hearth he grunted something unintelligible.

"You sound like one too," Valeria continued.

"Does your father never spank you for that impertinent mouth?" he grumbled.

Valeria turned her dark eyes on his broad back. She wrinkled her pert nose sarcastically. "Why should he spank me for telling the truth?" she said.

"Because even the truth can be bad manners, sometimes." He turned around and leaned against the counter, letting the heat flow up his back. For a few moments he kept silent, regarding her thin dexterous fingers as they split the long green husks and spilled the white beans into a black terracotta bowl decorated with pictures of racing Etruscan chariots. Valeria's hair, he noticed, had the same glossy black color. He reached over her shoulder and plucked a bean from the bowl, popping it into his mouth. It tasted slightly dry, but still sweet. "These are much better in the spring," he said.

"But it's not spring. It's winter."

"Unfortunately." Lucius quickly tired of her teasing. He knew she expressed affection for him in this adolescent way, but he could only take short doses of it. As he started to leave, she stopped him.

"Will you eat with us tonight, Lucius?"

"No thank you, Valeria," he said quickly, then instantly felt a twinge of regret. Too many meals alone made a man uncivilized, he could hear his mother say. But really it just made one lonely. Unwilling to take back his hasty answer he retired towards his rooms.

Pontius Cominus stood atop his serving tower pouring the final pitchers of wine and collecting money from the last few customers. As Lucius came out of the kitchen and around the side of the tower Cominus called to him. He climbed the three steps gaining entrance to the eight feet high wooded structure. As he came up the steps a patron appealed to Cominus for one last round.

"Hand me that pitcher, please, Lucius," Cominus said, pointing to the next to the smallest pitcher hanging on a peg on the back wall of the tower. He filled it with wine from an amphora beneath the counter, and poured the contents into a bronze funnel set in the front overhang under which the customer held a pitcher of identical size. "That's the last," he said. "I'd like to eat before everyone comes back to get away from their wives," he grumbled.

Fumbling underneath the counter as he straightened things up, putting stoppers in bottles and amphorae, he said in a low voice, "You have a visitor."

"Oh?" said Lucius. He pushed a large amphora back into line with its mates. "Who is it?"

"Publius Scipio."

Lucius jerked up, then quickly bent over out of sight. "For me? How long has he been waiting?"

"Calm down. He just arrived. Here, help me with this," he said, indicating an amphora stacked behind some others. "Although I don't think it's a social call."

Lucius easily pulled the amphora free and tipped it to fill a jug in Cominus' hands. "Take this with you," Cominus said. "It's the best we have."

"Thank you, Pontius. How much is it?"

"Let me worry about that."

"No, no, let me pay you."

"This time it's gratis," said Cominus.

Lucius chuckled quietly. "Nothing in Rome is gratis, Pontius."

"Eh," grunted Cominus. "I know that better than you."

Rising, Lucius saw Publius Scipio seated against the far wall with two other men. He put four cups on a tray and carried it to the table as nonchalantly as possible. Scipio rose from his seat and put a smile on his thin face. Lucius tried to read the purpose of the visit there but the dark, unflinching eyes said nothing. He knew that to read weakness in the small chin would be a grave mistake. His erect bearing and firm chin belied Scipio's fifty or so years. So did his handshake.

"Please sit down," Scipio said, indicating an open chair.

"To what do I owe the honor of this visit?" asked Lucius. He poured wine red as rubies into the four cups. A rich musty aroma wafted up. "Good health," said Lucius, raising his cup.

They joined him, sipping at the wine. Each of them raised their eyes in apparent surprise at the quality of the wine.

"Very good," said Scipio admiringly. "Where does it come from?"

"Somewhere in Campania, I think," said Lucius. "I'll find out if you'd like."

"Perhaps," said Scipio. He raised his eyebrows and his two companions excused themselves. "I'm sure you're wondering why I've come."

"The question crossed my mind," said Lucius. He tried to laugh but it died in his throat. Patricians, especially the older ones, were rarely seen in taverns. Socializing was done in private homes. A brief period of their younger sons' lives might allow for diverting themselves within the iniquitous confines of Suburan taverns, but after a certain (unspecified) age of responsibility it became unseemly. While a stop at the Tempanius farm would not have been unusual, a visit to Lucius' quarters constituted the extraordinary.

"I noticed this morning you were in the company of Aulus Vibulus."

"Yes?" Lucius said. He could not help noticing that Scipios bald head wreathed by dark hair, and small pointed chin gave him the appearance of a leek fresh from the garden.

"Are you dissatisfied with our relationship?"

Lucius stopped his cup in mid lift, and set it carefully back down on the table. "Aulus Vibulus has been a friend of the family all my life," he said, unable to keep a sudden cold violence from icing his words. "My father taught me well the value and meaning of friendship, and I sought only to honor him and his memory." Lucius struggled to maintain his composure, and civility. His father and Publius Scipio the elder had long ago established a client-patron relationship, and he was well aware of the obligations. Since his move to Rome, he had in fact paid some of those obligations by attending Scipio's entourage into the Forum, even serving as a personal bodyguard. But Publius Cornelius Scipio did not own him, and he would be no man's slave. "Have you found my services wanting?" he asked.

"Not at all…in the past." Scipio let the words drip, and his stare came back to Lucius equally icy. "Aulus Vibulus might be a good friend, but he is a threat to the Republic. Good men are obligated to discern when the good of the state must take precedence over friendships."

"Are you saying I'm obligated to drop my support from Aulus Vibulus?"

"I would never presume to tell a man what his conscience should obligate him to do. His own conscience should suffice."

Lucius drew himself up, squaring his shoulders. He put a look of utmost respect on his face, as a man of meager accomplishments compared to Publius Scipio. Nevertheless, as his father would have said, he was a free Roman. "Publius Cornelius Scipio," he began formally, "I have, and always will have, the utmost respect for you. Your family brought us to Rome as citizens, helped negotiate the price of half our present estate, and generously helped pay for my father's funeral. In this way you brought great honor to the Tempanii. These and many other things have you done for us. I say this, not because you need to be reminded, but to show you that I am well aware of our mutual bonds. And also to show that I do not take your words lightly."

"But…" Scipio interrupted him, a small but genuine smile on his severe face.

"But," said Lucius, as if cued by a piper, "you have put me in a difficult position. I am bound by many ties of faith—those to my family, to my family's friends, to you as our patron, and to those few who call themselves our clients. And, of course, to the Republic."

Publius Scipio took another drink of wine. It really tasted very good, not too sweet, not too dry. He could see, as he listened with amusement to the young man's assumed oratorical style that he had inadvertently put his back up.

Obviously, he misread Lucius Tempanius' lighthearted nature as a malleable one. His recent war exploits should have alerted him to a vicious streak of stubbornness and suggested another approach. He sighed as he set down his cup.

"Lucius," he said, interrupting the nonsensical circumlocutions. "The gods require faithfulness from us. I appreciate and respect yours. No man of honor turns his back on his friends. I would like to think that we are friends as well. In fact, one day perhaps I can help you acquire more suitable living arrangements." He held up his hand as Lucius began to protest. "Let me ask you to do me one favor; meet with your family and discuss what I've said. We need steady men like Valerius and Nautius as consuls, not demagogues like Aulus Vibulus."

Scipio stood up. Like hounds his two companions bounded to the door. "Whatever you decide I will respect your position. More I can not promise."

To Lucius the room became abruptly vast in its emptiness. The acrid smell of air torn by a nearby lightning strike filled his nostrils. Was it his fear and anger that put the sulfurous odor on his tongue? Or were the parting words of Scipio a lightning bolt themselves?

Draining his cup, he deemed the whole incident ironic, even comical. He had agreed to help Aulus Vibulus for no other reason than boredom. A political bone did not exist in his body, and what one man versus another might stand for—even supposing they expressed anything of the sort—held absolutely no interest for him. So there he stood, suddenly embroiled in a political firestorm. 'How can I get out of this?' skidded across his brain immediately. To be sure, he didn't want to offend a family friend. Nor could he afford to make an enemy of Publius Scipio, whose influence and patronage he might one day need. He also didn't have the skill to avoid doing one or the other. He felt certain of nothing but the ravenous hunger growling in his stomach.

"Does that offer for dinner still stand?" he bellowed, and stomped off to the kitchen.

+ + +

Publius Cornelius Scipio rode erect yet relaxed, his booted feet dangling below the belly of his black stallion. Beneath a hooded cloak of raw wool he wore two tunics, and leather cavalry breeches. His mount snorted, tossing its head spiritedly against the bit, impatient of the slow pace. Scipio held him back easily, in no hurry. Light fluffy clouds dotted the heavens in brilliant counterpoint to a cobalt blue sky. Jade green against the sky, the Alban Hills billowed before him. In the distance the high, snow covered peaks of the Apennines hulked like the walls of Veii. Between the Alban Hills and the Apennines spread a verdant valley overlooked by the Latin city of Praeneste. He felt like a drop of water running down the side of a great bowl toward a hole in the bottom. Though the grapevines were bare, and the elm and plane trees had lost their leaves and stood in stark bony outline against the sky, Latium remained green. Olive trees shimmered silver-green around gnarled trunks, grasses and vines put out emerald leaves. Fields green with legumes ran in neat ordered rows to well kept farmhouses, interrupted only by open tracts of land on which cattle and sheep placidly grazed.

"Rome is beautiful even in winter, isn't it?" he commented to his two companions.

Riding next to him Lucius Furius and Gaius Manlius voiced their assent. They had been selected by Valerius and Nautius respectively to serve as quastores if elected. The post essentially put them in charge of the treasury, as well as imposing judicial responsibilities. From that highly visible position they would then run for consul themselves the following year. Thus, campaigning for their friends also fell into the realm of self-interest, so they had agreed to come with Publius Scipio on a tour of rural voters.

When Scipio and his companions reached the Tempanius farm he reacted with surprise. He did not remember it as such a formidable enterprise. Oblong in shape and rising in two steps, the entire hill upon which the Tempanius farm sat pullulated in cultivation. On the west facing slope immature

199

olive trees, ranked in precise rows, ran to within a hundred feet of the cane lined stream at the bottom of the hill. The lower step, bordered by elm and poplar trees that provided fodder and bedding for the animals in the winter, was planted wholly in grapes. As they entered the stone gateway to the second step of the hill their eyes were met by a field divided into clover and legumes for the winter, a stone and brick farmstead with a large garden out front, clean pens for the animals, and an orderly yard for the marshaling of wagons and other equipment.

"Scipio whistled softly. "It's been too long since I've visited the Tempanii, I see."

From the rooftop where they were repairing leaking tiles Titus, and Didius saw the riders turn up the drive. "What can this be?" worried Titus, setting down a jar of pitch. Immediately he thought of Lucius, wondering what he had done.

Didius caught the unbalanced jar before it fell and spilled. "Ah, probably nothing more than a campaign visit," he said. "Elections are in a couple of weeks."

"That's right," said Titus, relieved. "I forgot."

"Oy, Petronius!" Didius called.

Petronius appeared in the yard from the tool room. "Oy," he answered, shading his eyes as he looked up.

Didius pointed. "Inform Domina she's got visitors."

Petronius spun around to look at the approaching riders as they passed through the stone gateway. "Looks like Publius Scipio to me," he said, as he disappeared into the house.

Titus looked around quickly as if a course of action might be to hand like a hammer, or a mattock. "What should I do?" he asked, a neophyte to entertaining, especially when the guest was no mere neighbor, but his patron. His father had taught him farming, letters, and numbers; the finer points of social protocol he gave short shrift.

Didius smiled. "He's just a man, Titus. Puts his tunic on over his head just like you. Maybe it would be good if you climbed down and greeted him, however."

By the time Titus descended the ladder Petronius had the horses in tow and led them around back to the stable. Scipio, Furius, and Manlius stood in the middle of the yard looking around with impressed expressions on their faces. Titus came towards them, reached out a hand, realized it still had black pitch on it and withdrew it.

"Forgive me, Publius Scipio," he stammered diffidently. "I wasn't expecting you."

Scipio clapped him on the back. "Of course you weren't. It's I that should apologize for coming unannounced. How are you, Titus?"

"Very well, thank you," Titus said, flattered that Scipio remembered his name. "And you?"

"I feel exhilarated, actually. It's been too long since I've been out of the city. But forgive me," said Scipio, noticing Titus' restless eyes moving back and forth to the other men. "I'd like to present Lucius Furius, and Gaius Manlius."

Again, Titus stuck out his pitch-stained hand and quickly withdrew it. He laughed nervously.

"Titus," Duellia called from an open window above. Titus spun quickly in her direction. "There are refreshments if your visitors would like. I'm sure they must be tired and thirsty."

"Thank you, Duellia," Titus said with relief. "Why don't we go inside and get out of the cold?" he said. He escorted them to the entrance where Didius held the door open. Drusilla stood at the top of the stairs, a welcoming smile on her face. "If you'll excuse me," said Titus, "I'll go clean up while my mother makes you comfortable."

When he returned, Titus found the three men comfortably ensconced in the dining room, enjoying a cup of wine and a variety of dried fruits and nuts. Duellia had just finished telling a funny story about Titus and his misadventures with a recalcitrant goat when he entered. He found his guests laughing comfortably and naturally, and his mother regarding Duellia with pride and admiration.

201

Other than her wedding day, when she had been obviously nervous and overwhelmed, Drusilla had never seen her daughter-in-law in a social situation. She had expected a flighty, nervous wreck, and instead discovered a self assured, entertaining woman who had easily put her guests into a relaxed frame of mind. She felt a sudden pang of regret for Duellia with the realization that buried out there in the country she would have few occasions to use the training she had so obviously received.

"Well," finished Duellia gaily, "since the famous goatherd has arrived, we'll leave you men alone." She rose to leave and Drusilla followed her out.

When they reached the kitchen Drusilla hugged her affectionately. "You were marvelous in there," she enthused.

"Oh, thank you, Domina," Duellia exclaimed. "It was such fun."

"Do you think," said Drusilla, almost shyly, "you could call me Mama when Titus isn't around?"

+ + +

"You have a most winning wife," Lucius Furius said.

"Thank you," said Titus. He poured himself a cup of wine and funneled some pine nuts into his mouth. To his right Publius Scipio sat staring contemplatively into his cup. Furius and Manlius, on his left, sampled the foods the women had set out.

"So," probed Scipio, "you take care of business on the farm while Lucius takes care of things in Rome?"

Titus chuckled uneasily. "Lucius prefers soldiering to sowing."

"Nicely put," said Manlius. He swept a lock of straight brown hair out of his eyes.

"It would appear you have an opposite preference," Furius said. His wide fleshy face suggested sensual license, amplified by a cruel mouth filled with small sharp teeth. "The quiet life seems to suit you."

Titus prickled with a feeling of distrust, and decided to be vague. "A Roman must be both soldier and farmer," he said. "Each has its season."

Publius Scipio looked Titus over with a critical eye. He did not have the tremendous width of his brother, was narrower of waist and taller. Even so the difference was like that between a horse and an ox. In one existed speed and power, in the other brute irresistible force. But this told him nothing of the structure of the Tempanius family, which had become a conundrum in his mind. Who actually directed the family?

"You've prospered out here on the frontier," Manlius said. "Do you get along with your neighbors?"

Titus thought the man looked like a fox, with close dark eyes, a pointed nose, and indeterminate age. Creases at the corners of his eyes bespoke of someone at least in his forties, but the taut ruddy skin of his thin face, and a full head of fine dark hair made him appear much younger. He did not trust this fox-man, either, and found himself wondering if his visitors had some evil intent. Caught up in these thoughts he didn't hear the question.

"I said, do you get along with your neighbors?" Manlius reiterated.

"Well enough, if you mean the Tusculans and Labicans," he said, guardedly. "They're allies, after all. Besides, our farm was once part of Tusculum, so…"

"And the land behind your little hilltop estate?" asked Furius, smoothing unruly curls of iron gray hair. "No one hinders your use of it?"

"Why should they? It's ager publicus back to the mountain. After that it's part of Tusculum. No one seems much interested in it, though, except to run a few goats and such."

His suspicious mind running free, Titus wondered if they had come to force him off the ager publicus. He had heard of incidents of outright combat over use of the public lands, but residing so far from Rome had always considered himself removed from such conflicts. Casting about for answers he could only think about how helpless he was against men of experience.

"You may recall," Scipio said, speaking to his companions, "Marcus Tempanius died heroically defending his land from the Etruscans. Not many people, living much closer to Rome, were willing to risk their lives so Rome wouldn't utterly starve."

Furius and Manlius nodded in eager agreement, and it seemed to Titus as if two wolf hounds had been called to heel. The power of his patron to give or take away had been deftly and perfectly displayed.

"Well, Titus," said Scipio. "I know you have much work to do so we'll get out of your way. I really just came by to ask if you would join us in supporting Lucius Valerius, and Gaius Nautius for consul at the coming election."

"Certainly," said Titus, immensely relieved that Didius had been right. "Thank you for the advice."

"Well then," said Scipio, expelling his breath with finality, "thank you for your hospitality." He rose from his chair. "But I missed seeing your brother. Antonius, isn't it?"

Titus gawked at the man's intimate knowledge and memory of his insignificant family. "Yes," he stuttered.

"Perhaps next time. If there is anything I can do for you, you'll let me know?"

"Of course. Thank you, Publius Scipio."

"You make me feel old, Titus. Please call me Publius. And express my thanks again to your lovely wife and mother."

Titus returned to his work in a daze as the three riders shrank into the gray-green distance.

"So?" said Petronius. "Who are we voting for?"

"Valerius and Nautius," said Titus mechanically.

"I thought so," said Didius.

+ + +

The only good thing about the Saturnalia as far as Aulus Vibulus was concerned, was that a man didn't have to wear a toga. How ironic then that it took place on December 17th when men searched high and low for more clothes to wear against the biting cold. The Saturnalia, first celebrated twenty years before with the dedication of the temple of Saturn, began as an amusing festival. It appealed to his contrary, iconoclastic personality because on that day Romans turned everything backwards. Masters waited on slaves, who treated them without respect. Everyone wore the pileus, the cap of the freedman, and slaves were allowed to gamble. Family and friends exchanged fake and worthless gifts, which Vibulus delighted in devising. Nothing was as it seemed. But first the novelty wore off, then the fun, and finally the acceptance. Combined with his nervousness over the election, which would follow less than a week after, he could not bear to stay at home. Instead, he piled on three or four tunics, pulled a hooded cape over them, and took his long legs down to the Boar's Tusk tavern. Without his toga.

A brisk business already consumed Pontius Cominus when Aulus Vibulus ducked his head through the doorway. "Hail, Aulus," he said, as he poured a pitcher of wine into the funnel under which a customer held his pitcher.

"Hail, Pontius," said Vibulus. "I swear, if you got a few more bodies in here it would almost be warm."

"So how goes the campaign?" Cominus filled a small pitcher, and handed it and a cup to Vibulus over the front of the counter. Vibulus barely had to reach up to take them, which amazed Cominus despite years to get used to the man's height. He wondered if any Roman had ever been as tall as Vibulus, or if he came from a race of giants.

"How much?" Vibulus asked, reaching into the many layers of tunics for a leather pouch.

"Gratis," Cominus said. "Don't worry about it."

"You're not Roman, are you?" laughed Vibulus.

"Maybe I spent too much time with the Greeks. You didn't answer my question."

"Well, Pontius," said Vibulus as he filled his cup, "you know how it is. I've been everywhere—to the farthest reaches of Rome. I've called on the ironmongers, the ceramists, the fullers. I've shaken hands with every citizen at least three times." He took a long drink and wiped his mouth with the back of his hand. "I've lined every road I know, and some I don't with signs. Even," he said aside, "taken a few down."

"Well, you've kept yourself busy, anyway," said Cominus.

"Yes," mused Vibulus. He surveyed the room with eyes that saw nothing of the physical, material world, but had abruptly turned inward to view unrecognizable thoughts bubbling randomly to the surface of his consciousness.

Cominus hastily served customers who came, not in a steady stream, but in intermittent waves that inundated him for brief periods of furious, chaotic activity, then waned to sporadic interruptions. He looked up to see Vibulus staring off into space.

"Are you looking for someone in particular?" he asked.

"What? No. Just…"

"Lucius Tempanius and some friends are over there in the corner if you want company," Cominus suggested.

"Why not?" said Vibulus.

Lucius sat with his back to the wall in the corner. Assembled around a small table his friends Cnaeus Considius, and Quintus Titinius, were engaged in light conversation. He saw Vibulus enter but decided not to say anything until Vibulus noticed him. As Vibulus approached their table, crushing chestnut shells still warm from roasting under his large feet, Lucius stood, and greeted him familiarly.

"Hail, consul Legumenus," he said, using Vibulus' nickname, and ascribing to him the title he had as yet not won.

Vibulus' large ears reddened against his stone-gray hair. The gap between his two front teeth made his self-deprecating smile comical. "Well met, Lucius," he said, waving limply to the rest. He drew up a chair and rolled his long body onto it with a soft moan.

"Say," teased Titinius, "did you have your ears repositioned?"

Vibulus chuckled. "I did," he said. "By a suburan surgeon disguised as a barber." He swept a long-fingered hand over his thinning hair, clipped extra short to look sophisticated.

"I think he attached two hands to the side of your head," Titinius continued unmercifully, "maybe you should get your bronze back."

"Thank you, Quintus. Of course, I assume this means I have the piper's vote."

Quintus Titinius slouched his small frame against the low backed chair. One arm dangled at his side, playing absently with the leather satchel that contained his pipe. His dark eyes, pinched closely together by a narrow skull, flashed with gaiety. "Our support was never in doubt," he said, revealing teeth jumbled tightly together in a small mouth.

Lucius, sick of politics, changed the subject. "We were just discussing Considius' good fortune," he said.

Vibulus poured the last of the wine from his pitcher. "Oh?" he said. "And how is that?"

A distressed look crept onto the fleshy, reddening face of Cnaeus Considius. His gray eyes dulled like two bruises in the pulpy flesh of an apple. He groaned.

"I was just saying what a good thing it is that Campania and Etruria had enough food to feed both Rome and Cnaeus Considius at the same time." Lucius reached over and patted Considius' ample paunch.

Considius lifted a walking stick in the air. "It's this knee," he said, displaying the cane as visual evidence. "It won't support my weight." He recoiled, and scrunched up his porcine face in expectation of the jibe he'd opened himself up to.

"Not many knees would," jumped in Titinius.

"In fact, at one point I think the consuls were going to send representatives to Sicily, and set up a separate granary for our friend, here," said Lucius. He laughed, guzzled his wine and refilled the cup.

"That would have been quite a diplomatic feat," laughed Vibulus.

"Had we only realized it sooner we could have shipped him off to Veii as a secret weapon," said Titinius.

"Oh?" sneered Considius. "How's that?"

"You would have eaten them to their knees!" Titinius guffawed, and slapped his knee. "They'd have begged to surrender just to take you off their hands."

A rectangular smile opened beneath Considius' broad squashed nose, exposing small uniform teeth. Genuinely good-natured, he played up to the teasing of his friends, pretending indignation, contempt, or hurt, depending on the required response. He enjoyed being the foil, and actually relished playing the role. It made him feel indispensable to the group's entertainment.

Vibulus, an outsider to this group, recognized the role each played. Lucius played the instigator, the fomenter of apparent discord, Titinius the attack dog seizing on the wounded animal played by Considius.

"What do you do to keep yourself busy?" he asked Considius.

Titinius jumped in again. "We're talking about making him a piper."

Considius scoffed at the thought. Peeling a hot chestnut, he said, "Why would I want to be a piper?"

"So you could march your knee back into shape?" asked Lucius.

"Because," Titinius leaned forward, "pipers play the music of the soul and the heavens."

Considius groaned. Lucius filled Titinius' empty cup. "Don't fall for it," he warned Vibulus. But Vibulus' interest had been piqued.

"In what way?" he asked Titinius.

"Are you familiar with the nine spheres of the universe?" asked Titinius.

"Vaguely," hedged Vibulus.

"Ah, well, let me refresh your memory." He took a drink and wiped his mouth. "There are nine spheres holding the whole construction together. One, the heavens, contains the other eight, as well as all the stars. Beneath it are seven other spheres. These all revolve in the opposite direction of heaven. They are, in order, the stars of Saturn, Jupiter, Mars, the Sun (which is in the middle), Venus, Mercury, and the Moon. Now all of these are heavenly and eternal. But below the moon all is mortal, and suffers corruption. That is, Earth, and it is the ninth sphere." He paused for another drink.

"I didn't know musicians were so profound," said Vibulus.

"They're not," said Lucius. "Those whose profession has no legitimate purpose are always quick to devise some religious reason for it."

Undaunted, Titinius continued on. "Now, as I said, Earth is the ninth sphere, and it is the lowest and heaviest, so that all the other spheres are drawn toward it."

Considius grasped his head in mock horror. "Are they going to collide?!"

"Some day, perhaps," said Titinius, distracted.

"Ah," said Vibulus, "so of course musicians keep the nine spheres from colliding."

"Yes," said Lucius, "in the same way they drive people apart with all their noise."

"You're all very funny," said Titinius. He reached into his satchel and pulled the pieces of his pipe from it. "Now listen," he said, as he assembled the two pipes into one mouthpiece. "These movements, the spinning and rushing of the spheres are precisely regulated along with the fixed intervals between them to create a harmony of high and low tones. Here's how it goes; the upper sphere containing all the stars revolves the fastest and emits a high tone. Like this." He played a high shrill note that stopped conversation in the tavern and turned all eyes momentarily their way. "Now the lowest revolving sphere, the moon, moves very slowly and produces a low tone; like this…" He played a note like the sound of waves heard underwater. "Here is the really interesting part," he said. "Two spheres move at an identical speed so that only seven tones are produced by the eight moving spheres. And seven, being a perfect number, is divine. So…" He played a combination of seven notes in a quick lilting melody that stopped the room again. "Music is divine."

Vibulus laughed, and clapped his hands in acclamation. "Wonderful, really wonderful. By Hercules, I think I've been keeping company with the wrong people all my life."

"A song, a song," someone shouted from another table, and the rest of the tavern took up the chant.

Titinius held up his hand for silence. "To the faithlessness of women," he announced. "The ballad of Tarpeia." As he played the melancholy opening notes a ragged smattering of voices began singing, then as others found the place the voices grew in strength and lustily filled the room.

When few were called the Romans, and Romulus was king

he kidnapped Sabine women and kept them under wing

The Sabine men still angry, thought to steal them back by night

and if so be to conquer, for they saw it as their right.

There lived a girl Tarpeia, her beauty held a fateful flaw

she loved the sight of jewels; and gold she held in awe.

In secret she was tempted and the torment drove her mad

succumbing she consented to sell her city and be so clad.

She asked for what a Sabine warrior wore on his left arm

and she would open up the city so none could spread alarm.

The night came dark and moonless as she crept up to the gate

and swung the port wide open and thereby sealed her fate

The Sabine warriors laughing crushed her 'neath their shields

upon the rock which bears her name where traitors all must yield.

For gold was not the only metal they wore on their left arms.

No one seemed to notice the day aging. Titinius played until he could play no more. The tavern exchanged customers like lungs exchange oxygen each time the door opened. Light and cold air swept into the dim confines, and squeezed out again as the door closed.

Having made himself a home in the Boar's Tusk Lucius went to the kitchen and put together a mixture of foodstuffs in bowls. He wrote an accounting on a wax tablet that he left for Cominus on the counter. Returning to the table loaded with plunder, he found to his disappointment that the conversation had turned to politics—that most odious of subjects. In silence, with a kind of hunger driven anger, he devoured a large share of the olives, figs, chestnuts, cheese, and hardboiled eggs he brought to the table.

"They are saying," said Considius, "that the gods will be angry if we elect a plebeian consul."

"Why should that make the gods angry?" asked Titinius.

"Because the priesthoods are all held by patricians," said Vibulus. "Of course, the gods couldn't possibly be happy if one of the leaders of the Republic wasn't a member of a priestly college."

"I suppose there is some truth to the argument," said Considius.

"Which truth would that be?" asked Vibulus.

"That the last time a plebeian was consul we nearly lost the Republic."

"The only truth that proves," said Titinius disdainfully, "is that the more you repeat a lie the more people will believe it."

"What are you talking about?" asked Lucius, breaking his silence.

"Spurius Cassius," said Vibulus.

"What about him?"

"He's being used by Valerius as an example of the gods' anger over electing someone not belonging to a priestly college."

"Why?" said Lucius. "What did he do?"

"He tried to make himself king," said Considius.

"Hm," grunted Lucius, as if that were commonplace, and of little concern. He filled his cup.

Vibulus laughed. "You don't know anything about him, do you?"

Lucius defended himself without taking offense. "I know there's the bronze column in the Forum with the treaty he made with the Latins."

"That was in his second consulship," said Vibulus. "Your father, Gaius Opimius, and I served in the legion under the other consul Cominius, along with Gaius Marcius Coriolanus when he earned his fame."

"Now there was a patrician blessed by the gods," sneered Titinius.

"You're too young to remember," said Vibulus, "but it was this very same Nautius running for consul now, who as consul then, blamed the commons for the defeats against Coriolanus after he turned traitor."

"I'm not too young to remember nearly starving to death because of Coriolanus and his ilk," said Titinius bitterly.

It seemed to Lucius that Titinius held a little too hard to his vehement dislike for the famous man. He himself had been but two years old when Coriolanus became famous for repelling a Volscian sortie and storming the gate from which it had come to take the town of Corioli. The subjugation of the city earned him the appellation Coriolanus. Lucius heard the story often in his childhood, for his father had been one of those under Gaius Marcius' command when they repulsed the sortie from Corioli. He also knew that his father respected Coriolanus, having fought with him on that and other occasions. But Coriolanus had been forced into exile a few years later for extortion. He fled to the Volscians and there embarked on a war of revenge against his former country that brought him to the gates of Rome in command of a Volscian army, only to be driven away by his wife and mother.

"What does that have to do with Spurius Cassius?" asked Lucius.

"Nothing, except Lucius Valerius was one of the quaestors that brought Cassius up for trial," said Vibulus.

The thread of the conversation seemed too hard to follow. Whether from too much wine, or lack of interest Lucius had either missed the point of this Cassius thing, or his friends had yet to come to it. Looking skeptically from under lowered brows he said, "Listen, how long ago was this?"

Vibulus closed one eye and calculated. "Oh, about eleven or twelve years ago."

"Ha," said Lucius triumphantly. "I was all of, what, eight, nine years old?"

"All I remember," said Considius, "is that he tried to give Roman land to the Latins and Hernicans."

Vibulus chortled, and shook his head in wonder. "It's amazing how their side of a story lives forever, and the other side dies with the men they kill."

"What does that mean?" growled Titinius.

"It means what you said earlier. That if you repeat a lie often enough people will come to believe it. If you want the whole story, ask Cominus some time. But I'll give you a short history lesson." He tipped a wine pitcher and scowled when nothing but a few drops came out. Twisting in his chair he tried to get Cominus' attention, then resigned himself to getting it himself.

"Here," said Titinius, reaching for the pitcher. "I'll get it."

"Spurius Cassius was consul three times," Vibulus began. "In the seventh, sixteenth, and the twenty-third year of the Republic. A man makes a lot of enemies when he's had that much success. This is important because only two other plebeians have been consul more than once, while the list of patricians who have repeated or passed the office down like a family heirloom is as long as my arm."

"Are you sure there's any room left there for plebeians?" laughed Lucius. "That's an awful long arm for such a young republic."

Mark Trapino

"Exactly, Lucius. There's precious little room left for plebeians. In fact, since Spurius Cassius there has been no room for plebeians."

"Perhaps you'll reverse the trend," said Cominus.

"I doubt it. Now will you let me finish the story? Fine," he said, when they dutifully fell silent. "Spurius Cassius, three times consul, celebrated a triumph in his first consulship for his victory over Pometia."

Titinius returned with a pitcher of wine, filled everyone's cup and sat down. "Now," he said, "where were we?"

"The second consulship of Spurius Cassius," Vibulus informed him. "In his second consulship he completed the treaty with the Latins that made them allies under Roman command. Of all our victories, none has increased our strength like the Cassian treaty. Yet the patricians looked suspiciously on Cassius ever after. Why?"

Though a rhetorical question, Considius answered anyway. "Because they thought he was trying to make clients out of all the Latins."

"No," said Vibulus. "That was later their excuse. The real reason was jealousy. Without shedding a single drop of Roman blood, Cassius increased our strength three or fourfold. Ask the old men around here what the fighting around Pometia was like. No quarter was given. It was savage and brutal. After that, Cassius knew we could not continue to fight alone. But more importantly he tried to extend Roman power without throwing away Roman lives. Now that was a new concept for our warrior class!"

"You must mean the Fabii," observed Titinius wryly.

"Well, curious you should bring that up," said Vibulus. He drank greedily, excited by the subject. "Until their recent disaster Quintus, Caeso, and Marcus Fabius between them shared a consulship virtually every year since the death of Cassius. There were never three more warlike men in Rome's

214

history. And don't forget, Quintus Fabius was consul when Valerius prosecuted Cassius."

Lucius yawned and stretched. "Sound like men after my own heart," he said. "Was there a point to this?"

"Yes," said Vibulus, "Cassius was tried and executed for his land reform bill—not because he tried to make himself king. They tried and executed him because he valued the blood of common Romans. Someday, Lucius," Vibulus said shortly, "this will be important to you."

"What about his third consulship?" asked Considius. "You haven't finished."

"You're like children," said Vibulus, shaking his head. "All right. In his third consulship Cassius made a treaty with the Hernici identical to that of the Latins. Same rights of commerce, marriage, sharing the spoils, all of it. Then, and here is where the truth became subverted, he proposed to parcel out ager publicus to needy Romans. But certain families held much of it illegally. So they created the lie that Cassius intended to parcel it out equally with Latin allies, and that's what turned the plebs against him. Of course, they accused him of trying to make himself king and that sealed his fate."

"Well," Lucius said, "life is a bubble, and if you meddle in politics, it's likely to get popped."

Vibulus laughed. "I'd like to see just how cynical you become by the time you're my age."

"Quit meddling in politics and you might be around long enough to see." Lucius smiled broadly, "I'm sure I will be."

+ + +

A stiff cold wind strafed the Campus Martius, pulling moisture from the Capraen marsh and flinging it into the faces of the voters assembled in centuries near the altar of Mars. Under stone gray skies Lucius and Titus sat on the damp earth discussing the possible implications of the vote. Lucius had not succumbed to the pressure of Publius Scipio, and continued to work for Vibulus' election. A lost cause if ever there was one, he thought.

Titus, unaware of his brother's actions until too late, chose early on to follow the wishes of the family patron. This put the brothers at cross-purposes, since things were not as simple as their votes canceling each other out. Attached to Titus as clients, among others, were Didius, Petronius, Primus, and theoretically Quintus, all of whose votes would go to the same candidates as Titus' vote.

Lucius had no clientele—except for the self-appointed Quintus. However, he did have notoriety from his military service, and this carried some weight with other members of their century who might be considered unaffiliated. All in all, it appeared that Titus' stone would spread the most ripples in the voting pool, and Lucius viewed the prospect with equanimity. What bothered Lucius were the possible repercussions on his standing with Publius Scipio.

"He hasn't severed all ties, has he?" asked Titus. His concern embraced two points; anxiety for his brother's future, and the ramifications such a falling-out might have for the rest of the family.

"No," said Lucius, playing with a blade of grass. "But he wasn't exactly understanding either."

"What did you say?"

"Don't worry, Titus, I was very tactful. I said, I was sorry if I'd made a rash decision, but it was based on the best of motives and in no way meant as a sign of disrespect."

"And?"

"And, I said, to prove it I would volunteer to serve with Valerius as soon as he's elected."

"That must have made him laugh."

"Why? I think I've proven to be a valuable soldier..."

"Not that," laughed Titus. "I mean the part about 'when' Valerius is elected."

"Oh. Well, even a blind man can see Aulus stands no chance. You wouldn't believe how much pressure these patricians have put on their clients to toe the line."

"Oh yes I would," said Titus.

"Well, anyway, I think he understood."

"And if he didn't?"

"Listen, first, I don't think it will have any effect on you. You've proven your loyalty. As for me, I'm nobody when it comes to politics. If I have to, I'll try to attach myself to someone else."

"What do you mean, 'if'?"

"I mean, Titus, what difference does it make? Why do I even need a patron? I live in a tavern until March, then I volunteer for the legions, and I'm gone until September or October. That's my life."

They fell silent for a time. Around them men milled about or formed pockets of conversation. On a dais near the altar to Mars the consuls with their lictors, clients, quaestors, and associates performed the various duties of augury, watching for omens, and organizing the election. The tribunes of the plebs, and the plebeian aediles observed the proceedings with critical eyes.

Titus inspected his brother closely, noting a pensive look on his round face. "You might as well spit it out Lucius," he said.

"What?"

"Whatever it is you're thinking."

Lucius grunted but said nothing.

"Let me help you out," said Titus. "You've been looking at property near the Anio river and you're actually worried that Scipio will try to prevent you from buying it."

Lucius stared in surprise at his brother. His mind raced but he could think of nothing to say. The color drained from his face. Titus laughed at his discomfiture.

"I'm not completely isolated out there on the farm," he said.

Stunned by the transparency of his plans, Lucius could think only of who might have shifted the veil to reveal them. He had shared the idea with Quintus Crispus, and no one else. And Quintus had been sworn to secrecy, an oath Lucius didn't think he would break.

As if his thoughts were chiseled into his forehead, Titus answered his questions. "I didn't find out from Quintus, if that's what you're thinking." The obvious relief on his brother's face pleased him. "I suspect living in a tavern has two sides. You hear all the gossip about who's doing what, and who's selling when. But there are also a hundred prying eyes watching you."

"You heard I was looking at property at the tavern?"

"A certain Flavolius mentioned he saw you out by the Anio 'inspecting' as he said, a property."

"Listen, Titus, I'm not trying to deceive anyone here. I just didn't want to say anything until I was sure of what I'm doing. But yes, I'm looking at some property and I'd like Quintus to work it."

"Actually," said Titus, "I'm glad. I think it's the wise thing to do. You need a steady income."

Lucius chuckled sardonically. "It's a small piece of property. I doubt I'll get any income out of it. But at least it will keep my property qualification up."

Trumpets blared from the area of the dais and a hush fell on the assembly. Nearly every adult male citizen over seventeen years old gathered on the field, waiting to cast their votes. Each man would vote twice, once for each consul. Tension and expectation charged the crowd with excitement. Criers went out from the dais announcing favorable signs and auspices for the election. Now, it only remained for lots to be drawn to determine the centuria praerogativa. The century thus chosen voted first, and the candidates selected by it considered blessed by heaven—especially the first man chosen.

Sixty pieces of clay, each with a number representing a century of the first class, had been placed in a large pot. One of the consuls would reach his hand in, pull out the numbered piece, and the century selected would vote first. Its vote would be announced, and then the other fifty-nine centuries of the first class would vote at the same time.

An official assigned to each century, called a *rogatore,* counted the votes, taken orally and in public. Representatives of each of the candidates hovered closely over this official to ensure the accuracy of his count.

Lucius and Titus stared fixedly at the dais. The gods would have to place the perfect marker in the consul's hand for Vibulus to have any chance, for he had few centuries committed to him. Curiously, neither brother could say how their century, the fifty-first, would vote. It had once been Vibulus' century before his property qualification moved him up to the equites, or cavalry. That fact gave him a kind of favorite son status, and might be enough to swing the vote his way.

On the dais the consuls drew lots to determine which of them would choose the centuria praerogativa. The honor fell to Verginius. Servilius took himself aside to watch and listen piously for signs from the gods. With much ceremony Vergilius reached his arm into the deep ceramic bowl, stirred it around innumerable times, then pulled forth the blessed numbered tile. Not a sound stirred the air. Every man tensed, as if to take a blow, and caught his breath. Verginius held the tile aloft for all to see, then brought it down to his eyes. He called out the number.

"Century thirty-four!"

The criers shouted the number in antiphonal response. A collective gasp went up from the centuries and an excited hum swept over the Campus Martius.

"That's exactly the number of years since the founding of the Republic."

"A sure sign from heaven."

Lucius looked at Titus with a stunned expression on his broad face.

"What is it?" asked Titus.

"I know that century is for Aulus," he said. Suddenly great possibilities catapulted into his brain. Vibulus could select him as a centurion in reward for his help. Perhaps even as tribune. He snapped his head to search the crowded dais for Vibulus.

Standing like a cattail over marsh grasses his expressionless equine face revealed nothing.

"How do you know that century's for Legumenus?" asked Titus.

"Because he has many clients and members of his tribe in it."

All eyes shifted to the rogatore counting the votes in the thirty-fourth century for the first consular position. Each man approached over a special plank bridge, gave his vote and returned. The process was then repeated for the second position. Each of the candidates dispatched representatives to jealously protect their interests, for no rules forbid the rogatore from influencing a man to change his vote.

The count took some time, for the century in reality contained more than one hundred men. On a wax tablet set aside for each candidate he made a mark for every vote. When the voting finished, he tabulated the results, handed the two highest totals to a runner who then brought the tablets to the consuls. A sudden burst of activity erupted on the dais and the consuls huddled in deliberation. Lucius thought he saw an exultant look flash across Vibulus' face, mixed with a lingering satirical pessimism. The delay put everyone on tenterhooks. Rumors flew, assertions bruited, and a restless turmoil flexed through the centuries.

The consul Verginius stepped forward on the dais again. "The first consul selected is Aulus Aquillius Vibulus." A rush of surprise blew over the gathering. "The second consul selected is Lucius Valerius." His election came as no surprise, and elicited almost no comment except in relation to his placement behind Aulus Vibulus.

The choice of Vibulus by the centuria praerogativa was a stunning development. Waves of excited conversation crashed about the Campus Martius. Not everyone expressed happiness. Controversies erupted amongst the centuries; angry outbursts rose above the surrounding noise as adherents tried to hold others to their previous commitments. Fortunes, honors, positions, futures were at stake if men's votes swayed and changed. Lucius suddenly found himself surrounded by a mass of men slapping his back, or reaching out to touch him as if he had become a talisman. Others glared angrily at him as if he were treason personified. Disorganization spread like plague. The other centuries should now have been called to vote but no one could settle the men down enough to do so, and the consuls hesitated to command continuance of the voting.

Suddenly trumpets rang out. The consul Servilius strode forward. "Citizens!" he announced. "Something unholy has taken place. While the vote was being taken, I heard thunder. This assembly is canceled so that we may take the proper steps of propitiation. The election will be rescheduled." Without waiting he, Verginius, their lictors, and attendants descended the dais and hastened into the city.

Vibulus surged forward, but two consular attendants restrained him, his angry protestations ignored and shouted down. The collected centuries collapsed in shocked silence. Ragged shouts of dismay rippled through the crowd, but no sustained uproar ensued. Who could argue with a religious omen?

Lucius smashed his fist into his palm. "Damn them!" he cried, enraged. Until that point the entire election had been a passing of time, a lark, a bit of play before the serious business of war came around. "Thunder!" he spat with contempt. "The only thunder they heard was the thought of losing the consulship."

"Come on," said Titus. "There's nothing we can do about it now." He put his arm around his brother's shoulder and led him back towards the city through the field of conical sepulchers at the foot of the Quirinal Hill.

"Never again, Titus," vowed Lucius. "I will never again subject myself to this kind of humiliation. They can keep their politics."

"I'd say that's exactly what they want."

A week later Lucius Valerius and Gaius Nautius were elected consuls by all the centuries. No ill omens marred the election.

Lucius Tempanius cynically volunteered for duty under the newly elected consul, Valerius.

# XIV

May 9-13, 474 BC

The Lemuria

Weak and desultory rain fell annoyingly from low sodden clouds. An impenetrable mist shrouded the Alban Hills behind the farm. Titus wished it would do one thing or the other. The rain came down just hard enough to splatter him maddeningly in the eye, or run in frigid balls down his spine. Like strands of coiled black rope his hair hung in his eyes, yet another annoyance, as he turned over ground in the garden with a spade.

He forced the point of the spade into dark soil with his foot, lifted a shovel full of dirt free, turned it over and broke up the clods. Working alone he labored without enthusiasm, forcing himself to maintain the monotonous motions of turning the earth, preparing beds in which he would plant asparagus. Usually the elements of digging, bedding, planting, and fertilizing left him satisfied and fulfilled. Not today. Today he felt hollow, breathless, and restless. He had an urge to take off running and not stop. It occurred to him to go to Rome, even though Lucius would not be there. Perhaps Antonius would like to go. The more he thought of it, the more the idea appealed to him. The previous consul, Servilius, had been brought up on charges by the tribunes for jeopardizing his legion by rashly attacking the Veientes on the Janiculum. In reality his obstructionist role in the elections lay behind the motive for the trial.

The long dour lines of his face lifted agreeably with his thoughts, and he worked the spade with renewed energy. Why not? Tomorrow was the last day of the Lemuria. He would drive the last of the *lemures* out, purify his house that night, and the next take Antonius to Rome. With the tossing of black beans and the clashing of bronze he enticed the shades of the dead to leave his house. He and Antonius followed them out the door.

Titus and Antonius stayed in Lucius' rooms in the Boar's Tusk. Titus found a barber first thing and had his hair cut for

1/8 of an as. He thought the price even more outrageous after he viewed his lopsided image in a planished bronze mirror.

Antonius observed his older brother with interest. More than usually animated and excited, he acted as if he must explain everything about Rome. Not that it distilled his happiness and excitement. He wore the toga praetexta with broad purple border and felt very cosmopolitan. The slow dignified walk required by the full-length toga made him feel solemn and important. On the farm he most often went barefoot, so that the feel of sandals slapping against hard paving stones gave him immense satisfaction. But his eyes could find no rest. So many shops existed in the Subura alone that he could not imagine how the city could hold more. Every lane, every street under the pale morning sky came alive with activity. Butchers, cobblers, iron smiths, armorers, barbers, leather workers, fullers, potters, all plied their trades in a jumble of small shops strewn chaotically around the quarter. Carts loaded with onions, garlic, beans, cabbage, lentils, and chard sold their produce in small plazas, or parked by crossroads shrines. Flower vendors carted their colorful panoply of sweet scented merchandise, pushing through rushing streams of playing children. Women carried water in pitchers on their heads from the fountains, or dumped pitchers of refuse into the cloaca maxima. His ears thrilled to the sounds of voices raised in laughter, shouted greetings, angry denunciations, bargaining cries of dismay. Wheedling, cajoling, scolding, joyful voices like a river of life flowing around him, filling him, carrying him away. He wanted to stop, look, taste, touch, but Titus pulled him on, dragging him out of the river of crowded alleyways.

Titus had a purpose. His will pulled Antonius up the Palatine through the old Mugonion Gate to the house of Publius Scipio. There they waited as the morning warmed. Swallows swooped and soared on scythe shaped wings, emitting shrill piercing cries as they flew swiftly past in close array. The sky darkened to the color of sapphire. More men arrived. Others, suppliants, came out of the large square brick house.

At last, the stream of visitors ended and Publius Scipio emerged. Somehow, he managed to know each man's name as he greeted those waiting to accompany him to the Forum.

"Well, Titus," he said, "how kind of you to come." He spread his thin lips in a smile and offered his hand. As they shook, Scipio noticed Antonius. "Ah, I see you've brought Antonius." He sounded genuinely delighted. "How old are you, now?" he asked, turning his attention fully on the boy.

Delighted and awed by the recognition, Antonius' voice broke embarrassingly. "Thirteen," he said, as he shook Scipio's hand.

"You're quite tall for your age, aren't you," Scipio observed.

Antonius blushed, looked down. "I don't know," he mumbled to his feet.

"Well, thank you for coming," Scipio said, turning away.

Instantly they were behind him as he greeted others waiting in line. A long procession of clients followed him to the Forum, so that everyone could admire the great dignity of Publius Cornelius Scipio.

Once in the Forum Titus and Antonius abandoned the entourage. They checked the white notice board mounted on the Regia, picked over terracotta pots in a potter's shop, and climbed the Clivus Capitolinus to the temple of Jupiter. From the Capitoline Hill they looked out over the Forum, and the seven hills of Rome stretching like mossy fingers into the distance. From the temple they walked to the precipitous face of the Tarpeian rock and looked over, down into the Forum Boarium, and the bustling docks of Rome's port. Though not nearly as high as the hills behind the farm, from which he could see the sea, Antonius enjoyed this bird's eye view of Rome. But more than anything he liked to see the terracotta statue of Jupiter in his four-horse chariot atop the red roof of the temple, as if racing the fiery dawn. From their eyrie they saw a crowd begin to gather near the *comitium*, the venue for the trial of Servilius. Time to fly down.

The Curia was situated on the north side of the Forum at the west end. Built mainly of wood and brick, with a red terracotta tile roof supported by wood beams running the length of the building, it sat solidly on a square stone pedestal. Here the senate and consuls normally met in consultation or to receive foreign emissaries. The trial took place out front in the *Comitium*, a circular structure that housed the Volcanal, the shrine of Vulcan, claimed as his father by King Servius Tullius. A sanctuary on the south side of the *Comitium* housed the niger lapis—the black stone which went back to Romulus and the founding of Rome. Incised with letters more Greek in appearance than Latin, the wording was so archaic no one knew what it said.

Thirty-two jurors had been selected at random from the sixty centuries of the first class and the six centuries of cavalry. They took their places while spectators filled most of the seats in the Comitium. Still, the tribune Genucius paced angrily. He wanted the trial held in the Campus Martius where the whole people could hear it. But the consul Nautius (Valerius being away with Legio I against the Sabines) decreed the trial be held in the Comitium on the grounds that it would be more manageable. Precisely why Genucius objected.

Titus and Antonius squeezed behind the back row of seats and stood to watch. A crowd of patricians entered wearing torn and dirty clothes of mourning, appearing disheveled, and unwashed. Nonetheless, space for them to sit instantly cleared. Cynical outbursts erupted from the crowd at this visual statement.

Down below, on a circular stage surrounded by jurors and spectators alike, Gnaeus Genucius and his colleagues shared one side of the floor, while Gaius Servilius sat haughtily on the other, representing himself. The prosecution began the proceedings. Gnaeus Genucius stood silently in the middle of the floor, stroking his large drooping nose pensively as he looked at the dark paving stones under his feet. He pursed thin lips and inhaled deeply through his small mouth.

"Citizens of Rome," he began, as if he had just decided on what to say. "I intend to prove that Gaius Servilius," he pointed at the accused with the short index finger of his right hand, "through negligence and over weaning ambition endangered, not only the lives of Roman soldiers by his reckless attack uphill against the Veientes, but Rome herself." He clenched his fist and his jaw flexed angrily. "But first," he drew himself up to full height, stroked his bulbous chin as if again uncertain how to proceed, "first I would like to address a separate but no less important issue.

"It has been said that this jury has been carefully selected to assure a favorable verdict for Gaius Servilius. If that is so it will not be foreign enemies to which our Republic falls. I personally put little credence in these rumors. However, it is not out of the question that some men may have already made up their minds. If such be the case, let me warn you, jurors, the people are watching. If we fail to deliver a just verdict, popular cynicism and discontent will only grow. If we make a mockery of justice and the law, shall we in the end escape the very justice we have postponed? I think not. To declare the innocent guilty, and the guilty innocent is an act of impiety sure to incur the gods' wrath. If we think to impiously save one man from justice so well deserved, we must accept a harsher judgement against our families, our friends, and our nation. Weigh carefully in your minds, gentlemen, whether you are willing to suffer such a fate. Indeed, our nation's very existence depends on a just outcome to such trials as this. So, I enjoin you, leave your minds open to the truth, and let truth alone sway your judgement."

Genucius strode in a slow stately circle as he spoke. Despite its abundant folds his toga could not completely hide the muscular build to which his gesticulating right arm gave evidence. Of average height, and with straight black hair tickling the top of his ears, he carried himself with a solemn dignity that lent weight to his words.

"Now, it is my purpose to convict Gaius Servilius of gross dereliction, and incompetence. And no doubt this could be satisfactorily accomplished simply by recounting the events that took place that day on the Janiculum Hill. Indeed, this will be done. But it will be done in such a way, and through the testimony of such a vast number of witnesses that only the most obdurate mind could sustain doubts of his guilt." He turned his back on the judges and picked up a scroll lying on the prosecutor's table. Holding it aloft he paced the circular floor as if each step were taken to punctuate his words.

"These witnesses," he said, lightly shaking the scroll, "will verify the ambitious, impatient, and egoistic manner with which Gaius Servilius used the legion Rome entrusted to his care. They will testify to the poor state of readiness, and the insufficiency of supplies. They will break your heart, gentlemen, when you hear of the hunger, of the interminable wait under a scorching sun without food or water, of the impetuous attack uphill against an entrenched enemy. And all the time you will remember in the back of your mind that Verginius was on the way. Verginius was near. Had he but waited, had he but kept the interests of Rome uppermost in his mind, two consular armies could have joined to destroy the forces of Veii and won a glorious victory for Rome. But then, Servilius' bright glory would have been diminished. He would have had to share it with another. As you will see, he thought it a better thing to risk his legion, and the safety of his country, than to risk sharing glory with his colleague.

"All of this, citizens of Rome, you will hear tomorrow."

Genucius sat down. Gaius Servilius slowly rose from his chair and stepped magisterially into the middle of the hard stone floor, his slender, knife blade body poised in brittle rigidity. His close-cropped hair, sprinkled with gray, gave his sharp face the look of a hawk. He turned his burning dark eyes on the crowd, an expression of contempt on his thin lips.

"I see," he said, "that many of my supporters have come dressed in mourning. Well they might." The words dropped out of his mouth in brittle, bitter chips. "It would seem that to take on the responsibility of the purple bordered toga is to invite calumny to be heaped upon your good name. It is no longer enough to be a man attempting to do his best. One must achieve the perfection of the gods or be condemned, driven into exile like Coriolanus, or to your death like our friend Menenius. Yes, you are right to wear mourning. If you aspire to the purple bordered toga and the chair of state, have your lictors carry not the rods and axes of your office, but the death masks of your ancestors. Indeed, your funeral will come upon you the moment you lay down the insignia of power.

"Fortunately for Rome good men will not heed my words."

He stopped briefly, turning a slow circle, taking in the judges and the crowd of spectators. A few hecklers denounced his claims as poor mouthing, clumsy attempts for sympathy. A few laughed outright.

"Of what am I accused?!" he cried, silencing the hecklers. "Of defending the city against a night attack; of hurling the enemy from our walls and putting him on the defensive in front of his own camp? I need no list of witnesses to defend me. I will call but one when the time comes, my colleague Verginius.

"But who are my accusers? Are they the fathers of valiant soldiers like Gaius Opimius, who died defending Rome?" Again, he spun a slow circle, looking the crowd over for affect. "No, I see them not. Are they soldiers who fought under my command and earned honors like Lucius Siccius, or Lucius Tempanius? No, like all patriots they are off serving their country—again.

"Who are my accusers?" He extended his long arm like a sword and pointed at the seated Genucius, his thin lips turned down in contempt. "These unofficial magistrates. These pretenders. These would-be tyrants. These sniveling tribunes! How have we come to this pass?

"They decry the limitations of liberty, but perhaps the truth is there is too much. It appears we have given over our liberty to tyrants who have no official office. The same tyrants who drove Coriolanus into exile and made an enemy of Rome's best soldier. Why? Because he expected the people to pay for the wheat the state imported. For this they made a monster and a criminal of him.

"Our friend Menenius, who had the misfortune to command men who did not have the courage of their commander, died of shame from being brought to judgement by these little kings. So soon did they forget the services of his father, without whom these—sacrosanct—tribunes would not exist.

"Frankly, gentlemen, I resent being tried by these plebeians who have no legitimate legal authority. Moreover, I refuse to submit to their tyranny. I promise you this, I will show no lack of courage in defending myself by whatever means I must. We will see tomorrow whose courage matches his words."

Abruptly Servilius stalked out of the Comitium, trailed by a protective entourage of supporters and clients. The Comitium burst into excited speculation as to the meaning of his last words. Titus looked down to see Genucius chewing his fingernails, a distant, distracted look in his eyes.

"Let's go," said Titus, pulling Antonius by the elbow.

Thrusting their way through the crowd they kept to the north edge of the Forum, sliding past the shrine of Cloacina where the Cloaca Maxima submerged beneath the Forum, then took the Vicus Suburanus back to the Boar's Tusk. Most of the shops were closed or just reopening because of the universal interest in the trial. At the Boar's Tusk they leaned against the wall waiting for Cominus to return and open up.

Though barely mid-day, the trial had created quite a thirst among those with nothing else to do, and soon a cluster of customers gathered like pigeons around the entrance to the tavern. Heated conversation revolving around the trial occupied the men's minds.

"Did you see all those patricians in mourning?"

"How cynical can you get?"

"They pretend to be the only ones who sacrifice for Rome."

"They sacrifice nothing. It's we who sacrifice."

"That's so."

"What do we get for our service in the legions? Death and debt."

"If a man's lucky he'll get killed."

"Well, I wouldn't go so far…"

"If it was up to them, we'd go back to the days of digging the great sewer."

"Excuse me, gentlemen," Cominus commanded, pushing his way to the door. He pulled a large iron key dangling from a cord around his neck and unlocked the door. As the men poured in, he unbarred and opened the shutters to let in light and air, climbed his tower, and began pouring wine. Wine flowed and so did the words, becoming louder, belligerent, bellicose. But in other parts of the city other men gathered also. And though their talk was quieter, it was far more dangerous and purposeful.

Titus and Antonius awoke early the next morning and again accompanied Publius Scipio to the Forum. If possible, a heightened sense of expectation filled the imaginations of Rome's citizens. A tremendous crowd gathered in the Forum. Even sparrows could find no room to land on the black paving stones, and pigeons, banished from the Forum, clucked unhappily from the eaves of homes and temples. Shops around the perimeter of the Forum selling cakes, sausages, and fruits did a brisk business. The smell of cooked meat brought saliva to Titus' mouth.

The Comitium filled with nervous, agitated judges. Servilius arrived early, a smug look of confidence on his hawk's face. A great host followed him. But this day the mourning clothes were put away, and hair and beards trimmed and shaved. A film of tension covered the Forum as the multitude awaited the arrival of the tribune Genucius, and his followers.

The Tempanius brothers, unable to force their way into the Comitium waited in the Forum like the rest. Squeezed back near the sacred olive tree in the middle of the Forum they stood on tiptoe to look down the Sacred Way in the direction of the Caelian Hill, from which Genucius would come.

But he did not come.

"Something's happened," said Antonius. His high cheekbones glowed with excitement, making his eyes look larger, darker.

"No," said Titus. "He's just making Servilius wait. It's a trial of nerves."

"Absolutely," interjected an old man, his voice harsh as a rasp. "Making him sweat."

The crowd grew palpably more anxious as the wait drew on. With restlessness came idle speculation, and wild conjecture. Every possible explanation passed through the crowd, caused a stir, and then died as another theory bore fruit. Some thought he had been bribed, or gone into exile out of fear; some called him a coward, others a wily litigator.

Antonius turned his mind elsewhere. He wondered about the great sewer comment he heard the day before. Thinking he should know this he remained quiet. Still, the question nagged at him, and he finally decided he must swallow his pride and ask.

"What did that man mean about returning to the days when the Cloaca Maxima was dug?" he asked Titus.

"What?"

Antonius repeated his question.

"I don't know. I suppose a return to the kings."

"I think it was more than that," said Antonius skeptically.

The old man leaned his lined, weathered face into their conversation. "No one's ever told you about the Cloaca Maxima?" His large hands, gnarled and twisted with arthritis, rested on bony knees.

"No," said Antonius. "Not that I remember."

"Well," barked the old man, "King Tarquin the Proud forced every able-bodied man in the city who wasn't otherwise employed to dig it. The work was so hard men hung themselves, or drowned themselves in the river to get out of it."

Titus pursed his lips in amazement. "I didn't know that."

"There's not many of us left who remember it," said the old man. "That was thirty-five or forty years ago, now."

"Did you work on it?" asked Antonius, uneasily. He found it difficult to look at the old man with his skin creased and wrinkled like a raisin. One milky eye, and the other red and weepy leered at him like some demon from the underworld. His lips seemed to have been sucked into his toothless mouth rendering his speech almost unintelligible. The old man wiped at his runny eye with a contorted hand, the nails long and yellowed. "That I did, young man," he said. "I wasn't much older than you, then."

Suddenly a roar of anguish and anger spewed from the crowd. Frantically word passed that friends had found Genucius dead. "Murdered in his own home!" Disorganized and undirected the crowded Forum swelled, pulsed, swayed with groups of angry people. Fearful and frustrated they had no place to direct their emotions until finally they melted away like snow from a furious March storm. The Tempanius brothers collected their things and headed home. The surviving tribune went into hiding.

Servilius and his supporters rejoiced, and celebrated. They may as well have admitted their complicity in the murder. But Servilius remained free. He had rid his house of lemures.

# XV

## June 9, 474 BC
## The Vestalia

An uneasy peace fell over Rome and the Tempanius household. Antonius became moody, lapsing into surly quiet. He ate little, and conversed less. He went listlessly about his work, though he could not be accused of neglect.

Titus thought the boy aimed his anger at him, though he couldn't say why. He recognized in Antonius a sensitive, intelligent spirit, and he knew the boy had taken the events in Rome to heart in some way. He accepted with equanimity the blame, real or imagined, for which Antonius held him accountable. Moping around all day might put people a little on edge, but as long as the work got done Titus wouldn't take issue with his brother's feelings. In good time Antonius would let it out and free himself (and everyone else) of the accumulating bile.

On another level, Titus found his brother's attitude humorous. After all, how many thirteen-year-olds took politics to heart? But he resisted the temptation to tease him and simply let him alone.

Drusilla, on the other hand, believed in intervention. The vision of her son, hollow eyed and bitter at age thirteen, revolted her. She did not feel compassion—that misplaced needy emotion enjoyed no dominion over her. She did feel concern, but not for his feelings. Her concern centered on the manner in which he expressed them. A Roman rejoiced in victory and took defeat with dignity.

"True defeat," she told him privately one evening, "occurs when a man loses control of his emotions."

Exasperated, Antonius contradicted her. "Only a man who is dead is without emotions. Do you expect me to just accept…"

Impatiently Drusilla cut him off. "Any man controlled by feelings is no better than a wild animal." Antonius attempted to speak, but she turned her fine head away from him and held up a hand for silence. Antonius swallowed his words like bitter herbs. Quietly, firmly, Drusilla lectured him. "Dead men are those controlled by their emotions. They are men of small souls, perpetually hunted by men of great souls. A wild animal has no choice; it acts according to its nature. But a man, Antonius, must choose how he will act. You must choose."

Antonius said nothing. Confused and conflicted he sought in his mind for what he knew, what he believed. But he found no philosophy, only feelings, and he knew if he spoke, he would begin with, "I feel…" Instead, he attempted to make a promise. Again, his mother cut him off.

"Make no promises one way or the other," she commanded. "I will know what you have chosen by what you become."

Small comfort resided in these words. Worse, he heard veiled recriminations of his father, whom he revered above all men. Did she mean to say his father had been a small-souled man because he refused to hide in Rome, and attacked the enemy when they ventured onto his land? The uncomfortable thought, existing alongside uncomfortable memories filled him with hopeless dread. He remembered the awful scene of his father's death. Heard Didius and Petronius beg him to come inside the wall. Heard his father's blood-lusting voice refuse almost joyously. Felt again the awesome swelling pride as his father called out a challenge to the doomed Etruscans. Saw again the bright red flood of life pouring onto the dry earth from his father's paralyzed body.

Over the following days he submerged the questions in the quotidian tasks of the farm. He preferred not to think about how he would become a great soul. He realized he did not possess the knowledge to plan such a thing. In some respects, his education had been cut short with his father's death. Marcus taught him to read and write, to work sums, measures, and weights. He taught him to plow a straight furrow, to know a weed from a bean, and to know the seasons for planting various crops. He learned the cycles of the stars, the sun, and the moon. He learned to leave ground that was *cariosa* alone until the rains soaked it thoroughly, and he kept his hands from timber until the dark of the moon. Still, much of his practical education had fallen to Titus, Didius, and Petronius after his father's death nearly a year before.

The finer points of learning resided in Drusilla's care. These remained few, and centered primarily on behavior and morality. She did what she could in the way of religious training, but this was rightfully the head of the household's duty as chief priest of the family. Titus and Lucius had much to learn in this regard themselves.

His age betrayed him he knew. It left him bereft of experience and the authority to pursue what he thought he might believe. As the days lengthened towards the solstice he gave up on his bitterness, plowed it under with the legionary red poppies, and made his peace with waiting.

Rome did not. In the city disturbances took place almost daily. Clandestine meetings took place nightly. At first, thinking they had cowed the plebeians, supporters of Servilius went smugly around the city. They exulted in the death of Genucius while denying complicity. But they minced no words in declaring his murder a fortunate occurrence, and what they supposed was the destruction of the tribunate as a boon to the Republic. Their swagger soon became a shuffle.

Open clashes took place outside the houses of the consul Nautius and the ex-consul Servilius between their clients, gathered for the morning salutatio, and their enemies, come to heap abuse and insults upon them. They walked to the Forum accompanied by two groups, one assembled to give dignity to the consuls, the other, louder, more strident, to shout insults, sing vile songs, or chant mocking and angry slogans. They were accosted in the markets, reviled in the Forum, shouted down in the law courts.

Outside the Curia groups of disenfranchised plebs congregated in raucous demonstrations, shouting, clashing brass and metal objects noisily together. To individual senators they threatened violence, destruction of property, and sabotage.

The ruling class got no rest. They spent sleepless nights listening to the cacophony of chanting, singing, and threatening outside their houses. Forced to hurry about always with an escort they began to feel like hostages in their own city. At last, the situation became intolerable and they decided something must be done. Putting the people under uniform always proved the easy means to discipline them, so they invented a raid by the Volscians and ordered troops to be levied. The ploy fooled no one. Worse, they aimed the levy at specific centuries, some members of which were known leaders of the 'rebellion.' No better way could have been found to antagonize the populace and bring about the opposite of the desired result.

At the foot of the densely forested Alban Hills, where wildflowers issued forth in a symphony of reds, yellows, and blues, where four petaled flowers wore a far more regal shade of purple than any consular toga, only faint echoes of this clash disturbed the ordered agrarian lifestyle. It was not a case of ignoring the troubles in Rome, but of being deeply involved in providing the stuff of subsistence. The farm required an immense amount of work. When Lucius moved to Rome, he essentially took Quintus Crispus with him, effectively reducing the labor force by one fourth. Then Sextus Crispus had been called up when Valerius raised his legion, and the available hands were further reduced. The obligations were not. Chickens needed feeding, goats pastured and milked, cheese made, fields plowed, gardens planted and weeded, fertilizer collected and spread, tools repaired, oxen fed and treated, hogs butchered and hams cured and sausage made, wood chopped and stacked, baskets woven, and myriad other chores that couldn't wait.

Titus was as civic minded as the farm allowed him to be. He found himself so wholly preoccupied with running it that in moments of utter weariness he caught himself envying those in the city who seemed to have nothing but free time. But then they were usually one of two classes; either the very wealthy who could afford Etruscan pottery, Greek wine, and hired laborers so they could spend their time in the city, or the very poor who were lucky to have a pot to piss in, drank bitter wine if any, and spent their time in the city. That both had a disproportionate say in Roman policy remained an irony lost on Titus. Overwhelmed by trying to run the farm at age eighteen, his mind was not bent toward appreciating the subtleties of political power. Then Quintus and Sextus came home.

The sky spread in a mosaic of azure and white tiles the day they returned. A cool breeze blew from the west, but in the sun the air hung heavy with humidity. For days word drifted in and out that a great battle would be fought, or had been fought. Every task was performed with an underlying anxiety. Impatient for news they worked, as it were, with faces averted, as if to catch the first glimpse of the messenger, or hear the first echoes of news.

Before Quintus and Sextus trudged half way up the drive they were surrounded. Questions came from every direction, and they tried to answer them all at once so that nothing intelligible came to light. As they reached the yard Titus called for quiet.

"You look tired," said Titus, observing their drawn faces, greasy hair, and tunics stained and spattered by weeks in the field. "Duellia, prepare them a bath. Domina; let's put some food out. We'll have an early lunch with everybody in the kitchen.

An hour later they came into the kitchen in clean tunics, chestnut colored skin ruddy from the hot steam of the bath. Seven eager faces already gathered around the table greeted their arrival. Sextus, taller and more muscular than his elder sibling, chuckled as he sat next to his father. Quintus ran a self-conscious hand through his wet, thinning hair and looked directly at Drusilla first. A half smile on his small mouth, and warm green eyes told her everything she wanted to know. He saw the worry drain from her high cheekbones, and the tense lift of her shoulders relaxed.

In front of everyone a large bowl of boiled wheat mixed with cheese, egg, and honey steamed. On platters in the center steeped boiled wild asparagus and onions drizzled with olive oil. Titus and Drusilla sat at the ends of the table.

"Well," said Titus, sprinkling raisins on his porridge, "we're glad to have you home safe and sound." Everyone greeted his avowal enthusiastically. "And how is my brother, Lucius?"

Quintus cleared his throat. He saw five pairs of concerned eyes turn on him as if he were an haruspex about to tell the future. "Lucius," he said slowly, savoring the attention, "has brought great honor to the Tempanius name." A whoop went up from around the table.

"Then we won the battle?" asked Antonius.

"Oh, yes," Quintus stated matter-of-factly. "The Sabines won't come out of the hills any time soon."

"Tell us about Lucius," said Drusilla.

"Lucius was the first over the enemy rampart when we took their camp," began Quintus.

Drusilla and Duellia dropped their wood spoons. Duellia clapped her hands excitedly. Antonius pounded the table as the others uttered words of admiration. Titus shook his head and smiled.

"But that's not all," said Quintus. He spooned a mouthful of porridge into his narrow mouth and let their anticipation build. "He also killed and stripped an enemy centurion in single combat."

A gasp of admiration rose from the diners, and they fell silent for a space, the click of spoons, or occasional slurping the only sounds. Drusilla broke the silence. "And how many wounds did he receive performing these heroics?" she asked.

"Like anyone who fights in the front rank he has his share of scratches," said Sextus indifferently. "But nothing serious."

Antonius chafed in the silence that followed over the dearth of details. A great battle had been fought, and all they could say was, 'we won' and 'Lucius did this or that'?

"There must be something else to tell," he said, unable to stand it any longer.

"Like?" asked Sextus.

"Like how the battle was fought. Where it was fought. You know."

Sextus shrugged. "It was fought like all battles. The only difference was this time we had allies. Our legion was in the middle, the Latins on the right, and the Hernici on the left. Of course, we," he pointed to Quintus and himself, "were out in front."

"And then?" Antonius insisted.

"And then we charged and they ran away. Just like always."

Titus laughed loudly. "Just like always," he repeated satirically.

Antonius glared angrily at the trivial answers his questions received as Sextus sucked a spear of asparagus between sardonic lips, staring glibly back with chestnut colored eyes.

"Have you been demobilized or just on leave?" asked Didius, pushing away his plain terracotta bowl. His intense green eyes washed over his son Sextus with warning waves of anger. He didn't like the way he baited the high-strung Antonius.

"They gave us a few days leave," volunteered Quintus.

Didius unlocked his eyes from his other son. "When do you return?"

"The day after tomorrow," said Sextus contritely.

"You must have gone to Rome first, then," declared Petronius. He wiped his bald head in a circular motion with his hand.

"Yes," said Quintus. "Lucius sent me to check on some of his interests."

"I didn't know a cup of wine needed watching," laughed Titus.

"Well, you know Lucius," said Quintus, "never leave the cup empty, and never leave the cup full." He looked down at his bowl, scraping it clean with a finger, and then popped an onion into his mouth.

Drusilla thought his furtive movements and his words lacked conviction. She decided to corner him later and find out what he was hiding.

"So, tell us about Rome. We hear it's in turmoil."

"Worse than that," said Sextus. He sniffed and ran a hand through raven black hair. His eyes, the color of oiled leather, glittered with intrigue.

"Worse?" Antonius' head snapped up.

"In what way?" asked Titus.

"The plebs," he tapped his stout chest inclusively with index and middle fingers, "are making life difficult for Nautius and Servilius…among others."

Duellia could not take her eyes off Sextus. When he smiled his full lips parted mischievously around straight, white as snow teeth. His nose fixated her with its nobility. She played with the rim of her cup, embarrassed by her thoughts. "Did you see my father?" she asked.

"No," said Quintus," but everyone is out day and night. The Forum is full, the streets are full."

"So what's it about?" pressed Antonius. "Are they going to try Servilius again?"

"I doubt it," said Sextus. "The quaestors are controlled by the consuls, so they won't bring any charges, and our tribune Veturius is too afraid."

"Of course," said Didius. Disappointment dragged the right side of his mouth downward into deep creases on his thin face. "He doesn't trust the plebs to protect him."

"Who can blame him," said Petronius. "They didn't protect his colleague."

"What are they doing, then?" asked Titus. "I mean, how do you take vengeance when you're not sure who's guilty?"

"At first," said Quintus, "the people just gave them the rough music. You know, insults, dirty songs, slanderous chants, that kind of thing."

Petronius laughed, vibrating the chest hairs sprouting out the top of his tunic like antennae. His deep bass voice, once clear, was chipping away to gravel. "Good clean fun," he said.

"You would think," said Quintus. "Except that it didn't end."

"So then," broke in Sextus, "the patricians got together and decided the only way to get control was to put the people under oath."

"A time honored tradition," sneered Didius. His small head shook slightly, barely moving the white hair that covered it, as if repressing emotions and thoughts too strong for expression.

"Maybe so, but it didn't work this time," said Sextus. "No one answered the levy."

Titus leaned forward and put his elbows on the table. A perplexed look dropped the sloping corners of his eyes lower. "What levy?" he asked. "I never heard of any levy."

Sextus smiled broadly. "Exactly," he said. "And that's why no one answered it."

"Is this some kind of riddle?" demanded Titus.

"It is for Sextus," said Quintus. "Because he enjoys twisting your brain into knots. What he means is, the consul informed the tribes to call up specific centuries."

"Obviously aimed at the men they considered ringleaders," interjected Sextus.

"But how unfair," cried Duellia.

"Yes," said Quintus. "That's exactly what everyone else thought too."

"We were there for this part," Sextus said with relish.

Antonius sat rigid with excitement. His swallow wing eyebrows gathered intently, and his wide full lips parted slightly in anticipation. Pushing his food impatiently aside, he said, "Would you get to the point? What happened?"

Quintus and Sextus exchanged looks, silently deciding who should tell the story. Quintus deferred to Sextus.

"Well," he began, "as we said, they ordered the call-up of certain centuries. So, two days ago the centuries assembled in the Forum as ordered. But there was a lot of talking and grumbling going on. Yet at first men answered when their names were called. You know how it is; nobody wants to be the first to refuse in case no one else does. Anyway, while they were calling names others were going around trying to convince men not to answer. One of those was Publilius Volero, who was very loud. So Nautius decided to make an example of him, and called his name."

"Which was insulting," interrupted Quintus, "because Publilius had been a centurion under Menenius, and now they were calling him as a regular legionary."

"Oh, it was beautiful," exclaimed Sextus, gleefully. "Of course he refused and didn't answer. So they called his name again, and he didn't answer again. So Nautius sent a lictor after him. Do you know Publilius?" he asked Titus.

Titus shook his head negatively.

"Well, he's built like an ox; like Lucius. So, this poor lictor had no hope of binding Volero and dragging him off. But he had to try, I suppose. Anyway, these two got in a tussle, and all the while Volero called for help from the people." He turned to Quintus. "Do you remember what he said?"

"He said there was no point appealing to the tribunes..."

"Ah, ah, that's right. He said, 'they'd rather see citizens flogged and beaten than be murdered in their beds by you.' Then the lictor became really violent and nearly tore Volero's tunic off him."

Drusilla rested her chin in the palm of her hand listening intently to the story. "And what was everyone else doing while this was going on?"

"It was chaos," said Quintus. "Everyone was arguing, shouting, running in circles, but no one stepped in to help. In fact, everyone backed away until they were alone in a circle like two wrestlers."

"Then what?" demanded the two women in unison.

"I think Volero was afraid no one was going to help," said Quintus. "Like Sextus said, he could've beaten the lictor alone; but then what? Finally, he threw him down, picked up his bundle of rods and broke them in pieces."

243

"He had to do something drastic; you see?" said Sextus, pursing the fingers of one hand together and vibrating it in front of himself for emphasis. "Something to make the people decide. So he broke the rods and yelled, 'don't be afraid of these lictors. They have no power but what you give them.' Then he picked up one of the rods and shook it and said, 'this is nothing but a stick. Why do you hold it in awe?' All of a sudden it was like ten thousand goats let out of a pen at once. Men were tripping all over each other to get at the consul and his lictors."

"They didn't harm the consul?" asked a horrified Titus.

"No," said Sextus, drawing the word out like he was paying out rope. "He knew well enough he'd lost. He ran just like the Sabines."

"Hm," uttered Titus. He chewed reflectively on a sweet crunchy fig. "Somehow the Sabines always seem ready for another fight."

# XVI

## August 19, 474BC

## The Vinalia

Times like this Lucius wished he'd kept at least one horse. Not that he hadn't walked twice the distance in full gear many times before, but horses would have made the day more pleasant. Instead, they walked under a blistering sun. The ground gave up its moisture in thick clutching humidity. Even the lightest tunic stuck uncomfortably to sweaty skin. Fields of ripe golden wheat awaiting the scythe surrounded them, broken in spots by brilliant green grapevines that sweetened the heavy air.

Two other men walked with Lucius from Rome to the Tempanius family farm, Quintus Crispus, and a Sabine slave named Restius. Long in the waist and short of leg, Lucius covered the ground not in long strides but with many mighty steps. He didn't so much walk as plow his way through space. The great breadth of chest and shoulders, and a head like a catapult stone lent him a stature he did not possess, barely attaining five and a half feet in height.

Quintus Crispus sagged under the weight of one of Lucius' muscular arms thrown across his shoulders.

"Well, what do you think?" Lucius asked. Despite the soaking heat, Lucius hiked exuberantly. A short successful campaign season sent his spirits soaring. "Are you ready to settle down and get married?"

"Well," Quintus stuttered, "I…"

"Listen, if you don't have anyone in mind, I promise you I'll find a pretty little thing to keep you straight for years to come."

Restius guffawed, stifled his laughter with a hand and choked it back, as if a slave were not allowed to hear and laugh at his master's jokes.

"Hercules!" exclaimed Lucius. "Don't swallow that laugh. You could injure yourself."

"Thank you, Dominus," said Restius, chuckling.

"Listen Restius," said Lucius, "my brother is a serious person. If he has a sense of humor no one's found it yet. He's not cruel, mind you, it's just that you'd better laugh while you've got the chance."

"I'll be sorry to leave your service, then," said Restius.

"No you won't," said Lucius. "I can't stand peace and quiet. With Titus you'll have regular meals, steady work, and the only danger will be from some randy goat."

"And Primus usually takes care of those," Quintus laughed.

The Via Labicana ran straight from the Esquiline Gate southeast to Labicum, perched atop one of the lower peaks of the Alban Hills. Numerous dirt paths, interspersed with immaculately paved drives spread away from the road as it rose and fell in gentle undulations. Diverse habitations divided the land irregularly. A large estate, given over to olive groves and grapevines dominated the rolling hills in one section, only to give way to clusters of small individual plots springing up like dandelions. About the midway point they passed through a crossroads village that existed as little more than a few cottages grouped around a central square, and a couple of small shops manufacturing pottery and leather goods. Behind the houses stone or cane walls divided vegetable gardens and fields of grain. A crossroads shrine and a fountain cooled in the shade of plane trees in the middle of the square, around which a smattering of women and children gathered. The three men stopped to rest and drink their fill of fresh cool water. Lucius adjusted his tunic, raising the hem to the top of his thighs, and retied the cord belt, blousing the tunic around his waist. He pushed his right arm through the neck hole so that the tunic now rested solely on his left shoulder. After a brief rest they moved on.

The landscape changed, the hills became higher, the ravines deeper. The undulations became steady climbs and steep descents. Fewer inhabitants spread themselves thinly as they approached the mountains. Hills covered in pine, beech, plane, and cypress trees fell away to streams lined with thick clumps of tall cane, or tangles of alder and willow.

The cleared, precisely ordered hill of the Tempanii rose high above the others, dominating the plain and visible from some distance. Lucius pointed it out to Restius.

"What's that larger hill to the left?" he asked, pointing to a knoll two miles to the east.

"Nothing, really," said Lucius. "There's a small village up there, but mostly it's just used to graze sheep and goats."

"This road cuts between that hill and the mountains. See there?" Quintus pointed up to the city of Labicum, white against the emerald green of coniferous forest behind. The road follows around the curve of the mountain and comes up to Labicum from behind."

"Then it must intersect with the road to Praeneste," said Restius.

Quintus began to answer in the affirmative when Lucius cut him off. "Don't be thinking about escaping, Restius," he said mildly, but with a deadly serious undertone.

"Of course not, Dominus," said Restius quickly. "I've just always had an interest in geography."

Tibia, wagging her tail joyously at the sight of Lucius, greeted them first as they crested the second rise on the property. Lucius petted her with rough affection, which she returned, biting at him playfully.

At the sound of the barking Titus came out of the tool shed, and Didius and Petronius emerged wraith-like from rows of tall tawny wheat. Didius gave Quintus a happy hug as they exchanged greetings.

"I've come bearing gifts," announced Lucius. "Well, one gift."

"Oh?" said Titus, scratching at a row of bug bites on his triceps. "What is it?"

"Restius, here," said Lucius, pointing at the Sabine slave. "At least he'll make up for losing Quintus to me." The broad satiric smile on his face dissolved as Titus spoke.

"Why do I need a slave?" he asked.

"I just told you," said Lucius. He looked at the others for support but they kept their eyes lowered to the ground. "You need the extra hands without me, and Quintus here."

"If I need extra hands, I can always hire Romans." Titus placed his large hands obstinately on his hips, and looked his brother in the eye.

Lucius smiled again. "Don't worry, Titus. You can still hire Romans for the harvest. But you can't afford any permanent help and you know it."

"Antonius and I have all the help we need," said Titus.

"Maybe you should ask them, before you get your back up at me for thinking about your welfare." Lucius' voice, flinty with offense, rose in volume.

Titus inhaled slowly. He did not want a slave. For a moment he held his silence, focusing on the musical chirping of birds in the trees, of bees buzzing industriously on their endless errands of pollination. A reddish-brown hen pecked at the ground at his feet. "Well?" he said at last, looking at Didius and Petronius.

Petronius sonorously echoed him, his round face and pointed nose looking up deferentially at him. "Well," he said, "I'd have to agree with Lucius. We could use the extra hands."

"Listen, Titus, Petronius and Didius aren't getting any younger. You can't expect the same amount of work out of them as they've done in the past."

Didius smiled crookedly, and ran a hand through the snowy hair capping his head. "I'm not sure I like the sound of that, but I suppose I have to admit to the truth of it."

Restius cast his green eyes furtively about. He suddenly felt a great fear of rejection. If a man's fate threw him into slavery, the best he could hope for was a kind master, and a good situation. This situation appeared to have both conditions. He stared down at his sandaled feet, thinking how, like a blacksmiths' tongs, his legs bowed. When Titus grunted, Restius looked up to find himself staring into strange, appraising gray ringed eyes. He scratched his nose, scooped like a bath sturgil, self-consciously.

Titus indeed appraised him. The very fact of this made Titus uncomfortable. The slave looked to be in his early twenties, about the same height as himself though not as muscled. Still, he appeared healthy enough.

"What kind of work did you do before?" he asked.

Restius cleared his throat. "I was personal attendant to Mettius Curtius, centurion and champion of the Sabines."

"That explains the light physique. How did you come to belong to my brother?"

Restius reacted with surprise to the question. "Your brother killed and stripped Mettius Curtius in single combat," he said formally.

"Ah," said Titus. "I'd forgotten."

Restius looked quickly at Lucius, a ruddy flush of embarrassment on his high cheekbones. Lucius smiled and tossed his head indifferently.

"Well," Titus said with reluctance, "we'll have to fix up a place for him to sleep." Fiercely to Lucius he said, "See, already you've created more work for us."

"Someday you'll thank me," said Lucius ironically. "Now I'm going to go in and say hello to Mama before we leave."

"You won't be staying the night?"

"I don't think so."

Quintus rolled his eyes and groaned.

+ + +

Pontius Cominus awoke with his mind made up. He splashed some water on his face from the bowl next to his bed, threw the first tunic to hand over his head, and lumbered down the stairs. It crossed his mind he should lose some weight. To his surprise he found Valeria and Lucius up and putting food out as the first flower of dawn opened in the sky.

"Well," he said, "I see the birthday girl can't wait to get the day started."

"Is it your birthday today?" asked Lucius.

249

"Yes," said Valeria. "I'm twelve." She emphasized the 'twelve' as if it were some kind of warning. Which it was. Twelve was the legal age of marriage for a girl in Rome. In her precocious femininity Valeria knew that at any moment her father could contract a marriage for her. But she also knew that he would accede to her wishes for a while. As the only child of a wife her father truly loved she enjoyed an almost unnatural fondness and attention from her father. Often female children were considered at best, a duty, at worst, an economic blight on the family—the sooner rid of the better. Despite her elevated status, she knew that a girl's duty called for marriage and children, and sooner or later her father would insist on her performing it. Not that she didn't share this desire. Her only reservation was that she would like to have a hand in the selection. A selection she had already made.

"How auspicious to be born on the Vinalia," said Lucius.

"Why? It practically left me an orphan."

Lucius set his pitcher of milk on the table. "You'd better marry her off quick," he said to Cominus. "Before she turns to vinegar." He thought it should be fairly easy. She displayed a nascent beauty with delicate features and wavy midnight hair.

Cominus, who had no intention of marrying his daughter off at twelve years old for quite selfish reasons, grunted his disinterest. "There's plenty of time for that."

"I suppose if her husband thinks with his back he'll avoid that stinging tongue," laughed Lucius.

"That would leave you out," said Valeria.

"Fortunately," said Lucius. He saw her flush hotly and look down at his innocent agreement. "I'm joking," he said softly, covering her shoulders tenderly with huge hands from behind.

Valeria smiled up at him gratefully, her dark eyes moist with a message that sent him into retreat. Quickly releasing her he sat down at the table, poured himself a cup of fresh goats milk and cracked and peeled a hard boiled egg. From a small bowl he took a pinch of sea salt and sprinkled it on the egg, then stuffed it whole into his mouth.

Valeria placed a small bronze pot of water on a low tripod over hot coals on the hearth for her father's morning herbal mixture. She sat down opposite Lucius and surreptitiously watched him as they ate.

When the water boiled, Cominus poured it into the cup that held his strange mixture of herbs. He allowed it to steep before he opened the conversation that had been running consciously and subconsciously through his mind for some days.

"I'm going to give you a birthday present today that you may or may not like. Either way, I think it's the best thing I can give you."

"What is it, Father?" Valeria asked excitedly, bouncing lightly on her chair.

"Starting today, or tomorrow if you prefer, you're going to begin helping me with our business."

Valeria had been aching to do just that for a long time, but Cominus had always refused. She wanted to proclaim victory, yet sensed something else behind the decision. "Is there something wrong?" she asked.

"Are you sure you want her out there with all those men?" Lucius butted in. He felt suddenly protective. Over the months he had become less like a boarder, and more like a part of their small family. He nearly ceased altogether from taking meals in his rooms, and ate with Cominus and Valeria instead. Often, when he had no commitments with Publius Scipio or friends he would help out in the tavern. His presence alone could quell an erupting fight, and when things got busy, he helped Cominus serve the customers. "I can help out more if that's what you need. Or maybe I could bring a slave back on the next campaign."

"No," said Cominus, "you are both jumping to conclusions. This tavern is all I have, and Valeria is my only child. It seems there's a certain symmetry there. If this is to be her inheritance, she must learn how to run it profitably, and deal with drunken men."

Valeria scraped her chair back and rushed to her father. "Thank you, Father. It's the best present I ever had," she said, hugging him fiercely.

Cominus put his arm around her waist and kissed her cheek with fatherly affection. "Well, you may not thank me in the future." He turned to Lucius. "I want Valeria to be free," he said. "The Greeks treat their women like dogs, and the Etruscans treat theirs as equals. We Romans are somewhere in the middle. I suppose it's a radical sentiment but I dislike the idea of Valeria being under the hand of a man she did not choose."

"My brother seems happy with the choice I made for him," said Lucius.

"That may be," said Cominus. "But is your choice happy with him?"

"I have no idea."

"There," said Cominus expressively. "Just so. Her happiness is not worthy of consideration. But Valeria's happiness is worthy of my consideration."

"But even so, Pontius, you'll have to find her a tutor," said Lucius.

"You're assuming she never marries," Cominus held Valeria as if putting her on display. "I think she will have no lack of suitors," he said proudly. "She's the express image of her mother."

Lucius agreed that Valeria was pretty. As a woman of property, she would certainly be a fine catch for a certain class of man. Maybe a moderately successful merchant would find it desirable to augment his income with the addition of a tavern. But still, she could enter into no contract to buy or sell without either a husband or a tutor to put his name on it. Lucius slid his thumb between his middle and index finger to ward off the evil eye. "What if, the gods forbid, you should die before she marries?" he asked.

"What an awful thing to say," declared Valeria, hugging her father protectively.

"No Valeria," said Cominus, patting her arm. "He's right to think this way. One must try to prepare for the future one least expects." Cominus paused, drinking his herbal philtre thoughtfully. In truth he had Lucius in mind for the role of tutor. If fate could be tempted, he wanted to wait and watch the young man's development before he took the step. It seemed to him that Lucius liked his fun, and could be frivolous, but a strain of honor had been inculcated in him that served to rein in his passions. He thought another year or two would tell the tale. He set his cup down softly. "No," he said, "I've thought the same thing, and you're right. But I must find someone absolutely trustworthy."

"Good luck," said Lucius, rising.

"Where are you going today, Lucius?" asked Valeria.

Lucius smiled. "You'll make someone the perfect wife," he said ironically. "If you must know, I'm going to the Forum to meet Publius Scipio and attend him for a while. After that?" He shrugged, "I'll probably go to the Campus Martius and exercise. A soldier has to stay in shape you know."

Publius Scipio hurried into Rome, took care of his business, and hurried out again. Oppressive heat scalded the air, and the ground sweated its moisture like steam rising from a pot. The humid air clung like a bad dream to the skin of those forced to remain in the city. Anyone who was able departed for the country to find cooler air. Except Lucius.

Lucius adhered to his schedule except for one minor deviation. After attending Publius Scipio on his official errands, essentially acting as escort and bodyguard, he used his free time to shop for a gift for Valeria.

The shops near the Forum, especially on the Vicus Tuscus carried merchandise beyond his budget. Fine Etruscan gold and silver jewelry, rich oriental perfumes, and fine linen clothes were sold in the shops there. Even so, he walked the main street of the Etruscan quarter and looked in the shops for the pure pleasure of seeing and touching such finely crafted handiwork.

With so many citizens gone from Rome fewer carts, litters, and people jostled in the roadway or vied for the attention of the shopkeepers. This raised the level of their courtesy despite his plain sleeveless tunic, and plebeian sandals that made obvious his economic class. Then a simple bronze comb attracted his attention. It rested in one of three shops built on the back side of a large house and rented to the merchants. The three shops were identical squares, fifteen feet by fifteen feet in a brick building sixty feet long fronting the street. One shop sold luxurious pillows, cushions, and mattresses, another fine perfumes and oils, the last ornate jewelry in bronze, silver, and gold. Outside, a carved block of tufa stone announced the shop of one Marcus Pulonius. Just inside the entrance a solid wood counter with shelves shielded by latticework on either end stretched across the room. A removable panel in the middle allowed ingress and egress. Only three or four feet of space in front of the counter kept customers out of the weather so plenty of light would reach the jewelry's natural beauty.

"Is there something in particular you're looking for?" asked the proprietor. He had a squeaky voice that matched his short thin frame.

Lucius glanced up. "Not really," he said. But he had spotted the comb. Such a simple thing, brightly polished bronze with delicate tines, and a clamshell crest embossed with five lions parading from right to left in two lines.

"Are you looking for yourself, or someone special?" asked Pulonius unctuously.

"I wouldn't say either," chuckled Lucius. "I'm looking for a birthday gift for the daughter of a friend."

"How nice." The man put a smile on his grim features. His nose swooped like an avalanche down his face to his mouth, a bitter tear dividing gaunt cheeks. "So, something nice, but not too expensive." Unerringly he picked up the comb and handed it to Lucius with fingers as fine as the tines of the comb. "This lovely Etruscan comb should hold her hair in place with modest luxury."

"How modest?"

The proprietor shrugged. "It's been a slow day," he said. "One as."

"It must need to be dead for me to afford anything here," said Lucius as he set the comb back on the counter. His lips turned down in disappointment. "Thanks anyway."

"Perhaps," said Marcus Pulonius, hating himself, "it's slower than I thought. I could let it go for a semi. But no less."

Lucius conjectured that there must be substantial profit in this merchandise if he could drop the price by half in the wink of an eye. "You're very generous," he said, "and I wouldn't think of asking you to go lower on the price, but as you can see, I'm just a common man. Thank you anyway." He turned to go.

"You're making a mile's delay for yourself," said the shopkeeper.

Lucius turned around. "Oh? How's that?"

"Just call it intuition," said Pulonius. He had been about to say 'you'll be back,' then thought better of it when a look of challenge lit like the first flare of a taper in the young man's eyes. He saw instantly that if he challenged him he would lose him for sure. "I simply sense that you've found what you want, and you'll be unhappy to settle for something else."

"If that's so, then you can be sure I'll come back," said Lucius. "For a semi."

"For a semi," smiled Marcus Pulonius.

What a life, thought Lucius, to have to wheedle and cajole people into buying your goods. It seemed somehow dishonest. He passed through the portal of the Vicus Tuscus, walked alongside the pond called the Velabrum, then turned right at the altar of Hercules to the docks.

Downstream from the Sublician bridge a widely spaced line of barges towed by oxen or straining gangs of day laborers slowly worked their way up the deep green Tiber River. The port clamored with the business of unloading barges, and loading the goods onto transport wagons or directly into warehouses. Men and animals raised their voices. Teamsters cursed, and cracked their whips as they drove their teams into position on the wharves. Arriving barges were guided to the appropriate wharves where the exhausted towline laborers received their pay. Lucius saw them look dumbly, empty eyed into the palm of their hands at the little bits of bronze for which they'd exhausted themselves. Bodies shaking with fatigue, sweat drenched hair, mouths wide sucking air, these were the coins with which they were paid. More laborers in loincloths unloaded a barge hauling Etruscan wine in tall clay amphorae with pointed bottoms. Another brought olive oil from the Greek cities of southern Italy. A barge riding low in the water with a heavy load from the salt flats of Ostia at the mouth of the river docked amid churlish shouting.

Lucius wandered the docks and warehouses looking for something to catch his eye. Sometimes one could buy directly from the importer and save a large sum. Heavy-laden men and animals strained at their labors. Oxen bawled, and men groaned in complaint. Mules brayed, and men cursed their miserable fate. He picked his way around baskets, bales, and the detritus of Rome, stopping briefly to inquire of a sneering overseer, or a tallying accountant attached like life to his wax tablet, and his inventory lists. The air hung heavy and hot under clear enormous skies. The docks smelled of fetid water, animal dung, and the sour sweat of men. He liked nothing he saw.

Still the comb burned in his mind like hot iron from the blacksmith's fire. He retraced his steps, parted with a semi, and went to the Campus Martius to play ball and exercise. But he took no joy in it.

Valeria squealed with delight, pulled his head down and kissed him on the cheek upon receipt of the gift. Immediately she began arranging her hair, trying the comb in front, then in back, as she experimented with different styles.

Lucius paid her no heed. A strange fear gripped him; fear that he would end up toiling at the end of a rope, wearing himself out for a few bits of bronze. Or worse, that he would have to lie, and argue, to make deals, and beg so people would buy his wares. He thought what a great fool he had been to give away his inheritance, while he procrastinated and spent the dowry he'd wrested from Marcus Duellius. One thought consumed him. Land.

"Pontius," he said.

"Yes?" Pontius looked up from the scroll that held him engrossed.

"May I borrow your mule and cart tomorrow?"

Pontius considered for a few moments. "That should be all right," he said. "Taking a girl on a picnic?"

Valeria glanced up quickly in imminent jealousy.

"No. I want to go look at some property."

Cominus raised his sparse eyebrows. "Oh? Whereabouts?"

"This side of the Anio River."

"What brought this on?"

"I've been thinking about it for some time, now. I just haven't done anything about it."

Cominus laughed. "So, you bought a girl a present, saw how much it cost, and thought land was a better investment."

Lucius smiled. "Something like that."

"I think it's a good idea. Just remember; always look at a piece of property three or four times before you buy it. It should look better to you each time."

"Well, I'm not sure I'll have that luxury. But I'll do my best."

"I'll pack you a basket so you'll have something to eat," volunteered Valeria.

Lucius suddenly felt better. He relaxed. "Let's have some wine," he said. "We'll celebrate the Vinalia."

"My birthday," contradicted Valeria.

"Of course," said Lucius gaily. "Both together."

+ + +

Lucius took to the road at first light. He picked up Quintus Crispus at the small one-room home he shared with his brother Sextus on the Oppian Hill, and together they went to inspect the property near the Anio River.

The Anio River flowed from east to west out of the Apennine Mountains, joining the Tiber a few miles north of Rome. It was a small river that flooded violently on rare occasions, but usually provided a steady supply of sweet water. On the north bank the Claudian clan held sway over large tracts of land ever since they moved en masse to Rome some thirty years prior from the west and central Apennines. Lucius gave this scant consideration, given his disregard for political calculation.

Fortunately for Quintus he took up scant space, for Lucius took nearly the entire seat of the two-wheeled cart. Little traffic impeded their progress, as if everyone were in hibernation from the heat. They made good time along the Via Gabina that ran parallel to the Anio, though some five miles distant to the south. Shortly after noon they turned off the Via Gabina onto a rutted dirt road heading straight north. In the near distance they could see the walls of Gabii. Farther up to the northeast Tibur reposed upon its hill.

Quintus laughed sardonically. "What is it about you Tempanii that you can't stand to own land near Rome?"

The wagon jounced, and the solid wood wheels slued along the rough unimproved lane. Lucius let the mule pick the way while he took in the surroundings.

"Does it make you nervous?" he asked. Plenty of wheat grew in tawny rows on both sides of the lane. Yet things seemed unkempt to him. The ditches alongside the road were overgrown or cluttered with trash. Wild growths of thorny blackberry vines, or breaks of cane interrupted the fields in disorderly fashion.

"No. It just seems inconvenient."

"We're poor plebeians. Can't afford property near Rome."

"So you make neighbors with all the other Latins."

"We've nothing to fear from them. They're allies." He handed the reins to Quintus. "You drive," he said. From a satchel behind him he pulled a map drawn by the property owner. "When you see a stone altar with a statue of Priapus on it turn left."

"Priapus?" said Quintus in surprise. "Is that some kind of joke?"

"I don't know. We'll have to wait, and see."

Priapus was considered the god of poor gardens. His unabating gigantic erection symbolized violent assault on any pest, spirit, or human who came near the meager crops. The rejected son (because of his deformity) of Aphrodite, he served mainly to protect small farms from thieves or the evil eye. Normally someone would carve his offensive image in wood, and place him in the middle of the garden, or the hollow of a tree. To be given status at a crossroads shrine reserved for the *lares* that protected these intersections might be considered sacrilege. Lucius inclined towards Quintus' viewpoint, a symbolic joke by the owner, who apparently didn't have much concern for the image such symbolism projected.

When the bumpy road finally gave out to an overgrown yard in front of a rundown house on five weed-choked iugera of poorly tended wheat fields Lucius knew he guessed right.

Quintus groaned. "It looks like we've wasted a day coming here."

Lucius felt unconcerned. "Listen," he said, "only the rich have the luxury of buying farms in perfect condition. We're going to have to settle for something less. Let's look the place over before we judge it."

Which they did. They poked at the walls of the house, constructed of a mixture of clay, rocks, and straw on a stone foundation, and found them reasonably sound. They climbed on the roof and inspected the tiles. Inside the two-room house the cold hearth still held the ashes of the last fire. Spider webs inhabited the corners, and the wood beams of the ceiling. A heavy, musty smell seemed to rise from the stone floor.

"Well," said Lucius, fingering the chalky ashes on the hearth, "now I know why Priapus is guarding the place."

"Why's that?" asked Quintus, as he tested the central roof beam for rot with the point of a knife.

"It's no longer a habitation. No lares or penates live here because no people live here. What do you think?"

"Well, actually the house seems to be in decent condition. At least the structure is sound."

"Let's go look at the land, shall we?"

Outside, the bright sunlight smote their eyes like fire. Heat, as if some divine alcahest, seemed to dissolve into their skin. Lucius hiked up his tunic to just below the groin, and belted it around his waist. He inhaled the sweet clutching smell of ripe wheat, and surveyed his surroundings. The property had few trees, a scattering of Mediterranean pines, some chestnut trees, and willows along the creek bed that ran along the western boundary of the property. Still, he felt undisturbed and predisposed to like the place. Going to the cart he pulled out their lunch basket and sat beneath the solitary plane tree near the house, shaded by its large three fingered leaves.

He mused and chewed in silence, letting the atmosphere soak into his subconscious. "It will need some trees," he said at last, "but overall, I think it's a good situation. The land faces south, there's the creek, a beautiful view of the mountains behind…"

"Lucius, we haven't even looked around," Quintus said. He discarded a moldy fig.

"No," said Lucius, reaching out for the fig. "We'll save that for Priapus when we leave."

"Don't be hasty," insisted Quintus.

"No, I won't," Lucius assured him. "But would you want to live here if I bought it?"

"I guess that would depend on your expectations."

"We've had this conversation," Lucius said impatiently. "My expectation is that I'll continue to meet the property qualification of the first class. If there's a surplus, we'll split it evenly."

"Then yes," said Quintus. "I think I could live here."

"Good," said Lucius, slapping his knee. "Then let's go look the rest of the place over."

By the time they finished, despite Cominus' advice, Lucius decided to buy the farm. He did not need another look, but desired only to get started. Already plans formulated in his head based on his observations of other farms in the locality.

"Maybe," he said, "I can pick up another of these properties in another year or two. By then you might have enough saved to buy your own place. We could get something good started here."

The words tumbled out far behind the thoughts in his head. Quintus took it all with a grain of salt. Lucius always could scheme and plan, but usually his carefree nature overruled his practical nature, and his schemes didn't reach fruition.

"You may have to share Sextus with Titus and your father," mused Lucius. "Should I see about another hand to help you?"

Quintus cast a quick appraising glance around, calculating in his head all the things that needed done, as well as all the items needed. "I'd like to say, yes," he said, finally. "But there are so many tools and supplies we need." He fell to thinking again of all the items he would need to make life possible.

It seemed almost impossible. There were shovels, hoes, mattocks, scythes, axes, shears, baskets, pots, hammers, rope, not to mention all the normal household goods. He would need to make plaster for the walls, and pitch for the undoubtedly leaky roof. Was he to plow next season with a hoe? No, he needed an ox, at least one or two milk producing sheep or goats, a dog and… He suddenly felt overwhelmed. Had he fallen hastily into a situation he could not handle, infected by the enthusiasm of his patron and friend?

Quintus looked up from his worried ruminations to find a grin rounding Lucius' bigger than life face. "A lot of work, eh?" he chuckled.

"Eh," grunted Quintus in agreement. But he could not repress a matching grin.

Lucius clapped him on the shoulder. "Look at me," he ordered, curling his arm and flexing his bicep. It bulged prodigiously. "I can do the work of ten men when I have a mind to. And you, by Neptune, you've out-worked me a time or two. If we can just get Sextus to keep up with us we'll have this place in shape in no time."

"What about an ox, and a goat or two?"

"Slowly, slowly, Quintus. If there's money left, no problem. But land is dear right now."

"I know, Lucius, but I'm the one who'll be out here."

"Listen, it's my property—or will be—so I'll be out to help as often as I can."

Quintus correctly understood this to mean as long as Lucius' enthusiasm lasted. Once that waned, he knew visits would become sporadic at best. It was in his best interest to push for as much as possible, and work to sustain Lucius' interest as long as possible.

"Well," he said, mustering as much excitement as he could, "let's take inventory of what's here. That way we can plan for exactly what we'll need in the future."

"That's what I like about you, Quintus. You turn my ideas into practicalities."

"Someone has to."

Later, as they turned out of the drive, Lucius left a couple of moldy figs for Priapus. Poor fare for a poor god.

+ + +

The news shot through Rome like a lightning bolt. No sooner had Lucius entered the Boar's Tusk upon his return than a chorus of voices demanded to know if he'd heard the news. Among the most strident were those of Titinius and Considius, who hailed him from their usual corner table.

"What's all the commotion?" asked Lucius.

Considius raised his considerable bulk off the stool as Lucius approached. His round fleshy face reddened with excitement as they shook hands. "An Etruscan fleet has been defeated off the coast of Cumae," he said breathlessly.

"By who?" asked Lucius. He started to pour himself some wine then realized he had no cup. "Hold that thought," he said. Moments later he returned with a cup and filled it from the pitcher on the table. "Now what's this about an Etruscan fleet?"

"Hieron of Syracuse has defeated them near Cumae," said Titinius.

"So, what does that mean?" teased Lucius. "That he's going to come and take up residence with the Greeks down by the docks?"

Amazed at such insouciance Considius gaped at Lucius. "This could shift the whole balance of power in Italy," he said. Suddenly Lucius, for all his battlefield prowess, became a person of no importance to Considius. That is, he could never be a complete person because he did not see beyond. He did not see beyond the next battle, the next cup of wine, the next woman.

"What balance of power?" asked Lucius.

"Between the Etruscans, the Greeks, and us and the Latins," said Considius. "If the Etruscans get pushed out of Capua, Nola, and Suessela we'll have the Greeks right at our door."

"Holy Mars!" exclaimed Lucius. "Before you know it their pottery will be in every home!" He laughed, and drained his cup.

"What he says could be true," said Titinius, his eyes squinted with amusement. "It's probably a little more serious than you think."

"You want to know what I think?" challenged Lucius. They nodded their heads affirmatively. Lucius leaned forward, elbows on the table. "I think the Greeks and the Etruscans are exactly alike. They're a bunch of cities that think only of themselves. So what if one Greek tyrant sinks a few Etruscan boats. He can't even control Sicily; how's he going to control Italy?"

Pontius Cominus had come up from behind Lucius and heard his analysis. "I think that's a fairly accurate assessment," he said, disappointing Considius. "But you've all left out what might be the most important piece."

"What would that be?" asked Considius.

"If the Etruscans are forced out of Campania, it might be the Volscians who have the will to move in. If that's so, they'll do their best to block trade between us, and the Greek cities to the south. We could be in for some hard times."

"Oy," called Lucius. "Who's minding the store?"

"Look," said Considius, pointing proudly to Valeria atop the serving tower pouring pitchers of wine. "Like she's been doing it all her life."

# XVII

## February 15, 473 BC
## The Lupercalia

Unfortunately for Lucius there arose an immediate consequence to the Etruscan defeat. Inexplicably land prices shot up and his coveted little plot of land cost him the remainder of the fifty asses he received as Duellia's dowry. Further compounding his suffering, the increase necessitated selling the armor he stripped from the Sabine warrior, leaving him nothing but the memory. This turn of events would have depressed him were it not for the amount of work required on the new farm. Titus graciously gave him a small pig and two goats, a black male and a white female, with which to begin stocking the small farm. Quintus immediately turned them loose on the grass growing thickly between rows of wheat.

Arduous days of harvesting, hoeing, trimming, stacking, cleaning, and repairing left them drained each night. Lucius did not see Rome for months. A torrential downpour in September exposed so many leaks in the roof that they had to remove nearly every tile and reset the roof. They had almost no help from Sextus, who was required by his father to labor on the original Tempanius farmstead.

Initially the work invigorated Lucius. He found that nothing replaced hard work for hardening muscles. Vitality surged through him like wine as he worked constructing a pen and shelter for the goats. His muscles rippled exultantly as he mowed tall grass, tied it in bundles, and with a mattock and hoe cleaned between the rows of wheat until there remained only the wheat and the dark brown earth turned over to a soft, spongy carpet. The wheat then fell to the crescent shaped scythe.

Quintus delighted to see Lucius so enthusiastic. The man knocked out tremendous amounts of work when motivated and approached the days energetically. But the lack of money limited supplies, and limited supplies meant a barn open to the west winds cobbled together just enough to keep the harvest from the autumn rains. Limited supplies meant nails and ropes, barrels and baskets were precious beyond belief. Limited money meant no oxen to plow the fields.

Yet Lucius remained sanguine. He felt sure the next campaign season would provide him the means to secure at least one ox. In the meantime, if he could not borrow a team for a few days there were plenty of men in Rome that needed work. Their labor cost much less than oxen.

As Quintus knew it would, the tedium of winter drove Lucius back to Rome. He had lasted longer that Quintus thought he would, but there remained much to do, and now he alone would be forced to do it. Quintus had to laugh at the excuse Lucius used to leave as January ebbed toward February.

"Well, Quintus," Lucius said, "I thinks it's time I went into Rome and found you a wife."

"Why?" asked Quintus. He pitched a forkful of grass into the goat pen. "Have I been looking at you funny?"

Lucius laughed. "Actually, I noticed the she-goat looked a little worried."

"That doesn't say much about your looks."

"And I'm genuinely hurt by that," said Lucius sarcastically. "But true friend that I am, I've taken it upon myself to find someone more pleasing to your eye."

"So, when are you going?"

"Tomorrow."

Quintus chuckled sardonically. "Can't get out of here soon enough, eh?"

+ + +

Despite her mother-in-law's encouraging words, Duellia harbored a persistent preoccupation. Until the birth of a child, consummation of a marriage in the eyes of the state had not taken place. She didn't know what was normal, but she felt certain Titus paid her the normal amount of attention. Still, she hadn't been able to get pregnant. Fear of barrenness, and that Titus would subsequently divorce her drove her to tears in his absence. Not that she would express those fears directly to him.

Titus, unaware of her thoughts, was in any case incapable of easing her fears even had he known them. Not that he was losing patience; it simply was a subject he did not feel comfortable discussing. As if one suddenly were no different than the goats and pigs. He assumed that when nature and the will of Juno intersected a child would be born.

Duellia sought a more direct approach, and to this end she broached the subject to Drusilla. Together carding wool in the weaving room, they sat facing one another, charcoal glowing in a brazier at their feet. A cool breeze blew in the west window, opened to admit light into the room. Beside them a vast pile of tangled wool awaited their tired hands.

"Mama," she said, her voice hesitant, "I think I should take part in the Lupercalia."

"Nonsense," said Drusilla. Adjusting the shawl around her shoulders she glanced out the window at gray lowering skies. "You're too young to be worried about such a thing."

"But it will be two years in May," persisted Duellia. Her large almond eyes glistened fervently. "There must be something I can do." She blushed hotly to the roots of the hair on her high forehead. Drusilla chuckled at the unintended innuendo. "I mean…"

"I know what you mean," said Drusilla. "Have you talked to Titus about this?"

"Oh no. I mean…not yet." Duellia's hands worked nervously at the wool. "I wanted to talk to you first."

"Surely you don't expect me to talk to him?" Drusilla raised her dark, arching eyebrows, her wide mouth compressed disapprovingly.

"Well…I…"

"You did!" Drusilla tsked several times like a lone cicada seeking company. "No, that's something you must do." She reached down for a clump of raw wool, placed it on the card strapped on her left hand, and with the fine nails of the other card began the laborious combing to straighten the yellow-brown fibers.

"But if I tell him I'm barren he might divorce me," wailed Duellia, combing fiercely at the bunch of wool between her hands.

"I don't think you're showing much faith in Titus," said Drusilla. "Has he said something to you?"

"No…"

"You see? He's not concerned."

"Why should he be? It's no disgrace to him."

"Duellia," said Drusilla, trying to calm the girl's growing hysteria, "I once had a friend who was married for five years and never had a child. When her husband was killed, she remarried, after a suitable time, and had a child the very first year."

"How?" asked Duellia, hopefully, then blushed again.

"Oh, I think in the usual way," said Drusilla. "But you see, sometimes it is the man, or perhaps the gods who are to blame."

"Thank you, Mama. But even so, I think I should go."

"Well, of course, it's up to you and Titus," said Drusilla. She spread her full lips in that wide infectious smile, and Duellia thought the sun had come out. "Maybe we can all go and make a true festival of it."

+ + +

Lucius held forth. In an expansive mood, he regaled his listeners with tales of his exploits. They gathered merrily around him at their normal corner table. Even Considius, who had held himself aloof, relented and showed up. Whether the sunshine and mild temperatures, a fresh bath and haircut, or the presence of his brothers put Lucius in his present mood he couldn't say. He spoke with broad bold gestures, and looked wildly from face to face. His broad face, sharp with excitement, looked like two jawbone scythes set on edge and leaning against a block of stone chin. In the middle an axe blade nose fresh from the blacksmith's fire cooled between glowing dark coals challenging anyone to refute his tale.

"This," he said, looking intently at Titinius, "you ought to put in a ballad."

"And what would I call it," laughed Titinius. "Death of a Sabine?"

"How about Lucius and the lioness?" offered Considius.

"No, no," said Valeria as she cleared bowls, and plates from the table. "The Idiot and the Oddity."

"Oh," groaned Lucius, grimacing. "I expect low blows from these low men. But you?"

"I know you better than they do," said Valeria saucily. She regarded him haughtily with laughing chestnut eyes as she took away the dishes.

Lucius saw Antonius follow her with hungry, stricken eyes, obviously enchanted. He logged the look in his memory. It might make a good match, he thought.

"No, you've got it all wrong," said Titus. "It's Lucius and the Expanding Sabine." A chorus of laughter greeted his words but he held up a hand. "But more; Titinius, you'd have to revise the song at every singing and make him larger and fiercer each time. Just to get the true flavor of the story."

Hoots and disparaging remarks greeted his words. Lucius, undaunted, carried on.

"Listen," he said, "he was taller than Aulus Vibulus and wider than Gnaeus here." He pointed to Considius and expanded his girth with his hands.

"Oh, two impossibilities in one person," cried Titinius, clapping his hands. "This isn't a song, it's a Greek comedy."

"You can ask Quintus Crispus," said Lucius.

"I'm sure he saw it all from the baggage train," laughed Considius, his ample jowls shaking.

"He was not at the baggage train. He was right behind me."

"You fought the Sabine behind the baggage train?"

"Very funny."

"It's no wonder there are no witnesses."

"I say you all would have run."

"It's always best to run from phantoms."

"What phantom?"

"The phantom Sabine."

"He was no phantom."

"But was he a fact-um?"

"I'll give you a factum," growled Lucius. He held up a clenched fist the size of a mallet. "I'll bloody all your noses if you keep this up." His smile told him false.

"Come on, Lucius, finish the story," said Antonius.

"Yes," said Considius, his face flushed red from laughing. "I'm worn out from waiting."

"No," declined Lucius with a petulant shrug. "You don't deserve that story. I'll tell you another."

Moans greeted the prospect.

"Did I tell you how I found a wife for Quintus?"

+ + +

Blackness, clinging in damp mists like the hoary fingers of spirits and demons froze her blood, slowed her step, and set her heart racing. The Circus Maximus lay supine on the floor of the Murcia Valley surrounded by altars and temples housing the mysteries of awe and sacrifice. Spectral in the pre-dawn darkness the altar of Consus, the temples of Mercury and Ceres, and the altar of Hercules Greatest wavered like pallid studs in the cincture of the oval meadow. Above, like a charcoal smudge against the inky darkness the baleful onyx eye of the Lupercal looked down from the lower slopes of the Palatine. This cave of wolf-men, this grotto where resided the terrible giant of her fearsome hopes, this cavern of awful blood-mystery suddenly terrified her.

She gripped Drusilla's arm tightly, shivering against the cold and fear, wondering how she had so lightly come to this decision as they felt their way along the enshrouded Via Albana. Lingering maddeningly behind the Apennines that hulked like a bank of storm clouds threatening the horizon, the sun tormented her with its slow rising. Would it never come up? Impatience fueled by fear gripped her as she squeezed harder on Drusilla's forearm.

Drusilla patted her hand encouragingly. "Come, come, Duellia," she whispered, "there's nothing to be afraid of." But she too felt the cold seeping through her stola, tickling the nape of her neck with scaly, slimy fingers. With her free hand she pulled her shawl closer around her shoulders. She took a deep breath and smelled the sterile, crisp nothingness of winter air. The girl's fear seemed to travel through her arm and into Drusilla's blood as if it were a physical agent transmitted by touch. To their left the gurgling of a small stream sounded like pursuing footsteps in the imprecise dark. She knew it was the stream, knew it submerged itself at the east end of the Circus and emerged from its subterranean travels at the west end before flowing into the Tiber. Sometimes knowledge and reason gave no help; the sound unnerved her. She felt Duellia grow icily rigid the farther along the road they moved.

"This is close enough," she said at last. "Let's wait here."

"Are you sure?" asked Duellia, her voice tremulous with fear and gratitude.

"Yes," Drusilla assured her. How much easier, she reflected, if they had only chosen a spot between the Velia and the Palatine hills. After all, the runners made the entire circuit around the Palatine. But Duellia insisted on being close to the start, so they had risen early, and made their way here in the dark.

They were not alone. Other women, childless and empty, fought their own desperate battles with fear to come to this spot in hopes of being blessed. More arrived every minute. Soon a low hum of subdued conversation rustled the darkness like the sound of dry leaves under foot. Now and then a high nervous laugh rippled through the solemn atmosphere, and died stillborn.

With tentative red knuckled fingers feeling the stony ridges of the mountains for handholds the sun began its lazy climb into the heavens. The sky grayed. Thick blackness gave way to soft shapes as trees, buildings, and hills materialized out of darkness.

Drusilla looked up to see the steps of Cacus climbing the Palatine directly in front of them. Here Hercules clubbed to death the giant, Cacus, who had tried to steal his oxen. Probably the Lupercal was the very cave into which he had dragged them backwards to fool the son of Jupiter, asleep in the meadow below. She turned around and looked behind and to her left. There, near a copse of trees she located the altar of Hercules, erected at the suggestion of Evander to consecrate the prophecy spoken by his mother of a great city's foundation. The same Evander who brought the written language, and with it civilization, to the rough shepherds of that time. She doubted the prophecy; Rome was small, haphazard, weak.

Maybe, in her basic, instinctual way, Duellia had been right about coming to this place steeped in mystery, history, and tradition. Here where Consus opened its mouth twice yearly to the underworld, here where Ceres presided over every phase of the growing season with her two helpmates, Liber and Libera. Here where the Circus served as holy allegory for the cyclical nature of life, here, maybe Duellia could find the answer she required to fulfill her calling as a Roman matron.

As she reasoned thus in the hopeful foreshortening of dawn, a parade from the direction of the Forum turned the corner around the Palatine, blocking the dark waters of the Velabrum from view. The procession, led by the consuls and the chief priests of Rome, Publius Scaevola the Pontifex Maximus, and Gaius Veturias, the Flamen Dialis of Jupiter, halted before a tripod altar set up at the west end of the Circus directly under the Lupercal. A considerable host followed behind them. Near the altar a banquet table piled with food sat in readiness for the celebrants.

Drusilla and Duellia had a good vantage point from which to watch. They stood on a rise below the worn tufa stone steps of Cacus, and could look down onto the Circus Maximus where the altar had been set up. The Lupercal gaped above them. They could easily see Gaius Veturius the Flamen wearing the gleaming bronze spiked apex helmet of office.

Behind them came the augurs in saffron robes, bright as suns against the dull green/gray of early morning. In two lines, escorting the representatives of their respective colleges, came the priests of the Lupercal. The Luperci had been divided since time immemorial into two colleges, the Quinctiales connected to Romulus, and the Fabiani connected to Remus. Naked save for loincloths the two youthful representatives followed their brethren for the only time that day. Prancing dutifully behind came two female goats, never sheared fleece washed white as snow, looking proud in their lovely apparel of boughs and red headbands. With them loped a large sleek dog, its white fur brushed to a flowing milky color and wearing the same boughs and red headband as the goats. All three strained happily at the tethers against which their handlers applied equal opposing force. Strung out behind them a host of incense bearers, pipers, priests of other colleges, and laurel crowned members of the senate spread themselves around the altar.

A fire kindled under a cauldron next to the altar flared to life, licking at the sides of the bronze pot. There seemed to be some confusion as the priests arranged themselves near the altar. Finally, a clot of men, goats, and the dog occupied the open space around the altar along with the semi-naked youths. The cauldron steamed.

Duellia's fear turned to anticipation as the sky lightened. High puffy clouds, scattered like sheep across a blue meadow, shadowed the earth in irregular patches. Drusilla sat on the grass next to her with her face towards the sun, turning her attention intermittently to the slowly unfolding proceedings below. Despite having been there for some time Duellia felt too nervous to sit. She played anxiously with the two bronze coil rings on her left hand, tugged helplessly at her dangling earrings, and fastidiously adjusted the mantle covering her head. None of this alleviated her nervousness. Around them men, women, and children continued to gather in an atmosphere of pious revelry. A constant stream of chatter rose and fell in eddies of ribald laughter. The two women talked little, Duellia's attention wholly fastened on events below. These events now began to move forward.

One of the goats was brought before the altar. She placidly munched on succulent leaves and grass at the altar's iron feet as men gathered around her. A priest stepped forward the tail of his white toga pulled up to cover his head. Accompanying him were a *camillus* bearing a box of incense, a piper, and three assistants. The priest washed his hands in a bowl of water and dried them on a clean white towel. A crier stepped forward and called for silence. As he did so the piper began playing to drown out any accidental noise. The priest took a bowl holding a special mixture of flour and salt called *mola salsa*, prepared by the Vestal Virgins, and sprinkled it lightly on the goat's head. She didn't seem to care or notice. From behind someone handed him a cup of wine that he ceremoniously poured on the altar as a libation, followed by incense that rose in sweet spirals of smoke. The assistants, their togas rolled down to their waists to leave their upper bodies exposed, stepped up and removed the boughs and headband from the victim. She shook her head mildly at this annoyance. The celebrant priest now took a long knife and passed it along the spine of the goat in consecration, then handed the knife to one of the assistants. Another assistant behind read from a scroll the formulaic prayer, repeated verbatim by the priest so as not to leave out the smallest word, which would render the sacrifice void. A pause, filled only by the plaintive notes of the piper followed the prayer.

"Shall I go ahead?" asked one of the assistants in a loud voice, displaying an upraised axe.

The priest gave his assent, and the assistant stepped in front of the goat, which looked up quizzically at him. Docilely she allowed the other assistant to cover her snout with his hand and pull her unblemished head down. In a flash the blunt side of the axe blade carved an arc through the air and smashed the goat between the eyes. Her legs wobbled, and her knees buckled. Instantly, the assistant holding her slashed her jugular vein and blood flooded from the stunned goat's neck into a bowl held by a third assistant. The goat collapsed without a struggle. A good sign.

Duellia breathed a small sigh of relief, and made the sign against the evil eye with her thumb. Any sign of struggle, or worse escape, by the victim meant bad luck.

The priest spread the rich life-blood upon the altar. When the other two victims had been similarly dispatched, they were opened up and their organs inspected for blemishes, or signs of corruption. Finding nothing unusual the animals were gutted by the assistants, their entrails sprinkled with *mola salsa* and placed in the steaming cauldron. While this *exta* simmered away the carcasses of the sacrificial goats were skinned.

The two half naked patrician Luperci came forward, grinning ear to ear. They could have been twins. Nearly identical in height with black curly hair, roman noses, and distinct jaws ending in knobby chins they could easily have been the young brigands Romulus and Remus. The sacrificial priest smeared their foreheads with blood from the goats, then dipped a wool cloth in a bowl of milk and wiped the blood off as the youths laughed with delight, as required. Each then donned the fresh bloody goatskins, sat down at the banquet table piled high with food, and laughed uproariously as they ate and drank their fill.

Duellia bounced up and down with nervous anticipation. Her time rushed upon her. Drusilla stood too, in anticipation, thinking she might be of some help to her young daughter-in-law, though unaware how. At last, the entrails finished cooking. As they were removed from the pot and chopped up on the altar, the two Luperci rose from the table with round bulging bellies. A priest handed each a strip of skin cut from the sacrificial goats called *februa* (that which purifies), and with their colleagues behind them began to run. Duellia shook loose of Drusilla and stepped out into the middle of the road. Her breath came in quick gasps through the parted heart shaped lips of her small mouth, a high feverish rose flooded her cheekbones, and her large eyes glowed.

Up the short rise loped the sleek muscled luperci wolf-men. Laughing with bared teeth, bellies bloated with festive food, they lunged, swinging the long strips of goat flesh. A train of tunic clad luperci trotted in two dust-clouded columns behind them.

Duellia waited in the middle of the road, trembling, her belly roiling in dreadful ferment. Her chest heaved. As if in a trance she raised her arms to receive them. They charged her, howling in ferous jubilation, these wolfish flagellants. The flailing goatskin *februa* raked her flesh like fangs, ripped across her face, and stung her arms into bloody welts. She laughed wildly into their rabid faces, feverishly inviting the fertile scourging as they butted her with brawny shoulders, spinning her round and knocking her down. She crumpled to the road in a heap; the runners parted, poured around her like water around a rock, and then were gone, bulling their way through hundreds of hopeful lacerated women. Like streaks of fire the welts burned her flesh, and she rejoiced in it lying disheveled in the roadway.

Drusilla rushed to her side, pushing through the stacks of people filling the road to watch the runners from behind. Gently she helped Duellia to her feet.

"Are you all right?" she asked, fingering the livid welts on the girl's cheeks and forearms.

"Oh yes, Mama," cried Duellia with manic exhilaration. "Wasn't it exciting? I've never felt so alive."

The next month her menstruation did not occur. She poured a libation, and said a prayer of thanks to Juno. Nine months later a male child lay on the floor waiting for its father to pick him up and accept him into the family. When he did, Duellia became a Roman matron in the truest sense of the word.

# XVIII

## March 1, 473 BC
## Dance of the Salii

Rome swelled with pregnant expectation. On the kalends the vestals cleaned out the sacred hearth of the city and rekindled the eternal fire. The great bronze doors to the temple of Janus swung open to war, and the Salii dancers, dressed in the garb of ancient warriors, retrieved the sacred shields from the Regia, striking them with sticks as they danced through the streets. However, external wars were not uppermost on the minds of Rome's citizens.

Despite all their influence and arm-twisting of clients, the patricians could not prevent the election of Publilius Volero as people's tribune. Since the plebeian assembly was essentially an extra-legal organization, it fell outside the boundaries of pontifical influence. This was a source of frustration to the patricians who were adept at manipulating the state religion in consular elections using signs or portents to advance or halt elections according to their ends. The commons exhibited such keen interest in these tribunician elections that voters, like Titus Tempanius, came from the farthest edges of Rome to take part, thus lessening the patricians' influence. The patrician strength in the plebeian assembly resided more in the control of the urban plebs, the rural plebs tending to more independent action.

Volero had done a good job of getting the vote out not only for himself but also for his preferred colleague, Gaius Laetorius. The two of them together made an intimidating sight. Both were large, powerful men in their prime. Both served in the legions as centurions, and were well known as brave, relentless fighters. These were the men with whom Lucius Tempanius entered into honorable competition when he served in the legions. He voted for both of them on the assumption that if they were in Rome playing politics, they couldn't be in the field winning military honors. And he harbored the express goal of eclipsing them in military honors. They could have the political laurels. He figured their head start of ten years could be overcome that much faster if they could be kept out of the field.

The patricians feared that Volero, who had successfully led the resistance against military service the previous year, would turn his anger against them and charge the outgoing consuls with capital crimes against the state. This seemed even more likely when his personally selected colleague also won election, thereby thwarting any possible influence by the patricians on the other tribune.

To oppose him they insured the election as consuls of Titus Quinctius and Appius Claudius, a man who seemed to have hatred for the plebeians in his bloodlines. When Volero brought his charge, Appius Claudius would not be afraid to defend his class.

Publilius Volero did no such thing. His attack on patrician power surprised them with its subtlety and character. Volero intended, not to charge the consuls with crimes, but to change the way tribunes were elected, and thus reduce the influence of the patricians on those elections. He called a meeting of the plebeian assembly for the day following the elections. But Publilius Volero made miscalculations of his own.

The usual group, gathered at their usual corner table in the Boar's Tusk, swelled with the addition of Titus, Antonius, and Aulus Vibulus. Lucius, ostensible host, wished they could go elsewhere. As a resident and unofficial member of the Cominus family he felt constrained to be on his best behavior when he remained at 'home'. He did not wish to be on his best behavior. Worst of all, the subject had turned to politics. As he leaned his bored bulk against the wall he wondered if he could quietly excuse himself and disappear. Now, he thought disgustedly, his only source of amusement would be watching his little brother Antonius moon over Valeria. A match intrigued him. Why not? They were close in age. Antonius would be fourteen in a month, and Valeria would be thirteen in August. Of course, he would have to talk not only to Cominus but his own family about a marriage. He knew his mother would object since all Valeria would add to the family was a tavern—not the most reputable of professions.

Lost in thought, his vacant stare did not take in the room full of men clad in tunics drinking, and eating. He gazed unaware of Valeria busily serving wine from the tower or Cominus waddling about the room delivering food and clearing tables. He did not hear the steady drone of conversation, the scraping of chairs, the ringing melody of a lyre player in the middle of the room, or the dull slap of wood against stone as the door swung open and closed. Nor did he smell the sweet pungency of wine mixed with the salty smell of pork sausages. He felt as if he were wandering among those nine spheres Titinius had once described. It seemed only right, then, that Titinius should call him back.

"What do you think, Lucius?" Titinius asked.

Lucius shook his large head, and looked at the rodent-faced man. "About what?" he said, scowling.

"Why would Volero call an assembly so soon?"

"He's got something on his mind, I suppose. How should I know?"

Titus dug an elbow into his brother's side. "That's my brother," he laughed. "Always ready with a profound answer."

"The only profound part of this discussion," puffed Lucius, "is how profoundly boring it is."

Cnaeus Considius grunted in disapproval. "You're hopeless," he said.

Lucius shrugged his massive shoulders indifferently. Considius had grown beyond the funny stage of fat. The bags under his eyes sagged like full wineskins, and his chin and jaw disappeared in a glutinous neck. His ravenous recessed eyes and pug nose searched endlessly to be satiated. That his knee had been destroyed in honorable combat was no excuse for allowing his body to become obscenely bloated. What further evidence of a weak soul did one need?

Quintus Crispus, seated between the two, looked emaciated in comparison. Lucius, although not tall, had a dominating physical presence with a chest broad as a river barge and arms like twin rudders. His wide ready smile and humorous dark eyes were a lie shielding the violence expressed in the strong nose shaped like the head of a sacrificial axe. A slight widow's peak in his curly black hair added an aggressive look to his bulky features.

But Quintus was not emaciated. Rather, he resembled a three-strand rope braided to add strength far greater than appearance would indicate. His strong jaw and resolute chin emphasized unwavering green eyes set close beneath a narrow forehead. "I don't see why he has to keep us here any longer," he said in a flat, flinty voice. "I've got work to do."

"Of course, the fact that you **are** here now couldn't have anything to do with it," said Aulus Vibulus sarcastically. Approaching fifty, Vibulus appeared to be physically caving in. His stooped shoulders cupped a sunken chest, and pushed his head forward at the end of a long neck. He had a large bald spot ringed by gray hair, and when he smiled a gold bridge flashed where his molars used to be. However, his mind remained youthful and vibrant, which led him to seek out these younger men when he'd had his fill of old friends.

"I don't understand," said Titus.

"Whatever it is he has in mind," instructed Vibulus, "he must feel he needs the votes of the rural plebs to get it passed."

Antonius took his hungry eyes off Valeria just long enough to comment. "I heard a rumor he wants to change the way we elect the tribunes."

Vibulus laughed, and placed a large friendly hand on Antonius' shoulder. "How is it you know more about civil affairs than either of your brothers?"

Antonius shrugged. "I don't know."

"I do," said Titinius, flashing jumbled, crooked teeth. "One's too busy sharpening his plow, and the other's too busy sharpening his sword."

Vibulus liked this image. "Well, Antonius," he said, "you keep sharpening your wits. They'll serve you better."

Antonius barely heard. His attention had already strayed to Valeria. Lucius observed him and laughed. "If he doesn't lose his wits first," he said.

+ + +

The tribunes called the concilium plebis, the plebeian assembly, to order on the Campus Martius under a gray, threatening March sky. A cold breeze blew up from the south into the faces of the men gathered before the altar of Mars. They assembled in no strict order, though they tended to gravitate to their tribes or centuries in which many shared friendships. The Tempanius brothers gathered with their clients, Didius and his two sons, and Petronius and his grandson.

Lucius shifted impatiently on his feet between Titus and Antonius. He wore two tunics, and a hooded wool cloak yet still felt chilled. Titus laughed at him, and Antonius marveled that a man of his size could be so susceptible to the cold.

"I hate March," Lucius snorted, dismissing their jests.

"It comes around every year," said Antonius. "Anyone with any sense would get used to it."

"Anyone with any sense wouldn't come out here if they didn't have to," retorted Lucius. He looked wistfully at the hills of Rome standing over the field, wondering why Antonius, who couldn't vote, would leave its warm confines to stand under these solid skies and listen to a sackful of empty words. In that moment he decided not to. "I'll tell you what," he said, poking Antonius in the chest, "you tell me later what all these chest-pounders said, and I'll go home where it's warm."

Before Antonius could overcome his surprise Lucius made good his words and stomped off in the direction of home.

As Lucius knew he would, Antonius took the charge seriously. Not that he found it difficult. Antonius had an active and passionate brain that found more excitement in political debate than he did in discussions of battles. He had been in battle at a young age, and had learned only fear, loss— and anger.

On a temporary platform erected for the purpose, Volero and Laetorius stood shoulder-to-shoulder preparing to speak. Behind them the two newly elected plebeian aediles stood. Around the dais were grouped various assistants of the tribunes and aediles, a cornicular with his curved horn slung at the ready, and a crier.

The cornicular blew his horn, the sound of a hundred horses neighing, and the crier called for silence. Publilius Volero stepped forward. Many ears perked up in interest, not all plebeian. Throughout the crowd of men patricians young and old wandered or stood listening. Laetorius, attentive to the fact that scores of men wearing the covered shoe of the patrician class had imposed themselves on a plebeian assembly, gesticulated wildly with his hands as he argued with someone behind the dais. Volero seemed not to notice or care.

"Citizens…fellow plebeians and comrades, we have called this meeting today for a matter of the greatest importance. I know that many of you are anxious to return to your homes, and it is for this very reason that we have hastened the process. For to vote on the bill I am about to propose without the full representation of the people would be, I think, a disservice to those who have taken valuable days away from families and farms."

Antonius regarded Volero with a mixture of awe and longing. With his left hand clutching one end of his toga, and his right hand passing slowly palm upraised inclusively over the crowd, he seemed the very image of dignity. His voice came in measured, sonorous tones, not monotonously or matter-of-factly, but with a cadence and stress that imparted dignity and seriousness to his speech. All around Antonius men listened raptly, and this impressed him more than anything.

"In fact," Volero said, "my intention, with the agreement of my colleague, is to make voting more equitably distributed so that you should not feel compelled to come to Rome for each and every vote when it proves inconvenient for you."

Titus leaned sideways, his arms crossed over his chest. "Beware whenever they say they're going to make things easier on us," he said quietly to Antonius.

"Isn't that the truth," said Petronius, who overheard.

"Shhh," hissed Didius. "He's coming to it now."

"I propose a complete restructuring of the plebeian assembly for purposes of voting by tribes." Volero paused as a flurry of noise passed through the assembly like wind in the trees. "I know that in the past we have always voted as individuals, and I am not seeking to dishonor our great tradition. But it has come to the attention of many that what our fathers found convenient has proven inconvenient in our modern age. A change to voting by tribe instead of as individuals may seem a drastic break with tradition, but it is really no different than voting by centuries, which we have done since the founding of the Republic in the centuriate assembly. The simplification will save days that for many of us could be better spent on our farms.

The crier called for quiet as arguments immediately filled the air. Volero allowed them to settle like pigeons disturbed into flight in the Forum, then began again. "How many of you have felt left out on an important vote simply because your farm demanded your presence? Is it fair that a disproportionate number of urban residents, tied to the patrician class as clients should so often determine the outcome of critical votes simply because your farm forbids your attendance? Friends, it is time we limited the undue influence of the patrician class on our affairs.

"You elected me to protect your rights and persons. I know of no better way to do this than to remove the pressure of patrician patronage from our electoral body by changing to a tribal voting system, so that every man truly has a voice and a vote."

No sooner had Volero finished speaking than a thousand debates began all over the great meadow. Everywhere Antonius looked men engaged in heated discussions. Except in his small group. Didius and Petronius, who had directly taken part in the secession of the plebs, and risked their lives to found the plebeian assembly adamantly opposed the group vote idea. The rest of the men in the Tempanius household shared their conviction. So instead of discussion a stolid, stubborn resistance encapsulated the small group of men as they faced the platform to hear the next speaker.

That speaker was Tiberius Coelius, newly elected plebeian aedile. He did not share the physical stature of the tribunes, had none of their brawny vitality. His fine hair drifted in the wind around his high apologetic forehead, and from thin lips came a raspy, choked voice. Yet his voice carried surprisingly well, and exhibited not the least bit of intimidation. Laced instead with gentle sarcasm, it held them spellbound.

"Friends, Romans," he said, looking over the gathered men with drooping sleepy eyes. "Do not heed the siren call of my friend, Publilius Volero's, proposal. However well intentioned it may be, it is in error. To say that there is some sort of proportional imbalance in our assembly is nothing short of calling you lazy and willing to delegate your voting rights to those who live closer. He claims that times have changed, and it is no longer so easy to be here for important votes. But I ask you, has Roman territory grown by so much as one iugera since our fathers marched to the sacred mount over twenty years ago?" He paused and let the murmuring grow then subside. "No; I thought not. Why then, except for sheer laziness, should it be any harder to come to Rome than it was twenty years ago?

"Then, my friend Publilius would have us believe that the interests of democracy are better served by having tribunes (and aediles, I suppose) elected by the tribes rather than by each man voting separately. Who can argue that counting to twenty-one takes less time than counting to ten thousand? Yet, my friends, there is no truer democracy than the equal importance of one man's vote with every other's. I need not go very far to prove my point. In fact, I will use the same example as my friend Publilius; the centuriate assembly. But first I must make a small digression, so that our minds may be perfectly clear, on the history of our assembly.

"When my father marched to the sacred mount," he hesitated, then forcefully punctuated his point, "Publilius Volero's father was not there! I point this out not to belittle or accuse my friend, but to illustrate the fact that the plebeian assembly was made up of the disenfranchised. It was made up of artisans, and craftsmen, of day and seasonal laborers, and of the small landowners who live every day under the threat of debt bondage, slavery, and death. It was devised by men who had no protection under the law, who were denied equal access to the public lands by those who controlled the law, and were considered of little import or intelligence. When the centuriate assembly met our vote was rarely needed, for the centuries of the first class, to which Volero's family belongs, had already decided the issue. So why weren't Publilius Volero's father and those like him with us? Because they still entertained hopes of winning honors and access to higher office. Needless to say, that hope has proven illusory, so now they come to us. And what is it he would have us do? Relegate ourselves to the same position we occupy in the centuriate assembly.

"I say, the man that votes for this measure is foolhardy. Only think about how our patrician 'fathers' influence the tribes now, and you will know which way your duty lies. If we give way on this, we will lose control of our plebeian assembly. Maybe not immediately, and maybe not in twenty or even fifty years. But ultimately it will no longer serve us, but the interests and ambitions of those who would rule us."

Heated debates erupted over the Campus Martius like fires that spread underground along the root system then burst out above ground on some tinder-dry bush. Other speakers mounted the platform and the fires died to smoldering embers until the speaker finished his harangue, then the opinion fires burst into flame anew. Laetorius delivered an impassioned speech against the patricians' tyrannical control of the urban plebs, imploring the men to vote for Volero's proposal as "the only way to ensure our liberty." Another in opposition took the dais. "Publilius rightly says we elected him to protect us. Let him do so then by pressing for codification of the laws, so that every man can read them for himself, and forget this bastardization of our election process."

Volero sat on the dais, square chin resting in hand, and dark eyes staring off into a place he had not foreseen. His hopes for immediate passage of his bill dissolved like salt in boiling water. In the distance the noon trumpet sounded, wavering, muted, unsure to his ears. Rising suddenly to his feet he gave an order to the cornicular who blasted the crowd to silence. When quiet lowered like the dull granite sky over the crowd, Volero calmly stepped forward and dismissed the assembly. Three comitialis days remained before the nones, and nearly a week of comitialis days before the Equirria—the feast of the cavalry. If he could not get his bill passed by then he would have to wait until the end of the month to try again. But today—today was no longer propitious.

Titus and Antonius returned to find Lucius working on his weapons, muttering curses under his breath. Two braziers filled with glowing charcoal sent thin streams of smoke drifting to the ceiling in acrid clouds. The stale air smelled like singed hair. Across his knees his breastplate glinted dully as he worked on the leather backing and straps.

"Your charcoal smokes too much, Titus," said Lucius by way of greeting.

Titus entered the dusky room, dimly lit by splinters of light angling through closed shutters. "You could always come back to the farm and take over the job," he said.

"What are you mad about?" asked Antonius, sinking into the straw mattress of Lucius' bed. He laced his fingers behind his head and closed his eyes.

"I'm mad because I only got five asses for the shield I took off that Sabine, and an armorer wants ten for one half the quality."

"I take it you're volunteering again?" asked Titus.

"Yes. I've already been to see Titus Quinctius. He's enlisted me as a centurion."

"Centurion!?" exclaimed Titus, surprised.

"Why not?" asked Lucius.

"You're a little young, aren't you?" said Antonius.

"I'll be twenty-four in May," said Lucius defensively. "And anyway, I've served almost every year since I turned seventeen. I've been in twelve battles, killed an enemy in single combat, won a corona vallaris, three torques, two armillae, and…"

"We know all your heroics," interrupted Titus, waving him off. "Who recommended you?"

"Publius Scipio and Lucius Valerius."

"Oh, I see," said Antonius. A laugh full of sarcasm and repressed anger left his throat like a growl. "And how will you be voting on Volero's bill?" he sneered.

"That has nothing to do with it," said Lucius, looking down at the leather straps between his thick fingers. "What difference would it make in any case? I'm one stinking vote."

"Well, who knows," said Titus, "maybe you'll be in the field before a vote is ever taken."

"So, Lucius," said Antonius, changing the subject. "How much for Valeria?"

Lucius' fingers froze in place, and his heart protector hovered just above the small table next to him. "What do you mean?" he asked darkly.

"You know," said Antonius casually. "For a night."

Lucius smashed his breastplate down and jumped angrily to his feet. "Why you little…" He advanced threateningly on Antonius, who remained outwardly relaxed on the bed. "I'd sooner sell you than ask Cominus such a filthy thing."

"Isn't that what you just did to be centurion?" Antonius blithely asked.

+ + +

Lucius spent the next few days chasing pleasures that gave him none. His anger at Antonius left a bitter taste at the back of his throat, and a fear in his gut that he might do him harm. That he should harbor such emotion against his own flesh and blood drove him to despair, and vain pursuits of the senses. He spent hours on the Campus Martius training, then wasted the nights in dissolution. The nones, which fell on the fifth day of the month, came and went.

Quintus refused to be dragged into his dissipate ways and went home. Too much work awaited him to spend the time wandering around the Subura from tavern to brothel to bath to tavern. Besides, certain danger waited in the wings of this brawling farewell tour Lucius engaged in, and Quintus did not want to be part of it. Lucius walked him to the Porta Esquillina the day Quintus left for the farm.

"It's unseemly to be so in love with your wife," he said, by way of goodbye, and patted Quintus affectionately on the back.

Titus and Antonius stayed on despite the strained relations, though each day Titus claimed to be his last. He could not leave the farm to two women and a slave indefinitely, he said, over and over. Finally, Petronius sent Primus back to the farm to help Restius, for whom Titus had become increasingly thankful. This allayed some of Titus' anxiety.

Despite his protestations, Titus found the Forum to be an exciting place. Perhaps the enthusiasm with which Antonius greeted every day's sojourn to the pulsing heart of the city had infected him. Or maybe it came from the milling throngs of citizens engaged daily in discussions far removed from the mundane considerations of the farm. Whatever, the atmosphere left a decidedly sweet taste in his mouth, and he finally had an inkling (or so he thought) of what attracted Lucius to Rome. Antonius laughed at the idea.

"Do you see Lucius anywhere near?" he asked.

They sat on a stone bench near the sacred olive tree, its trunk twisted and fissured, in the middle of the Forum under fickle March skies that on this day glowed like clear sapphire. A light breeze swirled indecisively, cool to the touch, like a woman whose promise means 'not yet'.

Not far away, near the Curia Hostilia the tribunes had erected a speakers' platform of heavy lumber. The tribunes placed it there by design so the consuls and senators, whether they wanted to or not, would hear the debates on Volero's proposal. A completely unnecessary precaution. For despite the fact the plebeian assembly had no legitimate standing, or perhaps because of it, the patricians kept a close eye on its actions. The simple truth was, the plebeian assembly had grown. What began as an organization of the poorest class of citizens, entirely geared toward self-protection, had expanded to include many members of the first class, and even a few of the equestrian order. Ironically, the patricians themselves had driven these more affluent citizens into the plebeian camp by gradually squeezing them out of the positions of state. The resultant inchoate political nature of the plebeian assembly infuriated many in the patrician class, and their petrosal response to any plebeian overture, meritorious or not, was entirely predictable.

Though by no means universal. The anfractuous politics of Rome, complicated by the obligations of class, friendship, family, clientage, patronage, religion, and patriotism made for a continuous shifting of alliances. Within this laminated communal context personal, and by accretion, family honors were highly prized, fiercely pursued, yet always subordinated to the glory of the city-state. Anyone who sought to elevate himself above the community brought suspicion on his person. Should he be accused, justifiably or not, of seeking the odious title of tyrant or king, his death lurked near at hand.

Volero was supremely aware of the peril of such an accusation. For that specific reason he had sought a colleague like Laetorius. Laetorius could serve as public scourge, whipping up the debate, while he worked calmly, as seamless as a toga, behind the scenes to effect a compromise. He saw with some surprise that he quite plainly misjudged the plebs themselves. Opposition to his proposal from the patricians any novice could have predicted. What surprised him was that the agents of the patricians within the plebeian organization were the least effective at resisting his bill. The plebs, firmly committed by ideology to the one-man-one-vote principle, wielded an unexpectedly strong influence. His delighted mind found the answer to the predicament in the figure of Appius Claudius.

The mutual hatred between Claudius and the plebs had been passed down from father to son. The son of the Appius Claudius who moved his entire clan en masse to Rome and fought against the establishment of the plebeian assembly, the current branch of the tree lived on the same sap of superiority flowing through his veins.

Volero decided to apply his scourge, Laetorius, to the back of Appius, and drive the plebs to his side. Yes, the whole concept delighted him.

Every class of people crowded around the speaker's platform. Titus watched in fascination as barefoot beggars in ragged tunics worked the crowd. They moved slowly with defeated eyes, dirty palms extended to the wealthy who waved away the mendicants with a gold ringed hand and then brushed at their light colored togas as if they'd been soiled.

Freedmen in their woolen caps mingled with poor citizens in patched dirty brown tunics and thin-soled sandals. Most, though, were like him. He wore simple open toed sandals that laced up to his calves, and a tawny wool toga without decoration. On the ring finger of his right hand he wore a bronze signet ring that he used on official documents, otherwise he wore no jewelry on his hands or hanging around his stout columnar neck. Though just approaching his twentieth birthday the makings of deep lines were in evidence at the corners of his gray ringed brown eyes that looked out with the sad acceptance of one to whom war and hard work were a birthright. That birthright reflected back in the long humorless lines of his darkly tanned face.

The inevitable question surfaced in his brain. How would the passage of this bill affect the lives of all those people? What changes would it bring to the youngsters like Antonius scrambling around in purple-bordered tunics or togas praetexta playing at the dreams they held for the future? What changes did it hold for him? He spun the question around and examined it from all the sides of the argument he'd heard over the last few days. But no clear picture came to mind. Then he boiled the arguments down, reduced them to their pure essence like he'd seen Etruscan jewelers do with gold. When the dross had been poured away there remained the original points of Volero and Coelius. He took them apart as he would butcher one of his pigs; a haunch of patrician influence here, the organs of the traditional individual vote there, the ribs of more equitable representation over there...

Antonius nudged him from his mental peregrinations. "Volero's going to speak again," he said. His voice filled with the excitement of the adherent.

Titus looked at him in surprise. "You agree with him?"

"Shh." Antonius made a downward motion for quiet with his hand.

Volero stood up slowly and stepped forward deliberately. With eyes down he smoothed his heavy black eyebrows pensively with the thumb and middle finger of his right hand. When he reached the front of the platform he stopped, dropped his hand, and breathing deeply straightened up. He surveyed the crowded Forum for a moment. Slowly he raised his hand in salute as voices stilled.

"Citizens," he cried, "I know we have made many miles delay for ourselves over the last few days. Most of us need to return home and put our houses in order. Well then, let us get on with it.

"I have listened along with you to many speeches, and I must say the entertainment value has been high." The crowd tittered. "That said, I won't bore you by going over them point by point. Instead, I would like to address what seems to me the greatest fear or desire expressed by opponents of my measure. And I must admit, as I have thought things over I am persuaded that in some sense my detractors are right.

"Now, before their heads swell with fevered thoughts of victory, allow me to clarify in what sense I mean. Certainly, it is not in any sense that my bill is detrimental to the people or the Republic. Indeed, I will go to my ancestors firmly convinced that the modifications my colleague and I have proposed are eminently just.

"Friends, we are depriving no one of his voice. Instead, we are trying to spread those voices more evenly and equitably throughout the whole populace. In fact, a man's voice is the more easily heard and of more effect when it is to his kinsmen that he speaks. Let the tribes then be the forums for debate, so each man's voice may carry more weight."

"Get to the point," muttered Titus. Exhaling, he stretched his arms and looked around. Suddenly he was tired of it all. If they didn't bring the thing to a vote today or tomorrow and decide once and for all, he would go home despite the ramifications. All this talk, and for what? He screwed his face up in chagrin as he saw Appius Claudius arrive preceded by his twelve lictors. Just like Appius, thought Titus, to have the rods carried high as a symbol of his authority and the majesty of his office. Quinctius always made his lictors lower the rods before the people, demonstrating his respect for their sovereignty. But Appius liked his imperium too much, and looked for every opportunity to display his power and dignity.

The crowd shrank away from the lictors that strode imperiously in single file. Titus could hear the clicking of the bones tied to their shoes as they parted the silent crowd. Behind them Appius walked head up, eyes forward, his clean-shaven chin like a block of marble aimed at the capitol. His white linen toga gleamed in the bright sunlight, and the purple border shimmered with each step.

Titus shifted his eyes to Volero to see how he was taking this interruption, but he seemed not to notice. Antonius cursed Appius for this deliberate display then laughed outright when he saw a quick smirk, and an amused glint in Volero's eyes as he continued his speech. As Appius took up a position near the dais Volero stopped and acknowledged him.

"How kind of you to join us, Appius Claudius," he said.

Appius waved his hand in a motion that was at once dismissive, and impatient for him to continue. Volero accommodated him.

"To return, citizens. It is simply not possible for two tribunes to be everywhere at once. While one is interceding for a citizen in the Forum, and the other is arbitrating a dispute between two others, a citizen in the Subura is taken off in chains. In this matter I will concede to my opponents that we have failed in our duty to protect you adequately. As a remedy we will amend our earlier bill, and provide for the election, by the tribes, of five tribunes at the next election. This…" he held up his hand for quiet, "this should also alleviate the fears of those who despair of electing a candidate to their liking."

Breaking waves of discord thrashed the crush of men. For some liberty and opportunity shone with the fulgor of the sun above their heads. They rejoiced in their efflorescent aspirations in discordant harmony to the lamentations of those who saw evil personal ambition at the root of this latest proposal.

The eruption drowned out Volero, and brought the other consul, Quinctius out of the Curia to see what the disturbance was all about. A covey of senators followed. Something like a melee verged on breaking out, and as Titus wondered how he and Antonius could escape Appius Claudius ordered a trumpet blown. The crowd quieted.

"Citizens!" shouted Appius, and quelled the last lingering bit of discussion among the throng. His square head rotated from side to side as he looked over the faces before him. His wide inimical mouth turned down in disgust, and a hot anger burned from his close-set black eyes. "Let us have no more of this disorder. I thought I'd seen and heard everything when I and those of my class were accused of influencing the vote in an organization which we not only have no part in but do not recognize as having any legal authority." A smattering of angry shouts splattered like trowels of plaster in response, but Appius shouted them down before they could stick. "Despite that, we have consented to allow the so-called plebeian assembly to exist in the interest of social harmony. But now we have this…disruption…"

Antonius grew spitting mad. How dare this man impose himself on the plebs business. Consul or not he had no right or authority to interrupt a meeting of the assembly of the plebs. And all these people just stood by and took it. Why? Because he had a title and a few lackeys (plebeians all) carrying the rods? He looked to the speakers' platform and saw Laetorius fidgeting angrily on his seat. His strong angular face clouded with rage, and his dark eyes fairly jumped out of his head as he clenched and unclenched his fists.

Appius read the anger shared by Antonius rippling through the crowd. "You think I have no business speaking to your precious assembly. But anything that concerns the welfare of Rome or Romans dependent on me is my business. You accuse me of using my clients to influence the vote," he turned in the direction of the tribunes, "well, if the poor are my clients then I am guilty. I am not so spiteful that I would willingly stand by and let Roman citizens be deprived of a voice in their own assembly. Something you, their protectors, seem anxious to do.

"But now, now I have heard everything. It is not enough that we have two tribunes stirring up sedition and inciting near riots like I just witnessed. Oh, no, now we must have five to wreak havoc on our Republic!"

Laetorius hurled himself furiously to the front of the platform. Antonius, watching Volero closely, saw a small discreet smile sneak across his face. In that instant he thought he knew Volero's mind.

"Friends!" screamed Laetorius. His barrel chest heaved passionately. He pointed a shaking finger at Appius Claudius. "How long will we submit to the tyranny of Appius Claudius? A man whose hatred for our class nearly every one of us can attest to? While he threatens and bullies and persecutes anyone who supports my colleague's bill, he accuses us of muzzling their voices. Did we elect a consul or an executioner? You need only to attend the courts to know that answer. Is that where you just came from Appius—devouring another citizen's life and property?"

On he raged in disjointed anger, spitting invective. Uneasy shifting coiled through the gathered populace as patricians and plebs separated into camps.

Titus saw men gird their togas to free their arms and legs, and a twinge of anxiety ran through him. Fear, anger, and excitement mixed on the faces surrounding him. Their eyes shifted ceaselessly like wolves on the prowl. Nervously he nudged Antonius. Caught up in the moment, his brother's face glowed excitedly, and a half smile glistened on his full lips.

"Let's get out of here," said Titus, looking around for an escape route.

Men flowed into the Forum like the Tiber in flood, converging from the area of the Vicus Tuscus, the Subura, and the Argiletum. Yet all remained relatively tranquil as Laetorius spouted off. Then he smashed the order and calm.

"I order all those ineligible to vote in the plebeian assembly to remove themselves from this meeting," commanded Laetorius.

The patricians in the crowd made no move to obey. Laetorius eyed a group of young patricians isolated near the bronze pillar inscribed with the Cassian treaty. "Arrest those men," he ordered, pointing in their direction.

The pillar stood uncomfortably close to where Titus and Antonius had positioned themselves. Titus fidgeted, hung back, but Antonius leaped immediately into the pushing match that ensued.

Appius Claudius, himself in a rage, shouted above the rising din. "You have no authority over anyone, least of all someone not of your class. Not only have you no authority, but this entire organization is illegal. Lictors, clear the Forum!"

The unexpected order brought an instant of stunned silence then a roar of voices as the two sides confronted each other. Shouting, and pushing, little battles broke out as the boldest on each side attempted to enforce the orders of their leaders. Increasing numbers of men were pulled into the fray as the fight expanded, and a general conflagration seemed imminent. Hard shoves, elbows in the ribs, the sickening splat of a fist against the soft cartilage of a nose, blood splattering bright red down tunics, flowing down chins the fight coalesced around Claudius and Laetorius.

Titus fended off bodies, searching the chaotic crowd for Antonius who had suddenly disappeared into the melee. Then like an isolated cloudburst it ended. Quinctius moved in with his lictors, senators, and clients and dragged a cursing Appius from the struggling mass.

Antonius stumbled back into Titus, a wide grin plastered on his face, bloody from a cut above his left eye. "Did you see it, Titus? Did you see it?" he cried, shaking with adrenaline.

"Jupiter," exclaimed Titus, "what have you done?"

Laetorius continued his bellowing but a large portion of the crowd lost interest and dispersed. Titus led Antonius out of the Forum towards the Boar's Tusk. "Here," he said, picking up Antonius' trembling hand and placing it on his bleeding eyebrow. "Press hard."

The following day, on the Campus Martius, the Publilian reform passed on the first vote of the plebeian assembly. Volero had his victory.

Appius would have his revenge.

# XIX

## March 23, 473 BC

## The Tubilustrium

The purification of the war trumpets on March 23rd marked the final rite in preparation for the war season. It followed the feast of the cavalry, and the purification of weapons in the martial order of religious observance. The men serving in the legions were now free to kill, rape, and plunder without bloodguilt. Titus Tempanius desired none of these freedoms, yet he stood in column with the others chosen from his century prepared to march. Favorable auspices had been obtained to commence the campaign when the consul performed the sacrifice on the great altar before the temple of Jupiter.

At the head of the column Appius Claudius gave final orders to his officers, the military tribunes, and marched the legion south out of the Campus Martius. Marching in column of six, preceded by the cavalry squadrons, the crimson and gold legionaries glimpsed a last look at family and friends lining the Via Albana from the Circus Maximus to the tomb of the Horatii. Flowers catapulted from the hands of a frenzied populace fell beneath their feet and were trampled into the dust. Punch lines to ribald jokes floated unheard onto the feathered crests of the men, and calls of endearment drowned in the noise of creaking wagons, scraping wheels, and neighing horses. The Volscians had raided Roman territory in the south, the Aequians in the east.

Who these people were became a question the frustrated Roman populace asked time and again. As if in doing so they could rid themselves of a plague infecting them for over twenty years. Twenty years of slow strangulation suffered at the hands of Italic peoples from some land north and east of Rome speaking a strange Oscan language. Worse, the Volscians had taken from Rome her colonies at Pometia, Cora, and even Velitrae on the south side of the Alban massif. From the Latins they had captured Antium, and the entire coastline south to Terracina. Under the command of the Roman exile, Gaius

Marcius Coriolanus, the Volscian advance carried to within five miles of Rome, devastating the Tempanius farm in the process. Ultimately repelled, it nevertheless left an indelible impression on the Roman mind for generations to come. These conquests, effected over a short time, left the Volscians in control of a vast area of the Pomptine Plain, and the front range of the Apennine Mountains to the east.

Other peoples were also on the move in Italy. In fact, it seemed to the Romans and Latins that Italy was a mass of migrating peoples. They were like the processions of dun caterpillars that dropped from pine trees, attached themselves to one another, and marched in long brown columns to a new tree. And just as dangerous. For if one stepped on them, just like the caterpillars, they gave off a poison that at best caused an itching rash, and at worst horribly swelled the eyes and olfactory membranes. To the Romans it appeared the whole of Italy teemed with these processions. They weren't far wrong.

The Greek cities of southern Italy were also under tremendous pressure from marauding migrants. Tarentum, a prosperous and important trade center on the sole of the boot, had fallen two years earlier to the Iapygians. To the west, the hard inhabitants of the rocky Lucanian hills looked to the Greek cities on the southern coast for a better life. And they had no interest in sharing.

With hordes of heavily armed men roving the countryside, trade between cities and regions became an ever more perilous enterprise, and dribbled off to sporadic forays when things seemed calm. An economic depression settled over the peninsula.

A different form of depression settled over Titus. He would have preferred to stay home and work, it's true, but he couldn't attribute his dispirited outlook to being pulled from the farm. Including Antonius, Petronius, Didius, and the rest there were enough hands to keep things going. Besides, as a good Roman he had no fear of doing his duty. If the campaign should prove successful, he might even return with valuable booty. In times of economic hardship plunder could be a tremendous benefit.

But therein lay the crux of the matter. Neither he nor the majority of his fellow soldiers had any confidence in Appius Claudius. Morale was low from the start, which boded ill and left him depressed.

Lucius headed in another direction, both physically and psychically. That Rome warred repeatedly with the same enemies concerned him not at all. One had to fight someone, and if they were close it reduced the miles of marching. This time the Aequians lay in wait.

In the Boar's Tusk and other taverns he had heard an endless line of doomsayers pronounce the imminent demise of Rome. Choked off, they said, by the Aequians, and Sabines to the east, the Etruscans to the north, and the Volscians to the south, it could only be a matter of time before they converged on Rome and wiped her out. Lucius did not discount this seemingly plausible theory out of ignorance, nor out of rank optimism, though he was optimistic by nature, but from an intuitive grasp of human nature. Especially the nature of the humans inhabiting the domains surrounding Rome.

The Etruscans were a single people only by race or ethnicity. Otherwise, their cities were as often at odds with one another as the Greek city-states, who could not resist attacking their brethren on the smallest pretext. As for the Aequians and Volscians, the one time they had actually combined forces against Rome they had a falling out and took to massacring each other instead of their quondam enemy, the Romans.

Only the Romans and the Latins, glued together culturally, religiously, and politically like the laminated layers of a shield had the strength to endure. He counted on this endurance as the means by which he would earn glory and honors as a soldier of Rome.

However, even Lucius admitted that Rome needed to win some real victories soon. As it stood, the Aequians had the initiative and the advantage. Sweeping out of impregnable mountain fortresses they stormed and captured Tibur, Pedum, and Praeneste, drawing a fortified knife across the throat of the Roman plain on the east. From these cities they launched attacks against Labicum, Tusculum, Gabii and the inhabitants of the Roman frontier, including the place of Lucius' birth, and the little plot of land near the Anio River Quintus Crispus worked for him.

Lucius seldom dwelt on these worrisome details, concentrating instead on his chances to win glory. Everyone took his own chances in life, he reasoned, and he took his. Now he marched as centurion of his century under a consul the men trusted. If only the Aequians could be brought to battle out in the open he would have a chance at glory, and a greater share of the plunder as a centurion than he'd ever known. He would be both rewarded and frustrated in his desires.

Quinctius moved his troops methodically and cautiously. The Aequians preferred quick-strike engagements in place of set piece battles where courage, strength, and will most often determined the victor. Quinctius refused to be drawn into a trap. He changed his marching formations regularly so the Aequians could never get comfortable with his methods and develop a strategy around them. One day he would put his men in a long column with the baggage train at the rear protected by the cavalry. Another day he divided the legion into three columns, or another he would place the baggage train in the middle and throw the cavalry out front as a screen. He made assiduous use of scouts to locate the enemy and avoid surprises. And he kept discipline in his army. Every day they built a fortified camp and kept a strict system of sentries.

At first Lucius found his duties stressful, almost overwhelming from sheer responsibility. It was his duty to supervise the construction of his century's section of the ditch and stockade that circumvallated the camp. As a regular legionary he had dug or hauled baskets of earth, set and tied sharpened stakes, all with good-natured camaraderie. Now he had to be aloof, keep the men at it, and make sure the work met standards.

He had to post guard details, arrange for the passing of the watchword for the day, and ensure a bugle sounded the beginning of each watch. These and myriad little details he had never thought of when he labored in the ranks wishing he had the easy job of centurion. He also began to learn leadership, and the duty a leader had to his men. As summer came on and he adjusted to his role he found he derived a certain pleasure from the responsibility. Still, his greatest responsibility would come in battle, and this test the Aequians refused to allow him to take. But the baggage train grew longer every day.

"How much longer you think they'll allow us to raid their territory without paying for it?" a legionary asked.

A long spit held a row of kettles suspended by their handles over a low hot fire. Above them stars in vast profusion glittered mysteriously in the onyx sky. The night air carried cool fingers to their backs from the mountains nearby while the fire felt like the August sun on chest and bare knees. A soldier stood and leaned over his kettle, holding the handle with a piece of cloth and stirring the steaming wheat with a wooden spoon. In the firelight his red tunic flared like a coal in the fire, and his face glowed white as smoke. The heavy smell of burning pine scented the camp.

Lucius looked out towards the rampart but the fire burned in his eyes and he could see nothing. "They won't attack unless they can trap us, and Quinctius won't be trapped. They're waiting for us to let down our guard," he warned.

Another man hoisted himself to his feet to check his pot of steaming porridge. "Ah," he scoffed, "they're waiting for someone like Appius Claudius who'll come barging in like a bull chasing a bee."

"Then they'll swarm all over him when he gets near the hive," said another, picking up the image.

"Grab your pots, boys," said the standing soldier. "Dinner's ready."

Every man with a pot hanging over the fire scampered to his feet and with the tail of a cloak held the hot handle of his bronze pot as one of them pulled the spit free. They ate in silence, mesmerized by the flashing teeth of the flames that consumed wood in lighter than air jaws.

"Well," said a soldier, with a satisfied sigh. "If they don't want to fight it's fine with me."

"Certainly," said another. "If they don't mind giving up everything without a fight, I don't mind taking it."

Lucius rose to his feet. "As soon as you're finished let's bank this fire and get some sleep," he ordered. "I'm sure Titus Quinctius has a nice walk planned for us tomorrow."

Overcome with sudden nervousness Lucius checked the sentry posts along the rampart. His century's ten tents were located at the end of the line nearest the palisade. If anything happened in the night, they would need to be the first to its defense.

All the talk of raiding unopposed unsettled him. At first the fun of it blocked his thoughts. But as they accumulated a huge herd of cattle, oxen, sheep, and wagons-load of pottery, bronze, and other valuables the thought bubbled in his mind that they had become a weight. With every addition the legion's progress slowed, and the light-armed troops detailed to protect the plunder drained its fighting strength. As long as they moved in unpredictable fashion and chose the ground, they were safe. Were they now becoming predictable? He struggled to keep his men vigilant, afraid they would grow lax and inattentive.

Then again, maybe Quinctius was holding all that plunder out as a temptation himself. The idea appealed to Lucius.

+ + +

The griping commenced almost immediately. Appius marched them six abreast in column with cavalry screens on the flanks. At quick time. They reached Lavinium, ten miles southwest of Rome, exhausted, only to find the inhabitants blithely going about business as usual. A few burned out farms on the outskirts of the city provided the only signs of the enemy. The next day the legion repeated the procedure to Ardea, gaining nothing but another twenty miles and stupefying exhaustion.

"I suppose he'll expect the corona obsidianalis for this heroic rescue," sneered one legionary.

"Is he trying to kill us or the Volscians?" panted another, guzzling the contents of an iron canteen.

Titus chopped furiously at the earth with a mattock, filled a wicker basket with the loosened dirt and rocks then bent wordlessly to hacking at the stubborn ground as a soldier hauled the basket away. Dread and fear-laden foreboding motivated him. He tore up chunks of earth as if he would dig a trench so steep and so deep as to make the palisade unassailable. He did not join his comrades in complaining, fearing some dire infection lived within those coarse and angry words. Yet when the consul strode by to inspect the work he stopped digging and leaned indolently on his mattock. Appius muttered something about tribunes and Voleros as he stomped off to his quarters.

The relationship did not improve as the legion crisscrossed the Pomptine plains in grudging search of the wraithlike Volscian army. Plunder was scrupulously guarded by the quaestors in charge, not from the enemy, but from the legionaries who captured it. A sure indication in the soldier's minds that Appius had miserly intentions for it.

Weeks drifted by in a haze of dust, sweat, and the boring sight of men's backs burdened with shield, helmet, basket, and tools. Appius allowed little to be carried by mule in the baggage train. Beards grew black, filled in. Skin turned nut brown from the soaking sun, and dark red tunics became drab with caked-on dust and grime. The leather workers kept busy repairing shoes, leather shield covers, and straps of endless variety. Then at last Appius found and cornered the Volscian army. He pinned it against the slopes of the hilltop town of Cora, once a Roman colony. The Romans pitched camp below them, blocking access to the plains. Appius ordered his soldiers to eat well and retire early. On the morrow they would come to grips with their enemy, and retrieve Cora in the process. Now they could turn their rage and hatred for him on the Volscians. Curiously to Titus, he got his best night's sleep in weeks. His fears evaporated. The enemy waited above him, and tomorrow he would meet them. All uncertainty melted away.

Like row upon row of blooming poppies they stood in wait, the black feathers on their bronze helmets like the dark tendrils in the center of the bright red flower. Out front, brown as desiccated grass, the velites approached the Volscian lines. Orders echoed down the lines and the heavy armed legionaries started up the hill behind the light-armed velites. Advancing up the steep irregular terrain the lines broke, flowed around boulders, trees or thick patches of sharp-toothed vines, and reformed. Up it moved, this bloody wave of poppies. Up, inexorably up under the bright noonday sun. Under pellucid cobalt skies. Under the eyes of a laughing, taunting, cursing enemy. Up they climbed, packed in red ranks ten deep and three hundred long ascending a funnel shaped rise at the narrow end of which the Volscians waited. The velites let loose an ineffectual barrage of stones and javelins at the Volscian lines, then retreated around the flanks of the advancing hoplites.

Titus, six rows back in the center of the line, carried his spear upright. Sweat ran down his face, down his back as he climbed up, up to the waiting enemy. On order the first four rows lowered their spear tips. The enemy followed suit. One hundred yards separated them when the trumpets blew the charge. Now they picked up the pace, climbing at the run, trying to gain momentum uphill.

At fifty yards the Volscians charged. Their battle cry roared like thunder. The gleaming metal points of their spears came at the Romans with terrible velocity, shattering the front rank. Fighting urgently the centurions restored order, kept the center intact.

Titus leveled his spear and pushed with all his might against the back of the man in front of him. Digging into the hillside that seemed to fall away beneath his feet he strained to push uphill. But the damage had been done. Pieces of the Roman line chipped away like red tufa stone under a mason's chisel.

Into each breach the Volscians poured, slashing at the Roman flanks until fear and confusion sent the soldiers running back in flight. Down, down the bloody terrible hillside. Down, down to the safety of their camp in stumbling headlong flight. With inimitable brilliance the centurions of the centuries in the center held their men together, repressed panic and directed an orderly withdrawal.

Every muscle in his legs ached as Titus backed slowly down the hill, resisting the pressure of the Volscians at the same time. Two red tunics still stood before him, but all he saw were the exultant faces, stabbing spear tips, and flash of slashing swords of a vast horde of Volscians. Jabbing with his spear, pressing himself against the man in front he fought with silent determination, left leg forward resisting the enemy advance. He felt neither anger nor fear, but an obstinacy that refused ultimate defeat. All around him men screamed, swore, cried out in fear and exhortation. But Titus' voice, choked by thirst and obduracy, came out in hoarse grunts as he panted and pushed, shoving his spear at a face or a flash of tunic or an exposed leg. Giving ground inch by grudging inch, willing the men around him to stand fast, to hold their ground.

Then suddenly it was over. The Volscians broke off, and Titus realized he stood only yards from the Roman camp. It came as a bitter realization. The Volscians, repelled from the camp, jeered the defeated Romans from a safe distance as the wilted poppies filed despondently into their refuge with drooping heads and silent voices.

Appius Claudius raged at the slump shouldered soldiers. He cursed them as cowards, accused them of losing purposely to spite him, adding insult to their grievous defeat. The absurdity of dying to spite him left the sour bile of disrespect for Appius Claudius in their mouths. Who ordered them to attack up this precipitous hill? Who wore them out with forced marches to nowhere? He forced this ignominious defeat on them, and then blamed them for it. As they ate a tasteless evening meal, they had no doubt they would also suffer at his hands for it.

+ + +

Lucius had second thoughts about acting as bait. The feeling of isolation and vulnerability wracked his nerves. Nervous sweat ran in rivulets down his temples, irritating his neck and chin under his helmet strap and cheek protectors. A portion of his century he spread out, scythes in hand, to harvest wheat in abandoned fields under the watchful eye of the remainder of his command, and the mountains looming nearby. In a low saddle separating the Praenestine Mountains from the Tiburtine hills the Aequian army occupied a strong tactical position. Quinctius hoped to draw them out, and to that end deployed Lucius' century to give the impression of an army grown careless. Screened by a thin line of soldiers the flocks and herds, raising thick clouds of dust, were used to provide the illusion of an army on the move. Meanwhile the main body of infantry, supported by squadrons of cavalry, lay in ambush along a ravine in a wooded area close by. A small number of his men he put to work looting the farmhouse, behind which he hid with thirty men, swords drawn. If the plan worked the enemy would be pulled piecemeal into a full-scale battle, forced to support punitive forays with ever increasing numbers of troops.

The men worked the fields like the experts they were, swinging half-moons of razor-sharp iron with one hand, stacking the felled stalks of blonde wheat with the other, while another coming behind tied them into bundles. Twice Lucius had to tell them to slow down, rest, and look like soldiers unconcerned with either the enemy or their commander.

Still they waited, the sun like a weight suspended above them, pressing down. Would they never come? His men shuffled nervously, guzzled water, adjusted this and that. The sun climbed yet higher, grew heavier, hotter, more intense. He allowed them to take their helmets off. The sky paled like a white-hot coal, and the air thickened with humidity and the sweet heavy odor of fresh mown grain. Bees, and black flies droned listlessly as if they carried in their wings the peculiar sound of stifling heat.

"Jove, I'm worn out with waiting," said Lucius. He rubbed his curly hair, matted like wet grass on his head. "Sit down. Eat something."

The men chuckled, put backs against the wall, and chewed on hard wheat cakes. Whooping like children with each new discovery the looters heaped bronze vessels, pots, and other valuable items in a pile in the yard of the farmhouse. Hopefully the growing pile was plainly visible to the Aequians in the hills not far away.

The dull thud of running feet pulled him from his lethargic ruminations. "They're coming!" cried the sentry as he came up.

"How many?" Lucius asked, instantly alert. Around him the soldiers also came alive, donning helmets, tightening chinstraps, hoisting shields.

"About a hundred, I think." The sentry panted with excitement. The run had not been far. His thin face, animated by excitement, glowed with expectation.

"Which way are they coming?" Lucius fought to remain calm.

The sentry pointed in a direction that would bring the Aequians across the front of the house. "There," he said. "They're following a cut in the forest that should bring them out over there." He shifted his pointing finger to the left slightly.

"Good." Lucius turned to his men. "Remember; on my command. We want them to go past us, then take them in the rear." He hissed at a member of the looting detail. "They're on the way," he said, as the man came over. "Be ready to run, but don't make it obvious you've been waiting. We want them to chase you." Turning again to the sentry Lucius sent him to pass the word to the harvesters.

It happened just as they planned. The Aequians burst into the farmyard from a tangle of purple drizzled cyclamens. The surprised looting soldiers scattered, running in the general direction of a distant dust cloud. Yelling as they ran, they pulled the harvesters upright from their hunched labors, and they too joined in the disorganized retreat. Hot in pursuit the

Aequians streamed like a roil of dust by the farmhouse in off-white tunics, leather jerkins, and round chest protectors.

"Charge!" bawled Lucius.

In close order the Romans sliced into the loosely spread Aequian troops, cutting them down from behind. Lucius led the charge, howling maniacally, swinging his sword at the enemy backs, crashing into surprised soldiers and bowling them over, then dispatching them with a savage thrust.

The Aequians peeled off away from the pressure, and fled. So completely had the Romans surprised them that though numerically superior they did not turn to fight, ruining the grand strategy devised by Quinctius.

A cluster of three Aequians sped off to his left and Lucius gave chase like a hound after a rabbit, following every twist and turn unrelentingly. One, a tall lanky soldier, stumbled and went down in a puff of dust, and a tangle of gangly legs. As he rolled to his knees, his round pot helmet skewed down over half his aquiline face. With his one uncovered eye he saw Lucius charging furiously at him. Instantly he threw his sword away and held his arms up in surrender.

"Me you win. Fair and square," he said in bad Latin.

Lucius came up short. He stared at the rangy figure, helmet askew, knobby knees bloodied, round shield held high in his left hand and his empty right hand clutching the air. He laughed.

"Fair and square?" he repeated. "What does that mean?"

"Me you win. I stop." The Aequian regarded Lucius with one blue eye. This Roman was so wide he blocked sight of the mountain behind him. He wondered how he got that huge fierce head in a helmet. "You don't kill," he said, smiling ironically.

Lucius laughed again, waved at the shield with his sword and said, "Put the shield down."

"What?" asked the Aequian, not comprehending.

Lucius pointed at the shield unequivocally. "Down," he ordered.

The Aequian prisoner hurriedly obeyed. "Certainly, certainly. Too heavy also," he said, again trying a smile.

Lucius smiled back as the prisoner adjusted the helmet on his head. "What's your name?"

"Me?"

"Yes, you. Is there anybody else here?"

"What?"

"You. Name."

"Ah. Graptus."

"Graptus."

"Yes, Graptus." Graptus pointed to his helmet and made motions of taking it off. Lucius signaled that he would allow it, so he hastily untied it and threw the helmet disdainfully on the ground. Making a face as if it were a disgusting item he said, "Too hot."

Lucius grunted ambiguously, collected his prisoner's discarded effects and led him back to the farmhouse.

+ + +

Titus Tempanius stood guard outside the consul's tent trying desperately to close his ears to the voices coming from inside. He could not.

The harsh stony voice of Appius Claudius came through like a snow laden north wind, chilling Titus to the bone. "This army is full of insubordination."

"But Appius," said a honeyed, placating voice, "if you do this, we'll lose them completely."

"I agree with Publius," said another sweet voice of reason. "Right now the goodwill the centurions have with the men is the only thing holding the legion together."

Appius' thick voice, scoffing. "Who, my tribunes, my Voleros?"

"But Appius, we're right under the eyes of the Volscians."

"This legion of miscreants must be taught some discipline."

A third mollifying voice said, "They have lost a battle. But if you order this you may as well take them back to Rome. They'll never fight for you again."

"They purposely disgraced me, and by Jupiter I'll see they're paid in full for it." His coarse voice shook with indignation.

A fourth voice, cold, factual, unrepentantly contradicted Appius. "It was your discipline that created the problem, Appius. You marched them half to death, then ordered them to attack an enemy in a superior tactical position. I will not support you in this, now—or in the future."

The barely veiled threat hardened Appius' resolve. 'You will parade the men in the morning. Goodnight."

Titus wanted to scream, to run through the camp shouting a warning. Instead, he stood rigid, calmly moving his spear aside to allow the consul's officers to exit the tent.

At first light the troops lined up on the parade ground in front of the consul's tent. They dressed the lines in meticulous straight rows and waited. Birds chirped and warbled as the sky brightened, but the men made no sound. They stifled coughs and sneezes, disciplined their muscles against movement and waited.

Appius came out of his tent in full dress. A high crimson crest floated atop his polished bronze helmet. Over his brilliant white tunic with broad purple border he wore a beautiful muscle cuirass with leather fringes at the shoulders. Strapped over double tied patrician shoes polished bronze greaves gleamed. He mounted a dais erected for addressing the legion.

"From the start of this campaign," he began, "I have put up with belligerent behavior, ceaseless complaining, and dilatory work habits. I have given you and your centurions ample time to correct these mutinous attitudes on your own initiative. But it seems to be beyond your abilities. You have instead become drunk with insubordination, competing with one another in slackness, corrupting one another in behavior unbecoming of Romans. Still, I relented from the drastic punishments others recommended, trusting your sense of duty would ultimately exert itself at the proper time.

"But yesterday proved how wrong I was to expect better of you. Your breach of military discipline was a disgrace to me, this legion, and to Rome. Through no effort of the enemy, you broke and ran…"

Titus' mind reeled under the castigating words. It wasn't true. It wasn't true. We fought hard. But he could not deny the inescapable truth—they had run.

"And so you leave me no choice but to decimate this legion."

Though no one moved Titus could feel the whole army stiffen. Like a prickling on his skin he could feel the thoughts and emotions stirring through the ranks. It wasn't just. They weren't to blame. But the ineluctable guilt of running in the face of the enemy hung over them like a shroud.

"Tribunes, start the count." Appius pointed to the end of the line on his left.

Titus held himself erect, immobile. His oval face lengthened, and his small solemn mouth turned down and hardened into bitterness, trembling imperceptibly, belying the impassivity he forced inside the gray rings circumvallating his brown eyes. Once a refuge, the camp had suddenly become an oubliette. Fate remorselessly dropped him into its inescapable confines. The count began. Down the long red line dread fate-filled numbers picked out the dead. One, two, three… the men counted off until the tenth man stepped forward, and the count started over. One, two, three… down the rigid line the numerals swept, at first faint in his ears, then growing steadily louder as the count drew closer. One, two, three… the insidious reckoning advanced and death was in its sum. His eyes strained to the right in a hopeless effort to tally his chances of survival. All he could see were the legionary next to him, and the tribune out front following the count. One, two, three…he tried to calculate his odds, but the tribune stood too far away. In what must have been a horrible, macabre relief, the men behind would know their fate before the men in front.

A dread silence, broken only by the dull, hopeless tallying of the ineluctable numbers oppressed the legion. "Step out," says the military tribune, pointing a twisted length of vine, the symbol of his office and authority, at the dead man. By some miraculous force of will the man would step out, as if he'd just been ordered to guard duty, nothing more. Closer and closer drew the deadly digits, advancing like the sharpened tempered spear points of the enemy towards his position in the line. Now the tribune took his stance just to the right of Titus and pointed his vine rod. Another victim stepped out. Frantically Titus attempted to count, but he could not see. One, two, three... he heard birds cheeping, and noticed the sound was somehow moist. He breathed deep, and despite the fear and tension that stung the air he could smell the grass, the pine trees, the sweetness of oaks. Four, five, six...A glance at the sky brought limpid aqua blue to his feasting eyes and he had a sudden urge to moan, to cry, to run. He stood still as a statue. How far away, how many spots was the number six? He could not tell. Ah, to have his fate hang in a number! The tribune moved not an inch. "Mars protect me. I will build you an altar and sacrifice a goat," he vowed under his breath. Seven... he made the sign with thumb between index and middle finger against the evil eye. "Eight," intoned the man next to him. "Nine," barked Titus hoarsely, a flood of relief and shame washed over him as the tribune pointed his vine.

"Ten," the soldier on his left said firmly. With grave dignity he stepped forward. Titus knew the man had not run in battle. They had fought shoulder to shoulder, holding their ground. Now he was condemned to die. The decimated.

"I'm sorry, Otorius," Titus whispered.

"Yes," Otorius said simply. Then added, "Will you tell my wife?"

"Of course. I'll make sure they know you honored your ancestors in battle and...death."

"Thank you."

Beheading three hundred men required the whole day. The ground swelled to soak up the blood but could not. It ran in sickening streams onto the feet of the soldiers lined up before the executioner's post under a scalding sun. Titus' boots carried the stain of innocent blood for many campaigns afterwards. The smell of it never left his memory.

# XX

## November 13, 471 BC
## Ludi Plebi—The Plebeian Games

Both Titus and Lucius considered the campaign season a success. Titus came away with his most prized possession—his life—intact. Lucius mustered out with two oxen, some cattle, a hundred pounds of bronze vessels and a slave. He sold the cattle, and most of the bronze, and with the proceeds bought another small parcel of land adjoining his. The remainder he kept to live on. Quintus reacted with joy when Lucius showed up with the team of oxen, but expressed a little disappointment when the slave, Graptus, was not left in his charge also. Lucius simply shrugged. "I have other plans for Graptus," he said.

Graptus was glad he did. Lucius put him 'on loan' to Cominus to help out in the tavern. In return, Cominus taught Graptus Latin. He proved an able, conscientious, and quick student. Within a few months he could express himself in the past, present, future, and conditional tenses with felicity. He also applied himself assiduously, if light heartedly, to the business of the tavern and soon became an asset. In his spare time, ironically, he attended Lucius.

Considering the type of work, again, Graptus felt a sense of gratitude. Only this time the gratitude was for the short period of time spent in attendance on Lucius. For he could not say he found pleasure in the duties Lucius pressed on him.

"Are there not better candidates than me?" he asked, in supplicating tones.

"Why? Are you afraid?"

The grin Lucius turned on Graptus looked wholly malevolent to him. The fearsome delight in his dark eyes confirmed it. The small ears pinned to the side of Lucius' head reminded Graptus of an animal whose likeness he had seen on a vase. A huge, blunt nosed four-legged beast with a horn rising straight out of the front of its face. He felt sure it represented a demonic version of Lucius from the artist's dreams. "Well, yes, I am afraid."

"Listen, it won't hurt. I just need someone to train with."

"Train?" asked Graptus, unfamiliar with the word.

"Yes. Practice," said Lucius, giving the meaning. "I'm wrestling in the games and I need to practice."

"Thank you. Wouldn't it be better to train with someone your own size?"

"In case you hadn't noticed, Graptus, you're taller than me," Lucius informed him.

They strolled under a cool blue sky through a portal in the earth rampart on the Quirinal Hill, and descended to the Campus Martius. Passing through the field of gray conical stone sepulchers seemed appropriate to Graptus.

"Yes, well, even so I'm about half your weight."

"Exactly!" exclaimed Lucius, as if Graptus had finally caught on.

"I see," said Graptus. "You want to chase me around the field. I'll be like those ducks," he pointed to the Capraen Marsh, a reed choked swamp in the middle of the Campus Martius where a large black dog paddled furiously through the water after the ducks, which seemed not to notice until the dog came close, then skittered away with a flap of their wings, and a squawk of annoyance. "And you'll be like that dog."

"Not exactly," smiled Lucius. Tossing his tunic to one side he stood before Graptus in loincloth only.

Graptus rolled his eyes at the sight of Lucius' huge chest, and powerful legs. He soon realized that the 'not exactly' part came when, unlike the dog, Lucius captured his duck, threw him to the ground and pinned him. Numerous times. Graptus was like a rope in Lucius' hands, he tied him in whichever knot he desired, and left him in a heap on the damp ground. Despite all his best tricks, feints, and dodges; despite dropping suddenly to take Lucius' legs out from under him, or using Lucius' weight and inertia against him, he could do little beyond delay the inevitable. Finally, he lay on the ground sucking the odor of damp smashed grass into burning lungs, and stayed down.

Lucius pulled his tunic on over his head. "You need to put a little meat on your bones," he said. "You're like this." He held up his little finger to represent Graptus.

"If I was like that," panted Graptus, "I'd outweigh you." He lay flat on his back, stomach muscles hurting from exertion.

Lucius picked up his tunic and flung it at him. "Let's go," he said. "I think you've had enough."

+ + +

The plebeian aediles put on the Plebeian Games with spectacular magnificence—thanks to the Aequians. Cattle, pigs, and sheep were sacrificed by the hundreds on the great altar in front of the temple of Jupiter—to whom the games were dedicated. The people feasted on the flesh, while Jupiter feasted on the life-giving entrails. Banquet tables laid out in every quarter of the city sagged under the weight of meat, cheese, eggs, fruits, nuts, vegetables, and wines imported from as far away as Greece.

As if the entire population sought to expunge the memory of the decimated legion, they ate, drank, and spent in excess. For weeks in advance potters labored to the last faltering rays of sunlight to fill orders for dinnerware, cookware, or decorative vases and vessels. Artificers in bronze and gold, inundated with orders recalling the most prosperous days of Rome under the kings, sweated and squinted to manufacture fine pieces of jewelry or decorative tableware.

Even the games exceeded all expectations, requiring an additional third day to accommodate all the contests. Men competed for prizes in long distance and middle distance foot races, as well as sprints. Long jumpers and high jumpers vied for honors. Competitions for stone throwers and javelin throwers gave way to wrestling and boxing matches. Finally, the games ended with everyone's favorites, the horse races and chariot races.

Vendor carts stationed around the Circus Maximus did a brisk business in figurine charms as people with bets on the line laid out additional sums to hex the opponents of their favorite, or bring extra favor from their patron god to the object of their bet. Bettors, including Sextus Crispus, sought out soothsayers, astrologers, and fortune tellers from whom they purchased pieces of lead or clay inscribed with curses or spells which they would throw onto the surface of the Circus when the person or animal took the field against their favorite. The curses and spells need not mortally endanger the opposition. They might simply call for a sudden shortness of breath or weakness in the arms or legs, a loss of balance, or an untimely fall. One desired only to win, not destroy.

Once again, the Tempanius clan reunited at the Boar's Tusk, staying with Lucius in his two rooms. With the addition of Graptus and Restius, the men's quarters grew crowded. The women had their own smaller addition in Titus' busy little two-year-old son, Marcus. The space seemed much smaller when filled with his boundless energy. When possible, they took their free time with Cominus and Valeria in the larger space of the tavern's kitchen.

"Papa?" Valeria said, as they sat around the large table in the kitchen.

"Yes?" Cominus looked up from the omnipresent scroll before him.

"Why shouldn't Drusilla Tempania sleep in my room? I could put a pallet on the floor in your room."

Drusilla looked up from a game of patty-cake with Marcus. "Oh, that's not necessary," she said. "We can manage. It's only a couple of days."

Valeria envisioned Drusilla as nothing short of perfection. Forty-two years old and still beautiful. Perhaps the most beautiful woman she knew. By comparison she thought herself ugly, and wished she had the same swallow wing eyebrows over large pleasantly spaced black oval eyes. She touched the tip of her petite nose self consciously as she admired Drusilla's strong straight nose, high cheekbones, and luscious full mouth. She saw Drusilla as boldly made, and she carried herself with calm, powerful assurance. Whereas she saw herself as timidly made, with a tiny waist, slim hips, and small features to match her bust. Now fifteen, she had not filled out at all in her own estimation.

"But no," Valeria insisted. "You are the Domina. You should have privacy. And besides, that way Titus and Duellia could have the other room together."

Duellia lifted her small chin and wide eyes hopefully in Drusilla's direction. Purple shadows of sleeplessness darkened the sagging skin beneath her eyes. The corners of her small heart shaped mouth turned down with disappointment. Drusilla wavered.

"Well," she equivocated. She wished Lucius were there. But all the men were out. "Only if we paid," she finished uncertainly.

"Absolutely not," said Cominus, coming up from his scroll again. "Valeria has offered her room out of hospitality."

"I meant no offense," Drusilla said hastily. Marcus began to whine as the patty-cake game ended before he was ready. "Hush!" demanded Drusilla. "Romans do not whine. I meant no offense," she repeated.

"None taken," said Cominus. He wiped his bald head with the palm of his hand and went back to his scroll. Drusilla made him nervous. His thoughts and feelings mirrored his daughter's, though tempered by maturity. He also had the uncomfortable feeling that to think about her amounted to a betrayal of his deceased wife. His divided mind acknowledged such a concept bordered on the absurd, yet it existed nonetheless. Reading was, by far, the easier choice.

The small company lapsed into silence, unsure of how to proceed. Duellia hoped her mother-in-law would relent. She had precious few intimate moments with Titus anymore. By custom, after the birth of a child Roman women avoided sex until the child was weaned. Titus had understandably become impatient of the custom on occasion, but honored it and slept in Lucius' old room. Duellia longed for him even if they did nothing more than lie side by side.

"Domina," Valeria said shyly, "you would do me a great honor by accepting."

Genuinely touched by the young girl's offer Drusilla capitulated. "Thank you," she said, smiling broadly at Valeria. "It is I who am honored." She wondered if the girl was betrothed.

+ + +

Titus watched with amusement as Lucius and Graptus worked out. If one could call it that. Mostly he watched Graptus get twisted into the air and slammed to the ground like a child's toy by his muscle-bound brother. Next to him Restius thanked the gods for motivating Lucius to give him to Titus.

"Does Graptus get any exercise out of this?" asked Titus with a laugh.

Graptus groaned. "Only if you count bruises."

"Don't encourage him," said Lucius. "He needs to learn the value of fighting to the bitter end."

"If I had done that before you wouldn't be having the fun you are now," said Graptus.

"He's learned his Latin well," said Titus.

"Yes," agreed Lucius with feigned weariness. "I asked Cominus to teach him Latin, and instead he taught him sarcasm."

Titus inhaled the crisp November air deeply into his lungs, savoring the tang of damp grass and mud carried by a whispering southern breeze off the marsh. Above them billowing clouds scattered like piles of chalk whitened wool across a deep azure sky. Between the gaps swaths of ineffable brilliance swept the ground.

At the bend in the river, near the village of Tarentum, a course the same oblong shape as the Circus had been set up. Here they found Antonius jogging in slow steady circles around the track. He stopped when he came abreast of where they stood watching.

Antonius had put off the toga praetexta of childhood, and taken the toga virilis of adulthood shortly after the spring levy. His brothers were understandably glad of the timing considering the course of events. He, in the certain immortality of youth, waited impatiently for his chance at glory, shrugging off the possibility of suffering the fate of the decimated soldiers by blithely claiming nine chances in ten of survival.

"Are you going to run all day?" asked Lucius.

Taking deep regular breaths Antonius considered his brothers, accompanied by their slaves. He smoothed his straight hair with one hand. "Are we in a hurry?" he countered. Loosing his belt, he let the hem of his tunic fall near his knees, then pushed his right arm through the armhole of the sleeveless garment.

"Big brother's always in a hurry where food and wine are concerned," laughed Titus. They began walking towards the city.

"That's the burden you take on when you have a slave in the city," said Lucius.

Graptus snorted. "Yes, the slave grows thin while the master eats for him."

"Where did you get this impertinent beast?" asked Antonius, cocking his winged eyebrows blackly at Graptus.

"Where else, the Aequians," said Lucius. "So," he said, changing the subject, "are you ready for tomorrow?"

"I think so," said Antonius. "You?"

They entered the Peteline woods near the river. Sunlight shattered as it struck leafless beech trees and long needled pines, scattering in brilliant fragments on the ground. A heavy smell of sodden leaves and bare earth trickled with the torpid water from the Capraen marsh into the Tiber. The small muffled sounds of the little wood silenced them, and it was not until they exited that Lucius answered the question.

"We'll find out tomorrow."

The next day arrived with sparkling clarity. Thin exiguous clouds spotted the clear cerulean sky as if, feasting with the Roman people, Jupiter had wiped greasy fingers on his celestial tunic.

Temporary wooden stands authorized by the plebeian aediles lined the Aventine side of the Circus Maximus. On the Palatine side the permanent stands of the senators and patricians filled as quickly. Vendors lugged wheeled carts into any open space they could find between the temples of Mercury and Ceres, and immediately began hawking their wares with loud voices. The early arriving crowd, enticed by culinary delicacies, baubles, charms, and souvenirs bunched around the rolling market stalls. Prostitutes, fortunetellers, and bookies plied their trades working the crowd for eleventh hour business. The stands filled with excitedly chattering people, overflowing to the grassy slopes of the Circus. Below them the great oval, six hundred yards long, was littered with contestants stretching, and performing warm-up exercises in anticipation of their event.

On this, the second of three days of the games the contestants were all human. Mostly Romans, with a few adventurous freedmen and foreigners mixed in, they matched skill, courage, strength, and speed in a variety of competitions. No slaves took part, though many acted in support capacities. It would have been unthinkable for a free Roman to be bested by a soulless slave, and so the possibility was not allowed. On the following day the Roman's favorite events took place, the horse races and the chariot races. Nothing compared in fervor to these. The mixture of power, speed, and impending calamity exerted a powerful emotive force and held a metaphysical fascination for the spectators. Fate, skill, luck, and the favor of the gods all came into play.

The first day of the games had been given over to throwing, jumping, and climbing contests, and like the second day's running, wrestling, and boxing events held their own peculiar attraction and excitement. Nearly everyone had a friend or family member among the contestants, and a tremendous amount of emotional betting took place. As they found seats, or spread togas on the ground the spectators speculated about each keenly anticipated event, comparing match-ups, discussing the strengths and weaknesses of the various slingers, javelin throwers or rope climbers.

Titus led the Tempanius contingent to seats midway up the tiers nearest the temple of Mercury. Besides Duellia, Drusilla, and young Marcus, the group included Petronius and his grandson Primus, Didius and his two sons Sextus and Quintus, accompanied by his wife. Cnaeus Considius and Titinius also joined with their gaggle of family and friends so that the group comprised some twenty or thirty people situated in various aspects of togetherness. Restius and Graptus served their masters down on the field of play.

As one of the rare venues where men and women gathered together in public, Titus carefully surrounded the women in his charge with the men of the household. He would brook no strange man's thighs coming in contact with those of his wife or mother regardless of innocent intent or the accident of proximity. He took seriously his responsibility to minimize the risks of immoral behavior in such promiscuous surroundings.

As they settled in the conversation quickly flowed around the subjects of Antonius' races (he had entered two) and Lucius' wrestling matches. They spoke around the shifting bodies of spectators moving in and out, precariously suspending baskets of food, or pitchers of wine as they spied an open spot and raced to claim it. Around them arguments broke out contending the antecedence of one group over the other in reaching a spot to sit. Bets were laid on the spot as talk of the attributes of one or another competitor turned to challenges of faith and confidence.

"Have you put any bronze on Lucius?" asked Petronius in his plangent voice. His bald head, round as the leather ball used to play harpastum, glistened like polished wood in the bright sunshine.

Didius, his thin face seeming to have sagged farther to the left with age, spoke out of that side of his mouth. "I expect he'll win easily," he mumbled.

"I never pay bronze for expectations," said Titus.

Drusilla nodded her head in agreement. "A wise policy," she declared. "Betting is a poor way to improve your circumstances."

"No worse than work," claimed Sextus Crispus, from his seat in front of them. His bruited observation drew ironic laughter from others who overheard. Thus emboldened, he added. "In fact, a smart man might improve his circumstances quite a bit."

"I take it you've made a bet, then," said Petronius.

A mad scramble for an open space just below them distracted their attention momentarily.

"Yes," said Sextus, as the altercation subsided. He twisted around to look at them. "I made a couple of them."

"On who?" asked Quintus, leaning over to look down the row at his brother.

"On Antonius, and Lucius Siccius," Sextus proclaimed strongly, as if expecting opposition. He judged well.

"You bet against Lucius?" said Quintus. "He's never lost yet."

"First," said Quintus, tolling off his fingers, "there's got to be a first time. Second, it's hard to lose when you don't enter; Lucius hasn't wrestled in two years. Third, Lucius Siccius is unbeatable." He didn't add that he'd also bought a spell against Lucius Tempanius.

"He's also seven years younger," warned Petronius.

"Another reason he'll win," shot Sextus. "More stamina."

Duellia nudge her husband. Aren't you even going to defend your brother?" she teased.

Titus pushed his lower lip out ambivalently. "Lucius can defend himself," he said. "Besides, Sextus might be on to something. Lucius Siccius has already earned himself quite a reputation as a soldier. He's not far behind our Lucius in awards, and he's only served three years."

"Quite impressive," said Drusilla. "Does his family have any daughters?"

Quintus, watching the athletes warming up on the green meadow below, remained interested in his brother's betting. "But you bet on Antonius," he stated.

"Of course," answered Sextus. "But only in one race."

"Oh?" queried Didius. He regarded his son with shimmering evergreen eyes, the drooping corner of his mouth hauled upward in a half smile. Of the six children his wife had borne, his two surviving sons, named for the order of their birth, were the joy of Didius' life. Despite the contrast in their natures, he favored neither, nor displayed more pride or disapprobation for one over the other. Instead, he accepted each son in his own right, and made few demands on their behavior other than an insistence on honesty.

Petronius found his lifelong friend's attitude strange given his solemn, one might even say penurious, character. Traits mirrored with some exactitude by Quintus.

"Why only one?" asked Petronius helpfully.

"Simple," said Sextus, flashing his bright mischievous smile. "There's nobody faster, so I'm sure he'll win the sprint. But I don't believe he has the stamina to win the longer race."

"Well," said Petronius, "I love Antonius like my own son, but I don't believe he can win either race."

"Why not?" demanded Titus. "Sextus is right. I've never seen anyone run as fast as Antonius."

"His feet are too small," insisted Petronius, thrusting out his pointed nose and small chin.

Didius exploded with laughter. "By winged Mercury, you must be joking. What possible difference could the size of his feet make?"

"It's obvious," said Petronius. "He has no base. His head will carry him over his feet and he'll lose his balance."

Derisive laughter greeted his words but Sextus quieted them. "No," he said thoughtfully. "If he was wrestling or boxing, I'd agree. But those small feet are exactly what make him so fast. There's less for him to pick up and move."

"Exactly," agreed Titus emphatically, though he wasn't too sure about the whole foot size theory in either case.

"So," pressed Quintus, "what about the distance race?"

A trumpet sounded, interrupting the discussion briefly as they watched the competitors leave the field for the west end of the Circus where the stables and dressing rooms were.

Sextus continued. "Well, Antonius was always sickly as a child, so I don't think his heart and lungs are developed enough to sustain him over a long distance."

"Now that you've broken my son into little pieces," said Drusilla tartly, as a second trumpet blew, "let's see how he fares."

Marked out by two swords shoved into the ground ten runners toed the starting line on the west end staring at the finish line two hundred yards distant, identified in the same manner. Some wore only a loincloth, others tunics girded up high on their thighs, and one arm free so that the tunic crossed the chest at an angle. Three officials watched over the race, one at the starting line to ensure a fair start, one at the finish line to judge the winner, and the starter with a trumpeter in the middle near the little stream that separated the two halves of the Circus.

Antonius crouched at the starting line facing the finish squarely, intently watching the starter. He shook his hands nervously, displeased with his position in the middle of the pack. Though direct interference was not allowed, the absence of lanes made jostling and surreptitious clutching commonplace. If a runner went down from 'incidental' contact, who could complain? Sandwiching him stood two taller men clad in loincloths. One turned almost parallel to the starting line, the other facing forward but upright. They eyed him warily. Antonius felt he had to jump away from them quickly to avoid getting manhandled. He tried to shut out all sounds, though the runners exchanged few comments anyway, and glued his eyes to the starter. When he saw him begin to turn his head towards the trumpeter Antonius tensed and took two or three deep breaths.

BRAHH... The horn split the air.

Antonius leaped out, gained free air space and looked left and right. Two runners, those on the ends, led him by small margins. They looked at nearly the same time, saw him and each other, and pressed forward. He pumped his arms, keeping close but letting them fight for the lead. As they reached the halfway point the three runners had inadvertently converged—a mistake on the part of the two outside runners, in essence lengthening the distance they would travel. Antonius felt good, strong, his breathing regular and free, his legs stretching comfortably. Confidence surged through him, and he increased his speed, pushing the leaders. They responded, and widened the interval. The ground flashed beneath their thudding feet.

A single continuous roar went up from the crowd as they jumped as one to their feet, screaming exhortations to their favorites. The Tempanius clan immediately began chanting, " 'Tonius, 'Tonius, 'Tonius," with wild abandon, jumping up and down, and pumping fists in the air. As the runners reached the halfway point the voices in the crowd changed as some cursed or wailed as their favorite fell behind, while those rooting for one of the three leaders screamed encouragement, made sacred vows, or cast the evil eye on their chosen one's challengers.

With fifty yards left Antonius asked his legs for more speed. They gave it willingly. The ground passed beneath him like a stream, rising to his feet as if propelling him along. He came abreast of the two runners, his eyes fixed on the finish. Now, he thought, now I'll run them into the ground. The two runners converged on him as if to bump him. Out of the corner of his eye he saw it, and reached down for more speed. His feet hammered the ground, his heart thudded against his chest, and his lungs burned at every intake of breath. He heard nothing but his thundering heart and pounding feet.

From the stands a gasp, a cry, a rolling wave of sound crashed from twenty thousand throats.

"They're squeezing him!" shouted Titus furiously, pounding his fist against his thigh.

"Go, go, go."

" 'Tonius, 'Tonius, 'Tonius," hoarse voices around him bawled.

Shoulders brushed him. Antonius stuck his elbows out, flinging them protectively as he ran, reaching for one more step, one clear space, one more burst. Suddenly he swept past. A strange gasping, intake of vast wind came to his ears but he focused his eyes on the finish crossing it with his hands exultantly in the air. He turned around, bent over and put his hands on his knees, gulping air in huge gasps. Raising his eyes he saw his two competitors in a heap on the ground, and two others from far behind finishing second and third.

The judges crowned Antonius with a wreath of olive leaves and presented him with a new dagger. A worthy prize. Up in the stands his family and friends exulted with him, and clapped Sextus on the back as an astute observer of talent. At least for that race.

As it turned out, his analysis of the second race proved accurate as well. Antonius, spent from the first race, finished far off the pace in the second.

The final two events, and by far the favorites of the day, were the wrestlers and boxers. No Tempanius had yet been fool enough to enter the boxing competition, though Lucius once considered it. But one look at the thick oxhide gauntlets, stiffened with brutal strips of metal, with which the boxers covered their hands sufficed to convince him otherwise. He could plainly see that his goal to become a famous Roman soldier might easily be imperiled by one good blow. But in years when a worthwhile prize had been announced for the winner, he tried his skill at wrestling. It paid him well. This year the prize was to be a young bull ox—a worthwhile prize indeed.

Titus soon saw that the wrestling Lucius had done with Graptus had actually served him well. Match-ups were not based on weight, age, or skill classifications. Rather, the interest for the Romans lay in contrasting pairs; pitting brute strength against speed, agility against size. They had no interest in so-called equal antagonists unless they should be the last two remaining. Each of these would have to win three matches to earn a berth in the final.

Lucius performed well. One tall, gangly opponent made it seem as if Lucius were wrestling a snake. Twisting, turning, seeming to wrap himself around Lucius, he at last succumbed when Lucius got hold of a leg and drove him head first into the ground. The second, barely larger than Quintus, fought with the speed of a fox, with tremendous balance and leverage, but Lucius simply overpowered him. The third opponent, closest to Lucius' size, took the quickest fall. He attempted to use brute force instead of technique, and Lucius turned this quickly against him and pinned him.

Lucius Siccius fared no less well. Strong, agile, and smart he made short work of his three opponents. The stage was set for Sextus' big moment. He threw his hex, with some embarrassment, onto the field.

Two more evenly matched antagonists would have been hard to find. Lucius stood five feet six inches tall and weighed one hundred and eighty pounds. At twenty-seven years old he had the advantage of experience. Siccius carried the same weight on a frame two inches taller than Lucius. His advantage lay in the vigor of youth, and a longer reach. Each man had supreme confidence in his ability.

The match started with both men circling, gauging, looking for an opening. Slapping away the other's dust powdered hands, or twisting oiled bodies quickly out of an attempted grip, they soon wore a circle of crushed grass beneath their bare feet.

In the stands spectators mumbled, a sound like hard rain on terracotta tiles, waiting for something to happen, ready to roar, as if their voices caught in the uncertainty of the wrestlers themselves.

Weaving, ducking, lunging, retreating, the two combatants continued their circling search for an opening. Suddenly they crashed together, butting heads, staring eye to eye, each with a hand on the back of the other's neck, the left arms doing a strange twisting dance looking for a hold. Incessantly shifting grips, over, under, searching by feel for a leverage advantage, shuffling quickly left, right, forward, back, their feet in step like dancers, but wide apart for balance. Locked together they pushed and shoved at one another, grunting, muttering, sweating. Breathing in quick gasps of effort, or panting in tense postures of rest the wrestlers worked and strove against each other.

Lucius' hands grew slippery with oil and sweat despite the coat of dust. Siccius had quick feet to match his toughness. He attacked with explosive power and acceleration, and it took every ounce of strength to fend him off. He found the longer reach of his opponent difficult to overcome when he went on the attack. They clinched again. Siccius drove his right leg forward, stepping between Lucius' planted feet. In the same motion he brought his left leg around as he dropped to his right knee, and attempted to wrap his arms around Lucius' thighs. Lucius threw his legs back before Siccius could bring his left leg around, and brought his barrel chest down hard on Siccius' head, to drive him to the ground. At the same time he swung his right arm up under Siccius' left to keep it off him.

In this attitude they remained motionless for some moments. Lucius, legs splayed out, practically parallel to the ground, and Siccius in a half crouch beneath him. Still, neither seemed able to gain an advantage. Each man made small adjustments until they incrementally worked their way upright and into another clinch, breathing hard, sweating profusely. Blood streamed from a split ear down Lucius' neck onto his chest.

As they clinched ear to ear, resting against each other Lucius growled in admiration. "I'll almost be sorry to throw you," he said, panting.

Siccius chuckled in between gasps. "You won't have to worry."

With lightning quickness Siccius pulled his head back and smashed his forehead against the bridge of Lucius' nose. Stunned, Lucius staggered, and relaxed his grip. Siccius smashed a forearm into Lucius' jaw and he went down in blackness. He felt his legs buckle but could do nothing to stop them. A suffocating weight fell on him and in the blackness he lay again on the Janiculum Hill, bodies piled on top of him, crushing the life from him.

"Get off me!" he raged. With a massive effort he arched his back and heaved the stacks of dead away from him.

Drusilla saw the blood gush in brilliant crimson from Lucius' nose as if someone had thrown it into his face. She gasped and covered her mouth in horror as his head snapped back from a forearm blow to the chin, and he crumpled to the ground. Wild clamoring swelled, reverberated off the hills, and crashed horrifically against her ears. Nearby Valeria screamed, "Get up! Get up!" Ejulation and exultation collided in a tidal wave of sound.

Lucius levered himself to his knees, chest heaving, fingers flexing automatically. Through a red mist he saw his adversary rolling away from him just feet away. Tossing his great head like a wounded bear he roared in answer to the crowd, and lunged for his prey. His shoulder caught Siccius in the middle of the chest just as he gathered his feet under him and smashed him to the ground. The back of his head hit the earth hard with a dull thud, and then Lucius landed on top of him. Siccius did not put up a struggle. He was out cold. So was Lucius.

+ + +

A flood of warm liquid gushed over his face and down his chest. He shot his arm upward to pull for the surface.

"It's all right, it's all right," said a soothing female voice. "It's just me."

Lucius squinted to see who 'just me' might be. He seemed unable to open his eyes completely. Again, the warm rush of liquid flowed over his face and down his chest. This time his vision cleared enough to see Valeria soaking a rag in a large clay bowl. Somehow, she looked different, he thought, but his brain was fuzzy, as if his head were stuffed with wool. He chuckled, raising himself to a sitting position on the kitchen table. Valeria had accused him of just that a hundred times over the years.

"What's so funny?" she asked, turning towards him with a dripping rag. She bent very close to swab his split ear and one breast gave against his shoulder. The realization that she had them struck Lucius like a thunderbolt. He had never ceased to see her as the child of eleven that she had been when he first moved to the Boar's Tusk.

"Where are we?" he asked.

"At home," said Valeria, wiping his cheek, like a wall held up by the cornerstone of his chin, free of dried blood.

Home, thought Lucius. It came so naturally. He thought he might protest her ministrations as the fog cleared, but gave up the idea knowing she wouldn't obey. And discovering he rather enjoyed the attention, anyway.

"How did I get here?" he asked, looking around the kitchen.

"They carried you," she said, reproachfully.

"Sorry to disappoint you." He shifted slightly on the table to get a better view of her.

Valeria stared at him, her hands in the warm blood-reddened water. "You didn't disappoint me," she said. "You scared me." The man was not only blind, she decided, he couldn't hear either.

"Who won?" he asked, as she doused his face once more.

"What does it matter?" she said. With every wipe the cloth came away bloody. His ear was split, his broken nose squashed over to one side, though Graptus had attempted to straighten it while he lay unconscious on the table. A cut over one eyebrow was so deep she thought she could see the bone, and his eyes were swelling and blacking more with every passing moment. And all he could think about was who won.

Lucius grinned. His head hurt, his face hurt, his neck hurt, and he felt sure many more parts of his body would hurt tomorrow. But now he was in the tender hands of someone he'd never seen before. "It matters," he said, "because I didn't go through all this," he pointed at his macerated face, "just for fun."

"What did you do it for?"

"A bull ox to stock our farm."

When she heard the word 'our' her heart nearly broke for joy and fear. Did he mean her, or was it just a casual use of the word? "You've got your ox," was all she trusted herself to say.

Lucius regarded Valeria through swelling eyes that were nonetheless new. There had to be something, some imperfection, he thought. It wasn't her hair, loosed and fallen in thick black ringlets, framing her face like a luxurious mane. Could it be her forehead, narrower than the bronze bracelet he wore on his right wrist, or the dark eyebrows that sloped slightly downward at the corners of her eyes? No, these attributes imparted a girlish innocence to her looks. She was, after all, only fifteen. Maybe it was her eyes, the color and suppleness of alder. Were they too large? No, they didn't dominate her face, nor pinch together. Instead, they were like two shimmering jewels perfectly set in an amulet.

"Where is everyone else?" he asked.

"They stayed to watch the boxing," she said, wrinkling her pert nose distastefully. "Apparently your blood wasn't enough for them."

Perhaps it was her nose. Too small? She had a thin delicate one, like an Etruscan statue, that divided the planes of her face as the sky is divided at sunrise between the setting moon and the rising sun. It reminded him just a little of the hill upon which he'd been born, standing above the plain like a noble crest.

Well then, it must be the mouth; too large? Too small? He had never seen such perfect teeth. Maybe her lips were too thin…no, that wasn't it. Her round chin and finely defined jaw weren't bottom heavy, or sharp like a scythe. He noticed the supple swelling of her body beneath her stola as she bent and stretched while caring for his wounds. No, he determined, there were no flaws worth mentioning. Her ineffable beauty stunned him, and he decided in that moment he must capture it for himself.

The idea surprised him. No woman had even infatuated him in the past. Suddenly he found himself in love with one. But though the idea surprised him he did not linger over it or analyze it. It appeared simply as a fact that he not only accepted at face value, but acted upon at the earliest opportunity. That very night, with purple swollen eyes and pounding headache he approached Cominus with the idea of marriage. Cominus delightedly agreed.

Ten days later, after the swelling around his eyes had gone down, they were married. His eyelids and the skin beneath his eyes still retained a deep vermilion color, and the whites glowed bright red in the corners. But his vision and his purpose were clear. Lucius chose the first day of the new week as propitious for a new beginning. It also carried the auspicious C of comitialis on the calendar. Cominus laid down a feast that any patrician would have been proud of. Aulus Vibulus presented Valeria with an ornate silver bracelet, while Quintus, Sextus, and Titinius together bought two Etruscan goblets with pornographic pictures depicting a joyful variety of sexual positions. Gaius Opimius also gave a present of fine tableware, though with more traditional subjects glazed on the black surfaces. From Titus, ever the farmer, they received a yearling sow and boar—which made Quintus extremely happy. The celebration lasted long into the night before Lucius carried Valeria across the threshold of his domus just across the hall from where she was born.

They put the goblets to good use.

# XXI

## August 23, 470 BC
## The Vulcanalia—Festival of Fires

Titus Tempanius built an altar of stone to Mars, as he had vowed, in the shade of a small grove of maritime pines on the south side of the farmhouse. Upon it he poured a libation of wine, offered cakes of spelt, and slaughtered a spotless goat submitting the entrails to the fire. Invoking the name of Father Mars, he asked the god to honor and accept the fulfillment of his vow, and sought protection for himself, his family, and his household; he requested protection for his grain and his vines, for his goats and their keeper, the oxen, the pigs, and even the chickens. He mentioned every item and aspect of his life specifically so that Mars would not forget or overlook anything. These rites he performed in the spring, and when he had accomplished them, he marched off to war with the consul Valerius. He hoped with better results than the previous season. In this, disappointment continued to hound him. Repulsed in an attack on the Aequians, Valerius loosed his soldiers to loot and plunder, but garnered little of value. Fortunately, happier events at home relieved some of his distress. The end of the campaign season revealed Duellia some months along in the happy state of pregnancy.

Antonius, taking the military oath for the first time, suffered the same fate against the Sabines. In his mind the fault lay wholly in the incompetent hands of the consul Aemilius. A sentiment echoed by many and at the core of much civil discontent.

Yet in some respects Rome's luck held. Her Latin and Hernican allies kept the rampaging Volscians at bay in the south. In the north the Etruscans stayed busy recuperating from their disastrous naval defeat of a few years earlier, while Veii thankfully honored her treaty with Rome. Rome aggressively pursued diplomatic goals with the Etruscan cities of Caere, Tarquinii, and Falerii, and these successes paid handsome dividends both in the short term and the long. In the short term they met two goals: to keep the Etruscan city-states out of alliance with her enemies, and to augment the economy with trade goods from Etruria. In the long term she kept the city-states of Etruria divided in their loyalties. There would be no comparable military success for many years.

The economy, such as it was in those rustic days, continued to shrink as Rome defended herself from foreign enemies. She fought alone or in league with her allies; but always she fought. Though only a marginal group of radicalized citizens longed for the days of the kings, many longed for the prosperity and prestige of Roman arms in those days of their grandfathers when the 'empire' of Tarquinius Superbus extended from the Tiber to Terracina, sixty miles south of Rome. At just under forty years of age, the Republic had fewer years than a good many of its citizens. These elderly reminders of days that had not yet achieved the low status of legend insured that their juniors should remember both the accomplishments and the tyrannies of Tarquin. By their presence alone they acted as goad and spur.

Little wonder that now, with a tenuous hold over merely half that territory, the citizens were in conflict. Accusations flew. The plebs accused the patricians of inept and oppressive leadership. The patricians countered with charges of seditious and ungrateful behavior. Wealthy non-patricians denounced the patricians for unfairly closing high office to them. Patricians indicted the wealthy for demagoguery. Foreigners visiting the city could only come away with two conclusions: Romans adored recriminating one another, and a republic so bitterly divided could not hope to stand for long. Their conclusions were half right.

Upon seeing his brother Lucius unexpectedly fall in love with Valeria, Titus admitted to but a single impossibility; that life in Rome could be boring. Only the most jaded inhabitants could have argued with him. The excitement stemmed not from wild or extravagant life-styles. On the contrary, the Romans on the whole lived in a conservative and austere fashion. Not that they didn't enjoy a good laugh and a cup of wine in the society of friends and relations. But they exhibited none of the licentiousness for which the Greeks held renown, nor the passion for banquets and gladiatorial entertainment that formed the essence of Etruscan society. Indeed, it would have come as no surprise if someone had told Titus that two centuries later Cineas, ambassador of the Greek general Pyrrhus, would mock the sour wine from the Alban Hills. In all probability he would have laughed and noted that the drinkers of sweet wine were suing for peace with those for whom sour wine served well enough.

Political turmoil generated excitement in Rome, and in this season the fomenters were two tribunes. Marcus Duellius, father-in-law of Titus, and Cnaeus Siccius, father of Lucius Siccius, brought charges against Appius Claudius for improper use of public lands, the ager publicus. While the accusation certainly had credence, no one could deny that revenge for the brutal manner with which Claudius had treated his legion motivated his detractors.

Thus, like the facets of a finely cut gemstone, the impending trial of Appius Claudius attracted the attention of the populace from many angles. Titus, with little competition for the ager publicus around his lonely hilltop on the frontier, took particular interest because he served in that ineffably humiliated legion. The poor, whose very lives and liberty depended on access to the public domain, looked on to see if their interests would be pursued.

Since his marriage to Valeria, Lucius Tempanius had acted in a perfectly contrary manner to Roman sensibilities. His friends could neither find him out carousing, nor entice him to go out. Not because such behavior signified moral weakness, but because he doted on his wife. They called him uxorious. They called him effeminate. They castigated him for enslavement to certain female body parts. He laughed with typical good nature as he tended to business in the tavern. Every morning the calendar allowed it he accompanied Publius Scipio in the Forum. And when Valeria announced she was pregnant, for the first time since his seventeenth birthday he declined to serve in the legions. His friends saw this as a sure sign of his moral decay. They predicted a wasting illness.

Lucius laughed them to scorn. His duty appeared clearly before his eyes, and he performed it. Simple as that. Since Cominus no longer required him to pay rent, and through Valeria he would inherit the tavern, he deemed it necessary to learn the business. Though not the most esteemed profession, he found it a profitable one. He took but passing interest in politics or the charges leveled against Appius Claudius, until Quintus arrived in Rome angry as a swarm of bees.

In the dog days of summer Rome lay with canine lethargy, prostrate, tongue lolling, panting from the heat. The wealthy fled to their country estates to escape the fetid air of the city unless public business compelled them to remain. Even the swallows took wing and deserted the city. Poverty held the rest of her citizens captive. For Lucius, the oppressive heat, intensified by thick humidity, was less bothersome than the rank deliquescent stench of human waste, and the accompanying clouds of black flies. Worst of all were the swarms of mosquitoes that signaled the beginning of the fever season. He worried inordinately about Valeria's health, and built flower boxes for each window, planting geraniums to repel the mosquitoes, and basil to keep out the flies. In the cooler confines of the kitchen where they spent most of their time he constantly drew plans for expanding the farmhouse.

"But how could we afford it?" asked Valeria. Slowly cutting slices from a yellow apple she chewed disinterestedly. She had a craving for cherries, which she could not satisfy now they were out of season.

Lucius turned his wide face expectantly on his father-in-law. "The first thing," he said, "is to return one of my rooms. We don't need all that space, and the rent would buy a lot of nails and tiles."

"That would certainly help," said Cominus. He pointed at Valeria's swollen belly. "Although living conditions might become a little tight. And what about Graptus?"

"We could put the baby in Valeria's old room," said Lucius. "And Graptus could sleep down here."

Valeria picked up a feather fan, waving it rapidly in front of her face. "Sweet Juno," she said, "it feels like I have a lighted brazier inside me."

A vehement knock on the front door roused Lucius from his seat. "I'll get it."

Grumbling at the intrusion he opened the door to find Quintus shuffling from foot to foot impatiently in front of the door. "Quintus," Lucius said in surprise, "what are you doing here?"

"We have a problem," Quintus said. He pushed passed Lucius without waiting for an invitation and seated himself at the nearest table. Worry lines in his thin face, flushed with exertion, drew his small mouth solemnly downward. Sweat beaded on his high forehead, and ran into the long-distance stare of lichen green eyes. "Do you have any water?"

"Of course." Lucius hurried to the kitchen and came back with a pitcher of water and a cup. He filled the cup and set the pitcher on the table near Quintus. "Now," he said, as Quintus drained the cup and poured himself another, "what's our problem?"

"Spurius Minucius," spat Quintus. He rose angrily, his body like a nail—thin, rigid, tough as iron. "He's trying to drive me off the ager publicus.

"How do you know it's him?" asked Lucius.

"I know."

Lucius pulled at the front of his tunic. "That's not enough," he said. In a cold, flat, matter-of-fact voice he said, "We'll find out for sure." Rising purposefully to his feet he strode to the stairs and called loudly to Graptus.

"What's Sextus doing?" Lucius asked when they'd all gathered around the kitchen table.

"I don't know," said Quintus. "I came straight here."

"What's the matter?" asked Valeria. She scanned Lucius' face worriedly for clues.

"Nothing serious," Lucius reassured her. "I just have to go out to the farm for a few days."

"You might get away with lying to your mother, Lucius," Valeria shot. "But not to me."

Lucius cast an impatient look at his wife then burst out laughing. A plump stranger's face stared back at him, red with indignation. Dark smoldering eyes scolded him, and firm compressed lips brooked no further attempts at subterfuge.

Cominus smiled. "I suppose I should have warned you," he apologized.

"It's nothing," Lucius said, flashing his paving stone teeth in a placating smile. "Just some trouble with neighbors. But it's my land so I have to settle any differences, don't I."

Valeria wanted to protest but gave it up. She knew Lucius too well, knew the stubbornness that locked him up. Never had she been more firmly instructed in his unshakable resolve than on her wedding night when she saw his naked chest up close for the first time. The wide expanse and the rippling musculature came as no surprise; one could imagine them even when he wore a toga. What took her by surprise were the scars. There must have been a dozen of them scattered about his chest and belly like leeches attached to his skin. Only then did she fully comprehend his reputation for obstinate bravery.

Lifting her chin proudly she declared, "I will soon be a Roman matron, and the wife of a centurion. You needn't lie to me."

Lucius gazed at her proudly. "What do you think, Graptus? If we had more soldiers like her all your Aequian brethren would have surrendered by now, eh?"

Graptus stuck his lower lip out in acknowledgment, and nodded his head. "Unfortunately," he said, "empires are won by the sword, and not by beauty."

"Don't be forward," admonished Lucius. "All right. Quintus, go see if Sextus is available. Are you staying in the city?"

"No," said Quintus. "Latinia is all alone so I'm going back immediately."

339

"That's a long walk," said Cominus. "Why don't you stay the night?"

"I just said why."

"I think that was an offer, not a question," said Graptus.

"It doesn't matter what it was. I'm going home tonight." Quintus turned to Lucius. "But first I'll stop by the house and see if Sextus is there."

"Good, we'll be there tomorrow." Lucius turned to Graptus. "Go see if you can find Titinius. I'd like him along also."

"How about Considius?" asked Graptus.

"No, he'd be no help. We'll see you tomorrow, Quintus."

They shook hands and Quintus sped off.

Titinius proved unable to join them so Lucius and Graptus set out alone at daybreak using Cominus' two-wheeled cart and donkey. They arrived under a sweltering sun at midday. Quintus and Sextus greeted them in the yard as they drove up. In the doorway of the two-room house stood Latinia, a worried expression on her almond shaped face. A large shaggy black dog barked laconically at her side.

Upon seeing her Lucius once again considered he had done Quintus a favor. Her lithe figure brought pleasure to the eye even in a loose stola. She patted at her ink black hair, loose coils of which escaped the knot on top of her head, wreathing her swarthy face.

"Good morning, Domina," Lucius said with a smile as he hopped down from the cart. "How is everything?" He threw the reins to Graptus.

"Very well, thank you," said Latinia. "And Valeria?" she moved to one side to let the men in.

"The midwife says she's due any day," said Lucius.

"I've set out a few things," said Latinia, her voice melodious as a dove cooing. "If you're hungry."

On a rough wooden table a clay bowl of hardboiled eggs, a platter of wheat cakes, and another bowl piled with apples were placed in readiness. A large pitcher of fresh cool water perspired in the middle leaving a damp ring darkening the table.

"Shall we wait for your slave?" asked Latinia as Lucius, Quintus, and Sextus sat on low backed chairs. "Or does he eat...elsewhere?"

"Oh, usually the impertinent devil eats with us. But we can start without him."

Litinia picked up a bowl of eggs, the traditional first course, and served each of the men, then selected one for herself. A short time after feeding and watering the mule Graptus drifted in.

"So, Lucius," Latinia said after a short silence, "If Valeria is due any day what are you doing here?" Her mellifluous voice somehow managed to chastise and soothe him at the same time.

Lucius bit into a wheat cake sweetened with honey and flavored with rosemary. Ground by hand with a mortar and pestle the wheat cake's coarse consistency required assiduous mastication. This gave Lucius time to gain control of his emotions, because he suddenly felt a terrible longing for Valeria.

"Unfortunately," he said, washing the last bits down with water, "my first duty is to my property, and my dependents. It would be selfish and irresponsible to leave you and Quintus at the mercy of a gang of thugs."

"That's nice of you to say," said Latinia, bowing her head slightly.

Lucius looked around the table at the glum faces of Quintus and Sextus, who had said virtually nothing since his arrival. "Besides," he said, "Valeria's sick of the heat in Rome, and told me to look into building an addition here."

A small cry came from the other room. "Well," said Latinia, "it's someone else's feeding time. If you'll excuse me."

Lying on the floor near him the dog licked Lucius' foot. He reached down and patted its side. "Very well," he said, "tell me what's happening."

Quintus swung his hooked nose from his plate to Lucius. "They threatened me again yesterday," he said. His green eyes brightened with anger. "They said they wouldn't be 'responsible' if I tried to harvest my wheat."

"How many were there?"

"Four," said Sextus. "But they had second thoughts when they saw Quintus and I with staves."

"Were they mounted or on foot?" The dog rolled onto its back and Lucius scratched her belly. She stared up at him with dark love-shy eyes.

"Mounted," said Sextus, flashing his infectious grin. "Otherwise, they wouldn't have gotten away."

Lucius reflected for a moment. "How were they armed?" he said at last.

"Lightly," said Quintus. "Just knives. They'd never seen anyone but me before. I think we surprised them."

"They'll come stronger next time," asserted Graptus.

"Yes," agreed Lucius, "and there'll be more of us, too."

"Maybe we shouldn't let them know that and prepare a little surprise," said Graptus. He smiled the simple inviting smile of the wicked.

Lucius laughed. "Finally, I've got an Aequian on my side."

The next morning after a light breakfast they crossed the road, and entered the wheat field through a gap in a hedge of broom, which no longer boasted the brilliant yellow flowers that scented the air in spring and early summer. Following a narrow dirt track that ended where the wheat field did, the four men divided according to plan.

Quintus and Sextus, tunics girded high up their legs and angled across their chests, wide-brimmed straw hats crushed on their heads, set down baskets which held scythes, twine made of broom, and water jugs. With staves lying close by they set to work reaping the field. Lucius and Graptus hid in the dense undergrowth from which Quintus had hacked and reclaimed the wheat field.

Graptus cursed himself for his bright ideas the instant he set foot on the uncultivated land. Spike-bearing weeds and long thorny vines whipped at his bare legs, tripped his feet, and snagged his tunic. The aptly named broom swept across his face and chest, but gave way easily to his efforts. Nettles left hot itching spots on his skin where the weed's insidious little needles stuck him. Scratching at the persistent itches he waited in a copse of beech trees.

The conflict over the little piece of property baffled him. He had walked the length and breadth of it in a few paces, estimating not three iugera comprised the entire field. Which made sense inasmuch as Quintus worked the land alone most of the time. Considering the savage nature of the land around the isolated wheat field Graptus wondered why anyone should care about or contest this small outpost of domestication. He took a swig of water from a bronze canteen and prepared to wait.

Sextus and Quintus worked well and hard. With smooth rhythmic strokes the curved scythes arced through the air, severed the stalks of wheat, and drew back for more. They cut until their backs ached from stooping, then gathered the golden stalks and tied them into bundles.

Graptus grew drowsy. The sun climbed higher, its heat penetrating even the shade where he hid. He began to hope that nothing would happen. Of course, that was a sure sign that something would.

Moments later the ground rumbled with the pounding of hooves. Four horsemen rode at the gallop straight at Quintus and Sextus brandishing flaming torches. They made a dash for their staves but were driven off by the horsemen who threw their torches into the wheat field. Like a lover waiting for her beloved the wheat burst into flame. Smoke roiled angrily into the air as Lucius and Graptus, extricating themselves from the tangled underbrush, came at the horsemen from behind, yelling their war cry.

Sextus charged and swung his scythe at the nearest horseman, at the same time reaching for the reins with his left hand. The rider sawed at the reins but the horse spooked, reared, lashed out with its hooves and struck Sextus on the side of the head. He went down in a heap and curled into a fetal position with blood streaming from his ear and a gash in his head. Quintus ran to his brother, abandoning the battle.

Lucius and Graptus yelled, assaulting the horsemen with swinging staves. The riders wheeled their mounts and bore down on the two men rushing at them on foot. Graptus raised his staff in both hands to bar the way of one of the riders but the horse veered willingly and left him staring at a wall of flames consuming the wheat field. Lucius ran straight at one of the riders as if he would collide with the horse. At the last moment he stepped aside. He took a mighty swing with his stave and unseated the horseman. Instantly he fell on the stunned assailant. The other three rode away unharmed.

Lucius hauled the man up by his tunic and screamed furiously into his face. "Who are you? Who are you working for?" He shook the dazed man violently, and threatened him with the very fire he helped set.

"Graptus!" shouted Quintus. "Graptus! Come and help." He knelt by Sextus who still lay curled in a fetal position, his legs drawn tight to his chest, his eyes clenched shut, and his breathing coming in shallow gasps. Behind them flames leaped into the black smoke as it joyously consumed the unharvested wheat and began to spread into the underbrush.

Graptus ran over, examined Sextus quickly then picked up his legs as Quintus grabbed his brother's arms. He was not particularly heavy but they were forced to avoid the flames of the burning field and more than once were forced off the path.

Lucius interrogated his prisoner, forcing information out of him with a few well-delivered blows and hard twists, then sent him back where he came from shamefully naked as the day he was born.

Sextus lingered three days without regaining consciousness. Quintus finally laid him on the ground so he could be in contact with mother earth and caught his last breath in his hands. In the field where he had fallen, they raised a funeral pyre and cremated his brave remains. As Lucius eulogized him an ironic thought surfaced in his brain. This wasn't exactly the intention of celebrating the Volcanalia.

Lucius wasted no time. As soon as he could arrange an audience, he went to see Publius Scipio. Graptus waited outside as a doorman ushered Lucius into the mansion situated behind the shops on the south side of the Forum between the Vicus Tuscus and the Vicus Iugarius. He gazed with awe at the interior. Even the vestibule, where he waited a few moments while the doorman announced him, advertised luxury. Padded seats accommodated weary guests. Plaster walls with colorful frescoes delighted the eye and inspired the spirit. Along both sides of the atrium life-sized terracotta statues of the gods were ranked in stately poses. Potted plants caught the sunlight from the compluvium—the open rectangular space in the roof that allowed in both sunlight and rain. An ornately carved stone basin caught the water. Private rooms lined one side of the atrium, while the other opened onto a private garden.

The tablinum, where Publius Scipio waited in a carved wood chair on a raised dais, was even more ornate. Twenty feet wide, and thirty feet long, all four walls were decorated with frescoes of heroic battles or events that formed the gaudy history of the Scipio clan. Next to Scipio sat his son, very much the likeness of his father, small mouth, bulbous head, short neck, and strong prominent nose. He had a solid build, though not to Lucius' proportions, and sat relaxed and upright, his hands resting easily on his thighs.

Scipio senior rose from his seat as soon as Lucius entered the room and greeted him warmly. The sign of respect heartened Lucius.

"Well met, Lucius," he said, pumping Lucius' hand. "Have you met my son?" They shook hands as Scipio senior introduced them. To his son he said, "Look at him," indicating

Lucius with his hand, "what a specimen." He shook his bald head in genuine awe and admiration at Lucius' physique.

The younger Scipio smiled casually. "Yes," he said. "It's fortunate we have him on our side."

"I dare say we could use a few more like him," said Scipio the elder. "Please sit down, Lucius." He indicated a chair in front of the dais.

"Thank you," said Lucius. Arranging his toga he sat and crossed his legs.

"And how is your wife? I hear she's to have your first child."

"Yes," said Lucius, flustered by the barrage of questions. "She's well, thank you."

"And Titus?"

"Titus is serving with Lucius Valerius. I hope he's well," he hesitated before finishing, "though the news from the army hasn't been the best."

"No," said Scipio thoughtfully. Scipio the younger started to say something but a slight raise of a finger dammed the words. "And your other brother, Antonius. I've never seen anyone run so fast. How is he?"

Lucius grinned. For a man pushing seventy he had a wonderful memory. "Antonius is getting his first taste of life as a legionary," he said. "He always has an opinion, so I'm looking forward to his return."

The Scipios laughed along with Lucius. "But you didn't serve this year. Why not?" The tone of Scipio's voice carried no condemnation. Yet something deeper than curiosity seeped into the words.

Lucius chuckled to himself. People always tried to ascribe deeper motives to his behavior than he could ever dream up himself. "That's simple," he said, "Valeria's going to have a baby, and I want to be there when my first son is born."

Scipio Sr. snickered. "You're confident it's going to be a boy, are you?"

Lucius drew himself up proudly. "The Tempanii have a long history of producing male children. Especially the firstborn. I expect I'll continue the tradition."

"Well," said Scipio, "it's always best to keep up our traditions." He smiled broadly—an oxymoron for the Scipio mouth. "Now tell me; how can I be of service to you?"

"My factor is having problems with a neighbor," Lucius began. He went on to fill Scipio in on the details of the harassment of Quintus and the death of Sextus. His voice rose steadily in volume and vehemence as he told the story. "I haven't fought the enemies of Rome for the last ten years just to be burned out by a fellow Roman," he finished.

"I see," said Publius Scipio. He patted his knee in rhythm to the thoughts drumming inside his large cranium.

"If I may comment, Father," said Scipio the younger, without waiting for permission. "The Minucii are a rather important family."

Scipio the elder murmured his agreement but said nothing further, keeping his own counsel for the moment.

Lucius decided to clarify his position. "I have come, Publius Scipio, in the hopes that you would convince Spurius Minucius that I have a right to use the ager publicus." He shrugged his broad shoulders indifferently. "If not, my family and friends are fully capable of defending that right—by whatever means."

An indulgent smile played across Scipio's thin lips. "As my son said, the Minucii are an important family in Rome. The matter is more delicate than you realize."

"I am no good at politics," said Lucius firmly. "But my father taught me right from wrong. I came to try and avoid bloodshed. On the other hand, I have no qualms about shedding it."

The Scipios looked at each other and burst out laughing. "Forgive us," said the elder. "I told my son we must avoid getting Lucius Tempanius' back up, and instead we've succeeded in doing just that."

"But you must see," said Scipio the younger, "that one does not easily make accusations and offend a family that boasts three consulships."

"I'm well aware of the family's history," prefaced Lucius. "I was born in the year Marcus Minucius held his first consulship, and the temple of Saturn was dedicated. If memory serves me, he and his brother Publius did nothing more notable in their other consulships than preside over a famine. Which seems about right, since now they're trying to starve me out." He flashed a mirthless, violent smile at the Scipios.

Publius Scipio Sr. chuckled and rubbed his eye with a knuckle. With the sagging jowls of old age and hairless scalp his head resembled a chunk of tufa worn into an uneven round shape. "I see your point," he said. "Still, as my son said, it's a little more complicated than that. With the present turmoil, and the fact they're a plebeian family…"

Lucius felt the conversation heading away from his objective so he boldly interrupted. "Forgive me, Publius, but this means nothing to me. First, the Minucii are no more plebeian than you are. This is why I dislike politics. We divide people into this camp or that camp. That way we can disregard what they say or do. I have come as a client to his patron to receive justice. It's as simple as that. You can call Minucius a Greek for all I care. My only concern is equal access to the ager publicus."

Publius Scipio made up his mind. "Well then, you shall have it. You're a forceful speaker, Lucius," he added. "One day I may call on you to use your talents in your tribal meetings."

Lucius looked down at his right hand and rubbed his thigh in embarrassment. "I'm just a little excited," he explained lamely.

A few days later the legion under the consul Valerius returned to Rome and demobilized. Valerius went about claiming the gods intervened to save the Aequians when a deluge halted his attack upon their camp and abruptly ceased as soon as he withdrew the troops. Taking this as a sign that the god's would not favor a continuance of hostilities, he piously marched his legion back to Rome.

Titus returned home only to find it necessary to travel to Rome to purchase tools that had worn out beyond repair. Naturally he stayed with Lucius. They sat outside the Boar's Tusk one morning taking the sun, leaning back against the wall as they idly observed the busy little plaza, built around a central fountain, that the tavern faced. Permanent small shops with living quarters above or behind sold used clothing, repaired and made shoes or cheap jewelry. A barber, a small butcher's shop that dealt primarily in eggs and chickens, with a few rabbits thrown in, a blacksmith, a harness maker, a fuller's shop, and a used furniture store lined the square. Other merchants wheeled in carts with flowers, cookware, small utensils, and fresh vegetables. A shop near a crossroads shrine sold clay pieces molded into eyes, noses, ears, fingers, penises, breasts, internal organs, and other anatomical members which the sufferer of a malady to that body part would cast before his or her patron god in hopes of a remedy.

In the Subura, the poor section of the city, the sexes mixed in public. Women shopped, filled jugs of water at the fountain, or stood in small groups talking, heads covered by palas of different hues. Lucius preferred the piazza to the Forum where women were seldom seen, and the colors were a uniformly drab array of beige and dingy yellow.

"Tell me about this divine rain Valerius tells everyone about," said Lucius.

"The only rain I saw," said Titus, adjusting his tunic, "was made up of stones and javelins. I wouldn't call it divine."

Lucius laughed through his teeth. "That's what I thought."

They sat briefly in silence, listening to the sounds of merchants hawking their wares, bartering with customers, or complaining to each other about business in general. The piazza filled with a wide assortment of people. Etruscan men in colorful togas and long hair like their women strolled arm in arm with their wives in a scandalous display of public affection. Ragged beggars pleaded with owners and customers for a crumb wherever food passed hands. Titus exercised his faculties to spot thieves, on the presumption that he would be less susceptible to their wiles if he could learn the techniques employed by the cunning.

"How's Didius holding up?" asked Lucius.

"He seems to have aged ten years. He really misses Sextus."

"I can imagine."

Titus turned his queer gray ringed brown eyes on Lucius. "Not yet you can't," he said. "Not until you have a son of your own."

"I suppose."

"What happened, exactly?"

Lucius recounted the story, including his interview with the Scipios. "You should have heard them giving me this, 'he's a plebeian' talk. I told them straight out Minucius is no more plebeian than they are. I think they were shocked."

Titus shook his head, chuckling at his brother's audacity. He scratched his shoulder lazily. "Someday your mouth is going to get you in trouble your muscles can't get you out of."

"I only told the truth."

"Sure. But so did they. Minucius isn't patrician."

Lucius snorted. "In name only. Listen, I guarantee he's got more in common with them than he does with the plebs. Besides, I don't see what that has to do with anything."

Cominus barged out the front door, his round face red as an onion and wild fear in his eyes. "Lucius, Lucius," he cried, "run get the midwife. No, no, you stay here, I'll get the midwife." He started and stopped indecisively.

Lucius jumped up. "You stay here," he ordered, "I'll get the midwife." He turned to Titus with a gigantic smile on his face. "Would you go home and get Mama? You can use the mule."

The baby exhibited the same indecision as its grandfather. It started, stopped, advanced, retreated. The midwife grew exasperated. Valeria, clutching the bronze birthing stand that kept her upright, grew tired. Lucius grew worried. Cominus closed the tavern and the men waited upstairs in his apartment for the baby to make up its mind. Valeria had the midwife, Drusilla, and Duellia for company and moral support. Lucius strained under the anxiety that twisted Cominus, and sent Graptus on myriad nonsensical missions that left the calm Titus shaking with hilarity.

"Relax," he said, "these things take time."

Lucius found the advice hard to take. The labor of giving birth to their first child carried on through the night. Even Valeria, in her exhaustion, dozed for short periods of time. Finally, the baby made up its mind.

Lucius knew something was wrong the instant Drusilla opened the door. No smile of congratulation, no words of joy came from her at all. He told himself she was simply exhausted, as he hurried to Valeria's room, but he did not believe it.

Titus and Cominus followed him timidly into the room. The anxious looks on the faces of Drusilla and Duellia told the story.

"What's wrong?" Lucius demanded. "Is Valeria all right?" He rushed towards his wife, who sagged against a pile of pillows that propped her up on the bed to which the women had moved her.

His mother reached out for his arm. "Valeria's fine," she said, restraining him. "It's your son." She made a motion to the midwife, who set the baby, wrapped in a small blanket, on the floor. Carefully she opened the blanket and exposed the baby.

Lucius looked down at the pink little creature. The umbilical cord had been tied off, and it had been washed clean of blood. A shock of black hair lay matted on its oblong head. He gazed, uncomprehending, as Valeria repeatedly asked for her baby. Red, wrinkled, with a sour looking expression on its tiny face, he saw nothing unusual about it at all.

Titus noticed first. "Look at its left hand, Lucius."

Lucius knelt down and opened the tightly curled little fist. There were the thumb, index, and middle fingers, and then…nothing. Maybe the first knuckles, but nothing more of the two fingers that should have been there. He straightened quickly, pulling his hand back as if he'd been burned.

Titus put a consoling hand on his shoulder. "I'm sorry, Lucius."

Valeria cried. "Lucius, Lucius. Please give me my baby."

Lucius looked at his mother's stricken face. "Has she seen it?" he asked.

Drusilla nodded.

"Yes, I've seen him," said Valeria. "Lucius," she pleaded, sitting up. "What does it matter?"

"It's deformed, Valeria," groaned Lucius. "Like…like an animal."

"He's not an animal! He's our son."

"Shall I take it out?" asked Titus, solicitously.

"No!" screamed Valeria. She clutched at Lucius' hand as he came to her side. "Lucius, please, he's our son. You can't expose him."

Lucius' dark eyes shot from one face to another, but only Titus' told him what to do. Inexpressible sadness teared in Duellia's large eyes, while from Drusilla he saw only compassion flooding forth. Compassion for him, her son. Compassion for Valeria, a poor young mother with whom she shared the knowledge of carrying a child for nine months, and of the excruciating pain and inexpressible joy of bringing life into the world. The awful, awful knowing of women. But she could offer her son no answer.

On Cominus' face too he saw concern, sadness, and relief that his daughter had not suffered the same fate as his wife. But no answer. Only Titus held firm to what must be done. While Valeria pleaded. Pleaded for his heart. Pleaded for his love. Pleaded for the life of their child. And when he looked at her with such unresolve in his eyes he saw utter, undying reproach blaze back at him from hers. His heart twisted in horror as the full knowledge of his choice became clear. If he denied the child, he would be denying her, and in that moment, he would lose not only the child but the love of his precious Valeria as well.

The baby cried, sending its own message into the air.

"Please, Lucius," beseeched Valeria. "Pick up your son."

Titus beheld the hunted look in his brother's eyes. Doubt, fear, the desire to run twitched across his strong features. Never in his life had he seen these emotions in his brother. Even as children when they had made their father explosively angry, Lucius took his punishment without fear. But now…

"It's deformed, Lucius," Titus said softly but with firm conviction. "If you keep it there will be no expiating this omen."

Lucius sought his mother. "What do you think?"

"It's only a baby," Duellia burst out.

"Duellia," Titus roared, suddenly angry. "Go outside. You have no right."

Duellia broke into tears and left the room in disgrace. Drusilla regarded her son, who had never seemed to need her as much as she needed him. Now, in his hour of need, she failed him. A vast suffering suffused her guilt-ridden glance.

"I'm sorry, Lucius, but a woman's heart can not make this decision for you."

"Lucius, you can have more children," said Titus.

"Oh, how do you know, Titus," hurled Valeria.

"You're strong and healthy, Valeria. The next one will be easier," answered Titus. He tried to be soothing but came across cold.

Valeria shivered as if an icy blast chilled the room. "Don't listen to him, Lucius," she begged. "He's our son."

"Don't fight against the gods, Lucius," warned Titus.

Lucius peered down on the tiny being kicking spasmodically on the floor. It seemed to be listening intently to the argument over its fate with imperturbable equanimity. As he contemplated, the tiny boy looked in his direction with unseeing eyes and smiled. Lucius' heart exploded in a gush of affection. Reaching down for the baby boy, issue of his and Valeria's love, he picked him up from the floor. Laughter filled his heart, and he vented it gladly. In a sweeping motion he held the child aloft.

"Welcome to the world, Lucius Tempanius," he cried.

The same night Appius Claudius died of disgrace in his home.

# XXII
### June 7-15, 463 BC
### The Vestalia

Lucius Tempanius the younger did indeed become a human being, alleviating his father's greatest concern. Despite Titus' warnings he had performed expiatory sacrifices, and these seemed to have been efficacious. Of course, he did his part as well. He strapped splints to the baby's legs so they would grow straight. Ankles, knees, hips, elbows, and wrists were kept tightly wrapped in swaddling bands and the hands forced open for the same purpose. Each day his son received a cold bath, at which time Valeria massaged his head to mold it into a round shape. She also kneaded his jaw, nose, and buttocks in like manner. At least in Lucius' presence. She felt less certain of the effectiveness of these ministrations, and tended to content herself with toughening her son for life with cold baths.

Lucius determined that his son, handicapped from birth with two missing fingers, should depart from the unformed savagery of infancy as soon as possible. To assure right hand dominance he required his left arm be tied to his side, allowing freedom to the right alone. He chastised Valeria for cooing at the boy like a pigeon, and demanded she speak to him in proper Latin. The boy would be forever *infans*—without speech—and therefore less than human if she did not teach him words.

Valeria went along with these policies because they were, first of all, proven traditional Roman methods for raising sons (daughters were another story). Beyond that, she was sensitive to her husband's unspoken thoughts, and knew that he dreaded the possibility that Titus had been correct. Now and then she caught him inspecting their son's left hand as if looking for evidence that the missing fingers were at last beginning to form. She knew he fretted over the idea that outer disfigurement indicated a hidden inner disfigurement. He sometimes cast worried glances at his son as if expecting any moment some manifestation of ether-worldly or bestial origin. She made frequent trips to the temple of Juno to offer prayers and sacrifice to the goddess, and when the temple of Vesta opened to women during the Vestalia she entered the sanctuary barefoot as required, and burned incense and prayed for the blessings of Vesta on her family.

Lucius the younger knew nothing of this. Before he could see he had looked at his father with adoring eyes, and he never ceased to do so. His mother he merely worshipped. Nevertheless, his father's son, he refused his mother's breast soon after his second birthday, and greeted his father with his first word—"Pater". A betrayal for which his mother instantly forgave him.

At the age of three his father took over his formal education and training. His first act addressed immediate concerns with his son's future, and to that end Lucius constructed a small shield of wood which he required Lucius Jr. to wield in proper fashion with his left hand one hour every day. As he grew older and stronger, the shield's weight increased in proportion.

Often accorded the rank of centurion during his many expeditions with the legions, Lucius had honed his judgement of men, and learned to recognize talent and aptitude. He therefore suffered no loss of dignity by enlisting Cominus to teach his grandson reading and writing, while Graptus taught him arithmetic. This left Lucius free to teach those things he knew best—fighting with sword and spear, wrestling, boxing, swimming, and running. He introduced his son to Publius Scipio, and together they often accompanied him in the Forum. Summers, while away campaigning, he shipped Lucius and Valeria to the farm on the Anio where the boy continued his education by helping Quintus and his sons with the work on the farm. Here he also learned to use the sling and javelin. Periodically Lucius gave in to his mother's protestations and sent Lucius Jr. and Valeria to stay on the original Tempanius farm, where the boy played with his cousins, and learned Titus' methods of farming.

Lucius Jr. felt conflicting emotions at these times. He loved his grandmother, and his aunt Duellia always doted kindly on him. His cousins, of which there were three, provided playmates, and the wild forests of the hills behind the farm a wonderful world of strange creations. But his Uncle Titus, though friendly and kind, seemed to withhold complete acceptance from him, and though he could not articulate the fact, on a visceral level understood it better than anyone else.

Titus tried. But every time he caught sight of his nephew's missing fingers a shudder of apprehension went through him. Often he searched through the wax tablets on which his father had recorded the many workings of the farm, from planting seasons, to prodigies, what work could or couldn't be done during which phases of the sun and moon. Cures for illnesses to both humans and animals, and the best dressings for all types of wounds were recorded haphazardly. No answers to his questions could he find however, on what to do about children with missing fingers or other deformities and what they might mean.

In all other ways his nephew appeared normal. He comported himself well and worked diligently at the tasks assigned him. He got along with his cousins, and like all boys enjoyed playing at war. Titus smiled to see the obvious signs of his brother's instruction in the martial arts. Although three years younger than his eldest cousin he gave Marcus a stiff contest when they fought on opposite sides and clearly dominated Titus Jr. Titus considered spending more time training his sons.

Where he would find it he didn't know. Didius died just short of his sixtieth birthday. The loss of Sextus had been harder on him than anyone suspected, and his health deteriorated rapidly afterwards. Petronius himself was fifty-nine, and afflicted with the many miseries of old age. Out of stubborn pride he insisted on doing his share, but that share shrank regularly. Titus replaced them primarily with seasonal laborers when need arose. Daily chores his children learned as they grew older, plus he had Restius, and Primus would apparently be content to grow old with the goats. He missed the knowledge and the mentoring that Didius brought to his life, and these he could not replace.

The biggest blow had been Antonius. Serving with the consul Quinctius some five years earlier, he had taken part in the assault and capture of Antium. Lucius won a *corona muralis* for being first over the wall, with Antonius right behind. When land outside the city was opened for colonization Antonius jumped at the opportunity. Drusilla pleaded, as she had with Lucius, for him to stay and suffered the same result. Antonius failed to see the irony in this, determined to strike out on his own. That he would be within spitting distance of Volscian raids left his family morbidly pessimistic about his chances of survival.

The call for colonists, despite the hunger for land, went unanswered by many in Rome. The land around Antium, well known as swampy and malarial, did not appeal to Romans who viewed the offer as a cynical and transparent effort by the powerful to rid themselves of a troublesome segment of the population. Antonius understood and agreed, but also believed that fewer settlers meant larger plots and greater selection. His mind made up, he put his name in and Titus Quinctius, one of the land commissioners and his commander, made sure he received a just reward for his bravery. Five *iugera* of fine land not far from a road, and with unoccupied land behind him constituted that reward. It even had a small cottage.

Even so, months of back breaking toil with the bare necessities for tools exhausted his energies, and left him wondering if he'd made the right decision. Another's misfortune boosted his when a Volscian named Tranellius wandered up asking for work. Antonius had little to offer but a pallet and whatever food they could grow, but Tranellius readily accepted. His plight was not unusual. Dispossessed of his property by the conquering Romans, he evaded capture and thus avoided slavery. Unfortunately, freedom left him homeless and in want. Antonius gladly took him in and a friendship soon blossomed.

With the addition of Tranellius the workload on Antonius lightened considerably, allowing his thoughts to travel. At twenty-five years old he began to think the time had come to look for a wife. His mind immediately went to Valeria, whom he'd always considered beautiful and wonderful. Now he laughed at his youthful infatuation and surveyed the problem in purely practical terms. A strong girl from a good family to produce strong Tempanii sons should be his main criteria, he told himself. If she happened to be pretty and intelligent like Valeria, so much the better. If not, it would be of small consequence. His mind made up he deemed it best if Lucius made the arrangements, so he decided to go to Rome as soon as opportunity presented itself.

Valeria, like most Roman women lived a bittersweet existence. In sum she could rightly claim her life tasted more of honey than of vinegar. Unlike most, her marriage had been made from love, not from social, political, or economic motives. Still, sorrow attended her like a faithful slave. In direct contradiction to Titus' words her success at delivering babies turned out to be abysmal. Two miscarriages were followed by the birth of a daughter who lived only a few months. Sex took on the specter of death, and her brain rebelled against her body's enjoyment, denying her fulfillment. She had her son, and her husband, and in these she found contentment, but at the age of twenty-two she felt already old. She attributed this not only to the deaths of her babies but equally to the constant danger to which Lucius committed himself.

Lucius, just turned thirty-four years old, decided to take a season off from war. Of the seventeen years since he became eligible, he had served in thirteen of them. Of the other four, two were years of peace when no levies were raised, one he spent recovering from wounds, and one he spent awaiting the birth of his son. The present season he needed to settle some business affairs. Quintus Crispus upon the death of his father inherited the family cottage in Rome, and with its sale finally had the means to purchase his own piece of property. Lucius, though happy for his friend and client, suddenly found himself in need of a new and trustworthy overseer for his small property on the Anio River. He found such a man in Furius

Villius, one of the legion of unfortunates for whom land was a passion, an essential component of their identity—and a distant dream. Regardless, Lucius felt it necessary to remain nearby, and visit the farmstead often in this first year of Villius' stewardship.

In June Antonius traveled up from Antium to visit and speak with Lucius about arranging a marriage. Lucius took the occasion to pay a visit to Villius. Hitching two mules to an open four-wheeled wagon they set off with Lucius Jr. and Graptus in the rear. All three men armed themselves with cudgels, long knives, and wicker shields as protection against bandits or, to a lesser extent, Aequian raiding parties. They traveled leisurely under a molten gold sun, and blue skies broken discreetly by flaxen clouds. The Gabinian Way ran before them hedged in by the luminous yellow blossoms of broom, filling the air with a sweet aroma. Small brown lizards with iridescent green stripes darted off the road at the sound of the bronze covered wheels scraping and grinding against the uneven surfaces of the black volcanic paving stones. The tall ears of the mules twitched in protest at the sound, and they snorted and blew in annoyance.

Lucius looked around at the fields already turning tan with growing wheat. Stirred by a light breeze the silver-green blade shaped leaves of olive trees reflected the light like fountains spraying round plumes of water into the air. The motion of the wagon jouncing on the road, and the sedate pace of the countryside relaxed him. He let the reins hang loosely in his fingers.

A lone argent winged seagull described a graceful arc in front of them. "Look, Papa," cried six year old Lucius Jr. pointing. "A seagull."

"Yes," acknowledged Lucius, "he's a long way from home, isn't he?"

"Is he lost?"

"Maybe. I don't know."

"I don't think animals can get lost," said Graptus.

"Why not?" asked Antonius. "Humans are far smarter than animals and they get lost all the time. Look at Titus, for example."

They all chuckled at Titus' notoriously poor sense of direction.

"I don't think it has anything to do with intelligence," said Graptus. "I think it's innate."

"What's in-nate, Papa?"

Lucius rubbed either side of his forehead where the hair receded, leaving a spear tip of hair in the middle. "Why did I let Cominus teach him Latin?" he agonized, referring to Graptus.

"It means inborn, instinctive," answered Graptus.

"I knew the answer," said Lucius forcefully.

"Of course, Dominus," said Graptus with a satirical smile Lucius could not see. "I was only trying to conserve your wind."

"How did you get such an impertinent slave?" asked Antonius.

"It's a curse, Antonius, a pure curse," lamented Lucius, with a broad paving stone smile Graptus could not see.

"Anyway," said Graptus. "I once knew a man who sold a flock of sheep along with the dog because the buyer thought the sheep would be easier to handle with a familiar dog directing them. But the dog, who was accustomed to sharing meals, and in every way treated as one of the family by his original master, so missed him that as soon as the sheep were delivered to their new pasture over a hundred miles away, he found his way back to his old home."

"Truly?" asked Lucius Jr. in wonderment.

"Yes," said Graptus. "And master and dog were so overjoyed at being reunited that the man sent a bronze *as* in payment to the buyer."

"Then what happened?"

"Well, it's very said." Graptus dropped his equine features mournfully. "After that the master was captured by the

Romans and made a slave, and he and his dog never saw each other again."

Lucius Jr. looked skeptically at the long faced Graptus. "I think you're teasing," he said seriously.

His father slapped his thigh and roared with laughter, startling the mules that kicked up their pace briefly, and then settled back down. "Listen, Graptus, you might pull the wool over my eyes, but little Lucius is a much tougher nut to crack," said Lucius.

They dropped into silence, sedated by the warm sunshine, and the heady smell of cultivated fields. Now and then the grating squeal of bronze bound wheels on stone set their teeth momentarily on edge. Antonius broke the silence.

"I think it's time I got married," he said.

Lucius lowered his voice in mock seriousness. "Oh yes, you're what, twenty-five now? Past time I'd say."

Antonius disregarded the jesting tone. "Will you help?"

"In what way little brother?"

Antonius scowled at the words. "By making a match for me."

"Ah. Do you have anyone particular in mind?"

"No," hesitated Antonius. "But I don't want just anyone."

"Well, that narrows it down."

"You know what I mean. Someone from a good family."

"What do you think, Graptus," Lucius swung his wide shoulders around and winked at his slave. "A scullery maid was good enough for the head of the family, but he needs someone from a 'good family'."

"But your eccentric taste in women is well known...Dominus," teased Graptus.

"By Jupiter, you'd better start thinking with your back before you open your mouth," stormed Lucius.

"Would you be serious," demanded Antonius.

Lucius clapped his slender brother on the back with a meaty hand. "Don't worry about a thing. I did all right for Titus, didn't I?"

Antonius nodded his head in agreement. "Well, then," Lucius continued, "I'll do the same for you."

"Thank you," Antonius said, raising his wing-like eyebrows uncertainly to the heavens.

"How soon do you want this to take place?" asked Lucius.

"About a year," said Antonius. "I have to get things a little more organized at home first."

"Good," agreed Lucius. He nudged Antonius with an elbow and gave him a leering wink. "I suppose you want a young one, eh?"

Antonius pursed his full lips in mild disapproval of his brother's flippant attitude. Sternly he said, "Not so young that she can't have children for two or three years."

Again, Lucius cast sidelong conspiratorial glances at Graptus. "He just doesn't understand, does he, Grap?" Noticing Lucius Jr. wide awake and listening he didn't elaborate. Graptus clucked his tongue in knowing agreement but said nothing. "Listen," Lucius went on, "I'll try to find someone for you. But most of the unmarried girls over fourteen are bound to be ugly or have some defect. Else they'd be married. Understand?"

"Of course. Anyway, as I said, I can wait a year."

"Good, then it's settled. Someone of senatorial rank or better."

"Very funny," deadpanned Antonius, looking away. To their right he saw the rise of the Alban Hills, incandescent green against the sea blue sky. From his perspective it appeared as if the ground rose in a gradual swell to the steep face of the mountains. He spotted the large hill east of his boyhood home, but could not make out the hill of his birth. "So," he said, "what kept you from volunteering this year? Getting tired?"

"Me? I've never been tired in my life." Lucius thumped his chest in proof of his soundness. "I just thought I should stay around and make sure my new factor works out."

"That's all?" His large dark eyes pierced Lucius, and a half smile played around his full mouth.

"No, it's not," said Lucius. "I didn't like the consuls. I know or have served under most of them in one way or another over the years, and these two I don't think much of."

"So, Titus could be in for trouble you think?"

"Poor Titus," breathed Lucius. A hissing laugh escaped through his teeth. "I've never known anyone that had such bad luck with consuls. It never seemed to fail that while I served under a Titus Quinctius, he got an Appius Claudius."

"He's taken part in his share of losing battles," agreed Antonius.

"Do you think he wants to lose?" asked Lucius Jr. His innocent question sparked an idea that Lucius had ruminated over before.

"No," he said. "But sometimes I can't help but wonder if he expects to lose."

"No," said Antonius emphatically. "Titus believes in Rome. He just puts it all down to bad luck and moves on."

They spent the evening and the next morning going over the farm with the new factor Villius, returning to Rome as the blood red sun sank into the low hills northwest of the city. Nearing the summer solstice, the ice blue sky faded to pale bluish-white before igniting on the red-hot coal of the sun, spreading across the horizon in bloody flame. Rather than hurry into the city, they lingered on a rise and watched the sunset in pious awe of the handiwork of creation.

+ + +

The burning ember of the sun as it sank behind the Alban massif represented to Titus the glowing coal of longing that burned in his guts; the steady longing for the simple pleasures of his family and farm. As they chased roving bands of Aequians and Volscians from Praeneste to Ferentinum, up and down the valley between the Hernican Mountains on the east, and the Lipini Mountains on the west he watched with aching heart as spring burst forth. As if the whole season were taking place without him. The consul Spurius Furius Fuscus, when he saw his men tire of fruitless chasing, changed tactics and plundered Volscian or Aequian territory hoping to draw the enemy into the open. Then at the first sign of activity he would go headlong after them like a hound after a rabbit. Now they encamped north of Anagnia next to a tributary stream of the Trerus River, in pursuit of yet another raiding party.

Sitting around a campfire eating pots of steaming porridge flavored only with a little salt, and playing a board game called 'thieves' the soldiers conversation turned to their leader's strategy.

Publius Opiter, a grizzled veteran with plenty of gray hairs salting his beard and short-cropped hair shrugged. "Well, we've seen a good part of the valley, collected a few nice things, and no one's got hurt."

Lucius Ambivius thought perhaps that point of view was a bit sanguine. "I thought we were enlisted to fight the enemy, not take a tour of the country," he said.

Heads nodded in agreement over bronze pots of gruel. The two players moving their pieces on a makeshift board of stone grunted approval.

Tiberius Pudens cast a tone of worry onto the board as he took one of his opponent's clay pieces. He had a face that seemed all out of proportion. His eyes, nose, and mouth scrunched together between a wide expanse of forehead and jutting chin. "I don't like the looks of it," he said. "All these different bands running around." He rubbed the back of his stubby neck with a large coarse hand as he thought over his next move. "I think they're setting some kind of trap."

"At least we'll have a fight, then," said Titus.

"Oh, we'll have a fight," retorted Pudens. He moved a piece and his opponent swore. "But it won't be on our terms."

Caius Gaberius laughed. "Ah, you always think the worst." He cleaned his bowl with a thick finger, sucking it clean, and shoved his squat body off the ground.

"Where you going?" asked Titus.

"To the river," said Gaberius. "I need a wash."

"Mind if I come along?"

"Not if you know the password."

"Mars Victrix."

"That's original," sneered Gaberius.

Titus followed the hunched shoulders of Gaberius through the north gate along a well-beaten path to the stream. A sliver of silver from the waning moon cast little light so they did not venture far away from the path. Dense undergrowth and large beech and pine trees closed around them, shielding the river from light, and prying eyes.

"This gives me the creeps," whispered Titus. He submerged his pot in the water without looking down. "Anybody could sneak through here."

"Don't worry so much," hissed Gaberius.

Despite his unease Titus unbelted his sword, released the thongs of the shoulder protectors of his leather jerkin, and pulled it and his tunic over his head. He slipped cautiously into the cold knee-deep water with his sandals on. Careful to limit noise, they gingerly lowered themselves into a sitting position and washed many days of dirt and grime from their bodies. The cold water flowed refreshingly over his body, and when he came out Titus felt invigorated, his skin taut and tingling in the warm night air. He slept deeply and awoke at first light rejuvenated. When the order came soon after breakfast to form up in battle formation a swift surge of hope, almost joy hurried his preparations.

The enemy dispelled any joy the Romans might have felt about finally coming to grips with them. As they filed out of their camp and formed into a phalanx, they could not help seeing the overwhelming numbers of Volscians, and Aequians filling the hills above them.

The Aequians in white tunics, round breastplates, shields, and simple bowl-shaped helmets held the right flank, anchored against the stream. The Volscians in triple disc breastplates and high crested helmets held the left, protected by a sheer rock outcropping. Strongly occupying the high ground, the enemy looked in no mood to relinquish it by coming down to attack the Romans.

In the lines, the legionaries could only wonder where they all had come from. It seemed as if every group they had chased multiplied a hundred-fold, and assembled on this mountainside.

Tiberius Pudens smiled, his top and bottom teeth meeting. "I told you we were in for a surprise," he muttered.

Titus agreed disconsolately, while in front of the legion the consul and his lieutenants hastily gathered in consultation. The velites were sent forward to test the impossible terrain while the hoplites could only look on with sympathy. Rock outcroppings, clusters of trees, thick tangles of thorny vines, and impenetrable bushes covered the uneven ground and hid ravines and hollows from which the enemy's light troops peppered the velites with lead, rocks, and razor-sharp javelins. With dispiriting ease, they drove them off the lower slopes. A jeering cheer went up from the enemy lines, which the Romans answered with stony silence.

Persuaded against rashness the consul ordered the recall sounded, and as the circular horns of the corniculars rent the air, the Romans retired to the safety of their camp.

The combined armies of Rome's two most persistent enemies rejoiced as they descended the mountain. Taunts and insults breasted the earthworks, filling the Roman legionaries with shame and anger. They manned the palisade, reinforced weak spots, stacked up large rocks and prepared for an assault on the camp.

Titus waited with grim determination his square jaw set in tenacious silence. Resting behind their fortifications his linemates hurled back the enemy's insults. Let them come, Titus thought. With all their numbers they would find it no easy thing to take a Roman camp.

The commanders of the enemy forces would have agreed with Titus. The Romans protected themselves with a ditch nine feet wide, and six feet deep. The dirt and stones from this ditch formed a wall three feet high on the inner edge of the ditch. Affixed in interlocking thickets sharpened multiple pronged stakes topped the earthworks so that they bristled menacingly in the face of any attacking soldier. From the bottom of the ditch to the top of the stakes the wall measured twelve feet in height, and each side measured one hundred feet in length. Pressed into this ten thousand square foot space were approximately five thousand defenders, plus baggage, animals, and equipment.

Still, the trapped and surrounded Roman army looked ripe for destruction, and the Aequian and Volscian commanders knew they could not let such an opportunity slip through fear-stricken fingers. As soon as their forces were organized, they ordered the attack.

Titus watched them come, emerging from the trees lining the river. Tiberius Pudens standing at his right shoulder muttered something about the end being near. Titus turned his gaze on him, the gray ring surrounding the irises glinting with petrosal fury.

"Yes," he said hoarsely, "for them."

The first wave of attackers came forward bearing ladders, grapples, mattocks; anything to pull down or scale the rampart the Romans had built. Slingers rained smooth stones, and oblong lead bullets at the defenders along the walls.

A wave of unyielding hatred welled up in Titus. "Not a ladder touches this wall," he shouted. "Roma!"

"Roma!" responded his section of the palisade, and the cry sped along the walls until the whole camp took up the chant, thundering it out in blood lust. "ROMA!"

The enemy answered the challenge and surged forward. Into the ditch and up the other side they came, a cascade of flesh and bronze. Titus lifted a rock in both hands over his head and hurled it down onto the head of an attacker, laughing as he crumpled. As he reached for another stone a javelin creased the air where his head had been. Again, he threw his stone, bashing another head, caving in a line of assailants. Still, on they came, clawing up the sides of the trench. Beside him

Pudens, Gaberius, Ambivius, Opiter, and the others of his century howled like furies, stabbing with spears, launching heavy stones, flailing with swords. Wave upon wave of Volscians hurled themselves at the Romans, ripping at the stakes separating them from their hated rivals, flinging javelins, charging madly up the steep incline with shields upraised, only to be repulsed, gutted, faces smashed, rolling lifeless into the ditch, taking their comrades behind with them. The writhing mass of living wildly extricating themselves from the dead made easy targets, and a torrent of stones and javelins poured down on them in a deadly rain, adding to the piles of slain warriors. Titus lifted his spear exultantly in the air uttering a feral animal cry at the enemy's retreating backs.

The commanding centurion came by, tolled off sentries, and ordered the remainder to sit and rest. Titus sat with his back to the palisade and drank his fill from the battered iron field flask that had accompanied him on so many campaigns. Dead and wounded were removed from the defensive perimeter and the gaps filled. Outside the camp the wounded and dying screamed and groaned in horrible harmony.

Basking in the fierce sun, his head tilted up to the washed-out sky he felt a strange contentment. Without looking at him he spoke to Pudens. "Think they'll be back for another try?"

Pudens' top and bottom teeth met in bloody smile. "You say that with such hope."

Titus rolled his head to look at Tiberius. As if for the first time, he noticed the man's lower front teeth had worn down to a v-shaped groove into which his upper teeth fitted perfectly. "Why not?" he chuckled maliciously. "They'd have to fill that ditch with dead before they took this camp."

"That'd be the most expensive victory they ever won," said Ambivius.

But the Aequians and Volscians decided in council that such a victory was not to their liking. They had the Romans where they wanted them. Let them fight their way out of it...or starve. Meanwhile, they themselves were now free to disperse raiding parties throughout Roman territory and lay it to waste. The siege began.

+ + +

369

News from the legion ceased like light extinguished in a lamp. The only couriers now were refugees from the country. Plumes of smoke rose from every part of the Roman plain. Soon the roads were packed with people and livestock streaming into Rome.

Lucius, worried about Villius, walked out the Via Gabina a short way and watched the procession from a small hill. Hastily laden carts piled high with valuables lurched and shuddered with bovine placidity in spite of the frantic curses and whippings of the drivers. Men, women, and children carried baskets strapped to their backs. Some carried a favorite lamb or a puppy in their arms, or walked with ox in tow at the end of a line. Flocks of sheep and goats, herds of cattle, and pigs jammed the road as anxious herders kept them together and moving with flicks of long switches. Dogs barked and gamboled about under foot amidst lowing cattle and bleating sheep.

Unable to watch any longer Lucius returned to the Boar's Tusk, deep creases of worry hardening the line of his wide mouth. He worried that in whatever catastrophe had befallen the legion Titus may have been killed. His mother's safety oppressed him. He fretted that Villius and his family may have been attacked and killed. And he worried that all his property may have been burned and his livestock run off. The thought of rebuilding the farm from the ground up turned his stomach. One fear was alleviated two days later when Villius pulled up to the Boars Tusk in a two wheeled cart loaded with family and valuables. In tow a bull ox and two pigs lumbered docilely behind.

"What about the other two oxen and the sheep?" asked Lucius.

"I told Scrofa to take them into the woods and hide," said Villius. "I figured they'd fare better there anyway."

"And the farm?"

"So far it's still in one piece. But they burned out a couple of places about a mile away, and I figured I was in line to be next, so…"

+ + +

As usual, indecision reigned on the Tempanius farm. Drusilla, having lost a husband defending her home, was now loath to leave it. Petronius vowed to stay if she stayed. Both of them encouraged Duellia to take the children to Rome where they could stay in comfort and security with their maternal grandparents. Restius dutifully loaded the cart with pillows, a trunk of clothes, a few valuables, and trundled happily off to Rome. Risking his life for a farm he had no stake in did not exactly appeal to him. His reprieve didn't last long. When Lucius heard his mother had only aging Petronius to defend her, he exploded in fury and sent Restius straight back. Restius consoled himself with the understanding that Lucius' anger arose from his own frustration at being unable to go himself since the consul Postumius held an emergency levy and called up every available man. Lucius included. At least he sent Graptus along. Lucius would have liked to send Antonius, but he had his own problems.

The first tingling of fear came to Antonius when he heard faint but unmistakable rumblings of discontent among the Volscian population of Antium. When fellow Roman colonists told him they'd been approached by Volscians who thought they might also be disaffected, he knew that such confidence could only be bred by the flush of victory. He immediately sat down with Tranellius and expressed his loyalty to Rome, and asked him pointedly if he had anything to do with those inclined to switch allegiances. Tranellius assured him that he'd had enough of politics and only cared about important things like wheat and goats and oxen. And someday, hopefully, vineyards and olive groves. Nevertheless, tensions remained high in the area. When the call-up from Rome for 'crisis men' came, he hesitated to answer for fear Tranellius, left alone, might get hurt and the farm looted by citizens with Volscian sympathies. Still, he could not refuse, so he gathered his equipment and hastened to the announced mustering post.

One would have thought every creature in Latium mustered in Rome, so crammed did the city become. In every quarter the braying of mules, the lamentations of sheep, and the bawling of oxen reached the ears at the same time as the smell of their bodily excrement reached the nose. No amount of geraniums or basil plants in the windows and doorways could keep the flies out or sweeten the air. Every inn, and every stable overflowed. In the Forum Boarium hundreds of animals were bunched together in makeshift corrals, and their complaining voices disturbed the fetid air every hour of day and night.

Nor was the noise from people any better. At the oddest hours voices raised in argument or song wandered the streets, echoed off buildings, and annoyed unwilling ears. Whole schools of wall philosophers came into being, and soon empty wall space for their graffiti became almost nonexistent. They railed against the patricians, the tribunes, the legions, and the enemy. They wrote crude jokes, fantastic accusations, or wry comments about life in the city.

Like an olive press, the pressure squeezed tighter. Yet the question persisted. Where was the legion? And where, besides all over the Latin plain, was the enemy?

Titus and his comrades knew exactly where the enemy lurked. All around them. They made desultory attacks to keep the legionaries on edge. They blew horns at all hours of day and night. They pelted the camp with whatever came to hand. They left the dead to putrefy in the ditch below the palisade so that the Romans could never escape the reminder of their wretched situation. To emphasize it they displayed the severed head of the consul's brother.

Desperate it was. The consul Fuscus lay wounded and bereaved in his tent. In a frenzied sortie to break out his brother lost his life, and the consul received grave wounds attempting to rescue him. Now he lay fevered and incapacitated in his tent.

Leaderless, nearly out of food and water, morale in the legion began to plummet. The tribunes took council together, and decided an effort must be made to get help. As a last resort the legion might try to fight its way out, but they held no illusions that such a rash course could save it from destruction. The three tribunes drew lots. The loser called his ten centurions to his tent and they drew lots. The loser picked two men whom he thought had a chance to evade capture and get a message to Rome. Spurius Romilius chose Titus, and Tiberius Pudens.

"Seriously, Spurius," protested Titus, "I can get lost in my own barnyard."

"Quit arguing, Titus," said Romilius. "I've made up my mind."

Titus and Pudens deposited their personal effects with the quaestor, who wrote a detailed list so they could reclaim them without question. They carried nothing but knives, and one satchel with enough hard tack to last two days.

The new moon provided hope and consolation for Titus and Pudens. They sneaked out of camp on their bellies like lizards slinking into the underbrush. Every movement sounded like an explosion of thunder in Titus' ears. Upon reaching the river they crawled into the bushes and waited.

Tiberius put his mouth next to Titus' ear and barely breathed his words. "We'll wait here a bit."

Titus nodded. On the other side of the stream they could hear the noises of camp life—sudden laughter floating on the still air. Horses snorted, pawed, snickered. Sparks from the campfires sprayed into the sky and died in blackness. Satisfied at last that no one was coming their way, Pudens squeezed Titus' arm lightly, slid silently into the water, and started off downstream.

Torturously feeling their way along, slipping, splashing, stopping, Titus thought surely they would be captured. To his ears they sounded like a whole army moving down the stream. Above them the stars laughed at their floundering, so clearly posted in precise locations, so clearly cognizant of fate's short reach. Through breaks in the overhanging trees Titus could see their glinting smiles, the flickering laughter in the cosmic eyes. He grimaced back, cursing their certainty, decrying their impervious nature. Fate's short reach, he knew, reached far enough to gather him in.

He reached out and grabbed Tiberius' arm, then sank slowly into the water. The soft padded clopping of hooves scudded past; a laugh receded like the faint whisper of a memory not wholly recalled. They waited. It felt good submerged in the water, away from the carnivorous hunger of the mosquitoes. They listened. The noises of camp life did not reach their ears. Had they gotten past the enemy lines? They looked, peering through the branches into the dark beyond, searching for the pale glow of fire, a stray spark ascending toward its distant brethren. Nothing.

Titus made motions of exiting the river, but Pudens shook his head fiercely in dissent. Titus relented and they continued feeling their way foot by agonizing foot, each step a potential disaster. They clung to branches or shrubbery for support, stepping gingerly, feeling for the bottom with toes numbed by the frigid water. Each slow, suspended step drained energy, requiring twice as much work as marching under full packs. They stopped and rested back-to-back on a boulder.

"We'd make better time out of the water," Titus whispered.

"Not if they catch us."

"We must be past their lines by now. Besides, we look like deserters."

"They'd kill us anyway. At the least."

"I know." Admitting it came hard to Titus. "Still…"

"You think it's safe?"

"I think we have to take the chance."

A long pause while they thought this word 'chance' over. Tiberius looked up through a break in the trees and found the big dipper poised to scoop the stars from the sky. From the end of the cup, he located Polaris, the North Star, and calculated they had begun to turn south. He made up his mind.

"Agreed," hissed Tiberius.

Cautiously, painstakingly they dragged themselves out of the water. Lying still on the south bank of the stream they waited and listened.

"Which way should we go?" asked Titus.

Pudens checked the stars again. "Anagnia is still southeast of us."

Titus twisted his head to find the North Star.

"It's straight ahead," said Pudens, a smile on his scrunched features. "But if we follow the river, we'll come to the road downstream a ways."

"The road's too dangerous," said Titus warily.

"Not by night. We'll hide during the day and travel at night."

This idea also gave them pause as they considered the merits.

"Agreed," said Titus.

They did not make good progress. Whipped by bushes, ripped by thorns, tripped by creeping vines, none of which they could avoid in the blackness of night they lurched and stumbled over the rugged terrain. When dawn stole into the sky, they found themselves short of the road. Gasping they slunk to the river, drank their fill, and considered the next move. Keep going, they decided, at least until they made the road. At the third hour of the day weary from tension, lack of sleep, and physically exhausted they finally descried the pathway to hope. Or so they hoped. They dove under cover, ate some hardtack, and slept by turns to replenish the energy depleted during their agonizing night march. When night came on, they roused themselves and took to the road.

Through the night they trudged, cringing at every strange sound, diving into the ditch along the road at a dog's bark. The sound of their footsteps crashed like thunder in their ears but they pushed on, forcing themselves to hurry, to disregard the pain and fear that coursed like fever through their bodies. As resplendent dawn rose in fiery glory, they discerned the high walls of Anagnia in the near distance. Joyfully they picked up the pace. At the gates of the Hernican city guards regarded them suspiciously, questioning them closely before they called an officer who escorted them to the town council. After they recounted their story to the city's senate, they were shown every courtesy. They bathed, received new tunics as gifts, and ate a lavish meal. Riders were immediately dispatched to Rome with information on the whereabouts of the missing legion and the forces besieging it.

A relief force left Rome the next day, and by forced march reached the trapped legion. Only to find the enemy had melted away into the forest like a spring snow.

# XXIII

## July 19-21, 463 BC

## The Lucaria—Feast of Clearings

Valeria felt vaguely disloyal. She knitted her sloping eyebrows in consternation—or perhaps in befuddlement. Anger overrode all other feelings. Of course, she felt glad the legion had been rescued, but it seemed hardly fair that Lucius, the one time he didn't volunteer should be called up nonetheless. Certainly, there were plenty of other men in Rome. Frankly, Rome overflowed with men—not to mention beasts. Well, she thought, a chuckle spreading across her perfect teeth, maybe they were one and the same.

Her brown eyes saddened, closing down the inchoate smile, depressing her joy. Joy had departed, crisscrossing the countryside in search of ravaging enemies.

"Come here my joy," she commanded Lucius Jr. and pulled him with unseemly affection into her lap. Stroking his wavy black hair and kissing his cheek. "Do you miss your father?"

"No Mama," Lucius Jr. said. He spoke as if no mere girl could understand. "He's fighting with the legions."

"Of course he is, but that doesn't mean we can't miss him."

Lucius Jr. struggled out of his mother's embrace. "Are you afraid?"

Naturally she was afraid. The only surprising aspect of the question was from where it emanated. All of her life Rome had been under attack. The few seasons of peace had been like gifts from the gods. In a sense she could barely remember a time when fear did not lurk at the back of her mind. However, only since her marriage had she known true fear. She realized that previously she experienced no more than a vague sense of disquiet. She had no brothers, and her father could no longer serve, so no direct threat to her life or loved ones disturbed her childhood sensibilities. Now, when she heard reports of savage battles she quailed. When she saw new widows and newly childless mothers parade in mourning through the streets, their heartrending wails froze her with apprehension.

377

"Yes, I am afraid," she admitted to her shocked son. "Your father is brave and strong it's true, but even the bravest and the strongest die in battle."

Naturally, she was afraid. Sometimes she climbed the Aventine Hill, if for no other reason than to ascend out of the stench that inhabited Rome. From the heights near the temple of Diana she could see smoke billowing from every point on the Roman plain. As if the whole of Roman territory were being razed to the ground. And maybe it was. The once promising golden brown fields went up in black roils like carrion crows of starvation. People said that thousands had been killed. Thousands! Would any good men be left to defend the city? Yet she imagined she could see squadrons of cavalry racing across a distant field, or vast columns of dust rising from the feet of marching soldiers. Theirs? Ours? She couldn't tell. Only the clarity of her palpitating worried heart, trying by some metaphysical means to see her husband marching strong and well in the midst of his comrades existed. Only that.

Lucius Jr. crossed his arms, tucking his left hand under his right biceps. "Papa won't die," he assured his mother.

"No," she said, wrinkling her fine, slightly pointed nose at him. "But I think he'd like it if you missed him just a little."

Lucius the younger looked at Valeria with the eyes he inherited from her. "No," he said, unafraid to contradict his mother. "He wants you to miss him. He wants me to carry my shield." Spinning abruptly, he ran off to do just that.

Valeria could have cried.

But there would be plenty of that later. She heard the first rumors at the salt merchant's. "So many funerals lately." The crowded shop on the Via Suburana abounded with strange voices and faces, as did the Subura district in general these days.

The proprietor, a thin shriveled man with salt desiccated flesh, hurried from customer to customer impatiently weighing small amounts on a bronze scale hooked over the fingers of one hand. Counterweight busts dangled like implacable accountants as he poured salt through whitened, cracked fingers into the pan, lifting the disembodied goddesses into balance. Larger amounts he scooped into measuring bowls cut into the countertop. "Semimodius is the limit," he reiterated, heedless of the astonished protesting voices. His voice dry as salt, restricted, immutable. "Quaestor's decree."

Valeria bought a semimodius and pushed her way out of the crush of flustered patrons. "You'd think the stuff was brought from Sicily!" indignant voices proclaimed.

The rumors persisted. "Three more last night." She purchased her beans and cabbage. Wary glances of strangers reflected like sunlight around the piazza. Residents pursed their lips while shooting arrows of accusation from their eyes at every strange face. She straightened her tan stola, adjusted the pala covering her head, and put her basket over her arm.

"Thank you, Domina," said the proprietor.

Valeria picked up her empty twin handled jug, gave him a half smile. "Goodbye."

At the fountain she filled her jug. Two friends greeted her, idly watching their small children as they leaned over the cistern and played in the water—pushing bugs, twigs, leaves, and other floating debris with handmade waves.

Valeria dipped her hand in the fountain and dabbed her forehead with wet fingers. The alarmed look that suddenly came to her friend's faces startled and puzzled her. "It's hot today." She thought she should explain.

"Do you feel all right?" asked Claudia. Her unusual auburn hair attracted attention, but her hooked nose and prominent front teeth disappointed.

"Yes," said Valeria. The tone of the question, imperative, searching, overly concerned, piqued her interest. "Why?"

"Haven't you heard?" Priscilla, pinch faced, large bosomed, with inquisitive darting dark eyes, was appalled.

"Heard what?"

"Plague," whispered Claudia, leaning close.

Valeria sucked in her breath, recoiled and brought her wet hand to her mouth. "Are you sure?"

"Is it any wonder?" declared Priscilla, wrinkling her knife blade nose with distaste. "The whole city stinks with all these animals."

"Yes," agreed Claudia. "Why don't these people go home?"

"Perhaps they don't have one anymore," offered Valeria.

"Then it's time they got busy rebuilding," insisted Claudia. "After all, the war is practically over."

"But it's only July," said Valeria. Patting her cheeks with cool water she looked up at the throbbing sun.

Black swallows careened through the cloudless sky in steep climbs, swooping, whirling, diving, sliding on thin cobalt air with shrill cries of joy. At her feet pigeons strutted, bobbing and tilting luminous green heads, argent wings folded back in disuse.

A band of shrieking children blustered by, chasing a solid wooden wheel, slapping it into motion with crooked sticks. Wobbly rolling from edge to edge, miraculously upright, the tottering wheel sent adults scattering before it like squawking chickens.

"I'm sorry," said Valeria, a frown creasing her narrow forehead. "What did you say?"

Claudia turned suspicious brown eyes on her again. "I said, rumor has it they'll demobilize two of the three legions, now that most of the fighting is done."

Valeria rose with supple grace, lifted the jug to the top of her head and balanced it there lightly with one hand. "I hope Lucius is one of them," she said.

Back at home she interrupted her son's Latin lesson to ask her father if he'd heard these rumors of plague.

"Yes," Cominus admitted. He rubbed at the coarse whiskers on his heavy jowls.

"Why didn't you tell me?"

"Because," he said gruffly, "I didn't want to alarm you with rumors. And I thought you'd hear them soon enough yourself, anyway. Which you have."

"Do you think they're true?"

"At first I wasn't sure…" he trailed off.

"But now you are."

"Yes. It's become evident."

"Then we need to close the tavern," she said.

"Well," said Cominus philosophically, "it's probably too late already. But I suppose you're right regardless."

Rumors for once proved true, and Valeria's hopes came true as well. The legions returned to Rome and demobilized. Lucius returned home to find the tavern closed. Worried something had happened he rushed upstairs to find things apparently normal.

"Why are we closed?" he asked.

"There's plague in the city, Father," volunteered Lucius Jr. importantly.

Lucius looked at Valeria with alarm. "Is that true?"

"Unfortunately," she said.

Now the consuls and the Pontifex Maximus confirmed the outbreak as well, and announced a feriae of three days. Criers went through the city, and notices were posted. All business, public, and private would cease for three days. Meanwhile all the temples opened for supplicants. Prayer and sacrifice were encouraged, work forbidden.

For many the prayers came too late. The city, once bustling with life, now became a festering pustule of death, fever wracked and vomitous. Day and night the temples welcomed the people, but brought no relief. Women swept the stone floors with loosened tresses. Altars smoked with the incessant burning of sacrifice and incense. Still the stench of death prevailed. At first funerals, especially those of the high born, were well attended. Clients and friends followed the funeral bier on which the dead man or woman reclined as if relaxing at a banquet. Mourners wept, and wailed inconsolably. But soon the whole city went about in mourning, dirty and disheveled, unshaven in tattered clothes, and no one had tears left to shed, or voice enough to cry. Blazing lights in the daytime sky and other portents were reported, and the people despaired.

Lucius paced irritably. He wanted to leave the city but he had nowhere to go. To go to his boyhood home might mean carrying the disease to his loved ones, and the house on his property had been burned to the ground. Even so, he thought, maybe it would be better to go live in a shelter of sticks and straw than to stay where death raged unchecked.

"But what would we eat there, Lucius?" asked Valeria. She desperately wanted him to offer practical answers to her questions, for she too feared death from which there was no defense.

"We would pack as much as we could carry. Villius and his family must be getting by."

"But that's just it. How many more people could the farm support as it is?"

"I don't know, Valeria. We'll eat the oxen if we have to."

"Well," said Cominus yawning. "I'm tired. I think I'll go to bed."

"Are you all right, Papa? It's awfully early."

"That's what old age does to you," he said with a half smile of chagrin.

Father time would not be blamed. The next day Cominus stayed in bed with a high fever. Valeria brought cooling water, soaking rags to put on his scorched forehead and forcing him to drink. His condition did not improve. He sweated a river then froze. His joints burned, aching as if he were being pulled apart in slow excruciating increments. The fever raged and delirium overtook him. He called out to his mother, babbling in the sweet dying voice of a child. Valeria wept.

Lucius made every remedy he could think of. He mixed dried wild cabbage in water. He boiled cabbage and put in honey, vinegar, and wine. He tried it with rue and coriander.

Valeria administered them all, but Cominus could keep nothing down. On the third day he seemed to rally and Valeria clapped for joy. He reached for her hand slowly and touched her lightly with clammy fingers. He tried to smile but the effort cost him dearly.

"Go," he whispered.

"Papa," she said, as if to a child. "I can't leave you now. As soon as you're better we'll go. I promise."

A sad, knowing, loving look of ultimate departure and separation filled his eyes. "You always..." he turned his head aside, closing his eyes against the effort.

"I always what, Papa?"

When he opened his eyes again, he could not see her.

Valeria stood slowly, turned stricken to her husband standing in the doorway. Deliberately she pulled the bronze comb from her long hair and loosed it as one frees a caged animal. Midnight curled voluminous around her soft slender face, draped her shoulders, flowed in galaxies down her back. Black pearls glistened with profound secrets in the long oval sockets of her sensuous eyes. Ineffable sadness, stirred up from the bottom of her heart, clouded the limped depths. She raised one slim arm to him, her bracelets falling with sybaritic chimes along the luminous taut flesh of her beckoning. She swayed, a feverish radiant glow, like polished bronze, emanated from her supple skin. Then her knees buckled, and Lucius caught her in his arms.

Valeria followed her father two days later. Screaming in rage at the awful pain of being torn apart over and over again. The disease threw her about on the bed, arching her back in spasms of agony, pulling her lips away from her teeth in a hideous snarl. She howled in rage at the terrible sun that bored a hole in her skull and burned behind her eyes inextinguishable, unquenchable by all the waters of the Tiber. She called to Lucius for mercy, but he watched helplessly as life wrenched itself from her clenched fingers.

Stunned with sorrow and remorse, Lucius presided over her rigid body with uncomprehending loyalty, like a dog waiting for its master to rise, not knowing he never would.

Though she had parted from him, he could not bear to part with her.

Lucius Jr. sat in his room alone, rocking his anguish back and forth, his heart twisted in incomprehensible grief. But he shed no tears. "Romans don't cry," he mumbled, repeating it like a prayer, a spell, a litany.

When finally he parted with her, Lucius parted with all of her. He tenderly carried her in his arms and placed her in the cart next to her father. Along with her lifeless body he piled every single one of her belongings, clothes, rings, bracelets, earrings, all their wedding gifts, anything that could remind him of his sorrow. He found a spot outside the city and used the wagon for her funeral pyre. With giant insufficient hands hanging in hopeless futility at his side he watched his love ascend in black ashes to the hard blue sky.

Father and son rode bareback on mules to the father's family home. Alone he climbed the steep sides of the mountain behind, and there in the cool environs of thick forest he cried out to the sky, and poured out his suffering in convulsive sobs. When he finished, he left the joys of his past there to wander in the dense lachrymal undergrowth, forever lost.

Like new ground he had been cleared by fire, and made ready to nurture a new crop.

# XXIV

## December 15, 462 BC
## The Consualia—The Opening of
## Granaries

They say that time heals all wounds. If true, Lucius Tempanius would require an eon. His family saw the change and could only hope that time would work its cure. When he shed his tears in the woods, he shed his joy as well. Like a molting snake he left the dead skin of his former self to rot, to deliquesce in the brambles and thorny tessellation of the forest floor.

From his boyhood home he sent Graptus, as soon as the plague had spent itself, back to Rome to reopen the tavern. Meanwhile, he and Lucius Jr. moved onto the property on the Anio with the bitter thought that if he'd insisted on going there before perhaps things would have been different. Once ensconced in a makeshift hut he, Villius, Lucius Jr., and Villius' two sons began building. They needed a house, stables, storerooms for tools, wheat, fruits, meats, fodder, as well as pens for the pigs and goats.

Lucius worked them from dawn to dusk, sparing no one, least of all himself. He took no joy in the work, instead viewing it as a kind of penance. He spoke little and laughed less. By winter they were all able to squeeze into the lower story of the house and stable the mules and oxen out of the cold. By spring they completed the stables, reinforced the temporary pens, and made progress on the storerooms. Wheat and barley were planted in March, after which Lucius decided the time had come to return to Rome. His body and spirit had become iron hard, forged in sorrow, tempered by bitterness.

No sooner arrived, he joined the legion under the command of the consul Lucius Lucretius. In a battle against the Volscians in the gullies and ravines near his boyhood home he fought with such savagery and abandon that his own comrades feared him. Though he won the civic crown for saving the life of a citizen, it meant nothing to him. He cursed the Volscians as a weak and womanly opponent, having given them ample opportunity to kill him.

Returned to Rome he found that even had he wanted to, taking up his former life would have been difficult. The dying in Rome had been widespread. Both consuls, the augurs, and the president of the ward-priests had all succumbed to the plague. Among the poor, an over abundance of labor no longer pertained. Graptus informed him of further losses.

"I'm sorry to say that Aulus Vibulus as well as your friend Cnaeus Considius died also," he said.

Lucius greeted the news not with indifference but with an acceptance that bordered on it. He shrugged his great shoulders. "I guess no one's exempt, eh?"

Graptus would have liked to say something consoling, sentimental. He said nothing, just gazed at Lucius. Maybe the close cropping had something to do with it, but it seemed to him the widow's peak had become more pronounced in Lucius' hair. The gray at the temples had definitely spread. Deep creases around his eyes the casual observer might attribute to years of sun and weather. But Graptus knew better. He also knew that consolation was unwelcome. Even his jokes fell flat. The man had grown so different it sometimes seemed to Graptus as if he'd been sold to another master. He couldn't get over watching Lucius, wearing so many military awards they would have bent other men under the weight, march with listless detachment behind the triumphal chariot of Lucretius. The day he lived for, the day he could impress all of Rome with his honors and his prowess, and he couldn't have cared less. His soul had indeed grown small.

"Shall I prepare something for your brothers?" Graptus asked.

Lucius shifted the brazier under the kitchen table, pulling it nearer with his feet. A small fire blazed on the hearth. In front of him two tallow candles in earthenware holders dripped yellow light in small pools over a wax tablet on which he composed a list of items for the tavern and the property.

"Yes," he said over the chewed end of a wooden stylus. "I suppose we ought to feed them."

Graptus knocked down the fire on the hearth, spread the coals between the bricks, threw on a few more pieces of charcoal, and set a bronze tripod over the glowing mass. He poured water into a terracotta pot, reached up to a shelf for salt and added two large three- finger pinches of it to the water. Into this he poured a bowl of husked and cleaned wheat, stirring as he did so. When he had it thoroughly mixed, he placed the pot on the tripod over the hot coals.

By the time Titus and Antonius arrived the mixture was boiling rapidly, the rising steam flowing out the smoke hole midway up the wall.

"Mm, smells good," said Titus, inhaling deeply as he entered.

"I'm starved," added Antonius. "When do we eat?"

"Soon," said Graptus. With a long wooden spoon, he stirred the mixture while slowly pouring in a pitcher of milk until it reached a thick creamy consistency.

Lucius looked up at his brothers. "Call Lucius, would you?"

"I'll do it," volunteered Antonius.

"Well, Titus," said Lucius, his hands spread like maple leaves on the tabletop. "Why didn't you bring Marcus or little Titus with you?"

Titus poured himself a cup of water and pulled up a low-backed chair at the end of the table. "They need to learn how to work first," he said. The cup covered his brown eyes as he drank the contents in one long draught. "Later they can learn to argue."

The candles guttered, throwing light in drunken splotches, avoiding the dark corners and glancing off faces as if embarrassed by ineffectiveness.

Lucius grunted ambiguously, and returned to his writing. Graptus set out four more cups and five wooden spoons. He ladled porridge into five bowls and set them around the table as Antonius and Lucius Jr. entered the kitchen. Lucius threw some wheat on the fire for the penates, the hearth gods of the house. Everyone remained silent until Graptus observed that the wheat had all been consumed.

"The penates have accepted the propitiation," he said.

For a time they ate in silence, Lucius left in sole possession of one side of the table.

"So, what did you learn today?" Antonius asked Lucius Jr.

Lucius Jr. sat with his left hand under his thigh, his right spooning creamy porridge into his mouth. He raised his eyes, the color of oiled leather, and looked engagingly at his uncle. "Nothing," he said.

His father shot him a stern glance. "Quit hiding your hand and tell your uncle what you learned today."

Reluctantly Lucius Jr. brought his deformed left hand up to the table. He raked his curly lava colored hair with it. "Today I learned about the rape of Lucretia," he said obediently, but without enthusiasm.

Antonius gave the boy his most encouraging smile. "Ah, that's a great story. Tell us about it."

The younger Lucius looked at his father, brown eyes pleading against the necessity of recounting the story. Lucius Sr. nodded his head and scowled at his son's reluctance.

Lucius Jr. took a deep breath and lifted his eyes to the ceiling. "Tarquinius Superbus was be…bes…besieging the city of Ardea," he began. "But it was a very long battle and everyone got tired. So, his son Sextus made a bet with some other men…"

"Which other men?" demanded Lucius.

"Umm, Lucius Tarquinius Collatinus and just some others. And they bet whose wife was best, and then they rode to Rome and found only Lucretia—Lucius Collatinus' wife—working. All the rest were just having parties. But Sextus Tarquinius liked her so much that one night he sneaked back to Rome and raped her. She was ashamed and told her husband what happened, and everybody said it wasn't her fault, but she killed herself anyway. Then everybody got very mad and made Tarquinius Superbus and his whole family leave Rome. And that's when the Republic started."

Titus clapped loudly. "Excellent," he said. His amphora-shaped face didn't so much widen as it did crack longitudinally from deep creases that ran from his drooping nose, cupped his small mouth, and disappeared into his chin.

Antonius also applauded, and spread his full lips in a wide smile of amusement. In a condescending voice he said, "Of course you know that's just a myth. But you told it well."

"Why is it just a myth?" demanded Titus. "Graptus, I brought a basket with olives and the like. Find it and break them out for us, would you?"

"Because things don't happen that way." Antonius widened his long eyes as if it were self-evident. His swallow wing eyebrows rose in flight. "It's too simplistic."

"Often times simple acts create complicated reactions," offered Graptus. Locating the olives in a basket at the end of the counter he spooned them into a bowl and set them in front of Titus. Returning to his chair he smiled to himself with the realization that Antonius would not acknowledge his comment.

"I agree, Graptus," said Lucius. "And just as often a simple act that follows a long history of bad behavior will set off a confrontation that seems all out of proportion. How many times has the same thing happened with your wife and children Titus?"

Titus chuckled at the thought. "Untold," he said sagely. He took some olives and passed the bowl to Antonius.

"I see," said Antonius. "An object lesson."

"Listen, I don't know what that means," said Lucius. "But if it means the story teaches that a man's behavior adds up to the man himself, then yes, it's a….whatever you called it."

Lucius helped himself to another bowl of porridge. Conversation lapsed. When he finished Lucius pushed his bowl away and shoved his chair back, stretching out his legs. "How about a little wine, Graptus. For the digestion."

"White or red?" asked Graptus. "For the digestion."

A tenuous smile hung on Lucius' wide face then fell. "Let's have some of that Etruscan red we bought in Caere. Well," he leaned back and surveyed his brothers in the dim light, "how'd the vote go today?"

"One interesting person," said Antonius.

"Oh?"

"Gaius Terentillus Arsa." Antonius moved slightly to let Graptus pour him some wine. "Mix it with water," he said, making a stirring motion with a stubby index finger. Graptus poured the cup half full with wine, then added water from the pitcher on the table.

With a smile.

"It's been said he'll try to get the laws codified," informed Titus.

"Think he'll succeed?" asked Lucius.

"I don't see how. The plebeian assembly has no power to pass laws, and the consuls will never propose it before the centuriate assembly."

"What's codify mean?" asked Lucius Jr.

"It means to write them down," said Lucius.

"How do they remember them if they don't write them down?" Lucius the younger asked.

Everyone laughed, even his father. Which made Lucius Jr. sad, because he wished he could make him laugh on purpose instead of by accident.

"You've cut right to the bone on that," said Antonius, but didn't elaborate. "The point is, Titus, they'll have to force them into it the same way Volero did. They'll have to obstruct the levy."

"I don't like that tactic," complained Titus. "It's not right to hold your own country hostage."

"Unfortunately, there's no other way for the common people to have a voice," said Antonius. He sipped at the wine, smacking his lips. "Very good. Sweet, unlike Roman wine."

"Roman wine is for libations to the gods," said Lucius. "Greek and Etruscan wine is for humans to enjoy."

"Assuming you can afford it," said Titus.

"The benefits of owning a tavern," said Lucius. He hoisted his cup sardonically in the air, and then drained it. Pouring another cup, he said, "Well, then, you're staying in Rome for the festivals?"

"Depends," said Titus. "I'm more interested in Terentillus' efforts."

"I thought you said he couldn't accomplish anything until the levy?"

"No, Antonius said that."

"Yes," said Antonius, "you said he couldn't accomplish anything."

"Nevertheless, I want to stay around and see."

"I have other reasons for staying," declared Antonius, and gazed significantly at Lucius.

"And that is?" said Lucius, feigning ignorance.

"It's been over a year and a half since you promised to arrange a marriage for me."

"Ah. Listen, a few things have gotten in the way recently. But I haven't forgotten. Besides, you said you could wait."

"Yes, but I expected to at least be affianced by now."

"Don't worry. I'm working on it."

"Do you have someone in mind?"

"I said I'm working on it," growled Lucius, quashing the discussion.

+ + +

Titus and Antonius remained in Rome to see nothing get accomplished. Terentillus did indeed make his proposals, whipped up some excitement among the plebs, and made no impression whatsoever on the consuls or their advisors in the senate.

Three festivals in succession then followed, the Consualia on the 15th, the Saturnalia on the 17th, and the Opalia on the nineteenth. The Consualia and the Opalia, agricultural in nature, celebrated the storage of food, soliciting protection of it, as well as celebrating the abundance of the harvest to carry the people through the winter. The Saturnalia was simply the day when nothing was as it seemed and licentiousness ruled. The courts closed, assemblies were forbidden, and all public business was suspended during this period. Titus tired of the city and returned to his beloved farm. Antonius returned to Antium single and without a fiancé`.

For Lucius, the winter passed as it usually did—too slow. It rained incessantly, and the cold passed through the walls and through his clothes as if they weren't there. He spent a small fortune on charcoal and still couldn't get warm.

On the other hand, business picked up. The victory over the Volscians garnered a weight of bronze breastplates, greaves, and helmets. These the consul generously distributed to his victorious soldiers. Many of them turned their gain immediately into cash—either by sale or melting their loot into bronze bars—which they willingly spent on wine, prostitutes, their wives, and other necessities of life. In the empty days of January, unencumbered with public festivals, politics and leisure reigned supreme. Each afternoon and long into the night, the Subura district hosted the city's revelers. Every class of citizen mingled in the taverns or 'specialty' shops of the district.

Graptus took on new importance as his role increased. In him Lucius discovered a business acumen he himself did not possess. It soon developed that Graptus enjoyed few hours of respite. His mornings were spent teaching Lucius Jr. reading, writing, and arithmetic. Later he prepared the afternoon meal, which often meant shopping for food and other household goods. At the eighth hour he involved himself totally with the business of the tavern. Since Lucius had turned over the bookkeeping to him as well, this often entailed working late into the night by a wicking tallow candle.

Not that Lucius sat back and collected the profits. He kept himself busy as well, and in his own way had a business acumen that complimented that of Graptus. Enamored of music and heroic stories and ballads, Lucius became a patron of musicians and poets. His un-Roman proclivity set his tavern apart, and its unique atmosphere, not to mention the wines he procured from Magna Grecia and Etruria thanks to his deceased father-in-law, drew customers from all walks of life. His iconoclastic way of life raised eyebrows within and without his family. Having the medals to prove his reputation for valor, courage, and ferocity, few outside his family said anything out loud. His mother and Titus were not so reticent. Thus it was that in January, forty-eight years after the founding of the Republic, the foremost 'enlisted man' of his time had to bear up under pressures from his slave, his brother, and his mother.

The fateful day dawned rainy, with a slate gray sky of congealed clouds. Lucius attempted to occupy himself, but without his morning exercise regimen and Lucius the Younger's training session on the Campus Martius a large hole opened in his daily routine. He lingered at the baths as long as he could stand, but the spartan facilities allowed little in the way of amusement and exercise. Returning to the Boar's Tusk he opened for business at the third hour instead of the normal fourth. Not that it made any difference, since mornings tended to be slow anyway.

Not long after Graptus finished his lessons with Lucius Jr. the two of them came downstairs into the main room of the tavern. Two customers sitting solitary and well apart made the room seem larger than it actually was. Lucius sat at a table near the serving tower, idly moving dust around with thick fingers.

"Morning Father," said Lucius Jr. He brushed his father's spiky cheek with a kiss.

Lucius wrapped a muscular arm around his eight-year-old son, who carried the same harmonious features as his mother. Roughly caressing the boy's curly black hair, his great paw covered his son's head like a helmet. "How did your lessons go?"

"Good," said Lucius Jr.

Lucius turned his gaze on Graptus to verify the veracity of his son's assertion. In reality he could not bear to look on the tremulous mouth, the chestnut eyes spaced in perfect balance on either side of a fine nose. To look on his son was to see Valeria and feel again the longing of his loss.

Graptus nodded approvingly. "He'll never be a poet, thank the gods, but no one will ever cheat him when it comes to sums, either."

"Good," said Lucius. "You can have a snack, then take your sword and shield to the stable and practice for an hour. Understand?" He turned his broad face, truculent lips pulled away from square teeth in a forced smile, to his son and sent him away with a pat on his backside.

"You're looking tired, Graptus. Feeling all right?"

Graptus pulled out a stool, and folded his lanky body onto it. He allowed his angular face to elongate with weariness and sighed not too heavily. "To be honest, Dominus…"

"Oh, Dominus, is it?"

"To be honest, Dominus, my duties leave me little energy."

"And what do you need extra energy for? Are you hiding a woman somewhere?"

"Well, not in the sense you're thinking…"

"I knew it!"

"It's not what you think."

"Tell me what I'm not thinking then."

"A woman did come by the other day…"

"And…"

"…her name is Demetria, and she lost everyone in the plague." Graptus hesitated, afraid of opening this wound, then plunged ahead. "She's absolutely desperate and, frankly, we could use a full time cook and housekeeper."

Lucius laughed through his teeth, a hissing, humorless sound. "If this is legitimate, I'll consider it," he said, searching

Graptus with critical eyes. "But if you're scheming with some ulterior motive in mind, I'll have your hide."

The wrinkling of sincere hurt in the sky-blue eyes that stared back guilelessly at him convinced Lucius. "All right," he said. "I'll take your word for it. Tell her I expect her to prepare dinner tonight. Titus and my mother will be here."

"Thank you, Dominus. You won't regret it."

"Eh. I suppose she'll need a room."

"Well…"

"Fix it up. You're going to send me into debt bondage yet."

Graptus hurried out before Lucius could change his mind.

Perhaps with a few regular meals her gaunt, wasted looks might soften to something more pleasant, but Demetria would never be anything more than plain. In matronly fashion she pulled her raven black hair into a tight ball at the nape of her neck. She had prepared the meal with large strong hands that performed their tasks with confident movements. Buried in a cabinet she found a shallow covered terracotta baking dish, obviously fallen into desuetude. After cleaning the oval dish, she allowed it to soak in water. When it had done this to her satisfaction, she placed a freshly plucked and cleaned chicken that she had rubbed with salt and infused with garlic, onions, and rosemary in the baking dish and put it in the oven.

Entering the kitchen, the aroma immediately set stomachs growling and mouths watering. Drusilla tried to help set the table only to receive a humble reprimand in a low husky voice from Demetria.

"Forgive me, Domina, but I think it is my duty to serve. Please," she waved to a chair, "sit down. Everything will be ready soon."

When all reached a state of readiness, Lucius threw a small wheatcake on the hearth fire to the household gods and Graptus announced the penates acceptance of the propitiatory offering. They ate the meal with gusto, accompanied by the steady drumming of cold rain outside. When they had finished, relaxed in the intimate warmth of the kitchen, Lucius called for wine.

As Graptus poured everyone, including himself and Demetria, a generous cup of violet colored wine Drusilla's thoughts turned to Lucius' future. A subject she had pondered often over the last year.

"Lucius," she said, "now that you have no reason to keep it, why not sell the tavern?"

"What do you mean, 'no reason'?" he asked. Taking a long drink from his cup, he stared over the rim at his mother.

"I mean," she said, ruffled but not about to be put off, "that since you are now, unfortunately, alone, there's no reason you can't sell it, and invest in more land. Even a nice house in Rome, if you wish."

"But I already have a house in Rome."

"I think what she's trying to say," said Titus, rubbing his fingers on the table, "is something more..." he made vague circles in the air with his hand, hunting for the word.

"Honorable?" filled in Lucius. A sardonic smile struggled across his face.

"I would say acceptable," said Titus. "But if you insist, honorable."

"I don't wish to play games with words," said Drusilla firmly. "The most honorable work for a Roman is farming the land."

"Then what would I do, Domina, since I wouldn't want to work it myself very often?"

The formal title coming from Lucius' mouth stung her. "I don't know. That would be up to you." Drusilla felt the hairs stiffen on the back of her son's head as if he still inhabited her body. Stubbornness exuded like oil from his skin. So like his father, she thought. "At least you would have the means to live as you wish."

"I already live as I wish. And I doubt I could get the same income off the land."

"Bronze, for all its value, is not the only thing," said Drusilla.

"You could probably be tribune if you sold it," said Titus, joking.

To Lucius the prospect of being tribune was of laughable importance. More, the office, such as it existed, held no interest for him. He laughed in cynical appreciation of Titus' joke.

"Now there's a dream I've always held. What has a tribune ever done for me?"

Titus, now goaded to defend his jest, took up the argument. "Well, at least they've extended the right of appeal. And if Terentillus gets his reform passed they will be responsible for even greater justice."

Lucius laughed indifferently. "If I need justice I go to Publius Scipio. Same as you."

"Could we return to the subject?" Drusilla interrupted.

"Mama," Lucius said with a tone of finality, "I'm not going to sell the tavern. I like it. It gives me something to do during the winter, and it keeps life interesting."

Drusilla shook her head and pushed her cup distastefully away. "Coriolanus turned away from the greatest victory of his life at the request of his mother. My son won't even part with a shameful tavern for his."

Titus raised one side of his dour mouth in a grimacing smile as their mother left the room in disgust. "Well," he said, with amused resignation. "I suppose this means I'll be going home in the morning."

# XXV

February 13, 461 BC
The Parentalia—Day of Honoring the Dead

Thunder crashed in cascading waves, rumbling down the hills in avalanches of terror. Stunned by the ripping concussions her owlish eyes blinked uncontrollably, and her heart thudded erratically against her breast. Rain fell in harsh, heavy sheets, splattering invasively against the house. The flash of yet another hammer blow lit the sky outside the open shutters of the window, and she cringed in anticipation.

"Duellia," soothed Titus, observing her fear, "it's only thunder." He sat at the kitchen table mending various sized pots using a mixture of wax, sulfur, resin, and gypsum.

"How can you say that?" said Duellia. Her voice trembled through thin lips compressed with anxiety. "After all those reports." Plangent peals of thunder pummeled the black sky.

"What reports are those?" asked Drusilla. With a thick bronze needle she mended a tear in a tunic for the slave Restius. "Oh Juno," she said, knitting her swallow wing eyebrows and peering down her straight nose. She moved the cloth closer, then farther away. "It's so hard to see anything I'm doing these days."

"Restius is perfectly capable of patching his own tunics, Domina," said Titus.

Another crack of thunder shook the house. The candles guttered, nearly extinguishing as if the air were being sucked out of the house. Duellia flinched, ducked her head. "They say it rained lumps of meat," she said, horrified. With shaking hands she wove a garland of laurel to hang over the hearth the following day. Every *kalends*, *nones*, and *ides* of the month she hung a garland over the hearth so the *penates* would feel welcome and stay in her home. The next day was also the Parentalia, the day of celebrating the family's dead ancestors.

"Well…" began Titus. His pursed lips pulled his long face into wrinkles of disbelief.

"And they say a cow talked," she insisted, her voice ascended in pitch.

The sound of her voice, pinched and tremulous with hysteria annoyed and spooked him. "Stop, Duellia. You can't believe half of what you hear."

"But you felt the earthquake yourself."

"Nevertheless, Duellia," said Drusilla mellifluously, "we must trust our priests know what to do."

Duellia stood suddenly, put down the garland on which she was working, and step- ped over to the hearth. She threw some fresh charcoal on the fire, banked it, and cleaned nervously, agitated. "Are you still planning on going to Rome after the Lupercalia?" she asked.

"Yes," said Titus.

"I wish you wouldn't. I have a bad feeling about you going. Besides, everyone will be here for the Caristia in a few more days."

Titus widened his mouth with a condescending smile. "There's nothing to worry about," he assured her. "It'll just be another market day."

Her fears were greatly assuaged by the good omen of clear blue skies and sparkling air. A smell of spring drifted comfortingly on a light breeze. Marcus danced by the solid wheels of the two-wheeled cart begging his father to take him with, only to be repulsed by a patient smile and, "not this time." Titus held firm to the conviction that Lucius had been introduced to the sybaritic call of Rome too early and too often. He would not make the same mistake with his son. Conveniently overlooking the fact that he also had gone along from an early age without adverse effects, he defended his decision by saying too much work needed done. He then exacted a promise from Petronius to keep the boy busy.

Patiently drawn on the flagstone road to Rome by a single ox, Titus had cause to wish, in retrospect, that he had the company of his son. His ox answered the lowing calls of her species drawing plows through the fields they passed, bawled in complaint to cattle leisurely cropping clover in meadows waiting to be furrowed. The image of rich loam roiling off his plow brought the strong scent of the earth to his nostrils. But he had no one with whom to share that joy inculcated in him as if by the earth itself.

When at last he reached Rome, his lower back ached from the constant jolting it took over fifteen miles of Roman road. The sun lingered, on the verge of vacating the sky, its day's work finished in cool splendor on the far edge of the sea. A sere veil of crepuscular light softened the stone, brick, and plaster buildings of Rome though Titus could still read the graffiti testifying to the political unrest in the city. Down the length of the Vicus Suburanus, starting at the Porta Esquilina he read the popular messages.

"Liberty without laws is tyranny!"

"Question: how many kings does it take to make a Republic? Answer: two." An obvious reference to the consuls.

"People can't obey what they're not allowed to read."

"Oppression begins with control of the law."

Others affected a more personal message, alliteration preferred.

"Tenacious Terentillus Triumphs."

"Sulpicius Serves Servility."

Volumnius Validates Venality."

The last two aimed at the present consuls as well, Titus chuckled to himself, admiring the creativity of the writers.

Upon arriving he pulled around to the back of the Boar's Tusk, unhitched the ox and guided her into a stall in the stable. He watered and fed her, speaking kindly as he rubbed her down with a handful of straw. She twitched her tail gratefully at his ministrations, now and then lifting her massive horned head to look at him with knowing dark eyes. These would be, she seemed to say, his last moments of peace.

One look around the inside of the tavern and Titus had to admit, that old ox knew what she was talking about. Barely had the sun descended than the Boar's Tusk came to life. A lyre player in one corner sang ballads of love and war. On the opposite end of the room Lucius filled pitchers of wine from the serving tower. Graptus ran back and forth to the kitchen carrying bowls and platters filled with food or the remnants of it. Voices and music thickened the atmosphere like flour thickens soup. The sweet smells of cooking meat and vegetables balanced the sour odor of spilled wine, and men packed tight conversing, singing, playing dice or bones.

"Need any help?" he shouted up to Lucius.

"Sure," said Lucius, looking around a pitcher, "want to buy a tavern?"

"No, I don't think so." Titus laughed.

"Listen, there's plenty of food in the kitchen if you're hungry. Ask Demetria and she'll get you something."

Titus enjoyed a simple meal of wheat porridge, preceded by a hard-boiled egg. As he spooned the honey sweetened gruel between thin lips his brother Antonius came in looking for something to eat. Antonius had come to Rome prior to the Parentalia and celebrated with Lucius the memory of their father and the long line of Tempanii ancestors whose memory, through honorable competition, they carried on.

"Well," said Titus, as Antonius sat down with a steaming bowl of creamed wheat, "it looks like I've been missing all the fun." He raised his eyes inquiringly; the iron bands restraining the brown irises gave them a greenish tint.

Antonius shrugged his spare shoulders, so different from his brothers; thinner, leaner, angrier. "You haven't missed much," he said. "Too many days nefastus. But now most of the days are comitialis, so your timing should be good."

"Fill me in."

"There's not much to tell." Antonius paused with a heavily laden spoon in front of his mouth. "Terentillus and Verginius are the two tribunes who do the most talking." He blew on the porridge then slurped it into his mouth.

Titus scraped the bottom of his bowl clean, pushed his chair back and from a shelf nearby retrieved a game board and dice. Noise from the main room of the tavern swirled through the kitchen like a single uninterrupted low note on the tibia.

"I don't understand," he said, setting up the pieces for a game of Twelve Lines. "What can they accomplish?" He shook the die in a leather cup and rolled them out on the table. "Seven," he counted, "the perfect number."

Antonius scooped the die into the cup, shook it roughly and slammed it onto the table, revealing the die slowly. "I think they're trying to put pressure on the consuls to propose the law to the centuriate assembly. Nine. I go first."

"Hmph. And the consuls?"

Antonius poured out the die and moved two pieces. "Oh, they're doing their best to ignore the whole thing."

Titus rested his chin in the palm of his hand, yawned, and rolled the die. "Two," he said disgustedly. He moved two pieces one space each. "They probably think it's best to keep out of it."

"That's ridiculous," said Antonius, dropping the die into the cup. "They're the chief officers of the State. They're inciting the people with their arrogance."

"That could be," speculated Titus as he rolled a three. "Jupiter!" he swore.

"No 'could be' about it," asserted Antonius, shaking the die vigorously with his hand over the mouth of the cup. "Rumor has it tomorrow they're going to drum up some excuse to call a levy and put the people under oath. Ha, Venus!" he exclaimed, rolling out two sixes. "I told you it'd come down to this."

Titus gathered the die into the cup as Antonius moved pieces around the board. "It's a little early in the year for a levy. But I guess we'll see tomorrow." He turned away from the table and bent forward, stretching his back. "Oh, my back," he groaned. "The ride here just murders it anymore."

The next morning Lucius and Titus dressed in their best tunics and cloaks and accompanied Publius Scipio into the Forum. Considering the rising tensions they did more than honor him, they acted as bodyguards as well. Scipio expressed his gratitude ingenuously, for their dress and the fact they met him at his door, instead of in the Forum, expressed their real concern for his safety.

Antonius escorted Titus Quinctius to the Forum in the same manner. He now considered Quinctius his patron since his quondam commander helped secure him a prime piece of property during the colonization of Antium.

With their respective patrons safely ensconced in the Curia, the three brothers reunited briefly. Lucius intended to depart almost immediately and return home to collect Lucius Jr. for his lessons in the military arts. After which he would work on his own training, then bathe and return to the Boar's Tusk to open the tavern.

"Aren't you interested in what happens here?" asked Titus, pointing at the black flagstones of the Forum.

Lucius pushed out his lower lip. "Not really. If I want to feel the wind I'll go to the mountains. Or the sea."

"You're too cynical for words," said Titus, shaking his oblong head.

"Exactly," said Lucius. "I'll expect you for supper." He waved goodbye as he crossed the Forum.

Directly behind them, near the sacred olive tree, the tribunes had caused a speaker's stand to be erected. Nearby stood the bronze pillar inscribed with the Cassian Treaty, tarnished to a dark brown color. A commotion informed them of the arrival of the tribunes who mounted the platform. Only two of them took to the dais, Verginius, a tall firmly built man in his mid thirties, and Terentillus, a swarthy stocky man in his late thirties. Colleagues in the tribunate, assistants, and clients encircled the platform in a protective ring. Terentillus stepped forward. He spoke with a powerful voice, rich in tone.

"Citizens, friends, I have come here today to ask just one question; how long must we suffer oppression and injustice? Consul may sound finer than king, but the truth is we have simply exchanged one king for two. For it is only kings and despots who hide from their subjects the very laws with which they crush them. Who but kings have unlimited powers defined only by their own lusts?"

Titus and Antonius edged through the crowd, trying to get closer, though they could hear well enough from where they stood near the shrine of Cloacina. They cut across the Forum at an angle, passing near the comitium.

Terentillus boomed on. "While we in ignorance proclaim our freedom to the world, our two consuls arrogantly claim we have no right to know either the laws by which they judge us nor the limits of the power with which they punish us. I say this is intolerable in a free state and must be changed."

A loud cheer rose from the multitude only to be strangled by the blare of trumpets from the Curia. Lictors poured out of the senate building carrying the bundles of rods tied with red leather cords against their shoulders. The consuls, bustling after, cut across Titus and Antonius' path, forcing them to halt, and climbed another rostrum erected on the east end of the Forum. Twenty-four lictors formed in two lines across the front of the dais.

"Silence!" called a crier from the stage. This platform, originally set up as a tribunal to hear court cases, now served another function. "By order of the consuls, upon advice of the fathers in the senate, the centuries will be called for enlistment in the legions." He thumped his staff against the wood flooring of the tribunal. "The levy to take place in four days time."

A roar of outrage tore through the crowd. Suddenly shifting aimlessly like a disturbed anthill men milled in every direction. Stunned, Titus looked at Antonius who wore a curious smile of justification. Or maybe vindication pulled those full lips and wide mouth into a smile. Beneath the swallow winged eyebrows gathered in martial flight his anthracite eyes blazed.

"What are they doing?" spluttered Titus.

"Starting a revolution," spat Antonius. His smile twisted into bitter contempt. "It's not enough…"

A cornicular stepped forward and blew his horn. Two martial notes gripped the air like blacksmith's tongs. The crier's voice hammered their iron ears. "Silence!" he boomed.

Volumnius elevated himself from his curule chair, adjusting the glittering vermilion stripe of his toga. In his early forties, of medium height and build, he had stark reptilian features, accentuated by a prognathous jaw that gave the impression of preening arrogance. Cut close to his head his gray hair glittered like scales, emphasizing the sharp features of his face. Close set dark eyes scanned the crowd as he held up a hand for silence. Gold on his finger and wrist reflected powerfully in the sunlight.

"The doors of the temple of Janus must be opened," he announced. "Opened by the perfidy of men we once called friends and brothers." He pointed with open hand in the direction of the Argiletum where the temple of Janus stood, its double iron doors closed in peace. "Citizens of Rome, Antium has risen against you, and it is for this that we have called for crisis men at such short notice."

"Lies!" yelled Antonius, sending a murmur of doubt rippling through the crowd. "Lies!" he screamed again.

"Who dares call me a liar?" challenged Volumnius, searching the multitude.

"I dare," answered Antonius. "Antium is loyal. I know it and you know it."

Now the tribunes took up the cry. Verginius stretched tall and raised his voice. "Do not listen to these false claims," he cried, aiming a muscular arm in the direction of the consuls.

Confused, conflicted, half scared, half resentful, the assembly of double minded men looked from tribunes to consuls, conferred hurriedly with one another. Verginius continued. "Just think, comrades. How, after the crushing defeat for which Lucretius was awarded a triumph, could the Volscians possibly threaten us again so soon? Only one of two possibilities can exist. Either the victory was not as resounding as was claimed (and if so, then why did we allow a triumph to

Lucretius?); or a cruel hoax is being foisted on us in an attempt to distract us from our just and reasonable demands."

Inchoate violence drifted like a mist, an infection polluting the bodies and minds of otherwise reasonable men. A space cleared around Antonius as he continued to yell in exultant defiance, "Lies!" at the consuls.

Volumnius succumbed first to the disease. "Lictor, seize and bind that man." Venomous rage pulled flushed skin tighter on his serpentine face. A shaking finger pointed at Antonius.

Titus, already feeling isolated, saw himself in a hopeless situation. Even as the crowd shrank away from them, he moved closer to his brother, determined that they would only arrest Antonius when he could no longer defend him. He wished Lucius had stayed.

"Thanks," he said sarcastically to Antonius.

A lictor, the bundled rods in one arm, pushed through the crowd towards them.

"It's nothing," laughed Antonius.

As the lictor approached Titus stepped in front of Antonius, shielding him from view.

"Let me by, Titus," said the lictor. Doubt, sadness, and duty mingled in his chestnut eyes. His muscular body stiffened, and his hewn jaw tightened.

"Sorry Lucius Manlius. You'll have to go through me first."

Manlius stepped forward. Titus shoved him back. Behind Manlius he saw another lictor dispatched in his direction. This one, he knew, was meant for him. Manlius came forward forcefully as if to bull his way past Titus. A punch in the stomach doubled him over and Titus shoved him backwards. Suddenly currents of men swirled around him, a human undertow of factions in violent conflict. Punches flew, hard hands thudded sickeningly, pushing, shoving, angry shouting spilled in blood-streaked faces around him. Clients and supporters from both sides converged on Titus and Antonius in increasing strength until a general melee broke out. In the confusion and chaos Titus lashed out at anyone and everyone until Antonius grabbed him by the tunic and pulled him backwards. Titus spun to confront his assailant only to find Antonius with an excited grin plastered on his face.

"Come on," he yelled above the tumult, laughing madly. "Let's get out of here."

Like fugitives they wove their way through the straining heaving mass of men until they reached the Vicus Suburanus. Antonius laughed delightedly as they hustled past the Mamilian tower and cut through the maze of houses, and shops in the lower Subura district to the Boar's Tusk.

"Well," said Antonius, breathing hard from the fight and his merriment. "I guess that takes care of the 'crisis' levy."

+ + +

The next day began the Fornacalia, which lasted three days. It celebrated the oldest organizational structure of Rome. According to tradition Romulus first divided the people into three tribes, the Ramnes, Tities, and Luceres. These were then subdivided into thirty curiae, ten to each tribe. Each curia had a name that, by tradition, derived from the Sabine women (or thirty of them at any rate) treacherously kidnapped by Romulus and his followers. Each tribe was obligated to provide one thousand infantry and one hundred cavalry, or one hundred infantry and ten cavalry from each curia.

By the time of the Republic the curiate system had given way to the centuriate organization, the tribes had increased from three to twenty-one, and it was now from the sixty centuries of the centuriate organization that the army was drawn.

Wedded as they were to tradition, rather than do away with the *comitia curiata*, the Romans simply added an extra layer with the *comitia centuriata*. The only duties the curiate assembly retained was to ratify adoptions, witness wills, and formally transfer power from outgoing magistrates to incoming magistrates.

So it came to pass that on the first of two days of the Fornacalia individual curiae reunited for what amounted to a picnic. The third day all the curiae met together. Romans called it the 'fool's day' because anyone who didn't know to which curia he belonged could then celebrate the Fornacalia. For to be human and civilized meant belonging to a community. Only animals and criminals lived outside the community, and for this reason Romans dreaded banishment more than death.

Despite the public nature of the festival the Pontifex Maximus determined the three days of the Fornacalia would continue as comitialis so that all public and private business could continue. Since their curia didn't celebrate until the second day the Tempanius brothers repeated their activities of the previous day.

Fewer men crowded the paving stones of the Forum, a large percentage having spread throughout the city to celebrate the Fornacalia with others of their curiae. Undeterred the tribunes Verginius and Terentillus continued to harangue the reduced crowds with the injustice of laws unpublished and powers undefined.

Titus and Antonius listened politely if less emotionally considering the speeches essentially covered the same ground as before. They had no sooner found a place to sit and listen when from the direction of the Palatine a mob of patricians and clients, led by a young man named Caeso Quinctius, came barging through chanting loudly. This force obviously had been organized as a tactical unit, and functioned as one. They bullied people out of the way, drowned out the speakers with raucous chants and catcalls, and sent opponents tumbling headlong. Caeso, a tall, strong man in his mid twenties beat one man, literally stripping him of his tunic as he drove him to the paving stones.

Antonius watched with boiling anger, yet felt torn. Caeso Quinctius was the nephew of Titus Quinctius, patron to Antonius. To attack Caeso would be tantamount to assailing his patron. Disgusted, he and Titus left the Forum—exactly the effect Caeso hoped for.

That night at the Boar's Tusk, as well as in dozens of other establishments and private homes, the subject of Caeso's violent clearance of the Forum passed everyone's lips. Surely, they said, his patrician elders put him up to it. But what to do…

The following day Caeso repeated his tactics, driving opponents from the Forum, accosting them openly, secure that few could stand up to his gang of thugs. All of it passed unnoticed by the Tempanius brothers who instead feasted with other members of the Velita curia. Tables, tents, and a small altar were set up on the eastern shore of the small lake between the Caelian and Oppian hills. Little in the scene of casually clad revelers would have given an inkling that five hundred years later the lake would be drained and a great coliseum constructed in which, in a much more sophisticated age, humans and beasts would be slaughtered for the amusement of the spectators, distant progeny of those gathered for a picnic on the scenic shore of a quiet little lake within the confines of the city.

A small stream halved the narrow valley between the hills, and flowed into the lake. Members of the curia Velita spread themselves out in the meadow on the south side of the stream. Dogs roamed the roasting pits in search of remains from the pigs, goats, and a sacrificial bull. Tables bore ransacked baskets of dried fruits, wheat and barley cakes, nuts, olives, and a wealth of vegetables. All over the meadow men and boys played games of field hockey with a hard leather ball and sticks. Groups of three played trigon, in which each player threw a small leather ball as hard as he could to one of the other players. They skipped rocks over the placid waters of the lake, or played hide and seek. Men and women congregated in separate groups renewing acquaintances and making new ones. Young boys flirted with young girls. Once again Titus regretted leaving his family at home. But Duellia had been upset by the omens, and he hadn't wanted to watch over the little ones all the time.

"Where's little Lucius?" he asked.

Strolling under mild blue skies the three brothers felt again the bond of blood, the comfort of family.

"Oh, he's off playing somewhere," said Lucius. He turned to Antonius. "So, are you ready to meet your future wife?"

Mark Trapino

"Why not?" said Antonius, easily. "What kind of dowry does she bring?"

Lucius laughed through his teeth, a habit he'd acquired as if he could no longer give himself over to unrestrained amusement. "That question is only for men who live close to Rome and have at least twenty iugera."

"Not to mention a house in town as well as on their twenty iugera," laughed Titus. "But don't worry," he slapped Antonius on the back. "If I know Lucius, he'll make up in looks for what she lacks in dowry."

Crushing emerald green wild grasses beneath their sandals they made for naked oak and beech trees lining the stream. Lounging on the grass around a toga spread out as a blanket a small group of people watched them approach. As they drew close one of them, a man in his late thirties, stood up.

"Well met, Lucius," he said, extending a strong hand.

Lucius took it, engulfed it with his own. "Gaius Concordius, my brother Antonius," he said, introducing them.

Antonius shook hands with his future father-in-law. If the father were any indication the girl would be typical Roman stock, black as pitch hair, dark brown eyes, large hooked nose, smallish mouth.

Concordius turned, motioned to a girl sitting with legs drawn under to come forward. As she did Antonius realized he couldn't have been more wrong. Just thirteen she carried her nubile figure with uncharacteristic grace. More, he found her visage, though not classically beautiful, nonetheless striking. She did indeed have black as onyx hair pulled back and gathered in three thick horizontal braids captured from underneath by a frame of hair twisted into a basket at the junction of her long neck and narrow shoulders. Her bold face attracted him with heavy black eyebrows, narrow oval black eyes glittering above high cheekbones. Her nose hooked commandingly and pointed to a wide mouth, full lips, and prominent chin.

This is Concordia," her father said.

"I'm very pleased," said Antonius, taking her hand.

Concordia met his eyes briefly, smiled to show him straight milky teeth, and then looked demurely down. They chatted for a short time then the brothers took their leave.

"Well," said Titus, "what'd I tell you?"

"One thing you have to say for Lucius," acknowledged Antonius, "he has good taste in women."

During the night a storm blew in from the north and fool's day ushered in a cold and rainy stretch of miserable days. A sparse turnout for the gathering of all the curiae on the Campus Martius did not deter men from frequenting their favorite haunts that evening. Once in the festive spirit it seemed senseless to stop until the last festival of February gave way to Mars' warlike month.

Due to the weather the Boar's Tusk filled early, forcing Lucius, Graptus, and Demetria to work harder than usual. Lucius declined offers of help from his brothers. Instead, they sat at a table and played a game of 'thieves'.

A lyre player tried to make himself heard above the hubbub of conversation. Lucius poured watered wine from his tower, and Graptus ran food out to the tables. A steady stream of customers going in and out turned the crowd over like fresh water entering a pond. As Titus and Antonius played their game at a corner table and listened to the lyre player recite the heroic ballad of Horatius holding the bridge a raucous gang of patricians plowed through the front door.

"Jove," exclaimed Titus, "it's Caeso Quinctius."

"He probably thinks there's some political meeting going on," said Antonius sarcastically without looking up from the game board. He took a drink of wine. "Where does Lucius get this wine?" he asked in admiration.

"Cominus is the one who made it possible," said Titus. "He made contacts in Caere, Neopolis, Capua, and a host of Greek cities down south. Lucius was just smart enough to keep them."

"I guess that's something," said Antonius, raising his voice against the volume of Caeso's party.

Customers crowded the serving tower, each of the three arches were two deep with men holding clay vessels under the funnel waiting for Lucius to pour wine from an identically sized pitcher into theirs. Caeso Quinctius shoved his way forward. Tall, broad shouldered, with a head shaped in the oblong form of a peltast's stone his presence commanded attention. Lesser men moved aside as he and his friends pushed to the front.

"So Tempanius," Caeso's voice boomed, "it's true. You're really just an innkeeper. I thought it was a joke." His dark eyes, hot with wine, glowed under thick black brows. Coarse laughter from his retinue followed his mocking words.

"That's right, Caeso," Lucius said calmly. "Now step aside, these other men were here first."

"These men gave way willingly to the greatest soldier in Rome," proclaimed one of Caeso's friends.

Lucius fixed him with a stare, saw him shrink, and smiled viciously. "The greatest soldier in Rome is serving the wine," he said. "And even if he weren't, Lucius Siccius holds a better claim than Caeso, here."

A contest of cheers and jeers clashed against each other as his words spread through the tavern and all attention focused on the front of the room. Even the lyre player silenced his instrument to listen to the battle of words. Titus and Antonius turned their chairs for a better view, slightly apprehensive of trouble, yet confident their brother could handle it.

Caeso laughed maliciously, insulted. "Imagine," he cried, "an innkeeper claiming to be a soldier." Another cheer of derision went up from his friends.

Antonius nudged Titus. "Come on," he said. "We'd better get up there."

Titus nodded agreement, and they casually moved towards the front of the room against a flow of men gradually clearing away from it.

"I suppose," continued Caeso, sneering, "serving wine to the consuls and tribunes out in the field might qualify in a coward's mind as soldiering."

Lucius flushed with anger as Antonius stepped impetuously forward. Caeso's words brought immediate silence to the room, and a wary cushion cleared around his cluster of friends.

Lucius stabbed Caeso with spite filled eyes, the widow's peak in his hair aimed like a spear at his heart. "You're not pushing around a commoner afraid of your family name," he threatened. He gripped the front edge of the service tower, showing off the muscles of his arms, knotted like clubs attached to the great hubs of his shoulders. He wagged his giant head chiseled in hard lines, wide mouth set like a livid scar above a granite chin. "Push me, and I'll rip you apart before you can say 'help'."

Antonius stepped into the cleared space, and Quinctius gratefully fastened his eyes on him. "Why if it isn't one of the traitors from Antium," he proclaimed. "Look at that, my friends. Innkeepers and ungrateful traitors—that's what the Tempanius family is made of."

Antonius jumped forward and shoved Caeso. At the same time Titus stepped forward, and Lucius came down from his tower. "Take those words back!" demanded Antonius, shoulder to shoulder with his brothers.

"Make me," challenged Caeso.

Lucius grabbed Antonius' shoulder but he shook him off. Looking back, he smiled at Lucius. "Just keep the rest off me,' he said. "I'll be all right."

"Guaranteed," said Lucius and Titus simultaneously.

Caeso waited with balled fists, a head taller and a good thirty pounds heavier. A nasty smile cut across his face.

Antonius stepped quickly forward, and Caeso swung. Antonius ducked, moved left bobbing. Caeso swung again, and again Antonius ducked the blow, stepped in and delivered an uppercut to Caeso's jaw, driving his head up. Caeso stumbled backwards, caught his balance and came back at Antonius who stepped sideways and drove a left hook into his kidney then followed with a right that Caeso blocked with the biceps of his right arm. They squared up. Antonius jabbed with his left, but his short reach made his punches ineffective, and Caeso brushed them aside with a smile of renewed confidence. The room played to his strengths and he knew it. Sooner or later, he would corner the smaller man, pin him against the crowd encircling them, or take advantage of a mistake in close quarters. Antonius fought unconcerned and unafraid. He moved left, then right, came in under a sweeping right by Caeso and laid into his body with a series of blows. Caeso kept coming, puffing hard, his face a purple mask of pain. Antonius smiled, knowing he'd hurt him. Caeso shuffled forward, his left extended to keep Antonius off, trying to pin him, to fix him, shuffling right with each step Antonius took. As Antonius backed up to the serving tower Caeso saw his chance and came forward swinging. Antonius slipped the punch, slid under Caeso's armpit and buried a combination of punches into his stomach, side, and kidneys. Caeso doubled over, and a ferocious uppercut snapped his head and sent him sprawling by the door.

Antonius laughed large, wild, exultantly. He stepped toward the fallen Caeso but he'd had enough. Caeso smiled faintly in resignation as he held up his left hand, fingers splayed open in surrender, and pushed himself to a knee with his right hand behind him holding a stool for support. He shook his head in awe, then swung the stool at Antonius' head with one powerful lunge and cracked his skull. Antonius dropped like a stone, and Caeso fled through the door with his friends acting as a rear guard.

Lucius and Titus charged the door with murder in their eyes, but Caeso disappeared like a mist into the night after a short chase. Rushing back into the tavern they found Graptus kneeling at Antonius' side. He looked up as they entered, immense sadness flooding his eyes and rolling down the long planes of his face.

"Damn him," Lucius cursed. He picked up his brother's limp body as if it were weightless and carried it up the stairs. "Titus, you'd better go home and tell Mama. We'll cremate him on the farm."

"She's going to take this hard," said Titus. The reality hadn't hit him yet, and he stared at his dead brother as if he were some stranger.

"She'll blame me,' said Lucius, his voice metallic with sorrow and guilt. "And she'll be right."

On the long empty road, under a vast sky littered with freshly kindled stars Titus wept. And swore revenge.

# XXVI

## March 1, 461 BC
## The Matronalia

The Matronalia rang like an indictment in Lucius' ears. The day when mothers filled the temple of Juno, and men stayed home to pray and gave their wives presents, caustically reminded him that his gift to his mother had been the death of her youngest son. And Caeso, bloody Caeso had jumped bail and gone into hiding. He cursed himself for not killing him when he had the chance. Two days after the fight he found him, but so did the tribunes. Lucius gave way when they promised to charge him with homicide and extorted an indemnity of three thousand asses against his flight from his father, Lucius Quinctius Cincinnatus, and ten other members of the senate. Worse, Titus Quinctius (Caeso's uncle) and Lucius Lucretius, two men under whom Lucius had prosperously served, and whom he respected, had gone about praising Caeso as if he alone won the battles in which Lucius earned the corona muralis, and the corona civica. He took it as a personal insult, and abjured whatever loyalty he felt toward these men.

Lucius sat in his empty tavern drinking wine and thinking in morose solitude. How convenient that mere days before the trial the augurs reported blazing lights had been seen in the night sky and declared a feriae of three days. All business, public or private was forbidden. Caeso opportunely chose this time to escape when religion forbade pursuit. Lucius spat on the floor. The patricians controlled the calendar, the auspices, and the priesthoods. They made and interpreted the laws. They divided the spoils of war and the lands annexed to Rome. They even decided when he could make money or not. And now they'd decided justice could be prohibited.

A single tallow candle pushed against the gloom of the shuttered room with a wavering yellow flame. Lucius slouched on a stool at one of the tables in the main room away from the cloying solicitousness of Demetria and the thin warmth of the hearth in the kitchen. How he detested March with its false promises and bitter reminders. He pulled the dark red cloak, under which he wore three tunics, tighter around his boulder sized shoulders. "I'd be warmer living under hides," he groused. He finished the cup of hot spiced wine and poured another, grimacing at its tepid temperature. Nothing could stay warm in this miserable month.

Lucius studied his hands, rubbing the knuckles swollen large as bronze coins. They had grown that way from years of work digging ditches, planting, harvesting, heaving stones and bricks and mortaring them into walls, and erecting defensive palisades. Carrying sword, shield, and spear he had killed men with those hands and cleaned their blood out from under the blunted nails. Now his hands longed for the blood of vengeance and justice denied. Just as the plebs were denied justice under laws controlled by a self-appointed elite claiming special access to the gods, and the abilities bestowed by them.

Oily smoke from the candle coiled serpentine into the grainy obscurity of the tavern's interior, giving off a vaguely rancid smell. An amber bubble of light floated around the tabletop casting abbreviated shadows into the dank environs. He poured the wine back into the pitcher distastefully. The plebs, he thought disdainfully, understood nothing. It would not make one iota of difference if every law ever devised were published for all to see, if they did not control the administration of them. One might as well wish for eternal life. Politics, he always knew, held no answers. Justice, like any other commodity, had a price. Apparently, it sold for three thousand *asses* in the Forum. Those who could afford it enjoyed it. Those who couldn't....

Lucius climbed the stairs to his apartment heavy footed, noisily announcing his coming. When he opened the door Lucius Jr. had his left hand buried under his thigh, aggravating his father. "Lucius, get your hand out from under your leg," he ordered.

"Yes, Father." Lucius Jr. exposed his hand, deformed by the absence of the ring and little fingers beyond the first knuckle. The defect earned him the appellation of 'three fingers' from other children, making him both self-conscious and angry. He knew well enough how to take that anger out on those who taunted him with the name. From those he called his friends he tolerated it, accepting the name on their lips as a mark of distinction.

At age nine he exhibited none of the bulk and prodigious strength of his father. In every way he resembled his mother, lithe, supple, graceful, and fleet as his uncle Antonius had been. He inherited her finely chiseled features, as if in his face a kind of divine harmony had been achieved in the balance of size and placement, angle, line, and fullness. But he had none of her nature. He seldom laughed and outwardly expressed little emotion unless goaded into rage. He viewed life with a detached curiosity that adults took as either precocious wisdom or arrogance.

"Pack some things," said Lucius. "We're going to Antium."

Lucius Jr. snapped to attention. "Me too?"

"You too. Graptus, I want you to make arrangements to rent two mules."

"Domitius Scaptius has a couple in the Forum Boarium, I think," offered Graptus, scratching his balding head with long fingers.

"Good. On your way out tell Demetria to pack us food for three days. Hard food, Graptus."

Graptus stood, stretched his tall lean body, his thin face split in a yawn. "I don't suppose we have time to go to the baths first."

"No." Lucius scratched at twelve days of thick black growth on his face. No blade had touched his face for the nine days of mourning, the other three for lack of interest.

"I thought as much," sighed Graptus. He pulled a hooded cloak on and clasped it with a bronze pin over the right shoulder. "I'll be back soon," he promised, hurrying out.

Outside, quiet hung over the dirt streets of the Subura. No one lounged outside, and most people's shutters remained closed against the cold. Not that it helped much. Regardless, Graptus kept to the middle of the street, avoiding the refuse on the sidewalks, and proximity to windows from which dangerous objects might hurtle down at any time. His shoes slapped the paving stones as he passed the crossroads shrine and stepped onto the Vicus Suburanus near the red brick Mamilian Tower. A light fog wove languorously around the edifices of Rome, pulling the menacing sky still lower. The city smelled sooty with smoke from inefficacious fires on hearths and braziers. He made quick work of his errand, hustling through the cold to the Forum Boarium and rousting Scaptius out of his uncomfortable slumbers to rent two mules.

By the time he returned he found Lucius in the stable behind the Boar's Tusk. He had his two mules squared away, one saddled, the other packed with a leather tent large enough to accommodate four men and their gear, cooking equipment, two leather satchels full of food, and various odds and ends. "You'd better put some leather breeches on," he said, pointing to his as evidence. "It'll be a long cold ride without."

Lucius led the mules around to the front, and contemplated the cypress branches warning of a family in mourning affixed to the door of the tavern. He had left them up longer than the nine days normally allotted for mourning simply to keep people away. Now he pulled them down and flung them into the street, trampling them under foot as the three travelers began their journey. Lucius hurried, keeping cadence in his head as if on the march, practically dragging the mules behind him. Though half a head taller with long striding legs Graptus labored to keep up, while Lucius Jr. trotted by his father's side, his struggle to stay abreast unnoticed or ignored. Graptus compassionately cleared his throat to speak up for the boy who ran without complaint, then swallowed his tongue at the sight of the ferreous set to Lucius' jaw. A slave thought with his back first.

They crossed the Cloaca Maxima, its smell of the waste of human civilization muted by the cold, and stopped outside the temple of Janus at the foot of the Argiletum. Lucius bought a stick of incense from a vendor outside, paid an admission fee and entered the temple. Even the gods were not free to the people. With cloak covering his head he lit the incense in sacrifice and intoned a prayer to the god of beginnings for a blessing on his new venture.

The falsely eirenic atmosphere of Rome grated on Lucius so they avoided going through the Forum, and instead climbed the Quirinal Hill heading for the portal by the temple of Semo Sancus. As they turned left off the Vicus Ficum by the crossroads shrine protecting the intersection at the Vicus Salutaris, Graptus spoke up.

"Wouldn't it be faster to go through the Forum and out the Porta Carmentalis?" he asked.

"You've lived here long enough to know that gate is called the Unlucky Way since the Fabius clan was nearly wiped out. I'm not leaving the city the same way they did to begin this new project." Lucius Jr. lagged behind as they climbed the hill, puffing and panting for breath. He ceased running and climbed at a laborious walk.

"What exactly is this venture?" Graptus yanked on the halter of the mule he led, which had slowed down for reasons of her own.

"Antonius left his property to me. We're going to see if it's worth keeping."

At the crest of the hill they stopped and waited for Lucius Jr. to catch up. Lucius smiled thinly at Graptus' obvious relief. "If I don't make him tough, he'll be eaten alive, Grap. You should know that. Rome is no place for soft souls." But when the younger Lucius caught up his father put him in the saddle on the mule and let him ride the rest of the way.

Descending the Quirinal Hill, they passed under the western cliffs of the Capitoline Hill and entered the Forum

Boarium. There they picked up the other two mules, and with everyone mounted climbed the Aventine on the Clivus Publicius.

No sooner had they left Rome than the sky cleared to a deep blue. Lucius took it as a sign of favor. Heading southwest towards the coast a crisp wind blew into their faces carrying a salty tang to their nostrils as they neared the coast. The humid air stung them and clung with icy fingers to the wool garments they wore in layers. They followed the coast south to Lavinium where they camped for the night. Next day they circled the walls of the city about the third hour after a breakfast of unleavened bread.

Lucius Jr. gaped in amazement at the slate-gray water stretching out to forever on his right. He marveled at the men who rode their wooden ships upon it, wondering how they ever found land again. He wondered if the sky and the water really blended together out there like they appeared to do from shore.

The well traveled road, smoothed and rutted from countless feet and laden wagons took them easily south. Once again, they had clear skies to travel under, but the humidity kept the air frigid to the touch. A bank of snowy clouds hovered on the horizon like ships in full sail making for shore. They let the mules choose the pace and settled into the steady swaying rhythm of their gait. Outside the gates of Ardea they stopped for the midday meal. Once again, a soldier's meal of flat-bread and water. As before at Lavinium, Lucius took them around the city instead of passing through.

It was a short ride from Ardea to Antium, and before they knew it the walls of that city grew out of the horizon. But as if he had acquired some aversion to civilization Lucius avoided the city and took the first dirt track he found leading east.

Lucius looked around and didn't like what he saw. Most of the farms looked impoverished, the land swampy, timber scarce. Pools of water lay fetid, cold, and stagnant around hummocks of spongy earth dotting the flat land like islands. Woody vines with long thorns occupied any patch of dry ground like an encamped army above the swampy earth. Forests of tall cane, thick stalks standing yellowish against sharp green leaves impeded his vision, blocked their progress. At least there would be plenty of material to make stakes. In the east, distant to the eye, the Alban Hills loomed in blue silhouette, inviting, imposing, mysterious. He thought if the land Antonius left him looked like this, he would sell it at the first opportunity. Graptus read his mind.

"Looks like an awful lot of work to drain these fields," he said.

"I bet it's cheap to buy, though," added Lucius Jr.

"If only mosquitoes were a commodity," laughed Graptus.

Lucius kept his own counsel, at odds in his thinking. On the one hand the soggy land looked overrun with tall grasses, reeds, and thick willows. On the other, he trusted Antonius' judgement and recognized in these same reeds and willows the materials that helped make a farm self-sufficient. If Antonius had put the few years he had to good use, the property might have some admirable qualities. He forced himself to be patient and open-minded. He would see soon enough.

A mile farther on they came across another dirt track heading south. Lucius consulted a map Antonius had drawn for him long ago and turned onto the road. Immediately they noticed improvement. The road was smoother, drier, and rose gradually in elevation. As they crested a small rise an improved drive took them east again onto Antonius' property.

Antonius had chosen his five iugera well. It rose in elevation from east to west and drained well. Along the northern boundary immature elm and poplar trees thickened, and on the east, behind the house willows had been tamed from their wild state. A low stone wall defined the western border, the direction from which they had come. Only the southern property line remained open.

The road divided the property in half lengthwise, and the house sat on the highest point of elevation about three quarters of the way in. A man behind a team of oxen looked up momentarily from his plowing on the south side near the property line, and then went back to work. He made the turn at the west end and started back towards the house. The riders stopped briefly to watch, listening to him curse or yell endearments to the oxen, flicking a long switch over their heads and holding the plow deep in the furrow with one hand.

Lucius rode to the house, dismounted and walked to the end of the row to wait for the plowman. One thing for certain, he could plow a straight furrow. As he reached the spot where Lucius stood, he picked the blade up out of the dirt, halted the oxen and laid the plow in its side.

"Something I can do for you?" he asked Lucius, wiping his gnarled hands on a dirty tunic as he came around the plow. He was shorter than Lucius, built like a brick, and with a round ingenuous face framed by black hair. He walked towards Lucius on bowed legs big as tree trunks, wiping dirt from arms like the lower limbs of old trees.

"I'm Lucius Tempanius," said Lucius, extending his hand. "You must be Tranellius."

"That's right. Antonius send you?"

"In a manner of speaking."

Graptus, and Lucius Jr. came up from behind. Tranellius eyed them quickly then turned his attention back to Lucius. "He decide to run for tribune?" Tranellius laughed, exposing a gap on the left side of his mouth where his upper teeth should have been.

"No. He was killed defending one," said Lucius, unwilling to discuss the exact particulars of Antonius' murder.

The gap in Tranellius' smile slid shut, and his heavy black brows knit together in a sad and bitter expression. He shook his swarthy head and spat. "I told him to stay out of politics. Politics never did a poor man any good. I ought to know." He reached down and grabbed a handful of earth, held it to his lips and kissed it, then crushed it in his fist. He wiped his mouth on a hairy bare arm, then opened his fingers and slowly let the dirt drift to the ground. Without a word he walked away and disappeared into the one room stone house. A few moments later he reappeared wearing a cleaner tunic, a brown cloak, and carrying a leather satchel.

"You want to check and see I'm not taking anything of your brother's?" he asked, holding the satchel open for Lucius to look inside.

Lucius shrugged. "I wouldn't know the difference."

Graptus could see him repressing a grin. That Lucius had made up his mind about the land was obvious, and Graptus thought he could guess his decision. "What kind of hospitality is this?" he asked rudely. "As soon as his master comes the overseer runs off to town to carouse with his cronies?"

Tranellius stopped. His broad face told all. Afraid to hope yet hoping still he gazed at Lucius, and waited for him to say something.

"As usual," Lucius began, "my slave has spoken out of turn."

Tranellius' face fell.

"He thinks he knows my mind before I do," explained Lucius. "But in this case, he's right." He waved his arm at the care and orderliness of the farmstead, missing the joyous look that flashed across Tranellius' face. "I can see you have a love for this land. I have no interest in working it myself. So, if you are willing, I need an overseer to stay on. However, I have some conditions."

Tranellius knew he had few options in life. He had no property and no family. Life being full of ironies, the irony of his life was that his only hope of having a family and property lay with the very country that had deprived him of the same. Nevertheless, dignity compelled him to ask. "What conditions?"

"I'm no longer interested in receiving a little rent from my properties. I intend to grow cash crops, and I expect them to do well."

"Like what, for instance," said Tranellius, gruffly.

"Like grapes for wine. Any objections?"

"None. I think the land is all right for grapes. I think Lucanians would do well here. We're a bit prone to fog so we have to be selective."

"I was thinking in terms of Murgentians," said Lucius.

"I was thinking of going inside," said Graptus.

Lucius raked him with a look of exasperation.

"I am a little cold, Father," said Lucius Jr. fearing that his father would club Graptus soon if he didn't intervene.

Lucius sighed. "All right. Graptus, unload the mules and see they're fed and watered. Rub them down too."

"Why don't you go inside and make yourselves at home," said Tranellius. He winced under the irony of offering the hospitality of his own home to Tempanius who was setting foot in it for the first time. "I need to unyoke the oxen and put them to bed for the night."

He led the oxen to the stable, a three-sided shelter constructed of stakes laced together with twine made from willow and open to the south. A mixture of leaves, willow, and straw spread liberally on packed earth made both bed and forage for the beasts.

"I don't think we'll have room for all these animals," observed Graptus. He yawned and stretched his long frame. "It's nice out here. Quiet."

Filtered through the sieve of the sun, diffused in limpid beams, twilight spread across the open fields, an ethereal unguent soothing the bruises of the day. Steam emanated from the massive bodies of the animals with a sickly-sweet odor. Their flanks twitched as the men rubbed them with handfuls of damp straw. A westerly wind picked up, spreading rumors of colder weather.

"Oh, my babies here are quite sociable," said Tranellius, patting the deep chest of one of his beasts. "They'll probably like the company, and they'll all stay nice and warm squeezed together."

The two men worked quietly for a while, rubbing the animals down, watering them, and fitting them into the stable.

Mark Trapino

"And what about your master?" asked Tranellius as he led one of the oxen into place. "Does he get along with everybody?"

"He used to. Get over there." Graptus shoved the hindquarters of one of the mules. "He's changed some lately."

"How so?"

"He used to be the fun-loving type. Now he's become serious."

"This happen since Antonius was murdered?"

"That's a strong word."

"It's the right one, isn't it?"

"Depends on which side you're on."

"You'd be wise to be on your master's side, I'd guess."

"Naturally. But to answer your question; Antonius was the final stone. It began when his wife died of the plague."

Tranellius finished with the oxen and moved into the yard where the plow lay. Dragging it to a stump he sat, flipped the plow over, and began scraping the blade clean. "Loved her did he?"

"Mmm," grunted Graptus. Patting at his tunic he stood watching Tranellius. "Doesn't seem typically Roman, does it?" They laughed.

"I don't suppose they're all that different from us."

Graptus scratched his jaw roughly, itching from three days growth of beard. "One day all of Italy will be in Roman hands because of that very thought," he mused. "They are vastly different from us."

"How so?" Tranellius stood, and together they carried the plow into a stone storage shed attached to the south wall of the house.

"First of all, they never let loose of a wrong done them. Vengeance is honor, vendetta a way of life. Second, they're single minded. You ought to know that from living here with

426

Antonius. When they get an idea in their heads, they pursue it without deviation."

"Perhaps you exaggerate."

"Perhaps."

Inside Lucius stoked the fire on the stone hearth built against the back wall. He prodded the moribund coals to life with an iron rod cast into the shape of a cupped hand at one end. Feeding wood that he found stored underneath the hearth slowly onto the fire, flames shot above the U-shaped bricks forming the fire pit. Smoke crawled through a small hole half way up the wall, forced back in by contrary swirling winds, blackening the stones and staining the thatch roof with soot. The unadorned interior greedily absorbed the reddish gold light of the fire, coating the gray stones of varied shapes and sizes mortared into walls that swelled thickly at the bottom. Lucius hung his cloak on a wooden peg mortared into the wall above the bed on which his son reposed. From a shelf near the hearth he grabbed a candle and lit it in the flame of the hearth fire. He threw a satchel onto the rough-hewn table in the middle of the room and sat on one of the four stools, posting the candle near him.

Lucius Jr. lay wrapped in his cloak on his uncle's narrow cot, relaxing on the straw mattress. He itched to open the closed cabinet at the foot of the bed, presuming it held his deceased uncle's weapons and armor, but contented himself with watching his father.

Graptus and Tranellius entered to find Lucius seated at the table with wax tablets strewn over its rough surface, tapping a stylus thoughtfully against his front teeth.

"All right," he said as they hung cloaks on the pegs over Tranellius' bed on the wall opposite the bed occupied by Lucius Jr. "We'll use Lucanian grapes. Provided you're sure you have access to vines."

"Not a problem," said Tranellius. He lit another candle and brought it to the table. "Two things, however," he said, sitting across from Lucius.

"Tell me."

427

"First, there's only five iugera here," said Tranellius. "I assume you're going to provide me at least one permanent hand here. When you factor in how much land it takes just to feed us, that doesn't leave much to grow your vines. Second, it takes at least three years before vines start producing." He paused, watching Graptus as he prepared the evening meal of wheat porridge. "There's some wine in a jar on the shelf to the right," he said.

Graptus pulled down the pitcher of wine and three cups, asking permission before he filled one for himself, then pulled up a seat at the end of the table as he waited for the water to boil.

Tranellius continued as if he hadn't stopped. "First, will you have the patience to give me the necessary time to make a profit? Second, and please don't be offended, but are you able to sustain losses until the vines prosper?"

Lucius put his elbows on the table and leaned forward. "I think we're going to get along fine. I like straightforward talk. Yes, I'll give you time, and yes, I can wait. Within reason."

"Good," said Tranellius. "I'll stay on." They raised their cups to each other and drank agreement.

"Now," said Lucius, "your other points are far more interesting." He flipped the wax tablets around so Tranellius could see them. "I've drawn the lay of the land as I saw it when we came in." He pointed at two empty spaces. "Here to the south and to the east are empty tracts. Here and here," he pointed to squares he had drawn adjoining the property on the north and across the road on the west, "are properties that are not prospering. What is the status of these? Are these empty tracts ager publicus?"

Tranellius held up a hand to stop him. "No need to go further, Dominus. I can tell you everything you want to know."

"Oh good," interjected Graptus, standing over a clay pot of water on the hearth. "Another mind reader in the family." His joke drifted out the smoke hole unheard.

"Behind us," said Tranellius, "the land is for sale. Not far away is a road your brother thought would serve the whole of Campania and the Pomptines in the future. If so, the property will be invaluable. The land to the south is ager publicus, but Rome's treasury is bare, so we hear, and Antonius thought we could buy some of it up. As for the two holdings you mentioned, you're talking about good Romans who've fallen on ill fortune. If you've got the stomach for it, you might buy them out."

"You see about the vines," said Lucius. "I'll stomach the rest of it."

+ + +

Five days stranded on the Pomptine Marshes in a one room stone shack wasn't exactly what Lucius Tempanius Jr. had in mind when they set out from Rome. Only thirty miles away, she might as well have been on the other side of the world. He missed the city desperately.

Most of the time he spent alone stuck inside the musty house with nothing to do except make quick forays outside into the incessant rain to fetch wood for the fire he kept burning on the hearth. Steeling himself to the icy cold he stepped out into ankle deep muck, wondering how much more water the viscid ground could take before it became a lake. Twice his father had not returned and Lucius Jr. spent the shivering nights alone in the black emptiness of his dead uncle's farm. Howling like lost souls the wind scratched and clawed at the thatch roof, and rattled the shutters. With clenched teeth he forced back tears of fear and loneliness, acting as if nothing at all were amiss when his father and Graptus returned the next evening. When finally told to pack his kit for travel the next day he did so with a repressed joy no nine-year old should be forced to disguise.

Graptus felt sorry for the boy. The changes that took place in the father twisted in the unpolished bronze mirror of the son. But the father saw none of it. In a fever to accomplish his plans they chased around the countryside inside and outside of Antium for five days. Graptus' back ached from hours in the saddle, and he feared he would never be dry and warm again. A great weariness descended on him, made heavier by the knowledge they were not headed back to Rome. He hoped he'd survive the trip—his normal good humor had already succumbed.

Lucius Tempanius the elder simply had a job to do and set about getting it done. In five days, he made arrangements to purchase two derelict properties and fifty iugera of public land at bargain prices. Including the property he inherited from his brother, he now had nearly seventy iugera to work with. He waited impatiently for Tranellius to return from his mission, visions of vineyards extending to the horizon and bronze filling his coffers exciting his imagination. Then, he thought, justice and equality could be had.

Tranellius returned with good news. Enough cuttings were available to plant forty *iugera* of vineyards. By his figuring he would need five field hands and a teamster.

"You'll have them," said Lucius. Turning to Graptus he smiled broadly. "We could use a good war this season, eh Grap?"

"Oh yes, Dominus. A war is always good for business."

For Tranellius the death of his friend Antonius came as a mixed blessing. Antonius had treated him as an equal, a good friend. Lucius Tempanius let it be known in no uncertain terms who owned the land and what Tranellius' status was. Yet if things went well, his prospects for the future looked far brighter working for Lucius. "Such is life," he sighed to himself, as he watched his new master disappear into the distance.

Lucius led his small party cross-country due east, excitedly pointing out to Marcus all the land that would soon be theirs. The mules snorted in complaint and snapped their tails in aggravation as they trudged laboriously over the swampy ground.

Graptus was in a mulish mood himself. A stiff wind from the northwest stung his face with needle sharp raindrops, and soaked his breeches. He turned his gaunt visage away from the wind, tilting his hooded head against the rain. His uneven teeth chattered, his nose ran annoyingly, and his fingers, numbed by the cold, could barely hold the reins.

They took an unimproved road north into the wind, a cold and bitter reminder to Graptus of his slavery. Only two types of men rode out in this kind of weather, those who chose to, and those who had no choice. He longed for choice in his life.

When they passed Lanuvium his heart nearly broke.

"There's still plenty of daylight," Lucius called back.

His words came back as another icy blast in the wretched face of Graptus, which seemed to grow longer with each passing mile. They passed the steep rise that outlined Lake Nemorensis and he wondered if Lucius would angle right and cut between the Alban lakes. He dreaded the thought of riding over arduous paths through thick forests of barren trees.

Lucius relented. As daylight faded they reached Aricia, a Latin town situated in the saddle between two volcanic lakes, Lake Alba and its smaller cousin Lake Nemorensis. They took a room above a tavern and slept, their clothes hanging around the room in a futile attempt to dry them.

The next day the weather gave them a break, and although the sun did not make an appearance the clouds held back the rain. Their path took them around the Alban massif, carving a ten mile crescent that brought them to the Tempanius farm on the north side at about midday. As they dismounted a flood of family members fell on them as if given up for dead. Restius greeted Graptus, glad to have company, and together they took the four mules into the barn. After the mules were stabled, they prepared a place for Graptus in Restius' quarters down the corridor.

Upstairs Lucius and Lucius Jr. felt the full brunt of family affection. Duellia doted on Lucius the younger, unable to get over how tall he had grown. She turned him back-to-back with her eldest son Marcus and compared them in height. "Look at that, Titus. Marcus isn't three inches taller, and he's three years older."

"So," said Titus, "what brings you out this way?"

"We went to Antium to settle affairs on Antonius' estate and decided to come back this way to visit," said Lucius.

"Well, you're timing is perfect," declared Titus. "You're just in time for dinner. Tempania," Titus gave his seven-year-old daughter a gentle push, "go tell Restius it's time for dinner."

The children and slaves ate in the kitchen, leaving the dining room to the four adult members of the Tempanius family. An undecorated bronze brazier, the three raised sides battered and blackened from years of use, provided insufficient heat. Lucius and Titus sat at either end of the table. Drusilla came in carrying a bowl of hard-boiled eggs shelled and sprinkled with salt and oregano, followed by Duellia carrying dried fruits, nuts, and pickled asparagus.

Lucius watched his mother closely as she served the eggs. She appeared to have aged twenty years since Antonius' death. Her hair, tied up and knotted behind her head, had turned almost completely gray with black streaks the only reminder of its original lustrous color. Her face visibly sagged, and her wide mouth turned sorrowfully down. As she set an egg on the plate in front of him, Lucius grabbed her hand and held it.

"How's my precious mother?" he asked tenderly.

Her dark, oval eyes widened momentarily, a spark of joy flamed then flickered out. "I'm always well when I have my sons near me," she said.

Lucius mistook for reproach the grave dignity of a woman from whom the sadness and suffering of too many losses had stolen her youth. Barely fifty, seven of her loved ones had preceded her in death including those children who had not reached maturity.

Titus chuckled, seeking to lighten the mood. "Perhaps you could persuade Lucius to move back here and become a country gentleman."

"You'd try to put me to work," said Lucius, releasing his mother's hand.

"Your father was certainly equally divided between the two of you," she said. "You got his love for fighting, and Titus got his love for the land."

"What did Antonius get?" asked Titus with immediate regret.

"His love for death."

"So," said Duellia, "what have you been doing in your travels?" She looked at Lucius with her great self-conscious eyes.

Lucius decided Duellia was not improving with age. His mother, twenty-five years older and miles more suffering, by far exceeded her in beauty. She looked like a cross between an owl and a mouse with her large eyes and aquiline nose dominating a small mouth and chin.

"Thank Fortuna," he replied, "it was a profitable trip." He stuffed the egg into his mouth. "I decided to keep his man Tranellius on as factor and made arrangements to buy another sixty iugera. We're going to grow grapes."

"How will you pay for all that plus the laborers until the vines start producing?" asked Titus, worried about the rashness of such a grand undertaking.

"I'm not going to pay laborers."

A troubled look darkened the weathered visage of Titus as he chewed the last bite of his egg and contemplated his brother's words. "So, you'll invest in slaves then."

Duellia and Drusilla left the room and came back with steaming bowls of porridge in which cheese and honey had been added. Lucius tasted the porridge.

"Slaves are cheaper," he said.

Titus blew on a heaping spoonful of hot gruel, the gray ring circling his brown eyes expanded and contracted with his ruminations. "They are also not Romans, who need the work."

"Yes, Romans I have to chase down every nundinae or feast day and beg them to work."

"How else are they to be part of the community?"

"Titus, how did you get such a plodding mind?"

433

With pitcher poised in mid air, and milk seeming to defy gravity as it reached the lip, Titus grunted in surprise. His callused hand imperceptibly gripped the handle tighter in anger as he stared at his brother. Then he calmly poured the milk into his porridge, stirring wordlessly.

Drusilla spoke first. "That is unfair, Lucius. You know as well as anyone that laws are only posted for three nundinae. Shall your profits take precedence over a citizen's responsibility to know the law?"

"Forgive me, Domina, but you know as well that these people come for gossip and a cup of wine. And if they read at all, it's the graffiti on the walls."

"You assume that since they're of the lowest class they have no interest," said Titus evenly.

"I assume that since they have no say it makes no difference." Lucius sucked an asparagus spear into his mouth. "We have precious little ourselves."

"How will they have a say if they have no work?"

"There's other work."

"Certainly," said Drusilla. "They could run a tavern full of violent men."

Lucius stuck out his lower lip but said nothing.

"But slaves?" said Titus, knitting a hedge across his forehead with thick eyebrows.

"Yes, slaves. They are there to work. They require only food and clothing. They don't have to observe all the festivals and the like so they're more productive. As you well know with Restius."

"Restius participates in all the festivals with us," claimed Drusilla.

"Slaves are also more dangerous," said Titus.

"In what way?"

"Haven't you heard?" said Duellia excitedly. Titus shot her a disapproving look and quashed her enthusiasm.

"A Sabine slave named Herdonius has seized the capitol with an army of twenty-five hundred slaves," said Titus.

"Impossible," expostulated Lucius.

"Nevertheless," averred Drusilla.

"What are they doing about it?"

"No one will do anything about it," said Titus. "The tribunes claim it's a lie. The people don't care if it is or not…"

"Of course not," interrupted Lucius. "Because they know they're one step away from the same fate. Why should they help save their oppressors?"

Titus casually poured a handful of pine nuts into his mouth. "That's a bit exaggerated, don't you think?"

"No," said Lucius facetiously, "I don't think. Have you forgotten our brother?" He saw Titus stiffen with the accusation and felt a certain satisfaction. Elated, he pressed the point home. "The only way we'll get justice for Antonius is if we exact it ourselves."

"Before you insult me again let me finish what I have to say," said Titus, glowering, his long face ruddy with anger. "I agree that if Caeso is not justly punished then we must do it ourselves. But first we should let the law run its course. Aulus Verginius has threatened to try Caeso in absentia, and his bail has been forfeited. Some say his father, Cincinnatus, has been made destitute."

"Ha!" scoffed Lucius. "More lies. It's well known that he intends to stand for consul at the next elections to secure his son's freedom. If he is destitute and living trans-Tiber as they claim, how is that possible?"

"It is not," said Drusilla. "Titus, in this I must side with your brother." Her mouth set and her chin jutted angrily as she stared at Titus. "The punishment for murder is death. And this family," she struck the table with the open palm of her hand, "will see to it that the punishment is carried out."

Lucius and Titus looked at their mother, then at each other, surprise written all over their faces.

"Come, Duellia," said Drusilla, her voice perfectly tranquil, "let's leave the men to discuss their business. We have children to look after."

"We have hot spiced wine for you," offered Duellia meekly. "I'll bring it in."

"Father always gave her free rein to voice her opinions," said Lucius. "But I've never seen her like that before."

"Truly."

Duellia returned with the wine and set it before them wordlessly. They drank in silence, lost in thought. The wine tasted tart and hot, giving off a sweet fruity aroma. Relaxed by the wine they appraised each other.

"You've changed," said Titus.

"Death will do that to you."

"Oh, I've had my share, I think." Titus sank his drooping nose into his glass and drank deep. "What else has happened?"

"I'll tell you what it is, Titus. I'm tired of being talked down to. I've served every consul I've ever fought under to the best of my ability (and that's better than most), and what's it gotten me in the end? There's only one way to be equal, and that's wealth."

"That's an illusion. You don't have the blood."

"Our bloodlines are as old as anyone's."

"Certainly," agreed Titus amiably. "But it's plebeian blood."

"And it will always be plebeian as long as we're content with our little hill."

"This little hill has provided us a pretty good living for some generations now."

"Sure. Right now you're lucky, out here on the edge where no one else wants to be. But someday these will be the cozy close-in environs of Rome and not the frontier. Then some patrician is going to want all that ager publicus we've used for all these years. Who do you think will win that fight?"

"You've become depressing."

"No, just realistic. All I'm saying is, let's beat them to it. I swear by Mars, Titus, that from now on when I go to war it's going to be for Lucius Tempanius every bit as much as for Rome."

Cries from the kitchen brought them off their chairs and into that much warmer room. Both the hearth and the oven below it had fires going, a waste that Titus ground his teeth over. On the large table in the center of the room the children cast bones, their mother and grandmother serving as arbitrators since Restius and Graptus had retired. Entering the festive atmosphere Lucius and Titus let the seriousness of their lives dissolve into frivolity. The children immediately lost interest in the game as the men walked in and clamored for a story.

"Papa," cried Titus Jr. excitedly pulling his father's tunic, "tell us a story. Please."

"War, war," cried the other two boys.

Tempania's face fell into a wistful knowing look of exclusion, wishing she had been born a boy.

"Ah," said Titus, pulling up a stool and drawing little Titus onto his knee. "What story shall we hear today?"

"Horatius on the bridge."

"The battle of Lake Regillus."

"The capture of the Sabine women," said Tempania hopefully.

"Ah, the capture of the Sabines," said Titus, filling his voice with awe. The boys groaned nonetheless at having to listen to 'girl's stuff', but Tempania clapped happily. "You know," continued Titus, "that incident led to a great war." The boys perked up.

"First," began Titus, "you must know what kind of city Rome was to understand why the story took place. In fact, in those days you could barely call Rome a city at all. It was more like a town. It was really no more than a cluster of huts on the Palatine. Of course, Romulus had a nice stone house that he called the citadel, but really there were no walls to defend the city. All that protected the city was a ditch and rampart between the Esquiline and Quirinal hills. Where the Sister's Beam is today at the Carinae was the eastern gate of the city. So you see, Rome was really very small.

"Now in those days Rome was made up of misfits, runaway slaves, petty criminals, and political outcasts. The homeless and the poor flocked to her in hopes of a fresh start—a chance to achieve honors their places of birth wouldn't allow them to earn. Unfortunately, most of them were men. Like all men they longed to have wives, so many fights erupted among them in the contest for what few free women there were. And also for the not so free because, human nature being what it is, many women found greener pastures away from their husbands.

"Romulus realized that his city was going to be torn apart before it ever had a chance to grow if he didn't correct the situation, so he called his most trusted advisors and together they came up with a plan. First, he sent envoys to all the neighboring cities proposing treaties of intermarriage. But these were all rejected and the envoys insulted."

"What's a envoy?" asked Titus Jr.

Titus shifted his son onto the other knee. "A messenger." Like a brown elm leaf his hand engulfed the cup that Lucius filled. He took a long drink and cleared his throat. "Where was I? Ah, yes, the envoys. They were all rejected. 'Why don't you open your city to runaway female slaves too?' those jealous cities scoffed. Romulus then put the other part of his plan in motion. He declared a celebration of the Consualia, and to show there were no hard feelings invited all the neighboring tribes to Rome. Now, in actual fact, not very many of them came. Maybe a few people from Labicum above us, and some from Tusculum, and maybe some from Crustumerium or Tibur. But for some reason, maybe because they wanted to get a good look around at the town and its defenses, a large contingent of Sabines came. And, of course, to make it look good they had to bring their wives and children.

"Good host that he was, Romulus made free with the wine and prepared an extravagant show. There were dancers, and mock battles, and chariot races, and they sacrificed a huge white bull with horns this wide." He stretched his arms out to their full width, drawing gasps from the children. "Then when everyone was involved in the spectacle he gave the sign, and all the Roman men," he made a lightning quick movement in the air as if catching a fly in his hand, "snatched the young women and ran off with them to their houses."

"Is that when the battle started?" asked Lucius Jr.

"Oh no. They had no weapons."

"That's kind of stupid," said Marcus.

"Stupid," echoed his brother Titus Jr.

Titus waved his index finger back and forth. "No, the custom was the same in those days as it is today. The gods forbid swords in the city."

"Then when did the war happen?" asked Marcus.

"Why didn't they just kill all the Sabines?" asked Lucius Jr.

"I asked first."

"So. Everybody knows what happened next."

"Shut up, three fingers."

"Don't call me that."

"You're a freak. You should have been exposed," Marcus spat.

Lucius Jr. went rigid, glaring hotly at his cousin as the adults tried to calm the unexpected outburst of emotion. With a feral howl Lucius Jr. hurled himself at Marcus. Chairs and bodies crashed to the floor in a tangled heap. The parents leaped to their feet but not before Lucius Jr. in one swift motion pinned his cousins' arms with his knees and pummeled his defenseless face with his fists.

Lucius and Titus reached the struggling boys at the same time, but Lucius shoved his brother aside as he reached down for his son. He picked him up, arms still flailing, and hauled him backwards until the table separated the two boys.

"Calm down," Lucius said sweetly into his son's ear as he pinned his arms to his sides in a supportive hug. "Calm down. It's all over now."

"It'll never be over," said Lucius Jr.

"How dare you offend one of your own family in this house," Drusilla railed at her grandson, Marcus, as his father restrained him. Neither boy shed a tear as they eyed each other heatedly. At his grandmother's words Marcus dropped his gray ringed brown eyes in embarrassment, suddenly contrite.

"I told you this would happen," said Titus in a low voice to Lucius. His words snapped everyone's heads up in surprise.

"Don't start, Titus," warned Lucius. His large face reddened.

"I told you this would divide the family if you didn't expunge the bad omen."

"Stop now, Titus, or any division of the family will be on your head."

"You've never seen your duty," continued Titus. "Everything you've ever done has been for yourself."

Lucius felt as if he were watching the scene unfold from a vast height. He observed himself standing stiffly erect holding his son. Saw Titus on the opposite side of the table, long face flushed with indignation, his rough hands resting on the shoulders of Marcus.

Duellia gathered her other children to her like a mother hen, backing up to the wall out of harm's way. He saw his mother, tense with anger, hold her ground and look from one son to the other with unbelievable repugnance in her olive shaped black eyes.

"Everything I've got I've fought for myself," he heard himself say.

Suddenly Drusilla stepped between them and brought him back to earth. Her wide full lips worked angrily, and her straight nose flared at the nostrils with hostility. "Both of you bring dishonor on this house," she said in a voice that rang with metallic fury. She turned to Titus. "Your words are a greater ill omen than any meaningless physical defect. And you," she spun on Lucius, "you think only of yourself. You pretend you sacrificed your ancestral home for the good of the family, but in reality you sacrificed your family so you would be free of any obligations to it. Your selfishness in the name of honor is wholly reprehensible."

The brothers' anger wilted before the vehemence of their mother. They felt puerile and inconsequential. Titus stepped forward to apologize—first to his mother, then to Lucius, and finally to his nephew. Lucius followed, and then it came the boys' turn. Marcus embraced his cousin, slurring his words around a fattening lip.

"I didn't mean those things I said," he assured Lucius Jr. "I was just mad."

"It's nothing," said Lucius Jr., the only one who didn't believe his own words.

Despite his family's protestations Lucius decided to head back to Rome. He sent Lucius Jr. out to inform Graptus who packed and saddled the mules with a sigh of weary resignation. The mules shared his feelings, exhibiting a decided reluctance to leave the comfort of the stable.

Lucius stepped out of the farmhouse to encounter clearing skies. Great rents in the clouds exposed brilliant swatches of lapis blue. Streams of effulgent light poured through the gaps, splashing in luminous puddles on the ground. Below them the Roman plain lay sectioned out in a patchwork of light and shadow, mottled like the bark of the plane tree in muted shades of green and brown. In the distance the mountains crowded bluish gray against the sky, pulling the horizon closer.

Graptus helped Lucius into the saddle. "Let's go," said Lucius in a flat, deadened voice, "before we lose the daylight."

# PART III

## XXVII

April 28-May 3, 450 BC
Festival of Flora—Goddess of Flowers

Like Rome, the fortune of Lucius Tempanius should have been growing. When he totted up his assets as Rome did her citizens an increase should have been obvious. Rome claimed 117,319 citizens after the last census. Lucius thought they must have counted the dogs and pigs running loose in the Subura, and maybe counted them twice at that, to reach such a figure. His growth proved just as mythical. His holdings were a tavern with living quarters and rooms to rent above it, ten iugera of land with a two-story farmhouse on the Anio River, sixty iugera of mostly vineyards near Antium, and a plot on the Aventine Hill. When all those were added up one would have thought he had built himself a strong financial portfolio. But what looked good on papyrus didn't necessarily get one into the class of equites.

Everything was in suspension; his plans for the Aventine; his plans for the vineyards in Antium; his plans for the Boar's Tusk; the tribunes' agitation; the senate's refusals; the constitution; what to do about Graptus. Vengeance for Antonius.

In other ways not much had changed. He still lived above the Boar's Tusk tavern in the Subura district. Rome still fought the Volscians and Aequians on a perennial, nearly quotidian basis.

Lucius had given up fighting in these annual campaigns a year previously. At forty-seven years old the fun had gone out of it. Now he diverted himself by sitting in his tavern and recounting the stories in glorified terms of the raiding, looting, and state sanctioned brigandage in which he had taken part. And if anyone challenged him, he brought out his mountain of medals to prove his claims. But now it was Lucius the Younger's turn to make war on Rome's enemies.

In fact, since his investment in the vineyards near Antium, Lucius had grown frustrated with the lack of resolution to these incessant conflicts. Increasingly he wished Rome could bring the Volscians and Aequians to a decisive battle and wring peace out of them, or come to some agreement with them. The economics of war were beginning to have an adverse effect on him, as well as on Rome as a whole.

His factor Tranellius worked diligently to bring the vineyards into production only to suffer depredations at the hands of Rome's enemies, making it impossible to sustain a regular income from the property. Costs, however, were as regular as the sunrise. Since Antium, with its large Volscian population, remained a highly contested city, Lucius thought it might be time to sell the property, and invest a little closer to home. He knew this would incur a large and precarious loss, and thus vacillated in making the decision.

As if that weren't enough, the troubles in the city made even Lucius Tempanius take notice. Much as he despised, distrusted, and otherwise ignored politics, he had come to pine for some resolution to the conflict between the plebeians and the patricians of the last ten years. But what started out as a promising compromise developed into something ugly, and mean. His worst fear was that he would be dragged into the fight.

What a shame to ruin a beautiful day with such dread thoughts. The Campus Martius sparkled with martial splendor. The Peteline wood glimmered with the tender green of new leaves. Wildflowers, scattered like jewels in the grass, glittered red, gold, purple, and delicate daisy white. Mimosa trees bloomed like golden terrestrial suns. From a clear cerulean sky the sun spread warmth like a thick wool blanket, as the earth gave off the fresh scent of renewal. Cyclamens danced in a light breeze swinging lavender flowers that lolled upside down like shy maidens swaying to a secret rhythm. Lucius looked across the field to where the sun glinted off the bronze helmets of legionaries in dark red tunics drilling in phalanx formation. He had lost track of Lucius Jr. when his musings took his concentration elsewhere.

"Do you see Lucius?" he asked Graptus.

Graptus pointed a long bony finger toward the sword posts set up north of the altar of Mars. "He's over there," he said. "Taking sword practice."

"Ah," said Lucius, shifting his gaze under the shade of his big hand. "I think you could use some of that Graptus. You're looking kind of skinny these days. Stick your arm out here."

Graptus obeyed. Lucius put his own axle-sized forearm next to it. "Look at that," he said. "You're like this." He held up his little finger to indicate Graptus' lack of girth. "You can't say I don't feed you enough."

Graptus retrieved his arm and wiped his bald, sweating pate with a thin hand. "No, Dominus. You feed me quite well."

"Are you sick?"

"No. At least, I don't think so."

"Maybe it's the work," Lucius grinned. Deep smile lines from broad nose to strong chin creased his wide face.

Graptus matched the smile with one of his own on his narrow peninsular face. "No, the work is mostly fine. Maybe it's old age," he offered.

"Then I should be wasting away to nothing," said Lucius. He patted a growing paunch. "As you can see, that's not happening."

"Am I feeding you too much?" asked Graptus, straight faced.

"No, I think you feed me just about right." Dark eyes laughed.

"Perhaps you could use some sword practice to firm up."

They laughed together, and Lucius draped a tree trunk of an arm over the narrow shoulders of his slave with affectionate familiarity. "I have a proposal I want you to hear."

"I know it's not completely unknown for a master to marry his slave, but I think in this case it might cause some consternation among the city fathers," teased Graptus.

"Very funny. That's why I've kept you all these years. Had you been one of those dour, humorless slaves you'd have been manumitted long ago."

They entered the city at the Porta Carmentalis, the Unlucky Way, near the river. Following the Vicus Iugarius under the Tarpeian Rock they entered the Forum in silence. Laughter died quickly in Lucius, though Graptus preferred the lighthearted conversation, and sought to prolong it. "You have to go abroad, across the Tiber to get the dour type of slave," he said, referring to the law that Roman citizens could not be enslaved at Rome. Because his joke assuredly mocked the Roman character, but it fell flat and he resigned himself to serious conversation.

Lucius might have laughed, and even feigned indignation at his slave's presumptuous comments had he not caught sight of three Decemvirs emerging from the Curia Hostilia each preceded by twelve lictors, and each bearing axes bound up in their rods in direct violation of customs that had been in existence since the beginning of the Republic. His lips froze into a hard line at this blatant sacrilege. Citizens fanned away from the Decemvirs with fearful deference. Those that didn't move fast enough the lictors knocked aside with rough arrogance. He followed their progress up to the capitol with angry eyes.

"It looks like we may be across the Tiber now," he muttered fiercely.

Making their way carefully through the labyrinth of the Subura, side stepping refuse, and evading defenestrated debris they arrived at the Boar's Tusk. Lucius locked the door behind them. He opened the two shutters to let light in, then sat at one of the tables while Graptus brought a pitcher of wine and two cups.

Lucius shook his big head, and laughed through his teeth. "What, no food?"

"I'm watching your weight."

"And I'm watching yours. Pour." He pointed at the cups. "I want to make you a proposition."

"So you said," Graptus replied, shoving a cup in front of Lucius. "Health," he said, raising his cup.

"Health," responded Lucius.

Motes of dust swirled in little cyclones in the gusts of air entering the windows. Sunlight hit the opposite wall in arched brilliance, illuminating the gray stone and mortar, splashing onto the floor and scattering in luminous droplets around the room.

Lucius took a drink and set his cup down hard. "First, I want you to know that I have always planned on freeing you." He waved off Graptus' thanks. "It's not such a great favor. I've had no kind of legacy to give you, so your prospects would be difficult at best."

"So…" said Graptus helpfully.

"So," repeated Lucius, but did not continue. He rubbed his face with both hands as if not knowing where to start. "So," he began again in a guarded tone, "here's the proposition. And if you refuse, I won't hold it against you."

"I'm itching all over with excitement, now."

"You've always been too familiar and too sarcastic to be a good slave,' Lucius said with feigned anger. "Now stop interrupting. My brother Antonius has been dead ten years, now, and has yet to be avenged. I intend to remedy that before I get too old. If you will agree to help, I'll not only give you your freedom, but I'll give you the Boar's Tusk, and enroll you as a citizen at the next census."

Graptus eyed his master closely as his brain pondered the ramifications of his answer. His master's face grew more round as the skin sagged along his jaw, and a profusion of white whiskers in his two-day growth leant an unhealthy pallor to his complexion. But Graptus was not deceived. Lucius Tempanius had the constitution of an ox, and he remained vital, strong, and capable.

"What can I do that you can't do yourself?"

"Find him. Everyone knows I want him dead. But they're all afraid to cross the Quinctii. It's like a wind has blown him away without a trace."

"I thought he went to Caere?"

"He did. Supposedly. Then it was Tarquinia, Faleria, Gabii, Praeneste. Jove, Graptus where hasn't he been? That's the problem, I need to know where he is."

"And why will anyone tell me where he is?"

"Because you're a slave."

"But I'm your slave."

"I understand. I didn't say it would be easy. But I think you're less easily recognized than me. If I write travel documents, you'll have legitimate authorization should any magistrates question you. If not…" he shrugged and raised his hands palms up.

"What would be my reason for traveling?"

"You're looking for new wines. What else?"

"And if I find him?"

With a backhand gesture of bitter disdain Lucius swept his left arm clean with his open right hand. "You come back and tell me. Then we'll avenge Antonius. Me, Titus, you, and whomever else I can dig up."

Graptus sipped at his wine. He stroked his equine face thoughtfully with one hand and drummed on the table with the fingers of the other. A part of him found it curious that he seriously entertained the offer. Lucius had assured him of his manumission whatever his decision, so why risk execution for someone else's vendetta?"

As if reading his mind, Lucius spoke up. "You know you'd be risking your life? If the magistrates think they have a case they can torture you to get evidence against me. I can't guarantee your safety."

"You could free me first," said Graptus. "Then they couldn't torture me."

"Yes. But it would make our story less believable."

447

All true. But what he left unsaid was the argument that filled his mind. He had developed a loyalty to this family, and especially to this man. With loyalty came responsibility. Now he had an offer of freedom, citizenship, and a financial future.

"Very well, I go from your slave to your client. Not much of a step up, is it?" jested Graptus.

Lucius raised his hand as if to strike him, muttering his usual refrain about thinking with his back, then moaned in mock despondency. "Why was I cursed with such an impertinent slave?"

"Because he's made you almost rich?"

Lucius scoffed. "I'm not an equite yet. And anyway, a good slave wouldn't leave his master 'almost' rich."

"Well, then I still have time to make good."

"Life's a bubble, Graptus. Redeem the time." Lucius shoved his stool back, swept his hands through thinning hair and yawned. "What do you say we take a walk? We'll go up the Vicus Ficum. I love to see the fig trees in bloom."

"We're not opening today?"

"Not today."

"How can I make you an equite if you don't open the tavern?"

"Tomorrow's a market day. Rome will be packed, and we'll be mad with work. Today I want to relax."

"Will your brother be in tomorrow?"

Lucius slammed the shutters shut and barred them, closing out the light. "I expect so," he said, opening the door and waving for Graptus to hurry. "He's been making a regular habit of it these days."

+ + +

Titus Tempanius lived on his hill, thirty Roman miles east of Rome, on ten iugera of quiet most of the time. He liked it that way. Mars had so far been a good protector, and the household lares were strong. The constant raiding between the Aequians, Volscians, and Romans had, with a few exceptions, missed his farm below the Latin city of Labicum. Almost every summer a Roman army, often with him in it, marched by on the way to the pass at Algidus on the other side of Labicum to fight one or both of Rome's perpetual enemies. At forty-three years old he had spent his whole adult life fighting these same peoples, broken by an occasional tiff with the Sabines or Etruscans. No, fortune had been with him out there on the perilous edge of Roman dominion.

On the flat ground behind his hill, he saw with satisfaction that the wheat planted there had taken root well and sprouted in luxuriant green sheaves. Weeding desultorily as he passed through the field, he began climbing the large hill that rose steeply a thousand feet like a defensive tower behind the farm.

Dense with oak, beech, elm, and plane trees, tall maritime pines were scattered like elegant parasols through the thick forest. Alder, and broom vied for growing room with wild blackberry and raspberry vines. On the forest floor wildflowers shone like porphyry. Titus moved through this other world with quiet caution, the sounds of his movement absorbed in its humid fecundity. Fulgent shafts of sunlight pierced the shielded darkness in random striations. The simultaneous sensation of tranquillity and menace filled him with joy, and he breathed deep the forest's heavy odor. A susurrant breeze weaving surreptitiously through the trees tickled his sweating skin as he followed a narrow game trail upward.

Though part of the territory of Tusculum, Titus thought of this uninhabited and ignored forest as his. His in its wildness as assuredly as the little hillock below was his in its ordered, meticulous cultivation. Here in summer he let his goats forage and his pigs seek in grunting satisfaction the cool wet earth. He hunted wild boar and collected nuts and berries, gathering all the natural abundance of earth that gave sustenance to his family.

In a clearing dominated by a rock outcropping the color of iron he sat on a cool flat spot from which he could see the Roman plain laid out like a game board in green and brown rectangles below. Across the plain the city of Tibur glistened like white mosaic tiles in the emerald green of the mountains. Here in this meadow, where only the hum and buzz of insects disturbed the quiet, he came to think.

Yes, life had been mostly good so far. Some losses had been suffered. He had caught the last breath of his mother, Drusilla two years prior, and his wife Duellia a year later giving birth to what would have been their eighth child. Neither one survived the ordeal, though they had tried by cesarean to save the child. His eldest son Marcus spent much of his time away with the legions, but he still had Titus Jr. and his youngest son Publius, now ten, still at home. And, of course Petronius Fuscus, now in his seventies, kept company by Primus and the slave Restius. He had given Tempania in marriage, and unwilling to have a house without women Titus betrothed Marcus to the daughter of Sextus Tullius. Tullia was a welcome addition, though Titus feared she might be overworked performing all the household chores herself and considered acquiring a slave girl to help out. But perhaps he should just find a wife for Titus Jr. who would be seventeen in a year.

Well, an easy problem, but there remained much to do. Besides the normal weeding, hoeing, and pruning, there were repairs to the barn, and animal pens, mending of harness, yokes, and fences.

The same held true for Rome. It had been a long winter of discontent. Ten years of discontent. The seeds of unity had finally been sown when representatives were sent to the Hellenistic cities of the south to research Greek law in an agreement between the patricians and the plebeians to codify the laws of Rome. Questions of nexum, or debt bondage, legal culpability for damage to private property, the rights of fathers and children, property rights, the calling of witnesses or filing suit against another citizen, laws regarding religious observance, laws of slavery, all these questions and more were to be written down so that every citizen should know his rights and responsibilities. A board of ten men, called decemvirs, took the place of consuls and tribunes so that no public or party agitation could take place until the laws were codified. Unfortunately, they had been unable to complete the task and so another board of ten had to be elected. That is when the troubles began. Appius Claudius, grandson of the original Samnite clan leader, rigged the election so that he guaranteed himself re-election to the board. Worse, this board of ten acted like despots, which obviously boded ill for the Republic. Titus fretted over this development, fearing an outbreak of violence in the body politic. Yes, much work remained to be done. And still Caeso ran free.

The sky paled as the sun passed midday and headed for the cool sea. Titus grunted as he levered himself off the hard stone. Tomorrow he would go to Rome for market day.

+ + +

It was market day, it was fasti, it was insanity. Men occupied every table, stool, and square inch of floor space. Demetria kept the kitchen steaming with food, and Lucius emptied amphorae of wine with inhuman speed. They set up tables out front in the piazza, and those too filled with customers.

Titus forced his way through a glut of togas and tunics to find Lucius behind the serving tower with a look of rage, panic, and frustration swirling on his wide face. Titus immediately broke into a sweat from the heat generated by the milling bodies. The room, even with windows and doors wide open smelled of hearth smoke, spilled wine, and humans. Titinius provided background music with his pipe to the fantastic volume of noise coming from men's throats.

Lucius took in the pained expression of his brother's long face as he poured wine through the funnel into a customer's waiting pitcher below. "Want a tavern?" he yelled.

"I suppose," Titus said, climbing two steps up towards Lucius and shouting to him, "this means you won't be free for a while."

"You're very perceptive," he called back. Matted and glistening with perspiration his thinning hair accentuated the widow's peak lancing forward on his forehead.

Graptus came rushing by. "I need two pitchers of red," he cried breathlessly, pushing between the gesticulating elbows of customers raggedly queued up around the tower. He looked up at Lucius and laughed. "Why Dominus, your normally calm self looks a trifle harried."

"And you're trifling with the wrong person," Lucius shot back.

In the blink of an eye everything changed. At first, with all the commotion inside, no one noticed the disturbance. But as news worked its way into the tavern men pushed their way outside to see what the trouble was. Soon shouts and sounds of struggle could be heard from outside and a mass exodus drew Lucius and Titus along with the crowd. Graptus stayed inside to make sure no 'stragglers' helped themselves to the goods.

Just off the plaza, on the side of the Boar's Tusk near a copse of plane trees confused sounds of fighting, shouting, and cursing rent the air. Fear and anger hung sizzling in the afternoon sun like a foul stench from the Velabrum. Lucius and Titus, shoulder to shoulder as if in battle formation, wedged their way through the horde of trembling spectators. As they reached the front a collective gasp went up from the crowd.

A decemvir, Marcus Cornelius Maluginensis, his fat barrel chest heaving with indignation beneath his purple-bordered toga, pointed his vine stick of office at a man struggling against two lictors. "Cease," he ordered.

"I appeal!" cried the citizen, from his knees avoiding the loop of rope a lictor attempted to cast over his head.

"There is no appeal," Maluginensis shouted. His flaccid clean-shaven face, and his large bulbous nose turned florid with anger. He pointed with small soft hands. "Go, lictor, and bind him," he ordered, thick vulgar lips pulled back in a bestial snarl.

"I appeal," the citizen cried again. His sere tunic had been pulled down over emaciated shoulders and scarred torso to reveal protruding ribs as he strained against the lictors holding him. Beneath black matted curls blue eyes glared with fear, and rage. Clearly overmatched, and puffing with exertion his hollow cheeks appealed for help more loudly than his hoarse voice.

"What's his crime?" Titus asked a bystander.

"Theft," he answered.

"The real thief is Maluginensis," someone else said. "One of his quislings covets Turpio's property."

With all his might the one called Turpio struggled to push his bony knees out of the dirt of the street, and stand on his feet. But one lictor held an arm and a handful of hair, while another twisted his other arm back and jammed a knee hard into his back. A third lictor untied his bundle of rods while the nine remaining formed a thin cordon around the violence.

Maluginensis raised his crows voice against the rising murmur of the crowd, seeking to overpower their objections with his authority and the awe of his office. "This man was ordered before the court to stand trial for a charge of theft. He refused to answer the summons, thereby confirming his guilt."

"Lies, lies," yelled Turpio.

The words echoed like tears in Titus' memory.

"On evidence given by Lucius Oppimius Pansa he has been found guilty."

"Lies," screeched Turpio again. But now the blood red cords holding the rods were untied and one came down hard on the back of his head. Stunned, the words died like a cough in his throat.

The lictors hurled his unresisting body to its feet, and slammed him face first against the leprous bark of a plane tree. His nose gushed blood, flowing crimson down his bare chest. Quickly they bound his arms around the tree.

"Punishment," croaked Maluginensis, "is confiscation of property, and beating with the rods."

"What did he steal, the whole house?" someone in the crowd                                    shouted. "Unjust," cried another voice.

As if with one mind the crowd closed in tighter around the decemvir and his lictors. Then Lucius noticed them. The

453

allies. He didn't know how he could have missed them before, but they were everywhere. In finely cut tunics a host of young patricians, and sons of senators bearing clubs and knives appeared as if rising out of the ground. Without orders they moved quickly to reinforce the lictors.

"In their mercy," spat Maluginensis, confidence filling his voice as the crowd step- ped back, "the decemvirs have spared his life, and not taken away his freedom." He turned to his lictors. "Commence the flogging."

Most of the crowd, unwilling to witness the beating, dispersed, heads down, eyes unwilling to meet, shame filling their hearts with bile. Lucius and Titus untied Turpio when the lictors finished with him. His knees buckled, his arms dangled slackly at his side, and his head lolled in unconsciousness as he dropped like a sack to the ground. His pulverized back stained the dirt. They carried Turpio into the tavern and laid him out face down on the kitchen table. A few diehard spectators drifted in with them and began ordering wine. Lucius angrily started to throw them out, but Graptus prevailed on him to allow them to stay and soon had a brisk business going. Nothing whets a thirst like blood and politics.

In the kitchen Lucius stoked the fire on the hearth and put a pot of water on.

"Have you any mild cabbage?" asked Titus.

"I think so," said Lucius. "Demetria," he called to his cook, "fetch me some mild cabbage, please."

"I think all we have is parsley cabbage, Dominus," she said, searching the larder.

"That will have to do then. Crush as much as we've got."

"Yes, Dominus," she said.

Titus took a sponge and gingerly began cleansing Turpio's back with the warm water on the fire. This brought him around some, and he moaned and writhed on the table. Lucius held him down as gently as possible. "It's all right," he reassured him. "We're just cleaning you up. Hold still, now."

Titus worked over him diligently, thoroughly flushing his wounds. As the dried cached blood and dirt flowed onto the table and stone floor, the raw open wounds and bruised flesh looked even worse.

"You're going to be sore a few days, I'll guarantee that," said Titus in a low voice as soothing as the unguent he was about to put on.

"No matter," gasped Turpio, "they've killed me anyway."

"How's that?" asked Lucius, his voice still tight with anger.

Grimacing against the pain Turpio raised himself up on one elbow. "Look at me," he said in protest. "You think I'm a bad farmer. But I once looked like you."

"Lie back down," Titus soothed.

Turpio ignored him, looking at Lucius with a spark of challenge in his sky-blue eyes. "I was like you," he insisted once again. "I have...had, two iugera near Fidenae."

Titus began to shush him again but Lucius stopped him angrily. "Let him speak. Maybe we should listen to this."

"Years ago," Turpio began again, "there was plenty of land for everyone there." Tears flowed from his eyes as he digressed and he choked on his words. "I was born there, as was my father, and his father." His pear-shaped chin trembled with emotion. "That land has been ours since Servius Tullius was king in Rome."

"So, what happened?" asked Lucius, impatiently. "The short history."

"What happened," said Turpio bitterly, "is our 'fathers' decided they needed all the ager publicus around my farm. They denied me use of any of it. How is a man supposed to feed his family on two iugera? How can he pay his taxes? And now look at me...a basket of bones. They should have finished me on that tree out there."

Demetria brought a bowl of macerated cabbage to the table and Titus persuaded the beaten man to lie down flat so he could finish dressing his wounds. He spread a thin layer of cabbage, crushed and chopped into a green paste, on the man's bruised, and lacerated back. He would have liked to apply it thicker, but he at least covered the man's back so that no skin remained exposed. As he wrapped Turpio in bandages he gave him instructions of further medical care.

"You need to renew the poultice twice a day. Will you be able to manage?"

"With what?" asked Turpio, sitting stiffly under Titus' ministrations. "I haven't a roof over my head. My wife and children are on the street."

"Are you listening to this, Titus?" asked Lucius.

"Yes," said Titus in medicinal, placating tones.

"No," insisted Lucius, "did you really hear? These men are no better than thieves."

"Yes, Lucius, I heard," said Titus emphatically. "Right now, the only thing I can do is help this man here." He turned solicitously back to Turpio. "Where will you go now?"

Turpio eased himself off the table, steadying himself against it until he had his legs under him. Words deserted him so he shrugged his shoulders, then gingerly pulled his tunic over them.

"Listen," said Lucius, his mind suddenly made up. "Do you need work?"

"Of course," said Turpio.

"Good. I'm building a house on the Aventine. You can build, can't you?"

"Anything that needs building, I can build."

"Fine. As soon as you're able, report to work. You'll find it on the south side of the Aventine above the Clivus Publicius."

Turpio expressed guarded thanks. He scratched the bump on his large nose with a callused finger, and pursed thin lips. "What are your expectations?" he asked. "Besides the actual work, I mean." He had good reason to ask. By accepting, he abjured fidelity to his former patron and attached himself to Lucius. Lucius had little to offer but his reputation as a soldier.

Then again, his quondam patron had not lifted a finger to help him, so cowed was he by the Decemvirs.

"My expectations," said Lucius, "are that when I need you or any member of your family, you will be there. Conversely, I will see to it that you have work and will assist you in any other way I can."

"Will you help me get my farm back?"

"I don't have that kind of influence. Listen, I'm not begging you. Take it or leave it."

"Thank you," accepted Turpio. "May I go now?"

"If you're able. If not, you're welcome to stay."

Although stiff with pain, and knowing that tomorrow would be worse, Turpio still had his pride. "I can manage. I'll be at work tomorrow."

When he had gone Lucius and Titus enjoyed a cup of mulsum wine, speaking little. A horde of thoughts pressed each man's mind, a hundred subjects vying for dominance. One consistently rose to the surface. Lucius, as usual, broached the subject first.

"I've made an agreement with Graptus," he said.

"What kind of agreement?"

"One that will help us finish our business with Caeso Quinctius."

"Is that safe?"

"Nothing is safe, Titus. But I trust Graptus."

"All right. How can he help us?"

"Listen, no one will give me a clue as to Caeso's whereabouts. But Graptus is a slave, and in a household the size of the Quinctii there's bound to be either a disgruntled slave, or one that can't keep his mouth shut. Graptus is a charmer—you see how he manipulates me. I'm counting on him to use the same skills to get information on Caeso."

"He certainly does control you," laughed Titus. "All right, if you're sure about it I'll go along."

+ + +

Summer came on. Rome panted under the heat of the sun and the cruelty of the decemvirs. The 'ten kings' as people came to call them, ruled Rome with an avaricious hand. More beatings, more confiscations, even executions took place. The weight of their tyranny, led by Appius Claudius, fell hardest on the plebeians, but even the patricians twisted uneasily. They thought at first that the plebeians would come crawling, offering untold concessions (primarily the tribunate) if the decemvirs could just be gotten rid of. They miscalculated. The plebeians saw the decemvirate as a tool of the patricians, and in no way trusted either party. Locked in this stalemate of mutual distrust and hatred Rome sat paralyzed while the decemvirs and their supporters prospered. Innocent men were accused of egregious crimes, denounced by men who coveted, and were awarded their property upon conviction.

Titus quit going to Rome every ninth day, instead making it every third nundinae. Even then, he sold his produce, his charcoal, or his baskets and left, lingering only long enough to bid his brother hello. He had too much work to do on the farm, and Rome had become depressing. Lucius thought the examples of Turpio and others were lost on Titus, but they were not. He simply did not know what could be done, and he feared someone would denounce him if he made his opposition too vociferous.

"You think because you have ten iugera you're safe," Lucius had accused him. To which there might be some truth, he conceded. One could certainly feed one's family on ten iugera. Most small holders had to feed theirs on a third of that or less. But could one buy all those items one couldn't make? Tools, jars, pots, braziers, shoes, and myriad other items a family needed? Highly doubtful. Rome needed a law guaranteeing access to the public lands, or at least limiting the amount any one family could control. The chances of that happening were about as good as the chances of wars ending with the Volscians and the Aequians. So, he stayed home and worked, controlling those things he could and leaving the rest in the hands of the gods. It seemed the better part of wisdom.

Graptus watched his master's rage and frustration grow with each passing day. Business at the tavern continued to thrive, however, and the potential to live well and free fired his imagination. Eventually men like Lucius would rise up and claim their liberty, he felt certain. If only he could keep out of the middle of it, he could profit handsomely from their courage.

His initial difficulty lay in locating and ingratiating himself with the right slave in the Quinctius household. He seduced a pantry maid, befriended a stable boy, and matched wits with the tutor all to know avail. When, finally, he found the key, he could have kicked himself. He met the wine steward in a shop on the south side of the Via Sacra opposite the Regia. Graptus had taken to wearing a threadbare tunic, and muttering complaints in the presence of slaves, but not so loudly that Romans could hear.

Wine stewards had a reputation of being connoisseurs, not lushes. This one didn't fit the mold. His jaw looked like two porkchops set on edge with the fat left on, and his fleshy lips pouted self-importantly.

"What did you say?" he asked, looking Graptus over distastefully with hooded eyes.

"Nothing," said Graptus, glancing furtively around. He breathed deeply. "Don't you love that musty smell of wine?"

The shop was a large one, two hundred square feet and built of red bricks. A counter ran three quarters of the way across the front of the shop. In the back were kept amphorae of wine, some marked with the name of a region, or a grower. On shelves along both side walls terracotta containers of various sizes waited to be filled. The shopkeeper was a small man, barely over five feet tall, and shaped like a bottom-heavy wine jug.

"I'll be with you in a breath, Graptus," he said, in a surprisingly deep voice. "Now, what will it be for the Quinctii, Axius?"

At the mention of the Quinctii, Graptus came alert. To hide his interest, he pretended to eye some of the pottery along the walls. In a reedy voice Axius read off the list on a wax tablet he pulled from a leather satchel suspended from a strap slung over his head, and crossing his concave chest. "Let me see, a congius of mulsum, a congius of Coan, and a congius of regular white wine."

"Must be quite a gathering they're having at the Quinctius house. I suppose you'll have to stay up all night serving the guests," Graptus observed.

"It's the duty of any slave," said Axius, carefully replacing the wax tablet in his satchel.

"Don't I know it. At least you don't have to do it night in and night out like I do. Isn't that right Oppius?"

Oppius Maelius tipped an amphora and poured wine into a shiny black jug. "That's your bad luck to be a slave in a tavern all right," he said, then changed Graptus' luck in the wink of an eye. "But at least you get to sample the goods regularly, eh?" he said knowingly.

Graptus could have kissed him. The red tip of Axius' long nose twitched with curiosity, and he suddenly assumed a congenial air. Graptus set the hook deeper.

"In fact," he said, "he's got a wonderful white wine from his vineyards in Antium that will soon be available in enough quantity to sell to you, Oppius. I swear by Ceres it'll make your mouth sing."

Axius cleared his throat. "Perhaps he has enough to sell to private parties for the time being. You say it's very good?"

"Oh, it's very good. And he sells it now to private parties out of the Boar's Tusk tavern in the Subura."

"Would it be possible to get a taste?"

"Do you mean for free? Nothing in Rome is free."

"Well, just enough to see if it might be something my master would be interested in." The hungry look in his eyes made Graptus smile.

Oppius set a large jug with a cork stopper on the counter. "That's the mulsum," he said.

Graptus skewed his smile into cynicism. He indicated his ratty, yellowed tunic with a sweep of his long-fingered hand. "You see how he outfits me," he complained. "Nothing is free in the house of Lucius Tempanius." He scrutinized Axius carefully for reaction to the name but got none. "But you're always welcome to buy a cup if you have any free time."

Another jug landed on the counter, and Axius said nothing. For a moment Graptus feared he'd gone too far and lost him. But Axius in his tedious way formulated what he thought would be a persuasive argument.

"Perhaps if you showed some initiative on your master's behalf he would treat you better," he offered.

"You might be on to something, friend. What do you say, Oppius?"

"You must admit," said Oppius, himself a freedman, "it sounds like a good idea. And you have been looking pretty ragged of late."

"Well, every *as* goes into the vineyards at Antium. You know, his overseer could be your brother. He's short and built like a squared block just like you. Smart too. He grows the vines against olive trees, and they're like horses and goats together the way they prosper."

The third jug hit the counter. "Well, what do you say?" asked Axius.

"Why not?" said Graptus. "And anyway, I like your face," he lied.

"Good." He handed the jugs to two slaves waiting outside. "Take these to the house," he said. "I'll follow in a short while."

The Quinctii lived in a fashionable section of the Quirinal Hill, its paved streets swept and washed regularly, the houses built of brick with beautiful gardens and atriums. Richly dressed people living amongst the splendors of the age. Down in the Subura another reality held sway. Few of the anfractuous dirt paths cluttered with stinking refuse, stray dogs, pigs, vicious rats, shards of razor-sharp pottery, screaming termagants, and violent men had names. Sometimes the people were the worst part of it. But most often they were just poor.

461

Graptus delightedly observed the tiptoeing, skirting, high stepping movements of his companion. Axius dug something out of his satchel and brought it up to his nose. Graptus could see in the constant sweeping of his bulging eyes that he had second thoughts about coming to the tavern.

"Almost there," he reassured Axius. "Perhaps we should send for a litter to take you home," he said, as he slipped the lock on the tavern door.

He opened a single shutter to light the cool dark interior. "Now," he said, I want you to try it in its different forms. We have it in mulsum for the dinner table—guaranteed to perk up the weakest appetite. We have it unadulterated for pure enjoyment, slightly watered to avoid inebriation, and spiced for after vesperna." All of which was true. He brought out four pitchers, and two glasses. Lucius felt justly proud of the wine made from the vineyards in Antium. He just could not keep a steady supply of it because of the constant raiding.

"You know," Graptus said, pouring a cup of the mulsum and pushing it in front of Axius, "the Quinctii don't exactly like my master."

Axius drank, slowly at first as if suspicious, then with longer draughts for the wine tasted good. He set the cup down. "It's quite good," he said, his eyes lusting after the other jugs.

"Ah, you like that. Well," encouraged Graptus, "I think the mulsum is the worst. Makes it too sweet. Try this." He poured a cup to the brim of undiluted wine.

Axius drank, and his thirst grew. The wine sparkled on his tongue, sweet and fruity, clear as water and just as refreshing. "When it comes to wine," he said, "perhaps they could put aside their differences."

Graptus filled his cup again. "Take it, take it," he said. "What do you say?"

"Very good. Maybe I should try the undiluted again just to make sure of the quality." His words began to slur and his eyes beamed bright as stars.

"Of course," said Graptus, pouring again. "And certainly, you're right. Personal differences should never stand in the way of commerce. Would you like some of the spiced?"

"Not just yet. Let's try another of the watered."

"Good, good. You're a true expert; I can see that. And after all, that thing with Caeso was a long time ago, and he's probably far away by now."

"Oh, not so far," sneered Axius. He lifted the cup and downed the remains.

"Here," said Graptus, "try this." He poured another cup of the undiluted. "What do you say?"

"Excellent. Really. I'm not joking. This is some of the best."

"You're too kind. Try some of the spiced."

"I haven't finished this yet."

"I'm sorry. Forgive me. I'm just excited now. How rude, I completely missed what you said about Caeso."

"He's in Tibur. Not so far." He drained another cup.

"Here, try this," said Graptus, and he felt as if he were serving his own wine.

+ + +

Graptus left Rome via the Porta Esquilina under a ferruginous dawn sky. The timing couldn't have been better. August blew on the city like someone with garlic on his breath. At his back were the putrid smells of decaying refuse, rotting corpses, and the swollen clutching humidity of Rome. In his saddlebags he carried letters of introduction and authorization from Lucius, as well as a small stipend or viaticum for food and shelter. He made good time under a limpid sky. The horse's hooves clacked against the paving stones with a steady rhythm. Riding along the Via Gabina, the mountains loomed tall and forbidding around him. He wondered how Lucius could be so sure that one day Rome would control them. How could you come to grips and defeat enemies like the Sabines, Samnites, and Aequians who would always hold the high ground and were at home in their mountain refuges? The Romans dwelt on the plains, and preferred to fight there where they could easily maintain their phalanx formation in battle.

"Of course," he said to his horse, patting its swaying neck, "the stupidities I fought with thought they should fight down here. Why make use of your natural advantages?"

His horse, a roan of easy temperament, twitched her ears at the sound of his voice, and snorted as if in agreement.

"Ah, true," said Graptus. "But you're much smarter than the generals I fought under."

The mare had a smooth rocking gait, her head swung side to side hypnotically, and his thoughts soon slid off to nothing in particular. The horse retrieved his attention now and then by shying at the sight of a brown lizard scurrying off the road. In the fields along the way men and boys bent to the work of harvesting tawny wheat. He passed a signal tower under construction by soldiers, and laborers from the proletariat class in the city.

Before he knew it, he reached the crossroads shrine marking the turn to Lucius' property on the Anio. He stopped in to visit with Villius, inspect the farm, and stay the night. On a wax tablet he made notes of work that needed done, and the crops being grown on neighboring farms, as well as their general condition. The next day he completed his journey to Tibur.

The ground rose in gentle undulations to the mountains that stood like fortress walls before him. Here also the land glittered with golden wheat, olive trees with spear tipped argent leaves, and luscious green grapevines. The air grew cooler as he climbed, and for a brief moment Graptus entertained the idea of continuing on and never going back. He breathed deeply, enjoying the herbal scent of the air.

Tibur walled up the top of a high hill at the foot of the Apennine Mountains and controlled about 135 square miles of territory. Though Rome held dominion over three times as much land, Tibur still represented a powerful threat to her security. About the eighth hour he passed through the western gate into the monotonous gray of the walled city, broken only by the reddish-orange terracotta tile roofs. He found a tavern with rooms above and rented one. The city reposed quietly while the inhabitants took their evening meal. Graptus plopped himself down on the straw mattress and took a nap.

He awakened a couple hours later to the strains of laughter and the delightful sound of his native tongue. A steady flow of foot and cart traffic passed beneath his room. He pulled a longer fresh tunic on over the shorter one he had worn for travel, and went outside. Next to the mountains the air smelled of pine and felt cool on the skin. He made his way to the town square that teemed with people and casually walked around looking at things as any visitor would. A fountain dispensing water in four directions provided him with a long refreshing drink. Around the edges of the forum, he found shops quite as nice as those in Rome. He bought some sweet honey cakes at one, and sausage spiced with fennel at another, then wandered over to the fountain for another drink. Looking for Caeso in his innocuous and patient way his perambulations took him to the temples around the Forum, to equestrian statues set up in honor of Tibur's heroes, while citizens strolled or talked in animated clusters around him.

Graptus was in no hurry. He knew Caeso to be a man of the city. He would not be one to sit quietly in a farmhouse, no matter how luxurious, outside the city walls. No, he needed the city like he needed air. Sooner or later, he would see him in the Forum, in a tavern, perhaps at a public bath. In the meantime, Graptus could speak and hear his native language to his hearts content, for the Aequians had taken Tibur.

Tibur, Praeneste, and Pedum had all fallen into Aequian hands nearly thirty years before. From these Latin cities the Aequians often issued forth to raid and war on Rome and her Latin allies. This strategic, fortified line blocked Rome's access to the mountains, and the true strongholds of the Aequian people. Graptus had come from Carseoli, one of these mountain cities. Now, hearing the Oscan language of the Aequi from the soldiers garrisoning the city he felt nostalgic for his family.

Suddenly, Graptus had a problem. He became a man of two minds. On the one hand he was working to create a future in an adoptive country, which despite his status he had come to appreciate.  On the other hand, the home of his birth was less than fifty miles away.  Two day's ride, and he would once again be an enemy of Rome, and Lucius Tempanius.  How strange to be a loyal slave, he thought, as he shoved escape from his mind.

The days passed pleasantly enough.  The agreeable climate and quality vines made his ostensible mission to find new sources of wine a diverting escapade.  But he made no progress toward his goal.  A week drifted by.  Daytimes he rode out to visit vineyards and farms.  Nighttime he prowled the streets of Tibur.

On a clear moonless night, the sable sky so full of stars Ursus Major appeared to have spilled them into the sky, he went downstairs to have a snack and a glass of hot spiced wine.  Few customers inhabited the wide shallow room so he had his choice of tables.  He chose one near a back room walled off with dark planks of rough unfinished wood facing the arched entrance.  Oil lamps, burning in nooks chiseled into the stone walls, cast deep shadows away from their misshapen pools of amber light.  He ordered a glass of hot, spiced wine from the proprietor's coquettish daughter, Lucretia.

"How much longer are you staying?" she asked, as she set a steaming bronze cup in front of him.

Graptus gave her a deceptive smile.  "Oh, about as long as it takes to win the heart of a pretty girl."

A pudgy hand, evidence of things to come, he thought, flew to her dark hair.  She checked the part in the middle then softly followed the hair that was pulled back and rolled into a wave at the back of her head, secured there by a bronze comb.  "Have you found one yet?" she teased.  She patted her hair brightly, and looked at him with frank green eyes.

Graptus tried to judge her age.  She had a slight figure and her complexion sported a pimple or two on her otherwise smooth cheeks. She wore a simple shift, and not a matron's stola, though she looked old enough to be espoused.

"And who are you espoused to?" he retorted.

"Why should I want to be espoused to anyone?" she said.

"I see, you'd rather serve wine for your father for the rest of your life. How old are you, sixteen?"

A pout shrunk her small mouth. "Fourteen," she shot back. "And I have many interested men. Some as old as you."

A confrontational fire lit her evenly spaced green eyes that Graptus found thoroughly enjoyable. For a moment his mind divided, and he had two simultaneous thoughts. One, that he might be the perfect age for such a lively young woman. The other, that she may have more knowledge of people in town than he suspected. He decided to act on the second thought.

"Oh, I can just imagine," he deadpanned. "I'll bet even the great Caeso Quinctius is on the list."

"He might be," she said haughtily. "He comes by often enough. But he's a Roman. He only lives here because they won't let him live at Rome anymore."

"I see. Why is he allowed to live here, then?"

She shrugged her shoulders and rubbed the side of her short straight nose. "Why should we care? At least the Romans speak the same language. Where are you from?"

"I was born in Carseoli."

"Aequi. I thought so. You don't speak Latin like you were born to it."

Graptus took a long sip of his wine, looking at the girl over the rim of the cup. He'd let the conversation get away from him, and struggled to think of a way to get it back. He decided to be frank. "Well then, you'd rather have the likes of Caeso ruling over you than the Aequi?"

Her thin eyebrows arched, and she regarded him quizzically. "You talk like you're one of them," she said. Glancing around the room quickly to see if anyone else needed her she settled back and looked at him. "I think you're hiding something," she said.

"Perhaps I'm looking for traitors," said Graptus, disconcerted by her perception.

"I'll ask my father is he's seen any." She spun around and left him, a swirl of cool air rushing off her cream colored shift.

At least he knew Caeso still resided here, he consoled himself as he sipped at the hot tangy wine. Instead of making him tired the hot wine and hotter conversation spun his mind into motion, so he went out to get some air. He didn't go far. Even in the smaller city of Tibur it might take him half the night to find his way back in the dark. Since the inn was in close proximity to the western gate he walked in that direction. Around the wall he could walk in the open space without fear of losing his way.

Above him the stars burst like sparks from the black caldron of the sky. Warm air, unctuous with humidity, spread itself on his skin like a soothing ointment. To the east the mountains bulked over the city, blocking out the sky. As he came closer to the wall, he ran his hand along the rough squared stones. A moldy smell came off them, tainting the air. Farther down he saw a bundle of lights suddenly erupt from a side street. A moment later the sound of a group of revelers reached him. Their torches cast eerie, gigantic shadows against the uneven stones as they swerved erratically towards him. Graptus ducked into a side street and found a deep shadow from which to wait for them to pass.

He had just seated himself in a dark archway when they came raucously by. Ten or twelve young men, half of whom bore blazing torches aloft, followed the line of the wall singing a bawdy Roman song about the rape of Lucretia. Confused, they stopped at the street where Graptus crouched in hiding. A momentary panic seized him, but he shoved it down and forced himself to watch. As they milled about, trying to decide which way to go, Graptus got a good look at them. Splashed garishly in yellow and red from the guttering torches, their tunics still bespoke of nobility and wealth. From his vantage point most appeared young, but there was one, taller than the rest, obviously balding, and significantly older. He waved his arms for quiet. A shout went up.

"Let Caeso speak! Let Caeso speak!"

"All right boys, let me think. Gods, you should know this city better than I." He spun around, looking up and down the length of the darkened wall trying to get his bearings. "Two more, I think, to the lovely Lucretia," he announced, waving his party forward.

So, Graptus thought, the Roman proverb was right, 'the Roman wins by sitting still'. He saw it as a confirming omen, for he had sat still and waited like a good Roman. As the strains of merriment receded in his hearing, the stars glittering above in patient brilliance, he committed himself to becoming a Roman. All things would come to the Romans; he felt it as strongly as he felt his heart pumping. Then another realization struck him, and he made quickly for the inn.

He walked through the door to a festival in full swing. Caeso held court at the same table where Graptus had sat, his broad back against the wall, screened by his friends. On his left knee, his left arm firmly around her waist and his hand up under her breast, sat Lucretia. He supported her as if she weighed nothing, bouncing her on his knee like a babe. "How much?" he asked in a loud voice, tossing back his balding head molded in the form of a grape.

Squinting myopically, and wringing his fleshy hands in anxiety her father, an ingratiating smile on his rotund face tried to make light. "Why, Caeso Quinctius, how would I ever betroth her afterwards?" he said in a worry constricted voice.

Graptus slid inconspicuously into a seat by the door, but saw the reproach in Lucretia's eyes when she caught sight of him. He let his eyes drift away.

"Betroth her to who?" said Caeso contemptuously. "Some old sack of wind who can't remember the last time he tried to make sons?"

A big laugh went up from the gathered sycophants. Caeso raised a crooked smile at Lucretia who recoiled as best she could in his iron grip. "Or some young roe buck that can't teach her to like the ways of men?"

"You have bad breath," said Lucretia loudly. "Even the youngest man knows to freshen his mouth with mint before he attempts to seduce a girl."

469

Led by Caeso the revelers laughed heartily at her riposte.

"Could I get a cup of wine, here?" asked Graptus acidly.

Lucretia's father took the clue and moved his bulky figure forward a step. To extract his daughter from Caeso's clutches he accused her with an angry tone. "Come now, Lucretia, quit playing. We have a mountain of work to do. Fetch our guest here a drink."

Graptus felt Caeso's eyes shift to him, but he steadfastly kept his gaze on the innkeeper demanding service. Partly in shadow where he sat, he did not want Caeso to get a full view of him, nor get an inkling that his interference might be out of personal interest.

Slowly Caeso released his grip on the girl and set her free. She set a cup of wine down contemptuously in front of Graptus.

"I suppose," she said through clenched teeth, "that's what passes for gallantry among the Aequi."

"He didn't seem like such a pig when you spoke of him earlier," Graptus replied.

"One day Tibur will be free of Aequians and Romans," she challenged.

"That's dangerous talk," he said. "And worse, unlikely."

When she left, her father made sure he kept her too busy to return to the public room. Later he thanked Graptus for his intervention.

"It's nothing," said Graptus, and then extracted every last grain of information about Caeso the innkeeper had stored in his memory as payment

# XXVIII

August 27, 450 BC
The Volturnalia

The interminable wait nearly drove Lucius mad. Day after day no word came. Unable to stand it any longer he closed the tavern and escaped the oppressive heat and ennui of Rome by traveling to Antium to visit his vineyards and celebrate the Volturnalia with Tranellius. They erected umbrae, made sacrifices to Volturnus in order to secure his protection of the grapes from scorching late summer winds, and talked over Lucius' ambivalent plans for the future.

It didn't help. The sea at Antium and the low-lying marshes of the Pomptine plain saturated the sweltering air with glutinous moisture. With little to keep him busy Lucius could not take his mind off the mission he'd given Graptus, and fretted day and night over all the scenarios his fevered brain dreamt up. He fled back to Rome only to find it morbid and depressed.

He blamed the decemvirs. They had driven all the fun out of the city along with the patricians. In a long continuum of ironies, it seemed that nothing stimulated business so much as oppression. If any part of the day were fasti, the Boar's Tusk was full. But then, why not? Setting foot on the perilous pavement of the Forum courted bullying at the hands of the decemvirs and their minions, or worse, accusations leading to confiscation of property, liberty, or life. Better by far to spend one's time in amicable company quaffing sweet wine.

At the end of another long day Lucius relaxed with friends. They pulled two tables together, lit some tallow candles and sat around talking. Demetria brought out a platter loaded with grapes, figs, and wheat cakes as Lucius brought a large pitcher of mulsum to the table.

"Will there be anything else, Dominus?" asked Demetria. At first glance, with her stone gray hair pulled back in matronly fashion she looked quite plain, but closer inspection revealed the beauty of her youth lingering on her face.

"Do we have any meat? Some sausage or salted pork? I feel like some soft food tonight."

"I'll find something," she said with a smile.

"Thank you, Demetria."

"You should marry that woman, Lucius," stated Turpio sagely. "Those great big eyes of hers see only you."

Lucius poured five cups of wine, smiling indulgently.

"And look at the fine set of teeth she displayed," chimed in Titinius.

"Yes," agreed Publius Ambrosius. "So straight and white. Are you sure they're real?"

"Who cares," said Sextus Cluellius, "just take them out…"

"All right, pipe down," interrupted Lucius. He slapped his leg, laughing at his pun, for all but Turpio were pipers. No one else laughed. "I'm a man among boys, here," muttered Lucius. "Listen, you leave Demetria alone. I don't need your advice on women."

"Well, your own doesn't seem to be working very well," said Titinius. Naturally they all chortled loudly at his statement, which wasn't even funny.

"So, tell me," said Lucius, "what is the collegium of pipers up to these days?"

"Actually," said Publius, "we're considering going on strike."

Lucius cringed. He wanted to keep the conversation light and had purposely changed it from one that dredged up bitter memories to one he thought would be funny. Instead, he realized he had opened a subject that would elicit serious discussion from at least three of his friends.

"That's so," said Sextus, nodding his head. His wide, open face and appraising gray eyes surveyed his companions. He shifted his considerable weight and cleared his throat. "We're talking about the Ludi Romani."

"Not really?" said Lucius, genuinely surprised.

"Yes, we are," Titinius vehemently asserted.

"But that will stop the games completely," marveled Turpio.

"That's usually the idea of a strike," Sextus snidely stated.

"Exactly," cried Publius, crashing his cup on the table. His small hand lost control of it and the cup spun off the table and broke on the floor.

"You're too little to drink wine," Sextus said, a taunting smile dividing his face.

"So. You're too fat," said Publius.

Demetria hurried in with a fresh cup, then swept the broken pieces out the front door.

"It's not that he's too little," asserted Titinius, "it's that he should be drinking from that great beak of a nose instead of that tiny mouth. He takes in too much air, and the wine goes straight to his head."

Laughing with the rest, Sextus clapped Publius on the back and said, "So why are we striking lead piper?"

"You know as well as I do. You tell."

"How do you all play the same tune together?" asked Lucius. "It's a virtual riot with just the three of you in the same room."

"Ah," Sextus said, "it's nothing. Publius has been mad ever since they told him the spear weighed more than he did, and he couldn't serve in the legions."

"That's a lie, you gray headed old bear," said Publius, but a jumble of yellowed teeth poked out of his small mouth in a mulish smile.

"But tell us about the strike," said Turpio.

"The strike," said Titinius, "is because the Decemvirs refused to allow us to celebrate the Quinquatrus Minores in the temple of Jupiter."

"Which we have done since the time of Ancus Marcius, I might add," said Publius Ambrosius. "He, at least, understood the importance of the sacred pipers to religion."

"The temple of Jupiter wasn't even begun until the reign of Tarquinius Priscus," scoffed Turpio, disputing the accuracy of Publius Ambrosius' chronology.

"On what grounds did they refuse you use of the temple?" asked Lucius, restoring the subject.

"Since when do they need grounds?" groused Publius.

Demetria returned bearing another platter with slices of sausage, salt pork, boiled eggs, and cheese arrayed invitingly, and topped with sprigs of parsley or basil. She took away the empty wine jug.

"You asked for soft food," laughed Turpio, for whom hard work and regular meals had done much to restore firmness and girth to his body. "If you eat like this too often people will start talking."

"I'm touched by your concern," said Lucius. Sandwiching a basil leaf between slices of cheese and sausage he said, "good appetite."

"Exactly," said Sextus, liberally helping himself to the victuals. "The risk of being called a sensualist is a small thing in the face of such fare."

"There's no risk for you at all," said Publius. "It's already well known."

"The news goes before him every day," laughed Titinius, patting his large friend's belly.

Demetria's slim hand appeared long enough to leave a refilled jug of watered red wine on the table, then disappeared again as if she had been but a wish. The men ate with relish, the good food quelling conversation.

"Where's Graptus these days?" asked Titinius, finally sated.

"Good question," said Lucius. "I sent him out to the Anio to inspect my properties, and see what else might be available. But I'm beginning to think he's run off."

"Not really?" said Titinius. He had been friends with Lucius and Graptus, in whom he'd found a kindred spirit, for over a decade. In his easy going way he was an excellent judge of character, and the thought of Graptus running away seemed unlikely.

"No," said Lucius. "It's just been over three weeks, and I'm tired of running the tavern myself."

"Do you think it's safe sending him so near the Claudii?" asked Turpio. "What I mean is, the last thing you want to do is call attention to yourself. With their thirst for property they'll have you accused, convicted, and your property confiscated before you can walk from here to the Forum in a tunic. Just like they did to me," he finished venomously.

"I hadn't thought of that," said Lucius. He shifted uncomfortably under the thought that surfaced in his mind, but kept the true nature of Graptus' expedition secret. "How long after the expulsion of Tarquinius Superbus did Appius bring his clan to Rome?"

"Let's see," said Titinius, counting on his fingers. "That was during the consulship of Publius Valerius and Titus Lucretius…" He re-counted his fingers. "It must have been the fifth, at most the sixth year of the Republic."

"And this is what…" hesitated Lucius, worrying his lower lip with his thumb.

"The fifty-ninth year of the Republic," responded Publius quickly.

"Can it be that our republic will only last three generations?" Lucius asked.

"It will as long as a man can be deprived of his property for no just reason," spat Turpio.

"Is everything about property with you?" asked Sextus, who had none but the small house he lived in.

"Property is power. Property is liberty. If a man can be deprived of his property by the whim of another, then he has no freedom."

"Elegantly put," said Titinius.

"You joke," Turpio continued heatedly. "But when does your century vote?"

"Almost never," offered Publius. "The issue is already decided before it gets to us."

475

"Of course," said Turpio. "Musicians are put in the infra classem. But what about you, Lucius? When do you vote?"

"I vote with the rest of the classis centuries."

"By next census you'll be rated with the equites, and won't associate with us infra classem," teased Sextus.

Turpio would not let go. His thin lips turned white and his nose darkened with anger. A twitch had developed near his right eye. With a pointed index finger, he encompassed all the others. "Yes," he said, "and so you decide for us what will be."

Lucius took umbrage at the implication that he wielded power over their lives. "I imagine that didn't bother you much when you were assessed as a member of the classis," he shot. "Besides, I'm also in the front line of battle while the pipers wait in camp, and the proletarians wait here." He stabbed his finger emphatically on the table top. "Who else should decide if I must risk my life?" he demanded.

"Perhaps if we were all equal, and every man's vote counted the same as it used to in the plebeian assembly, then we would all share equally in the dangers as well," said Turpio.

"And maybe the state will give us each a hundred iugera and four teams of oxen to work it," laughed Titinius. "You think too much, Turpio."

"I suppose," said Sextus, "that you opposed Volero's reforms. Because naturally, as a farmer who cared more about philosophy than farming, you found it easy to be in Rome on every occasion the assembly met. You must be Greek."

Turpio half rose with both hands on the table and leaned into the blithely smiling face of Sextus. "Are you saying," he menaced, "that I lost my farm because I spent my time in Rome?"

"I'm saying," said Sextus, still with a smile and not the least intimidated, "that you think with your feelings and not with your head."

"And you think with your belly," Publius Ambrosius said, attempting to defuse the situation.

"It's a better gauge of the truth," Sextus laughed.

Lucius pulled Turpio back into his seat. "You are right about one thing, Turpio, wealth is power. Our ten kings prove that to us every day."

With smoldering blue eyes, the right side of his face working uncontrollably, Turpio locked onto Lucius and held his gaze. They stared intently at one another for a moment then Turpio looked away and wiped his hands on his brown tunic. "You see," he muttered, "but your sight leads you astray." He stood slowly, deliberately. "You think to become one of them," he said, his solemn tone like that of an haruspex, "knowing that to possess the land is to possess your liberty. But once you have become like them you will think no one else has the same right. For you will, in truth, have become one of them."

+ + +

Graptus returned, his equine face a healthy bronze, his eyes bright with happiness, and a bounce in his long gait. His hands waved like plumage as he spoke. "He's in the palm of our hand," he told Lucius. "He's succumbed totally to sensuality and become utterly effeminate, chasing anything on two legs under seventeen."

"You mean he takes no precautions?"

"Oh, well, he hasn't become that debauched. He always has someone with him. But we'll have opportunity. He's returning to Caere the week of the Ludi Romani. We can ambush him on the way like bandits. There won't be the least bit of suspicion."

"Hmm, when shall that be?" mused Lucius. He stopped near the grove of oak trees by the open-air altar of Hercules, watching disinterestedly the activity on the docks.

"Is that a rhetorical question, or has everything I've said gone past your ears like a woman's whisper?" laughed Graptus.

"You know Graptus, it's too bad there's no place in Rome for poets. Maybe you could start a collegium."

"Perhaps I will. Will you sponsor it on the Aventine?"

"Why not." They turned and started for the Clivus Publicius. At the crossroads shrine protecting the intersection with the road leading over the Sublician Bridge he left a small token in sacrifice.

"So," said Graptus, as they ascended the Aventine Hill, "I heard the decemvirs finally produced the last two laws."

"Yes." Lucius looked up at a royal blue sky. Great piles of milk white clouds seemed suspended from invisible strands of cosmic line on the polished surface of heaven.

"That makes twelve."

"Yes."

The autumn rains had come, washing the city clean of the stifling heat of summer. Yet all remained green, verdant, almost as if spring returned for an encore. The air sparkled, and the sunshine felt pleasantly warm. They climbed the Aventine and passed the temple of Diana on the crest, then descended the south side of the hill.

"But they have not stepped down," said Graptus.

"No. They still have to submit the twelve tables to the centuriate assembly for ratification."

"And the piper's strike?"

"Nobody knows."

"Will they postpone the Ludi?"

Lucius stopped and eyed Graptus closely. Eager expectation creased the long lines of his face, and he held his mouth open like a horse anticipating battle chews the bit. "What is it you want to say, Graptus?"

The question surprised Graptus. He resorted to formal language. "Forgive me Dominus, but you seem suddenly strange. Have you changed your mind?"

"To be honest, I don't know. Maybe I'm getting old. Sometimes I just want to enjoy life again. Like this very moment, Graptus. To feel the sun on my skin, to see the green of the trees, and the colors of the flowers. To let a good wine linger on my tongue and the sweetness of a fig burst in my mouth."

Graptus chuckled. "Maybe you should start a collegium of poets."

"Listen, I have already outlived my father. How many more years do I have left? What's the point in dying with bitterness and anger on your lips?"

"And Antonius?"

They turned off the Clivus Publicius and took a small dirt street to the construction site of Lucius' new home on the Aventine. A house he had no legal right to build on land that technically belonged to the state. Many others had done the same, and the Aventine bustled with building activity. Given patrician intransigence the plebeians had taken it upon themselves to distribute state land on the Aventine. Proposed by the tribune Lucius Icilius, the Lex Icilia passed the plebeian assembly and the plebs swore a sacred oath to protect those who built on the Aventine. The State officially sanctioned the law, and the peoples' right to the property five years later in exchange for the suspension of the tribunate and the institution of the decemvirs. A bronze plaque legitimizing the building was mounted in the temple of Diana.

"I haven't forgotten Antonius," he said, as they made a supervisory circumnavigation of the building. "Nor have I forgotten you."

Satisfied that nothing had been vandalized or destroyed they returned the way they had come. Lucius remained in a reflective mood. "Think about it, Grap," he said. "I was born when the temple of Saturn was dedicated. I was two when the temple of Mercury was dedicated and the plebs seceded. Since then, I've seen the temples of Ceres, Castor, Fortuna, and Semo Sancus built. Rome has changed incredibly in my lifetime."

"So, what are you saying? That you're responsible?"

"You are the embodiment of every argument against slavery." Lucius shook his big head wryly.

"What slave isn't?"

"Those who are obedient and treat their masters with deference."

"Those slaves," said Graptus pointedly, "are less than human. I may be of a different status by rule of war, but I consider myself no less equal as a man. I too have a soul."

"You will when you become a citizen," said Lucius.

They entered the Forum from the Vicus Tuscus and sat on the steps of the temple of Castor. In silence they watched the comings and goings in the Forum. Supplicants entered the temples, clerks and scribes hurried to the temple of Saturn, or the Curia, or up the hill to the Capitol. From the direction of the Argiletum a procession made its way into the Forum, attracting the attention of nearly everyone. A desolate man, seated on an ass and naked as the day he came into the world, suffered being led through the Forum. Tears of shame streaked his distraught face as he wordlessly implored his fellow citizens for understanding. None was forthcoming. People stopped what they were doing to laugh, jeer, mock, and hurl insults at the adulterer.

"Better to remain single, and frequent whores than to be pilloried for your lack of self control," said Lucius, watching the disgraced man make his painstakingly slow progress through the heart of the city.

"I would venture to wage his crime is of the heart," said Graptus.

"No matter," said Lucius. "Adultery is a crime against man and gods."

"That's the one aspect of you Romans I've found most difficult to understand. That man could take out his lust on any slave in his household, male or female, and you wouldn't say a thing. But fall in love with a free woman and be caught, and you suffer the opprobrium of the whole city."

"I don't know why I let Cominus teach you Latin," said Lucius, scratching his head.

From the Curia the midday trumpet sounded. Lucius felt his stomach growl and stood up. They headed for the shops nearby to find a snack. He nudged his way through a few indecisive customers and came away with two honeyed cakes.

"What you fail to understand," he said, handing one of the cakes to Graptus, "is the difference between satisfying a bodily desire, and giving yourself over to it." He chewed a large mouthful of the sweet gritty cake. "An uncontrolled movement of the soul, in this case the man's passion for a freeborn woman, is the sign of a base animal nature. It's symbolic of weakness and effeminacy."

"You mean by being caught." Graptus broke his cake and gave half to Lucius.

"Listen, a man is always caught out in his weakness." Lucius accepted the proffered cake, and stuffed it in his mouth. "Take me, for example." He patted his stomach. "It's becoming easy to see that I've fallen under the sway of my appetite. A man who cannot tame his appetites is no man in truth. In fact, starting tomorrow we begin exercising daily on the…"

He stopped speaking as another procession made its way into the Forum, this time moving along the Via Sacra. The decemvir, Quintus Fabius Vibulanus, preceded by twelve lictors, strutted in his purple bordered toga and palm embroidered tunic. His double-knotted patricians shoes slapped the paving stones. A contingent of young patricians, obviously acting as bodyguards, surrounded him on three sides. One of the lictors clutched a rope, the other end of which looped around the neck of some unfortunate soul. Following behind stumbled a smaller group of citizens in the torn clothes of mourning, dirt poured upon their unkempt hair, and wailing in sorrow.

As their lachrymose howls burst over the disparate groups a shudder ran through the Forum. Without a word an anxious crowd surrounded the mourners, the lictors, and Quintus Fabius in the middle of the square, bringing the cortege to a halt. Packed close, necks craning to see, people fired unanswered questions at each other. Lucius and Graptus fought for elbow room in the tight crowd. Graptus looked over the heads of the crowd and apprised Lucius of what transpired.

"Lucius Quinctius Jr. is among the patricians," noted Graptus.

"Why am I not surprised," breathed Lucius.

"Romans," shouted Quintus Fabius, "how long will we allow the lawlessness of a few to pollute the body of Rome? This man, Veturius Flaccus, given every chance by the esteemed Lucius Quinctius, nay given third and fourth chances to repay long delinquent debts has this very day refused to pay that which he rightfully owes."

"Not true," cried one of the mourners.

"And worse," said Fabius, raising his voice to drown out the opposition. "It's not that he can't pay. Any man can understand if circumstances prevent an honest debtor from paying, and make allowances. But Veturius Flaccus is not an honest or honorable debtor."

"Scandalous!" cried one of the mourners. "How long shall we endure these ten kings? Veturius Flaccus is well known to all of you. He has served his country faithfully. See his chest, the scars of battle reside there as evidence of his honor. How can any man pay when year after year the enemies of Rome burn the crops, butcher our cattle and sheep, and make off with our precious oil? How long must we endure war on Roman soil? Do our 'fathers' protect us? No, they pursue the enemy with ineptitude and lay the blame on us. As if we were our own leaders."

The crowd stirred angrily, assenting to the words of the speaker.

"Who is that speaking?" demanded Lucius.

"Lucius Icilius,' said Graptus.

"Lictor," cried Quintus Fabius, "go and bind him for his treasonous talk."

The crowd pushed in around Icilius, blocking the lictor and the patrician bodyguards from accosting him. Threats to their persons followed. No one moved.

Icilius went on unperturbed. He pushed his stout body forward, and glared with close set penetrating eyes surmounted by beetling black brows. His strong voice commanded attention. "Do you blame the decemvirs?" he shouted, and when a wave of assent began to build, he suddenly quelled it. "You err. When was the last time we had land to distribute so men could feed their families? Our fathers in the senate lament that they can't afford their fine Greek tableware—then take the food out of the mouths of Veturius Flaccus' children. They weep under the whip of their wives' tongues because they cannot buy a new vase—while hundreds of Romans, like our friend Flaccus, have no seed to sow in their fields.

"Do the patricians want?" he cried.

"No!" answered the multitude.

"Are they hauled before the courts, strangled by a rope with blood running from their eyes?" He pointed at Flaccus who had indeed reached this state. His swollen face darkened to eggplant purple, blood ran from his ears, nose, and bulging eyes, yet he managed to croak in supplication, extending his hands.

"How much is his debt?" cried Lucius suddenly, moved with tremendous anger. He pushed at the brown togas in front of him.

Quintus Fabius would not answer, but shouted instead. "There is no appeal. The sentence will be carried out."

Infuriated, Lucius shoved his way through the crowd. "How much is his debt?" he insisted, his muscular frame planted firmly in front of Fabius. "I will pay it by bronze and scales." He looked hard in Fabius' eyes and dared him to refuse.

The crowd received this news with acclamation, and Quintus Fabius found himself cornered. "Thirty asses is his debt," he said. The crowd gasped, the amount seemed farfetched. Lucius widened his eyes at the extortion, knowing Fabius had invented the figure. "Bring the scales," he shouted angrily. He sent Graptus home for the bronze, as others ran to nearby shops for a set of scales. When Graptus returned with the money Lucius held it aloft for all to see, then struck the scales so hard the sound rang across the Forum. "By this ceremony of bronze and scales," he cried, "your debt is paid. You are a free man Veturius Flaccus"

The lictor let loose the rope around Flaccus' neck, and he fell at Lucius' feet, clutching his knees. In a hoarse, barely audible voice he proclaimed Lucius his savior and swore eternal fidelity to his family.

Icilius came up, clapped him on the back and said, "I guess all those things I heard about you were wrong. We need more men like you."

Lucius stared quizzically at him. "Thank you," he said, without knowing why. He turned and walked off, followed by Flaccus and a host of others offering words of admiration. Lucius heard none of it. One thought filled his brain.

"I want you to go get Titus tomorrow," he told Graptus through gritted teeth. "We're going to finish our business with Caeso."

# XXIX

## September 4, 450 BC
## Ludi Romani

Faustus Ventriculo lived off a squalid little alley in the Subura in a one room conical cob shack with a wife, two kids, and the mice that inhabited the leaky straw roof. He smiled disingenuously at Lucius with rotten blackened teeth, and just managed to brush the mat of dirty hair out of his heavy lidded, sleepy eyes.

"Sure, I know who you are. My old man told me some day you'd come. Or one of your family." He tilted his stool and leaned back against the peeling wall, staring up at Lucius, back-lit against a blue sky. He held a small knife and a half completed carving of Priapus slackly in thick stubby fingers. A young man about Lucius' son's age, as disheveled as his father and dressed in a stain spattered russet tunic patched with successive hems to accommodate his growth, rested against the door jam.

"I have a job for you," said Lucius. "Will you take it?"

"I owe you for a basket o' charcoal and no more," said Faustus.

"I'll pay the difference," said Lucius.

"What kind o' work we talking about?"

"I'm taking a trip, and I need an escort."

The hooded eyes narrowed and he rubbed a blunt nose with the back of a dirty hand. He pointed to his left leg with the tip of the knife. "Ain't had the use o' that leg in fifteen years." Pushing out a thin lower lip in his gaunt, sun bronzed face he shrugged indifferently. "Escortin' people gets dangerous."

Lucius nodded at the young man in the doorway. "What about him?" he asked.

"Him?" Faustus reached out a paw and jerked the boy forward. "Ain't sure he's worth a basket o' charcoal. But it's yer choice."

485

"Can you keep your mouth shut?" Lucius asked, looking the boy straight in the eye.

"Yes sir." The youth returned his gaze without blinking.

"I'll take him with me now," said Lucius.

Faustus went back to his carving. "Pay first," he said.

"You said he wasn't worth a basket of charcoal."

"That's what yer call a figger o' speech."

"You're an educated man," said Lucius.

"I knows the value o' things, all right."

Lucius reached into a leather pouch inside his tunic. He flipped a bronze coin at Faustus. "One *as*," he said.

Faustus Ventriculo grunted, content with his day's wage.

Lucius put the boy under the care of Demetria who cleaned him up, cut his hair, and found an old tunic Lucius Jr. had discarded as well as a pair of sandals. He wolfed down a bowl of wheat porridge, a large slice of cheese, a handful of olives, and a boiled egg. When he finished, she turned him back over to Lucius.

Taking in his skinny arms and legs, the features sharp as a knife, Lucius figured it would take a month of such meals before the boy put on any weight. "What's your name?" he asked, taking a seat across the kitchen table from the young man.

"Faustus."

"What weapons can you handle?"

Faustus shrugged his narrow shoulders as if the question were unnecessary. "Same as every runt in 'a Subura. Sling 'n knife."

"Can you ride?"

Faustus snorted. "I can hold on," he said, a wry grin pulling one side of his mouth.

+ + +

It took three days for his small army to collect in a grove of maritime pines off the Via Caeretana northwest of Rome. Though the plangent breaking of waves against the shore sounded with the rhythmic beat of a lover's heart in their ears, they took no notice. Quintus Crispus brought his second son, Gaius, with him from their farm in the rolling hills southwest of Rome. Titus brought his second son, Titus Jr. and their slave Restius. Turpio, Flaccus, and Titinius came alone.

Lucius, Graptus, and Faustus waited under the pines that bloomed like giant green mushrooms with corrugated ferruginous stems. He would have preferred to have more men but Lucius had learned to make do. His son Lucius Jr. and Titus' eldest son Marcus were both serving with the legions, and Furius Villius had age against him.

Even so, eleven riders and pack mules easily raised suspicion so they stayed off the road, traveling north on small tracks, or cross-country. A few miles from Caere, Lucius found a spot to his liking. Two hills shouldered hard against the road at the bottom of a steep descent from both directions. Caeso could either die or fight his way to safety, but he could not run from the constricted killing ground.

They waited two days through chill nights without a fire. Lucius worried that Graptus had received poor information, or Caeso had changed his plans. Then on the third day Titus Jr. from his perch on the heights above the road whistled a warning. Soon a group of riders came into view. The Tempanius brothers and their clients took their positions.

They devised a simple plan. Titus, Titinius, and Turpio would block the road back towards Rome, while Lucius, Graptus, Quintus, and Flaccus blocked the road north to Caere. Titus Jr., Gaius, and Faustus were to pour a rain of stones down from the heights. Restius guarded the mules.

Caeso Quinctius rode to Caere just as Graptus said he would. In his arrogance he had but four companions, none of whom wore armor, though they all had shields thrown over their backs and swords belted around their waists. Joking and laughing they rode in confidence towards the ambush. A skin of wine passed between the five riders. They regarded the scenery not for the dangers that might lurk behind its bushy undulations, and rocky outcroppings like compound fractures of the earth's bones, but with eyes that sought only pleasure.

Graptus lay behind a bush ten yards from Lucius, who held the end of their short line. Sweat rolled down his forehead into his eyes. He had second thoughts as he released the sword from his sweating hands for fear it would slip out when the time came to use it. The sun bore down like an olive press, and his sweat poured out like oil. Lying in the dirt, weeds, and stiff grass caused itching all over his body, but he didn't move. With his face pressed close to the ground the heavy smell of earth suffocated him. He looked at Lucius who looked back and smiled broadly as if having the most enjoyable time. Well, why not, thought Graptus, he'd been in nearly a hundred battles. The last battle Graptus fought he'd been captured by this very Roman. Now, he consoled himself, one small battle and he could free himself to be a Roman. He smiled back at Lucius, and nodded.

As he watched the riders enter the south end of the narrow gorge his spirits rose. Caeso was lackadaisical and outnumbered—a deadly combination. Nevertheless, it seemed an eternity before the horsemen fully entered the one hundred feet long stretch of killing field pinched between the two hills. On his left Quintus and Flaccus in brown tunics blended in with the rocky ground, but he spotted the gleam of Flaccus' helmet, and a sudden twinge of fear went through him that they would be spotted. He turned his head back to see Lucius put his helmet on. Rubbing his hand in the dirt to dry the perspiration he gripped his sword and tensed. He wished he had a helmet.

Lucius bunched like a sprinter ready to run. He gripped his sword firmly but did not strangle it. The voices of the riders wafted indistinguishably to his ears. Twenty yards of ground stretched between him and the road to close the trap. Not much distance when you're twenty, but at forty-seven it seemed half way to Rome. His keen brown eyes swept the riders vigilantly. In a glance he took in their short riding tunics, breeches, and sandal shod feet dangling at ease. Two of them wore wide brimmed straw hats against the sun; the others went bare headed. They rode unprepared for battle, laughing and joking. Lucius hated them. They believed in their position and status, in their divine right to privilege. He lifted himself into a crouch.

"Now!" he shouted, leaping to his feet and running for the road.

From the bluff above the road a barrage of stones whistled through the air with deadly accuracy, bruising riders and horses with dull thwacks. Taken by surprise the horsemen reined in their skidding, whinnying mounts, fighting for control of the beasts while at the same time drawing swords and bringing their shields around to protect themselves. A straw hat sailed off the head of one rider, and he fell hard to the road, stretched out by a second rock. Caeso shouted above the confusion of wheeling, rearing horses, and the battle cries of men, trying to organize his comrades.

Graptus churned his legs pushing sand, and gravel, slipping on grass, struggling to rise and move forward. Flaccus, Quintus and Lucius covered half the distance before he got his feet under him and started for the road.

Titus, Turpio, and Titinius swarmed over the riders from the rear, dispatching the fallen rider and crashing into the terrified horses with shields upraised and swords flashing. A horse reared, spilling its rider. Turpio fell on him with utter savagery, plunging his sword into the man's gaping mouth, blunting the point on the paving stones as it exited at the back of his neck. A fountain of blood shot onto Turpio's legs and he screamed in exultation. Titus, and Flaccus dragged a rider from his mount and disemboweled him as he writhed in resistance. He stared in dismay as his intestines snaked across the flagstones. In the midst of the sanguinary melee Caeso spun his horse in a mad circle, swinging his sword wildly at every flash of face, or glint of metal. He shouted to his last surviving companion, and together they spurred their horses forward. Graptus hurled himself into Caeso's horse at full speed, aiming his shield at Caeso's knee that gripped the side of his steed. The horse stumbled, pitched sideways as Caeso lashed out with his sword, striking downward at the charging Graptus. Graptus felt something slap his back as he went down in a tangle of flailing hooves. Before his horse could gather speed, the attackers swarmed over the last rider and murdered him. Caeso kicked free of his horse, and clutching his knee picked himself up and started running. Lucius and Titus tore after him and dragged him down from behind. Vengeance surging through him, Lucius jammed his knee into Caeso's back, grabbed the thin shock of hair on top of his head in his left hand and pulled back hard. Caeso screamed against the pain, but not for long. With a giant swing of his sword Lucius beheaded his hated enemy. He surged to his feet holding the bloody head aloft as Caeso's flopping body gushed blood onto the black paving stones. "Antonius!" he cried, shaking the bloodied face at the heavens, "you are avenged."

Behind him on the road Titinius cradled Graptus' pale head in his lap. Tears streamed down his face as he rocked his friend back and forth.

"You'll be all right," he insisted to the weak smile Graptus gave back.

Slippery pools of Graptus' life flowed over the road, clotting in the gaps between the paving stones. Lucius rushed up.

"Ah, what have you done now, Graptus?" His broad face drooped with concern.

"I think," he said, raising his hand weakly and measuring a small space between thumb and forefinger, "your plan had a little flaw."

Lucius knelt beside him. "Listen," he said, choking on the words, "you've always been a horrible slave." Graptus smiled and nodded slightly, staring hard at Lucius. "But you've been a true friend. And a great soul."

Graptus grimaced, and arched his back tightly. "At least," he gasped, "I'm free." His head rolled, his eyes stared unblinking at a clear blue sky and his mouth fell open as if in amazement at its beauty. Titinius sobbed openly.

# XXX

May 9-13, 449 BC
The Lemuria


Echoing off the brick walls of empty patrician domiciles, the voices of the criers calling the members of the senate to assemble hung in the air like a word on the tip of the tongue— just out of reach of memory. Citizens stopped what they were doing to listen, as if the criers' voices invoked pleasant memories, as the smell of chicken roasting with garlic and rosemary calls forth the comfort and security of a mother's kitchen. "Those who are fathers, and those who are enrolled," the criers proclaimed, rapping their staffs on the flagstones. But no one answered. The senators had left the city. Then the pleasant sensation popped like a bubble when streams of refugees poured into the city bearing tales of murder, rape, and destruction at the hands of the Aequians. Peace came to a sudden end.

A delegation from Tusculum hurried into the presence of the decemvirs worriedly convened in the Curia. There they received news the Aequians threatened Tusculum and Labicum from the Algidus Pass area. The news came as no surprise. For years the cut on the east side of the mountainous ring called the Alban Hills had been used as a staging area for the Aequian armies. From it they could slice through the heart of the ancient volcano's cone and attack Tusculum, and Labicum, or circle around and attack Roman territory. Why no one ever fortified Algidus against the Aequians the soldiers who had to force them from it could only wonder. In their minds it proved their complaints of corrupt and inept leadership.

In this spirit the usual group assembled at the Boar's Tusk for the morning salutatio. At least that's what they called it, all being clients of Lucius Tempanius. He preferred to think they came for a free breakfast. Demetria had set out a pitcher of milk, thin wheat cakes, and cheese when Lucius descended the stairs from his second floor apartment accompanied by his son. The five men rose as soon as they heard his footfalls on the lower stairs.

"Hail Lucius," they saluted in unison.

"Do you want accompaniment today?" asked Flaccus solicitously. Every market day since Lucius had paid his debt and saved his farm he had come to Rome and attended Lucius wherever he went. Often, he picked up Turpio on his way and together paid their respects.

"No," said Lucius waving for them to sit. He had gone gray after the death of Graptus, and he seemed to have aged ten years in the eight months since the tragedy. Lucius not only missed his slave, he blamed himself for his demise. By his reckoning that made three innocent victims of his stubbornness and malice.

Before the five men sat, they all shook hands with Lucius Jr. and greeted him deferentially as well. He returned their greetings with reserved warmth. His chestnut brown eyes, wizened over the last eight months regarded them coolly. Forced to take over many of Graptus' duties, to his father's delight he discovered he had an aptitude for business. He stood casually behind his father his lean frame attentive, relaxed. He did not have his father's barrel chest, or forearms the size of pork shoulders, but his solid build served him well, and he had courage to go along with it.

Titinius looked at Lucius Jr. with paternal concern on his perpetually young face. "Do you think you'll be called up for the levy?" he asked. He shook his tightly coiled mop of silver hair, and raised v-shaped eyebrows in consternation.

Lucius Jr. shrugged. "I'm sure they'll think a levy is necessary." He had a rich, syrupy orator's voice. "The situation being what it is I doubt they'll exempt any centuries."

"You can't go," said Flaccus forcefully. "This is the time to put a stop to these ten kings."

Lucius Jr. smoothed an eyebrow with his left hand. "There is no appeal. I think," he said, his unctuous voice carrying a hint of castigation, "it would be better to risk battle than be executed for treason."

"I think you're getting ahead of yourselves," said Lucius. He picked up a wax tablet from the table, held it at arms length, and squinted deep creases into the corners of his eyes. "What is this?" he asked, looking over his shoulder at his son.

"That, Papa, is the list of things you need to do today. At the top of which is recording the sale of the Antium property with the plebeian aediles."

"He thinks," Lucius said, "that he can order me about because he's my sole heir." The men laughed. Lucius Jr. ignored his comments.

"Second," said Lucius Jr. "is registering the purchase of the Anio properties."

"So," said Turpio, interrupting, "do you think there may be a settlement before a levy is called?"

Lucius pondered the question momentarily. "Listen," he said, "elections should already have been held, right?" They all agreed. "And now they've summoned the senate, right?" Again, they nodded their heads in agreement. "On what authority? Their term of office ended May fifteenth when we should have had new magistrates."

"What do you mean, on what authority? They've been the authority for two years," Turpio spat.

"Your indignation is marvelous to behold, Turpio," Lucius needled. "But you lack subtlety. If they are the authority, why are they summoning the Senate to legitimize it?"

"Exactly," said Flaccus, "and that's why no one should answer the levy."

"Certainly," said Gaius Apronius. Slate gray eyes glared earnestly from the craggy face of the tenant farmer. He had a large nose squashed down onto his upper lip, and a chin that rose to meet it, giving him a comical expression even when angry. "Now is the time to use our leverage to force concessions."

"What concessions would those be, Gaius?" asked Lucius.

"Why," he said, his voice seeming to bubble from his nose, "the return of our tribunes. What else?"

"There might be many things," said Lucius Jr., running a hand through waves of coal black hair.

"For example?" prompted Turpio.

"For example," said Lucius Jr. "why should the plebeian assembly not have the right to enact laws?"

"And why should the moon not shine as brightly as the sun?" said Furius Villius. "It's the nature of things."

Lucius Jr. looked condescendingly at Villius. A large man, bald on top of his head, and older than his father, he had been a good soldier in his day. The land he managed for Lucius always produced. But his mind worked in traditional circles. "It's good that nature is constant," Lucius Jr. began. "Because we can then know the best times to plant, to harvest, to dig a trench. We can find our way because we know the orderly movement of the stars. But men change, and the seasons of men change." He laughed. "Why look at yourself, Furius Villius, you once had hair and a full set of teeth." Everyone laughed except Villius who recognized an insult when he heard one even if disguised by a joke.

"If my mind had gone along with my hair and my teeth, young Lucius Tempanius, I should think your words witty, and wise."

"Listen, my friends," Lucius said, "the sun is up, the birds are singing, and this old tavern is colder than a Sibyl's heart." He got to his feet. "I'm off to the Forum to take the sun and see what our Tarquins have in store for us today."

Turpio and Flaccus accompanied father and son to the Forum beneath a burnished blue sky. Unhindered by clouds the sun spread warmth like tepid honey, and even in the Subura the tantalizing smell of efflorescent spring dominated the air.

"Truly now," said Turpio, as if everything before had been in jest, "do you think the Senate will take our side?"

Lucius chuckled. "The Senate will never take our side. But they might be forced to accept some of our demands when conditions are right."

"Like now," said Flaccus. "When they're in the same boat as us."

Lucius sighed and shook his big head. "Listen, they're never in the same boat as us. If they stay away today then, then it may signify that they've found it in their best interests to side with us."

"And if not?" asked Turpio.

"If not, then they have other ideas."

"Who, exactly, is 'us'?" asked Lucius Jr.

"That's the crux of the matter," said Flaccus despondently. "We're never organized."

Lucius stopped at the crossroads shrine at the intersection of the Vicus Cyprius, and the Vicus Suburanus and left a small sacrifice to the lare protecting the crossing. "No," he said, as they continued down the Vicus Suburanus alongside the Cloaca Maxima, "you've got it wrong. We're well organized. We have the plebeian assembly, the plebeian aediles. We have our tribunes, our collegiums, our tribes, and our centuries. What we don't have is recognition and power."

"Do you hope to be appointed to the Senate, then?" asked Flaccus.

Turpio spat into the sewer. "That group of gutless snivelings."

"My education in politics came late," said Lucius, "but I think I understand things right. First, don't underestimate the Senate. Any man who tries to act independently of its approval is doomed. Look at Spurius Cassius. It's true, Turpio, that many just put their signet ring to whatever the consuls want, but you also have to remember that they have many ties of friendship and kinship amongst each other. You and I would be just as duty bound to support one another as Titus Quinctius and Lucius Valerius are."

"Certainly," said Turpio. "Better to be a tribune where you have some independence of action."

"Tribunes are like a voice without a body," scoffed Lucius Jr. "They can do nothing but make noise."

"What then?" said Turpio, in exasperation. "Will you become patricians?"

"In a sense that's exactly what must happen," said Lucius to the groans of impossibility rising out of Turpio and Flaccus. "Listen, of course it's impossible. But if plebeians want equality, they'll only get it through the magistracies."

"You mean the consulship," prompted Lucius Jr.

"They will never relinquish the consulship," said Turpio.

"Why not?" asked Flaccus. "They agreed to the decemvirs."

"Because," explained Turpio, "the consuls control the land. They decide where colonies will be, how large each plot will be, and how many settlers there'll be. What could be more clear? Control of the land is power, and the patricians won't give up their control."

"But Turpio," said Flaccus, "there have already been plebeian consuls. Why, Brutus, the first consul was plebeian."

They halted at the shrine of Cloacina, guarding the great sewer that passed beneath the Forum at this point. A terracotta statue, piously dressed in a flowing stola, and modeled after a particularly beautiful vestal virgin, rested in an arched brick alcove of the otherwise open-air shrine. Turpio leaned against the altar and crossed his arms.

"Yes, yes," he said, waving off the whole idea of plebeian consuls. "Here and there a so-called plebeian consul has been elected. But none in the last five years, and except for Spurius Cassius none have supported our need for land or debt relief."

"You are too cynical for words, Turpio," said Flaccus, tiring of the conversation. He chuckled dismissively.

"Really?" said Turpio, unwilling to let go. "And what would you call the eleventh table if not cynical?" he demanded.

Flaccus tried again to extricate himself from the conversation. "You can't marry a patrician anyway," he teased. "You're already married."

"You joke, but this law against intermarriage is another way of keeping property in their hands. Are not sons and daughters considered the property of the paterfamilias under the law?"

Lucius Jr. tired of the conversation and wandered off in the direction of the Curia. Lucius Sr. listened to his two friends quietly. He tended to agree with Turpio, but thought his client's thinking did not go far enough. While Turpio understood the concept of property rights as fundamental to liberty, his ideas stopped at the two and a half iugera he unjustly lost at the hands of the decemvirs. Lucius understood that this minuscule amount could not even guarantee subsistence, to say nothing of liberty, and that the commons would remain perpetually in debt to the aristocracy as long as they aspired to nothing more. He cleared his throat authoritatively.

"Turpio," he said, "we've created a mile's delay for ourselves with this discussion. Why don't you go make sure the masons are getting something done on my house. I'll come by a little later."

Turpio took his leave and headed for the Aventine to supervise the construction of Lucius' house, a position he had acquired when Lucius fired the original contractor for shoddy construction practices. Flaccus departed as well, heading for the vegetable market where his son minded their produce until his return. Lucius suddenly found himself alone.

He strolled up the north edge of the Forum to the Curia. A great crush of men crowded into and around the Comitium as senators in purple edged togas worked their way through the massed togas and tunics. Lucius sensed an atmosphere he couldn't define. An air of accommodation, of studied civility existed in the handshakes, the kind words, and the courteous comportment of the senators as they made their way into the Curia.

The atmosphere abruptly changed when Gaius Claudius, uncle of the decemvir, Appius Claudius, edged his way through the crowd. Hissing and booing immediately rose like the putrid steam from the nether regions of Puteoli.

"Shame!" came the cry.

Someone gave him a shove. A shoulder set firmly bumped him as he passed. A hand mussed his iron gray hair disrespectfully. Spittle wet his ears and cheeks. "Lackey of the Tarquins!" Shielded from the worst by the men of his household, dressed in crimson- bordered white tunics, he kept his gray eyes straight ahead.

Anxiety flowed out of the Curia like sweat from the multitude. Lucius could smell both of them. Decemvirs flitted around like seagulls after crumbs of spelt, until Appius Claudius stood to speak. Lucius forged his way through the crowd to the front near the doors of the senate house, which had been left open regardless of the protests of the decemvirs.

"We have called the senate together to put forward a motion to handle the current threat to our nation..." His protruding eyes swept the gathering of senators who sat on their benches in attitudes varying from distrust to combativeness.

"You have no authority to call the senate," a voice from the back benches loudly protested. Hoots of agreement went up from the people outside the door who heard the comment, and as the words were passed back through the Forum the cry grew to a chant.

"In order," Claudius raised his deep voice, "to have a united people to oppose the depredations of foreign enemies."

"Our domestic enemies are worse!" A voice in the crowd drew derisive laughter.

"We ask the Senate to join us in a call to raise troops for the defense of Rome," finished Claudius.

No sooner had Appius Claudius seated himself stiffly on his curule chair than senators jumped up to speak. Lucius watched with amusement as they disregarded long-standing rules of procedure. They did not defer to older distinguished members, nor did they wait for the decemvirs to ask their opinions individually. Lucius Valerius Potitus demanded they address the political situation—by which he meant the decemvirs illegal continuance in office. The decemvirs refused. What a surprise, thought Lucius cynically. Marcus Horatius Barbatus called them the ten Tarquins to their faces and harangued the senators and the decemvirs on the illegality of the decemvirate in general and the tyrannical nature of this group in particular. A deep current of agreement rolled through the assembled multitude outside the Senate House. The brother of the decemvir, Maluginensis, stressed the military threat to the Republic, which caused another huge outburst of ironic laughter from the citizens gathered near the door. Finally, Gaius Claudius rose and, perhaps influenced by his rough treatment, delivered an impassioned speech imploring the decemvirs, and particularly his nephew, to step down and announce elections. The decemvirs listened politely and ignored him completely. Again, a call for raising troops and tabling any debate on the state of the nation was made; again, Valerius and Horatius declared their obdurate opposition to the legality of any proposal by the decemvirs. A scene of near violence erupted as Valerius made for the top of the steps to address the people directly. Appius Claudius, his face a wedge of darkening anger, ordered him arrested, but was immediately convinced to retract it and allow Valerius to speak.

A space cleared around him as he approached the top step of the Curia. Lucius looked up at him from two steps below as he spoke of tradition, history, and of his family's long association with the commons—thus the appellation of Publicola (friend of the people) that had long been attached to the name Valerius. He besought them for help in restoring the Republic and protecting his person. They listened politely and disregarded him completely.

"Where were you when Veturius Flaccus was hauled to court for a debt he didn't owe?" shouted Lucius. "Or when Publius Turpio was beaten with rods and dispossessed of his farm?"

"Have you protected one citizen in all this time?" another shouted.

From every direction crimes against citizens came flying at Valerius, and he had nothing to answer but a pledge that things would be different. Few believed him.

"It's enough to make you puke," spat Lucius to a stranger nearby as the crowd began to disperse.

"You notice he didn't mention our tribunes," the man responded.

Lucius heard his name called and looked around to see a solidly built man in his early thirties squirming through the mass to get to him. He had a thick head of wavy black hair and an anxious look on his open face. Lucius recognized him as the former tribune Lucius Icilius.

"Hail, Lucius Icilius." They shook hands. "I hear congratulations are in order."

"Ah yes, thank you."

"You're a lucky man. Verginia is quite beautiful."

Icilius was obviously happy with his betrothal as well. "And that's the least of her good qualities," he said, with a giant smile lighting his handsome face. "Will you come to the wedding?"

"I'd be honored. Thank you."

"My pleasure. However, that's not what I wanted to speak to you about."

"Let's walk together, and you can tell me what it is." Lucius headed directly for a fruit stand on the other side of the Forum.

"I think things are about to turn," Icilius said, helping himself to the cherries in a basket Lucius offered.

"Things are always about to turn," said Lucius, spitting a seed to the ground. "Then it always seems like the patricians keep what they had and divest us of a little more of what we had."

"I agree with you to some extent," Icilius hedged.

"If you mean your law to guarantee our right to the land on the Aventine, you have my thanks. But getting the patricians to ratify something the people have already done and safeguarded with oaths, and getting them to share power are two different things."

"The task is more difficult, no doubt. But there seems to be a growing consensus among the present group of senators that the decemvirs must go. Especially among the non-patricians."

"What a surprise. And what will replace them?"

"That's what I wanted to talk to you about. We need to formulate a program so that when the time is right, we can present it. Along with your war record, your confrontation in the Flaccus affair has brought great respect to your name. I think you could be influential in drafting a plan."

Lucius started to decline, then stopped himself. "Come," he said, "let me show you what your Lex Icilia has allowed me to build on the Aventine." He thought about the offer as they walked past the shops of the Vicus Tuscus, exited the portal and held their breath past the dark still waters of the Velabrum. All his life he had detested politics. That revulsion hadn't really changed. However, as he planned and schemed to increase his wealth, he had to admit that the power it bought him was inherently political. As they climbed the Aventine, he broke his silence. "I've spent a lifetime avoiding politics," he said. "Now, if I'm not mistaken, you want me to help draft what amounts to a new constitution."

"You ceased avoiding politics when you paid the debt of Flaccus."

"Ah. That did earn me a few enemies."

"Word has it that you rid yourself of one or two also."

"Rumors are rife in Rome. Most have no more weight than a mote of dust."

"Well, if I see Caeso Quinctius floating in the air I'll let you know," Icilius laughed.

Lucius inspected the high pitch of laughter for signs of a threat but could find none. "I'll think about it," he said. "I must admit, against my better judgement my interest has been piqued by events of the last few months."

Turpio came running up as he saw Lucius and his guest approaching up the drive.

"Wonderful," said Icilius. "Is this your house?"

"Yes."

"It's very nice. My compliments to the architect."

"Thank you. I accept."

+ + +

The levy took place as expected, and Titus got lost, as usual. His son Marcus, frustrated, bit his tongue as his father led them through the labyrinth of Rome. Why they couldn't have followed the Via Labicana straight to the Vicus Suburanus and gone directly to his uncle's tavern in the Subura he had no idea. Except that his father had decided he needed to know more than one or even two ways in and out of the Subura. Now they wandered a maze of dead ends, alleyways, and streets that circled back on themselves, apparently just as lost as his father.

"Maybe we should ask directions," he suggested, as they passed a crossroads shrine somewhere on the Viminal Hill for the second time.

"How are you going to learn to find your way if you're always asking directions?" said Titus, puffing with the exertion of climbing another hill. He stopped, bent over and rested his hands on his knees, breathing deeply to catch his breath.

"Are you alright?" Marcus asked, adjusting the reed basket on his father's back.

Titus raised his eyes without lifting his head. Perspiration beaded on his forehead. From beneath wrinkled brows he looked at his son standing expectantly without a sign of fatigue. He breathed easily despite carrying all his military gear. He had inherited his father's looks and build, so that when he gazed solicitously with brown eyes circumvallated by an argent ring at his father, they each saw themselves at different ages. Titus what he once looked like, five feet eight inches tall with wide shoulders and narrow waist. He carried himself with natural athletic grace and could run like a horse. Marcus saw himself in another twenty years, a full head of hair streaked with gray, the drooping nose pointing at a strong chin, and small mouth cupped by deep creases at the corners.

"Papa, are you well?" Marcus asked again.

"I'm fine. I'm just trying to get my bearings."

"Did you lose them on the ground?" Marcus asked.

Titus shot a scathing look at his son, saw the absurdity of the moment reflected back at him in the mischievous smile, and laughed. "If you're so smart, you lead the way."

Marcus gladly did so, and they soon strode to the front door of the Boar's Tusk. Lucius sat on a stool leaning his back against the wall as they walked up, Marcus in red tunic burdened with his military gear, and Titus in a worn tan tunic with a basket of personal effects strapped to his back.

"Why didn't you bring a cart and sell some vegetables while you're in Rome?" asked Lucius by way of greeting.

Titus grunted, slinging the basket gratefully on the ground. "I thought I should leave it for Tullia and the boys in case they have to evacuate the farm."

"Ah," said Lucius, eyeing his brother closely. "How is it you've kept your hair?"

"Clean living," Titus said, smiling.

"You couldn't tell by your clothes. Look at you. Your tunic looks like you just came in from the fields, your shoes are full of muck. Where have you been?"

"I was fine," protested Titus, inspecting himself self consciously, "until I got to Rome."

"We've been exploring all the side streets of the Esquiline and the Viminal," said Marcus. He flashed his winning smile at his uncle.

"I see," said Lucius. "Your father was lost again."

"I was not lost. I knew exactly where I was."

"Oh yes. Somewhere in Rome." Lucius stood up. "Take those filthy shoes off and you can come in. Demetria will murder us both if you track that stuff inside."

"I see you've moved up in the world," said Titus, as he untied his shoes. He nodded at the off-white linen tunic Lucius wore.

"They're more comfortable in summer than wool," said Lucius. "I'd let you wear one of my extras but I'm afraid they'd be too short and offend your modesty."

"You do like to wear yours right on the edge of decency."

The tunic Lucius wore stopped two inches above his knees. Titus wore his at knee length and considered anything shorter immodest. However, neither the length of Lucius' tunic, nor the wide leather belt studded with bronze rivets that cinched it around his thick waist were the point.

"How is it the rest of Rome can't pay their bills, and you're out buying flaxen tunics?" he asked.

"Because even in the worst of times people drink wine and talk."

"I still don't see how you can prefer this tavern to working your own farm. It lacks dignity."

"Dignity can't buy linen tunics or property on the Anio. The truth is, Titus, I grow and sell more crops than you do."

"The difference is, I do it myself."

"I'm going to the Campus to report for duty," broke in Marcus. This conversation had been going on for longer than he could remember. He couldn't tell if they enjoyed it and so rehashed it whenever they were together or what, but he did know it always made him uncomfortable.

Titus embraced his son. "The gods be with you," he said, tears choking his voice.

"Don't let them see your back," said Lucius, shaking the young man's hand.

Titus and Lucius went inside, which immediately made Lucius nervous and restless. Ever since Graptus had died he had been unable to relax in the Boar's Tusk, as if the place were no longer his. He ordered Titus to sit while pacing the floor himself. He fetched wine and cups then left his untouched. That he promised the place to Graptus then got him killed wasn't really the point. Risks are a given in life. He knew it, and Graptus knew it. No, he had begun to associate the tavern with death. Valeria, the one love of his life, and Graptus, perhaps his dearest friend, both were inextricably tied to the

Boar's Tusk. Without them the tavern became empty and void of meaning. He felt like an interloper in this inn of ghosts.

"Well Titus, you won't have to worry about it much longer. As soon as I can move into my new house, I'm going to sell it."

"What?"

"The tavern…what have we been talking about?"

"That was…never mind."

"But not for the reasons you said," Lucius insisted. "I've just lost interest. The place isn't fun anymore."

"Whatever the reason, I think it's a good decision."

"Listen, put on your toga and we'll go to the Forum. I'll run upstairs and get mine and be right down."

"So why haven't you replaced Graptus?" asked Titus as they crossed the little plaza in front of the tavern.

"Two reasons," said Lucius. "One, he was my friend. You can't replace a friend. Two, slaves are definitely out of my price range now that I'm no longer soldiering."

"If we don't break out of this pen the Volscians and Aequians have us in we'll all be beggars," said Titus with a shake of his head. "And now the Sabines have joined in."

"True. What scares me most is they've got better leaders than we do. We just might lose, Titus."

+ + +

Though registered in the same century Marcus Tempanius and Lucius Tempanius the younger were selected to serve in different legions. Marcus served with Quintus Fabius against the Sabines, and Lucius Jr. served under Marcus Cornelius and a host of decemvirs against the Aequians.

Hurled against the Aequians on Algidus the Roman phalanx, unable to keep order over the uneven terrain, was routed. They fell back on their camp but the Aequians stormed and took that, giving no time for the Romans to prepare a defense. From their camp the remains of the legion fled to

Tusculum with what few items they could carry. The Aequians busied themselves plundering the Roman camp rather than follow up their victory and destroy the Roman legion. Lucius Tempanius Jr. broke his spear defending the camp, and retired to Tusculum with the rest of the dispirited army. In the three aching fingers of his left hand he clutched his shield. He felt like a child again.

In Legio I the political cancer also ate away at morale. The first night in camp along the River Allia, Marcus sat around the fire with members of his century discussing the straits Rome had gotten herself into. Their centurion, Lucius Siccius, now forty years old and big as a wagon, shocked some with his seditious talk. Then again, for those who had been tribunes it seemed to come as naturally as breathing.

"You know, I once wrestled your uncle," he said to Marcus.

"Yes," said Marcus, flashing his disarming smile, "you lost."

"He cheated," said Siccius. His blunt face split in a smile as wide as a spear wound.

"That's what he says about all your medals."

"Jealous is he?" Only Lucius Siccius could have said such a thing. Eight times he had emerged victorious in single combat. A veteran of 120 battles, he had not a single scar on his back, although he had forty-five of them on the front of his body to testify to his courage. Not even the coveted corona obsidianalis had eluded his grasp. And he could still serve six more years if he desired. Lucius Tempanius had fallen just short of being the finest soldier of his time.

"I guess you could call it jealousy. He claims the consuls gave you all those honors to keep you quiet as tribune."

Siccius spat into the fire. "Truth is I was more of a man then. At least I stood up for our rights. By all the gods we ought to refuse to serve as we did then."

A bubble of naysayers mumbled of the impossibility of such action. No appeal. They'll decimate us.

"Don't be such women," Siccius chided. "We should elect tribunes and make our demands. If we stand together, they're powerless."

The debate went on into the night until they turned in. An uneasy peace fell over the camp as the soldiers slept.

The next morning a picked group of men led by Lucius Siccius received orders to make a reconnaissance patrol. Marcus and his comrades thought it odd that no one else in their century was included and warned Siccius to be careful. Some hours later, wild eyed and covered in blood and dirt, the remnants of the patrol stumbled into camp with a tale of ambush. Four of their comrades, including Siccius were killed. Marcus immediately sought permission to find the bodies and bury them. Twenty men were given orders to go, and after receiving directions from the survivors set out.

Slowly, cautiously they moved forward, picking their way through the woods. At the river they crouched, waited, watched. Marcus led five of them across, scouted the other bank then waved the rest forward. They melted into the trees, moving stealthily, freezing at every sound. When they reached the clearing Marcus waved them all down then sent five men around the clearing to the right, and five to the left. Two birdcalls informed him the area was secure and he moved his men into the clearing after posting guards in the woods around it.

Lucius Siccius lay still, his hand gripping his sword in death. Around him three other legionaries sprawled, all still in their armor with swords near where they had fallen. A chill went through Marcus as he surveyed the scene. "Look at this," he said, sweeping his hand over the bodies. "It was an ambush, all right. But not by the Sabines."

"Not one of them has been stripped," observed a comrade.

"Gaius," Marcus ordered, "look for any sign of dead or wounded being dragged away."

"I doubt we'll find any."

"This smells worse than the sewer in August."

"They got more than they bargained for trying to murder Siccius."

"I'll wager our commanders are behind this," said Marcus.

"Who's the snitch in our century, is what I want to know."

"We're not going to let them get away with this, are we?"

"Not this time. Gaius, did you find anything?"

"Not a sign. This was a murder, Marcus. Pure and simple."

"All right. Let's make a litter and take Lucius Siccius back with us."

"What about the others?"

"Leave them for their brothers the vultures," said Marcus.

Their return to camp brought a near mutiny. Anger pervaded every tent, and the patrician officers they treated with contempt. Hoping movement and the enemy would keep the men in check, Fabius ordered them to break camp. The men refused and sent a message through their centurions demanding leave to take Siccius' body back to Rome. The thought of such an enterprise brought serious alarm to the commander's tent. Rome, he knew, would convulse with anger and probably erupt in revolution. To forestall such an event, they decided to give Siccius a full military funeral at public expense. This did little to assuage the soldiers' anger, but it did prevent them from spreading it to Rome.

Fabius gave the order to break camp again, and this time the men obeyed with a grudging lassitude. Near Eretum, in the Apennine foothills east of Rome they fought dispiritedly and gave ground to the Sabines until they had been pushed back all the way to Fidenae. There they fortified a camp on a small hill and allowed the Sabines to advance no farther, fighting only hard enough to save their lives.

+ + +

Lucius and Titus could smell it. It had the acrid odor of fullers' brine, a mixture that included human urine as one of its ingredients. The rotten stench of corruption permeated every quarter of Rome, mingling with the smell of fear as news flew on ominous wings from the legions to Rome. Concern for the lives of their sons grew with each passing day. And each day they hurried to the Forum for more bad news. Caught in a terrible cycle, they couldn't stand to miss the news they couldn't bear to hear. So once again they ate a hasty breakfast and made their way to the Forum, each step ponderous with foreboding.

Golden tines of sunlight poked at the Forum, glancing off the Samnite shields of the moneychangers on the south side. A procession of lictors in red tunics with broad white sash belts carried their bundles of rods into the Forum. Dangling from the tops of their crimson shoes, bones carved into half moons and circles clicked softly like the scattering of dry leaves across flagstones at each step. Behind them Appius Claudius walked with regal, measured steps, his double knotted patrician shoes flashing beneath the purple-bordered toga. On his sharp visage a look of stern confidence was anchored. Heedless of comments or entreaties his head remained steady, his eyes fixed straight ahead. He made immediately for a tribunal erected on the east end of the Forum and seated himself on the ivory curule chair of office. With an imperious wave of a hand, he ordered a crier to announce that all those who had a case to present could bring it before the court.

No one knew what to think. The incongruous image of lictors attired for war while Appius dressed as if peace reigned, unsettled the citizens. How could the city be at war and peace both?

"I guess he wants us to feel like he has command of every situation, no?" Lucius observed.

Seated outside a shop's rectangular post and lintel under a thick cotton awning eating honeyed cakes on the south side of the Forum they viewed the coming of Appius with spiteful eyes.

"Either that or he doesn't know which is proper, so he does everything together," said Titus.

Lucius laughed between his teeth. "That's probably closer to the truth." He pushed a platter closer to Titus. "Have another cake."

"No thanks. I've had enough."

"You eat like a bird. Pretty soon you'll be like this." He held up his little finger.

"Don't worry, you'll make up for both of us the way you're growing."

"I exercise every day on the Campus Martius," protested Lucius. "I can still throw you I'll wager."

Titus looked carefully at his brother, who had become indolently portly to his mind. "I just might take you up on that wager."

They lapsed into silence, content to watch the comings and goings of the populace in the subdued atmosphere of the shops. With two defeated armies in the field few people were in the mood to buy anything other than necessities. Male and female slaves made the rounds of fruit and vegetable stands, spice merchants, or salt dealers for the great houses of Rome. Titus made a game of identifying which families they belonged to by the color of the tunics they wore. Blue for the Quinctii, yellow for the Fabii, poppy red for the Valerii. Tiring of the game he shifted his attention to the tribunal where Appius Claudius held court, which brought to his mind the question of the twelve tables. The decemvirs had yet to bring them before the people for ratification. Although everyone knew they lied, the decemvirs insisted the final two laws were not yet ready. Ostensibly this provided the rationale for not relinquishing their positions. Titus along with the rest of the citizen body knew quite well not only that the last two laws had been written, but exactly what they were. The eleventh law, banning intermarriage between patricians and plebeians, so obviously aimed at keeping the magistracies out of the hands of the plebeians by maintaining the purity of the patricians' genealogy, became a constant topic of debate in the Forum. Titus wondered that the decemvirs could so stubbornly cling to their false claim.

"What effect do you think the law of nexum will have on you?" asked Titus.

"Which part?"

"The part that says a father can only hire his son out three times before he automatically becomes emancipated."

"Not at all."

"What do you mean? Most of your field hands are exactly those sons, aren't they?"

"Certainly, some are." He blotted up a few crumbs with a wetted index finger. "However, you fail to see two points. First, there will always be more debtors than creditors in Rome. Second, where will those sons go? Their fathers may not be able to hire them out, but they'll still need work."

"But then you'll have to pay them."

"Listen, Titus, as long as we're fighting on our own soil, people will need seed, or sheep, or a dowry, or what have you. I have them. Right now, I have nearly fifty clients. Did you know that?"

"No," said Titus, truly impressed. "I had no idea."

"No, and neither does anyone else. With their dependents I could call up a century if I needed. That in itself provides a fairly stable labor force for me, and every year I add a few more clients. Best of all it reduces my cost of living because I can buy most of my produce and meat from my own tenant farmers at a much lower price. Now, that may not sound like much to the Fabii, or the Claudii, but it's a good start for a Tempanius."

Titus appraised his brother, somber brown eyes alight with curiosity. "Do you hope to contend with the likes of the Fabii, and the Claudii?" The very thought astonished him, and he feared his brother suffered delusions.

"Contend?" Lucius asked rhetorically. "No Titus, you need to understand things better if you want to survive. Do you think the eleventh table is designed to prevent plebeians from competing with patricians? Not at all. It's designed so that plebeians can't join them; understand?"

"I fail to see the difference." Titus broke the last remaining cake in half. He wasn't hungry but the sitting made him nervous, and the eating gave his hands something to do. He wished he'd stayed home and been content with the simple life of his farm.

"The difference is that as long as we plebs are obligated as clients to the patricians, power will always flow through their hands."

Titus plowed his hair with sausage sized fingers. "And so…" He did not see anything new in this concept, so he did not entirely grasp the depth of Lucius' meaning. There had always been patrons and there had always been clients. By his own admission Lucius had a clientele of his own. And so did Titus, although much smaller. A patron spoke for his client in the law courts, provided him seed when he had none. He made land available to his client's sons, or provided a small dowry for their daughters. In return a client attended his patron when he came to Rome, or spoke for him at his tribal meetings when his patron ran for office, or worked for him during planting or harvest. It had always been thus, and to Titus' mind it would always be thus. "…would you change the structure of society altogether?"

Lucius reflected a moment, picking at stray balls of wool on his toga. "No," he said. "At least, not in the sense I think you mean. Listen, at the beginning of the Republic there were a number of consuls of plebeian birth, right?"

Titus agreed reluctantly, fearing a trap.

"As time went on there were fewer and fewer until there have been none for the last five years. Right?"

"Yes," said Titus grudgingly. "But at least three of the decemvirs are plebeians right now."

Lucius waved off the argument with his hand. "A political expediency of a second decemvirate. Listen, where do you think the family of our friend Lucius Icilius was when Father and the rest of the plebs seceded forty years ago?"

"I have no idea," said Titus, still fearing a trap. "I suppose with the rest of the plebs."

"Wrong. They were in Rome. It's only since the patricians have squeezed them out of the consulate that they've become plebeians."

"I thought you were friends with Icilius."

"I am, but that doesn't mean I close my eyes to the truth."

"Which is…?"

"Think, Titus. The likes of Icilius were too rich to be part of the 'great unwashed' that walked out of the city, and didn't have the blood to be patricians. As long as our 'fathers' were content to share power they accepted the status quo. But since they've been excluded, they have only one way to gain access to the offices of state; that's to expand their own clientele among the plebs."

"And you intend to control a portion of that clientele."

"Exactly."

"So that, in sum, you can become patrician."

Loud voices from the direction of Claudius' tribunal carried into the brother's conversation. Titus glanced at the source of the noise then disregarded it.

"No," said Lucius, his eyes on the gathering crowd around the dais. "So that I have the same opportunities as the patricians."

"I see," said Titus, scratching his jaw. "And what about the rest of us commons with our two to five iugera of land?"

Lucius stared at his brother with a flinty hardness in his dark eyes. "Don't be one," he said. He stood and stretched his back. "Let's see what the excitement's about at Appius' court."

A large and vocal crowd had gathered around the platform where Appius Claudius held court. Lucius and Titus pushed their way into the center of the throng then asked a bystander what all the fuss was about.

"Marcus Claudius," said the man. "He's a client of Appius Claudius."

"So, what's his complaint?" asked Titus.

"He claims this girl is his slave."

"How can he judge a case that his own client brings before the court?" hissed Lucius.

"Who's the girl?" asked Titus. He shifted his feet as other people jostled him seeking a better view. Whistles and catcalls flew from the crowd.

"The daughter of Lucius Verginius."

"Verginia?!" exploded Lucius. "He can't be serious."

"It's worse than that," chimed in another onlooker. "This is all the doing of Appius. He's tried every way he can to get her into his house."

"But she's betrothed to Lucius Icilius," said Lucius, pushing his way to the front.

"That doesn't mean anything to Appius," said the man to Lucius' back.

"What kind of hideous crime is this?" demanded Titus under his breath. He followed his brother forward.

Were it not so serious, the scene might have been comical. On the bottom step of the dais, tugging on one of Verginia's arms Marcus Claudius claimed in a loud voice that she had been born a slave in his household. Pulling on her other arm the girl's slave, with terror distorting her face, cried for help. Verginia, her face full of conflicting emotions—fear, doubt, amazement, anger—didn't know which way to pull, and so became the rope in a tug-of-war.

"Calm down, calm down," Appius Claudius shouted, waving his arm. "Let loose of the poor girl's arm, Marcus Claudius," he ordered. "Before we have a riot on our hands."

Appius looked dispassionately at the young woman as if he were a neutral judge interested only in the truth, but Titus thought he could see lust soaking through his eyes. Desire for the girl was understandable. Released from the plaintiff's grip she drew herself up to her full height, a statuesque five feet seven inches. Her raven black hair had come loose in the struggle and long wavy strands of it fell to the small of her back. A finely sculpted nose divided rosewood colored eyes. Perspiring under the intensity of the moment, her dark complexion glowed hotly, and her breast heaving with panic swelled her maiden's stola with the nascent sexuality of a fourteen-year-old.

When a degree of calm had been restored, Appius spoke again. "First, be assured that this claimant has a legal right to state his case before this court. So let us not get all excited here, and we'll get to the bottom of this.

"Verginia, approach the court please."

With timid steps the girl approached, casting longing glances backwards at her nurse and the sympathetic faces of the crowd.

"Now, Marcus Claudius," Appius said, seating himself on his curule chair, "state your case."

Lucius felt the familiar burn of anger, like wheat when it begins to boil, rising in great spitting bubbles. He saw Appius Claudius sitting with knees apart, and he imagined them looking like the legs of his curule chair, carved in the shape of a wolf's hind legs. Like a god, hands on his knees, he sat on the padded leather covered chair, polished brass rivets glinted like stars in his heaven. Appius combed his dark brown hair forward in flowing waves, and his hooked nose and block of stone chin were raised with judicial haughtiness. Lucius could sense the relish with which Appius wielded his power over this girl's life. Worse, when he examined his hatred for the man, he found at its core a deeply painful envy and covetousness.

Marcus Claudius, weak chin, smooth black hair, thin framed and small voiced tried to sound impressive. "This girl was born in my house as a slave. Her mother was a slave."

"She doesn't have your ugliness," shouted someone.

"And," he raised his shrill voice, "and was stolen as an infant."

Derisive laughter ascended from the crowd. "Come Appius," shouted Titus, "couldn't you think up a better fable than this?"

Appius rose from his chair. His lictors moved forward. "Quiet," he demanded. "We will hear this case."

"How she was palmed off on Lucius Verginius I cannot tell," Marcus Claudius continued. "But I have incontrovertible evidence that she was."

Lucius turned to Titus. "Someone needs to go tell Lucius Verginius what they're about to do to him."

"Where is he?"

"With the legion at Tusculum."

Despite Appius' warning the crowd grew more vocal. Now Marcus Claudius had to yell to make himself heard above the restive audience. "While I have compassion for Lucius Verginius, who has certainly been defrauded worse than I, I can prove before any court and Verginius too, that his so-called daughter is in truth a slave."

"Will no one speak for this poor girl?" implored her crying slave, reaching prayerfully out to the crowd.

"Titus, see if you can find Lucius Icilius," said Lucius. "Meanwhile I'll try to stall things here."

"I ask the court for the rightful possession of my property," Marcus Claudius declared.

Lucius stepped forward into the space before the tribunal. He had never been there before. Suddenly he felt the eyes of literally hundreds of people trained on him. A surge of hot adrenaline flooded through him, his hands shook, and his voice wavered with a constricted sound he did not recognize.

"I think," he said, clearing his throat, "I think it would be a miscarriage of justice to let this," he turned and pointed at Marcus Claudius, "this barking dog take possession of the daughter of Verginius on his word alone." His voice grew stronger as confidence warmed him to the subject. "After all, who is this whining pup who scratches his head with one finger and hides behind the stolas of Rome's maidens while Lucius Verginius risks his life in honorable defense of our country?"

The audience encouraged him with laughs, shouting its approval. He lashed out more venomously at the character of Marcus Claudius, and by association at Appius Claudius. Appius sat on the tribunal, his face a darkening thundercloud of anger.

"Why indeed is this young man (I use the term loosely) in Rome? Has he served even ten years in the legions? I have over twenty campaigns and a hundred battles to show; how many has he? Yet he would demand possession of this girl whose rightful father is away with the legions and cannot defend her honor. How perfect is this coward's timing, how fittingly dishonorable.

"Surely, Appius Claudius, you cannot allow this to happen. The fact that you sit in judgement of your own client defies tradition, though we would like to trust in your impartiality. The laws of Rome, which you yourself helped design state that the defendant must be allowed to make his case before his property may be taken from him. If there is justice in Rome, Lucius Verginius must be allowed to defend his daughter before she is given into the hands of this...this cowering dog."

He paused, looking around to see if Titus had returned with Icilius. The spectators, and even Appius seemed to be waiting for him to say more. A vast majority of those crowded round were on his side, but he assessed this correctly as due less to his oratorical skills than to sympathy for the girl's plight.

Sweeping the crowd with his right hand held aloft and spinning in a slow stately circle, he continued to plead for Verginia's freedom. "Can anyone here have any doubts as to why this scurrilous claim has been made now? Is this the first time Verginia has walked in public with her lifelong nurse? Come, we all know the answers. Of course it's not. Many times have I seen her nurse walk her to school—and I've served most of my life in the legions. It can hardly be the first time Marcus Claudius, who hangs around the streets of Rome like some over-aged prostitute, has seen her. Why has he said nothing before? It is patently obvious that he has chosen this time (if indeed it was he) because the girl's father, a man who has the courage and honor to face his enemies, could not be present to defend her virtue.

"If the bestial man lusting for this beautiful young girl can rein in his passions—a difficult task, I know, for a notorious dog who wags his tail indiscriminately all over Rome—Lucius Verginius can be here in two day's time. If there is still justice in Rome, surely you must return this frightened girl to the hearth of her family until the case is proven one way or the other."

A hush fell over the multitude as Appius Claudius, chin resting on curled fingers, contemplated the arguments of both sides. In hushed whispers they debated among themselves the merits of the case and the speakers, for this held every bit as much importance as the facts of the case. The general consensus held that Lucius Tempanius should win the day.

Appius Claudius stood to pronounce his judgement. At the same time Titus returned with Lucius Icilius and Verginia's uncle, Publius Numitorius. He had found them at the temple of Ceres going through some records. When he told them of the trial, they sent servants to find Icilius' brother and Numitorius' son, who were immediately dispatched to the Legion's camp near Tusculum to inform Verginius of his daughter's peril. Icilius rushed up flushed with anger as Appius prepared to speak.

"First, let me commend Lucius Tempanius for his fine defense," Appius began. "For someone untrained and unskilled in the art of public speaking he acquitted himself quite well...all things considered. You may rest assured that justice will be done, and that the law you mentioned will be applied without respect of persons. The case we have before us is not as simple as you would make it out to be. We have both a seemingly legitimate claimant, and an absentee father. It seems to me that the court must then split its judgement, as it were, until the case can be resolved. Here is our ruling. A final ruling will be reserved until the father can be sent for and appear before this court."

A murmur of approval rippled through the crowd. Appius held up his hand. "However, since the father is absent there is no one to whom the master can turn over custody. Therefore, it is the court's decision that the claimant shall take charge of the girl. He must promise to produce her before this court in two day's time, when the person of the said father must also appear."

Stunned by the ruling the crowd fell into a mumbling disquiet, but made no move to prevent Marcus Claudius from taking hold of the stricken Verginia. A flush of anger darkened Lucius' broad face, and he stepped forward threateningly. Behind him a lane suddenly opened in the crush of spectators and Lucius Icilius and Publius Numitorius strode towards the dais. A lictor stepped out.

"Judgement has been rendered. The case is closed," he cried.

The words no sooner left his lips than Icilius moved passed him. The lictor shoved Icilius. He spun, shoved the lictor hard, and the man went down. Enraged, Icilius turned on Appius. "You dare attack me in the Forum? Then you had better do it with steel." He pointed at Verginia. "I am betrothed to that girl, and I intend to have a virgin for my bride."

With a motion of his hand Appius called all twelve lictors forward to surround Icilius. In their blood red tunics of war, and bundled rods they struck awe and fear in the people. The front rows of the crowd backed away. Lucius girded his toga for a fight, and in an instant Titus, Numitorius and a few others stood beside him. Icilius stood defiantly in the middle of the circle, girding his toga with a vicious smile on his face.

"Bring all your lictors Appius Claudius," he taunted, by which he meant the 120 lictors of the decemvirs together. "I for one am not ashamed to fight your tyranny alone. Kill me now, so my death can be an example to the rest of these people to throw off your yoke of slavery."

The whole Forum flexed with tension, awaiting the outbreak of violence. Appius hesitated. "This is not about your defense of Verginia, Icilius," he pronounced, hoping to dispel the hardening resolve of the populace to defend the girl, "but against your words to incite a riot. This is a fine excuse for you to stir up trouble."

Regardless, a formidable knot of men coalesced around Lucius, and Icilius. The realization that a confrontation now might stir up an insurrection caused Appius to rethink his position. He decided it would be better to assemble his forces on the day of his choosing, so he could control events as he pleased.

"However," said Appius, in conciliatory tones, "to show the court's mercy we will allow the girl to return to her father's house if you will provide surety. Be forewarned, if her so-called father fails to appear tomorrow this court will not be afraid to rule in favor of the plaintiff.

"And believe me, I will not need to send for any of my colleagues' lictors to ensure the peace." With that he ordered the crier to call the next case, and sat on his curule chair to wait.

Like the windlass and beams of an olive press the pressure on Rome ratcheted tighter and tighter. The legions hovered close to mutiny, while the city held its breath over the case of Verginia. The riders sent to the legion near Tusculum nearly killed their horses to bring Lucius Verginius back to Rome. Icilius' forethought proved providential for as soon as the law courts closed Appius sent a messenger to the commander of the army ordering him to deny Verginius leave to return to the city. By then he had already gone.

Tallow candles splashed saffron light late into the night at the Boar's Tusk as Lucius, Titus, Icilius, Numitorius, and Verginius huddled to discuss strategy for the next day's trial. Verginius, haggard, hollow eyed and physically weary said little. He could hardly believe the events described to him could take place. In military tunic, his dark curly hair matted from the helmet he held in his large hands he listened as ideas and strategies passed around the gathered tables like bones in a game. Finally, he pushed his stool back and stood up.

"Friends," he said, his deep voice sonorous with fatigue, "thank you for this showering of concern." His wide mouth split in a grisly smile. "I know I can count on your support tomorrow when I defend my daughter's chastity in whatever way I must." He hushed the expressions of affirmation with a raised hand. "You must know that my sole intention is to free my daughter from the clutches of Appius Claudius. However, you may also be assured that I have no intention of allowing injustice to be carried out unhindered." He drew a hand over his face. "But for now, I must get some sleep in the few hours that remain."

The meeting dissolved. Torches dispersed like giant fireflies into the night. Lucius and Titus began picking up, having sent Demetria off some hours before. Icilius stopped and grabbed Lucius warmly by the arm.

"Thank you for what you did today," he said, "and for the use of your tavern tonight. Both of which took a mountain of courage."

Lucius looked into the eyes submerged beneath wave-like black eyebrows. He thought they glowed too hotly for this time of night. The strong nose that walled off Icilius' dark eyes flared with excitement at each breath, like a war horse awaiting the trumpets.

"It's nothing. I'm sure Appius will have heard of it regardless."

"I almost hope so," Icilius declared.

"You look altogether too eager for battle," Lucius observed with a smile of amusement.

"Men who love freedom are always eager for battle."

"Men who love freedom choose the most propitious time for battle."

"Then this is not about Verginia at all to you," said Titus, coming up from behind.

"Her freedom is our freedom," Icilius responded, half turning to admit Titus into the conversation.

"A nice speech," said Titus. "But Appius was right when he said your words were aimed at causing a disturbance."

"Does that bother you?"

"My brother is always concerned with the purity of motives," Lucius chuckled.

"You are betrothed to this girl," said Titus. "Yet not once have I seen any genuine compassion for what her fate will be if judgement goes against Verginius tomorrow."

Icilius squared his feet, and his amiable face hardened. "Every citizen denies himself for the good of Rome," he said tightly. "If I seem callous to Verginia's fate it is because I can accept no outcome other than her freedom."

"Yet if there is such an outcome you are more than willing to use it to political advantage."

"You know, Titus, that's the problem with you," said Lucius. "You can't see that philosophy and politics actually affects people."

"We have laws," insisted Titus.

"We do not have laws," Icilius cried, smashing his fist on a table. "We have tyrants who make laws to gratify their own lusts, and enrich themselves at other's expense."

Lucius abruptly burst into laughter and clutched Titus and Icilius each by the shoulder. "Oh, I can't believe it. You're both neophytes. It's the nature of those who govern to reap profits from the governed. When has it ever been different? Do you think Numa, or Servius Tullius our so-called good kings didn't profit from the people? Didn't they live in a palace behind the Regia? Who do you suppose provided that?"

"You're the most cynical person I've ever known," said Titus. His smile sent waves of wrinkles across his long face.

"I figure there are three types of people," said Lucius, "tyrants, cynics, and fools. We have an overabundance of two of the three, and I'm in the minority."

Icilius laughed also, and moved towards the door. "And what exactly does that mean?" he asked, although not expecting an answer.

Lucius rose to the occasion. "It means that anyone who believes government has the good of the whole people in mind is a fool; and anyone who believes government can provide all the solutions is a tyrant. So naturally the only safe road is that of the cynic, who, I might add, will always find a refuge at the Boar's Tusk."

Dawn nudged darkness to the ends of the earth. Awash in the diffused rose color of sunrise the Forum began filling. Citizens clustered in excited groups. Senators and former consuls in purple bordered togas and palm embroidered tunics gathered around the tribunal. Women stood out as splashes of bright color against the drab redundancy of tawny togas and tunics worn by the common man. Conspicuous to everyone was the presence of Valerius and Horatius who had continued to assault the legitimacy of the decemvirs. A palpable air of excitement and anticipation hung over the Forum as the multitude eagerly awaited the arrival of Verginius. They were not disappointed.

The procession entered the Forum from the Via Vesta, passing forlornly in front of the sacred circular temple of Vesta. The message could not have been more clear. Chaste and pure Verginia, face tear streaked and dressed in the rags of the powerless, followed behind her father whose toga, rent in mourning, tugged at the heart of his fellow citizens. Into the Forum they came with slow saddened steps, followed by her maids, also dressed in mourning and weeping inconsolably. Behind them Icilius, Numitorius, Lucius and Titus Tempanius, and a host of friends, clients, and well-wishers paraded in noisy lamentation.

Verginius, disheveled, hair hanging in greasy ringlets, face unshaven for days and stinking of stale sweat reached a filthy hand out to every person he came near. "Don't let injustice fall on me," he begged. "Have I not been standing in the line of battle to protect your very wives and children? Has Rome become a brothel, that they can take our virgin daughters and debauch them on a whim?"

A murmur and a hissing went through the multitude like a corporate shiver. At the next group Verginius pleaded again. "Should I beg for your support? But why? Have I not until yesterday been protecting your families, while mine," he stopped and pointed at his weeping daughter, "was being viciously attacked within the walls of my own city?

"Friends, help me. You mustn't allow this horrible crime." He tore the front of his toga, exposing the scars of battle on his chest. "No man has out-shown me in courage or valor in doing my duty. See the scars I carry as the price of defending your wives and your virgin daughters."

Once more he took hold of Verginia's hand and pulled her towards the tribunal. She followed with stumbling footsteps, her limp body powerless. Her long black hair fell unbound and cascaded in flowing waves to her waist. Like a frightened doe she cast her large oval eyes beseechingly at individuals in the throng and wiped her delicate nose, rouged by tears. As they neared the platform on which Appius Claudius imperiously sat Lucius Verginius raised his voice another notch. "But now what price must I pay for my patriotism? Wounds and hunger, thirst and weariness these I spent gladly, must I now watch as my daughter suffers the horrors of a captured town? Defend me friends, as I have defended you!"

Appius nodded to a crier who came forward and ordered the crowd quiet. Marcus Claudius stepped forward to speak.

"Yesterday," he said, his pinched effeminate voice cracking, "I was deprived of my property by an unwashed mob of bandits." He lifted his beaked nose and sniffed the air distastefully. "I find it repugnant that a law-abiding citizen like myself should have to suffer injustice at the hands of such an unruly mob who have no respect for the rule of law. Now today they come in even greater numbers, no doubt to intimidate the court in order to steal from me the property that is rightfully mine."

Catcalls, whistles, and lewd comments pertaining to Marcus Claudius' more personal proclivities flew from the crowd. Then to everyone's surprise, including Marcus Claudius, Appius stood up and raised a hand for silence.

"While it might be diverting to hear further comments, the court and the people's time is precious. Evidence has, moreover, come to my attention that makes a decision immediately possible. This incontrovertible proof forces me to rule in favor of the plaintiff. Marcus Claudius, you may take possession of your property."

A roar of indignation and disbelief crashed like thunder from the populace. A dense crowd of men and women encircled Verginia protectively as Marcus Claudius tried to push his way through to claim his property. Tears began to flow in earnest from the women and Verginia, horrified, shrieked angrily, "Get away from me!" as she caught sight of Claudius working his way towards her.

Lucius Verginius shook his huge fist furiously at Appius Claudius. "I betrothed my daughter to Icilius, not you. I meant her for a marriage bed, not a brothel. Are men and women to copulate like goats and rabbits? Whether these people will allow it I don't know, but I will never allow your perverse lusts to sully my daughter while I have breath."

Incensed by the monstrous decision the citizens hung on the verge of violence. They shoved and jostled Marcus Claudius with growing ferocity as he tried to claim his prize. Appius ordered a trumpet blown and uneasy silence fell over the mob. Lucius and Titus tensed for a battle. Along with Icilius and others they stood in front of Verginius and his daughter prepared to battle the considerable forces of Appius Claudius. Lucius became increasingly aware of a mass of Appius' clients forming up in the crowd, and passed the word along. He had no doubt that unless the citizens took up Verginius' cause they would lose a straight fight as the clients of Appius heavily outnumbered those of Verginius.

"Won't this be ironic," he said to Titus out of the corner of his mouth. "To get killed in the Forum by our own people after all the years fighting our enemies."

Appius Claudius gazed down on the knot of men contending his dominion. "Yesterday Icilius, and today you Verginius come to this court and threaten violence. I have further evidence that throughout last night secret meetings took place at a tavern in the Subura for seditious purposes. Forewarned being forearmed, I have come so, with an armed escort should anyone attempt to disturb the peace. No law abiding citizen will be hurt, but I will brook no violence or threatening.

"Lictor, clear the crowd. Let the master through to take possession of his slave."

A lictor rushed forward and the crowd shrank back, leaving the small island of supporters adrift in the vast sea of the Forum. Verginius watched bitterly as his support melted away. He made a last-ditch effort to save his daughter's virtue.

"Wait, please," he said, holding his hands up in supplication to Appius. In yet more conciliatory tones, he addressed the tribunal. "If I have said words in anger, Appius Claudius, forgive me. It is only because I can not understand how my daughter, whom I laid in her mother's arms, could not be my daughter. Add to this my fatigue from being on duty all these days, and I can not think straight. Please, leave me alone with my daughter and her nurse so that I can get to the truth of this matter and at least bid her farewell."

Appius looked around, mulled the request over for a moment, then reluctantly gave his assent. Verginius cupped his daughter in his left arm, pulling her close. He guided her near the shrine of Cloacina to an open butcher shop. They entered in hopes of a little privacy. How appropriate, Verginius thought. Passing under the rectangular door frame they entered into the arched brick interior, and stopped in front of the counter that ran across the shop. Plucked chickens, wide eyed with embarrassment, and rabbits skinned save for their lucky rear feet, dangled in their faces. Rolls of sausages hung from pegs cemented into the walls. On the counter a whole suckling pig was displayed. The smell of dead flesh and fresh blood, of meat gone ripe filled their nostrils. To their right as they entered the proprietor put down a long carving knife he was using to slice a shoulder of smoked pork. No doubt, Verginius thought, in anticipation of a lucrative business following a sordid trial. Soft food for soft souls. The butcher wiped his fatty thick jointed fingers on a soiled linen apron. Verginius did not like the looks of him. His bald porcine head and jiggling rotundity were evidence that he partook of too much of this soft food. Probably a freedman, he thought. What did he care for Rome, or her institutions of freedom, as long as he had money?

The butcher smiled, showing a hodgepodge of teeth, no two seemingly together—more evidence of a soft souled life. "May I help you?"

"Sir," said Verginius politely, "forgive our intrusion. But if we may have just a moment of privacy in your shop."

"But certainly," said the butcher kindly, for his view of the proceeding had not been totally obstructed.

"Thank you."

"It's nothing," said the butcher, retreating to the back of the shop.

As Verginius consoled his daughter and discussed the situation with she and her nurse, Titus watched from a distance and wondered what he would do. He tried to place himself there with Tempania. How could he allow her to be debauched by Appius Claudius? Rape and plunder were a part of warfare, which by definition made this an act of war by a magistrate against his own citizens. If that were true then overthrowing the decemvirs became an act of defense, and not revolution. Yes, he thought as he watched Verginius embrace his daughter, we must come to the defense of the Republic.

Verginius looked out into the Forum. Just outside a line of lictors, Marcus Claudius, and behind them a great mob of people stared into the shop in fascination. He turned back to his daughter, pulling her tighter against him with his left arm.

"Verginia," he said softly.

"Yes Papa," she answered. Her voice echoed the hollow future of never calling him that again.

"You know that I love you?"

"Yes, Papa."

"And that I would never do anything to hurt you?"

"Yes, Papa. But why must I..."

"Shhh. No one is going to hurt you. Do you trust me?" He reached out his right hand softly, tenderly caressed her cheek with the back of his fingers wiping away her tears, then dropped his hand to the counter.

"Yes Papa."

"Good. I won't allow Appius Claudius to touch you."

"Oh, thank you Papa!"

"Now, let's show them all the courage of free Romans." His left arm released its tight grip on her and as she moved slightly away, looking with grateful eyes at her father, he picked up the butcher knife in his right hand. In one swift motion he brought the knife up under her ribs, piercing her heart. A tremendous sob burst from his throat.

A look of surprise lighted Verginia's beautiful face for an instant, then her heart gushed blood in a hot torrent out onto her father's hand. He grabbed her tightly with his left arm as she collapsed, clutching her to him in a final embrace, feeling her warm blood soaking his toga, running strong along his arm, smearing his bare chest.

Verginia's nurse, her lifelong slave and companion, screamed and reached out in horror to the eviscerated girl. Verginius, still clutching the knife, picked up his lifeless daughter and carried her out into the Forum.

Stupefied by the act, Titus shrank away from Verginius with the rest of the crowd as Verginius, covered in gore, approached the tribunal. He laid his child gently down on the paving stones for all to see. Facing Appius Claudius, he stretched his arms out wide so that the full extent of his bloody deed could be seen.

"Appius," he cried, "may the curse of this blood be upon your head forever."

"Go, lictor, and bind his him," Appius ordered.

Verginius brandished the bloodstained butcher knife. "I have shed my own daughter's blood today. Don't think I'll hesitate to shed yours," he warned the lictor as he came forward. The man stopped in his tracks, having no stomach for this fight.

Lucius and Titus muscled the lictors out of the way who suddenly had become listless themselves. A deathly quiet crushed the Forum, and a horrible feeling of impiety froze citizens and officials alike. Taking advantage of the temporary paralysis they escorted Verginius out of the city by way of the Vicus Tuscus, and with a mass of people following, started walking towards Tusculum. Behind them they heard a roar like a sudden wind and knew the people had come alive.

In the Forum Icilius and Numitorius lifted the body of Verginia into the air for all to see. Shouting people milled about in horror. A group of young patricians, the escort he had spoken of earlier, surrounded Appius protectively awaiting his orders. Confusion reigned. Women tore their hair loose in mourning and gathered around the slain Verginia wailing with grief. Icilius and Numitorius stomped about proclaiming that none of this would have happened if plebeians still had their tribunes. Their words took effect, and the mob began to coalesce and focus on the tribunal when Appius decided to act. He ordered the trumpet sounded, and in the momentary quiet called Icilius to appear before the court, accusing him of inciting a riot.

"I will appear before no court of yours, Appius Claudius," he swore contemptuously. Turning to the crowd, he shouted. "Could there be a more illegal court than this?"

The crowd surged forward angrily. Appius commanded his lictors to arrest Icilius. A battle of pushing, shoving, and punching broke out as the crimson clad lictors fought to break through a cordon of men in tan and brown tunics protecting Icilius. Like a general, Appius led reinforcements, his patrician escort, charging into the fray. The tide of battle began to turn. The supporters of Icilius were forced backwards, when suddenly a group led by Valerius and Horatius attacked Appius' men from the flank and drove them off. Now the two groups stood facing each other breathing hard, awaiting the next clash.

Appius Claudius thought he had one more chance. If he exerted all his authority perhaps the power and dignity of his office would over awe his adversary's supporters and yet give him victory. Panting heavily, his face dripping sweat, he raised himself to his full height and put all the force of the majesty of his position in his voice. "I order this man, Icilius, arrested by the authority vested in me by the Senate and People of Rome. Go Lictor, and bind him."

"You will arrest no one," Lucius Valerius said, stepping forward. "We will not allow it. You have no official standing from the Senate or the People of Rome, Appius Claudius. And if you resort to force, you will get a belly full."

Appius retreated to the tribunal, shouting orders that could not be heard for the people shouted him down, and pressed dangerously in on him. Valerius ordered the lictors to refuse any command Appius gave them since he had no official standing.

Appius covered his head and fled past the temple of Castor into a house on the Palatine, his power and his dignity broken.

# XXXI

June 13-15, 449 BC

Quinquatrus Minores—Pipers Festival

From the legion's encampment below Tusculum the disorderly column resembled a procession of snails crawling slowly along the Via Tusculana. Lucius Tempanius Jr. first descried the jumbled host as he took the sun outside the camp. Taking in the scenery his eyes roved from the verdant valley below to the towering tree covered mountain that confined Lake Alba across the narrow valley. He shifted his gaze west to the rippled horizon of the Tyrrhenian Sea and spotted movement coming from the red roofed hills of Rome. He called to some comrades, and they sat in the hot sun listening to the buzz of insects, and watching the dark snaking line draw closer.

"It's not military," said Sulpicius Rufus.

"Yes, too disorganized," agreed Fulvius Metrucius.

A military tribune came out and ordered them back inside the camp, but they ignored him. He came back with another tribune, hoping apparently to have twice the authority.

"Do you see any Aequians about?" asked Rufus snidely.

"I wasn't asking for a scouting report," said the tribune. The horsehair plume on his helmet shook angrily with each word. "I ordered you into the camp."

"I have a feeling the decemvirs won't be giving orders to anyone soon," said Lucius Jr. "Look."

The assembled soldiers sighted along his finger down onto the lower slopes of Tusculum where the host of civilians began climbing the hill. Lucius Verginius came clearly into view wielding a glinting object in expressive arcs and circles, before the road curved and took them out of sight into the forest. Now the sound of the mob reached them, and they listened with itching ears to the noisy excited babble. Legionaries poured out of the western gate or lined the palisade to see the strange sight of a legion of civilians marching on Tusculum. The wild assembly debouched from the woods a hundred yards from the camp, and its strangled guttural sound and sanguinary appearance overpowered all military restraint.

Verginius, girded toga hanging in blood encrusted shreds, led an irate mob pouring out a cacophony of encouragement, recriminations, and lamentations. A host of auditory confusions set the soldiers' mouths agape, not knowing if they should laugh at the spectacle or take up arms. Near the front of the crowd Lucius Jr. recognized his father and Uncle Titus. He knew at once that something drastic must have happened in Rome.

Nearly the entire legion crushed against the camp gates and in contravention of orders brought the civilian host into the camp. The state of Verginius' appearance elicited a plethora of excited questions that he at first could not answer for the sobs tearing his breath. Lucius Jr. pinned his father down immediately to learn the facts.

"He killed his daughter to keep her out of the hands of Appius Claudius," Lucius informed him.

Soldiers jostled to get a better vantage point to hear and see, all the while hurling questions at Verginius. He held up his blood encrusted right arm, glaring madly at the blood-blackened blade stabbing upward at the soft underbelly of the sky. Silence fell like a stone from a wall.

"Friends, comrades, I come bearing the grief of a father whose daughter has been violated. Yes, this is the blood of my own daughter. And, yes, it is this arm that shed it." He shook his brawny limb viciously. "Just as you have heard. But before you pass judgement, I beg you to hear me out." Verginius reached both arms to heaven in supplication, swearing an oath to the veracity of his tale. Aghast with disbelief the soldiers listened, now and then whispering hurried questions to the intermingled civilians for clarification or confirmation.

"Fellow soldiers," Verginius concluded, "don't blame me for this hideous crime. I acted only to preserve my daughter's honor against dishonorable men. How could I allow her chaste behavior to be corrupted by the perverse nature of Appius

Claudius? Which of you would not have done the same?" He paused momentarily to let them answer the question for themselves. "I urge you, do not repeat my mistake." The voices of men who suddenly thought of their own daughters and expressed the fear that leaped into their heads overpowered his words. Verginius held up his bloodstained scepter and quiet spread again. "Oh yes," he cried, "I blame myself. I waited for someone else to rid our country of leaders who live without morals and consider high office a right. As if integrity and honor didn't matter. And now," his voice choked, tears started in his eyes. He swallowed, pushing his heart back down into his chest. "Now I have found out too late just how much they do. But you who still have wives, daughters, sisters to defend, do not let them be carried away like slaves to the brothels. My poor Verginia is dead, but the lust of Appius and his ilk still lives. While you yet have something to defend, let us make certain they are safe and secure in liberty."

Aroused to anger, the camp boiled into turmoil. No expression of kindness or threat of horrible punishment could give control back to the commanders. The entire night the men spent clustered in groups, going from campfire to campfire, discussing what should be done. In the end, the enemy on Algidus being of lesser concern, they decided to march back to Rome. Next day, led by their centurions, they formed in exquisite order and marched in column six abreast to the Aventine Hill and set up camp.

The decemvirs who had been in command hurried back to Rome in disgrace without their army. Fabius and his subordinates, whose army, driven back to Fidenae by the Tiburtines, united with their brethren on the Aventine, soon joined them. The Senate and the decemvirs convened in the Curia, although much talking and debating could produce nothing more than a resolution to treat the plebeians carefully.

Seated outside a tent erected for Verginius, Icilius, and Numitorius, the men huddled there greeted the news with disdainful laughter.

"How else would you treat eight thousand men armed to the teeth?" laughed Titus.

"They treat us like slaves then are surprised when we act like men," said Lucius.

Icilius looked around the circle with his dark expressive eyes. "My friends," he said, "let's be cautious in our ridicule. First of all, it's dangerous to ascribe inferiority to your enemy. It more often leads to a lack of vigilance and defeat instead of victory. Second, don't think that because we seem to have an advantage it will cause them to act as if it were so. We must strongly press it home if we hope to gain our liberty."

"Icilius is right," said Verginius. "We must have our demands ready and be ready to defend them."

"They'll be sending representatives soon enough," said Numitorius.

"Yes," agreed Lucius, "but not to negotiate. They'll want to see our organization first, and learn what our bottom price will be."

"Very astute," Icilius said. "What we need to do is get the tribes together and elect tribunes. Then we can put a program on the table."

"How shall we do it?" asked Titus. "How many tribunes? Two?" He had never agreed with the expansion of the number of tribunes and hoped to return to the original number.

"Why not by tribes?" suggested Numitorius. "That way every tribe will be represented."

"I like it," said Icilius. "It gives us the broadest consensus and therefore the greatest strength."

"And endless debates," objected Lucius.

"That's a risk we'll have to take," said Gaius Sicinius, son of the first tribune.

Marcus Duellius, Titus' brother-in-law, found something to say. He knit his bushy eyebrows, wrinkling his small forehead. "Tribunes by tribes is best," he said. He described a series of blocks in the air with his hands. "That way we also have a command structure in the event a military situation develops. Also," he said, scratching the thick pelage-like whiskers on his face, "we should elect two as supreme commanders."

They finalized arrangements for the plebeian aediles to hold elections in two days. The meeting then broke up as they went to find the divisores and curatores of each tribe to pass the word and organize each tribe for the coming vote.

Lucius and Titus relaxed, basking in the warm sun outside Icilius' tent like old dogs luxuriating in the penetrating heat. Returning from official business Icilius threw off his toga and reclined on the grass in a linen tunic with the two brothers.

"Is this what happens to old soldiers?" he teased. "They camp out like small boys pretending to be legionaries?"

"Worse," said Titus, "they dream about it."

"Worse yet," said Lucius, "they collect at the tavern and relive it."

"I'd say anyone that survives twenty years of service deserves it," said Icilius, implicitly showing his respect for the two brothers.

"Speaking of camp life," said Titus, "why are you sleeping in this tent instead of in your house?"

"Actually," Icilius laughed, "I had thought to stay at Lucius', but he tells me it isn't finished yet."

"Disappointing, isn't it?" laughed Lucius. "It's right in the vicinity too." He pointed towards a clump of trees below the southern crest of the hill. "It's just over there."

"At the rate it's going up, his son will be lucky to live in it," said Titus.

"That's politics for you," said Lucius.

Icilius turned away, attracted by movement to his left. Duellius came up quickly with short springy steps.

"Looks like they've sent some emissaries," he said.

Icilius sucked his teeth in consternation. "We're not ready yet."

"Nevertheless, we need to put together a delegation," said Duellius. "I'll get Sicinius, and Verginius, you find Numitorius, and we'll see what they have to say."

"Excuse me, gentlemen," said Icilius, heaving himself to his feet. "Enjoy the sun."

Lucius and Titus got up slowly and ambled behind their self-appointed temporary representatives. Three senators climbed the hill, all former consuls wearing purple striped togas and double-knotted patrician shoes. No lictors preceded them, though the three stood close together and straight as a bundle of rods. The instant they were spotted, interested men surrounded the Senate's representatives so that they had no idea if any individual or a group of persons acted as spokesman. Typical plebeian mob.

"The Senate inquires as to the meaning of this mutiny," said Gaius Julius. His severe mouth puckered in accusation as he furrowed his broad forehead and looked down his long straight nose. "By whose orders did you desert your posts?"

"And just what are your intentions," added Publius Sulpicius, "now that you've captured your own city?"

The words, issued haughtily with an undertone of threat drew whistles, catcalls, and invective riddled threats of their own. Icilius addressed them formally.

"We will only talk to Valerius and Horatius," he declared.

The gathered men thought this an excellent riposte and echoed it with one voice, rejecting the authority and dignity of the emissaries from the Senate.

Lucius and Titus laughed at the discomfiture of the three patricians as they timidly picked their way through the throng of armed men.

"That ought to set some tongues wagging," said Titus.

"Those three probably left their friends talking about how they would divide up the spoils. Now they're going back empty handed."

The scene around Titus pulsed with a breathless, diffused quality. Men milled about the temple of Diana in full uniform.

From up on the hill the river looked like a thick black snake, motionless save for the sunlight glinting off its scaled back. It seemed surreal, dreamlike. Civilians came and went as they pleased, but the soldiers maintained strict discipline, remaining in their units, posting sentries, using passwords as if encamped in enemy territory. With good reason.

A siege mentality prevailed in the city. Thousands of loyal patrician clients manned the ramparts, and the cavalry, dominated by the patricians, remained powerfully intact. The Senate debated heatedly what their course of action should be. Some advocated a direct assault on the encampment on the Aventine, disregarding the threat from foreign enemies. Their willingness to risk the Republic to gain victory for their class excited the bold, caused trepidation in the timid, and disgusted those who sought a civil solution. The rest bemoaned their fate of being born in such awful times.

The citizens that remained seldom left their neighborhoods. The Forum represented the shame they felt for their country. Friends spoke in private or in small groups around the public fountains and local market stalls. Few took pleasure in the center of their city.

"Does this seem real to you?" asked Titus.

Lucius chuckled. "Do you feel like Lars Porsenna occupying the Janiculum?"

"I didn't think of it that way," Titus said. "What I mean is those senators were right. We have captured our own city, yet we sit here waiting for an offer. Not a sword has been raised in the city."

"Ah," said Lucius. "You mean, why don't we just march on the Curia and take what we want?"

"Well, it wouldn't be that simple, and that's not what I'm advocating, but no one else seems to be either, and that's what makes everything seem so unreal."

"It would seem we have more respect for law than our 'fathers'."

"Maybe that's it. Maybe the measure of a people is if they can settle their differences without bloodshed."

"Or maybe we're still too afraid to take the patricians head on. It could be, Titus, in our hearts we really think we are inferior."

Titus laughed heartily and gave his brother a light shove. "You've never believed yourself inferior to anyone. In fact, to prove it I think you should put your name in for tribune of our tribe."

"Where will I get a white toga?"

In the following days the twenty-one tribes met, compiled their lists of candidates, and voted. The tribe Voltinia elected Lucius Tempanius tribune, the first elected position of a Tempanius in the history of the family. For Lucius it confirmed the blessing of Mars so many years before and the conviction that a man must have a name and a clientele to get ahead in Rome. For his clientele assuredly made the difference.

"Not bad," said Lucius, "for only a second generation citizen."

"No," said Icilius, "unless you consider the Claudii, who had a consul within five years."

"Listen, if I had his clientele, I'd have been consul long ago."

The wrangling began. Hotheads among the plebeians were just as ready to go to war as their counterparts in the Senate. Others desired only to go back to the way it was before the decemvirs. Some thought only true democracy, like that in Greek cities, would guarantee liberty. Vociferous, hard fought, and vehement, the debates raged until Greek style democracy and outright war were eliminated.

Manlius Oppius, one of two tribunes elected as consular tribunes, called for order. "Let us first note," he said, "that we are unanimous in our demand for the restoration of the tribunate."

Universal consent followed, and he recognized Numitorius as the next speaker. Numitorius faced his colleagues. "I think we must protect ourselves further, gentlemen. Certainly the tribunate and the right of appeal are the foundation of our liberty, but this has not proved adequate. I need not remind you of the threat of reprisal once we have come to terms. Make no mistake, if we do not demand amnesty for all those considered leaders in our enterprise (of which each of you is now one) lives and fortunes will no doubt be forfeit. We must also extend this to every legionary."

A wave of approval met the motion, and the aediles duly noted it for a final vote. Another tribune demanded trial and punishment of the decemvirs, a position also quickly seconded.

Manlius Oppius next recognized Lucius Tempanius.

"My friends," he said, "it seems to me we are not going far enough by half. What do we gain by a return to the status quo? If our view of liberty is restricted to the right of appeal then this fight will occur over and over again. Time after time we have pledged our lives to defend the sacrosanct persons of our tribunes and the few plebiscites they have enacted. Many of us have houses on this very hill that our friend and colleague Lucius Icilius made possible by his Lex Icilia. Yet even that, although the Aventine has been sacred to the plebs since the foundation of Rome, had to be guaranteed by a lex sacrata. Nor was it officially recognized by the patricians until we used it as a bargaining chit when the decemvirate was first proposed.

"Our friend Publius Numitorius rightly stated that the tribunate is the foundation of our freedom. But which of you is content to live on the foundation of your house without the walls and the roof it supports? Yet that is what we've been doing for fifty years in Rome. Gentlemen, it is time to add the walls and roof to our liberty, that we might have liberty indeed."

His speech garnered enthusiastic applause from his fellow tribunes and the citizens in attendance. Unfortunately, he hadn't proposed anything concrete so they soon fell to arguing over just what the walls and roof of their freedom should be made of. Still, the days passed and no one heard from the senators and patricians. Finally, Duellius brought news that the Senators were sitting on their hands, shouting recriminations at one another and proposing nothing in the way of constructive reforms or reconciliation. Frustrated by patrician intransigence the people's tribunes put the drastic proposal before the concilium plebis to evacuate the city and retire to the sacred mount. The vote resulted in near unanimous approval.

Duellius' report held elements of truth but fell far short of the whole truth. After all, the Aventine could be reached by a short, leisurely walk from the Forum. Many residents of the Palatine could look from their houses and see much of what transpired. Security measures did not restrict the people's access to the temple of Diana, or their homes, and so a constant flow of traffic between the Aventine and the city took place daily. The patricians had their spies, and though they could not know every proposal discussed and voted on inside the palisade of the camp, they had a working idea of some of them. They knew the return of the tribunate, the right of appeal, amnesty, and trials of the decemvirs were the commons' main negotiating demands. But time had always been on the patrician's side, so they waited. When the plebs voted to march through Rome as a show of their frustration, the patricians received this information with mixed emotions. Some viewed the tactic as one of last resort, a sign that if they waited a little longer the plebs would capitulate. Others saw it as a sign of the people's resolve and braced for a protracted struggle.

The pipers demanded time to celebrate their festival before any move should be made. Lucius teased Titinius and other of his friends among that sacred collegium, but they solemnly insisted that religion, not three days of drunken feasting, was utmost on their minds. For three days the temple of Diana reverberated with the music, laughter, and raucous behavior of the quinquatrus minores. Finally, the army could march.

A little the worse for wear, the pipers led the army off the Aventine Hill playing marshal tunes that set the cadence for the march. The long column descended the hill in step, six abreast, polished and shined to glittering crimson and gold perfection. As the pipers reached the portal entering onto the Vicus Tuscus, soldiers still descended the Aventine. Past the altar of Hercules they stepped, the ringing of their footsteps echoing off the heights of the Palatine as they marched past the algae edged Velabrum. Into the Forum they came, the deafening peal of hobnailed boots reverberating with marshal ardor off hard paving stones as the legions passed the temple of Castor. In front of the Curia on the order, "eyes left" they snapped their heads to face the Senate house with a thunderous crash as spears struck shields in the same instant.

Senators gaped in awe as citizens, wild with excitement at the magnificent spectacle, lined the streets in cheering masses, throwing flowers at the soldiers as they marched with their high plumed heads held proudly in the air. Helplessly the senators watched Rome's hoplite infantry climb up the Quirinal Hill on the Vicus Ficum, and exit the city. Behind them followed an aroused and jubilant citizenry carried away by the splendor of their men in arms, and the awesome discipline of their march. Three miles north of Rome they ascended the same low hill overlooking the confluence of the Tiber and Anio rivers that their fathers had climbed forty-six years before. There they waited.

In Rome an eerie quiet oppressed the city. Even the stray dogs seemed to have disappeared, or wandered bemused, aimlessly looking for their normal benefactors. The few proprietors who remained, mostly freedmen, sat outside their shops taking the sun, doing desultory business with the women and old men left in the city.

The Senate met with renewed concern, but with the same indecision. They could not abide the situation as it existed, nor could they abide the concessions they would have to make to correct it. A few old men, all that could be seen in the Forum these days, laughed them to scorn as they made their quotidian trek to the Curia.

The *decemvirs*, still nominally in power, refused to step down, clinging to the excuse that the twelve tables had yet to be ratified. This fiction so infuriated a large number of senators that substantial discussions began to be held. Lucius

Valerius, and Marcus Horatius, scions of two storied families, finally overcame the paralysis engendered by the terrifying thought of the tribunate. Valerius scathingly reminded the senators that their cruel treatment of the plebeians gave rise to the very office they so abhorred. How much longer would they wait? Until the citizenry rose in armed rebellion? "Do you prefer the collapse of Rome to the humiliation of restoring the tribunes to the people? For shame gentlemen, to value prestige and power above the good of the Republic."

Their will broken, the *decemvirs* and senators agreed to a three-pronged approach; the restoration of the office of tribune, in exchange for ratification of the twelve tables, and amnesty for the *decemvirs*. Little did they know the plebs had seen them coming.

Valerius and Horatius arrived at the little hill early in the day. Thin ragged clouds stretched in sere streams across an azure sky, clinging to the gray concave face of austere Mount Janus to the east. A derisive shout of acclamation, which at their funerals would be retold as 'heartfelt', greeted the Senate's representatives. Each brought with him two unarmed attendants. They had expected private meetings, but instead Sicinius directed them to a platform erected facing a large square outside the regulation military camp. On the platform Lucius Tempanius sat with twenty other plebeian tribunes. Valerius and Horatius took seats next to him as Icilius rose to speak.

"Lucius Valerius Potitus, and Marcus Horatius Barbatus, the people of Rome formally thank you for your presence before them. We wish first of all to allay any fears you may have for your personal safety." He swept his arm over the vast expanse of soldiers and civilians covering the square. "As you can see," he said, with a broad sardonic smile, "you are well protected."

Valerius and Horatius nodded their heads, half smiles on their otherwise impassive faces.

"We wish you also to know," continued Icilius, "that while we regret the necessity of a second secession, we are even more adamant in our determination to carry it through if a just resolution cannot be reached. We extend our hands, therefore, in hope, that hope might bring concord, that concord might bring justice, and that justice might restore to Rome her loyal citizens." Icilius sat down.

Horatius pushed himself to his feet and strode to the front of the dais. His tall strapping frame commanded attention in his close-fitting tunic, and the thick black hair of a man in his thirties exuded the full flowering of virile manhood. He spread full lips in a self-deprecating smile and extended his muscular arms. "Citizens of Rome, thank you for the warm welcome." He turned and bowed slightly to Icilius. "Lucius Icilius, thank you for the fine speech. You may rest assured that we not only take your secession seriously, we hold ourselves responsible."

In the audience Titus stood with his son Marcus, and his nephew Lucius Jr. close to the speakers' platform. "I never thought I'd hear that," said Titus.

"If my father has his way, he'll pay for it too," said Lucius Jr.

"The demands have already been decided, have they not?" asked Marcus.

"Maybe so," said his cousin, "but if they show weakness, we should exploit it. They should call a recess before they discuss terms."

"I think," said Titus, "if we get what we agreed on in the concilium that should be enough."

"I mean no disrespect, Uncle, but it is never enough if there's more to be had."

"That's a hard code to live by, Lucius. One that could lead to an awful lot of sadness," said Titus, returning his attention to Horatius.

"But let us now come together as citizens of the same country and reconcile our differences," Horatius said. "We have come as representatives of the Senate to discuss these very terms." Without saying more, he sat down next to Lucius. Leaning over he quietly asked, "Do you think that can be done?"

"I would say that depends on you," responded Lucius with a shrug. "If you're willing to give up a little, you may gain a lot."

"That's a rather ambiguous answer," broke in Valerius.

"It seems to me," quipped Lucius, "politics is a rather ambiguous business."

Icilius again stepped forward to speak. "It may surprise you to note, esteemed senators, that the people have already put together a detailed program."

"Now watch their faces," laughed Marcus, speaking to his father and cousin. "They can't be ready for this."

"No," said Lucius Jr. maliciously, "they're sitting there smugly thinking they only have to give back the tribunate."

"Look at Valerius," said Titus. "He looks worried. I think your father may have given them the idea our demands are not as simple as they thought."

"First," elucidated Icilius, "as you must obviously know, in order to protect themselves from oppression, the people demand the restoration of their tribunes."

A tremendous roar went up from the crowd at these words. Icilius raised his hands to suppress the noise. "Along with our tribunes, the right of appeal must naturally flow. However, to avoid a recurrence of another decemvirate we also require that no office should be created that is exempt from the right of appeal.

"Next, that the position of tribune shall be sacrosanct, as well as the plebeian aediles, and the board of ten judges. That is, all plebeian magistracies shall be held to be sacrosanct, and anyone who assaults one of their persons shall be punished by death or exile, and their property sold at auction and deposited in the plebeian shrine of the temple of Ceres."

From the equanimity on their faces Lucius could see that Valerius and Horatius had come prepared for these demands. It came as no surprise to him. Little could take place in secret in Rome. A hiss of laughter escaped through his teeth at the thought of their reaction to demands he felt sure secrecy had prevailed to keep from them. Both men shot a querying look at his short burst of laughter, but he merely smiled.

"Next," said Icilius, itemizing the plebeian demands, "we must be guaranteed complete amnesty for all military and civilian personnel involved in the struggle to restore our liberty.

The plebs cheered as he delivered each point, and the shock wave of their voices washed over the senators like booms of thunder.

"Next," shouted Icilius, "we demand that all laws passed by the consuls in the centuriate assembly be delivered in writing to our plebeian aediles in the temple of Ceres so that every citizen may know the exact nature, and extent of every law.

"Next, that the tribunes shall have the right to veto any measure deemed contrary to plebeian liberty.

"Next, that any resolution passed by the plebeian assembly must be recognized as law by the senate and be binding on the whole people of Rome."

Both senators blanched and went rigid at the shock of the last two demands.

"Does that take care of some of the ambiguity?" asked Lucius, a huge smile bouncing off their disconcerted faces.

"Next, that the decemvirs be surrendered to the people for the administration of justice. They are to be tried, and if found guilty burned alive.

"Those, esteemed senators, are our demands. I'm sure you'll find them reasonable and just."

Valerius and Horatius took themselves back to Rome to confer with their own advisors. This did not necessarily include the whole senate or the *decemvirs*, for the two men had their own agenda. The next day they returned to give their answer.

Valerius, descendant of a popular aristocratic family, took his boyish good looks to the front of the speaker's platform. His roan-colored hair hung straight and fine, blowing with misleading insouciance in a light breeze. When he addressed the people and their tribunes, he did so with an ease and confidence that Lucius admired.

"Friends and citizens, fellow soldiers, I must confess that one or two of your demands caught us by surprise. Yet we must also confess that they exhibit a degree of judgement, resolve, and reserve that is admirable, and welcome. I would caution, however, that one or two of your points have been dictated by a passion that perhaps must be tempered. However, let me first address those points that have obviously been the result of careful thought, and debate."

Titus, with his son and nephew beside him in military tunics, felt the happy swell of pride in community, breathed deeply the air of brotherhood and listened intently to Valerius. A low buzzing, like bees working a meadow of clover, hovered over the throng as his words were passed to those out of earshot.

"As to the tribunate and the right of appeal, they are so equitable that we should have granted them of our own initiative. For by these you seek only to secure and safeguard your liberty."

On the dais dreams assaulted Lucius in such profusion that he almost didn't hear the words of Valerius as he conceded nearly every point of the plebeian agenda. For the first time he saw the squared blocks of opportunity for his family. His heart swelled with pride in his wagon sized chest as he thought of his own election as a tribune, however short term it might be. He was the first, but he resolved he would not be the last. Then Valerius demonstrated what true power meant.

"Now let me address those items whose temper is perhaps too brittle," he said. "First, that our city should not devolve into one of rule by vendetta we must not allow the members of the decemvirate to fall into the hands of your understandable anger. Do not now place yourselves in the position of tyrant, out from under which you have justly brought yourselves. Instead, in order that our country's wounds should fully heal, we must extend to the decemvirs the same amnesty extended to your leaders.

"Next, you must ratify the twelve tables as currently composed.

"Lastly, we must also adjust your demand for the power to promulgate laws. Not…" The buzz grew angrier and louder, but Valerius held his hands up and quelled the swarm. "Not to deny it, for why should the people who must live under the laws not be able to advance their own ideas. But to ensure the favor of the Gods we propose that laws passed by the concilium plebis will be given the force of law only after they have been inspected for proper religious language by the Senate and chief priests of the State, and when they have been ratified by the comitia curiata.

"However, to secure this you will need to ensure that my colleague Marcus Horatius, and I are elected consuls. For we can only promise what we can perform, and opposition to this will be fierce and unremitting. If you will help us become consuls at the next election, we will see to it that these goals become reality.

"And now, CITIZENS, in the name of your country, may she and you forever prosper, we invite you to return to your homes, your wives, your children."

A roar of excitement went up from the multitude. Over the entire field men congratulated one another with handshakes, backslaps, and hugs. No joy of victory on the field of battle could have been more complete or sweeter, after the long and bitter trial. Now, finally, their discipline began to break, and men ran to their tents to collect their things and head back to Rome. They did not march to Rome so much as celebrate a triumph.Titus, with his son and nephew sought out Lucius behind the speakers' platform. They found him shaking hands with well-wishers, wagging his great head happily and an unseemly smile plastered on his broad face. In his tan toga, among all the blood red military tunics he looked an incongruous sight. Yet to Titus he appeared completely in his element. He marveled at the change in his brother.

"Congratulations," Titus said, taking his brother's hand. "You've won a great victory for the people today."

Lucius pumped his brother's hand vigorously and looked him sternly in the eye. "We've won a great victory for the Tempanii," he corrected.

"Yes," said Titus, a ripple of apprehension passing through him, "you've brought honor to the Tempanius name."

"Let's hope it's just the beginning," said Lucius.

+ + +

Lucius lost his election bid for the office of tribune. Valerius and Horatius fared better, gaining the consulships to which they aspired. True to their word they instituted the reforms to which they had agreed. The patricians swallowed hard, with great angry faces to make the medicine go down. These laws were known to posterity as the Lex Valeria-Horatia, and were considered down to the end of the Republic as the cornerstone of the Roman constitution.

Titus, happily returned to his farm, came to Rome for the ceremony of mounting the Twelve Tables. Lucius seemed a bit down, but he thought that understandable after the high excitement of the previous months. As they stood in the Forum near the sacred olive tree where the Twelve Tables, inscribed in bronze, were affixed to a pillar for all to read, Titus thought to cheer his brother up.

"Well," he said, "now I can die feeling like I've done something for Rome."

"That's funny," said Lucius. "I was just thinking I was born a generation too soon to accomplish what I want."

# THE END

# Acknowledgements

While my research of the Roman Republic extended to approximately 100 books, there are a few I would like to mention as particularly important and influential, especially for the time period in which The Gift of Mars take place. At the top of the list are The Beginnings of Rome, by T.J. Cornell, and, of course, The Early History of Rome, by Titus Livy; however, many others were instrumental in putting bone and sinew to the republic: The Roman Republic, by Michael Crawford; The Roman Assemblies, George W. Botsford; Republican Rome, by A.H. McDonald; Social Conflicts of the Roman Republic, by P.A. Brunt; The Making of the Roman Army; From Republic to Empire, by Lawrence Keppie; Public Order in Ancient Rome, by Wilfred Nippel. I found a wealth of information on religious festivals and rites in Roman and European Mythologies, by Yves Bonnefoy, and on the Roman diet in Le Abitudini Alimentari dei Romani, by A. Dosi and F. Schnell, and on agricultural matters Cato and Varro On Agriculture, by M. Porcius Cato and M. Terentius Varro, Loeb Classical Library

If I am able to continue the subject as a series, perhaps at a later date I will compose a complete bibliography, but for now I hope this will suffice.

A few notes:

1 iugera of land equates to approximately ¼ hectare or 6/10ths of an acre; so, 4 iugera would equal 1 hectare and 5 iugera would equal about 3 acres.

1 Roman Mile was 5000 Roman feet, equivalent to 4860 modern feet or 1481 meters

During the era in which this novel takes place, Rome did not have official currency; purchases were made either through barter or by weighing out pieces of bronze and later, silver.

Made in United States
Troutdale, OR
07/02/2023